P9-BYN-842

Praise for <u>Hope</u> by Lori Copeland

"Hope *is another fun, inspirational outing from seasoned writer Lori Copeland. Who else but Lori would include among her characters an ornery goat, a stolen pig, a mule called Cinder, and a man named Frog? It's easy to see why romance readers are circling their wagons around the Brides of the West series!"* —**Liz Curtis Higgs,** *author of* Mixed Signals

"*I just loved this book! Only Lori Copeland could weave a knee-slapping tale with such a beautifully redemptive message. Her characters are delightfully funny and unpredictable, and her plot is full of refreshing twists and turns. I can't wait for her next book!"* —**Terri Blackstock,** *best-selling author*

"Lori Copeland concocts just the right mix of faith, romance, and humor in Hope. I started chuckling right away and didn't stop till the end. A cheering, uplifting story of God's wisdom and love." —**Lyn Cote,** *author of* Whispers of Love

"*Lori Copeland's third book in the Brides of the West series,* Hope, *is such a delight! I laughed, I cried, but most of all I thrilled to see how spiritual truths could be woven into a rollicking good story! Lori's light and lively voice makes for good storytelling! This one's a keeper!"* —**Angela Elwell Hunt,** *author of* The Silver Sword

"*This tender and funny page-turner will tug at your heart from start to finish. Hope's journey to love kept me cheering, sighing, and chuckling as I read.* Hope *is Lori Copeland at her very best!"* —**Diane Noble,** *author of* When the Far Hills Bloom

What readers are saying about Brides of the West

"Faith *is one romance that will sit on my limited shelf space and be read over and over."* —L.C.

"*Your new book in the Brides of the West series is wonderful! Keep up the fantastic work!"* —P.G.

"*I love stories that are both uplifting and realistic, and* Faith *and* June *really fit the bill. God bless you and may you continue to brighten people's lives with your God-given talent!"* —K.L.M.

"*Thanks for a quality story, well-written and uplifting! I'll spread the word and recommend this book to others. I'll also check into the other HeartQuest books with anticipation."* —J.B.

"*I truly enjoyed your books,* Faith *and* June. *I am looking forward to more of your books. My husband (a bookworm) is impressed that I have actually read two books in three weeks!"* —S.T.

"*Absolutely magnificent! The stories are fresh and exciting and inspire me to greater faith and service for God. God has anointed you for a mighty work through your wonderful novels."* —K.M.

romance the way it's meant to be

HeartQuest brings you romantic fiction
with a foundation of biblical truth.
Adventure, mystery, intrigue, and suspense
mingle in these heartwarming stories of
men and women of faith striving to build
a love that will last a lifetime.

May HeartQuest books sweep you
into the arms of God, who longs for you
and pursues you always.

Glory

Ruth

Patience

Glory

LORI COPELAND

Brides of the West 1872

Romance fiction from
Tyndale House Publishers, inc.
WHEATON, ILLINOIS

To four very special men in my life:
my grandsons, James, Joseph,
Joshua, and Gage

Acknowledgments

Writing is a solitary act, but no book is written without the help and encouragement of others. A big thank-you to my editor, Diane Eble, for her strength and vision for my work. Working with you, Diane, is a blessing.

Thanks to the HeartQuest team—Becky Nesbitt, Kathy Olson, Anne Goldsmith, Diane Eble, Danielle Crilly, Jan Pigott, and Catherine Palmer—for cheering me on. And thank you, Travis Thrasher, for too many things to list! You do Tyndale proud.

I want to thank my family for allowing me time to write and overlooking my sometimes shameful preoccupation with work. I love you guys.

Thanks to Janet Colliate, who forfeited retirement time to proofread and offer suggestions on this book in its early stage. I value your friendship, Janet.

April 6, 2000

Chapter One

Well—well, the least you could do is stay for supper!" Glory choked on dust as Ralph Samuels's buckboard spun out of the yard on one wheel. Sighing, she glanced toward the shanty, hoping that was squirrel she smelled frying and that Poppy had cooked enough for two.

Bending over, the petite young woman with a boyish frame picked up the knapsack holding her extra pair of denims and shirt. *Poppy isn't going to be happy about this,* Glory thought. It was the third time in as many months that an almost-husband had brought her back. The eager suitor would call on her proper-like; then Poppy would propose marriage. The besotted swain always agreed, only to go back on his word before vows were spoken. Glory didn't understand it. This time she'd nearly made it through the whole day before this fickle lout got cold feet.

Men were just too picky. Yes, she'd corrected Ralph a few times this morning—only *corrected* the man. So what? She hadn't said that she knew everything. He was thin-skinned and took her harmless observations for a sign of bossiness. Bossy? Her? She wasn't bossy—just happened to have more knowledge about turnips than Ralph could ever hope to have, and it was his pained expression, not hers, that put a blight on the outing.

She glanced at the shanty again, wondering if Poppy would be upset with her for coming back—or being returned—a third time. He shouldn't be. Seemed to her that she was lucky to have discovered Ralph's headstrong tendencies now rather than later. Wouldn't it have been dandy to be hitched to a man who couldn't discuss *turnips* without blowing up?

"Poppy!" Glory sniffed the late afternoon air, her eyes traveling to the piece of metal pipe stuck through the tin roof. Only a faint waft of smoke curled from the chimney. *Odd,* she thought. That was meat she smelled frying.

Climbing the steps to the porch, she kept a firm grip on the knapsack. Wasn't any need to unpack. When Poppy had gotten it in his mind a few months back that he wasn't going to live much longer, he'd set out like a man possessed to get her married off. No amount of arguing could have convinced him otherwise. She didn't need a husband; she was able to take care of herself. Been doing it since she was knee-high to a grasshopper. But the old hermit had argued—something Poppy didn't do that often. He'd fretted day and night about how she couldn't live in these parts alone—not these days. He'd contended that if Indians didn't stir up trouble, men with no-good intentions would.

How could Poppy worry? Glory could fire her old Hawkins rifle better than any man; Poppy couldn't dispute that. She could haul water and chop wood and skin a bear in less time than it took to talk about it. She wasn't much on cooking and cleaning, but Poppy did all of that. She knew all she needed to get by. She didn't want any man telling her what to do.

Why, if she hadn't fallen off that wagon when she was a baby and if Poppy hadn't found her lying on the trail, she probably could have raised herself.

Her resolve stiffened. She had to talk Poppy out of this foolish notion of marriage; it wasn't going to work.

"Poppy?" Glory pushed the front door open a crack and peered inside. Late-afternoon sunlight fell across the dirt floor. A remnant of morning fire had turned to white ashes. The iron skillet was on the stove, and the scent of frying meat—and burnt bread—teased her nose.

Squinting, her eyes shifted to Poppy's cot across the room. Poppy, hands across his chest, lay sleeping peacefully between the rumpled blankets.

Shoving the door open, she came inside. Sleeping at this time of the day! Poppy would be up all night. Pausing beside the cot, she smiled down affectionately on the only father she'd ever known. She didn't know her real pa's name, but when she'd fallen off that wagon and nobody had noticed, Poppy had become her family from that day on. If her real ma or pa had come back looking for their infant daughter, they hadn't found her. Poppy said he'd stayed around the area for over a week, waiting for someone to come back to claim their baby girl. Then bad weather had set in and he'd been forced to bring the infant to his shanty, and that's where she'd lived ever since, with Poppy; Molasses, the old mule; a cow; and a few settin' hens.

For years afterward, every time a wagon rattled by the shanty, the old hermit would flag it down and ask if anyone was looking for a lost child. The weary travelers would shake their heads, saying how sorry they were to hear about the tragedy, but they hadn't known anyone who was missing a young'un. So Glory had stayed, and the years had passed, and now the old man was worried about dying and leaving her all alone.

"Poppy?" She gently shook Poppy's shoulders. "Wake up, sleepyhead. It's gonna be dark soon, and you'll not sleep a wink tonight."

The old man lay deathly still, his blue-veined hands resting lightly across his frail chest, a faint smile on his weathered features. "Poppy?" she repeated, her breath catching as she bent to press her ear to his upper body. Her heart sank when she realized that he wasn't breathing. The beat that was once hearty and strong was silent now.

"Oh, Poppy." Tears smarted in her eyes, and she gathered the kind old man into her arms. "Why did you have to go and leave me?"

Sunbeams stretched across the shanty floor and gradually faded to shadows. Glory sat on the cot and cradled the old man like an infant, rocking him gently back and forth, singing a lullaby that he'd sung to her so many times before: *Sleep my little child, sleep and run no more. Someone who loves you holds you tight and will forever more.*

Poppy was gone. Memories flooded her heart: memories of how the old hermit had taught her to hunt and fish, to track wounded animals to either put them out of their pain or attempt to heal their wounds. He'd taught her to laugh at herself and to care about others, though it was a rare treat when they ever saw another living soul.

They lived deep in the Missouri hills with only animals and each other for company. Poppy's brother, Crazy Amos, came around occasionally looking for a handout. Glory was scared of the ferocious-looking giant. He stood heads taller than Poppy, and his massive hands were as big as the hams Poppy had hanging in the smokehouse. Poppy didn't cotton to his younger brother either. Said he was a freeloader, and Poppy didn't hold with freeloaders. Had "gold" in his eyes, Poppy contended; all Amos ever wanted was money. Poppy said if'en a man was able-bodied but didn't work, then it weren't fittin' he should eat. Amos lived a spell away and came around only once or twice a year, but that was enough to sour Poppy's disposition for days.

Tenderly smoothing her hand over the old man's forehead, Glory buried her face in his hair and cried. "What am I going to do without you?" She was alone now—completely alone. She'd never had anyone but Poppy, and the cow, the old mule, a few chickens. And now she didn't have Poppy.

It took her two days to dig the grave. Glory washed the old hermit and dressed him in a clean shirt and pants. Afterward, she set his battered hat on his head, tilting it at a rakish angle the way Poppy liked it. Stepping back to survey her work, she smiled. "You look mighty perky, Poppy." Then she dissolved into tears and couldn't do a thing for the next few hours.

She didn't know how to let Amos know about Poppy's passing; the thought brought only relief. The farther away Amos stayed, the better she liked it. He wasn't right in the head, and worse, he was mean. Once she'd seen him hit his mule so hard with one of his big hands, the animal wore the mark a week later. He'd boasted about the men he'd killed and the women he'd mistreated. Glory didn't think he should be proud of his actions, but they seemed to amuse him.

Amos would pin her with a black-eyed stare until she'd squirm in her chair, heat igniting her cheeks. Finally, he'd laugh and look away but not until he was satisfied that she was weak from fright. He was an evil man, and she hoped she'd never have to set eyes on him again.

It took all of her might to get Poppy from the shanty to the grave-side. She didn't weigh much, but she was sturdy. Poppy had been proud of her strength, and today she worked hard to live up to his praise. Grasping him under the arms, she dragged Poppy's lifeless form down the ravine, careful to keep his pants and shirt as clean as possible. The journey to the grave site thirty yards away took most of the afternoon.

She shoveled the last spadeful of dirt onto the grave and mounded it up. Straightening, she listened to the silence. The stillness overwhelmed her. No Poppy's voice calling her to supper, no sounds of him putting the animals down for the night.

Not one other living soul to share the empty days.

"I cain't help but feel like I'm leavin' something undone," she said to no one, pondering what that something might be.

She remembered the time Poppy brought home a picture he'd found, saying it'd probably fallen out of a passing wagon. It showed some people standing around an open grave. The women were weeping into their handkerchiefs, and the men held their hats over their hearts, real respectful-like.

"Surely they must have spoken a word or two over whoever was in that hole." Glory thought long and hard. "Well, I reckon I ain't rightly sure one way or the other. . . . I would sure hate to find out later I was supposed to say something and didn't."

She tried to gather her thoughts as she kicked at a rock. Seeing as how she didn't own a handkerchief, she took off her hat and held it over her heart.

For a moment she searched for words. "Don't rightly know what to say. . . . Poppy, you was a good man, and you sure was good to me. I thank you for pickin' me up off that trail when I fell out of that wagon. Weren't something that just any ole body would've done . . . well, guess most anyone would've picked me up, but not everybody would've kept me and loved me the way you did. I'm much obliged, Poppy. I loved you too—a powerful lot—and I'm gonna miss you something fierce." She had to stop now because tears were choking her.

The cow waited nearby, wanting to be milked. Molasses, the old mule, munched on late summer grass near the lean-to. A couple of hens shook their feathers before flying to the nest to roost. Everything seemed normal, yet nothing would ever be the same.

Sighing, she laid a clump of sunflowers on the fresh dirt, wishing for a proper marker. Rocks would have to do for now, but she fashioned them in the form of a fish. Poppy loved to fish. She'd spent many a day on the riverbank catching catfish with him. She carried the shovel back to the lean-to and stored it before she milked Bess, who by now was looking a mite uncomfortable.

After the burial, days blurred. She got out of bed at the same time, did the same chores, listening for the sound of Poppy's voice. Every night she visited the grave site and wept from loneliness. It was the first time she'd experienced separation, and the empty feeling deep inside her hurt something awful. She had no one to talk to, no one to explain the hollowness.

"I don't know what to do, Bess," she whispered, leaning against the cow's warm flank while she milked. The fragrant smell of Bess's coat and the warm milk hitting the cool bucket gave her a measure of comfort. This animal was a friend, someone she knew when the rest of her world was void of anything familiar.

Warm weather gave way to blistering heat. Fireflies kept her company at night. By day, she hunted her food and cared for the animals in silence. At night, when the isolation felt as heavy as an iron blanket, she talked to the mule for companionship, sharing stories of her day.

"Though it don't seem it, winter will be here in a few months, and I'm afraid," she whispered to the old mule. "Saw a woolly worm this afternoon. His coat was black and thick; it's going to be a bad winter."

Poppy had taken to town a few times, so she knew there was one not more than a couple days' ride. Should she leave the shanty before the snows came? The thought terrified her. Life in the woods was the only thing she knew. Squirrels and chipmunks were her friends; she wouldn't know how to live around other people. But she wasn't sure she could survive a brutal winter alone in the woods, either.

One night Glory sat straight up in bed, reaching for the rifle when she heard someone pounding on the front door and shouting, "Let me in, girl! I know you're in there!"

Amos! He continued banging on the door with his enormous fists, muttering drunken threats between poundings.

Sliding out of bed, she crouched beside it, her fingers tightening around the gun's stock. When Amos was drinking, he was mean as a wolverine. Poppy had warned her to never let him in when he was in such a state.

The heavy bar across the door rattled. "Come on, Glory girl! Open up the door and let Uncle Amos in! It's hot out here!"

He wasn't her uncle—he was no kin to her, and now that Poppy was dead, she didn't have to pretend that he was. What did he want? Why was he here in the middle of the night pounding on her door? Her heart thumped in her throat. Had he found out that Poppy was dead? How could he know?

Amos's voice dropped to a menacing growl. "Open the door, Glory. I've come for my money." He shoved his weight against the oak, and Glory slid under the bed. Her fingers closed around the trigger, fear choking her.

He knew. Somehow he knew Poppy was dead, and he was here to take the gold Poppy kept hidden in a pouch beneath the floor.

Amos slammed his bulk against the door, trying to break it down. Glory closed her eyes, silently praising Poppy for building the shanty out of strong oak. Trembling, she listened to Amos's repeated attempts to enter. Over and over, he threw his weight against the door. She could hear him swearing violently under his breath, threatening her with unimaginable, vile acts.

Trembling, she gripped the Hawkins until her hands hurt. Other than hunting food, she'd never shot another living, breathing thing, but she intended to shoot Amos if he broke that door down. She could hear her own breath coming in ragged gasps as his threats became more threatening and vile now.

She kept her eyes shut and waited. If he gained entrance, he would kill her and take the gold. Images raced through her mind—images of the rage burning in his dark eyes, corn liquor coursing through his veins, his big hands doubled and ready to hit, greed spurring him to madness.

"I want that gold, Glory! It's mine and I mean to have it!"

She kept quiet, refusing to answer. *Give up and go away, Amos. You're not coming in!*

Then there was silence, and the night seemed endless. It sounded as if Amos had left, and then she knew he was back. She could hear him chopping at the door with something, but the oak still held. A bottle shattered on the porch, and he bellowed in rage. The stench of corn liquor drifted under the crack beneath the door.

Fueled by whiskey, Amos slammed against the door—over and over until Glory was certain he would come flying into the room at any moment.

Getting out from under the bed and standing up, she positioned herself a few feet away from the doorway, waiting for him. She hefted the loaded rifle to her shoulder, squinted, and took aim. The room was dark. She couldn't see a thing, but she knew where to point, and there weren't many better with a gun than she. If Amos came through that door, she'd drop him like a hot rock.

Suddenly silence fell over the cabin again. The pounding stopped. Straining to hear, Glory eased closer to the door. Had he given up and left? Long seconds passed while she waited, conscious only of her frayed breathing.

The windowpane behind her shattered. Whirling, she fired, aware of the sound of more breaking glass. Her heart threatened to leap out of her chest as she dropped to her knees and crawled toward the front door. He was at the back of the house now; she had to escape. If he trapped her in the cabin, she wouldn't have a chance.

Bounding to her feet, she lifted the bar, threw open the door, and bolted outside. The night was pitch black, a heavy cloud cover obscuring the moon. Racing toward the lean-to, she bent low, her bare feet covering the ground silently. He wouldn't be able to see her, not in this blackness.

The smell of hay and cow dung rushed over her when she slipped inside the crudely built shelter and threaded her way to the back of the stall. When she was a child, she'd hidden here from Poppy many a time when they were playing hide-and-seek. She could hear Amos shouting her name, cursing as he staggered about in the dark searching for her. The hunt went on for hours. Toward dawn, he finally staggered onto the front porch and collapsed from drunken exhaustion.

Seizing her chance, Glory shot from the lean-to and raced to the back of the cabin. She climbed through the broken window and hurriedly gathered her knapsack with her extra pair of pants and shirt, a jacket, some bacon and a few cold biscuits, and the pouch of gold that she took from beneath the shanty floor. She quickly pulled on her scuffed leather boots.

Amos's besotted snores filled the cabin as she carefully eased the front door open and gingerly stepped over his sprawled form.

His right hand snaked out and latched onto her ankle. "You're not going anywhere, girlie."

Bringing the butt of the gun down on his hand, Glory broke his hold. Howling, he struggled to sit up, but Glory swung the rifle a second time and knocked him cold. With a moan, he slumped to his side and lay lifeless, blood seeping from a wound on his head.

Scrambling off the porch, Glory raced to the lean-to and swung open the door. "Shoo!" she yelled at Bess.

The chickens started on their nests, squawking as she raced through the coop and opened the back door. She drove the cow out, making a clear passage for the hens' freedom.

A moment later, she fastened a bedroll and her knapsack on back of the mule and swung aboard. The last she saw of Amos, he was sprawled on the front porch, lying amid the remains of a shattered whiskey bottle.

She didn't know if she had killed him or not. But by now, she didn't rightly care.

Chapter Two

Oh, Molasses!"

Hands on her hips, Glory stood beside the lifeless mule a day and a half later, feeling helpless. She'd depended on that mule to get her to—well, somewhere. They weren't very far from the cabin, and she was sure that Amos would try to follow her, once he regained consciousness. *If* he regained consciousness. Had she killed him? The thought gave her a bellyache. She hadn't intended to kill him, just escape him. When it came to gold, Amos was determined.

She studied the dead mule. Molasses, on the other hand, had never been determined about anything, except going to the barn.

"Well, ole friend, you gave us the best you had, and I thank you for it." Glory knelt and patted the mule's rough hide. Poppy had brought Molasses home one day when Glory was very small. He'd bought him from a down-on-his-luck trader. Now Molasses was dead, and she was afoot.

Hefting the bedroll, her pack, and the Hawkins over one shoulder, she struck off. She was not sure where she was going, but she knew she couldn't sit in the middle of the road and twiddle her thumbs. Poppy had headed this direction every spring when he'd gone to town for supplies. To her way of thinking, there had to be people in this direction, and where there were people, there was opportunity to start a new life. A new life was what she needed the most right now.

That and a mule.

She plodded along the faint trail for some time, shifting the pack from one shoulder to the other until hunger made her stop and dig into her meager cache of supplies. She was glad she had fried up the last of the bacon and made that batch of biscuits the day before Amos arrived. She'd have enough food for another day or two if she was careful.

Sitting down on the pack with her rifle across her knees, Glory munched on the bacon and biscuit slowly, trying to make it last. The sun was straight overhead when she heard the creak of wagon wheels. Both excited and apprehensive, she waffled between the choice of flagging down strangers or hiding until they passed.

"Better a ride than blisters on your feet," she decided, quickly jamming the last bite of biscuit into her mouth. Wiping her face with the back of her hand, she peered down the road, waiting for the wagon to come into sight. She hoped it wasn't Amos—if it was, she'd bolt like a jackrabbit.

The tall ribs of a prairie schooner with a double hitch of oxen came over a rise. Glory's mouth went dry. A man—a big man—much younger than Poppy, sat on the driver's seat; his hat was pulled low over his face.

The mid-July sun was hot, so hot she could hardly breathe. Swallowing, she eased out in the road, thankful that it wasn't Amos and hoping it wasn't something worse.

◞◞◟

Coughing, Mary Everly leaned forward on the wagon seat. "Is that someone standing in the road?" she asked, squinting.

Jackson Lincoln was wondering that himself.

"The owner of the dead mule we passed aways back, I'd venture."

Jackson smiled at the earnest youngster who hovered near his shoulder. He'd had his doubts when he left Westport a few days ago to escort five women to Denver City to be mail-order brides. It was the most unusual assignment he'd ever undertaken. When he'd first seen his charges, he'd almost backed out of the job; they seemed awfully young to be traveling such a long way. They were orphans, too old to be adopted and, therefore, an unwanted liability. The head of the orphanage had allowed the girls to sign marriage contracts with Tom Wyatt, a broker who had promised to secure a good husband for each one of them.

But a couple of days into the trip his worries had been proven false. The girls were pleasant and helpful, passing the time amicably. Mary was fifteen, he guessed. Patience, Ruth, Harper, and Lily—all around the same age. Not one of them was certain about anything except that she had no home unless he could safely deliver her to Wyatt in Colorado.

Jackson suspected why some of the girls had never been adopted. Mary was sickly and pale with a persistent cough. Patience, at sixteen, he figured, was gentle in nature but addled at times. She'd stop talking in midsentence to think about something, and he'd found her more than once conversing with a bird on the limb of a tree.

Harper was a hard one to figure out. Her mother had soured her on all men, leaving Harper tough as leather. Thought to be fourteen, she was the youngest and a clear-cut troublemaker with a razor-sharp tongue. Harper looked out for herself and tended to irritate people. Just the opposite of Patience, who would mother the others, making sure everyone was comfortable before she took to her own bedroll.

Then there was Ruth—the serious, most educated one, who looked on the positive side of the worst circumstance. Ruth was certain a wonderful new life lay over the next rise. Jackson wasn't so sure of that. Experience had taught him otherwise. Caution made him one of the best wagon masters around, even if there was only one wagon on this assignment.

Ruth's opposite was Lily, who laughed easily, her eyes dancing with mischief. Jackson strongly suspected that this fifteen-year-old was bound for trouble before the trip was over. She was too full of life for him to think otherwise.

"Who is it, do you suppose?" Lily leaned out of the wagon over Jackson's left shoulder, straining for a better look.

"I don't know, but we're about to find out."

Hauling back on the heavy reins, Jackson drew the team alongside the thin youth. Clearly, the teenage boy had outgrown his dirty cotton trousers. The hems crowded the tops of his scuffed leather boots. Jackson's eyes touched on the faded flannel shirt that was too big across the shoulders. The brim of the battered leather hat hung down over his forehead, obscuring half the youth's face. One thing for certain: he handled the Hawkins like someone accustomed to having it close at hand. The wagon rolled to a halt, and the boy shuffled his feet.

"Got a problem?" Jackson asked.

The wiry youth squinted up at him, and Jackson noticed his smooth cheeks. He wasn't even old enough to shave, and he looked almost feminine under all that grime.

"Mule up and died on me."

"Where're you going?"

"To town."

The boy was young; Jackson noticed his voice hadn't dropped yet. "Climb aboard, but the rifle goes in the back."

The stranger hesitated briefly before handing it up. Jackson passed the weapon back to Lily.

The youth fixed him with a stare. "I want it back."

Jackson met his troubled gaze, then scanned the dirt on the youth's face. "You'll get it back once you reach where you're going."

The girls didn't like handling guns, which suited Jackson just fine. Then he didn't have to worry about their getting hurt. But the boy was another matter. He could be an outlaw, or he could be down on his luck as he claimed. Jackson wasn't taking any chances.

The boy slung his bedroll and pack up into the storage box and shinnied up beside Jackson, who caught a whiff of the young man and regretted the invitation. The kid stunk—smelled as bad as rancid meat. The girls, who had crowded to the open flap at the front of the wagon to eye the stranger curiously, immediately moved farther back. Mary joined them. Jackson hoped he could keep the boy downwind as much as possible.

Slapping the reins over the rumps of the oxen, he kept an eye on the newcomer from the corner of his eye. "Lost your mule, huh?" The loaded wagon slowly traversed the rutted trail.

"Yes, sir. Died on me clean as a whistle."

"Where's your family?"

"Don't have any. Mostly just had the mule and Poppy. Poppy died a few weeks back."

"That right."

The boy watched the road. Jackson noticed he was gripping the seat like it was going one way and he was about to go the other. When the lad noticed Jackson staring, he turned to eye him and asked, "Where're you heading?"

"Colorado."

"Colorado. Is that far?"

"A dreadfully long way," Mary declared from the back of the wagon. "We're going to Denver City to be mail-order brides."

The youth turned to look over his shoulder. "Brides? You're gonna marry someone you've never met?"

Mary nodded, a friendly expression in her hazel eyes. "A gentleman by the name of Tom Wyatt is paying our way. Mr. Wyatt arranges marriages for young women. We've signed a contract with him, and he in turn will provide us with suitable husbands."

The boy turned back to look at Jackson, who was working the reins to avoid a deep pothole.

"How far have you come?" Patience asked the boy. The girls all gradually shifted back to the front to join the conversation while keeping upwind of their guest.

"Don't know . . . left the cabin 'bout two days ago." The boy kept his eyes trained on the road. "Buried Poppy there . . . dug the grave myself."

"Poppy?" Harper poked her round, coffee-colored face over Lily's shoulder. "Who on earth's Poppy?"

The boy blinked as if he'd never seen a dark-skinned person before. "Don't rightly know—just a man, I guess. He found me on the trail when I fell outta my pa's wagon and took on the job of raising me."

"Found you?" the girls chorused.

Lily's eyes widened. "Where are your real folks?"

The boy stiffened. "Don't know that either. It's always been just me and Poppy." The boy shifted as if he'd rather not continue the discussion.

"Then you're an orphan like us," Ruth said.

"Don't know about that, but I'm mighty glad you came along."

Jackson smiled as he listened to the friendly chatter. The boy was so candid.

"What happened to your Poppy?" Ruth asked.

"Went to sleep and never woke up. Guess that was good. He didn't suffer, I suppose."

"You buried him?" Jackson asked. "And started off on your own?"

"Yes, sir. Off to find me a new life."

"So are we." Mary scooted closer. "A new life, with husbands and hopes for families and children one day. They told us at the orphanage that more and more people are moving west and building towns with stores and houses."

"It's an exciting adventure," Lily bubbled, "and we can hardly wait to get there. But Mr. Lincoln says Denver City is a long way off."

Jackson grinned. "A very long way, ladies. With any luck, we'll be there in plenty of time before the snows."

Right now, that was Jackson's main concern—to complete the six-hundred-eighty-five-mile trip to Denver City before late September, and he wanted nothing to slow them down. What concerned him most was getting through the high divide between the Arkansas and Platte Rivers before snow, even though it was now July and snow seemed a long way off. It was a crucial pass, and wagons were advised to get past the spot as early as possible.

"I'll just be riding to the next town," the boy said.

Jackson nodded. "Should be there sometime tomorrow."

Late that afternoon Jackson pulled the oxen off the road and went another mile before stopping in a grassy field beside a running stream. "Black Jack Creek is a good place to camp for the night. Good grazing for the animals with fresh water nearby."

"Why, it *is* almost evening," Ruth said, surprise registering on her flushed features.

The afternoon had passed pleasantly enough. The boy had warmed up to the girls when they'd stopped for a half hour to rest the team and let the group pick the blackberries growing thick along the roadside.

Jackson got out of the wagon and unhitched the team. The boy leaped down nimbly, dragging his bedroll and pack with him.

The girls quickly set about making camp. As they did their chores, the newcomer pitched in to help. Jackson was happy to see the youth was no shirker. The young man gathered wood, and by the time Jackson had watered the oxen, he had a fire going in a circle of rocks and a coffeepot bubbling to one side.

Jackson staked the oxen where they could graze during the night, then joined the others at the fire. The boy jumped up to pour him a cup of scalding black coffee.

Jackson smiled and thanked him. "I didn't catch your name."

The boy glanced away, and Jackson wondered if he was shy.

"Glory."

The wagon master's smile slowly faded. "Glory?"

"That's right. Name's Glory." The kid looked straight ahead.

"Glory." Jackson took a sip of coffee. He hadn't expected this. "What's your last name?"

"Don't have one. Name's just Glory."

Lily burst into laughter. "You're a girl?"

"Of course I'm a girl," Glory spit out. "What'd you think I am?"

Mary blushed. "Well, your trousers—"

"And the way you look . . . all dirty—"

"Harper!" Ruth scowled.

"You thought I was a *boy?*" Glory sprang to her feet, ready to fight, until Jackson calmly reached out to restrain her. The waif's eyes moved to the simple gingham dresses the others wore, and she frowned. "I ain't no boy."

"We can see that now." Patience smiled. "We just didn't expect to find a girl alone on the trail."

Glory glanced at Jackson, then back at the girls. "Well, I didn't expect to see a covered wagon with five girls and a man in it either, but I recognized a wagon when I saw one."

Lily giggled, and Mary smothered a cough. The tense moment passed, and Jackson poured himself a second cup of coffee.

"How come you don't have a last name?" Lily asked.

"I've been *trying* to get one. Poppy tried to find me a husband, but that didn't work out."

Jackson choked on a swallow of coffee that went down the wrong way. Glory leaned over and whacked him on the back until the spasm passed.

"Married?" he choked.

Glory nodded. "Been trying to get married, but men are fickle. They keep bringing me back."

Patience's eyes widened with surprise, and the other girls snickered.

Jackson pinned them with a stern look. "Ladies."

Glory shrugged. "Poppy found three likely candidates before he died, but each one brought me back home before the day was out. Almost made it to supper with one, but Ralph didn't like it when I told him he didn't know beans about turnips. So, I've got just *Glory* for a name."

She pulled off the battered hat and thrust her hands into the released mass of curly, cinnamon-colored hair. Jackson frowned. If she'd taken off her hat earlier, he'd have realized that she was a female. She was a comely young woman, perhaps a bit older than Ruth, with slightly tilted gray green eyes in an oval face. Despite the dirt, Jackson noted a few freckles sprinkled across a finely carved nose above a neatly defined mouth. If only she didn't smell so bad. Poppy clearly hadn't emphasized regular baths and clean clothing.

"Well, far as I know, there's no law about not having a last name." Jackson finished the coffee and pitched the grounds into the fire. "Best we get supper over with early. We leave at first light."

Weary from the day's journey, the group ate supper and washed dishes. Each girl took a bedroll from the back of the wagon but seemed hesitant on where to spread her blanket. One waited for the other to make a decision. Jackson spread his bedroll at the front of the wagon, giving the girls privacy.

Standing upwind, Ruth glanced at Glory. "You get first choice on where to sleep."

Glory's eyes surveyed the possibilities, and she shrugged. "Don't rightly matter."

Lily licked one finger and held it up in a clear effort to determine the direction of the slight breeze. Then the girls spread their blankets upwind from Glory.

Glory wondered if she'd done something wrong. She'd been real polite, answered all their questions best she could, and she thought they were getting along right well for strangers. But clearly nobody wanted to sleep near her.

Jackson issued a gentle reminder from the front of the wagon. "Ladies, it's getting late."

Tucked in her bedroll, Ruth opened a leather-bound book and smiled at Glory. "We were reading in Psalms last night. Psalm twenty-three."

Glory listened to Ruth's melodic voice as she read words that Glory had never heard before, beautiful words. She didn't understand what they meant, but they kept her attention. She'd seen a book like that once. Poppy had brought it home and said a lot of people put store in the words, but since neither she nor Poppy could read, they didn't know what it said. She glanced at Jackson, who lay listening to Ruth read. Did he know what the strange words meant? Did he count them useful? He must, she decided, because he didn't make Ruth stop.

When Ruth finished reading and closed the book, the girls bowed their heads and Patience began to speak. "Lord, we thank you for a safe journey today and for food tonight. We thank you again for Jackson, who is taking us to a new life in Colorado. And we pray for a restful night of sleep and a good day tomorrow. Amen."

The other girls echoed, "Amen."

Ruth started to put the book back into its waterproof pouch.

"What is that?" Glory asked.

Ruth turned. "This?"

Glory nodded. "It has pretty words."

"Why . . . it's a Bible. Haven't you seen a Bible before?" Mary asked and then dissolved into a fit of wheezing and coughing. Glory noticed that Mary coughed more as the sun went down. She seemed to have a powerful affliction.

"Don't reckon I have. . . . Poppy had something like it that he'd found on the trail." She looked away. "Couldn't neither one of us read."

Patience looked shocked. "I thought everyone knew about the Bible and read it."

"Well, I didn't. And I ain't read it," Glory admitted softly.

Harper's head popped out of her bedroll. "You can't read? Even *I* can read. Some."

Ruth leaned closer to Glory. "Don't pay any attention to Harper. I'd rather hear someone read the beautiful words that God has given us than read them myself."

"Dawn comes early," Jackson called. "Time to turn in." He doused the lantern, and the girls settled down for the night.

Poppy had said that same thing every night before blowing out the lamp. "Time to turn in." The familiar phrase reminded her of her loss as she rolled into her blankets. She lay on her back and stared up at the stars and wished that she could have Poppy back. Knowing that she couldn't, she wished she were already in "town" starting her new life.

"Good night," Patience whispered.

Rolling to her side, Glory smiled. "Good night."

For the first time in weeks, she wasn't alone, and it felt good. So very good. And she'd learned a few things this day. Not all people were as bad as Amos; and if she tried, she could walk a long, long way.

Oh, Poppy, I wish I was back home in my own bed and you were sleeping across the room. Her eyes stung, and she rubbed them. The wind must have kicked up some dust. She coughed, mumbling under her breath.

Jackson's gentle voice drifted to her. "Go to sleep, Glory."

"Yes, sir. Thank you for giving me a ride. I'm much obliged."

"You're welcome."

If nothing else, Poppy had taught her manners, but she suspected there was a lot Poppy hadn't, or couldn't have, taught her.

Closing her eyes, she listened to the fire crackle and burn lower. It was good that she'd run away. If Amos had followed her, maybe he'd given up by now and gone back to wherever he'd come from.

And it was good that this wagonload of girls and Jackson had come along when they had. Real good. She didn't feel so alone now.

She fell asleep thinking how nice it felt to be with people—people who talked and laughed and knew about places called "town."

Chapter Three

The sun was below the tops of the trees when the prairie schooner rolled into Squatter's Bend the following evening.

Glory was dumbfounded by the bustling activity; she couldn't do anything but stare openmouthed at the wide, dusty street and all of the funny-looking buildings. She'd only gone with Poppy when she was a young child, before she could be left alone at the shanty. She didn't remember the buildings being so tall and odd looking, as if they were more of an afterthought than an honest-to-goodness intention.

Mary leaned over to tap Glory's mouth shut. "You'll catch a fly. Haven't you ever seen people before?"

"I've seen a few, but never this many in one place."

Glory couldn't get enough of the strange sights. She was reminded of the picture Poppy had of all those men standing at a graveside, all those women crying. She had thought it was really something and had stared at those bawling folks for hours on end. But gawking at a picture full of people had been nothing like the spectacle playing out before her today. In her eyes, Squatter's Bend bested a burying scene any day of the week.

If she and Poppy spotted a passing wagon twice a year, they were lucky, leastways she'd thought so. Then there'd only been a ma and pa and a few young'uns in it, never this many people and never all bunched in one place. Fact was, she hadn't known there were so many people in the world! On second thought, she decided that there weren't any more people; they all had to be here in Squatter's Bend.

Buggies and wagons pulled in and away from the fronts of buildings, their wheels rattling on the dirt road, kicking up dust. Men whistled to their teams and threw friendly shouts at each other as they rode off. Mamas, their arms full of fat bundles, herded small children across the street like protective hens. Glory strained to get a better look at the packages. What could they have bought? Probably most anything they liked. And the smells! She sucked in drafts of mouthwatering aromas, most notably that of baking bread, wishing with all her might that she could smell butter, too. Her mouth pooled at the thought of hot bread and butter, and she swallowed repeatedly, craning her neck to try to see everything at once.

Mr. Jackson Lincoln sawed on the reins, and the wagon rolled to a stop in front of the tallest building, which sported a wide, white porch. After setting the brake, he carefully wrapped the reins around the handle before he turned to the girls. "Stay close. I don't want to have to hunt you up when I'm finished."

"Yes, sir, anything you say, sir." Harper's dark eyes flashed back at him as if he'd said something he shouldn't have. Glory wondered if the girl plain flat out carried a chip on her shoulder. This morning at breakfast, Jackson Lincoln had asked Harper to pass the butter, and she'd told him to get it himself—she weren't his servant. Jackson had gone on eating like the butter wouldn't add to the biscuit, but Glory had known it would. She had jumped up and gotten the butter for him herself. Even dug around in the box and found some apple butter to go with it. No, it just seemed to her that Harper didn't like taking orders from a man—least of all Jackson Lincoln.

"It won't take me long to get staples ordered. We'll pick up the supplies before we leave town in the morning." He glanced at Glory. "You gonna be all right here by yourself?"

"Yes, sir." Glory swallowed the sudden, growing lump in her throat. "I'll be just fine. Thank you, sir."

Leastwise, she sure hoped so. She'd never been away from the shanty, and she didn't know what to expect. Fact was, nothing she'd ever known had prepared her for this, but she guessed now that she was on her own, she'd learn to handle it.

The wagon master smiled, a right nice smile, and she noticed a dimple in his left cheek. She couldn't say his age—hard to tell. But he was older than she and probably forty years younger than Poppy. As she watched, he jumped lithely from the wagon to the ground and disappeared into the general store. A bell over the door tinkled when he opened it, a sound Glory had never heard before but liked. It made a nice, welcoming noise that she thought sounded peaceful.

Harper climbed onto the seat Jackson had vacated and sniffed the fragrant aroma of baking bread. Closing her eyes, she grinned, her even white teeth flashing in the early morning sun. "Now don't that smell like paradise?"

Glory thought it smelled better than anything she'd ever smelled before, especially since she hadn't eaten much lately. With Poppy gone and supplies running low, she'd gone to bed hungry more often than not the past few weeks. And there hadn't been an abundance of vittles since she'd left the cabin. Shooting game hadn't seemed worthwhile, and then she'd accepted a ride with Jackson Lincoln and the girls, and she hadn't wanted to be any more trouble than she already was. That thought reminded her of why she was here with Jackson Lincoln: Amos.

A shudder leaked out when she thought of her narrow escape. Was Amos trailing her? Of course he was. Last night she'd told herself he'd give up, but she didn't really believe it. The more likely question was how long would it take him to find her? And when he did, he'd take her pouch of gold and leave her with nothing to her name. She wouldn't have the slightest means to start a new life. She didn't know how to do anything but hunt and fish, and from the looks of things in Squatter's Bend, there wasn't much call for the like.

Mary coughed, and Patience leaned over to gently arrange the shawl more snugly around her thin shoulders. "Put your handkerchief over your mouth, Mary," she said softly. "The dust will make your cough worse."

Mary nodded and complied. Glory could see the two girls were fond of each other.

Harper squirmed on the seat. "Shouldn't we get out of the wagon? Mr. Lincoln might be awhile, and I'd surely like to stretch my legs."

"Me, too," Ruth agreed.

The girls climbed out and Glory followed, her gaze drinking in the frantic bustle that didn't stop. Up the street, fire billowed from the blacksmith's pit, and the even rhythm of his hammer as he pounded the hot iron into shape echoed up and down the rutted street. Poppy had done what shoeing was necessary at the shanty; she'd tried her hand once but hadn't been good at it.

Glory edged closer to Mary, her bewilderment overwhelming at the moment.

"Don't be afraid," Mary whispered, clutching the hanky over her mouth. "Towns are always noisy places."

Glory didn't want the others to know how frightening the town was to her. She wasn't a baby—she could hold her own. "Ain't afraid. Just like to be near you." To prove it, she joined hands with Mary. Only seemed proper, seeing how nice they'd been to her.

Holding hands, two by two, the six young women ventured down the sidewalk, Glory gripping Mary's hand tensely. The girls paused in front of a dress shop to admire the array of pretty store-bought dresses and other goods in the window.

"Ain't those pretty," Harper breathed, and Glory thought maybe she'd forgotten her usual fierceness in the excitement.

"I had a red dress once," Ruth said softly. "It wasn't near as pretty as this one, but I liked it, and it fit better than most." She sighed. "I loved that dress."

Glory didn't want to mention that she'd never owned a dress in her life. Dresses like her new friends wore seemed to be the thing most young women wore instead of trousers. Another thing she learned from being in town.

"What happened to your red dress?" Lily asked Ruth.

"Wore out," Ruth replied wistfully. "Wore it until one day when I washed it, it fell clean apart."

A murmur of sympathy passed among the girls.

"How come you couldn't get another one?" Glory asked.

"When you live in an orphanage, you get what other people don't want," Patience explained. "Sometimes folks pass on things that are better than others. Occasionally a dress or coat that still has a few wearings left in it will be donated, but not often. An orphanage depends on the goodness of others, except folks couldn't afford much goodness at the one we came from."

"We learned to take what we got, make the most of it, and be grateful," Ruth added.

Glory studied the shiny material displayed on a form in the window and wondered how women could stand to wear such things. Why, getting through the brush with all that material dragging behind would be nigh to impossible. And the wind would whip up that skirt right smart-like.

"Never had a dress," Glory murmured, almost before she knew she was saying it.

"Never had a dress?" Lily moved to stand beside Ruth, upwind of Glory.

"No."

"Not ever?" Harper frowned. "How come? I thought every girl had a dress."

"Not me. Never had much use for one."

The women on the wagons who had come by the cabin wore faded dresses that more often than not hung loose on them, the hems sometimes ragged. None wore anything like what she saw in the window or even like those the women in this town wore. This dress was a pure wonderment. All that frilly lace and rows of ruffles would choke a horse.

Glory spied the boots sitting beside the dress in the window and grinned, pressing her nose against the cool glass. Now there was something she could use. Her boots had holes in the soles. She'd patched them with a bit of leather, but nothing lasted long, and the stitches let in water.

If she was careful where she stepped, she could wear her old boots out in the woods, but thick briars punched through the patches and the leather was soon eaten away again. When the snows had come, she'd padded the soles with rags to make do, but that was powerful lumpy to walk on and caused hurtful blisters.

Eyeing the durable leather boots, she thought about the gold in Poppy's pouch hidden under her belt. She didn't know how much it amounted to, but it was enough to get Amos riled. She could spend some of the money on a new pair of boots, but she didn't dare show it. If Amos was so bent on getting the gold, then others would be too. Besides, if she were to begin a new life without any skills, it would take every bit of the gold she had to stay alive until she figured a way to make a living.

"It is quite remarkable handiwork," Ruth observed, her eyes fastened on the window display. "Look at the fancy stitching along the bodice, and the way the skirt hangs so beautifully from that point in front."

Harper made a disgusted noise. "Where would anyone wear something like that?" But Glory noticed Harper didn't look away; she just kept staring at the pretty red dress like it was a pork chop bone and she was a hungry pup.

Jackson Lincoln came out of the mercantile and whistled shrilly. Glory jumped at the sound, but the girls, apparently accustomed to this signal, turned immediately from their daydreaming and started back toward the wagon. Glory trailed behind.

Jackson grinned as the girls approached, and Glory admired his right fine-looking eyes. They were blue, the color of eggs she'd found in robins' nests each spring. And when he smiled, his white teeth flashed and his cheeks creased like he smiled a lot. "All set, ladies?"

Ruth nodded, smiling back at him pretty as you please. "Got the supplies ordered?"

He chuckled as if he really liked her, and Glory felt funny inside, kind of empty.

"They'll be ready first thing in the morning." He glanced at Glory, and his smile reappeared, making her feel warm inside. "Had decided to buy our staples when we reached this point of the journey. We'll be camping right outside town tonight. You're welcome to stay with us."

"No," Glory said, dying inside to accept his kind offer. She wasn't looking forward to seeing that prairie schooner leave without her. "I'm starting my new life, so I might as well get to it."

Swallowing against a dry throat, she glanced up the street, her gaze taking in the orange glow of the setting sun. Things were settling down a bit, not as busy as they'd been earlier. Loud music now spilled from a doorway; men were coming and going from the building.

Gunshots rang out suddenly. Glory jumped, automatically crowding closer to Jackson. The crowd scattered like buckshot, ducking behind posts and water troughs. Then two men wearing tin stars on their shirts appeared from another building and quickly took in hand the two men who'd been staggering down the street and shooting off their guns. Glory didn't understand what was going on, but she'd just as soon it hadn't happened.

When the excitement cleared, Jackson took her arm and steered her down the street. "You're sure you won't stay the night with us? This town looks kind of rough."

"You don't have to start your new life this very minute," Mary encouraged. "You can spend the night in camp with us, then return in the morning when we come for our supplies."

The other girls chimed in to agree, and Glory felt real proud to have such good friends. She'd never had even one friend before, unless she counted Poppy, and now she had a bunch. But she couldn't accept their generosity. She'd already declared her independence, and Poppy would expect her to take care of herself.

There wasn't a better place to start than here, right now, in this town . . . among all these strange people. "Thank you much, but I'll be staying here tonight."

"All right then, load up, ladies. It will be dark soon."

Before they got into the wagon, each girl gave Glory a parting hug. She would have liked for those acts of kindness to go on longer, but the girls kept the friendly embraces brief.

Handsome Jackson Lincoln swung himself onto the wagon seat, as the women scrambled aboard. Ruth claimed the bench seat beside Jackson, Glory noticed, and she didn't blame her. That's the spot she'd have chosen.

Then it was time to leave. Glory stood on the edge of the road, waving until the wagon disappeared from sight, trailing a faint cloud of dust. She drew a deep breath to settle her quivering stomach and tried to ignore the wave of loneliness that washed over her, the likes of which she'd never felt before.

Squaring her shoulders, she sighed. Wasn't nothing left to do but get to making her new life.

She set off down the walk, having no idea where she was going or where she'd spend the night. Smells coming from a building with a wide window drew her. She peeked in to see people, happy people who smiled at each other, eating at long tables. Her stomach knotted with hunger. Her noon meal had been a biscuit and bacon left over from breakfast, and it had satisfied her at the time, but that had been a long time ago. Wondering just how one got to eat in there, she forgot where she was until a gruff-looking woman with gravy stains on her white apron came out to shoo her away.

"Get on, girl. Quit annoying the customers."

Hurt, Glory turned and strode down the planked sidewalk, head held high as if she had somewhere to go. Before long, she slowed. The rough planks hurt her feet through the thin soles of her worn boots. She hadn't noticed before, but a wind had sprung up, a wind with rain in it if she knew the signs. And it was getting dark. She pulled her thin jacket closer, wishing it fit better. It wouldn't do much to block out dampness. She scanned the black sky. If it rained, it would take days for her clothes to dry, and wearing wet clothes was miserable, even in July. She'd gotten caught in storms a few times while out hunting, and she didn't look forward to it again.

She kept moving, following sounds and dodging threatening-looking men who eyed her either with pity or with another look she didn't understand at all. One threw her a coin. At first she was insulted and refused to pick it up, but then she decided that maybe the man would be upset if she didn't accept it. She didn't want charity, but then she'd never known anyone who had enough money to throw away. So she picked up the coin and stuck it in her pocket, hunched her shoulders against the dampness, and continued on down the street.

When she felt water well up in her eyes, Glory blinked hard and reminded herself of Poppy and how ashamed of her he'd be if she couldn't make her own way. She couldn't keep feeling sorry for herself. Stiffening her spine, she crossed the street and hurried toward a white clapboard building where men and women were gathering. Expensive buggies and fine-looking teams filled the yard, where a mellow light shone from lovely narrow windows. As she approached, the first stinging droplets of rain spattered on the dry road. The scent of rainwater hitting dry dust filled her senses.

A laughing couple carrying a baby entered the building, allowing warm light to spill out the door momentarily. A woman's lilting laughter and children's happy voices drifted to her, and she wished with all of her might that she could be a part of the festivities inside. Overhead, a bell tolled from the tower, its sweet sound filling the stormy night. She paused to look up, blinking rain out of her eyes. That sound called out to her, its friendliness beckoning to her. *Welcome, welcome, welcome,* it tolled. But then one of the finely dressed men spotted her and smiled, shooing her out of the way when he and his family passed. He was eyeing the Hawkins rifle she still clutched in one hand.

"Run along now," he said. "Services are about to start."

His little girl stared back at Glory with wide blue eyes before her mother pulled her forward and they disappeared inside the building.

Glory backed away, and the man pulled the big doors closed. A moment later, singing began, singing like she'd never heard before, and she was caught by the sound. How wonderful it was! The melodic sweetness washed over her like rich, thick honey as she stood in the rain and listened. Shutting her eyes, she pretended that she was in the warmth and light, singing the beautiful songs with all those nicely dressed folks.

Rain peppered down harder, reminding her that she was not part of what was happening inside, but still she hesitated to leave. The music was so beautiful. Finally, the thunder and lightning drove her to seek shelter, and she hurried across the street toward a row of tall buildings. Water soaked through the shoulders of her jacket and began seeping through the soles of her boots.

Driven into an alley for protection against the blowing rain, Glory found a large, wooden crate that offered temporary cover. Scrunching into the box, she ate a cold biscuit from her pack and watched the rain turn the street into rutted strips of mud.

Oh, Poppy, I miss you so much. Her heart ached nearly as much as the chill in her bones.

She wondered what Mary was doing tonight. She imagined her sitting by a warm fire, eating some of Ruth's fine cooking. Salt pork and brown beans. And, of course, the girls would be talking and laughing. Then, due to the rain, they'd go into the wagon to sleep. It might be close quarters, but they'd be dry and cozy, having each other for company.

Leaning against the back of the crate, she pulled her feet in tight and closed her eyes. Gripping her rifle tightly to her body to keep it dry, she thought of handsome Jackson Lincoln with eyes the color of robins' eggs. He'd been good enough to give her a ride into town, and he hadn't charged her a cent. How lucky Mary, Patience, Ruth, Harper, and Lily were to be traveling with a fine man like Jackson Lincoln, who would protect them and make sure they get to their destination, their new lives.

She drew a shaky breath and wished she were going somewhere, too. Wished with all her might that she had somewhere to go. Maybe she should have accepted one more night of their hospitality. It wouldn't have affected her independence. At least she would have been dry. It was still up to her to find her own way, to make a new life, but she regretted starting out on her own on this night, this cool, rainy night. A few more hours with her new friends would have been nice. A few less hours of being so alone.

A fierce wind rattled the brittle crate, and she pushed farther into the corner. Curling into a fetal position, she listened to the rolling thunder, her fingers still gripping the rifle, her teeth chattering more from fright than from cold. Men ran in and out of the building with the loud music, passing by the end of the alley. Women laughed louder. One woman had come out to roll a cigarette, the lantern light catching the red in her hair. She looked strange. Glory heard strains of the other music from across the street—the sweet, pure music coming from the building with the warm light. It seemed the two sounds warred with each other. One, loud and disturbing; the other, sweet and comforting. The sweeter singing told about a place called heaven and how they were all going to go there someday and walk on streets of gold.

Streets of gold. She closed her eyes.

Just imagine.

Gritting her teeth to keep them from chattering, she tried to find a comfortable spot. She'd heard Poppy mention that town called Heaven once. He'd said it was a place some folks hoped to go when they died, but he wasn't sure how they planned to get there. For days after, she'd lie in the grass in front of the shanty and stare up at the sky, trying to figure a way up there. It would take a mighty tall ladder, taller than any she'd ever seen, taller than any ever made.

Keeping her eyes shut, she listened to the glorious voices coming from the warm building, hoping that Poppy had gone to live in that town called Heaven and that someday she could go visit him. Wasn't likely, though. She didn't know where this Heaven was or how to get there. Right now, she wasn't overly fond of Squatter's Bend and not so sure it was where she wanted to start her new life.

And truthfully, she couldn't imagine how Poppy could have gotten to Heaven, because he certainly wasn't going anywhere the day she'd buried him six weeks ago.

She dozed, huddled against the blowing rain. Sometime during the night the music from both ends of the street stopped. Toward dawn, the rain slowed to a foggy drizzle.

It was full daylight when Glory awoke with a start, nearly dropping her rifle. Soaked to the skin, teeth chattering, her hair falling into her face, she crawled out of the crate. Stamping her feet, she tried to get the feeling back. She looked like a drowned rat and felt worse. If her new life was going to be anything like the past few hours, she hoped she would die young.

The town was strangely quiet, nothing like the day before. Creeping to the mouth of the alley, she watched from the shadows to see what was happening. Vapors of fog rose from the muddy streets, and the stillness was almost as frightening as the rowdiness of the day before.

Not many people were about. The few who stirred were shopkeepers removing shutters from store windows. The blacksmith's fire was flaming up again, fanned by bellows pumped by the same big man who had worked there yesterday. The thin man at the livery stable yawned sleepily as he scooped grain into a bin for the horses.

Glory turned at the sound of a lone wagon rolling into town. The prairie schooner appeared through the gray mist, and she almost cried out with relief when she spotted the tall form of Jackson Lincoln on the driver's seat and Mary's pale face peering over his shoulder.

A more welcome sight Glory had never seen. She longed to rush out to greet them, but she didn't. Instead, she shrank farther into the shadows, wishing she could hide somewhere until the traveling party collected provisions and left town. She couldn't bear for Jackson to see her like this: her boots sucking water, her clothes soaking wet and muddy, her hair stringing in her face and dripping inside her collar.

Frightened, Glory held onto the corner of the building and ignored the hunger gripping her belly.

"Glory?"

She recognized Ruth's voice and quickly shrank farther into the shadow of the alleyway.

"Glory!"

But she wasn't quick enough. Seconds later a strong grip lifted her to her feet. She peered up into Jackson Lincoln's handsome face, and she felt faint with embarrassment.

He eyed her condition; his cleanly shaven jaw was set with anger. "What did you do? Sleep under a downspout?"

Before Glory could respond to his query, the girls arrived, all talking at once.

"Glory!" Ruth exclaimed. "Why, you're wetter than an old hen!"

"Come, get out of those damp clothes before you catch your death," Patience exclaimed.

"Girl? What's *wrong* with you?" Harper's hands sprang to her hips. "Don't you know enough to get in out of the rain?"

Jackson interrupted the girls' excited babble. "Girls, you can ask Glory all the questions you want later. Right now, she needs dry clothes and, by the looks of things, hot coffee, and some eggs and bacon are in order." He turned back to eye Glory. "That won't slow you down but an hour or so, getting on with your new life, will it?"

Glory nodded meekly. No use lying to him now. He could clearly see that the first night of her new life hadn't exactly been a bragging success. "No, sir, hot coffee and eggs and bacon sounds real nice—thank you, sir."

He leaned close enough that she could smell the scent of his shaving soap as he chided gently, "The name is *Jackson*."

Glory glanced at the other girls. Mary nodded. "It's all right—we all call him Jackson."

Glory smiled between chattering teeth. "Yes, sir. Jack . . . Jack . . . Jackson."

She allowed the girls to lead her to the wagon, which Jackson had hitched to the rail in front of the mercantile. The girls helped her into the back, and Patience wrapped a light blanket around her shoulders.

Ruth rummaged in the food box and handed Glory a biscuit and bacon. "Here, have these for now. You must be starving," she said.

Glory's stomach clenched with hunger, but she forced herself to accept the food without snatching it out of Ruth's hand. "I'm all right," Glory said.

"No, you're not. You should have stayed with us."

Glory folded the whole biscuit into her mouth and chewed. It wasn't mannerly, but she wasn't in a mannerly mood this morning. She was mad—plain mad that she couldn't take better care of herself. What did Jackson think of her now? He probably thought she was a helpless, sissy female too foolish to get in out of the rain.

"My, it's a wonder you didn't catch your death last night," Lily scolded as she fished inside a trunk, sorting through clothing. "We slept warm as toast in here."

Patience toweled Glory's wet hair while Mary stripped her out of her wet clothing.

"Why didn't you come looking for us?" Lily asked. "We were camped just outside of town. You could have found us easily."

"Didn't need to find you." Glory wedged a fat strip of bacon into her mouth.

Lily and Patience exchanged a look that Glory couldn't make out.

Clearing her throat, Patience smiled. "Why don't we go over to the hotel and get you into a hot tub of water? Cleanliness is next to godliness, you know."

Ruth shook her head. Her penetrating gaze seemed to silence Patience. Glory wondered if Ruth knew she felt they were ganging up on her.

"Nowhere in the Bible does it say such a thing, Patience."

"Oh." Patience blushed. "I'd always heard—"

"Well, if it don't, it should," Harper grumbled.

Ruth gave her a stern look.

Lily reached for the dry clothing, and Glory shook her head and wadded another piece of bacon into her mouth. "Already had my bath."

Lily's face fell. "You did?"

"'Course." Glory felt both resentful and puzzled.

"You did *not*." Harper towered above her, hands on hips. "You slept in that alley in the rain. That's how come you smell like a wet dog."

Glory refused to look at her. She'd already decided they weren't go-

ing to be friends, though Glory felt beholden to her for her help. "Did
too—had one the day I buried Poppy, and before that I had my spring
bath, same as usual."

"Well . . . you can put these on." Lily handed Glory a dry shirt and a
pair of trousers. "I used to wear these when I helped in the orphanage
garden. They should be about the right size."

Glory hoped her eyes conveyed her appreciation. The last thing she
needed was to fuss with one of those dresses on top of all her other
troubles.

Jackson Lincoln emerged from the mercantile as Glory climbed from
the back of the wagon wearing Lily's trousers and shirt. They'd fit
someone who ate more biscuits than she did, but Glory wasn't complaining. The warm clothing was a heaping sight better than her wet
ones. Harper intercepted the wagon master on the sidewalk, her dark
eyes flashing.

"You know Glory slept in that alley last night? Sat there in the rain
all night."

"I suspected as much." He fixed Glory with a tolerant look, setting
his Stetson more firmly on his head. "You got a hankering to be a
duck?"

Glory hastily braided her hair and stuck the braid under her hat. "No,
sir, just don't want to be a burr under your saddle."

He patted the top of her head, then picked up a box of supplies and
loaded it into the back of the wagon. "You let me worry about that,
short stuff. The only burr under my saddle is getting these ladies to
Colorado ahead of winter snows." He stored the box and turned back to
face the girls. "Mary, take Glory to the café and get a hot meal in her.
Ruth, Patience, Lily, Harper? You help load supplies. It'll take most of
the day, so let's get about it."

Mary and Glory set off for the café, and the others started toward the
mercantile.

"We tried to bathe her," Lily whispered when she passed Jackson on
the way into the store.

He frowned. "No luck?"

"Said she had her bath the day she buried Poppy and one last spring."

A laugh started in Jackson's throat and bubbled up into an amused
rumble in his chest. The girls paused on the mercantile porch and
turned to determine the source of his amusement.

"Ain't funny," Lily whispered, struggling to keep up with the wagon master's long strides. "She just plain *stinks*." She pinched her nose daintily.

"The dousing she took last night didn't help?"

Lily made another face. "Made it worse—she smells like an old dog when he's been out in the rain too long."

"Well, we can't hurt her feelings. If she doesn't want to take a bath, we can't make her. If she won't join up with us, guess it won't be a problem come morning."

"Yes, sir, suppose it won't. She's right sweet—a shame she won't agree to come with us. I'll bet that nice Mr. Wyatt could find a husband for her, too. Can you talk to her, Jackson? She hasn't got anywhere to go, and I think she's afraid but too stubborn to admit it."

"She's a grown woman, Lily. She's welcome to come with us, but I can't force her."

"Yes, sir. I suppose you're right."

Jackson opened the door to the mercantile and gave the young woman a lopsided grin. "But on the off chance that she changes her mind and decides to come with us, keep after her about that bath. OK, Lily?"

Lily shuddered. "Intended to do that anyway, Jackson."

Chapter Four

Shove that barrel to this end!"

"There's room for another pound of bacon over here!"

The Lincoln party worked until the sun hung like a red-hot globe over the town. Sweat poured off temples, and tempers cooled as quickly as they flared. At the end of the day, Lily collapsed on the general store's porch step and declared that her back was near broke. Worn to the nubbin, the others agreed. Every last one of them.

Perched on the stoop, the travelers shared dippers of tepid water from the rain barrel and looked back on their long day. Bacon had been stored in boxes surrounded by bran to prevent fat from melting away. They'd packed fat slabs of pork in the bottom of the wagon to keep them cool. Flour had been stitched inside stout, well-sewn, double-canvas sacks, twenty pounds in each bundle.

Ruth had stood over an iron pot behind the store, preserving butter by boiling it thoroughly and skimming off the scum as it rose to the top until it was clear like oil. She'd placed it in tin canisters, and Jackson had soldered them shut. Mary had sacked sugar and put it in a dry place.

Dried and canned vegetables were stored in tins for travel. Lily said she would make pemmican later: buffalo meat cut into thin strips and hung up to dry under the sun or over a slow fire.

It had taken the better part of the day to prepare for their long trek from Westport, Missouri, to Denver City and eventually to the foothills of Pike's Peak where Tom Wyatt lived.

As far as Glory was concerned, it had been the most exciting day of her life. Helping out made her feel like she was part of a family. At times during the day she found herself daydreaming. She longed to go with her new family, to witness sights she hadn't known existed until today. The women chattered as they worked, excited about the prospect of new lives, exhilarated at the thought of sturdy young men awaiting each of them at the end of the long, hard journey. Glory was tempted to forget about independence—especially when Mary and Lily kept after her all day to join them. She hadn't mentioned a word about Amos, and she didn't intend to. Wasn't any use to upset anyone, and besides, Jackson Lincoln and the girls would be gone in the morning, and they wouldn't have to know that she'd struck Amos, taken the gold, and run away. That was stealing to some folks, but the way she figured it, she hadn't had much choice. It was Poppy's money, and though she wasn't his blood kin, Poppy had meant for her to have it if anything ever happened to him. Of course, Amos thought the gold belonged to him because he *was* blood kin—guess that's where they had a fuss. She didn't care a whit about the gold, but right now she was in no position to be giving anything away to Amos or anybody else. She was on her own, and she had to take care of herself first.

"There's nothing keeping you here," Mary had argued when they'd stored the sugar.

"Nothing but pride," Harper had said.

Glory hadn't let the remark rile her; pride had nothing to do with her feelings. If she left, she'd never see Poppy again—leastways, his grave. He might be gone, but right now she knew where she could talk to him if she needed to. She might buy a horse and ride the distance back to the cabin occasionally. Likely she wouldn't do that for a good long spell because of Amos, but she'd go back sometime. If she traipsed off to Colorado, she'd never see the likes of these parts again, and it didn't seem right to leave Poppy lying there, day after day, without her visiting. Especially considering the way he'd looked after her all these years.

"Pride don't have a thing to do with it," she'd argued. "I got to start my new life. If I went with you, before long I'd be depending on you, and Poppy raised me to fend for myself."

"It's going to get real lonely around here," Ruth had murmured. She carried a pan of bacon to the back of the wagon. "Once we're gone, you'll have no one to help you—no one who cares deeply about you."

Glory had already considered that; there wouldn't be a soul she could call on if she were to get sick, so sick she couldn't look after herself. Wasn't likely that she would; she'd always been healthy as that old mule.

When she'd caught a chill, Poppy had rubbed bear grease on her chest and put a steaming cloth hot from the fire over her heart. Phew! The medicine had stunk like all get-out, but it had done the job. By morning, she'd usually felt fit as a fiddle. But the old mule had given out, and she supposed she'd go the same way someday.

She'd thought plenty about all the advice the girls had given throughout the packing: why she should go with them, and how she shouldn't be alone. But she had to give independence a try. Wouldn't seem right otherwise.

Glory did concede to have supper with the traveling party that night. Jackson shot and dressed some squirrels by the stream just before dark. Glory perched on a nearby rock, watching him work.

Jackson Lincoln was a mighty handsome man—not that she'd seen that many men in her life. She'd spied a couple when they hunted near the shanty during the winter. One had been older than Poppy, and the other one had passed by so quickly she'd hardly gotten a glimpse of him. Poppy had told her not to be thinking about men, and she hadn't because she didn't know what she was supposed to think.

But Jackson Lincoln was different from those other men—handsome, strong, real gentle-spirited, it seemed. She had the feeling she was coming down with something every time she was around him—something feverish and bad. Like right now, her mouth was dry as day-old bread, and her stomach felt like she'd eaten something sour though she'd barely eaten at all.

Glory studied his large hands gutting and cleaning out the squirrels' entrails, pitching them aside for a wild animal to find later. Her mind worked furiously to think of something interesting to say—she wasn't much on conversation and didn't know a lot about many a thing. Sometimes she and Poppy sat for days on end and never said a word; reckon they'd about said everything there was to say before he'd died. But there were a lot of things she didn't know about Jackson Lincoln. A lot of things she'd like to know.

"Did you know that Lily wanted me to take a bath today?" She eyed Jackson at a slant to see if he thought the idea was as outrageous as she did.

"That right?" He pitched a skin onto the bank.

"Told her I'd had my bath—bathed *twice* this spring already. Once at the usual time and once the day I buried Poppy." She'd thought that was proper in view of the sadness of the circumstance.

Jackson smiled and kept working. "The girls take a bath once a week and take a sponge bath nightly. They even wash their clothes twice a week in that big tub hanging on the side of the wagon, if the weather cooperates."

Glory turned to look at the object. "Once a week?"

"Once a week."

"Don't that plum wear their hide clean off?"

"Nope." Jackson rinsed the blade of the knife and then washed his hands in the stream. "Their skins are pretty as a picture. The young ladies like to keep themselves smelling good."

Glory stared at the gurgling water. Did she smell good? She'd had those two baths—surely she did. "If I was to change my mind about coming with you, would I have to wash once a week?"

Jackson grinned and handed her a pan of fresh squirrel. "Yes, you would."

Well, then, that was one more reason for her to stay put.

She trailed him up the steep bank, and an hour later the party was sitting around the fire, lazy and replete from fried squirrel and gravy that Ruth had prepared. Lily picked up a guitar and strummed it, joining with the chorus of night creatures enfolding the camp in peaceful solitude.

Glory saw Ruth open the Bible and read to herself for a few minutes. That Ruth was real regular with her reading. She was smart, book smart. Glory admired that, though she didn't have any book learning herself.

Glory nodded in Ruth's direction. "Why does she do that every night?"

Mary stirred, her cough more pronounced tonight. "Ruth loves the Lord; she wouldn't miss reading his Word." Getting more comfortable, Mary laid her head on her forearm and stared at Glory across the fire. "You don't know much about the Lord, do you?"

Glory shook her head. She'd heard Poppy mention the name when he talked about that town called Heaven.

"He's our heavenly Father," Mary murmured. She closed her eyes, and Glory watched the fire pop. Everyone seemed to know about that town except her. Her eyes roamed the sleepy group. Tonight was a far cry from the terror she'd felt last night; she wondered about each of her friends, where they'd come from, what they hoped to find once they reached Colorado.

"Mary? Tell me about the others."

"Ummm," Mary said softly. "Well, Ruth came to the orphanage about a year after me. We'll be sixteen on our birthday. Ruth's folks and two brothers died during an outbreak of cholera. She was the only one left. A Sioux warrior brought her to the orphanage and left her on the doorstep.

"Lily came when she was five. Her ma couldn't keep her after her pa was killed in an accident." The girl's eyes shifted to Harper, sitting away from the others, huddled in a blanket.

"Why is she so cross?"

"Just her way. She really isn't so bad once you get to know her. She keeps her distance—scared, I suspect. Her ma didn't know who her pa was."

"What happened to Harper's mother?"

"Potter, the man who tended garden at the orphanage, didn't want Harper's ma coming around much. Seems she took men home with her—men she didn't marry. After a while she stopped trying to see Harper. Don't anyone know what happened to her. She left one day, and nobody's seen her since."

Turning, Glory smiled at Mary. "And you? What happened to your folks?"

Mary sighed. "The cough. My folks were on their way to California, and I was so sick they couldn't take care of me. Ma was afraid I'd die, so she wrote me a note and told me how much she loved me, but that she loved me enough to want me to live. They went on, and I stayed behind." Glory thought she saw moisture in Mary's eyes now. "Don't blame them—I cough all night and keep everyone awake."

"Must have been a real hard decision for your ma and pa."

Nodding, Mary huddled deeper into her blanket. "Patience's folks were killed by a band of renegade Indians when their farm was raided. A young squaw brought her to the orphanage one day. She knew she was in danger of being killed herself, but she brought the baby anyway. Patience was scared and had dirtied her britches. Took a long time for her to warm to folks. She likes to talk to birds—you noticed that?"

Glory nodded. She'd seen Patience talking to a sparrow behind the mercantile earlier that day. Her eyes moved to the one in the group who interested her most. "What about Mr. Lincoln?"

Mary smiled, opening her eyes. "Nice-looking man, isn't he?"

Glory shrugged. "Guess so."

"Nice-looking and kind. The kind of man a papa would want for a daughter."

"Is he married?"

"No, he's soured on women. We consider ourselves lucky to have him leading us. Supposed to be the best wagon master around. Don't think he would have taken the job at all if he hadn't been a close friend with Mr. Potter. Jackson leads large trains—hundreds of people—to California and Oregon, but Mr. Potter wrote and told him about our situation and how he needed to get us to Colorado safely because Mr. Wyatt had good husbands waiting for us. The orphanage is too crowded for us older ones. I suspect Jackson didn't want the job or the responsibility of five young women, but Mr. Potter had done him a favor once, and Jackson nearly had to agree. Think he's afraid that we've gotten off to a late start, and he's worried about early fall snows."

Glory frowned. "Is it time for the snows to come?" It seemed so hot; it was hard to think about cold weather.

"No, they're months away, but Colorado is a long way off, and it snows early in the Rockies."

Jackson got up and turned down the lantern. Glory knew it was time for her to leave. Getting to her feet, she said good-bye for the last time, knowing she would never see the group again. The thought hurt almost as bad as losing Poppy.

Jackson saddled his horse and took her the short distance to town. Concern filled his eyes when she slid from the animal to the ground, clutching her pack. Gazing up at him, she wished with all of her might that she didn't need her freedom so bad. His eyes fixed on hers and caused that funny feeling to erupt in her stomach.

His features sobered. "I respect your decision, but I think you should come with us, Glory. Squatter's Bend is no place for a young woman alone."

"I'm much obliged, Mr. Lincoln—"

"Jackson. Remember?"

"I remember. Jackson." She took a deep breath, liking the sound of his name on her lips. "I need to do this on my own."

Nodding, he tipped his hat. "You're a mighty brave young lady." Flanking his horse, he gave a friendly wave and rode off.

Not brave at all, she corrected, turning around to view the town of Squatter's Bend. It looked as scary as it had the night before, only scarier now, since she knew that not a mile down the road were a warm campfire, new friends, and Jackson Lincoln. The building that had been filled with warm light last night was now dark and quiet. Loud music spilled from the brightly lit building, where men and women were laughing and dancing. She drew another long, fortifying breath and trudged toward the music.

Glory took a few halting steps down the uneven plank sidewalk. The rising moon shed a narrow strip of light beneath the building eaves. Careful to remain in the shadows, she slid her right hand along the rough walls, while keeping the Hawkins tucked firmly under her left arm.

If she were to begin her new life in this town, she might as well learn her way around. She wondered if she could make friends here—friends like Ruth, Patience, Mary, and Lily. Even Harper's companionship, despite her sharp tongue, would be welcome now. Glory thought of Jackson, his strength and calmness. A lump crowded her throat. She'd spent her life trying to be self-sufficient, but at this moment, the quiet protectiveness of Jackson and the warm consideration of the girls would be a comforting haven.

Unaccustomed to the kindness of strangers, Glory wondered if the people in this town would be as generous and caring as Jackson and the girls had been. If that were the case, she might be able to start her new life here.

A short distance ahead, a couple emerged from a shop. The handsome boy and girl appeared to be no more than a few years older than Glory. Shyness swept over Glory, making her drop her gaze.

Seconds later, a thread of hope caused her to glance up. Maybe these two well-dressed folks would introduce themselves and offer her kindness like the girls and Jackson had done. The couple strolled casually toward her, eyeing her curiously and whispering to each other as they drew closer.

Perhaps six feet away, the girl suddenly pressed a lace handkerchief to her nose and turned away. The boy cast Glory a disapproving frown. Grasping the girl's elbow, he steered her sharply around Glory, then quickened their pace.

"Whew," he muttered, "you'd think a girl would take more pride before mingling with decent folks!"

Glory dropped her chin and rushed to the first alley she saw; she scampered around the corner, craving solitude. She kept moving until she found a dark corner. Wedging herself between two abandoned crates, she slid down the wall and folded her arms around her knees.

What did that boy mean by "take more pride"? Glory couldn't count the number of times Poppy had accused her of having too much pride for her own good—"stubborn pride," he'd called it.

Glory wasn't sure what the boy had meant, but she was certain of one thing: rejection. The young couple had forsaken her at first sight. She didn't have to understand the meaning of his words to interpret the looks of disgust and revulsion on their faces. Why, the girl had acted like she was too superior to breathe the same air as Glory.

Stung and humiliated, Glory buried her forehead against her knees. Pain pricked the backs of her eyes like needles, and an unfamiliar wetness slipped down her cheeks.

So much for starting a new life in this town. When people her own age wanted nothing to do with her, there wasn't much chance of being accepted by older folks. How could they be so quick to find fault? She hadn't spoken a word. She hadn't done a thing to them. Who did they think they were?

Glory tossed her head back and sniffed, wiping her cheeks with the backs of her hands. Well, if they didn't want her, she didn't need them! There had to be other places she could go where people were nice like Jackson and the girls.

Although she'd spent only a short time with the party, they were never far from her thoughts. How could she have fooled herself into believing that others would be as considerate as they had been?

More likely most folks were like Amos. Her heart pounded at the memory of her narrow escape from him. What if he found her here? She shivered at the thought.

Shadows lengthened in the muddy alley, and a dampness rose from the ground, sending a chill through her thin clothing. She gazed at the strip of stars overhead. It was clear, no rain likely, but definitely a cool night ahead.

She heard manly voices at the end of the alley near the street. Cautiously, she peered over a crate. She saw silhouettes of men passing by, a few in pairs, others alone, all headed in the same direction. Each looming shadow looked like Amos. Throaty laughter and harsh shouts reminded her of the vile man and his taunting threats, his promise that she could never escape him.

Glory wanted to spring to her feet and run for her life, but she was frozen with fear. If she left her hiding place, she could likely run smack into him. One of those men could be him. If he tried to grab her, would anyone stop him? She remembered the young couple. Not likely anyone in this town would come to her defense.

Behind her, through the wall, she could hear a tinny piano and the clink of glasses, followed by loud voices and the scrape of furniture pulled across wooden planks.

She crawled into an overturned crate, similar to the one where she'd sought shelter the night before. It was tight and cramped, but she'd be safe here. Maybe her luck would hold out again. Her fingers tightly gripped the rifle stock. She'd never shot a person, but if Amos appeared, it might have to be her last resort.

She remembered his rage. Surely Amos was in pursuit. Greed had sent him to Poppy's cabin. He'd been prepared to do whatever it took to get his hands on Poppy's gold.

Now something more would drive his search: revenge. She had escaped, and in the process she had hurt him. She knew that he would never tolerate that. Even when Amos had visited Poppy on earlier occasions, even when he'd acted friendly upon arrival, his good humor had always exploded into rage when Poppy had refused his demands. Poppy had warned her that his brother was evil. At the first sight of Amos, Poppy had sent her to the shed or anywhere so that she wouldn't be around him.

A week before his death, Poppy had demanded that Glory promise him never to share the gold with Amos. The whole conversation had made Glory uncomfortable. She hadn't wanted to discuss a life without Poppy, but he hadn't been satisfied to drop the subject until she'd given him her word.

At this point, Glory was tempted to give up the gold in exchange for her safety, but she could never break her promise to Poppy. He'd asked so little of her over the years. Only one promise. He'd insisted that he'd saved the gold for her, to give her the start she deserved.

She'd gladly trade all the money to have Poppy back, to go back to her life with him in the cabin. She sighed; she couldn't go back to that life. Poppy was gone forever. And Amos? Would he ever give up trying to find her and the gold?

She shook her head sadly. Not likely Amos would ever give up. She'd been foolish to think she could start a new life in this town. It was too close to Poppy's cabin, only a few days' ride. Sooner or later, Amos would show up here . . . if he wasn't here already.

The thought filled her with dread, and a realization dawned on her.

She had refused to continue with Jackson Lincoln and the girls, not because this town appealed to her. It had been because she knew that when Amos found her, and she had a scary premonition that he would, he would not hesitate to hurt her or anyone with her.

Her heart ached for the girls and Jackson, but she felt protective and loyal where they were concerned. They were the only people besides Poppy who'd ever been good to her.

The noise in the building behind her grew louder, the voices more raucous. Drunken shouts like those she'd heard from Amos startled her.

Poppy had mentioned that Amos spent most of his nights in saloons. Just her luck. In her embarrassment, she'd darted into the first alley she'd seen. Of all things, it was next to what had to be a saloon, and probably the most likely place for Amos to visit if he'd chosen to stop in Squatter's Bend.

The night seemed endless, and sleep impossible. It was too dark to travel, only a sliver of moon. Glory vowed that she would leave this town at dawn's early light.

As the noise diminished and the crowd thinned out, Glory allowed her eyes to close for just a moment. They felt so dry, they ached.

Through the thin wall behind her, she heard a sudden crash. Her body jerked convulsively, and her head thudded the top of the crate. "Ouch," she muttered, rubbing the growing bump.

"Hear somebody?" a man asked, his words slurring.

Glory's eyes flew open in alarm. Shuffling feet sounded nearby. She must have dozed, and someone had moved into the alley without her knowing.

"Yeah," someone said gruffly, kicking over an empty barrel. "Suppose we got company?"

"Could be."

Glory clutched the rifle in her stiff fingers. Her body hadn't moved for hours, and she felt rigid. Cold fear made her shrink back into the crate as far as she could.

Closing her eyes tightly, she strained to hear footsteps drawing closer. Her eyes flew open again when she heard the crash of another barrel, this one very near.

"Come out, come out, whoever you are," a man's voice sang out in a mocking tone, followed by rumbling laughter. A howl echoed down the alley as someone kicked an empty crate. It tumbled until it crashed into the crate where she was hiding.

Desperately, Glory scooted out of the crate, her stiff knees slowing her down. She scuttled backward until she hit something hard. She pushed herself to her feet. Drawing the rifle to her hip, she called out hoarsely, "Stop. Don't come any closer; I'll shoot."

The two men paused and swayed in the early light of dawn. They looked too thin to be Amos, but instinct told her that they could be equally dangerous.

"Sounds like a kid," the tall man muttered, squinting in the shadowy light.

"More like a girl, if you ask me," the short man chortled. "Well, well, now," he said smugly. "This could be our lucky day."

The two shared a meaningful chuckle as they spread their arms and shuffled toward Glory to block her escape.

Glory glanced over her shoulder. At the end of the alley was a fence, flanked on either side by doors to buildings, most likely locked from the inside. No time to test them, she knew. The men were effectively closing off her only avenue of escape.

"I'm warning you," she said, panic lending her a menacing tone, "I'll shoot you, both of you."

"Oh, my," mocked the short one, "I'm s-o-o-o scared."

"Me, too," the other agreed with a raspy laugh.

As they drew near, the short man lunged toward her, landing heavily on both feet. "Boo!" he hollered.

Instinctively, Glory swung out and caught the side of his head with the butt of her rifle. The man staggered, then keeled over backwards.

The tall man sank to his knees beside his companion. "Charlie? You all right?" He touched the side of the man's head, then jerked his hand back and stared in stunned silence at the blood on his fingers.

Glory seized her chance and raced past the two, keeping as far away from them as possible.

The tall man on his knees looked up as she raced by. "You killed Charlie," he declared. "You killed Charlie Gulch!"

Glory raced down the middle of the street without looking back, but the man's last cry came clearly to her as he shouted, "You'll hang for this, you hear me? You'll hang!"

Chapter Five

Wе're burning daylight, ladies!"

Jackson saddled the mare while the women finished breakfast. Overhead, the first pink rays of dawn filtered through oak branches.

Ruth took a pan out of Harper's hand and extended it to the wagon master. "Care for the last biscuit and bacon?"

Jackson smiled, patting his flat abdomen. "The way you've been feeding me, I'll have to start walking beside the wagon instead of riding in it."

Ruth flushed beneath his praise. "Figure a man needs a square meal under his belt if he's going to see a group of women safely cross-country."

"Well, you're going to make some lucky man a fine wife." He grinned at her as he tugged the saddle cinch tighter.

Color flooded Ruth's cheeks, and she turned away to dump the coffee grounds on the fire. "Seems the least we can do for you, Jackson."

The girls pitched in, gathering up the plates and cups. Patience tucked the remaining strips of bacon inside the last biscuit and folded a napkin around it. "For later," she murmured as she handed it to Jackson.

"Thanks." He tucked the napkin into his shirt pocket, then shook out his coffee cup, his eyes scanning the hills behind him. A movement in the brush some hundred yards away caught his attention, and he froze. Was someone trailing them?

Casually he turned back to the group and handed his cup to Harper, who stood at the bucket rinsing the dishes. "Thank you kindly," he said quietly.

"Yeah," she replied without a glance. "I'm just a real sweetheart, ain't I? Gonna make some man a real fine wife." She threw back her head and laughed.

Jackson turned toward the hills and bent to pick up his gear, keeping an eye on a thin line of brush running the length of the ridge. This time he saw a speck of fabric and the quick bob of a head. He groaned as he looked down and shook his head. Glory. Now why on earth was she following them?

"Something wrong?" Ruth asked.

Jackson considered telling her that Glory was following them, but he dismissed the idea. No use getting the girls stirred up. If Glory was following instead of joining them, she must have her reasons, though he couldn't imagine what they would be.

"Just falling behind schedule," he said. "Let's get a move on."

Sighing longingly, Glory parted the thicket for another look. The aroma of frying bacon still scented the air, and her stomach knotted with hunger. What she'd give for a serving of that breakfast. When the wagon started moving, she was going to search the camp for scraps. Her shoulders slumped. She knew that Jackson and the girls were careful not to waste food or leave anything behind.

She couldn't run down the hill and join them, much as she wanted to. She'd told Jackson that it was time she started a new life on her own. Of course, then she'd thought she would stay in Squatter's Bend. That was before she figured out that people didn't like her there. Truth was, she didn't like the people. And now she'd killed one of them. She sighed heavily. She could still see the two men who'd cornered her in the alley, the spurt of bright red blood after she'd struck one of them . . . could hear the snarled threat: *"You'll hang for this!"*

Not only would she have to hide from Amos, who was surely pursuing her for Poppy's gold and his own personal revenge, but now she would also have to dodge the law.

Hiding here in the dark woods, she had considered returning to Squatter's Bend to explain to the sheriff what had happened in that alley. It had been a desperate act of self-defense. She'd never meant to hurt anyone, only to get away from those awful men who'd given her no means of escape. But would anyone believe her? She doubted it. Surely the folks in Squatter's Bend would believe otherwise.

She was a stranger, and the tall man obviously lived there with Charlie. "You killed Charlie. You killed Charlie Gulch!" that man had shouted. She swallowed the lump in her throat as she corrected herself: the man who *had been* Charlie Gulch.

No one would believe her, and if she went back now, it wouldn't bring the dead man back to life. If she returned, Amos would likely be there ready to tell his story, a pack of lies about her stealing gold that belonged to him.

No good could come of her going back. She gazed wistfully at the wagon below as the girls scrambled into the back. How she wished she could race down that hill and join them—let Jackson Lincoln protect her. The small party had provided the only warmth and security she'd felt since Poppy had died.

She shook her head and sank back on her heels. She couldn't drag them into her troubles. Amos was on her trail, maybe lawmen, too. Jackson had enough problems. Besides, when he'd offered to let her join them, she'd flatly refused, told him she could take care of herself—been almost high-handed about it.

"Well, I've done a fine job of taking care of myself so far," she muttered ruefully to herself as she watched Jackson climb onto the wagon seat and gather the reins, ready to leave camp.

As if he'd remembered something, he handed the reins to Ruth and hopped to the ground, then strode back to the campfire, now just a pile of damp ashes. With his back to the wagon, he took something out of his shirt pocket and set it on a large flat rock. He returned to the wagon and swung onto the seat. Without a word, he took the reins from Ruth and gave them a shake, setting the team on its way.

Moments later, Glory crept toward the abandoned campsite, keeping an eye on the disappearing wagon. She knew before she touched it what was inside the tightly wrapped item Jackson had left on the rock. The aroma was unmistakable. Bending down and snatching up the small package, she pulled back the corners of the napkin and inhaled the pungent tang of bacon seconds before sinking her teeth into the delectable meat. She sat on her haunches, chewing. Her eyes scanned the area nervously.

She darted into a shadow behind the trunk of an oak. In a moment, she had devoured the biscuit and was beginning to feel better. She sensed that she was completely alone, other than the scurrying squirrels and the noisy birds.

Eventually she padded down to the creek and sipped several handfuls of cool water. For a moment, she examined the napkin that had contained the biscuit.

Why had Jackson left food behind? Did he know she'd been out there, watchful and hungry? Usually she could outwit her prey, moving quietly and undetected through the woods, but Jackson was no fool. Somehow, he must have sensed her presence or the presence of someone he thought might need the food.

She warmed the napkin in her hands, grateful for the wagon master's kindness. Bending down, she dipped the napkin into the cool water and wiped it across her forehead and over her cheeks and mouth.

Feeling better now, Glory decided to follow the wagon, keeping out of sight. She could shadow the traveling party all the way to Colorado, remaining far enough behind to keep them from seeing her but close enough to not feel so alone.

"Looking for something?" Ruth asked as Jackson scanned both sides of the trail.

"Just enjoying the fine weather." He winked at her. "The trail is full of surprises—need to keep an eye out."

When they'd stopped for a noon meal, he thought maybe he'd spotted Glory in a grove of sycamores. When he'd looked again, no one was there. He'd resisted the urge to leave food behind. If he made it easy, she wouldn't make herself known. He didn't need another girl along, another responsibility, but it would be easier for him to have her with the others than to worry about her out there trailing the wagon.

He berated himself for having left the biscuit that morning. Feeding strays was sure to make them hang around. At the same time, something about the homeless waif brought out his protective side. Could it be pity? he wondered.

In many ways, she had been very sheltered. She could move through the woods, hunt like a man, and put meat on the table, but she was unprepared for the world and its threats. She'd made him want to shield her . . . until he'd encountered her stubborn pride. That was a nuisance he could live without.

That night they made camp at Rock Creek. Jackson checked the perimeter of the rolling terrain where he'd tethered the stock to give them access to the lush grass. However, he saw no signs of Glory or anyone else for that matter. Bidding the girls good night, he turned in early. If Glory decided to join them, it was going to have to be on her own terms.

Several days later, Jackson saddled the mare instead of tying her behind the wagon. They'd crossed Dragoon Creek late yesterday; about a mile up was Second Dragoon. After the girls had broken camp and climbed into the wagon, he handed the reins to Ruth. "Think you can handle the team by yourself?" he asked.

She smiled. "Yes."

He returned the smile, grateful for her quiet competence. "Good girl."

"Ladies," he announced a moment later.

The girls poked their heads out of the wagon behind Ruth, who was sitting on the driver's seat.

"Up ahead, we'll encounter another stream. Usually has a rapid flow over a sandy, level bottom. But with recent rains, it could be out of its banks. It might be a tough crossing. I'll ride beside the team to steer them to solid footing. Ruth will drive. Harper, be ready if she needs a hand. Everybody stay in the wagon and do as I say."

"We're ready," Ruth called cheerily. "I've yet to see the righteous forsaken, and I'm fully confident that the Lord will see us safely to the other side."

"Yes, ma'am! He's never failed me yet." Jackson scanned the group, and every head nodded.

"Yes, sir," Harper added with a trace of mockery in her tone. "Like Ruth said."

"Let's move out!"

Jackson glanced around, hoping he'd made his announcement loudly enough for Glory to hear. He'd seen no sign of her this morning, but he'd felt compelled to leave their scraps behind in a small bundle beside the campfire before dousing it. He couldn't let the girl starve.

When they reached the stream, Jackson studied the swollen waters and swift current. It was worse than he'd imagined. The girls watched in silence as he reined his horse up and down, studying the bank. At one point, he clucked to the mare and tapped her with his heels. The horse responded, leaping into the water that swiftly rose to her shoulders. He maneuvered her against the current as he carefully threaded their way across and up the opposite bank.

"We'll cross here," he shouted from the other side, a distance upstream.

Ruth sawed the reins and clucked to the team of oxen, guiding them upriver as Jackson made his way back across to them. In a few minutes, he helped her line up the wagon.

"Got everything secured in there?" he called.

"Got everything tied down," Lily shouted.

"And knotted twice," Patience added, poking her head out between the canvas.

"Could get bumpy, ladies, so find something solid to hold on to."

Ruth glanced back over her shoulder and then bobbed her head. "Ready," she announced.

"Let's move out," Jackson called as he took a position close to the team. The animals slid down the bank into the river, the wagon wobbling behind.

Jackson kept an eye on the wagon as the oxen stretched their necks to keep their heads above water and dug their hooves into the sandy bottom. Slowly they worked their way across, Jackson reining his mare and pulling on the oxen's harness, and Ruth sawing the reins to support their direction.

As they approached the other side, Ruth slapped the reins and Jackson hauled on the oxen as they scrambled up the muddy bank. Safely across on dry ground, the wagon master turned to face Ruth. "Everybody OK?"

"Everybody's OK here." Ruth glanced overhead and added, "And we thank our Lord."

Jackson bowed his head respectfully and sat back in his saddle for a moment. When he looked up, his heart leapt in his chest. "Oh, no," he muttered, kicking his horse into action.

In a flash, the mare bolted back into the water and under Jackson's urging swam toward the center of the swollen stream, her eyes wide with fright. The girls leaned out the back of the wagon to see what had gotten into him.

"Glory!" the girls shouted in a chorus when they spotted her a few feet from the far bank, her head barely above water as she struggled to hold her rifle above her in one hand while treading water with her other hand.

Glory moved farther into the river where the current strengthened, making it impossible to maintain her balance. Her eyes rounded in panic. When she opened her mouth to call out, she gagged on a gulp of muddy water.

Jackson guided his mare downstream, anticipating the inevitable, hoping he'd reach Glory in time. Her head disappeared beneath the surface of the water and then bobbed to the surface.

He urged his horse into what he prayed would be the path of the girl as the river clutched her in its undertow. He would have only one chance to grab her. If she got by him, the current would take her faster than he could follow.

The mare grunted as something solid collided with her broadside. Jackson plunged his hand into the water and grabbed the first thing he felt. Up came Glory, held tightly by the hair of her head. She sputtered and howled in pain as Jackson drew her up behind him astride the mare.

For a moment the horse thrashed for a solid foothold under the added weight, then scrambled forward. When he was able, Jackson turned the animal in a slow circle and headed toward the bank.

The girls had climbed out of the wagon and were anxiously pacing the bank. As the mare drew near, Patience and Lily grabbed the bridle on either side and helped haul the horse up the slippery bank.

Weakly, Glory slipped off the horse and collapsed on dry ground, struggling for breath. When she lifted her head to look gratefully into the eyes of the man who had saved her life, Jackson seared her with the heat of his scornful gaze.

"You could have been killed," he muttered between clenched teeth. He had nearly missed snagging her in the churning water. For a few seconds he had felt helpless to save her, and he hated feeling helpless; it was something he could ill afford when he was responsible for the lives of others.

"I'm sorry," Glory choked out, gagging on dirty water.

"I'm tired of your games." The rebuke came out harsher than he'd intended, but the little twit had scared him senseless. "Get yourself into *that* wagon and *stay* there before you get your fool self killed!"

Glory met his gaze squarely, her quivering chin the only sign of how much the effort cost her. "I can't," she replied in a small voice.

"Can't or won't?" he snapped. He tossed a look to the sky. "Keeping an eye out for you has slowed us down for days. Thanks to the delay you've brought us, we won't make Council Grove this week."

"Will that be a problem?" Ruth asked.

Jackson shook his head. "It could be." He shot a glare at Glory. "We'll make better time if you're with us than letting you traipse along behind, slowing us down."

"I'll only bring you trouble."

"Trouble?" Jackson muttered, glancing away. "What do you call what just happened?"

"Trouble—but I was trying to stay back!"

Ruth knelt beside her and brushed matted hair off her face. "Glory, you have to listen to reason. We understand your need for independence, but you must cooperate now. Let's get you into some dry clothes. After a bite to eat, everything will look brighter."

Glory grasped Ruth's arms. "I can't join you. Bad things follow me. I'd only bring you harm."

Patience touched Glory's shoulder. "You're talking nonsense. Now let's get you into dry clothes before you catch your death."

Glory shook her head, staring at Jackson, who was gazing stonily ahead. He knew she realized he thought of her as a burden. She wanted to prove she could fend for herself, but after what just happened, how could she blame him for doubting her ability to survive on her own?

She struggled to her feet. "I have to go."

Ruth reached out to cajole her. Jackson saw the stubborn pride in the tilt of her chin and knew she had a will that would be nigh onto impossible to break. He had two options: He could tie her up and haul her aboard against her will, or he could let her go her own way. The last thing he needed was for someone to accuse him of abducting a young woman and holding her against her will. Drawing a deep breath, he knew his choices. None. He'd have to let her go until she made up her mind to join them.

He glanced at the others. "Well, ladies, you heard her. Let her go. We've wasted enough time."

The girls stared at him in disbelief, but the set of his granite jaw effectively stated his case. Eyes downcast, the girls rose and shuffled toward the wagon.

Ruth hung behind, whispering to Glory. "I'll leave you dry clothes and food. Please, think it over and change your mind. You must walk by faith, Glory."

"How do I do that?" she questioned, puzzled.

"By being sure of what you hope for and certain of what you do not see."

"I'm not so trusting as I can do that." Glory was deep in thought. "Leastways, not right now."

"Sure you can! You have to practice at it. Like putting one foot in front of the other, knowing that when you do so, eventually you'll get to where you're going. The more you practice walking by faith, the more natural it will become. Pretty soon, it will get downright easy." Ruth's eyes reflected deep compassion. "Besides, it's impossible to please God without faith."

"Oh." Glory's mind was bombarded with weighty thoughts. Poppy's gold. Crazy Amos. And the voice in the darkened alley echoing, *You killed Charlie! You'll hang for this, you hear me? You'll hang!*" Glory didn't even think to ask who this God was that Ruth spoke of.

"Please think it over and change your mind. You can't look after yourself. Come to Colorado with us. Please, Glory!"

"I can't, Ruth, but thank you just the same." Glory shot an un-friendly look in Jackson's direction, which he shot back.

Ruth hurried to the wagon, and as promised, she set a few items on the ground before climbing onto the seat to take the reins.

As the wagon rumbled over the hill, Glory pushed herself to her feet, frowning at her boots that squished with muddy water. It was then that she realized her rifle was missing. She turned to stare into the dark, surging waters and remembered. When she'd slipped underwater and felt the undertow, she'd released the Hawkins to fight her way to the surface with both hands. It was long gone now, downstream by a mile at least. She was alone and unarmed.

Defeat washed over her. How long could she last without Jackson's protection?

Chapter Six

Afew nights later, Jackson sat opposite the fire, deep in thought. The damp air held a renewed promise of rain. Ruth picked up the plate of fried apple pies and walked around the fire. "Have another one, Jackson. You only ate two at supper."

"Thanks, Ruth. I've had enough." He got up and handed her his cup with a warm smile. "I have some business to take care of. I'll be back in a few minutes." He picked up a lantern to take with him.

Lily frowned. "Where're you going?"

"Be back in a few minutes, girls. Nothing to worry about."

Ruth followed him to the clearing where he proceeded to saddle the horse. Worry dotted her youthful face. "Where are you going at this hour?"

"Don't worry, Ruth. I'll be back in a few minutes." He dropped the leather strap through the cinch ring and drew it up tight, then mounted his mare, whirled her in a circle, and rode out of the clearing.

A shadow of the moon darted in and out of the clouds. The horse picked her way slowly through the overgrown path. Holding the lantern aloft, Jackson searched the bushes for the object of his nocturnal search. Glory still trailed the wagon, hanging back in hopes she wouldn't be discovered. Was she playing some strange, childish game? Was she trying to get on his bad side? If she was, she was doing a fine job.

A deer darted out and leaped across a gully up ahead, momentarily spooking the mare, causing her to shy. Jackson tightened the reins in his left hand. "Easy, girl."

Where was Glory hiding? She'd been on his tail for days, so where was she now? Was she crouched in a bush, hungry and scared? The mare settled down, and he gently nudged her flanks. He'd seriously considered letting her remain out there tonight. He'd asked her twice—no, three times—to join them, but she refused. If the fool girl was headstrong enough to refuse his help, he didn't have time or patience to worry about her.

That's what he'd considered, but his conscience wouldn't let him do it. Rain was brewing, and she didn't have a lick of shelter. The nights were unusually cool for early August, and she had no protection from the elements. She seemed proud of her self-preservation skills, but he doubted that she'd ever had to use them for an extended period of time. The old hermit had kept her sheltered, teaching her only the basics of self-survival, certainly not enough to remain on her own in the wilderness. She'd proved that when she'd taken a river dunking.

Weather could turn on you fast this time of year, and she barely had adequate clothing. Chances were, she had a minimal food supply, if any. The way he figured it, the Lord had just appointed him Glory's keeper, whether he liked it or not. And he didn't like it—not one bit.

Lord, I'm not questioning your judgment; I'm asking for patience. Patience to take care of these women and get them safely to Denver City. If you want me to look after Glory, grant me fortitude, because right now my supply is running low. Amen.

The moon disappeared behind a storm cloud, and the night was blacker than sin. Holding the lantern aloft, he scanned the thicket. If he yelled out, he'd startle her. She'd bolt, and he'd never find her. He didn't want a death on his hands, though he was tempted to wring her neck like a Sunday chicken. Why was she being so stubborn about joining them? He didn't need a sixth girl to look after, but neither did he want Glory's safety on his conscience.

Something darted across the road, and he hefted the light higher. The bushes rattled, then stilled. A deer? A two-legged one? He chuckled at his own humor. Glory was anything but funny to him. He was using valuable sack time to hunt her, and he didn't like it.

Nudging his horse's flanks, he eased closer, his hand resting on the butt of a Winchester. He reined in, listening. Silence. Clucking softly under his tongue, he squeezed the mare's flanks. The horse took another step.

Stillness surrounded him.

His eyes skimmed the darkness, instinct telling him that she was there. He tightened his thighs, and his horse took another step. *Playing games, sweetheart?*

Minutes crawled by. The rustle of leaves and the sound of his own breathing filled his senses.

Flanking his horse, he burst into the bushes. Glory screamed and bolted. Hoisting the lantern higher, he threaded the mare through the underbrush, following the sound of trampled thicket. Glory, spooked now, ran straight for a clearing, and he had her.

He wheeled his horse and galloped back to scoop her squirming form up with one arm. Madder than a hornet, words spilled out of her mouth no lady would be caught dead uttering.

"Put me down!" She took a swing at him and missed as he cantered back to the overgrown path. She hauled off and swung again, letting him have it. This time she connected. Tightening his hold, he grunted, wondering what he'd done to deserve this.

"Settle down! You've been a nuisance for days, lady. You're sorely testing my patience."

"You saw me!"

Yes, I saw you, he silently mimicked. Watched her trail the wagon three days, and it had gotten on his nerves. "You're going to get yourself hurt out here alone."

"I can take care of myself—" She squealed as he hoisted her up in back of him and rode toward camp.

When the mare galloped into the camp, the girls ran to meet them.

"Glory?" Mary ran alongside the mare, her eyes wide with bewilderment.

"Don't run, Mary," Glory warned. "It'll make you cough!"

Jackson reined in his mare and reached back to give Glory a hand down. She slid to the ground, shooting him a resentful look. Mary, Ruth, Lily, and Patience gathered around; Harper waited close to the fire.

Mary was breathless now. "Glory? What in the world?"

Glory glanced at Jackson, and he shook his head. The girls weren't aware that she'd been trailing them. They'd assumed she'd traveled on alone; he'd let them think what they wanted. They couldn't spend their time worrying about a pigheaded girl, and neither could he.

Glory nodded, her eyes reflecting her gratitude. He nodded back. He'd spared her one embarrassment; it was up to her to tell the girls why she was hanging back.

Lily alleviated the need for an immediate explanation. "You've changed your mind! You've decided to come with us after all."

Glory looked at Jackson. "I've decided to come with you after all!" Glory glanced at Ruth, her smile was a tad sheepish. "Figure this is as good a time as any to start walking by faith." Draping her arm around Lily, she walked the young woman back to the campfire.

Lily smiled, discreetly squirming out of the hold. "I'm so glad; we've been worried about you."

Ruth's face lit with elation. "I'll read you the book of Hebrews. It's full of Scriptures about faith."

Glory nodded in agreement. She hadn't meant to stretch the truth to Ruth. And maybe in the long run, she wouldn't be. She'd sure give this faith thing a try. Especially if it meant having Ruth read to her from that mysteriously wonderful book.

"I wasn't worried," Harper announced. "Should have come with us in the first place. Knew you'd have to join up eventually."

Glory shrugged off the remark. "Worried? About me?" She laughed, still avoiding Jackson's eyes. Squaring her shoulders, she crowed, "I can take care of myself."

Jackson handed the mare's reins to Patience. "Ruth, get Glory a plate of supper, please."

"Yes, sir. Right away." The girl hurried off to do the wagon master's bidding.

Jackson listened to the girls' chatter as he unsaddled his horse and stored the rifle in the back of the wagon. Glory had been fortunate; he hoped she realized it. Tomorrow he'd have a talk with her and get the rules straight: As long as she traveled with him she'd give up her independence. And she was going to travel *with* them—no more hanging back and drinking a gallon of muddy river water. She wasn't going to like the rules, but then he didn't like the extra trouble. Now he had six women to safely deliver before the first snow.

All she had to do was follow orders.

Seemed to him he'd gotten shortchanged.

"Mr. Lincoln?"

He turned to see Glory standing in the shadow of the clearing. Her face was dirty, and she had corn-bread crumbs around her mouth. He turned back to the horse. "It's late. You'd better get some sleep."

"Yes, sir . . . I'm going, but I was thinking maybe I'd better thank you first."

"No need for thanks. I'd have done it for anyone." He didn't want her thinking she was special; she wasn't. She needed a bath and was ornery and more trouble than she was worth. She was older than the others, maybe had as much as three or four years on them, but that still put her young enough to be trouble. All he needed was to get personally involved with her or any of the girls. He'd seen the interested look in Ruth's eyes and had done everything he could to erase it. Ruth and the others had husbands waiting for them in Colorado; he wasn't the marrying kind. Ma had seen to that. When he'd been a kid, she'd run his pa off and denied Jackson the pleasure of a normal upbringing. The betrayal had left a bitter taste in his mouth.

Glory stepped into the clearing, fishing in her right pocket. "If I'm going with you, then I'm going to pay my way."

"No need—Tom Wyatt will pay your way when I deliver you."

"Well—" she paused—"that's the thing, Mr. Lincoln."

"Thought I told you to call me Jackson."

"It doesn't feel right yet—when it does, I'll do that, sir."

He picked up a brush and began to curry his horse. "I'm sorry I yelled at you. I was upset, that's all. I shouldn't have lost my temper. Go on to bed now."

"Don't have any hard feelings, sir."

When she continued to stand there, he turned around to look at her.

"What if I don't want a husband?"

"I'd say you'd better give it more thought. You got no kin and no way to support yourself. A husband's not a bad idea at this point. A good man can give you a home and food on the table."

"If I pay you to take me to Colorado, then I can make up my own mind whether I want such a man. Wouldn't that work?"

The brush paused. "I suppose it would, but where are you going to get that kind of money? Tom Wyatt pays a good price for his mail-order brides."

She took a pouch from her pocket and approached him. Extending the poke, she asked softly, "Have I got enough in here to pay my own way?"

Jackson stared at the bulging sack. By the looks of it, she had enough to buy half the state, with money left over. "Where did you get that kind of money?"

She drew the sack to her chest, looking cautious now. "It's mine. Poppy gave it to me—I didn't steal it."

"Let me see that." He took the sack from her, untied it, and spread out the gold ore in the palm of his hand. "How many people know you have this?"

"No one . . . except Poppy's brother . . . but he doesn't care."

Jackson shook out a small nugget, examined it, and then stuck it in his pocket. Yanking the string on the pouch closed, he met her expectant gaze. "One nugget is all I need, and I'll owe you some at that."

A relieved grin broke across her freckled face. "Then you'll take me with no strings attached? I don't have to take a man if I don't want one?"

"You've paid your way; I have no say over what you do when you get there."

She flashed another grin. "No, sir. You don't." She whirled and started off, turning back around when his voice stopped her.

"I may not have any say when you get there, but as long as you're in my care, you play by my rules, agreed?"

Glory's grin faded, but she nodded. "Agreed."

"And another thing. Don't be showing this money to anyone, you hear? Not to Mary, or Patience, or Ruth, or Harper, or Lily. No one— do you understand? You keep it hidden somewhere where no one but you can get to it."

Young, rich, and naïve—he couldn't think of a worse combination for a woman alone. He couldn't think of a worse combination for him. Now he had to worry about the girls' safety and roughly twenty thousand dollars worth of gold ore.

"Yes, sir." She cocked a brow. "Figure I can start a new life in Colorado as good as right here."

His features sobered. "I'll get you to Colorado. Once we're there, you'll be responsible for your own protection." He turned back to the horse, but she stuck her hand out and insisted that he shake on it.

"We got us a deal." Her eyes searched his in the lantern light.

"We got ourselves a deal," he murmured without much enthusiasm.

She started off for the fire but turned a second time. "Mr. Lincoln?"

"Yes?"

"This Colorado town—is it anything like Heaven?"

"Heaven?" He frowned.

"Yes, sir. One night in Squatter's Bend, I heard these people in a building singing about a place called Heaven. Sounded real nice, real pretty—sort of like Colorado, I'd imagine. Is it?"

He turned around to face her. Was she serious?

"Well?" she asked.

"Colorado isn't a town; it's a territory. It's real pretty, but I don't imagine it can hold a candle to heaven."

"Really? You been there?"

"To *heaven?*"

"No, to Colorado." She frowned. "Sounds to me like it's a tad harder to get to than Heaven." She looked up, studying the sky. The building storm shot fingers of light in the distance. "Wonder what it's like there in Heaven."

"I imagine no one complains."

"Yes, sir. Imagine they don't." She hitched up her britches with a look of satisfaction. "Well, I feel a whole lot better about everything. How about you?"

Actually, he felt a whole lot worse, but he was hired for a job he intended to complete, no matter what happened. The gold nugget weighed heavy in his pocket.

Lord, I don't know what you're doing here, and I still don't like it. Sir.

⟡

Glory walked back to camp feeling a sight better. Thunder rolled in the distance, and she shivered. Truth be told, she was glad Jackson had come after her. Loneliness was a powerful thing, a hurtful thing, and she'd just as soon be through with it. Now that Jackson didn't expect her to take a husband, it made things a whole lot easier. Once she got to Colorado, she'd get busy making a new life. Until then, she'd enjoy her new friends with no false expectations on their part. The others might want a man in their life, but one would only clutter up hers.

She looked up as she walked, studying the sky. She'd never thought about having a home of her own or babies—never seemed to need it. Poppy had been her life, and the animals her friends. Now they were all gone—but where? Where'd a soul go when the body died?

To Heaven, silly. Isn't that what the song said? The tune hummed in her head: *"When we all get to Heaven, what a day of rejoicing that will be! When we all see Jesus . . ."*

Jesus. Now who was that? Since Poppy had died, she was finding out there were a lot of folks she didn't know. Had Poppy known about these things and neglected to tell her? She made a mental note to ask Ruth about Jesus. Ruth read from the black book each night and seemed to be real knowledgeable about it. Ruth was much smarter than she. Glory hardly knew anything she should know, and she'd proven it today. Falling in the river, nearly drowning . . . she could swim as well as a fish; why hadn't she been able to swim this morning? The current was swift, but she was strong, able to swim the width of the river when she and Poppy had gone fishing. Her heart ached when she thought about how Jackson had dismissed her as a careless fool. She cringed when she thought of the anger she'd heard in his voice this morning. She didn't like him to be mad at her. She might not be as smart as Ruth, but she wasn't a fool, and sometime during the trip to Colorado, she was going to prove it.

When Glory returned to the fire, Mary glanced up from her sewing. Her cough was worse tonight; Glory could hear the dry rasps a distance away. Ruth was reading the Bible; Harper was putting a pan of bread aside to rise for breakfast. Patience and Lily were bent over the tub, washing out a few things by hand.

"Going to rain," Glory announced.

Ruth glanced up, scanning the sky. "Still a few hours away." Her gaze switched back to Glory. "Where's Jackson?"

"Tending the horse." Glory sat down before the fire, warming her hands.

Harper covered the pan of bread with a cloth and then straightened, pressing her hand to the center of her back. "A bath would feel mighty good right now."

The others murmured in agreement—all except Glory who stared at the fire, her mind still on the day's events.

Ruth glanced at the other women. "Doesn't a bath sound good, Glory?"

"Told you, took my bath a few months back," she said absently, then looked up, still deep in concentration. "How did Jackson get his name?"

"Get his name?" Lily laughed. "Why, I suppose his mother gave it to him. Why?"

"No reason. Just thinking aloud." Jackson Lincoln. The name fit him: a good strong name for a good strong man. She thought about the play of muscles she'd seen in his forearms as he brushed the horse and wondered if Jackson Lincoln had a woman of his own. Didn't matter, she guessed. Spoken for or not, he'd never look at her the way he looked at Ruth or most likely any other woman.

Ruth pulled her light wrap closer. "His mother named him after two of our presidents: Andrew Jackson and Abraham Lincoln. President Jackson served our country in her father's time, and Mr. Lincoln served her state in the Illinois House of Representatives from '47 to '49. I believe his mother's father knew Mr. Lincoln personally and thought highly of him. When he was elected president of the United States in '61, Jackson said he and his mother attended the inaugural festivities."

Harper turned to stare at Ruth. "How do you know all of that?"

Color dotted Ruth's cheeks. "Jackson told me. Seems he and his mother don't get along anymore. He rarely talks about her."

The admission caught Glory's interest. "He told you they don't get along?"

Ruth shrugged. "Not in so many words, but I could tell by the things he was saying."

Harper sniffed. "Lots of folks don't get along. Don't mean a thing."

"Ruth? Things such as . . . ?" Lily asked.

"Such as she's domineering and complains all the time. They had words a few years back, and he hasn't seen her since. Said she drove his father away when he was a young boy. It's such a pity—mother and son losing contact with each other. She must miss him something terrible."

The girls fell silent, contemplating the situation. Glory finally broke the hush. "What's a president?"

Lily and Patience giggled. Ruth shot them a disapproving scowl. "You don't know, Glory?"

Glory blinked. "Is it something bad?"

"Bad?" Harper scoffed. "Girl, you been livin' under a rock?"

"Harper," Mary rebuked softly, "Glory hasn't had our advantages." She turned to Glory and smiled. "A president is a man whom the people elect to run the country."

"What's a country?"

Ruth stopped the astonished looks with another stern look. "Lily, tell Glory what a country is."

"Well . . . a country is where we live. We live in the United States of America. Actually, our forefathers first set sail to this land in 1492. But it took a war with the British to gain our independence, and we became a country on July 4, 1776. We are the people of this country, and the people elect a president every four years. All told, we've had seventeen presidents."

"Did you know these presidents?"

"Oh my, no!" Ruth laughed. "Most of us were infants when Lincoln served, and Mr. Jackson was elected in 1829 and was our president until 1837. President Lincoln was assassinated by a man named John Wilkes Booth while he attended a play at Ford's Theater on April 14, 1865. It was a terrible loss for the whole country."

Glory stared at her blankly.

"Assassinated—shot to death," Ruth informed her.

"Oh." Glory didn't know anything about assassination. It sounded downright mean-spirited to her, but now she knew what a president was. "You reckon this Mr. Lincoln went to Heaven?"

"President Lincoln was a fine Christian man. I believe heaven is his new home." Ruth smiled.

"And Jackson's mother favored Mr. Jackson and Mr. Lincoln particularly."

Lily nodded. "It seems that way. She named her son after them. His full name is Jackson Lincoln Montgomery, but we call him Jackson or Mr. Lincoln."

"Jackson Lincoln Montgomery." Jackson had three names, and she had only one. She looked up and grinned. "It's a fine name." And it confirmed what she'd known all along. Jackson Lincoln was different from other men. Why, he was almost presidential.

Regardless, he shouldn't feel bad toward his mother. Glory didn't know what had taken place to anger him, but whatever it was, it couldn't be bad enough to cause a parting.

"At least he had a mother," Harper murmured.

"One that didn't give him away," Mary said, shifting and adjusting her blanket. "If I have a child with a cough, I'll love it no matter what. I'll never give it away."

Ruth glanced at Mary. "Perhaps there was a reason your mother felt she couldn't keep you, Mary. I suspect that if she could have, she would have kept you. It can't be easy for a mother to part with a child. I've never known anyone who did things without a reason, and I'm sure your mother had a very good reason."

"Maybe," Mary conceded. "But I would never leave my child."

"Never say never, Mary. None of us knows what lies around the corner."

Scooting closer to the fire, Glory thought about the girls and their lives. She'd never once felt bad toward her real folks. She'd thought about them once in a while, wondered where they were and if they were sad about losing her. But Poppy had treated her well and given her enough love for two parents. She guessed a woman didn't have to carry a child in her stomach and birth it in order to love it as much as her own.

"Guess we all wish for things we can't have." Patience stood up and stretched. "I feel like Ruth. I wish my pa would have lived and my ma could have kept me, but since that didn't happen, I'm thankful for people like Mr. Potter and the others at the orphanage. They were kind to us, gave us a home when we had none."

"Amen," Ruth seconded. "I wish my parents hadn't died so young, but they did. Our lives could be a lot worse."

"A lot worse," Glory conceded, her thoughts returning to Squatter's Bend. Hers would likely get a lot worse if Amos or the man from Squatter's Bend caught up with her.

Chapter Seven

When Jackson returned to camp, Glory was putting dishes in the dry box. He noticed the other girls were clustered upwind. He shook his head. There was no getting around it; something needed to be done about the stink. You'd think after a near-drowning in the river she'd smell a sight better. If anything, she smelled worse. Without soap, wet only made things worse.

He busied himself checking the harness for damage from the river crossing, grinning when he heard the girls dropping hints Glory should be able to catch.

"You know, Glory," Mary began gently, "after all the bruises you got in the river today, a pleasant bath in the stream with some nice castile soap would feel mighty soothing. We have an extra one-pound bar that could be yours."

Glory shook her head. "I'm fine."

Ruth smiled warmly. "Why, I haven't seen such a lovely stream in a long time—nice pools, not too deep."

Glory shook her head tightly. "Seen enough water today to last me for a long time."

Locating a tear in the leather harness, Jackson bent over his box of tools, looking for the right one, trying to appear as if he wasn't listening.

The girls sighed as they knelt for evening devotions. This evening someone made mention that cleanliness was next to godliness, but Ruth didn't bother to correct her. Jackson noticed the subject seemed to be lost on Glory.

A moment later, he left to check on the animals. When he returned to the campfire to turn in for the night, he noticed that the girls had their bedrolls tucked under their arms. Once again, the girls were reluctant to lay them out. They'd given Glory her bedroll but were waiting for her to pick a spot first.

"Go ahead, dear," Ruth said. "You pick wherever you'll feel comfortable. We insist; you first."

Glory looked around uncertainly. "I don't rightly know where." She shrugged. "It doesn't make any difference to me. Wherever you girls like to be is good enough for me."

Ruth shot Jackson a pleading look, and all eyes turned to him. He was not one for shirking responsibility, but he was bone weary, and the last thing he needed was a bunch of feuding women on his hands.

An awkward silence developed as the girls looked expectantly at Jackson to lay down the law to Glory. He looked back at them, figuring a delicate subject like personal cleanliness should fall to the women to discuss privately. The girls had tolerated Glory's odor when she'd been a temporary guest; now that it appeared she'd be with them for the rest of their journey, they wanted relief.

He took a deep breath and slowly released it. He'd handled just about all the challenges he could stand for one day, and he was fresh out of tact. Not that he'd ever had much to begin with, he thought wryly.

Ruth sighed. "Well, someone needs to do something."

The women prepared to take an evening dip before turning in, and Jackson discreetly moved to the other side of the wagon. Glory bounded to her feet and rushed to his side.

"Care if I join you?" She slanted her head and nodded in the direction of the others. "They're going to the stream to bathe *again.*"

He stepped back, giving her room. "Look, Glory. You sure you don't want to join those girls?"

"No, sir, I want to stay here, help you with chores and the like." She smiled. "Remember? I took my bath a few months back." Then she apparently remembered her manners. "But thanks for thinking of me."

He looked at her, and for the life of him, he couldn't think of a way to explain the situation. In short, there wasn't one. "Well," he said, rising to his feet, "we tried. Sorry, Glory, but you stink."

Leaning forward, he grabbed Glory around the knees and tossed her over his shoulder like a feed sack. His long striding gait covered the distance down the ravine, straight for the stream. "Cover up, ladies," he announced loudly, "you're about to have company."

He kept his head down and his eyes shut as he flipped Glory over his shoulder and into the pool. Then he spun on his heel and trotted back to the safety of the wagon.

Glory broke the surface, spitting water, her eyes as wide with shock as those of the women who'd paused in their lathering to watch the spectacle. She slapped the water in fury.

"Jackson Lincoln! I'm sick of you grabbing me and throwing me around!" she shouted, sending a spray after his retreating back. "I'd like to throw you around—see how you like it!"

The girls stared at Glory in shocked silence.

Glory glanced at them. "What? No one ever dared to talk to Mr. Lincoln like that?" She glared at them, deciding they were probably in cahoots with the wagon master, since none of them looked sorry that she'd just been manhandled.

To retaliate, she splashed water at them in a big plume. A playful water fight erupted, and the tension dissolved into giggles. Soon, Glory was having a great time, feeling fully accepted into the group for the first time.

By the time Glory climbed out of the stream, tired but clean, the girls had persuaded her to strip off her dirty clothes, scrub from top to bottom, and rub her hair with soap until it squeaked.

Ruth had fetched a fresh outfit for Glory, and when Glory walked into camp, she looked like a different girl. Eyes aglow, freshly scrubbed hair falling to her waist—she was a sight to behold. Jackson ventured a glance from the far side of the wagon but kept his distance. He planned to give her overnight to cool off. Yet he had to smile at the transformation.

Glory looked lovely wearing one of Patience's dresses, her skin radiant and glowing, her green eyes dancing as she laughed. Her mass of cinnamon-colored hair glistened as Mary carefully brushed it dry in the firelight. As he stared at her, something stirred in him—something he didn't care to identify.

That night Glory noticed that the other girls moved their bedrolls closer to hers. When the light went out, she rolled to her side and whispered. "I have to admit," she began, compelled to show her appreciation, "this is the best I've felt since Poppy died."

"Tell us about Poppy," Mary urged gently.

"Well, he was the closest thing I had to a family."

"Was he like a real daddy?" Patience spoke in hushed tones.

"Poppy was good as gold to me, raised me from a youngster like I was his own. Fed me, taught me to hunt and fish, taught me everything he knew."

"That's nice," Mary said wistfully. "I always wanted to be adopted by a nice couple."

"Not me," Harper declared. "I knew better. Knew better than to wait around for somebody to pick me out like a cur in a litter. All I ever wanted was for folks to leave me alone."

It was the most Glory had ever heard Harper say at one time; there was a pent-up force behind her words, like a sudden thunderstorm. Glory shook her head in the darkness. "Poppy told me he found me in the road, figured I'd fallen off a wagon when the wagon train had passed through on their way west. Said he waited at that very spot for days, in case my family came back to find me. He figured they'd have come if they could."

"He just took you home to raise by himself?" Ruth asked with a trace of amazement.

"Said he had a wife once, but she died giving birth. Baby died too. After that, he lived alone because he said no one could match her. I miss Poppy a lot, but it's better now." Better now that she felt a kinship with these girls, safe under the protection of Mr. Lincoln.

"So," Harper hissed, "you fell off a wagon headed west, and now you're in another one headed west."

"Guess I'm meant to ride west in a wagon," Glory said with a sigh.

"Well, try not to fall out this time," Patience whispered so earnestly that the rest of them broke into giggles.

"Pipe down, ladies," a gruff voice reprimanded from the far side of the wagon. "Miles to make up tomorrow. Get your rest."

The group fell silent, and Glory snuggled down under her fresh-smelling blanket. As she closed her eyes, she reached out to capture Mary's hand in hers and give it a reassuring squeeze.

"Don't worry, Mary. I know your ma loved you. And even if she didn't, I do."

The pleasant aroma of castile soap still clung to her clothing when Glory opened her eyes the next morning. Rolling to her side, she stared at Mary, who slept opposite her. Sighing, Glory realized that she'd gotten a mite upset last night—wasn't used to being waylaid like a common criminal. A bath *this* time of year! Seemed a waste of good soap and water. Still, she had to admit it felt good to have the dirt off.

An unexpected thought popped into her mind. Had Jackson noticed? Guess he would have since he was partly responsible for the ambush. He'd said she stunk. The words still made her cheeks burn. Well, someone could have told her something earlier if she smelled all that bad! She didn't powder herself or wash with soap until her skin looked plumb raw like the other girls. She sniffed the air and decided they'd expect her to smell like this all of the time. Well, if it was so all-fired important, then she'd bathe every night like the rest of them and hope her skin didn't wear out.

Mary opened her eyes and returned Glory's sleepy smile. "Good morning."

The sun was not yet up. Birds chattered noisily overhead in tree branches as daybreak rose over the camp. Glory shut her eyes and savored the smell of strong coffee perking. A smile touched the corners of her mouth. Jackson was up a full half hour ahead of the others every day. It was nice to wake to the sound of another person.

But Jackson and coffee weren't the only things on her mind this morning. These were her friends, and she was putting them in the way of danger. She hadn't mentioned Amos because until now there'd been no need to tell them about Amos or the man she'd killed in Squatter's Bend. Now she was part of their group—a real part—and being part of someone or something meant you had to be honest. You had to share.

She wasn't prone to lying. Poppy wouldn't have it, but Glory could stretch the truth as well as anybody. Didn't do it all that often, but she could when she needed to. However, this wasn't the time for fibs. It was the time for truthfulness, painful as it might be. Jackson and the girls needed to know what she'd done.

She shivered deeper into the blanket, trembling when the voice that haunted her day and night echoed inside her mind. *"You killed Charlie! You killed Charlie Gulch!"* She'd never meant to kill anyone—wouldn't kill anyone unless she saw no other way out, and she hadn't seen another way out that night.

"Penny for your thoughts." Glory opened her eyes to see Mary still smiling at her opposite the fire.

"They're not good ones." The others were still sleeping, oblivious to the girls' softly spoken conversation. Glory could hear Jackson moving around the wagon, checking the harness for the long day's travel. Her heart ached for what she was about to do.

Would Lily and Mary hate her once she told them the truth? Seemed like they would. Killing was wrong, no matter how a person tried to excuse it.

Lily, awake now, too, reached for Glory's hand. "What's wrong? You look sad this morning. Are you still mad about the bath? Because you really need—"

"I killed a man."

The dazed silence was as loud as a gunshot.

Glory stared at the crackling fire, waiting. Apparently Lily and Mary were trying to think of a response.

"Did you hear me?"

"You said you . . . killed a man," Mary repeated.

"I did . . . and I stole money from Poppy's brother—leastways he thinks I did." Her words tumbled one over the other now. "I didn't steal that gold, because Poppy told me that if anything was to ever happen to him, I was to take the money—it was supposed to be mine." Glory rolled to her side, grasping Mary's hand. "I'm scared, Mary. I'm scared that Amos is following me and will take the gold. And the man I killed? That wasn't my fault, honest. He and his friend was tormenting me, saying awful things, wanting to do awful things, and I spooked. Before I knew it, I'd hit him."

You killed Charlie! You killed Charlie Gulch! You'll hang for this!

Lily, wide-awake now, with eyes as wide as saucers, pressed a hand to her mouth. "When? When did this happen?"

"The second night I stayed in Squatter's Bend."

"Oh, dear." Daylight filtered through the camp. The girls lay in the stillness, Mary holding Glory's hand.

"Do you hate me?"

"Hate you? Goodness, no." Mary squeezed her hand reassuringly. "I know you'd never kill anyone unless you felt you had to. The good Book tells us not to kill—"

"I wouldn't, honest, Mary." Glory's voice came out in a shaky whisper. "Honest. What should I do?"

The girls thought about it for a long while. Finally Lily said, "I guess you'd better tell Jackson."

Oh, she *hated* to have to tell Jackson. "Isn't it enough that the two of you know? You can help me keep watch for Amos and the dead man's friend. If we're lucky, they'll not catch up with us."

"They'll catch up with us," Lily predicted. "If Amos lives in these parts, he'll ask around and discover you hooked up with us. If the other man is behind us, he'll catch up too. You don't have a choice really. You have to tell Jackson. He'll know what to do."

Glory felt like bawling like a baby. New friends. She'd not have a one after today. When the others found out that she'd stolen *and* killed, they would leave her beside the road and not look back. And who could blame them? Loneliness washed over her already, and she held back bitter tears.

"I don't want to tell him. He'll make me leave."

"No, he won't. He can be gruff at times, but he's fair, Glory. You tell him what happened and ask him to help you."

She'd sooner walk over hot coals barefoot, but she knew Lily was right. She had to tell Jackson; it was the only fair thing to do. "All right. I'll tell him first thing this morning."

The promise was a hard one to keep. During breakfast she watched the others laughing, having a good time, even putting up with Harper's bad mood in a charitable way. The sun rose, hot as a new-formed blister. The girls broke camp while Jackson hitched the team.

Lily sent her supportive glances, but Glory hung back, reluctant to destroy the only remaining shred of her newfound security. Still, there came a time when she couldn't put it off any longer.

"Mr. Lincoln."

Jackson glanced up from tightening a harness strap. Freshly shaven, wearing a blue broadcloth shirt that matched the color of his eyes, he looked so confident, as if he had the world by its tail. She'd be grateful for a little of his confidence this morning.

"Shouldn't you be helping the others break camp?" he asked.

"We're done." She shuffled closer, eyeing the oxen. "Fine team."

"Yes, they're good animals." He went about his business, glancing up a moment later. "Did you want something, Glory?"

"I killed a man."

It came out mighty harsh sounding, even to her ears. She'd rehearsed more tactful versions, but somehow they all came out the same. She'd killed a man. No way to sugarcoat it.

"And a man thinks I stole money."

Jackson's face drained of color. She'd known that it would. Could have bet on it, but Poppy didn't hold with wagering either. She'd been nothing but a thorn in Jackson Lincoln's side since they'd met up, and she'd just made it worse—lots worse.

Silence built. He stood there, leather harness in hand, staring at her, probably trying to figure a way to shoot her and get away with it.

"Well . . . aren't you going to say anything?"

"You killed a man and stole his money."

"It wasn't exactly like that." She explained what she'd done as simply as she could, if murder could ever be considered simple.

"Are you sure the man was dead?"

"You killed Charlie! You killed Charlie Gulch!"

"Yes, sir, he was dead." When she saw resentment and then anger cross his rugged features, she sighed. "I'll get my things and be out of your way." She turned to step to the back of the wagon when his gruff voice stopped her.

"The way I see it, you didn't steal the money. Your guardian gave it to you, so put Amos out of your mind. We can deal with him. However, killing is a serious thing. If the man threatened you, you had a right to defend yourself. If you shot him point-blank without a reason, that's a different story."

Glory took a step toward him. "I didn't shoot him! I hit him. Him and that other man was up to no good; that's the only reason I hit him!"

"That may be, but you should have gone to the sheriff and reported the incident."

"I was scared. All I could think about was getting out of that horrible town." If she never saw Squatter's Bend again, it would be too soon for her. And truthfully, all she'd thought about that fearful night was getting back to Jackson and the girls.

It wasn't right, but that's what she'd done, and now she'd have to pay for her behavior. She should have gone to the sheriff and tried to explain. Maybe he would have taken her side, and maybe not. Either way, she wouldn't have the killing hanging over her right now, choking her like a heavy rope.

Jackson was right; the money was hers, no matter what Amos claimed. But had she been honest from the beginning, she might have been spared the frustration evident in Jackson's eyes right now.

She faced him, lifting her chin. "Do you want me to leave?"

He viewed her somberly. "Do you want to leave?"

No, she didn't want to leave. She'd do most anything to stay, to be a part of their group on the long journey west. But she wouldn't cause him any more trouble, even if that meant she'd be on her own again.

"I'd . . . be beholden if you'd let me stay." The admission hurt, but that's the way she felt.

Stepping back to the animals, he laced a leather strap through a brass ring. "Seems only fair that I'd talk it over with the girls. We'll all be affected by your decision."

Nodding, Glory stepped aside. "Seems only fair. I'll wait right here."

She watched the group huddle for a short meeting. The disdain in Harper's tone clearly carried over the other voices, and Glory's heart sank. They didn't want her to stay. They didn't want to be peering over their shoulders, running from a crazy so-called uncle, from a man seeking revenge for a friend, maybe even from a lawman or a posse.

Quietly she eased toward the wagon and reached inside to fumble for her pack and bedroll. Might as well go ahead and leave, make it easier on everybody. Tears welled in her eyes, temporarily blinding her. Didn't seem fair. Charlie Gulch had intended to hurt her; she'd had no choice but to defend herself. And Poppy told her she was to take the money if anything happened to him. Well, something happened to him and to her, too. Something neither one could stop.

Lily caught sight of Glory as she turned from the group, and she shouted, "Glory! Wait!" Breaking from the huddle, she ran to meet her. "You can stay! Everyone agreed that we want to help you."

A smile broke across Glory's face. "They did!"

"Of course. You're ours now." Lily draped an arm around her.

The other girls gathered around, adding their support. Even Harper gruffly conceded that she could stay as long as she kept out of her way. Glory didn't care; she'd keep out of everybody's way for the entire trip, just so long as she didn't have to be alone. Mary and Patience hugged her, and Lily patted her back. When she saw Jackson watching the exchange, she broke away and cautiously approached him. "I won't be any more trouble," she promised.

He nodded, his demeanor more sober than she'd ever seen it. "You keep your eyes out for trouble."

"I will, sir." She'd watch harder than she'd ever watched. She wouldn't cause him a lick more of trouble.

"Jackson. How many times do I have to tell you? It's *Jackson*." He glanced up, giving her a grin that melted her heart.

"Yes, sir. *Jackson*." The name suddenly felt right on her tongue.

He winked at her, then stepped around the front of the oxen. "Girls! We're wasting daylight!"

And as easy as that, Glory put her pack back into the wagon and prepared to walk the ten miles of travel that day with Jackson.

Chapter Eight

The wagon traveled across level prairie until it passed Big Turkey Creek three and a half miles up the trail. The rest of the day the Arkansas River Valley was in sight. The frequent rains left pools of water along the road. Late afternoon, Jackson spotted a wagon in a clearing up ahead and slowed the team. It was too early to stop for the night, but the girls would enjoy sharing supper with company.

Observing no activity around the camp as he drew near made Jackson uneasy. Reining in the team, he assessed the area: no one in sight, no animals, campfire in ashes, belongings scattered. Dread replaced the uneasy feeling.

"Hello," he shouted. "Anyone here?"

Ruth sat beside him on the wagon seat; the other girls peered from behind the curtain, trying to get a look.

"Let's go say hello," Ruth suggested. "They can't be far."

"Stay here." Jackson turned on the seat, his glance taking in every curious face behind him. "All of you," he added firmly. "I'll have a look."

He sprang lithely to the ground and slowly approached the campfire. Squatting beside the ashes, he passed his hands inches above the remains. Cold. When he straightened, he noticed the dishes and four bedrolls spread out around the camp. "Hello," he called again and waited—no response, the silence eerie.

Unable to see anything around the others, Glory raised the side canvas a few inches. "Hey," she whispered, "I can help—"

Jackson lifted his hand to silence her without turning around. His deliberate manner stopped her midsentence, but she and the other girls continued to squirm for a vantage point from inside their wagon. No doubt the prospect of meeting other travelers, maybe young people their age, filled the girls with anticipation.

Jackson moved to the back of the deserted wagon and took a deep breath before lifting the flap. Sunlight spilled over his shoulder into the dark corners as his gaze moved over the faces inside—a man, a woman, between them a young boy and a small girl. All dead. Their bodies close, embracing each other.

He stepped back, dropping the flap as he turned and strode to the edge of the clearing. He released a breath and filled his lungs with fresh, cleansing air.

"Is something wrong?" Glory called.

He dropped his head briefly before he lifted his gaze. The women's eyes were wide and inquisitive. Covering the uneven ground in efficient strides, he returned to stand beside his wagon. Glory drew back slightly at the look of despair on his face.

"What?" Ruth whispered, speaking for all of them.

"Cholera." His tone was flat.

"You sure?" Ruth's eyes flew back to the infected wagon.

Jackson nodded, his expression resigned. "Seen it more times than I care to remember."

"Are they . . . ?" Patience began and then seemed unable to finish.

He nodded. "All four of them."

"We can't take a chance of catching this sickness," he said grimly. "Do exactly as I tell you—nothing else." He made brief eye contact with each of the women. "Understood?"

Each responded with a vigorous nod.

Ruth's eyes returned to the wagon. "What do you want us to do?"

Jackson stepped to the back of the wagon and reached inside for the box of matches. "Move our wagon to the edge of the clearing and wait for me there. I have to burn their wagon. Only way to stop the contagion."

"Can we get down?" Glory asked. "Look for their stock? If they're tied up and left behind, they might starve."

He considered for an instant and nodded. "Do *not* go near their wagon."

"We should hold a memorial service for them." Patience looked to Ruth. "It's not fitting to . . . it's not fitting to go this way."

Worry creased Jackson's brow as he glanced back at the silent wagon. "I can't afford to risk your safety."

"We can't afford to leave them without saying words from the good Book," Ruth said quietly. "I promise we'll be brief."

Jackson nodded. "I'll scout around to check for their stock."

⟨⸺⟩

"I'll help." Glory scrambled out of the wagon, relieved Ruth was going to be otherwise occupied. She could help Jackson; the thought was pleasing though the circumstances were anything but happy.

Jackson and Glory searched a wide loop around the family's wagon while the girls moved the wagon. He led the way down a slope to the Arkansas River, where tethered nearby they found a nice team of red mules still under harness, tied so they could graze on the heavy bottom grass and also reach water.

Glory murmured soothingly to reassure the two large animals as Jackson freed them. She trailed behind as he led them uphill. After tying the pair of animals to the back of his wagon, he and Glory joined the girls, who had formed a loose circle a short distance from the burned-out campfire. Glory and Jackson bowed their heads.

"Ashes to ashes, dust to dust," Ruth murmured.

Glory's gaze drifted over the neat bundles near the campfire: bedrolls, folded clothing . . . people's lives. Her eyes focused on a scrap of black leather left out in the open not far from where she was standing. She stretched her neck for a better look. Beneath the black cover, she saw a flash of gold. It reminded her of the good Book open in Ruth's hands. She glanced up. Sure enough, the two looked practically same: black leather covers, pages edged in gold.

Her eyes widened. Could this book be a valuable treasure like the one Ruth handled with such care? she wondered. She glanced up to capture Jackson's attention, but his eyes were closed as he stood silent with head bowed.

"Amen," Ruth intoned, and the others followed.

"Amen." Jackson glanced up and frowned at Glory, who was staring at him. When he raised his brows questioningly, she pointed to the black book on the ground not far from her feet.

"Can I . . . ," she began haltingly, "would it be OK if I picked it up?"

Jackson's gaze traveled from the Bible back to her eager eyes.

"Sorry, Glory. I can't let you have it. Cholera is a powerful sickness. We have to burn everything."

Glory's face fell. She'd give anything to have a book like Ruth's. She couldn't read it, but she could hold it and feel the power of its words in her hands.

Stepping away, Jackson walked to his horse and loosened the leather strap on his saddlebags. He withdrew a book, secured the flap, and walked back to the gathering. He handed the book to Glory, his features grave. "You can have my Bible."

Glory stared at the book, then up at him. He was giving her his Bible?

"I couldn't take your Bible." She handed the book back to him.

Seconds later, the black book was back in her hands. "I want you to have it."

She opened the front cover and saw lines neatly penned in black ink. With a sigh, she passed the book back to Jackson. "What does it say?"

"You can't read?" he asked gently.

Glory shook her head, unable to meet his eyes, feeling suddenly inadequate and strangely disappointed.

Jackson's eyes softened. "It's the family Bible, Glory. The names and origins of my family's tree are recorded in the front." He leaned closer, his breath warm on her cheek. "See here? My closest relatives live in Illinois."

"Illinois," Glory murmured, staring at the feathery script. No doubt Jackson's kin had written the information for future generations.

"Perhaps you and I can write Jackson's relatives in Illinois and tell them about our trip," Ruth suggested, "so they'll know where Jackson is and what he's doing."

"Thank you, Ruth. That's a real thoughtful suggestion of yours." Jackson gave Ruth one of those smiles Glory envied.

He studied the book in her hands for a moment. "I'm placing my Bible temporarily in your care, Glory, with one important condition."

She nodded. "Whatever you say." He was actually entrusting her with something of his. She'd never owned a book before. Neither had Poppy, though he'd always put a lot of store in such. She couldn't believe her good fortune!

"If you want to keep this book, then it will be your responsibility to care for it. I think Ruth's suggestion is good; you and Ruth will write to the names in the front of the book and tell them about yourself and how you came to be with my wagon." He met her gaze directly. "This book is important to me, Glory. I wouldn't entrust it to just anyone."

She felt color spreading to her cheeks. "I can't write." He must realize that, so why was he embarrassing her all over again?

"Then you must learn to read. And write."

Now she couldn't believe her bad luck.

"*And* write?" Read *and* write. He might as well tell her to rehang the moon . . . or find an easier route to Heaven.

She sighed. For some reason, she wanted this book more than any earthly thing she could recall because it was his, but it came with strings attached. She sensed this reading and writing deal was going to be work, the kind of work she didn't like, the kind of work where you had to sit still and think. She looked at the book, felt the weight of it in her hands. At that moment, she knew she would agree to most anything to keep it.

She nodded. "OK."

"We have a deal then?"

"Deal," she nodded, sticking out her right hand while gripping the book tightly in her left.

Jackson took her hand and gave it a firm shake, then turned to face the girls. "Ruth, I'd like for you to teach Glory to read and write."

"Of course, Jackson. I would be happy to tutor her."

Harper lifted her brows and crossed her arms. "Teach her to read? Are you addled?"

"I don't believe so," Jackson replied, meeting Harper's surly look with one of his own. "Other than you, Harper, no one has thought to question my common sense."

Harper looked Glory up and down, her eyes dark with resentment. Glory felt her face grow hot under Harper's scrutiny; she felt she was being judged like a cow taken to market.

"I-I'm not stupid," Glory stammered.

"There's times when—"

"Harper," Ruth cautioned.

"I can do it," Glory straightened defensively. She wasn't an imbecile. There were just a whole lot of things she didn't know. And reading and writing happened to be two of them.

"Well, Harper, I know you'll want to get in on Glory's education. You can teach her to cook," Jackson said.

"Cook? Her?"

"Maybe you're not as smart as Jackson thinks," Glory stated, crossing her arms smugly. "Maybe you can't teach anybody to cook."

Harper uncrossed her arms and crossed them again. "I can teach *anyone anything* if I set my mind to it. My ma was intelligent. That's what Mr. Potter said. Very intelligent. He said that's where I get my smarts."

"Ha."

"Ha."

The girls faced off hotly.

"Then it's settled." Jackson seemed eager to move on. "Harper, you'll teach Glory to cook, and Ruth will teach her to read. Ladies, return to our wagon and move on down the trail about a hundred yards. Wait for me there."

The girls followed his order, loaded up, and started down the trail. They were over a hill and down the other side when Ruth reined in the team to wait for Jackson. They could no longer see the family's campsite, but minutes later, they saw smoke rising in the sky and knew what was happening.

When Jackson topped the rise and approached, they could see the sadness on his face. He stowed the matches, then joined Ruth on the wagon seat. Without a word, he took the reins and gave them a shake. The oxen leaned into the yoke and trudged on down the trail.

Glory turned to stare out the back of the wagon, clutching the worn, black book to her chest. Jackson had loaned her his Bible. She thought she was going to burst with the joy of it all.

⌒〜⌒

After supper that night, Ruth sat with Glory beside the campfire, going over the alphabet. Jackson suspected that Glory would have preferred to spend her time skinning rabbits, cleaning a fish, even washing dishes, but she appeared determined to prove herself a capable student.

He smiled at the frown of concentration on her face as she carefully repeated after Ruth. Beckoning to Lily and Patience from the other side of the wagon, he got their attention.

"Ladies," he whispered when they joined him, "I would appreciate it if you'd teach Glory some household skills. You two do a fine job of it, and those are skills she's going to need in the future."

"Of course," Lily said. "I've been thinking the same thing."

"Couldn't be that hard," Patience agreed. "If Ruth can teach her to read and write, and Harper can show her how to cook, Lily and I can hone her domestic skills."

"I'd be much obliged." Jackson nodded with a conspiratorial smile. "And, ladies, let's just keep this among ourselves, shall we?"

Patience and Lily glanced briefly at each other and back to him. "Of course."

Later, Jackson found a moment to talk privately with Mary, and she agreed to teach Glory to sew. Each of the women was more than willing to help, and all had agreed to keep their arrangements with Jackson confidential. After all, they told him, they wouldn't want to hurt the young woman's pride.

Jackson grinned as he set the wagon in motion the next morning, feeling downright proud of his accomplishments. He glanced over his shoulder, his smile widening. Glory was in the back of the wagon, leafing through his Bible. There'd be no walking until she satisfied her curiosity, and that would take awhile.

A girl would be ill prepared for marriage unless she learned basic domestic tasks. Whether she liked it or not, before the trip was over, Glory would be qualified to make some man a good wife, even though somewhere in that stubborn brain of hers, she still thought that she was going to make it on her own.

Cooking. Now Jackson was set on meddling in her business. Glory picked up a long-handled fork and approached the fire warily. There were a hundred things she liked better than cooking. Sore bunions, for instance, or an earache would be better than standing over a hot skillet of spitting bacon.

She had more grease burns on her arms than she had freckles on her face. Uttering a bad word, she turned a piece of bacon, jumping farther back, spouting another unsavory word. Frowning, Lily shook her head. "We don't say those words around here."

Glory eyed the popping skillet, shoving it away from the fire. "I can't help it, Lily. I'm not a cook. Don't even like it. Can't I do the wash? Or shoot something for dinner like a rabbit or a squirrel?"

"You ate when Poppy was alive, didn't you?"

"He did all the cooking. I made sure he had stuff to put on the table." If Mary or Lily asked her to skin a deer, she could do that. She could shoot a jackrabbit or wring a hen's neck to throw in a boiling pot. What she couldn't do was fry a strip of bacon without burning it or make a drinkable cup of coffee! She jumped back again, sucking a burnt finger.

The group gathered at the back of the wagon to eat breakfast. Eating had turned into an ordeal Glory would just as soon avoid. For three weeks they'd been on the trail now, and for some reason table manners seemed suddenly more important.

The girls eyed Glory disapprovingly when she sopped up gravy with bread. Why? You were *supposed* to sop gravy with biscuits, not eat it with a fork like Patience. If she tried to eat gravy with a fork, it would take her all day to get a decent bite.

Jackson approached the wagon, removing his hat. The girls bowed their heads, and he blessed the food. "Lord, we thank you for this bounty and ask that you be with us today on our travels. Amen."

Ruth and Lily unfolded their napkins and laid them in their laps. Ruth's eyes followed Jackson, and she hurriedly reached for the plate of bacon and eggs. "You must be real hungry this morning."

"Thanks, Ruth. I can always eat Harper's biscuits."

I can always eat Harper's biscuits, Glory mocked silently. Envy coursed through her. He'd never told her that he liked her cooking. Of course, she couldn't blame him. She didn't like her cooking, either.

She felt the girls' eyes on her as she dug into her eggs, anxious to be on her way. The long days were full of new adventures, and she looked forward to each new day and to the knowledge it would bring her. Breaking a biscuit apart, she dunked it in gravy. "Good thing we ain't—"

"Haven't," Ruth corrected.

". . . haven't," she amended dutifully, "come across any more families who caught the cholera."

Ruth passed Jackson the pan of biscuits and filled his coffee cup a second time. Her hand lingered a moment longer on his than what Glory thought was proper. Ruth smiled. "Jelly?"

Jelly? Glory watched the exchange, assuring herself that she didn't care. These new feelings were worse than having a shoe fit too tight. Ruth had been good to her, real nice, but Ruth clearly had her sights fixed on Jackson, and clearly he wasn't complaining.

Glory didn't like the hurtful twinges Ruth's maternal clucking caused, partly because she didn't understand them and partly because she wanted to be the one doing the fussing. Jackson didn't seem to mind who clucked over him. He took the mollycoddling in stride, like it was his due.

Scooping a bite of eggs into her mouth, Glory wiped her chin with the cuff of her sleeve. "What do you think we'll see on the trail today, Jackson?"

Yesterday they'd spotted a big ten-point buck standing along a ridge. He'd stood there proud as a peacock, sniffing the air. Glory had studied the beautiful animal as Jackson rode to the back of the wagon and eyed her sternly before he spoke. "By the size of his rack, he's been around a few years. Unless the meat is needed, nobody in this train kills for sport."

Glory wouldn't have shot the buck for any reason; Jackson didn't need to look at her that way, as if she were loaded with evil. Poppy had said it was wrong to kill for sport, and she'd never dream of felling that magnificent creature.

The rest of the day she'd kept busy watching geese lifting off of ponds and colorful birds taking flight, wishing Poppy could see all the new wonders.

They'd stopped at Big Timbers long enough for Jackson to check the harness, and she'd watched Patience talking to a couple of bluebirds on a fence post. When she'd asked Patience if they'd said anything back, Lily gave her a weary look. Well, Glory didn't talk to birds. How was she supposed to know if they talked back to some folks?

Jackson glanced up from his breakfast plate, disturbing her musings. "We'll be at Apishapa Creek in a month. At that point, you'll be able to see the Huerfano Mountains and Spanish Peaks in the distance."

"Huerfano?" Glory asked awkwardly, trying out the different sound on her tongue.

Jackson nodded. "Means 'orphan' in Spanish."

"Like us," Lily murmured. The girls felt an immediate kinship with a range of orphan mountains.

"Yes," Jackson said, lying back to rest. "The Cherokee Trail comes in from Arkansas near Bent's Fort and leads to the gold diggings at Cherry Creek."

"That's in Colorado," Ruth said.

"Wow," Glory murmured in awe. She shook her head, marveling at her good fortune. She'd already been farther than she'd ever dreamed possible and seen things she never knew existed, and Jackson said they'd barely begun the long trip, and they were less than halfway there.

That day they walked only ten miles, but the trail had crossed high, broken terrain. The going was slow and difficult, and the wagon had gotten hung up several times.

For weeks, Jackson had warned them that there would be many tedious days like this one, not to let themselves be spoiled by some of the earlier days when the road had been flat and worn down by previous travelers.

Again, Jackson reminded them of what lay ahead. "The road is just as bad up ahead," he told them as they gathered around the fire that night. "Don't look for easy travel."

Glory listened to the warning, bone weary tonight. Her sore feet agreed that the road had been hard today, though she had found previous days exhausting as well. She ladled lard into the skillet and set it on the fire to heat.

The others eyed the skillet bleakly.

Glory noted their leery looks and determined to make them eat their uncharitable thoughts. Ruth had put her in charge of cooking tonight, and they were going to see that she was improving. She cut up an onion and threw it in the hot grease. The spicy aroma added hot fuel to the late August air.

Lily sniffed the pleasant smell, rubbing her swollen ankles. "I'm just too plain tired to eat."

Glory smiled to herself as she mixed brown beans and potatoes in a bowl. Lily might think she was too tired to eat, but once she got a taste of Poppy's recipe, she'd come alive. Poppy had fixed it twice a week—had vowed it was good for what ailed you.

Rummaging through the staples box, she located the bundle of hot peppers. There was nothing better than a dose of Poppy's Blazing Fire stew to get the blood circulating. That should get them back on their feet.

While the others dozed before the warm fire, Glory added seasoning to the skillet, humming as she worked. The mixture in the pot bubbled merrily over the red-hot coals.

Ruth finally stirred and went to the back of the wagon. Glory glanced over her shoulder to watch Ruth climb into the wagon. She wondered if Jackson would follow, but he didn't. He sat by the fire, hat tipped over his eyes, resting from the long day.

Wiping her hands on her apron, Glory went in search of Ruth. She found the young woman taking a sponge bath in the privacy of the sheltered wagon. Ruth glanced up when Glory rounded the corner.

"Oh!" She quickly drew her bodice back into place.

"It's me, Ruth. Sorry, didn't mean to scare you."

Ruth smiled and returned to her nightly grooming. *I swear, she's going to wear a hole clean through her skin,* Glory thought. But she envied Ruth's scrupulous good habits . . . and even more, she admired the way Ruth was so happy and satisfied, so sure of what she wanted. Glory longed for Ruth's peacefulness and inner beauty, and she had a hunch it had something to do with the Bible. Ruth understood life and what was expected out of a person more than most folks. Whatever it was that caused Ruth's glow, Glory wanted it.

When Glory continued to stare, Ruth turned to look over her shoulder. "Thought I'd freshen up a bit while supper is cooking."

"You're not going to take a bath in the river?"

"No, it's rather shallow here. I'll just freshen up a bit in the wagon." She flashed a wholesome smile. "Care to join me?"

"Can't. Supper's cooking." But she would later. It was getting to where she didn't sleep well unless she was spanking clean. As far as she could tell, the daily baths hadn't hurt her skin.

When Glory continued to stand there, Ruth frowned. "Did you need something from the wagon?"

"No, needed to ask you something." It was a thought that'd been going around in Glory's mind for weeks. The only way she knew to get rid of it was to come right out and ask Ruth directly so she wouldn't be thinking about it day and night.

"Ask away." Ruth's slender fingers refastened the front of her dress.

"You like Jackson, don't you?"

Ruth's brows lifted curiously. "Like him? Yes, he's very nice."

"No. I mean, you *like* him."

When the implication sank in, Ruth's smile gradually faded. "Don't you like him?"

"I like him a whole lot, but he doesn't like me."

"Nonsense." Ruth laughed. "He's been very good to you, Glory. What a thing for you to say. He's been kind and considerate and most thoughtful of all our needs."

"He doesn't like me like he likes you, Ruth."

"Nonsense." Ruth picked up the round basin and emptied her bath water in the bushes.

"But you do like him, don't you?"

"I don't think that's a proper thing for you to be asking."

"Why not?"

"Well . . . because. Whom I like and whom I don't like is a private matter. Besides, Mr. Wyatt has arranged for me to be a mail-order bride. Even if I were to find Mr. Lincoln attractive—"

"And you do?"

Ruth glanced away. "Even if I did, he isn't free to return my sentiments."

Glory couldn't let it go. It was like a worrisome hangnail that just got worse with too much handling. "But you want him to like you as much as you like him."

Ruth feigned indifference, but Glory knew better. "I can't say that I don't find Jackson a desirable man, not only in appearance but in various other ways."

Glory nodded. She knew the other ways. Confident, self-assured, powerful—he attracted Ruth all right, and Ruth's feelings amounted to more than like.

Ruth turned to face her. "Seems to me he's rather partial to you. After all, he entrusted his family Bible to your care."

That was true, he had. And it still was hard for Glory to believe.

Ruth consulted a small mirror on the back of the wagon. "Does that answer your question?"

Nodding, Glory studied the brush Ruth was pulling through her hair. The thick tresses were shiny and as black as coal. "You're in love with him."

Didn't matter, really. Glory figured most every girl on the wagon trip was in love with him, except Harper, who didn't like men, period.

"But he can't return my affection, so it doesn't matter," Ruth repeated, her tone gentler now. "Now, if I'm not mistaken, I smell supper burning."

"Yes, probably so."

When Glory returned to the fire, Harper was stirring the bubbling concoction with a large wooden spoon. Her dark eyes surveyed the pot curiously. "Girl, what in the world is this?"

Moving her out of the way, Glory replied, "Never mind. You're going to like it."

And like it they did. Jackson ate four servings, and Glory noticed with considerable satisfaction that even Ruth went back for seconds. When Lily scraped the skillet clean, Glory thought she would burst with happiness. Maybe cooking wasn't so bad after all.

The moon rose high over the campsite. After some time, however, the girls left the wagon, one by one, and ran toward the creek.

Eventually, Jackson staggered from his bedroll and beat a path to the bushes. By dawn, the whole party was lying on the riverbank, gripping their stomachs.

"What did you put in that devil's brew?" Harper moaned. She rolled to her side and heaved.

Lily, Patience, Ruth, and Mary wet towels and put them over their eyes.

Lying prostrate on the ground, Glory mustered enough strength to reply, "Just some beans . . . potatoes . . . chilies . . . and grease."

Grease—lots of thick, heavy lard. Guess she must have gone a lot heavier on the grease than Poppy did. She'd never paid much attention to how much of each ingredient he'd used.

Lily doubled over, holding her stomach like something was about to fall right out of the middle. "Oh, mercy!" She moaned in agony. "In all my life I've never felt so close to death."

Patience groaned. "We may all be in heaven before too long."

"Except for those of us bound for the alternative!" Harper's glassy eyes burned feverishly in her head.

Glory felt the ground spinning beneath her as she continued to lie belly down. Oh, no. They couldn't all go to Heaven tonight and leave her! She'd been sicker than this before, though it was hard to remember exactly when, but she knew she was nowhere near dyin'. And what was that alternative thing Harper was talking about? Glory didn't even know what the word meant.

She winced when she heard Jackson struggle to his feet and make another dash for the bushes.

Well, she thought, closing her eyes against a wave of nausea, if they were so fired up about teaching her to cook, they'd have to suffer the consequences.

Jackson wasn't talking. No one was, and no one wanted breakfast, even though Ruth offered to cook it. They sat around the fire, wrapped in blankets, making periodic sprints into the brush. The whole incident cost a day of travel, and Jackson wasn't too happy about it.

Glory wasn't any happier, but the way she figured it, she could have killed them all—almost did. She'd lain there on the riverbank, holding Jackson's worn black book and looking up at the sky, where she'd pleaded with someone to please not let Jackson die.

And while you're at it, I'd sure appreciate it if you'd spare the other girls' lives, too.

Someone had answered her prayer, and Glory was truly beholden to the source.

On the other hand, Jackson didn't miss the chance to tell her that it would be a cold day in August before he ate *that* stuff again.

Chapter Nine

In the next couple of days, the party recovered enough to eat solid food again.

But Glory was anything but a quitter. For the next few weeks, she watched Harper's cooking methods attentively, followed her directions as well as she could, and prepared a few dishes under Harper's close scrutiny.

Glory was itching to try something on her own without the teacher's continual criticism. The others were leery about what she fixed, giving her recipes a wary eye. For that reason, she'd decided not to ask Harper for help. This time she'd try a tasty treat that she *knew* was one of Jackson's favorites: apple pie. If she couldn't make a simple apple pie, then she was a plain disgrace to womanhood.

During the noon break, she'd walked the horses to the stream to water them. On the way back, she'd discovered a wild apple tree. It had reminded her of the autumns she'd shared with Poppy. Early September had always brought golden days, crisp nights, and delicious apples. She'd filled her apron with ripe, tart fruit and hidden it in the wagon upon her return.

That evening as they set up camp Glory peeled, cored, and sliced the apples the way she'd seen Poppy do so many times. Now for the crust. Poppy had let her help with the apples, but he'd always fixed the shell himself. Said it was easier to do himself than to teach someone how. Claimed you had to have a feel for it, an instinct that told you when to add more water, when to add more flour, when to let it rest, how to roll it out just so.

Glory shrugged. How hard could it be? Didn't everyone say "simple as pie" when they thought something was easy? Poppy never measured ingredients, so neither would she. She began with a scoop of flour, a splash of water, a pinch of salt, and a generous handful of lard.

Everyone was busy setting up camp. Mary paused on her way to the stream, carrying dirty clothes to wash. She studied the mixture, brows arched. "What are you making?"

Glory spun around. "Nothing." She shoved a lock of hair out of her eyes with the back of her hand, and a sprinkle of flour sifted down like the first flecks of an early snow.

"Baking?" Mary smiled. "Are you making Harper's famous biscuits?"

"Hmmm," Glory smiled. "They're the best, aren't they?"

"The very best." Mary glanced around, her eyes searching for Lily.

She wants Lily to help so I won't make them all sick again. But Lily was busy gathering firewood.

"Well . . . need any help?"

"No. I can do it alone."

Shifting the basket of dirty clothes into her other arm, Mary frowned. "Best get these clothes washed—"

"Better do that." Glory spun back to her pie dough. Interruptions and distractions she didn't need. "Where was I?" she mumbled. "Oh, yes." She grabbed a wooden spoon and began stirring.

The dough formed a sticky ball. She nodded, remembering seeing this step in Poppy's process. It was now that he got his hands into it. She dumped the ball onto the wooden board with a satisfying thud. Working it with her hands felt good at first, but then it got too sticky. She tossed in a few handfuls of flour and worked harder. Pretty soon, the dough got too stiff.

She rummaged around until she found the rolling pin. Now things would go better. She shoved at the dough, but it resisted her efforts. Leaning on the rolling pin, she bit her lower lip. This was harder than it had looked when she'd seen Poppy rolling it out.

Maybe some water would soften it up. She reached into the bucket and scooped out a handful and tossed it onto the mound of dough. "Oh, no," she muttered when she saw specks of dough floating in the water bucket. She glanced toward the others. "I'll have to get fresh water before supper," she murmured, making a mental note for later.

Now the dough was softening up. It was also sticking to the rolling pin and her hands and her elbows. She was so exasperated she could scream. Hearing the girls' laughter alerted her that they were on their way back from the stream. She rolled faster. She had to get this done.

Grabbing the pie tin, she slapped the dough into it. Desperately, she pushed at the dough with her hands to spread it. It required so much force that the tin flipped up and down and spun like a top to the edge of the board. With a lunge, Glory caught it before it dropped to the ground.

"Enough of this," she muttered as the sound of laughter grew nearer. The dough would probably spread nicely when heated. She tossed the apples on top of the dough, and then added a generous scoop of sugar, three tablespoons of flour, a gob of butter, and a dash of cinnamon. The top crust! She closed her eyes, and her head rolled back. She'd forgotten about the *top* crust. She remembered how Poppy had laid neat strips of dough across the top of his pie, weaving them, humming while he worked.

"Next time," she muttered, "next time we'll have neat strips." For now, she'd have to make do with a few stray lumps of dough that had previously escaped the pie tin. She tossed them on top of the pie and hurried to the fire.

The girls were close now. Glory spied the large cast-iron pot Patience had used to boil water. Glory had seen her pour the water into a bucket and take off with it. Obviously, she was finished with it, so Glory slipped her pie into the pot and clamped on the lid. Carefully, she settled the pot down into the hot coals.

Wiping her hands on her apron, she straightened. By the time supper was over, her pie would be baked to perfection. A triumphant smile spread across her face. *Won't everybody be surprised,* she thought with smug satisfaction. Poppy had been right as usual: cooking was a matter of instinct. You had it or you didn't. Tonight she'd show them all. She had it.

As the group sat around the fire finishing rabbit stew, Patience stood and reached for the pan. "Anyone care for seconds?" she asked.

Jackson extended his plate. "I would."

Glory glanced up. "Better save room for dessert."

"I didn't make dessert," Harper said. "Too much washing to do."

"What's this?" Patience asked, pointing down at the iron pot nestled in the ashes.

Glory bounded to her feet. "Allow me." She wrapped a cloth around the handle of the pot and pulled it from the coals. Carefully she removed the lid and lifted out the pie. It didn't look like the apple pies Poppy had made, but she figured in the future they would look better.

Patience approached, peering over her shoulder.

"It's not how it looks that's important," Glory began defensively. "What matters is how it tastes. Jackson, if you'll pass your plate over here, I'll serve you first."

After a slight hesitation, all eyes turned to Jackson. Harper reached her hand across the circle. "Here," she said, with a beckoning wave. "No need to get up. I'll pass your plate over."

Jackson paused a beat before handing his plate to Harper. "This isn't like Poppy's Blazing Fire stew recipe, is it?"

Glory's hand shot to her hips. "I don't want to hear another word about Poppy's stew."

Harper returned his plate to him; it was laden with a huge slice of pie. "Eat up, Mr. Lincoln." She grinned.

Jackson nodded, eyeing the pie. "Looks . . . mighty good."

He cut into his pie, while Glory continued to fill one plate after another. "Oh my," she exclaimed when the pie tin was empty. "I forgot to save a piece for myself."

"Here." All plates extended toward her.

She waved their plates away, smiling. "Oh, I couldn't."

"I wish you could," Harper murmured, staring bleakly at the wad of crust on her plate.

Glory looked at her friends, beaming now. "I have to admit I didn't want to learn to cook, but fixing this surprise for you has taught me the true meaning of . . . what's that saying? 'It's better to give than to receive.' Never made sense to me before." She shifted, settling her hands back around her waist. "Now what else can I get for everyone?"

"Water," Jackson managed to choke out. He coughed, and Glory prayed that a chunk of dry crust wasn't wedged in his throat.

"Coming up!" She quickly filled his cup from the dipper in the bucket and handed it to Ruth to pass to him, all the while keeping her eyes on the others as they slowly ate their pie.

"What's this?" Ruth asked, staring at the white blobs floating on the surface of the water.

Glory leaned forward to look. "Oh." She'd forgotten to get a fresh bucket of water after she'd dipped her hand into it. Clumps of dough were floating in the bucket and in Jackson's cup.

"What is it?" Mary echoed, staring into the cup as she passed it to Jackson. Wide-eyed, she looked up at Glory.

Glory shrugged and snatched up the bucket. "I'll get some fresh water from the stream." She picked up the lantern and disappeared.

When she returned, she was happy to see that every plate was empty. *They must have loved my pie—not a single scrap left behind,* she mused. She would have enjoyed hearing their praise, but she guessed the moment had passed while she was at the stream.

When the last dish was cleaned and put away, Mary asked Glory to help her with the mending. Glory didn't make an excuse but willingly sat down to learn. She'd proven she could make a pie, so domestic duties weren't so bad, certainly not as exciting as hunting and fishing, but necessary just the same.

She intended to do her share of work. Truth was, she was beginning to find satisfaction in doing nice things for others. Her pie had been a hit, why not darn Jackson's socks? He'd appreciate having those unsightly holes repaired.

"Perhaps you'd want to practice mending tea towels first, dear," Mary suggested gently.

"No, I like doing things for Jackson." The words were out of her mouth before she even realized she'd thought them. Embarrassed, she bent her head to her task, drawing closer to the fire, hoping that anyone looking would believe the warmth of the flames was causing the redness in her cheeks.

One morning a couple of weeks later Jackson chose to walk a few miles beside the wagon, carrying his rifle and scanning the hills. For days they'd been crossing flat spaces where he could see for miles. Now they were moving along the river road that ran up to the old pueblo at the mouth of the Fontaine qui Bouille Creek.

They marched through lush, rolling hills where a man could be ambushed. Jackson doubted the law was tracking them, but he was concerned about Amos. Greed could make a man do strange things.

After noon break, he climbed onto the wagon seat and took the reins. Amos or not, he couldn't walk another step. His feet were killing him; it felt like he'd been walking on rocks all day.

After a few miles, he handed the reins to Ruth and tugged off a boot. "No wonder," he muttered, running his hand across the bottom of his foot. "Been walking on knots the size of Texas." He glanced at Ruth. "Who did this to my socks?"

Ruth continued to stare straight ahead. "Don't ask," she murmured.

He groaned, staring at the rumps of his oxen. "Whose idea was it to have her learn all these domestic skills?"

Ruth chuckled. "Yours."

That evening they made camp early beside a narrow stream and a stand of trees. They needed fresh meat for their meal. While the women gathered firewood from the ample supply surrounding the campsite, Jackson set off on foot with his rifle. Glory followed not far behind, carrying his shotgun.

An hour later, they returned with six pheasants—two of them shot by Jackson, four by Glory.

"Might as well clean those while I clean mine." She reached for his two birds.

Awkwardly he handed them over, unaccustomed to having someone do his work. "You need some help with them?"

"No, sir." She headed toward the water.

Steamed, he watched her trotting off, happy as a lark.

"I'll be down after I feed the stock," he hollered. "The mare has a sore tendon that needs rubbing down."

"Already did it," she called over her shoulder.

He caught up with her in a few steps, spinning her around to face him. "You've fed the stock?"

"Of course not, Jackson. They're too hot to feed when we first break for camp." She shook her head in disbelief. "I rubbed down your mare's left foreleg with liniment on the noon break. She's still limping, so I think you're wrong about her problem being in her tendon."

He looked up and then away. "Then why don't you tell me what you think it is," he said tightly. "And don't feel like you have to break it to me gently."

She grinned. "Oh, I get it. You're kidding, right? Of course I'll tell you what I think directly, man to man, so to speak."

"Yeah, I'm kidding." He didn't like her taking over his chores, and he sure didn't like a woman telling him how to run his business.

"Good, then I can tell you straight-out I think your mare is limping because she has a stone bruise."

"A stone bruise," he repeated. His eyes met hers. "I knew that."

"I know you did. Not much we can do for that but rest her for a while."

She was right. The mare would only get worse if they didn't rest her.

Now she was sore. If he rode her, she would become lame. Just one more delay he couldn't afford.

"It's not my fault," Glory reminded him as she scanned his grim expression.

"Yeah, well, I'll feed the stock now."

"All right." She headed to the stream.

"And from now on I shoot the game," he called.

She turned to look back at him. "But I was only—"

"From now on *I* shoot the game! Understood?"

"From now on *you* shoot the game. *I'm* not deaf."

He watched her slide down the embankment, the birds bundled in her hands, his shotgun under her arm.

Women.

He was in charge, deciding what to do, when to do it. He was the wagon master, and he didn't want a woman dogging his steps, cleaning his birds, diagnosing his mare, and doing his chores.

He shook his head. It was the first time he'd thought of Glory as a woman. A girl, yes. A waif, yes. A kid, yes. A woman, no. Why, he didn't think of the other females as any more than girls, either. He trudged up the hill. He didn't need anything to upset the balance. Best to distance himself from Glory before . . . he refused to consider what he was about to think. He was feeling uncomfortable enough as it was.

Lily cooked the pheasants, and the weary travelers ate the first fresh meat of the week. Afterwards, the girls started on the dishes. Glory washed slowly, knowing it would not be long before Ruth would expect her to settle down by the fire for her lessons.

She wasn't eager to begin her studies tonight. She glanced around and saw Jackson disappear around the wagon, carrying his toolbox. *Bet he's going to repair that squeaky wagon wheel,* she thought. *Bet he'd appreciate some help.* It wasn't like she was going to shoot any of his old birds.

Jackson was running a hand over the edge of a broken spoke when Glory squatted beside him. For a moment, neither of them said a word. She stared at his hands as he worked, admiring his strength. Funny, seemed to her that he was getting more handsome every day. His robin's egg blue eyes sparkled when he smiled, and the reddish gold lights in his hair when the sun shined on it nearly snatched her breath. And it was pure pleasure to talk to him about things they both understood. She enjoyed being with the girls, but she didn't have as much in common with them as she did with Jackson.

He was trying to hold both ends of the spoke while he slathered tar between them. She could see what needed to be done. Without waiting to be asked, she quickly reached out to support one end of the operation. The backs of their hands brushed and their shoulders bumped. Jackson scooted away like he'd been scalded.

"Shouldn't you be studying or something?"

Grunting, she held the spoke in place. "Not till the dishes are done."

"Wouldn't they be done sooner if you helped?"

"Might be." She let go of the spoke and straightened. "Thought you could use my help more." She stood there for an instant, expecting he'd realize how much he needed her and insist that she stay. Clearly, he could use another set of hands.

He kept his eyes on the spoke. "I think you'd better join the others."

Her chin dropped. He had no cause to be so unfriendly. She'd never heard him talk to Ruth or the others like that. Sure, he gave orders, but when he talked to Ruth, it was always in gentle tones, like she was his equal. Now that she thought about it, he'd been acting strange all evening. From the time they'd gone hunting to now, he'd acted like she was bothering him, like she was stepping on his nerves.

"Go on, Glory. Those dishes won't wash themselves."

Spinning on her heel, she marched back around the wagon. She had no idea where she was headed, but she felt a powerful urge to be alone. When she strode past the campfire, she felt a tug on her elbow. She looked back to see Ruth.

"It's time you practiced your writing," she said, gesturing to the Bible, paper, pen, and ink she'd laid out by the fire.

"Don't feel like it," Glory announced, trying to hide the quaver in her voice.

Harper frowned across the fire as she looked from Glory's face to the other side of the wagon, where Jackson could be heard working. "You're bound for a heap of trouble if you don't do your studies," Harper murmured. "A whole heap, girl."

"Oh, all right!" Glory spun around and tramped back to drop onto the blanket. It was better to cooperate than to let Harper announce to the others that she'd been annoying Jackson. "Where were we?"

Ruth took a seat beside her. "You were practicing your handwriting by writing the Ten Commandments. I believe you left off with the last one: coveting."

"Figures," Glory muttered. Ruth had briefly explained the implications. They fit Glory to a tee. Jealousy. It was a feeling she experienced all too frequently these days. It wasn't good. She thought about the other nine commandments. The one about not killing ate away at her. *"You killed Charlie! You killed Charlie Gulch! You'll hang."* She'd already broken two; how many others was she wallowing in or capable of committing? If the other sins left a body feeling as miserable as killing did, and this awful thing called envy—which she couldn't for the life of her seem to shake—she wasn't sure she could endure the pressure. More and more she was feeling like a sinner, but she didn't know the remedy or even if there was one.

Guilt assailed her. She never meant to kill Charlie Gulch, but she was a living example of someone who constantly broke the tenth commandment. Every time she saw Ruth and Jackson smiling at one another, laughing together, talking like old friends—it was as if a spike were being driven into her heart. These were two people who had been kinder to her than anyone else; she should be happy for them, want them to find happiness with each other. But she didn't, and she despised the hateful feeling inside her.

"Let me see," Ruth said, leaning over to examine Glory's efforts. "Very good, your best handwriting so far."

Glory sat back and sketched whatever came into her mind. She had no idea how to rid herself of ugly feelings like jealousy, but she knew that if she let her mind wander and let herself draw beautiful images, it would help.

"What are you drawing?" Ruth leaned over for a second look.

Glory handed her the paper reluctantly.

"Angels?" she asked. "You like to draw angels?"

"Makes me feel peaceful to draw them."

Harper glanced up. "I like pictures of things that are real, like trees and mountains. Don't see why you'd waste your time on something that isn't even real."

"Angels are real."

The young woman eyed her skeptically. "Now how do you know that? Have you seen one?"

Glory shook her head. "Poppy saw them. Saw them hovering over the bed of a dying child. Next day, the child got better. Kept getting better until she was well. Poppy gave credit to the angels."

"Do tell. And you believe in them because that old hermit believed in them?"

Glory shrugged as she reached for her drawing. "What he believed is good enough for me."

Believing in angels was a sight better than feeling envy; even Harper couldn't argue that.

"I believe in angels," Ruth said quietly. She handed Glory a clean sheet of paper. "Let's try writing the ABCs once more, beginning with the letter *A*." She smiled. "For angels, for surely they are watching over us this very night."

Ruth continued. "The Bible is full of stories of angels. The birth of Jesus had lots of angels involved: telling Mary and Joseph what was to happen, singing before the shepherds. Why, even Jesus was helped twice by angels—once after he was tempted by Satan, and also in the Garden of Gethsemane."

"Jesus?" Glory asked. "Even he was tempted? You read to me about his birth and some of the stories he told. But I don't understand why, if he was God, he had to die the way he did." Ruth had read the story of Jesus' death before, and Glory had a hard time grasping the concept that if Jesus was God, he could die.

Ruth replied after a small pause, "It was because of our sins. God had to punish someone for sins. Jesus willingly took on the punishment for our sins, so we wouldn't have to face God's punishment."

Glory thought about breaking the tenth commandment and how guilty she felt. "So how does a person know if Jesus died for his sins?"

"You believe in faith that he died for you and ask him to come into your heart."

There it was again, that word: *faith.*

Glory lay in her bedroll later and stared at the stars. If angels were up there, why hadn't she seen one? She supposed it had something to do with faith. The Bible said that taking things on faith meant believing that just because a body couldn't see something didn't mean it wasn't there. She couldn't see the wind, but she felt the whisper of it on her face.

Rolling to her side, she closed her eyes, thinking about all the things she couldn't see but knew existed. Like love. She had seen the evidence of love, but she'd never touched it. Peace. That had come into her life the day she'd joined up with Jackson and the girls; but she couldn't touch it. Security. Joy. She felt those every time she looked at Jackson and his handsome features and his gentle ways, but she couldn't physically touch security or joy. Some folks might say the bag of gold she kept hidden under the floorboards of the wagon represented security and could buy a whole lot of joy. But it was only a bag of nuggets, and once they were gone, there'd be no security or joy. Look at Poppy. When he'd died, he'd taken the only thing that counted in the Lord's eyes: his soul. The gold had remained hidden beneath the floor of his cabin.

She lay there counting the things she'd have to accept on faith, until she finally drifted off. There were enough to keep her awake long after the others were sound asleep.

Chapter Ten

Blistering late-summer heat plagued the travelers as the prairie schooner slowly wound along the creek of Fontaine qui Bouille. The calendar that Mary kept with her personal belongings said that it was September, but the relentless sun beating down on their heads refused to give way to cooler temperatures.

They had been on the trail nearly two months, and the extra roominess in Glory's shirt and pants, and the growing holes in the soles of her boots testified to her long hours spent walking.

This morning the only conscious thought in her mind was that the walk would be shorter today. Over breakfast Jackson said that over the next ten miles the trail was rough and uneven, but that there would be an abundance of wood, water, and grass where they would make camp early tonight. The tight lines around his eyes reminded Glory that he was worried about breakdowns and additional delays.

First, crossing the river had held them up. Then, Poppy's Blazing Fire stew had kept them abed and not far from the bushes for one whole day. Last week they were detained a day and a half when an axle broke and they had to hunt up a blacksmith to fix it.

With each new setback, the lines around Jackson's eyes tightened even more. It seemed powerful important to him that they reach Denver City before late fall, so it became Glory's primary goal, too. She did everything possible to be helpful and not be underfoot.

Wildlife was sparser now. She'd seen an armadillo yesterday, a strange-looking creature with a hard shell covering its shoulders and backside. The funny-looking animal with short legs moved quickly, its strong feet and thick claws burrowing with surprising speed.

Jackrabbits were plentiful, but the meat was tough. Glory longed for the tender flesh of the small rabbits found in the woods surrounding the shanty.

At times, she even found herself missing the old cow and the mule, Molasses. Poppy had brought the little mule home before it had been weaned. Glory had had to get up twice every night to feed the animal, but because of her mothering, a strong bond had formed between the animal and herself.

She looked forward to the new life awaiting her in Colorado, but she missed her old life something fierce, with its lazy days hunting and fishing with Poppy and its cool nights lying on her small cot, the sounds of cicadas and pond frogs drifting through the open window.

If it weren't for being with Jackson, seeing his smile, listening to the stories he told around the campfire at night, she might be tempted to turn back. Because the shanty, in spite of her new friends and Jackson, was all she'd ever had to call home.

Shortly after noon a harness broke. Glory paused in back of the wagon, listening to Jackson mutter under his breath, wincing at his sharp expletives.

My, he surely isn't listening when Ruth reads the part about not cursing. Seemed to her there was something in those worn pages about not taking the Lord's name in vain, and the words that were coming out of Jackson's mouth this morning most assuredly weren't holy. The only time she'd heard words like that was when Molasses had stepped on Poppy's infected toe. He'd whacked the old mule upside the head and talked to him something awful.

Besides, just last night Ruth had read about being angry and not sinning. Glory would be the first to admit she didn't know much of anything about what was or wasn't a sin, aside from the Ten Commandments. But to her blistering ears, Jackson sure sounded like he was mad as a wet hen and doing some powerful sinning while he was at it.

Shoving her hat to the back of her head, she joined the other girls as they walked toward the wagon master cautiously. Glory knew full well that when Jackson's face was red and bad words were as plentiful as weeds, he wasn't in any mood for socializing.

The travelers stood in the middle of the trail, staring at the torn strip of leather as if staring would miraculously repair it. The sun seared through their bonnets as the women shifted stances, eyes switching periodically to Jackson.

Lily finally broke the strained silence. "What do we do now?"

"Fix it."

"But that will take all afternoon!" Glory exclaimed.

Jackson took off his hat and wiped a stream of sweat dripping off his forehead. "Do you have a better idea?"

"We could switch teams. Use the mule team today and repair the oxen's harness tonight."

He nodded, but his grim expression didn't soften. "We could do that, *if* the mule team's harness hadn't broken when I went to hitch them this morning." His tone was louder and harsher than usual. "All our leather has taken a beating in this heat. I wipe it down with conditioning oil at night, but the salty sweat and the wear and tear have taken their toll."

Glory didn't have another idea, good or bad. She stared at the thick leather, then at Jackson. "So we stop and fix it now?"

"I guess we don't have a choice."

Jackson disappeared into the back of the wagon for the repair kit. Glory stayed put, knowing he didn't want her help. For the next few hours, he sat under a shade tree and patched the broken harness.

Ruth offered to help, but he brushed her efforts aside, saying he could complete the job faster by himself. However, Glory noticed he was thoughtful enough to thank Ruth for her offer.

The girls spread out, each pursuing her own activity. Ruth and Lily caught up on mending; Harper read a dime-store novel that she kept tucked out of sight in her satchel. Patience sat in the shade and fanned herself, her young face flushed with heat.

Midafternoon, Mary climbed into the back of the wagon and slept, her coughing more pronounced today.

Glory asked, "Why does Mary cough so much?"

"Dust," Ruth explained. "She has asthma."

"What's that?"

"It's a powerful affliction affecting the lungs. Doctors don't know much about it, so it's difficult to control or treat." She glanced at the wagon, shaking her head. "Poor Mary."

Glory nodded. Poor Mary. She listened to Mary's dry coughs at night, hurting for her. Mornings, Mary's ribs were sore from coughing, and she struggled to draw each breath. When the attacks refused to let up, Ruth heated water, and Mary put a towel over her head to inhale the vapors. Sometimes that was the only thing that kept Mary breathing.

Late afternoon, Glory wandered over to the tree where Jackson was repairing the harness. She studied the tool he was threading through the leather. "What's that?"

"An awl."

"What does it do?"

"Pokes through leather so you can sew it."

She stood for a moment, waiting for an invitation to join him, but it never came. So she sat down without one. Lately, he didn't seem to mind her company as long as she didn't talk too much or ask too many questions. She thought maybe he was getting used to her.

Jackson glanced up from his mending. "Where are the other girls?"

"Keeping out of your way."

He flashed a tolerant grin. His temper had cooled, but Glory noticed the worry lines were still evident around his eyes. The delays were happening more often, it seemed. Guess he had a right to be concerned.

"We'll walk faster," she promised. "We'll be in Denver City before the first snow."

"I hope you're right."

They sat in companionable silence, she watching his long, capable fingers thread the rawhide strips through the harness straps. Mary's worsening coughs filled the silence.

"You shouldn't talk bad, you know," Glory said evenly.

He bent his head, pretending interest in the harness, but he didn't fool her. He was ashamed of himself for talking that way in front of the others, and he should be. He was a good man who had let his anger get the best of him.

"There's women present—Ruth says a man isn't to talk that way in front of a woman."

"Ruth's right. I'm sorry."

"It's all right." She wasn't one to hold grudges. "I'll remind you when you do it again."

He gave her a sour look. "You do that."

Settling back, she crossed her arms over her chest and stared at the faultless blue sky. "Do you believe in angels?"

Jackson glanced at her from the corner of his eye. "Never thought much about it. Why?"

"Ever met one?" Glory turned to perch on one knee, watching him work. Her discussion with Ruth still lingered in her mind.

"For certain? No, I don't think so, though I wondered a few times."

"Really? You think you might have met one?" If he'd met an honest-to-goodness angel she wanted to hear about it. Harper didn't believe in angels, but there wasn't much she did believe in.

However, angels fascinated Glory. It was only a couple of nights ago Ruth read where God gives his angels charge over you, to protect you, to guide you. One appeared to Mary in a blaze of light to tell her she was going to have a baby. And a whole bunch of angels sang in the sky to the shepherds. Now that'd be plumb scary—get a body's attention all right. The suggestion that there was an all-powerful God and watchful angels looking after her seemed imaginary, yet when Ruth read from the black book, Glory wanted to believe it. Wanted to believe it with all her heart. The pretty words spoke to her—made her long to know this all-powerful being, made her want him to know her. But how could he know her? Except for Jackson and the girls, no one knew her, and it wasn't likely God would ever find her out here on the trail.

Jackson worked the tool through the leather, lost in thought. "Met a man once. I'd been shot trying to defend a friend; I was left lying beside the road. I thought I would bleed to death, but a stranger came along and tended my wound. He got me to a doctor, and before he left, he told me that I would live."

Jackson paused, staring at the piece of rigging in his hand. "There was something about his eyes. . . . At the time, the doctor shook his head, and I could see he didn't think that I would make it through the night. Infection set in, and I was out of my head with a high fever for two weeks. Then one morning, I opened my eyes. My fever was gone, and I was hungry enough to eat a bear."

Glory sat up straighter, leaning toward him. "Was it because of that man? You think he was an honest-to goodness angel?"

"I don't know who he was, but that day he was my angel."

Glory sat back, mulling the story over in her mind. Poppy could have been her angel—hadn't she fallen out of the back of a wagon, and hadn't he been there to rescue her? She knew their prairie schooner traveled for days, sometimes weeks, before meeting another soul. Poppy's shanty was even more secluded, so why had Poppy been there that day, that hour, that moment?

She glanced back at Jackson. "You never talk about your life. Why not?"

"Not much to tell."

Glory didn't believe that for a minute. He was an interesting man with an interesting life. She bet that he had all kinds of stories to tell, adventurous stories, like meeting that angel—if it had been an angel.

"Actually, I'm boring." He laid the mended harness aside and flexed his hand. "Lived a pretty normal life."

"But you take people across country every year." She'd heard Ruth and Lily talking; Jackson was one of the most experienced wagon masters around. Folks paid a bundle of money for his services.

"That doesn't make me interesting." He smiled, and her heart leaped at the familiarity in his eyes, and she wanted—oh how she wanted—to sit here all day and talk to him. She thought about what would happen to her when they reached Colorado. He'd go one way, and she'd go another. She didn't much like the thought. The feelings that went with it grew more painful every day.

"What about your mother?" She knew she was out of line now. Ruth had already told her that he didn't get along with his mother and didn't like to talk about her.

His features tightened. "My mother lives in Illinois."

"Do you see her often?"

"Not often." He leaned back, resting his eyes from the hot sun. Grasshoppers lifted in a dark cloud; others flitted back and forth across the road, their spindly legs whirling. He was silent so long she thought he had forgotten her question. Or maybe he was sorting out his feelings.

"No more often than necessary," he finally murmured.

Glory couldn't imagine not wanting to see Poppy. She'd loved him, wanted to be near him, though he wasn't perfect. Far from it. Cantankerous as a woodpile rattler at times, but that didn't make her love him any less. She could be a mite trying herself if the situation called for it. Yet she couldn't understand why a son wouldn't want to keep in touch with his mother. Didn't seem natural.

Jackson's eyes remained closed. "Go ahead."

Glory pulled a strand of weed. "Go ahead what?"

"Ask what you're fairly bursting to ask."

"I'm not bursting—not much, anyway. I was just wondering why a son wouldn't want to be with his mother as often as possible."

"You haven't met my mother."

She knew he was right. She hadn't met his mother, didn't know a thing about her, but she'd like to see the woman who'd produced such a fine specimen of manhood. For Jackson, with all his swearing and impatient flare-ups, was a good man. Other than a few bad words in trying situations, he was a true gentleman. He also seemed to have faith like Ruth's Bible said. He often reminded the girls about their evening devotions and prayers before each meal.

She'd seen the way he dealt with others less fortunate whom they'd met along the way. He'd given a man and his wife and infant child two sacks of flour—flour that would be needed for their own journey—but Jackson had said that they were all getting fat and could eat less for the duration of the trip.

Another time he'd given a fellow traveler a pair of boots, boots Glory knew Jackson favored. But the man had no boots, and Jackson said he had two pair. Jackson seemed to go out of his way at times to prove otherwise, but he had a good heart.

He met her eyes and sighed. "My ma ran my father off when I was a little boy. I didn't think much of her from then on."

"Ran him off? Like, 'Shoo! Go on, get out of here'?"

"No, like she complained and nagged until he couldn't take it any longer. One day he up and left, and I never saw him again."

"And you're mad at *her*?" Seemed it ought to be the other way around. Glory didn't know much about mothers, but she'd heard Ruth read something about children respecting their parents.

"Doesn't that book say something about the way we're supposed to treat parents?"

"It's not 'that book'; it's the Bible, Glory. And, yes, it does say how we're supposed to treat our parents, but sometimes it's hard to live by those teachings."

Glory thought about that. She expected that he was right; no matter how hard she tried, she messed up. And those rules Ruth read were mighty lofty goals for people. She sat, twirling the weed in her fingers, thinking about all the troubles a body faced.

"I don't know much, and I don't know anything at all about your mother, but seems to me folks would be better off trying to right their own problems than stewing about the wrong in everybody else."

Reaching for the harness, he glanced at her. "How old are you? Fifty?"

She shook her head. "Don't rightly know, but I don't think I'm *that* old."

He grinned. "That was meant to be a joke."

"Oh." She grinned, relieved. She was hoping her almost nightly baths made her look right nice, even nice enough for him to notice.

His eyes softened, and he leaned over to brush a lock of sweat-soaked hair off her cheek. "How old *are* you?"

"Best I can figure—eighteen."

"You don't know?"

"Can't know. Poppy could only guess how old I was when I fell off that wagon." Her eyes fused with his, and the sun suddenly felt like a fiery furnace. "How old are you?"

"Turn twenty-eight this spring."

Twenty-eight. He was mighty old. A lot of years separated them, but the age span blurred for Glory. When he looked at her the way he was looking at her right now, those blue eyes boring into her soul, she didn't care how old he was; she could love a man like Jackson Lincoln if he were twice her age.

"I'm too old for you," he stated, and she wondered if she'd spoken her thoughts aloud.

"Ain't looking for a husband," she reminded him. The only thing she needed was a life free of Amos and to be rid of the awful burden of knowing that she had killed a man.

His smile was crooked. "You *aren't* looking for a husband."

"That's what I said."

They stared at each other, unable to break contact. Glory wondered what she saw in the depths of his eyes. Respect? Affection? Trouble? Regret that he'd even asked her to ride along that day?

Mary's cough broke their visual standoff.

Gathering the mended harness, Jackson stood up. "See if Mary needs your help. She sounds worse this afternoon."

"Yes, sir." Glory struggled to her feet, brushing dirt off the seat of her trousers.

"Jackson," he reminded. He winked at her.

Jackson. Her heart sang as she hurried to the back of the wagon to look in on Mary.

Fiddlesticks. Twenty-eight wasn't *that* old.

Chapter Eleven

The prairie schooner swayed along the Fontaine qui Bouille Creek. The travelers walked long into the night, trying to make up for lost time.

During noon breaks, Jackson would unhitch the oxen and tie them to the back of the wagon. In their place he would hitch the mules they'd rescued from the family who died of cholera; the mules could withstand the heat of the afternoon sun better than the oxen. Switching teams made it possible for the animals to work longer than they could have otherwise.

Sunday was a day of rest, except when rains plagued them during the week and muddy conditions forced them to stop. Then they would travel even on the Lord's Day, after a short worship time. Jackson said the Lord would understand.

Glory helped with the stock as often as he would permit her, and Ruth took on as many extra duties as she could, but the weight of responsibilities fell directly on Jackson's shoulders, which were beginning to ache on a daily basis.

He silently prayed for the weather to hold as his eyes searched the clouds. It had rained every night for the past week, bad thunderstorms with wolves howling in concert. Shoving his sweat-soaked hair off his brow, he was tempted to curse the relentless heat that raged every minute the sun was up, but he knew that it was better than the blizzards that would halt them on the trail if he didn't make up time somehow.

And cursing wouldn't set well with the Lord, whose favor he sorely needed.

Lord, Jackson prayed, eyeing the ominous sky, *please help the weather hold. I won't even complain about this cursed heat if you'll just help us to not lose any more time.*

The mare's stone bruise had healed, and he'd ridden her every day, ranging ahead to check the trail or falling behind to be sure they weren't being followed. Amos was never far from his thoughts.

On a few occasions he'd seen wisps of smoke from a fire not far from their camp. When he'd ridden out to check it, he'd found freshly doused ashes, but no one present. There was no doubt in his mind that someone was trailing them. It was one more worry, but there was a more immediate concern on his mind that afternoon as he tied his mare to the back of the wagon for the noon break.

No matter how far he'd ridden from the wagon that morning, he'd been unable to avoid hearing Mary's racking coughs as she'd tossed on her fever-soaked pallet inside the wagon.

The inescapable dust that billowed around the wagon, penetrating its canvas and even the dampened cloths placed over Mary's face, made her ailment worse. There were alarming moments when Mary was wheezing so badly that everyone waited, praying that she would catch her next breath.

Ruth disappeared inside the wagon to spoon bites of milk-soaked corn bread into the girl's mouth, but she was coughing so hard that she was unable to keep the food down. As the hours passed that afternoon, Mary grew weaker.

That night when the wind finally died, Ruth successfully fed Mary thin soup that seemed to ease her raw throat and give her a small measure of strength. When she could manage a few words, Mary's concern was that her condition was slowing them down.

"Nonsense," Lily soothed. "It's the road, not you, holding us up."

Lily climbed into the wagon to stay with Mary, and Ruth joined Jackson. They spoke in quiet tones as they walked a short distance away.

"She won't last much longer at this rate." Ruth drew her shawl tighter around her shoulders. After sunset, a penetrating chill had settled over the flatland. "She needs a doctor."

Jackson nodded. "Dodge City is half a day's ride ahead." He stopped to face Ruth squarely. "We'll find someone there to look after her."

Ruth gazed up at him. "Mary's concerned that she's creating another delay. She knows it's important to make up for lost time. And now—"

"Let me worry about time," he said. "Assure Mary that we're doing fine." He turned to head back to camp, refusing to meet Ruth's inquisitive eyes.

"Would that be the truth?" Ruth probed gently.

"Get some rest, Ruth. You've been working double time."

"I'm not the only one." She glanced at the others gathered around the campfire stealing casual glances their way.

"Leave it to me, Ruth. I'll get you to Colorado safely."

The next afternoon they detoured into Dodge City, and after making inquiries, found that it had a physician, of sorts. They arrived at his office where Jackson carried in a weak and feverish Mary. The other women trooped in behind him, crowding the cramped quarters until there was scarcely a breath of air.

"If you don't mind," said the elderly, stoop-shouldered doctor, casting an encompassing glance around the room, "I would like to examine the patient privately."

"I'll stay," Ruth volunteered. "It is customary for a woman to remain present while another woman is being examined, isn't it?"

"Very well," the doctor conceded.

Jackson gave a terse nod, and the other ladies filed out, their eyes lingering on Mary as they shuffled to the door. Jackson turned to follow them, pausing to speak to the doctor quietly. "You will step out to speak with me after your examination." It was a statement, the kind the wagon master often made, that was never mistaken for a request.

"Indeed," the doctor replied as he placed his glasses on his nose and bent to his task.

Jackson closed the door behind him and took a seat on the first bench outside the doctor's office. He watched Glory lead the mules to the water tank and return them to their positions behind the wagon.

It didn't bother him anymore to see her helping out. At first, he'd been worried that she would get herself hurt, but now he realized that she was as good a hand with the stock as he, probably better. He watched her soothe his riding mare, stroking her neck, then lifting and checking each hoof for rocks or other debris. The mare was calmer around Glory than she was with him. The girl caught him watching her and flashed a friendly smile.

He felt a tug on his heart. It was easy to like her. She was natural, honest, and too open for her own good. She used none of the feminine wiles that he'd seen in others. She could be stubborn, even confrontational, but there wasn't a calculating bone in her body. Not like his mother. Now there was a woman who could use and abuse others to suit her own selfish purposes. Amelia Montgomery could manipulate practically anyone into anything until she grew tired of the game.

Glory was nothing like his mother. Still, he kept his distance. The last thing he needed was to get involved with the orphan. He might be just a wagon master, but it was the life he'd chosen. Not a job he planned to do forever, but for now it suited him. He was taking care of people who would be otherwise helpless, and he liked his job. No commitments, no woman to run his life or run him off when she tired of him.

He watched Glory rub down the mare and decided she wasn't helpless in the wilds or anywhere else for that matter, but there were people who wouldn't hesitate to take advantage of a woman alone on the frontier. Ten years stretched between this girl and him, years that represented a world of experience. And yet there was something about her that drew him out of his shell. She could make him laugh or make him want to tear out his hair—and sometimes both at the same time.

Technically she wasn't a mail-order bride, and she swore she didn't want to be. But she'd have no choice in the matter. She had youth and natural beauty. Once Wyatt saw her, Jackson had no doubt he would want to arrange a suitable marriage for her. The prospect bothered him the few times he let himself think about it. He was trying to make sure that she learned the skills she would need as a wife. Her reading and writing were coming along faster than he'd anticipated; her domestic skills needed improvement, but then she'd had no role models until she'd joined the girls on this trip. He hoped her future husband would appreciate her spirit and not try to break it. She was a special woman, and he couldn't stand the thought of her being mistreated.

Glory stepped onto the porch and dropped down on the bench beside him. Looking up at him in that trusting way of hers, she grinned. "Heard anything about Mary?"

He shook his head. "Not yet." He was close enough to overhear the doctor's easy voice inside but unable to make out his words.

The door opened, and the doctor motioned to Jackson, who rose to join him. Glory hopped up and started to follow, but the doctor closed the door, effectively shutting her out.

The day dragged on. Jackson took turns with the girls sitting with Mary, holding her hand, encouraging her to take small sips of soup the woman from the café sent over. Folks here in Dodge City were a good sight friendlier than those in Squatter's Bend, Glory decided.

She sat on the doctor's porch, hands on her chin, staring at the activity going on around her. Across the street a man and a youth loaded grain into the back of a wagon. Two women standing in front of the millinery chatted between themselves, admiring the display of colorful bonnets.

Farther down the street, music drifted from an establishment with wildly swinging doors; Glory figured the business was another one of those places with painted women and boisterous men, who drank until they had to be carried out by their arms and legs.

Her eyes caught sight of a striking young couple coming out of the general store. The woman had long, dark hair that fell to her waist; the man couldn't take his eyes off her. She laughed, smiling up at him as he carried her bundles and beamed like a besotted fool.

Sighing, Glory watched as the couple crossed the street and walked down the plank sidewalk toward her. Would a man ever smile at her that way, wear his heart in his eyes for the whole world to see? She'd told the others she didn't want a man in her life, but she supposed that wasn't exactly true. She didn't want just *any* man, but if Jackson were to decide—

She caught her wayward thoughts and dismissed them immediately. Wasn't likely Jackson would ever smile at her the way the tall, dark-haired gentleman was smiling at his lady.

The couple drew closer, and Glory could hear the two sharing another laugh. Drawing her legs back so they could pass, she smiled.

The gentleman returned the greeting, tipping his hat politely. "Good afternoon."

Glory's smile widened. "Afternoon, sir." Her eyes fixed on the beautiful lady, and Glory realized that she was not much older than she. The young woman wore a gown of lavender blue and a matching hat, and her violet-colored eyes resembled pools of cool, deep water. She slowed when she saw Glory. "Hello," she said. "Isn't it a perfectly lovely day!"

Glory thought it would be lovelier if Mary were better, but she nodded. "Yesterday was cooler."

The couple exchanged a personal look, and the woman giggled, color dotting her pretty features. Glory didn't know what was so funny about her innocent observation, but the man and woman found it amusing. Squeezing the gentleman's arm, the woman extended her hand to Glory, beaming. "Please excuse us; we're newly married."

"Oh!" Glory jumped to her feet, admiring the handsome gold band on the third finger of the woman's left hand. "It's very pretty."

Still laughing, the woman held her hand in front of her, staring for what Glory suspected wasn't the first time at the symbol of her husband's love. The couple exchanged another look, and Glory realized they'd sooner be alone than chatting with a stranger.

The man recovered first, clasping the woman's hand tightly. "Forgive our giddiness. We've been married less than a month." He lifted his wife's hand and lightly kissed it. "We're Dan and Hope Sullivan."

The couple locked gazes with each other, and Glory envied the adoration she saw in their eyes.

Mrs. Sullivan turned and looked at Glory. "My husband's work has brought him to this area, but when it's finished, we'll be on our way home—well, not home, but to Michigan to visit my aunt. Hopefully, my two sisters, Faith and June, will be there with their new husbands, and we can have a family reunion before Dan and I begin our new life in Virginia."

Hope then told Glory about her sisters and Aunt Thalia in Michigan, and how her name had been Kallahan until a few weeks ago. Before Glory knew it, she was telling the Sullivans about Mary's asthma and about Jackson Lincoln, how he was taking five women to Denver City to be mail-order brides. But not her, she insisted.

"Mail-order brides?" Hope exclaimed. Both she and the man seemed to find that quite humorous. They laughed, and Dan leaned over to steal a brief kiss from his wife.

"Not me," Glory reiterated. "I've paid my own way, so I don't have to marry. Only Patience, Ruth, Lily, Harper, and Mary." She turned to look at the doctor's closed door. *If Mary doesn't die.*

She couldn't bear the thought of losing Mary to death. It wasn't fair. Death had worn out its welcome with her. Mary was young and alive, looking forward to the day when she would have a husband.

Please, God, please spare Mary's life. The prayer came so naturally she didn't realize she'd thought it.

Hope leaned closer to Glory, smiling conspiratorially. "My sisters and I were mail-order brides. We were all supposed to be, but Parker Sentell came along and June fell in love. Then Dan happened along for me. Only Faith married her intended, Nicholas Shepherd, and—well, it's a very long, very complicated story. But I'm happy for your friends, and I'm so sorry about Mary's illness. Is there anything Dan or I can do to help you?"

Glory shook her head, aware of how her appearance contrasted with Hope's. Glory was wearing trail-worn pants and a shirt, and her hair was stuffed under a wide-brimmed hat. The lovely Mrs. Sullivan was all sweet smelling and looking pretty as a sunrise. The comparison only served to remind Glory why Jackson would never look at her the way Dan Sullivan looked at Hope.

"The doctor is with Mary now. We're taking turns sitting with her. Nothing much anyone can do but wait, but thank you for offering. You're very nice."

The young woman took her hand, and Glory saw so much warmth and caring in her eyes that she felt as if she'd made a new friend. "I'll ask God to watch over her," Hope volunteered.

"Thank you," Glory murmured. "I'd be much obliged. And . . . could you ask him to help Jackson, too? He's worried about reaching Denver City; he's especially concerned about getting to the Arkansas and Platte Rivers' divide before the first snow. Seems like it's one delay after the other, and now there's Mary's sickness . . ."

"Of course I'll pray for your friends. And don't worry—" the young woman squeezed her hand—"when all looks the darkest, God works his greatest miracles if you have faith."

Glory watched the young couple continue down the walk, Dan Sullivan's arm protectively shielding his wife's small frame. She watched until they disappeared into the hotel. The scent of Hope Sullivan's perfume lingered, as sweet as the words she'd spoken. No wonder Dan Sullivan had such love in his eyes. If Glory didn't know better, she'd think she'd just met an angel.

⌒

The other girls joined Glory on the bench, and they sat quietly, lost in their thoughts, waiting for the door to open again. It seemed that hours went by. Glory grew restless and left the bench to thread her way between the mules tied behind the wagon.

Her thoughts were taking her places she didn't want to go. She sat on the back of the wagon, stroking Jackson's mare between the eyes. Jealous thoughts spiraled through her. For the brief instant that she'd stood outside the doctor's office, Glory had seen the look of relief in Ruth's eyes when she'd seen Jackson entering. The bond between them was obvious. They treated each other like trusted equals. Glory couldn't help but believe there was tenderness between them; oh, Jackson didn't look at Ruth the way Dan Sullivan had looked at his ladylove, but he still looked at Ruth kindly. Glory cared for both Ruth and Jackson and hated these angry feelings that threatened to overtake her. She reached for Jackson's Bible and held it tightly between her hands, hoping that the anger and hurt would go away.

"Glory! Glory!" Glory glanced up to see Lily rounding the wagon, looking up at her curiously. "Can't you hear me? Mary is asking for us, wants you to bring Jackson's Bible with you."

Glory scrambled down and rushed toward the doctor's office, the Bible tucked under her arm. She filed in after the others. Her eyes fell upon Mary's face as she entered. She'd never seen her friend look so pale; her face blended into the white pillowcase. Jackson and Ruth were on the other side of Mary's bed.

The doctor turned to pour water into a basin, where he began to wash his hands. The room was steamy, the air heavy with the fragrance of eucalyptus and other oils she couldn't identify.

Mary's eyelids were heavy and her face damp, but her coughing had eased. Her breathing was raspy, yet she seemed stronger. "Please," she whispered, looking directly at Glory, "the twenty-third psalm, my favorite."

Glory fumbled with the Bible nervously, but Harper tugged her elbow and turned the book to the correct page. Mary's gaze remained steadfastly on Glory. With a nod, she made it clear she wanted Glory to read to her.

"Uh," Glory said uncertainly. She glanced at Ruth.

Ruth nodded. "Go on. I'll help if you need me."

Nodding, Glory began haltingly. " 'The Lord is my shepherd. . . .' " The words were slow and awkward as she read, glancing from time to time at Mary's face. The girl's wan smile gave Glory courage, and she continued.

The room was silent except for her tentative words and Mary's audible breathing. Surprisingly, Glory read to the end of the lyrical passage with minimal errors. " 'Surely goodness and mercy will follow me all the days of my life.' "

Glory glanced up to see Ruth and Jackson, standing side by side, watching her with pride shining in their eyes. Glory swallowed hard against the lump in her throat, and she felt her tension ease. At that moment, she felt jealousy and anger leave her heart, replaced with a sense of peace.

When she closed the Bible, Mary smiled her thanks, and Glory took her hand and squeezed it gently.

"You did a good job, Glory," Jackson said quietly. "You've studied well." He looked around the solemn group. "The doctor wants to keep Mary overnight for another vapor treatment. He says if she has a good night, she can continue with us tomorrow, provided we keep up with her daily treatments and a liquid diet for a few days. Ruth has agreed to spend the night here to look after Mary's needs. We'll make camp at the edge of town."

The girls sighed with relief and expressed hushed words of gratitude to the doctor as he brushed past them. "I'm headed upstairs for a light supper," he stated at the stairway. "I'll be back down to treat her in an hour." Looking exhausted, he turned and left them.

At Jackson's nod, the girls whispered good-bye to Mary and began filing out. Glory waited till last. "Ruth, if you want your things, I'll bring them from the wagon before we leave."

"Why, thank you, Glory. I'd appreciate that."

Glory nodded and left, glad to be able to look at her friend without the awful jealousy that she'd been feeling so much lately. She glowed in her newly found peace. She also remembered a Scripture Ruth had shared about how God sent his Word and healed them. She was so excited she could have spit. But she knew now that sort of thing was no longer an option, seein' as how it wasn't ladylike.

Glory still wasn't quite sure who God was or if he knew who she was. But she now believed he was real. She'd listened to the other girls pray, and a couple of times she'd added her own amen. But she had never asked him for anything until she'd prayed for God to heal Mary. And he'd answered! Now she wanted to pray more, but she wasn't real sure how to go about it, since it was only her second time.

With childlike faith, she looked up to the heavens. He sure must be a long ways up there, she reasoned. 'Cause for as far as she could see, she still couldn't get a glimpse of him.

As if he were hard of hearing, she leaned her head way back and yelled, "Thank you! Thank you much for what you did for my friend Mary!"

And she meant every word with all her heart.

Later, when she handed the personal items to Ruth, Glory smiled and teased, "Wouldn't want you to miss your nightly scrubbing."

Ruth chuckled. Her face was tired, but her eyes brightened with mischief. "And I trust you won't miss your nightly scrubbing just because I won't be there to remind you."

" 'Course not," Glory responded playfully. It felt good to shed the tension between them. Over the past few weeks, Glory had found it difficult to talk to Ruth, to share her feelings with her like she had at the beginning of their trip together.

As Glory returned to the wagon, she hoped her jealous feelings would stay away. As the wagon rumbled down the street toward the edge of town, Glory resolved to read the twenty-third psalm every day if that's what it took to feel peace in her life.

By the third day the doctor pronounced Mary well enough to travel.

Jackson watched Patience and Glory help the ailing girl into the wagon and settle her on a pallet, wrapping a soft blanket around her skeletal frame. She'd lost weight this past week, weight she couldn't afford to lose.

The prairie schooner rolled out of Dodge City at daybreak, heading west. Midmorning Jackson handed the reins to Ruth and stepped into the wagon to check on Mary. The girl's drained features were pale as death, dark circles ringing her sunken eyes.

Harper sat beside Mary, dipping a sponge into a water bucket, bathing the young woman's face with infinite tenderness.

"Are you comfortable, Mary?"

Mary's eyes fluttered open, and she smiled wanly. "I'm fine, Mr. Lincoln—don't mean to be a bother."

Jackson patted the frail, white hand lying limp on top of the blanket. "You're no trouble, Mary. Let me know if you need anything." He met Harper's eyes. "Get her to drink often and as much as she can."

Harper nodded, rewetting the sponge as Jackson stepped to the back of the wagon and parted the canvas. His eyes skimmed the thick underbrush for signs of trouble. Glory chose to walk in front of the wagon this morning, chatting with Lily and Patience. His rifle was tucked under her arm out of habit. Lately, she was careful to point out game birds and remind him a squirrel, quail, or pheasant would taste good, but she let him provide the meat for their table.

Jackson's biggest concern at the moment was that one of the girls would wander out of sight. Should he remind them that Amos might be following and they were to stay close? He weighed the possibilities. If he did, Ruth would be scared, and then Patience would sit up all night stewing if she knew Glory's uncle was close by.

Jackson could deal with Amos if he could see him. It was the long stretches of road when he couldn't that kept him awake nights. An ambush worried him; so did the possibility that Amos could kidnap a girl if she wandered out of sight. Despite his concerns, Jackson decided to keep quiet and see what the day brought.

Stepping down from the wagon, he mounted the saddled mare tied to the back. Loosening the reins, he cantered the horse alongside the wagon. "Ruth, I want you to keep the other girls close. No one walks more than a few feet from the wagon!"

Ruth nodded, urging the team along the rutted trail. "Are you going somewhere?"

"Up the road a piece. I'll be back shortly." Whirling the horse, he galloped off, tipping his hat to Glory, Patience, and Lily as he rode past.

Patience frowned. "Wonder where he's off to in such a hurry?"

Glory watched his tall form disappear down the road. "Don't know, but I wish I was going with him."

Late that afternoon, Glory ventured farther down the trail. The road was washed out, and Ruth was busy concentrating on maneuvering the wagon through the rutted channels. Jackson was out of sight and couldn't help. The oxen balked, their heavy bodies straining to pull the load. The old wagon rocked back and forth, rattling pots and pans and banging the tin washtub against its side.

When Ruth spotted Glory drifting farther away, she hollered, "Jackson said to stay close."

Glory acknowledged the shouted warning with a friendly wave over her shoulder but kept walking. Keeping pace with the wagon was tiring; it was too slow, and she felt the need to stretch her legs and walk faster.

Up ahead, a covey of quail took flight, startling her. Her hand automatically switched the rifle to her shoulder, and she took aim. But the image of Jackson's scowl brought her up short. *I shoot the game. Understand?* She lowered the rifle and walked on, peering over her shoulder at the quail that skittered across the road and thinking they'd look a whole lot better in a frying pan.

The wagon bogged down again; she could hear Ruth and Lily yanking the harness, trying to drag the animals now. Voices grew fainter as Glory veered off the trail and headed for a grove of saplings. The sun was blistering hot; a few minutes in the cool shade would feel good before she tackled those stubborn oxen. She was a good half mile up the road, but Ruth hadn't noticed. Glory dropped down under a tree and sat there, listening to the girls wrestling with the team, feeling a little ashamed. But the shade lessoned the guilt. She was exhausted. She just had to rest a spell.

It was cooler here, quieter. She leaned back and closed her eyes, listening to a blue jay chattering overhead and enjoying the peaceful reprieve. She could still hear the oxen snort and Ruth, Lily, and Patience talking to each other.

A twig snapped.

She opened her eyes slowly and froze. Standing not twenty yards away was a deer. A small doe, nibbling grass in a clearing. Sunlight filtered through overhead branches, putting the deer in a perfect light.

Glory lay quiet as a rock, observing the animal. A deer that size would last the party for a good two weeks. Lily could make fresh jerky; there'd be venison roasts and thick tasty steaks. . . .

The animal lifted her head, her tail fluttering up and down. The doe had caught her scent.

Glory's fingers slowly closed around the rifle butt.

The deer stamped her front foot, snorting.

Glory eased to a sitting position, settling the weapon onto her shoulder, taking careful aim.

Jackson whirled when a shot rang out. Kneeing his horse, he galloped back to the wagon.

When Ruth heard the shot, she started, almost dropping the reins. "What was *that?*"

Lily and Patience spun around, eyes seeking the source of the gunfire. "I thought it was Jackson hunting."

"It wasn't me," Jackson declared as he rode up. His eyes scanned the road ahead. Glancing over his shoulder, he searched for Glory. "Where are the others?"

Ruth followed his eyes. "Harper!"

"Back here, with Mary."

Ruth glanced at Jackson. "Glory!"

Silence.

Jackson cupped his hands to his mouth. "Glory!" He glanced at Ruth. "Where is she, Ruth?"

"The last time I saw her, she was heading up the trail. I assumed she came back, though, and was with Mary. I warned her not to go off."

Ruth looked to Patience and Lily. "Have you seen her?"

The girls shook their heads.

Patience and Lily rounded the wagon. Both girls cupped their hands to their mouths and yelled for their friend: "GLOOOOOORY!"

Wheeling the mare, Jackson took off, shouting, *"Glory!"*

Jackson rode the trail, searching side roads and overgrown paths until darkness closed in, forcing him back to the wagon. Without a lantern, he was wasting his time.

Jackson found the girls huddled around the wagon. They were hungry, scared, their eyes dark with fatigue.

Ruth anxiously stood up as he approached. "Did you find her?"

"No." He dismounted, dropping the reins so the horse could graze. The girls were silent; only Mary's occasional cough broke the stillness.

"She stayed close to the wagon most of the day," Lily ventured.

Ruth leaned forward. "We were busy with the animals. I'm sorry, Jackson. I thought she was with Mary. I never thought she'd go off on her own."

Jackson took off his hat and ran a hand through his thick hair. "Did anyone see anything? Did you see anyone following the wagon?"

One by one, the girls shook their heads. "There's someone following us?" Harper exclaimed. "I didn't see anyone; 'course, I was in back with Mary most of the day."

"I didn't see anyone," Lily agreed. Her voice caught. "Is it Amos?"

"She'd have said something if she thought Amos was following," Patience said. She struck a match and quickly lit the lantern. "Are you worried that Amos might be trailing us, Jackson?"

"I don't want to worry you, but someone's been trailing us for the last few days. Nothing I can't handle, but you need to stay close. Ruth, I told you that no one was to wander more than a few feet away."

"I'm sorry, Jackson. My mind was on the animals."

Jackson released a pent-up breath. Where was Glory? Lying somewhere wounded, unable to help herself? Had the fool girl gotten herself shot? Had Amos shot her?

They stood in a circle, looking at each other, afraid to voice their growing fears. Ruth sank to the ground, wringing her hands. "What do we do? We can't leave her out here alone, maybe injured."

Harper bounded up onto the wagon seat, her dark eyes wide with fright. "Maybe she wandered off and got lost."

Jackson didn't believe that for a minute. Glory knew her way around the woods. She had a tracker's instinct and a familiarity with nature that he envied. She could spot a trail quicker than he could, and he'd pit her sense of direction against a Sioux's any day of the week. "She's not lost."

He glanced at the girls and knew they were near the breaking point. They hadn't eaten since noon, and they'd traveled over twelve hours of rough road today. They'd gone as far as they could go.

His eyes scanned the edge of the trail. They had no choice but to camp where they were. At first light, he'd search the area. If Amos was out there, he wasn't going anywhere either, hindered by the same conditions. No one was leaving until morning.

"We camp here tonight."

"Here?" Ruth stood up, her eyes skimming the area.

"There'll be no fire. Ruth, Lily, can you fix a cold meal?"

Lily nodded. "We have bread and cheese."

Jackson would give a month's pay for a cup of hot coffee, but food didn't interest him. "Fix what you can—"

"Hey, you!"

The party whirled, eyes searching the darkness for the source of the voice. A lone figure with a rifle slung over a shoulder came down the road, whistling.

Jackson took a step, reaching for his shotgun.

"Well, you going to sit here all night?" Glory walked into the ring of light. "Hi, folks." She grinned. "What's taking you so long? Had supper ready for half an hour."

The group, speechless, simply stared at her. Then confusion broke out. Ruth sprang forward and grabbed Glory around the neck and hugged her. Lily, Patience, and Harper jumped up and down, waiting a turn to express their relief.

"Is that Glory?" Mary called weakly from the wagon.

Jackson watched the exchange, his exasperation rising. Wading into the middle, he parted the women until he reached Glory.

She grinned up at him. Her shirt was splattered with blood, and her hair was loose from her cap. "Hey, how ya doing, Jackson?"

Jackson set his jaw. "*Where* have you been?"

She stepped back, her smile receding. "Waiting for you. Where have *you* been? It's dark."

"Where have *I* been? I've been scared half out of my wits, looking for you for the last hour!"

She frowned. "Scared? Why would you be scared? I wasn't but a half mile up the road." She turned to point the way. "Right up there."

All eyes pivoted up the road. Straining, they could see a faint light glowing in the far distance, a light that they hadn't been able to see in the twilight.

"Got a surprise for everyone."

She struck off, and the girls scrambled into step behind her, while Jackson got Mary and put her on his horse. Glory led them to the clearing, where a side of venison browned over a rosy fire. The smell of roasting meat flavored the air. She stood back, hands on hips, looking pleased with herself. "Shot me a deer. Thought you might enjoy something other than beans tonight."

Squealing, the girls attacked the meat, juggling the hot pieces in their hands as they tried to eat it.

In the midst of the chaos, Glory approached Jackson. Head hung low, she murmured, "Didn't mean to cause a scare. You were off somewhere, and the wagon wasn't going anywhere, so I decided to take a rest before I helped. I meant to come back . . . 'til I spotted the deer." She sighed. "I know I promised to let you put meat on the table, but you were busy and—but you have to admit meat will taste mighty good tonight."

Jackson wanted to wring her neck. And he wanted to draw her into his arms and hold her until the fear left him. She'd scared a year off his life, but he was so relieved that she was safe that he had a hard time staying mad.

She slowly lifted her eyes to meet his. "Don't be mad at me, Jackson. I'm only trying to help."

Removing his hat, he knocked the dust off on his wool-clad knee. "Right now, the only thing I'm mad about is the fact that you don't have hot coffee to go with that venison," he said gruffly. He didn't want her to think she could pull this a second time.

Her sunny smile resurfaced. "I can fix that. If you let me use your horse, I'll go back and get the coffeepot. I'll have a pot made by the time you bring the wagon around."

He caught her arm as she was about to skip off to jump on his horse. Meeting her gaze, he said softly, "Don't ever do that again, Glory. You scared me to death."

"Yes, sir," she replied. Then she flashed a grin. "Honest?"

"Honest what," he snarled, looking away.

"Honest you were worried about me?"

"I was worried," he conceded shortly.

"That makes me feel real good." Riding off with the lantern, she turned to wave at him over her shoulder. "I am going to write your folks, just as soon as I learn to write better!"

Shaking his head, he reached for a piece of venison before he set off to follow her on foot. He'd been far too worried; she was becoming more important to him than he cared to admit.

Chapter Twelve

Afearsome windstorm came up on Saturday, banging pots and pans against the side of the wagon, threatening to rip canvas and spook the animals.

The girls and Jackson battened down their belongings, shouting at each other above the gale. Lily made Mary get inside the wagon and close the flap, securing it tightly to keep the dust out. The wind blew so hard as they worked that at one point the party was forced to run for cover among some bushes. With the wind came rain. When the storm finally abated, they were all soaked to the skin, grateful for their lives. Ruth stood in the middle of the road, arms held aloft, praising God for safe delivery. Glory had climbed a small rise to watch the storm whirling off into the distance. Two small twisters rose into the clouds moving off, leaving a sky now stunningly blue.

The next morning Glory woke with a fearsome chill, her teeth chattering as she pulled on a heavy sweater Jackson had lent her. They walked eighteen miles that day. By late that night, she was huddled in a blanket in the wagon, too feverish to eat her supper. Mary shared some of her tea, but it left a bitter taste in Glory's mouth, and she pushed the cup aside.

She rode most of the next day on the back of one of the mules tied to the back of the wagon. Every time she tried to drink or eat anything, it left a brackish taste in her mouth. But she refused to slow the group down because she felt poorly.

Every day brought them closer to Denver City; yet every day the remaining distance seemed formidable. Glory's thoughts turned to the time when she would say good-bye to Jackson and the others. Sometimes she couldn't bear the idea; other times she was filled with trepidation. What would she do when she was no longer a part of the daily lives of Jackson or the girls? The girls would marry; Jackson— well, she didn't know what Jackson would do. Maybe he would marry Ruth, and they would return to Illinois and buy a small farm, start a family. She wanted that for Ruth, truly wanted it, but try as she might, she didn't want it for Jackson. In her heart she couldn't hand Jackson over to another woman, though Ruth had insisted there was nothing between her and the handsome wagon master.

Something in Glory wanted to hang on, to pretend that it was real interest that she saw in his eyes occasionally, maybe even a special look meant just for her, the kind a man gives a woman when he thinks she's not watching.

But Jackson was mad at her these days. She'd given him a dose of his own medicine, and he hadn't liked it. It had happened two days ago, when she'd rounded a corner and found that a skunk had him cornered against a big rock. Jackson had been pinned there like a gnat; the area around the rock stank something fierce. That skunk had fired off several pernicious rounds, and Jackson looked a mite shaken though he hadn't been touched.

When she'd walked past, Jackson had waved his arms, trying to get her attention. She'd paused, sizing up the situation from a safe distance. She felt ornery that day—real ornery. The way she figured, he needed to notice her a little more and find fault a little less.

He'd mutely implored her to shoot the animal, motioning toward the rifle and pretending to pull the trigger.

She'd motioned back, shaking her head.

He'd scowled. "Why not?" he'd mouthed.

"Can't kill anything—you'll get upset." She grinned, hoping the Lord wasn't watching.

His scowl had darkened. "Kill the skunk!" he'd mouthed, jabbing the air with his finger to emphasize his demand.

She'd slowly wagged her head, pantomiming someone choking her around the neck, and her falling to the ground, dead. She'd lain there, pretending to be out cold.

A vein had pulsed in his neck. "Stop playing around and kill the skunk!" he'd mouthed.

Shaking her head, she'd gotten up and walked on. She'd been in enough trouble for shooting out of turn, thank you.

Of course, that skunk would leave a powerful smell, one they'd all have to suffer with for a few days.

"*Glory.*" The voice of conscience boomed in her head.

Heaving a sigh, she'd turned around and fired the gun in the air. The skunk bolted and ran for safety.

"I was only funnin'," Glory explained. She glanced at Jackson and grinned, noticing he wasn't laughing.

They passed fewer wagon trains now. When they reached the fork in the road, Jackson explained that most travelers chose the large Indian trail that crossed the main creek and took a northwest direction toward Pike's Peak. Jackson said the longer one would be safer, but he preferred the less traveled road because it had more water and better grass along it. He believed that his route would cut off some miles. Glory and the others were in favor of the shorter route.

Jackson pulled his horse to a stop and raised his hand to halt the wagon. "We've been pressing hard, following this stream for days, but I believe this route could save us a week or more. So if you'd like, we can detour a couple of miles and follow the Indian trail where I can show you the mineral spring that gives the Fontaine qui Bouille Creek its name: The Fountain that Boils."

"Yes!" came a chorus of feminine voices. The girls were eager to take a break from the routine for a little sightseeing.

When they arrived, they hopped out of the wagon and scrambled over large ledges to see two springs bubbling up out of solid rock. Following Jackson's example, they scooped up a handful of water to drink. Though strongly infused with salts, it was fun to taste.

Glory giggled as the tiny bubbles tickled her nose as she tried to sip. She glanced up to catch Jackson watching her. The warmth in his gaze was more exhilarating than the bubbles tickling her tongue.

As they doubled back to the fork in the road, Glory watched Jackson's handsome form riding ahead of their wagon. Their little excursion to the springs was a memory she would treasure in her heart. She savored the look in Jackson's eyes, his pleasure in her delight.

The following Sunday dawned disagreeably. The October wind was blowing hard, and it was bitter cold. Large flocks of snow geese flew overhead, getting a late start for warmer climates. The women wanted to observe the Sabbath today, but the incessant rain had slowed them. They decided to walk on, only not so far today. Tonight they would have services and go to sleep early.

Jackson was keeping an eye out for signs of early snow. The worsening weather made Glory think it couldn't be far off. *Please, God,* she prayed as she walked ahead of the wagon, winding her scarf tighter around her neck, *Jackson said we needed three more weeks, that's all. Three weeks, and we'll be in Denver City. Can you please hold back the snow until then?*

They passed herds of buffalo and antelope grazing in the fields. The wind whistled across the expansive valleys.

Late one afternoon, the wagon came upon a crossroads trading post. The adobe building crouched beneath a watery sun looked lonely to Glory. Not having seen a fellow explorer in days, the girls were eager to stop.

"All right, ladies." Jackson steadied his mare as he brought her even with the wagon. "We'll make a brief stop. The animals need water." He glanced back at the road they'd traveled. "Be careful now. Keep your eyes out for trouble."

"We will!"

"Thank you!"

The inside of the trading post was a wondrous delight. Glory's eyes roamed the crowded room, and the sights fascinated her. Eight or nine male Indians sat around a large woodstove fashioning crafts. Some wove colorful baskets, others strung jewelry using glass beads, and still others worked with a reddish metal.

"Copper," Ruth whispered over her shoulder. "Isn't it lovely?"

A beautiful young woman moved from behind a counter to wait on them. *"Je t'aide?"*

Glory and Ruth smiled, moving on down the aisle. "What did she say?" Glory whispered.

"I believe it's French for 'help.' She wants to know if we need help."

"She's so pretty."

Ruth nodded. "Like someone you'd see in a picture book."

Turning ever so slightly, Glory checked to see if Jackson was in the building. She was relieved to see that he was busy outside watering the animals. Her eyes traveled back to the beautiful girl wearing a beaded dress sewn from buckskin. That was the kind of woman Jackson deserved: large dark eyes; waist-length, raven black hair; a body slender and strong.

When Jackson came into the post, the girls had browsed through most of the merchandise. Everything was so pretty Glory couldn't decide what she liked the most. Lily and Patience made a game out it, going through the rings and bracelets like excited children. Mary chose a shiny bracelet made from red beads and an eagle feather. Lily decided on a copper bracelet that fit around her tiny wrist. Patience liked the beadwork and chose a necklace. Harper favored the woven blankets, sorting through the colorful patterns several times before deciding on a favorite. Ruth fell in love with the pottery: vases and containers painted the colors of the desert.

Glory loved everything. Beads, bracelets, pottery, and blankets—it was impossible to choose a favorite, but she relished the game, thinking how wonderful it was to simply be in such a grand store.

"Do you like it?"

Glory jumped when she felt Jackson's warm breath on her cheek. He stood looking over her shoulder, staring at the beaded mirror she was admiring.

"It's very pretty." She'd never taken a close look at herself in a real mirror. The image had surprised her. She had freckles across her nose, and her eyes sparkled like dew on a frosty morning.

"Then it's yours."

"Oh, no!" She whirled, thrusting the mirror at him. "I couldn't spend money on that."

He grinned at her, his eyes softer than she'd seen them lately. "I'm buying it for you. A pretty girl should have a mirror to look at herself." Turning to the other girls, he called, "Pick out one gift apiece, girls. My treat."

The male Indians winced as the girls' squeals of delight filled the adobe.

"Are you sure, Jackson?" Ruth asked. "This is so generous of you. . . ."

"I have nothing better to spend my money on than beautiful women. Pick anything you want—just don't break the bank." He winked at Glory. "Especially you."

Glory felt a blush color her cheeks. She didn't know how to take his teasing, but she liked it, liked it a lot. And he was doing it more often lately. The lovely clerk behind the counter smiled, coming over to help the girls make their selections.

Glory had never had a more exciting time. Why, it felt like Christmas when Poppy would put an orange and a peppermint stick in her stocking hung by the stove! The clerk wrapped the gifts in soft cloth for the girls.

When the wagon pulled away from the trading post half an hour later, Lily held her wrist aloft, admiring her new copper bracelet; Patience preened in her beaded necklace. Harper had a red, blue, and black striped blanket on her lap while she ooohed over Mary's shiny beaded bracelet with the eagle feather. Ruth happily sat on the seat beside Jackson, cradling a large pottery vase painted like the desert.

Glory, too excited to sit still, walked behind the wagon, staring at herself in her new mirror.

All in all, it had been the best day of the journey, maybe the best day in her whole life. Certainly one she wouldn't soon forget.

<hr />

Days later, Mary's condition took a turn for the worse; her deep racking coughs echoed as the wagon lumbered between boulders. Her coughs were sometimes as painful to hear as they must have been to experience. Walking beside the wagon, Glory found herself wishing that she could accept Mary's affliction for a few days so the poor girl would have a chance to rest and regain her strength.

Jackson rode past Glory without looking at her as he headed to the rear of the wagon. She turned her head to watch him canter by. He'd been circling the wagon for the past few hours.

"Whew," Glory muttered, waving her hand in front of her face, "as if we don't have enough dust flying, he keeps it stirred up. Mighty antsy today." She wondered what was bothering him and then figured it must be his concern for Mary as the girl fell into another fit of shuddering coughs.

Glory decided to spell Patience, who was caring for Mary today, and turned to walk to the back of the wagon. She was ready to climb inside when she spotted three riders down the road about a quarter mile. Surprised to see anyone out in the middle of nowhere, she raised her hand to shade her eyes and squinted through the dust. Three dark silhouettes loomed on the horizon.

"Hey, no gawking," Jackson warned as he brushed by her on his mare. "You're falling behind. Get in the wagon."

"Look!" Glory pointed at the riders.

"I know," Jackson said gruffly. "Been following in plain sight for two hours. Get in that wagon. Now."

Glory reluctantly complied. Grabbing on, she swung over the tailgate. Once inside, she stared at the three figures who sat astride spotted horses. The horses walked steadily, keeping pace with the wagon.

At first she wondered if one of them might be Amos. She dismissed that notion quickly. None of the figures was large enough to be Amos, and to her knowledge, Amos had never ridden this far in his whole life.

As the prairie schooner topped a rise, Glory could see above the dust cloud and realized the figures were actually Indian braves. At that moment, she heard Jackson call to Ruth, his signal that it was time to pull off for the noon break.

When Ruth reined the oxen team to a halt near a stand of towering pines, Jackson pulled his mare up behind the wagon. "Glory, change out the teams now. I want fresh mules harnessed and ready to go."

Usually Glory swapped the teams at the end of their break, not the beginning. Her gaze shifted to the riders, who had stopped for a moment on the rutted trail, watching them. Without his saying it, she figured Jackson wanted to be ready to make a run for it if necessary.

"Who are they?" Glory asked as she dropped the tailgate and scrambled down.

"Shh," Jackson replied, shaking his head. "Ladies, we're taking a shorter break than usual. Just get out the leftover biscuits and what's left of the water."

Ruth joined Jackson at the back of the wagon. "I see them," she said evenly, keeping her eye on the three figures on the road. "But we're going to have to get Mary out of that stuffy wagon and into the shade for some fresh air, and we have to heat some water for her tea."

"OK," Jackson conceded, "let's make it snappy."

He dismounted, tied his mare to the wagon, and pulled his rifle out of the scabbard. Handing the Winchester to Ruth without a word, he climbed into the wagon. "OK, ladies, time for a short break." He scooped Mary into his arms and carried her to a tall pine, where he gently settled her against the trunk.

The girls climbed out, squinting in the noonday sun, moving to their chores. Lily had gathered an armload of firewood when she glanced up to see the visitors. The sticks tumbled from her arms. "Who's that?" she cried in shocked dismay.

"Indians," Glory replied matter-of-factly, pausing with a towering red mule standing on either side of her.

"Indians!" Lily exclaimed, her jaw slack. Even Harper looked worried.

"Are they going to scalp us?" Patience whispered, her hands flying to the thick blonde bun coiled at the nape of her neck.

"Calm down, girls." Jackson took the rifle from Ruth's grasp and tucked it under his arm. "Go about your business. Don't stare. Act like they're not there."

The girls tried to comply, but their movements seemed awkward and jumpy. After hitching the team, Glory knelt in the shade beside Mary. The girl began to cough harder, her eyes wide with fright. "It's OK," Glory soothed. "Jackson won't let anyone hurt us."

Glory rose to her feet and walked to the campfire to get the mug of tea that Lily was brewing for Mary, but Lily's hands were shaking so badly that she nearly scalded herself trying to pour the boiling water. "I'll get it," Glory volunteered, bending to steady the cast-iron pot.

When she straightened, her heart sprang to her throat. The Indians had now dismounted their horses and were walking straight toward them.

"Jackson!"

Jackson stepped into the middle of the road, lifting his right hand, palm in front of him, pushing it forward and back.

The Indians stopped abruptly. Silence settled over the area.

Jackson continued to signal with his hand. "I do not know you. Who are you?"

The lead Indian flashed a succinct signal.

Shaking his head, Jackson raised both hands and grasped them in the manner of shaking hands.

The Indian responded in kind.

Glory sidled up closer to Jackson. "Who are they?"

Placing a hand on each side of his forehead with two fingers pointing to the front, one of the Indians fashioned the narrow, sharp ears of a wolf.

"Pawnees."

"What do they want?"

"We're about to find out."

The oldest Indian, a middle-aged man, stepped away from his two younger companions and moved closer. His eyes looked past Glory at Mary, who was bent double, coughing in spasms.

Glory studied the look in his eyes. Until a few months ago, she had been unable to read or write; she had spoken with few people besides Poppy. Her communication skills had been largely nonverbal. Poppy had taught her to observe closely and trust her instincts. He'd warned her that men could twist their words to mislead, but if observed carefully, they would eventually give themselves away.

"*Trust your instincts,*" Poppy had always said, like woodland animals that depend upon their intuition for survival. If a rabbit senses danger ahead, Poppy had said, it doesn't say to itself, "oh, well, it's probably nothing," and then proceed—not if it wants to live another day.

Glory observed the Indian—his body language, his eyes, his facial expression—for clues to his intentions. She saw no hostile pose, no aggressive move; his eyes were filled with curiosity and . . . concern. She sensed no danger.

The Indian slowly removed a leather pouch from his belt and extended it toward Glory.

"Glory," Jackson warned in a low timbre, "take the pouch."

Glory nodded, stepping closer to meet the Indian.

"Easy," Jackson said softly.

"It's OK, Jackson." Glory accepted the leather pouch in both hands. "They mean us no harm."

Glory looked straight into the Indian's eyes, and she saw wisdom and kindness there. With a roll of his hand, he gestured that the pouch was for Mary. Glory peered inside the bag and looked at the Indian with raised brows.

In a lithe motion, the man moved to pick up an empty mug beside the fire. Gently, he took the pouch from Glory and shook out a small amount of the powder from the bag into the cup. He imitated the motion of adding water from the pot boiling over the fire. Glory carefully filled the mug from the pot as the Indian held it out to her.

They moved slowly, carefully, as in a dance, trusting each other in small increments. He handed the mug to Glory. With a swirl of his fingers in the air, he communicated that Glory should stir the brew, which she did with a spoon. With a halting gesture of his palm, the Indian signaled that she should wait. She sniffed the concoction, figuring that the wait was to let it steep, like tea.

The Indian pantomimed bringing a cup to his lips and drinking from it. Then he pointed to Mary.

"Oh," Glory said, for the first time unsure. "He wants Mary to drink this."

Jackson balked. "No one drinks anything until I know what it is."

The Indian seemed to understand the doubt apparent in their voices. He held up both hands, grasping them in a shaking manner, as Jackson had done earlier. Every eye rested on him. He pointed to Mary, then clutched his own throat and pretended to cough, harsh racking coughs like the ones that had come from Mary all day. Then he pointed to the mug in Glory's hands and then to Mary. He pretended to drink from the mug. Then he stroked his throat in a soothing manner and inhaled long, slow, audible breaths and exhaled them with ease.

"It's for Mary," Glory announced, "to make her feel better."

"Yeah," Jackson said cautiously, "but I still don't know what's in that powder. Maybe medicine, maybe not."

Glory looked at the Indian, pointed to the leather pouch, and shrugged, lifting her palm in the air, trying to ask him what it was.

The Indian nodded and moved to one of his companion's side. He opened a bag strung over his companion's shoulder. Carefully, he removed a dried flower with its root still intact. He pointed to the root, imitated a grinding motion, and then to the pouch.

"What is that flower?" Glory asked. "Looks like a daisy, only it has a bigger center."

"Coneflower," Jackson said. "The Indians grind the root and use it to ward off illness, especially breathing ailments. They've used it for years, trading it from tribe to tribe. I'd forgotten about it."

"Then I think we should give it a try," Glory said.

"Not so fast." Jackson restrained her. "Mary hasn't had solid food for days. She's weak and exhausted. What if this medicine gives her a belly-ache or worse? I can't risk that."

The women nodded their agreement at the wisdom in his caution.

"We don't know these men," Ruth warned.

"How do we know they really mean to help?" Harper seconded.

Glory looked around, taking in their fixed expressions. She shrugged, figuring it was the least she could do for these folks who'd done so much for her. "You're right," she announced. "We should test it." She raised the mug to her lips and took a long swallow.

"Glory!" Jackson snapped, knocking the cup aside. "You are the most impulsive, *stubborn*—do you realize what you may have just done?"

"I helped my friend," Glory retorted defensively.

"You should have asked me. There's nothing I can do now. If something happens to you. . . ."

The women looked at him, startled. Ruth looking curiously from Jackson's distraught expression to Glory and back again. "Seems if she wanted to put herself at risk, it's her choice, Jackson," Ruth whispered.

"She should have *asked* me." His gaze scanned the group. "We should have voted on it, at least. I'd be worried if *any* of you had decided to do a fool thing like that."

"Hmmm," Ruth said, lifting a brow. "Do tell."

Uncomfortable with the tension rising around them, Glory blurted out, "Well, no harm done. I'm fine, feel better than ever. Seems like a safe medicine for Mary to try."

"I don't know," Jackson said.

"I do," Mary said in a small voice, beckoning the Indian to come to her.

Glory met Jackson's scowl with lifted brows. She didn't want to lead the Indian to Mary and then to have Jackson shoot him. Jackson released his breath in a long, defeated-sounding sigh and nodded.

Glory refilled the cup with the powder and water and let it steep for a couple of minutes. Motioning for the Indian to follow her, Glory led him to Mary and handed her the cup. Mary tipped the cup to drink, looking into the Indian's eyes over the rim.

When she finished, she set the cup aside and held out her wrist. With her other hand, she untied the rawhide that held the new bracelet with red beads and an eagle feather. She gestured toward the Indian's arm in a request for him to extend it. He leaned down, bringing his arm close to her hand. With a small smile, she tied the bracelet around his wrist.

The Indian's eyes lit up. He touched the shiny beads with reverence, then nodded to her.

As the three men turned to leave, Ruth approached them, carrying a five-pound sack of sugar. She extended it to them with a murmur of appreciation. They nodded as they accepted the token from her.

The ladies broke camp quickly, and when they returned to the trail, the Indians were nowhere in sight. And though no one mentioned it, Mary's cough seemed to have subsided.

Chapter Thirteen

That evening the group camped on a small plateau. The air was windless, the sky full of stars, except for along the north, where a long bank of growing clouds glowered.

"Storm's brewing," Jackson muttered. Scanning the valley below, his gaze pinpointed a narrow wisp of smoke rising from a campfire less than a mile away, and his heartbeat accelerated. Whoever had been trailing them was closing in. Many a morning before dawn, Jackson had doubled back to corner the culprit, but instead, he'd always discovered a doused fire and an empty campsite. He needed to take care of business now, before any storm hit and they became more vulnerable.

Tonight he was going to ride under the cover of darkness and surprise the intruder. Was it Amos? He felt sure of it. He'd catch him off guard and get the drop on him. He knew he needed the advantage that darkness could provide. By day, his group was too cumbersome to flee, and there weren't too many places ahead where he could avoid an outright ambush.

The girls didn't seem to notice him saddling his mare that evening. Some were busy fixing a late supper; others were beside the campfire, reading and mending. He slipped his rifle into his scabbard, checked his Colt pistol, and strapped on his holster. He'd had a bellyful of Glory's uncle, and tonight he intended to finish this once and for all. He'd send Amos on his way and be done with it.

Glory didn't need the crazy old coot on her trail for the rest of her life. He'd leave camp and return before anyone missed him. Quietly he led his mare out of the camp, keeping to the far side of the wagon, so as not to be seen.

"Where you headed at this hour? Storm's a-brewing," Glory reminded from not three feet behind him.

Jackson jumped and spun around, his hand resting on the butt of his Colt. "Don't go sneaking up on me like that!" His heart was pounding like a blacksmith's hammer. Hearing her voice right behind him scared a year off his life. He'd better be more adept at sneaking up on Amos than he'd been at slipping away from her.

Her eyes widened. "What's going on? I've never seen you wearing a side arm."

Jackson looked the other way. "I'm going for a little ride, Miss Nosy." He reached inside the wagon, grabbed his shotgun, and handed it to her. "Look, I didn't want to upset anybody here, so I was hoping I could come and go without an interrogation."

"What's that big word mean?"

"It means you ask too many questions."

"You don't have to get so cranky about it," she said, disappointment in her voice. "You've told us to stay alert. I was just following orders."

"Oh, yes," he murmured, "you're good at following orders all right." When he saw the hurt look on her face, he softened. "Look, I need your help." He noticed that she immediately brightened. "I need to check on something. Do me a favor: Stay here and guard the camp with my shotgun. Only please don't upset the others. They'll never get to sleep if we get them stirred up, and Mary needs all the rest she can get."

"You got it," she said, her eyes bright even in the low light. "Where are you—oh, that's right. I'm not supposed to know where you're going."

The corner of his mouth lifted in an involuntary smile. "I shouldn't be too long," he said, turning away. Then spinning back around, he added, "But no matter how long I'm gone, you stay here. That's an order."

"Yes, sir." She gave him her best rendition of a salute.

He shook his head and swung into the saddle. One touch of his heels, and the mare took off in a soft trot.

He was careful to approach the campsite from the woods. He tied his mare to a tree and walked the last quarter mile, staying low and moving stealthily. When he neared the campfire, he stayed behind a low bush, from where he could spy one man, squatted low, pouring himself a cup of coffee. There was only one bedroll on the ground and one horse tethered nearby.

Slowly, Jackson drew his Colt from his holster and waited. Ten minutes passed as he waited to make sure there was no one else around.

The man looked to be around thirty, slim and broad-shouldered. Jackson focused on his gun belt. Somehow, he didn't think this man fit Glory's description of Uncle Amos, but the girl tended to exaggerate at times, and Jackson was taking no chances. He waited till the stranger had both hands busy, his coffeepot poised in the air ready to refill his cup.

"Put your hands in the air nice and easy," Jackson called solemnly from the underbrush as he cocked his pistol. "Try something foolish, and I'll shoot."

The man set his cup on the ground and the coffeepot beside the fire. His eyes narrowed. "You might join me for a cup and a chat," he said in a measured, even tone, slowly unbuckling the belt of his holster and removing it. He tossed it aside a few feet. "Might be, we could straighten things out before somebody gets hurt."

"Could be." Jackson lifted his head and scanned the clearing. "You alone?"

"Usually am. Tonight's no exception."

Jackson paused, listening intently. Hearing no sign of anyone else nearby, he stood and slipped through the underbrush into the clearing. "We'll start with your name."

The man raised his hands and looked Jackson up and down. "Name's Dylan McCall." He paused for a beat. "U.S. marshall."

Though he tried to maintain a neutral expression, Jackson knew his eyes registered surprise. "Don't see a badge. Wouldn't have proof of that, would you?"

The corner of the man's mouth lifted a fraction. "Right here," he said, dipping his chin to his left, "in the pocket of my vest."

"One hand—slowly remove it and slide it on the ground my way."

The stranger complied, his eyes never leaving Jackson's face. He seemed to be assessing him calmly.

"Have a seat," Jackson said, preferring the man not be in a crouched position, ready to spring. "And keep those hands high."

The man sat down. "Mind if I take a sip of my coffee before it gets cold?"

"Not yet," Jackson kept his gun trained on him, while squatting to pick up the flat leather square the man had tossed on the ground. He opened it and dropped a quick glance down. The silver star flashed in the firelight. Opposite the badge was a card identifying one Dylan McCall, U.S. marshall. Jackson locked eyes with the stranger. "Looks real enough," he said, smoothing his thumb over the star. "How do I know it's yours? Could be you took it from an unfortunate Marshall McCall after you met up with him?"

"Well, take a look at my horse, bears the U.S. brand on his hip. Check out my gear, strictly government issue. And in my saddlebag here, you'll find an extradition order to fetch one nasty little gunslinger from Denver City back to Kansas City to stand trial."

Jackson promptly dragged the saddlebag to his feet, reached inside, and drew out a long envelope. His fingers lifted the flap and withdrew the paper inside. With a flip of his wrist, the paper unfurled. Quickly he scanned the contents. He looked up and assessed the man across from him. "Well, you look as official as the documents you're carrying."

The man nodded. "You're not the trusting type."

"You've been tracking us for weeks. I'd like to know why."

"I haven't been tracking you. This happens to be the only halfway reliable trail in these parts. I've been about my business, checking in with the county sheriffs as I pass through their territories, sometimes escorting some unsavory types to their new quarters in jails and penitentiaries along the way."

Jackson looked at the man for a long moment, made a decision, and uncocked his pistol. After slipping the Colt back into his holster, he motioned toward the coffeepot. "Believe I'll take you up on your offer and have a cup."

Dylan reached inside his pack, drew out another cup, and filled it. As he handed it to Jackson, their eyes met.

"I owe you an apology, Marshall. I'm not in the habit of sneaking into camps with my pistol drawn."

"Call me Dylan. And I don't get the feeling you're a dangerous felon on the loose."

"Lately," Jackson chuckled, "I'd have to believe that would be an easier life. I'm Jackson Lincoln, wagon master, escorting a group of mail-order brides to Denver City."

"Women?" Dylan exhaled. "That would tend to make a man a little jumpy."

Jackson nodded. "Especially since one of the girls has a crazy uncle who's threatened to do her harm. That reminds me, I can't leave the girls alone for long. I need to get back. I am sorry for busting in on you like this. Least I can do is offer you a meal. The ladies will have supper ready by now. I'd feel better if you'd join us. You can share our camp for the night. Storm's brewing and it feels like a bad one."

Dylan paused for a moment, then shrugged. "Thanks. I'm tired of my cooking, and I could use the company." The marshall loaded up while Jackson went for his own mare.

A short time later, the two men rode into camp. The girls beamed when they saw they had company. Male company. After introductions were made, there was a flurry of activity as everyone rushed to accommodate their handsome guest, everyone except Glory, who stood staring, eyes wide, the shotgun still tucked under her arm.

Jackson quietly moved to her side and gently confiscated the shotgun. "I think we can put this away for now."

She glanced up at him with a small furrow between her eyes. "What's a U.S. marshall doing in these parts?"

She looked so serious he succumbed to teasing her. "Here to bring back a dangerous murderer." He wondered only briefly at the frown that clouded her face as he hurried to the back of the wagon to stow his guns.

After supper, everyone lingered around the campfire, eager for conversation with a new face, and such a handsome one at that. "I feel safer knowing we have Marshall McCall in our camp tonight," Mary announced, and there were affirming nods all around.

"Call me Dylan," he said with an inviting smile. He pronounced the name *Dill-an*.

"Dylan," Lily purred, trying out his first name before the others, "I can't imagine what could bring you to this desolate place."

"The job, ladies. Where there's a felon to be apprehended or transported, I'm your man."

"Then you travel this trail regularly?" Ruth asked.

The handsome marshall rested his eyes on her. "As regularly as weather permits, ma'am, but you could say I know every mile and every town from Westport to San Francisco."

Glory felt her heart begin to thump wildly. If this lawman knew every town on the trail, then he'd surely been through Squatter's Bend and heard of the female murderer who was still at large. She was surely on his list of felons. She shrunk back in the shadows.

Her crime was never far from her thoughts, especially during her nightmares, and more recently during her evening prayers. The more she read the Good Book, the more she realized the enormity of her sin. She had killed another human being. She had broken a commandment: "Thou shalt not kill." Those words haunted her. She'd killed Charlie Gulch. And according to his friend, she would pay.

She only halfway listened to the banter and giggles surrounding her. No one seemed to notice her, except Jackson. When she glanced up, she caught him staring at her quizzically. It was then that she made her decision. She couldn't tarnish the reputation of a good man like Jackson Lincoln by letting him continue to harbor a fugitive.

"I'm a murderer," Glory announced in a clear voice.

The chatter around her ceased. Gazes flew in her direction.

She extended her wrists, ready for the handcuffs. "Arrest me." She lifted her chin resolutely. "I just want to say that these people had nothing to do with my escape. They are totally innocent, especially the wagon master, Mr. Lincoln."

"Uh, just a minute, Dylan," Jackson began, looking intently at Glory in that way she'd come to understand meant that he wanted her to shut up. "This girl is overly tired and just a little dramatic at times. We've been pushing her to read, and I think she's gotten some crazy notion—"

"Please don't try to cover for me, Mr. Lincoln. I'm of sound mind, and I know what I've done. It's time to confess my sin. Every night I've prayed for God's forgiveness, but it's time for me to pay society for killing Charlie Gulch."

There were whispers all around, but Ruth cleared her throat to silence them. "Marshall McCall, this innocent girl was attacked by an evil man; she did . . . what she did . . . to protect her virtue and her life. It was clearly a case of self-defense."

Mary spoke, her voice thin but clear, "I don't think you should take her in, Marshall . . . uh, Dylan, that is. She's a good person who deserves another chance out West."

Dylan raised his palms in the air to stop the remarks that were beginning to pour from all sides. Even Harper was shaking her finger at him.

"Ladies, ladies," he began; then glancing at Jackson, he added, "and gentleman." His authoritative tone settled a hush over the group. "Let's clear up a few things before we jump to any more conclusions, shall we?"

There were nods all around.

"Good. Then I'll ask the questions, and Glory will answer first. Then if anyone has a comment, we'll speak one at a time. Clear?"

Glory sat up straight and tall, feeling as pale and luminous as the moon above. She nodded that she was ready.

"Glory," Dylan began, "could you be speaking of Charlie Gulch of Squatter's Bend?"

Her eyes widened in surprise and then sadness. "Did you know him well?"

Dylan nodded. "Still do, if I'm correct. He's the town drunk. Everybody knows Charlie Gulch."

"No, sir. I killed him three months ago."

Dylan shook his head. "I shared a card game with him two months ago, and he was very much alive that night, I assure you."

"But," Glory said, confused for a moment, and then certain as the memory sprang to her mind, "I hit him with my rifle. His friend touched the blood that was everywhere. He said—I'll never forget his words as long as I live—he said: 'You killed Charlie. You killed Charlie Gulch. You'll hang for this. You'll hang.' "

"And that was three months ago?" Dylan asked incredulously. He shook his head. "I remember . . . around three months ago Charlie was wearing a bandage around his head. Claimed he'd been hurt when he'd apprehended a gang of thieves trying to rob the bank. But his sidekick said Charlie got frisky in a dark alley with a girl who whopped him up-side the head." Dylan's features colored. "Excuse me, ladies."

"No offense taken, Marshall," Ruth assured him.

Dylan nodded, returning to his story. "Town was pretty evenly split over which version of the tale to believe. I figured there wasn't a shred of truth to either one. Most likely Charlie had fallen down drunk and banged his hard head against something harder."

There was an audible sigh of relief around the campfire, but Glory still looked confused. "You mean he isn't dead?"

"No, ma'am, not unless he's passed on in the last several weeks since I stopped in Squatter's Bend. I think your conscience can be clear, young lady." Dylan smiled at her. "The deceased is probably tipping his glass as we speak."

Glory felt an enormous relief. A terrible burden had been lifted from her heart. Then she looked at Jackson, who was smiling at her, and she felt foolish. Once again, she'd done an impulsive thing without checking with him first. She sighed and looked down as the girls around her reached to hug her.

Glory met Jackson's eyes over Ruth's shoulder as Ruth embraced her, and he was shaking his head and grinning at her.

Starting first thing tomorrow, Glory resolved, she would never do another impulsive thing. Never, ever would she give Jackson Lincoln another moment's grief.

Later that night, Glory dissolved into tears, crumbling into Ruth's arms. The past few hours had taken an emotional toll on Glory. To be free of the awful burden of taking another person's life left her feeling drained.

Holding her tightly, Ruth soothed her, tenderly consoling her as Glory poured out her heart.

"I've been so afraid, Ruth." Glory sobbed, hot tears washing away three months of misery and self-recriminations. She hadn't killed Charlie Gulch, and Amos wasn't following her. Could *he* be dead? No, he had been breathing when she ran off. *Thank you, Lord,* she silently cried.

"I know, dear. I know."

Patience and Lily drew near. By now, sleet pelted the sides of the wagon, but inside, the girls were warm and cozy.

Draping her new blanket over Glory's shoulder, Harper scooted closer into the friendship circle. "Now don't go crying," she sniffed. "You'll have us all bawling, and we should be celebrating. Won't have to worry about some lawman breathing down our collars when we reach Denver City. And it looks like that mean uncle of yours just plain gave up on finding you."

"I know, Harper, and I'm grateful, honest. It's just that what if I had killed a man? The Bible says 'Thou shalt not kill.' " She'd written the Ten Commandments over and over until she knew them by heart. Killing was powerful wrong; how would she have explained to God what she'd done?

"Oh, Glory, the Lord understands if we kill in self-defense," Ruth consoled. "He wouldn't hold you accountable for defending your life."

Glory sniffed, wiping her nose on the handkerchief Mary discreetly pressed into her hand. "You're always so confident, so sure, Ruth. Why can't I be more like you?"

"You are like me." Ruth's smile was close to angelic in the dim lantern light. "We are all nothing, the lowest of sinners, without God's grace." She took Glory's hands, holding them tightly in her own. "Grace—the love and forgiveness of God—is a gift. You have everything you will ever need to claim his love."

Frowning, Glory sniffed. "I don't have *anything* except the clothes on my back, you, and Jackson's Bible." Her eyes traveled the circle of friends, meeting eyes that looked back at her with love and affection. "And you, and you," she whispered, reaching out to touch the hands of each one of them.

At that moment she realized that she *did* have everything: people who loved her, the knowledge that she wasn't alone in the world. A worn Bible entrusted to her care by a man she admired more than any other.

Her eyes returned to Ruth. "But you have something more, an inner peace, a contentment, a joy. You never get upset or mad or yell or scream or cry, even when you have every right to fuss. You hardly raise your voice to the animals. How do I get to be like you, Ruth? How do I get up each morning, sure that whatever happens, I will have the peace that the Bible speaks about, the peace that passeth all understanding?"

Smiling, Ruth touched the Bible resting in Glory's lap. "The key is right here, Glory. All you have to do is read it and accept it."

Laughter mingled with tears as the girls shared a group hug. Tonight they felt their bond grow even closer. The next day they would reach the high divide between the Arkansas and Platte Rivers. Once safely through, their time together would come to an end. The thought weighed heavily upon them all.

"We'll write each other," Lily promised.

"Every month," Patience echoed. The girls held hands tightly as Patience verbalized the pact. "We promise to write each other every month, and if we should be confined or otherwise unable to correspond, we promise to have a loved one write and inform the rest about the other's welfare. We pledge to pray each day for each other, for our soon-to-be husbands, and the children we will bear." They sealed the accord with a unanimous tight hand squeeze.

When they opened their eyes, Glory gazed at them. "What about me?"

Mary smiled. "What about you?"

"I . . . won't be marrying—leastways, not anytime soon. I paid my own way, and Jackson said I'm not obligated to take a husband."

"Well," Lily said, biting her lower lip, "you will someday, perhaps." Her youthful features sobered. "What *will* you do, Glory? You can't live out here alone. Colorado is a harsh, unforgiving land. The winters are long and hard. You won't know anyone, and you have no skills."

"I do now!" She could read reasonably well, thanks to Ruth's tutoring. Harper had taught her to cook; folks didn't clamor for seconds, but she was getting better, and she hadn't made anyone sick in weeks. Thanks to Lily, she could sew a decent stitch. Mary had taught her to add and subtract. Seemed to her she was as qualified as anyone else to find work.

Harper, who'd been silent, said softly, "Maybe I could get a job, pay Mr. Wyatt back, and then you and me could stay together."

The girls turned to look at the mahogany-skinned girl. Ruth frowned. "Why, Harper, I thought you wanted to get married."

Harper's words were barely audible. "No, I never wanted to get married. The orphanage said I had to. Don't like most men," she said, her voice dropping lower. "Most men—they're mean to a body."

"Mean?" Ruth leaned over and took her hand. "Why ever would you say that?"

Shifting to her hip, Harper lifted her blouse and showed them her back, crisscrossed with deep white scars.

Patience's soft gasp covered the stunned silence.

"Dear Lord in heaven." Lily turned away.

"You never said anything," Mary whispered.

"Wouldn't have done no good. Folks at the orphanage knew about it, said they wouldn't let Ma have me if she came back. She brought men home—"

Glory's cheeks burned hot. "They had no right to do that to you. Poppy said a man who'd beat a woman was no better than a rabid animal."

"Men are mean when they're drinking," Harper whispered, tears pooling in her dark eyes as she trembled beneath the heavy blanket. "I've . . . I've been thinking that I don't want to get married to some man I've never met. I don't want no man beatin' me every night till I bleed. Glory and I can get us a place—"

"Oh, Harper." Mary hugged her, switching turns with the others as they comforted her.

"Not all men are bad," Glory argued. "Look at Jackson. He's kind and protective, and I can't imagine he'd lift his hand to a woman. We've all seen him about as mad as he could be, and he didn't treat us bad."

Dabbing her eyes with her handkerchief, Harper managed a weak grin. "Guess that's true, Glory. He'd have beat you silly weeks ago if he was turned that way."

That brought a laugh from everyone. Glory's reputation for stepping on Jackson's nerves was legendary.

"I'll bet Mr. Wyatt has a wonderful young man waiting for you," Mary said. "Handsome, strong, just itching to be a proud papa and a loving husband to you."

The girls shared a nervous laugh this time. Glory, for one, wasn't so sure about marriage. If she'd been stuck with any of those men that Poppy had tried to pawn off on her, she wouldn't be happy about it.

"Harper, you'll be just fine. We pray that Mr. Wyatt will be a kind man and that he'll find a good husband for you. It's Glory we have to worry about." Lily reached up and turned down the lantern, and the girls settled into their warm blankets. Gusts shook the wagon, and sleet peppered down on the canvas.

Closing her eyes, Glory thought about Jackson sleeping under the wagon, wondering if he was warm enough, if his pillow was soft enough, if his bedroll sufficiently heavy to withstand the cold mountain air. She'd like to do so much for him: wash his clothes, fix his meals, and be the last one he talked to before his eyes closed in sleep.

Lily snickered.

Pretty soon Patience giggled.

Lifting the blankets over their heads, the two girls dissolved into guffaws. Before long, they were all giggling.

"What are we laughing about?" Ruth squeaked, her shoulders heaving with suppressed laughter.

"I don't know," Mary sniggered. "Shh, keep your voice down. Jackson will hear us."

The wagon rocked with the girls' ill-concealed giggles. Glory's sides hurt from trying to keep quiet. The last thing she wanted was to disturb the old bear, Jackson.

"Girls!"

Too late. Slapping her hand over her mouth, Glory's body shook harder, tears rolling down her cheeks now.

"Yes, sir?" Harper called, bending over double, pulling her knees to her chest.

"It's late!"

"Yes, sir!"

The six girls, tears rolling down their faces, laughing so hard their heads hurt, made every effort to sober. Each attempt failed miserably, and they burst into renewed peals of laughter. Burying their faces in their pillows, they gasped, chortled, sure they would die if they couldn't stop.

Eventually, the spell passed, and none too soon. They expected to see Jackson part the back curtain and yank a knot in their tails.

Lying on their backs, they wiped tears from their eyes, hiccupping.

"What was that all about?" Ruth whispered.

No one knew, but the thought produced another brief round of snickers.

"I know," Patience whispered.

"What?" they said in a hushed chorus.

"It has to be those silly rules Lily was teaching Glory yesterday."

Glory sat up, wiping her eyes. "My lands, I'd forgotten those—" She started giggling.

"What rules?" Mary scooted closer to Glory.

"Some old rules Lily thinks I should learn so I can be a proper lady."

By now the girls were sitting up, eyes brimming with curiosity, dying to know what was so funny.

"What are these rules?" Harper asked.

Glory glanced at Lily, and they both grinned. "You tell them, Lily."

"OK." The girls lay back down and got quiet. "Promise, no one laughs?" Lily fumbled for a match, lit the wick, and then took out her book.

They all promised to stay quiet, certain Jackson would skin them alive if they woke him a second time.

"All right. This book, I think it comes from Boston, but I'm not sure. It has rules men and women are supposed to abide by."

"And they are?" Ruth plied.

Clearing her throat, Lily began to read: " 'Ladies and gentlemen, when meeting on the sidewalk, should always pass to the right. Should the walk be narrow or dangerous, gentlemen will always see that ladies are protected from injury.' "

"That doesn't sound so bad."

"It gets worse. 'Ladies should avoid walking rapidly upon the street, as it is ungraceful and unbecoming. Running across the street in front of carriages is dangerous and shows want of dignity.' "

Glory giggled. "That lets me out."

" 'When walking with a lady, a gentleman should insist upon carrying any package that the lady may have. Before recognizing a lady on the street, the gentleman should be certain that his recognition would meet with favor.' "

"How would he know?" Glory asked.

"An educated guess, maybe?" Harper ventured.

" 'No gentleman should stand on the street corners, hotel steps, or other public places and make remarks about ladies passing by.' "

Patience snickered. "Especially about her weight."

"Or the size of her caboose," Harper whispered.

" 'Upon the narrow walk, for her protection, the gentleman should generally give the lady the inside of the walk, passing behind her when changing corners. A gentleman walking with a lady should accommodate his step and pace to hers. For the gentleman to be some distance ahead presents a bad appearance. And last but not least, the gentleman accompanying a lady should hold the door open for the lady to enter first. Should he be near the door when a lady, unattended, is about to enter, he will do the same for her.' "

"What's wrong with that?" Glory murmured, getting sleepy from all the merriment. "I think that's nice."

"Me too," Harper said. "Better than letting the door slam in her face."

That brought on another round of giggles, but the long day finally took its toll. Soon the wagon settled down, the lantern was turned down, and the occupants rested quietly, listening to the howling wind.

Just before Glory drifted off to sleep, she thought about the rules and decided that Jackson would observe every one of them.

Because Jackson Lincoln was a gentleman.

Chapter Fourteen

Marshall McCall stayed the night, sleeping under the wagon beside Jackson.

The next morning the sleet had changed to a steady snowfall—big white flakes that Glory tried to catch on her tongue.

"Hop back in this wagon, girl," Harper warned her. It was Glory's habit to be the first one dressed and out every morning. "You can't go out there in those worn-out boots."

Glory scrambled back into the wagon. "I put on my flannels, wool dress, and jacket," she explained.

"Well," Harper said, "that's good, but you can't wear those thin boots. Time to be wearing your winter boots."

"Don't have any." For most of the trip now, Glory had been wearing whatever change of clothes another girl wasn't wearing at the time, but she had only the holey boots she'd been wearing when she'd joined them.

"Lucky thing." Harper handed her a pair of dark leather boots. "Jackson picked up a spare pair when we stopped at that trading post some time back. Thought someone might need them, and we all wear close to the same size."

Glory's eyes widened in surprise. Jackson seemed to think of everything. Despite all the trouble she'd caused him, with all the responsibilities he had, he still kept her—well, all the girls'—needs in mind. A rush of tenderness for this man filled her heart. To think he cared enough to be sure the women had what they needed, even clothing. Even for her.

"Thanks," Glory murmured in awe, lacing the boots up to her calves. She couldn't remember ever having a good pair of boots to keep her warm and support her ankles on the rough trails.

Moments later, Glory was helping Jackson harness the oxen. When he walked around the team to join her on her side, she glanced up at him warmly. Time to show him her gratitude. She reached down and gathered her skirt with both hands and hefted it up to her knees. "Well," she said with a big smile, "what do you think?"

Drawing a thick strap over the ox's broad back, he paused to glance over. When she looked down, his eyes followed hers to the pair of shapely legs she was revealing to him. "Good grief," he muttered, glancing up to her face incredulously and back down to her legs again, seemingly before he could stop himself. "What are you doing? Drop your skirt, girl." His eyes shot left and right, looking for a safe place to look, his expression guilty. "What will people think if they see you—you can't go around hiking up your skirt and asking a man what he thinks!"

Glory's shoulders stiffened. "I'm asking *you* what you think of the new boots," she huffed. "What do you *think* I was asking about?"

"Well, I . . . uh, you kind of took me by surprise," he stammered. "I didn't rightly know what to think." His tone turned defensive. "You should be more specific when you're asking questions."

"It's a sad thing when a person can't thank another person for her new boots without him getting all cranky." She looked away, feeling stung by his reaction. If anyone else had tried to thank him, she felt sure he would have been gracious. "I declare sometimes you are fussier than Poppy after two weeks of snowed-in cabin fever."

She turned on her new heel and marched to the back of the wagon to saddle the marshall's horse. Why was it, she thought in a fit of pure frustration, that she couldn't even try to return a kindness without Jackson taking offense?

Ruth banged two pots together to signal it was time to gather around the campfire for a hearty breakfast of biscuits and gravy. They crowded around to warm themselves and share a meal that would have to hold them through a cold morning's work. Ruth said the blessing and began serving, handing the first plate to their guest.

"Dylan," Jackson began, studying the marshall over the rim of his coffee cup, "I'd sure be appreciative if you'd accompany us for the next several days."

The girls watched the handsome lawman expectantly, their smiles inviting. Harper shoved another biscuit onto his plate before he could refuse, and then followed it with a ladle of cream gravy. Mary refilled his coffee cup before he had a chance to ask.

"Thanks," he said with an appreciative nod. "I must say, Jackson, if I hang around too long, I'll get fat and spoiled."

"I don't think that'll happen too soon. The girls and I will have all we can handle today climbing to the divide." He glanced at the threatening sky. "If possible, I'd like to be through it before nightfall. Having you with us will increase our chance of making good time."

"Seems the least I can do for the kind hospitality you've shown me."

Glory stepped up with the reins to Dylan's black gelding. "I saddled your horse, Marshall. I know we'd feel better if you rode along with us."

He smiled at her in a teasing way. "I imagine you feel better knowing you won't be wearing my handcuffs today."

"Yes, sir," she replied, blushing quickly, her gaze dropping away. Everyone chuckled and smiled at Glory sympathetically.

Dylan looked at Jackson and then glanced around to include the ladies. "I accept your invitation."

"Good." Jackson nodded, looking relieved. "Let's gather round," he began. "We've got maybe our toughest day ahead of us." A gust of wind whipped around them, sending up sparks from the campfire to swirl with the snowflakes. "The weather is going to make it slick going. Each of you will have to walk as much as you can to lighten the load. The animals will struggle just to pull the weight of the wagon." He sent a meaningful glance in Glory's direction. "And stay close. Don't wander away even for a minute. If you need a break, let Dylan or me know, so we can stop the wagon. Too easy to get lost in a snowfall, and it will get heavier the higher we go."

The girls murmured their agreement and dropped their heads as Ruth, then Jackson, led them in a brief prayer for safe passage.

Because she didn't have her stamina back, Mary was chosen to sit on the back of a mule tied behind the wagon. Glory gave her a boost, and Mary scrambled aboard, clutching the mule's heavy leather collar for support. Patience climbed aboard the other mule to keep Mary company. The girls planned to alternate throughout the day with one or another of them sitting on the back of the other mule tied next to Mary's. It gave them an occasional rest from walking, and the gentle mules accepted their slight weight without a problem.

On the trail, Jackson ranged ahead to check conditions while Dylan rode beside the wagon. Ruth was at the reins, and three girls walked beside the oxen, helping her keep them in the middle of the trail.

As the trail grew steeper and slicker, Ruth slapped the reins and called encouragement to the oxen that trudged slowly, leaning into the traces, dragging the wagon behind them. Glory and Harper smacked the oxen on their wide rumps and pulled at their harnesses when they veered off the rutted trail.

Glory kept an eye on the marshall, who was riding alongside the wagon and staying real close to Ruth. As the wagon climbed higher, the wind almost snatched their breath away. Glory moved to the back of the wagon.

"Care for a break?" Dylan asked Ruth amiably, touching the brim of his hat with his right hand. "I can climb aboard and take the reins for a while. Your arms have to be tired."

Ruth turned her head and looked into his crystal blue eyes framed by lashes dampened from the blowing snow. She stared for a long moment, then blinked suddenly and looked away. It was then that one of the oxen stepped in a hole and nearly jerked the reins out of her hands. "Ouch!" she exclaimed at the sharp tug on the leather that pulled her shoulders and lifted her off the seat for a second until she could lean back.

"Got him!" Harper shouted as she pulled up on the ox's halter until he regained his footing.

Ruth huffed a moment, catching her breath. Then she gasped in surprise as Dylan settled his weight on the seat beside her. He leaned away to secure his horse to the side of the wagon and then turned to reach across her. His gloved hands wrapped around her gloved hands on the reins.

"I-I can handle it," she stammered defensively, stiffening her arms to lean as far away from him as she could.

"Just trying to keep the tension on," he said, his hands tightening on hers. "Just ease out from under me."

Glory punched Harper, who'd joined her behind the wagon, and the girls grinned.

"Looks like the marshall's sweet on Ruth," Harper whispered.

"It surely does," Glory said. "Sweet as honey."

Ruth pulled her hands out from under his as quickly as she could, but his firm grasp slowed her. "You can loosen your grip," she said sharply.

"Let's take it slow. Wouldn't want those oxen to take a crazy notion and run off now, would we?" He chuckled. When he glanced her way, their faces were scarcely inches apart.

She cleared her throat and slid to the far edge of the wagon seat. "I hardly think the oxen could run anywhere at this point." Ruth's face flushed despite the icy snow pelting it.

"I'm kidding, Ruth," he said reassuringly. "It is Ruth, isn't it?"

"It is." She rubbed her shoulders with her hands.

"You OK?"

"Oh yes, fine," she said quickly. An awkward silence stretched between them. "Uh, I want to thank you for the way you treated Glory last night."

He nodded. "She seems like a fine girl, more sincere than most folks I meet."

Ruth's eyebrows shot up. "You mean more sincere than most criminals, don't you?"

"I generally say what I mean, ma'am," Dylan responded evenly.

"Well," Ruth said with a sigh, "it's a good thing you know this Charlie Gulch." She paused a beat before continuing, "If you hadn't, I dare say you would have arrested her, right?"

"I . . . I hope it wouldn't have come to that. I'd have had a long chat with her."

"An interrogation, I believe it's called."

His head swung around, but Ruth's gaze was fixed on the snowy trail ahead. "It would have been more of a conversation," he explained, "much like the one we had last night."

Ruth nodded. "So after you'd arrested her—"

"I don't think it would have come to that."

Ruth shrugged. "If you'd arrested her," she persisted, "you would have hauled her back to Squatter's Bend."

"Where she would have been cleared and released."

"Then she would have been separated by hundreds of miles from the only friends she has. It would have been too late to make the journey to Colorado this year. As it is, we're hitting the passes a little late."

"It's my job." He snapped the reins. "I don't always like it."

Glory punched Harper again. "That's real nice of Ruth to take up for me like that."

Harper nodded. "Push!"

Ruth ignored his remark and continued, "On the other hand, if

Charlie Gulch had died from the head wound she gave him, what would've happened to her then?"

"I think they would have weighed the circumstances."

"Of course, he's a town resident; she's a stranger."

Dylan whistled to the oxen to move them up the steep slope. "I'm not the judge and jury, ma'am."

"No," Ruth agreed, "but it's not hard to see her motivation. Glory makes no pretenses. It would be your choice to let her go."

He shook his head. "Not my call."

"And if she found herself at the end of a rope?" She looked at him directly. "And you knew in your heart that she was innocent of murder, despite what she claimed in her statement?"

He shifted his shoulders, looking somewhat uncomfortable. "If it had come to that, I would've spoken in her behalf."

"That girl is no threat to society, no matter what happens to the likes of Charlie Gulch."

"Not the way the law works, ma'am."

"Hmmm. I imagine there are a goodly number of fugitives who move out West to start a new life and do so successfully."

He nodded. "I imagine so."

"Unless, of course, they are arrested and taken back to stand trial."

"You're a hard woman, Ruth."

"On the contrary, Marshall McCall. I happen to believe that vengeance belongs to the Lord."

"Well, miss, it's not within my authority to choose whom to arrest and whom to let go."

"Forgiveness is appropriate in some circumstances, don't you think?"

"I'd have to agree, but in our country that's up to a court of law." He lifted his shoulders. "Just stating a fact, miss. Don't shoot the messenger."

Suddenly the oxen hit an icy patch. As their feet began to slip, they balked. The wagon wheels locked and started sliding sideways. Dylan slapped the reins and shouted, but the oxen were paralyzed with fear. Glory and Harper jumped aside as the wagon slid another couple of feet and a back wheel dropped off the edge of the trail. The undercarriage of the wagon slammed down on the ice at a precarious angle.

Dylan grabbed Ruth to keep her from falling out as she looked down to see that the drop-off was hundreds of feet straight down the mountain. "Oh, my," she exclaimed, desperately throwing her arms around his neck.

Harper and Glory were up front now, pulling on the oxen to no avail. Jackson galloped back to the wagon. "Hang on," he shouted as he shook out his lasso, tied it securely to the back of the wagon, and looped it around his saddle horn. He backed his mare, keeping the rope taut as Glory rushed to his side. "Hold my horse steady," he told her as he slid to the ground.

Mary and Patience had slid down off the mules tied behind the wagon. "Untie the mule team, girls," Jackson ordered as he moved to the back of the wagon. "Bring them to me. Now back them up and hold them steady." Jackson secured the mules' harness to the corner of the wagon where he'd tied his rope to stop the slide. "Now, girls, lead those mules toward Glory. Steady, steady," he repeated, as the mules began to pull the wagon as far back onto the trail as the dropped wheel would allow. "Whoa," he called. "Hold them right there."

With that, he untied a long wooden pole strapped to the side of the wagon and pried it under the corner of the wagon that was resting on the edge of the precipice. Leaning hard, he applied all the pressure he could. Harper and Lily joined him. Pushing down on the end of the pole together, they got enough leverage to lift the corner of the wagon. When it was high enough, Jackson called to Glory, Mary, and Patience to lead the mules a couple of yards farther, which pulled the wagon the rest of the way onto the trail.

Everyone was exhausted from the effort. Dylan climbed down from the wagon seat and helped a shaky Ruth to the ground. Jackson and Glory switched the oxen for the mule team to pull the wagon the last hundred yards to the summit.

The snow stopped shortly after they passed the summit. They made camp that night a few miles down the trail under a clear sky. After a warm supper, an air of hope and celebration filled the air. Dylan took out his harmonica and played a square-dance tune, and Jackson took turns dancing with each girl, one at a time, saving Glory for last. As she twirled in his arms under a million stars, she felt like the happiest girl alive.

Ruth, Patience, and Glory were the last to bed that evening. The wind shifted, and clouds rolled in for a second time that day. As she changed clothes inside the wagon, Ruth had talked nonstop about Dylan. Dylan this and Dylan that. The conversation itself was unusual, especially since Glory usually had to pry a discussion out of her after a long day. Seemed she thought the handsome marshall was overly arrogant and overly confident. Seemed to Glory that Dylan was only doing his job, but she'd been too tired to argue.

"I think I'll check on Jackson—see if he's warm enough." Before anyone could object, Glory slipped out the back of the wagon and closed the canvas.

Frigid air blew up Glory's skirt as she hurried toward the front of the wagon. Sleet fell in prickly sheets, howling through the boulders. She'd never seen weather change so fast, and dresses were nothing but a nuisance! If her two pairs of trousers weren't so dirty that they could stand alone, she'd never have consented to wearing Patience's hand-me-downs. The bodice was too tight, and the dress made her look girly— too girly—but it was much too cold to do wash.

Rounding the schooner, she spotted a light in the distance. *Jackson must be visiting with Dylan.* She supposed that he was enjoying time with a peer—especially since he'd been confined to female companionship for the past four months. Jealousy suddenly surged through her, but she pushed it aside. *Lord, I'm trying hard to be content with what you give me and not be envious of Jackson's time with others.*

Lately, she'd found it easier to talk to the Lord in a natural way, as if she'd known him as well as Ruth did. In many ways she was creeping closer to Ruth's certainty of belief. Sometimes Ruth spent extra time with her reading lessons; nowadays she could understand the words in almost half a Bible chapter without stumbling. Stories about the women in the Bible—Miriam, Deborah, and Esther—fascinated her; she never tired of reading about them.

Shivering, she pulled her jacket tighter, thankful that the Lord had answered her prayer and seen them safely through the high divide. With the worsening weather, even one day would have made the passage more difficult, if not impossible. Denver City was only two days away now. Two days was all the time she had left with Jackson.

She paused, wincing as icy pellets struck her, watching the light of the lantern bobbing toward her. Jackson's tall form, bent against the wind, came into view. When he spotted her, he quickened his pace, his boots crunching atop the thin icy glaze.

"You should be in the wagon," he scolded as he approached.

"I wanted to check on you—I saw your light. . . ."

Taking her forearm, he steered her beneath the makeshift awning strung near the fire. Wood chunks blazed brightly in the midst of red-hot coals. The air was warmer here, sheltered from the blowing wind.

Retrieving the coffeepot, Jackson poured two cups, the fragrant aroma pleasantly mingling with the arctic air. Taking both her hands, he closed them around the steaming cup. "You should be in the wagon. It's not a fit night for man or beast."

She nodded, meeting the warmth of his eyes. "Is Marshall McCall comfortable?"

"Comfortable as anyone can be in this kind of weather." They edged closer to the fire, standing shoulder to shoulder. She noticed he wasn't eager to seek shelter, and she could only hope it was because of her company. They shared the silence, taking sips of coffee. After the next two days there'd be no more sharing coffee or late-night conversations. She wondered how she'd pass the hours, with no friends, no more Jackson Lincoln to argue with or hash over the day's events.

Jackson broke the stillness. "Were you frightened this afternoon?"

"No." She was never scared when he was around; only scared when he wasn't. A wagon hanging over the side of a mountain was nothing. She doubted there was anything that he couldn't fix or mend or make work, and she told him so.

He chuckled, a low male resonance that stirred the pit of her stomach. "Your trust could be misplaced. There are a lot of things I can't do or wouldn't attempt without the help of a higher source."

"You mean without the Lord?" She didn't know why folks found the source so hard to identify.

He nodded, taking another sip from his cup. "Been doing a lot of bargaining with God about that pass."

"Were you honestly worried that we wouldn't make it?" She couldn't imagine that he'd fear anything. He seemed in control of every aspect of his life.

His expression sobering, he focused on the crackling fire. "I was concerned. Even a day's delay could have meant that we wouldn't have made it through until spring. That spot is prone to sudden and severe changes in weather. One of the worst snowstorms I've heard of happened here in May of '58. We're coming through it at the end of October, but with this weather. . . ."

Glory was smart enough to know what he hadn't said, that death would have been almost certain if a blizzard had set in.

She sidled closer to him, slipping the coffee cup into one hand and her other hand into his. The act felt as natural as rain. His large hand tightened around hers protectively. They were both foolish, standing out in a cold sleeting rain, but she wasn't inclined to leave, and neither was he, she noticed.

She looked up at him. "Guess you were happy to have Marshall McCall along to help."

Jackson nodded. "Seems to be a good man." He glanced at her and smiled. "What's between Ruth and him?"

"You noticed, too?"

Their soft laughter mingled with the popping fire; they kept their voices low so they wouldn't disturb the others. Ruth wouldn't appreciate them talking about her, but it was plain to see Ruth had gotten downright flustered around the handsome marshall.

Suddenly aware of the proximity of the others, Glory gently removed her hand from his and wrapped both hands around her cup. She moved closer to the fire and sat down. Jackson came and sat next to her. They took another sip of coffee, huddling deeper into their jackets. Sleet hit the canvas, icy pellets dancing lightly in the air. Wind shrieked through the pass, howling like a banshee.

"Two more days to Denver City?" she asked wistfully.

"Two more days," he verified.

"Guess you'll be glad to be relieved of your responsibilities."

"Not necessarily."

She took a deep breath, dreading to ask the next question but knowing that she must if she were to sleep a wink tonight. "Then what?"

He glanced at her, then back to the fire. "I'll make sure you ladies are settled, and, depending on the weather, I'll either stay around for a few weeks, or I'll start back to Illinois."

"I wish you wouldn't." The admission simply slipped out. She'd meant to thank him for his care and safe passage. Instead, she'd spoken her thoughts aloud. Did he think she was being forward?

If he thought anything of it, he didn't show it. "You thought about what you'll do?"

She shrugged. "Begin my new life."

"And that will be?"

"I don't know. Guess I'll have to see if there's work available in Denver City." She found it hard to look at him now, her emotions close to the surface. "Thanks to you, I'm a sight more capable of finding employment now than I would have been earlier."

"No thanks to me," he corrected softly. "Lily taught you to sew. Harper taught you to cook. And Ruth taught you to read and write."

162

He turned to meet her eyes. "You were a good student; you learned your lessons well." A teasing light entered his eyes. "Do you realize that I am close to eating one of your pies without choking or dipping dough out of the water bucket?"

She accepted his good-natured ribbing gracefully and tossed a measure of it back at him. "And you can shoot a squirrel at thirty feet and still have enough meat to put on the table. Aren't we amazing?"

"Thanks to you," he conceded. They shared a smile. "We make a good team," he said softly.

"We sure do." She wished it were a permanent team, like man and wife. . . . She stopped her train of thought. She didn't need a man or a husband. What was she thinking? She was sad only because she knew how little time they had left together.

He picked up a stick and stirred the fire. "Haven't changed your mind about marriage, have you?"

She shook her head, her chin firming. "Going to make it on my own. Well, I'll need the Lord's favor, but he's the only one going to tell me what to do."

"I understand." He watched the flames. "Feel the same way about taking a wife. Don't need a woman around, making life miserable."

"Like your mother?" she supplied.

"Like my mother."

They fell into a companionable silence.

"Not all women nag and complain," she reminded him.

"How would you know?"

"Don't for certain. Just know I wouldn't be like that."

"You wouldn't?"

"No. When I marry, I'll make sure I don't nag or complain. And if I do, I'll give myself a sound talking to, like I do when I get in your way. Remind myself that I'm lucky to have a good man, and he's lucky to have a good woman, and folks are just folks. Never met a perfect person, and seems more likely every day that I won't. So when a man and a woman marry, they ought naturally to expect there'll be times when they get on each other's nerves. Considering no one's perfect, they ought to make up their minds right off to forgive and go on." She took another sip of coffee, avoiding his gaze. "Don't you think?"

He sat for a long moment, apparently considering the likelihood. "I suppose so . . . if a man and woman love each other."

"And if they don't," she said simply, "then it's not likely they'll overlook a thing. They'll always be getting in each other's hair, looking for a way out, in which case, no one can help because it's up to the person whether he chooses to overlook fault or find fault. If anyone's looking for fault, he's going to find it; and if he's looking for good, he's likely to find that, too. Poppy used to say, 'Be happy with what you got before you get a whole lot worse.' " She studied Jackson out of the corner of her eye. "Can I ask you something?"

"Is it one of those things you're bursting at the seams to ask?"

"Might be." She dropped her gaze, cradling the coffee in her hands. "What's the question?"

"Are you sweet on Ruth—are you going to marry her?"

His jaw dropped. "What?"

"I see the way you two look at each other, all soft and caring. You never look at the other girls that way, so I think that maybe you've fallen in love with her and you're hoping to marry her once we reach Denver City."

Strained silence closed over them. A twig snapped, shooting up a shower of sparks. Glory lifted her cup for another sip. Finally, she couldn't stand the awful suspense. "Well?"

"Where would you ever get the crazy idea that I'm in love with Ruth?"

"I told you . . . the way you look at her, the way you talk to her—"

"I look and talk to Patience the same way."

"No, you don't."

He took a sip of coffee. "Your imagination is working overtime, Glory."

"You don't look at Lily or Mary that way, either."

"You don't look at me like you looked at Dylan this afternoon. Does that mean you're in love with the marshall and you dislike me?"

"Of course not. I didn't look at Dylan in an unladylike way."

He turned to face her, lifting a brow. "Every single *one* of you has looked at him in an improper way. All day long."

They turned back to study the fire.

She held her ground. "You're avoiding my question."

"How can I answer when the question doesn't make sense?"

He understood the question only too well, and he didn't want to answer. His reticence confirmed her worst fear: What he felt for Ruth was personal, and he didn't care to discuss it with her.

"OK. I don't believe you," Glory said.

"Fine," Jackson answered.

"Fine with me, too."

They sat for a few more moments.

"If I married Ruth," he said teasingly, "I'd have to borrow the money from you to pay back Wyatt."

"That's not true and you know it."

The hour grew late. Sleet pelted the overhang, and wind rattled the canvas. The coffee warmed her insides, but the long day finally claimed her. Slumping against Jackson's broad shoulder, she realized that Ruth would say she was being too forward, but his shoulder was too tempting. Although he didn't look at her the way he looked at Ruth, tonight he had talked to her the way he talked to Ruth.

Jackson glanced over, smiling when he saw her nodding off. In the past few months, she'd gone from a dirty, orphaned waif to a lovely, desirable woman. She had no idea how lovely or how desirable. There were times lately he'd had to remind himself that she was his charge, not his soul mate. She matched his zest for life where no other woman had ever come close. Was he in love with Ruth? The thought amused him. Ruth, like the other girls, claimed a part of his affection, but the girl whom—he was startled by his thoughts and surprised by their intensity. What was he about to think? That walking away from Glory wasn't going to be easy? He shook the thought away. The cold was numbing his brain.

Dumping the remains of his coffee, he turned and removed the cup from her small hand. She stirred slightly, snuggling closer to the warmth of his body. He carefully eased her back into a sitting position. Then he stood up, bent down, and lifted her tiny frame into his arms.

Pausing at the back of the wagon, he tapped on the closed canvas. A moment later, Patience poked her sleepy head out. When she saw Glory in his arms, she spread the opening wider, and he laid the drowsy girl on her pallet. Settling the blanket over her sleeping form, he gently tucked her between the soft covers. What did he feel for this woman-child?

Lord, help me—what do I feel?

"Good night," he whispered.

"Good night," Patience whispered back. She quickly secured the back canvas against the whistling wind as he turned to leave.

Turning his collar up, he adjusted the brim of his hat. By morning, the ground would be a solid sheet of ice. That meant no traveling tomorrow.

It also meant one more day in the company of a woman who was about to cost him a night's sleep.

Chapter Fifteen

Storm clouds built overhead as Jackson led the prairie schooner along Cherry Creek to the main street of Denver City on the first day of November. Six expectant faces peered out of the wagon.

Marshall Dylan McCall, riding behind the wagon all day, nudged his horse into a trot to catch up with Jackson at the front of the wagon. They rode beside each other in silence until Dylan pointed toward the sheriff's office. "Here's my stop, friend. I leave you now to meet my new traveling partner, and I'm sure he won't match the pleasant company I've recently enjoyed."

The two men reined to a halt and shook hands, and the wagon stopped behind them. Jackson met the marshall's even gaze. "I appreciate your help this past week, Dylan. Don't know how we could have gotten through the high divide without you."

"Would prefer present company to my next companion, I assure you." Dylan circled his horse to face the wagon. His gaze met Ruth's as she sat straight and stiff on the wagon seat, watching him. "Farewell, ladies."

When Jackson moved on, Ruth paused a moment. "Farewell," she finally replied. She lifted her chin and shook the reins. Grinning, Dylan tipped his hat as the wagon passed him for the last time. The girls leaned out from under the canvas to wave and call good-bye, a soft sadness filling their eyes.

Excitement broke out as the party traveled the remaining distance to a house several miles outside Denver City. Chatter faded as their eyes scanned the crudely built structure.

"Is this it?" Lily asked.

"Seems rather . . . bare," Patience murmured.

Ruth smiled, and the girls reached for each other's hands. "It will be fine. Perhaps our soon-to-be husbands are already waiting for us."

"Mercy, let's hope so." Harper's eyes took in the shabby farmhouse.

Jackson dismounted, and the girls slowly climbed out of the wagon, each clutching her valise. Stepping on the porch, he rapped on the door and waited until a harsh voice responded, "Come in. It ain't locked."

The door creaked on rusty hinges as Jackson swung it open and stepped inside to hold it for the six girls who slowly filed past him. Their eyes cast about, taking in the broken chairs and filthy bedrolls scattered on the floor. Three unkempt men sat around a table piled with poker chips.

A blond man with long, matted hair folded his handful of cards and laid them facedown on the table as he stood up. "You must be Jackson Lincoln," he rumbled.

Jackson nodded. "I am." An awkward silence followed as the wagon master waited for the man to identify himself.

"Name's Wyatt." The man's pale eyes narrowed. "Been expecting you for two weeks now."

"Had some delays on the trail, early snow in the high passes."

Wyatt grinned at his two unshaven companions. "Yeah, that's what we figured the first week, didn't we, boys? Along about the second week, we figured you'd decided to keep the girls and go into business for yourself."

The two seated companions roared at this. "Good one, Pa!"

"Excuse me," Jackson interrupted coldly, "but there are ladies present."

This prompted a few more hoots until the men took in the granite expression on Jackson's face. The laughter subsided, and Wyatt's mouth thinned. "Oh yeah, well, I'll get your money, and you can be on your way."

"I know it's getting late," Jackson began, "but I was hoping to meet a couple of the prospective husbands you've arranged for these five ladies."

Wyatt lifted his head to survey the women. "I count six." He grinned at his companions. "You throwing in a bonus?"

"Not exactly." Jackson frowned, and Glory moved up behind him to peer at the men. "I was hoping you could arrange work and proper quarters for a young lady we met along the way."

"Which one is that?"

Jackson shifted Glory around to his front, keeping a hand on her shoulder. "Her name is Glory."

Wyatt's eyes skimmed the comely girl. "Won't have no trouble finding her work; she can join the others. Got us a nice little silver mine—always need a few more to sort rocks. Can you cook, honey?"

Glory mutely wagged her head.

A slow grin spread across the man's malevolent features. "Don't matter if you can. You can load rock, can't you?"

She shook her head.

Jackson's shoulders stiffened. "A mine? These women are mail-order brides." Behind him, the girls drew together in a tight knot, their arms wrapping around each other for support.

"Really?" Wyatt's tone took on a confrontational tone. "No mention of that in your contract."

"Your letter said—"

"Things change." Wyatt shrugged as his right hand dropped to rest on the butt of the pistol strapped to his hip. "All your contract says is that you will bring me five orphans from Westport for the amount agreed upon. I'll even throw in a bonus, seeing as you've brought me one more. Whatever my letter to Potter said," Wyatt shrugged, "well, now, a letter ain't a binding contract, is it? Now these ladies signed a contract, and a contract is nice and legal."

"Why you—"

"Jeb, get me the strongbox." Wyatt's eyes hardened. "Let's pay this man, so he can get back to town before dark. He looks a bit road weary. Long trips can make a fella disagreeable. Round here a man can get hisself killed if he don't take a proper tone with the locals."

Grinning, the man called Jeb slammed a heavy box down on the table. Wyatt lifted the lid, took out a large pouch, and set it on the table. Glancing at Glory, he selected a smaller pouch and placed it beside the large one. "Put the box away, Son." He turned to the other man. "Luther, make yourself useful and show the wagon master out."

Wyatt threw the money bags at Jackson with enough force that he had to catch them or be bowled over by them. When Jackson looked up, Wyatt and Luther had their pistols drawn. Jeb had joined them, carrying a sawed-off shotgun.

"Now let's not quibble over details," Wyatt said, his pale eyes icy.

"Mail-order brides or mine workers, either way these unwanted, too-old-to-adopt orphans are going to have to work off their expensive passage west. When they've done that, why, you can ask my boys here, I'm a reasonable man. The girls will be free to go wherever their little hearts desire."

Jackson met the cold gaze with a clenched jaw. "You bought these women to work in your mine?"

"Well, now, that's a little harsh. As I said, once they pay off their passage, they're free to go."

"But that would be hundreds of dollars," Ruth argued.

Wyatt smiled. "Ain't it ridiculous what prices are these days?"

"It will take years for us to work off the debt," Lily exclaimed.

Wyatt chuckled, a humorless sound. He gestured toward the door with the barrel of his pistol. "Better be on your way, wagon master. After dark it's hard to see in these hills. Easy to mistake a man for a thief or an intruder. A fella could get shot." Wyatt's gaze dropped to the pouches in Jackson's hands, and his brows lifted with interest.

Jackson's eyes moved from pistol to pistol to shotgun.

Glory's gaze flew to Jackson. "Shoot him, Jackson. He's plain no good."

Shrugging, Jackson backed toward the door, holding his hands up in surrender. "Ladies, I've done my job. You'll have to talk to Mr. Wyatt if you have a complaint."

"Jackson?" Glory exclaimed in shocked disbelief, reaching for his arm as he opened the door. "Are you nuts! You can't leave us here with this—this polecat!"

"You can't," Ruth begged, as Lily and Patience clung to her sobbing.

"Please, Mr. Lincoln," Mary wheezed, despair flooding her face.

"That's it, run like a yellow-bellied coward." Harper stepped in front of Jackson and blocked his path. Her eyes locked with his. "Just like a man. All those nice things you did for us—just an act. Once you got your money, you run out on us. So high and mighty in front of us, then some flea-bitten curs point a gun at you, and you're gone."

"Hey, who you calling flea-bitten curs?" Jeb shouted.

"Well," Wyatt said coldly, "she's right about one thing. Money changes a man. Say good-bye to your knight in shining armor, ladies."

Jackson opened the door, tipped his hat to Harper, and left.

Glory listened to the jingle of harnesses. After three and a half months, she knew it was the sound of the prairie schooner pulling out. As the sound faded, cold dread filled her heart. She couldn't believe what had just happened. Jackson hadn't lifted a hand to save them. She looked at Ruth, who turned away, handkerchief pressed to her mouth.

"Hey, Daddy, you want me to show these women their new temporary quarters?" Luther asked with a salacious grin.

"Why, that's right good of you, Son, right hospitable." Tom Wyatt grinned, revealing broken, tobacco-stained teeth. "You do that, boy. And ladies? Better get to bed right after supper. Got a lot of rocks waitin' for you in the morning—say around four-thirty?"

Jackson Lincoln was furious. Blood pounded in his temple, and his chest hurt with tightness. His face was dark with rage.

Halfway down the mountain, he secured the wagon and teams in a protected grove. Saddling the mare, he bounded aboard and rode into Denver City with a crisp wind at his back. Pewter-colored clouds promised a heavy snow by nightfall.

Springing out of the saddle in town, he strode to the sheriff's office and entered with the rage of the impending blizzard.

"Whoa." Dylan McCall whirled to identify the commotion behind him. "Montgomery?"

"Marshall, am I glad you're still here." Jackson grabbed hold of Dylan's arm and took a deep breath.

"Looks like I'll be around for a while. Seems my prisoner hanged himself in his cell rather than share my company on the trip back for trial. I just sent a telegram to my superiors, requesting my next assignment."

Jackson turned to the sheriff. "I need your help." He quickly told the two men about his encounter with Wyatt and his sons, and what Wyatt intended to do. "We have to get back there before he puts those girls to work in the mine."

Dylan frowned. "Where's Ruth?"

"She's with the others. Wyatt won't move them until morning, not with bad weather closing in."

The whipcord-thin sheriff shook his head. "Not so fast. We know about Wyatt and his boys. Already contacted state authorities, and they're sending investigators to check Wyatt out for fraud. We've heard similar stories about other kids he's brought into town. No doubt Wyatt is a snake, but what he's doing may not be technically illegal. The experts from the state will figure that out."

"We can't wait for experts!" Jackson exploded. "Those girls are up there scared to death. They think I walked out on them."

The sheriff shrugged. "You can't interfere with a state investigation. Tell him, Marshall."

Dylan laid a hand on Jackson's arm. "Easy, friend. Let's hear him out."

The sheriff continued. "Seems we have a pattern so far. From what we've heard, Wyatt contacts a slick solicitor in a territory, who then makes the arrangements at a local orphanage, offering to take the older children off their hands while greasing a few palms. Then he tells the girls that he represents a fine man who has assembled some eligible bachelors willing to pay their passage west to meet them. He tells the young boys that he has high-paying jobs waiting for them. Then he whips out contracts so full of legal wording that the kids have no idea what they're signing. After that, he makes arrangements with a wagon master to bring them west."

Color drained from Jackson's face. "That's how I was brought in on the deal. I was doing Frank Potter a favor."

The sheriff shook his head. "I hate to add to your troubles, but you may have a more immediate problem."

Jackson frowned. "What could be worse?"

"There's a man here in town," the sheriff began, "by the name of Amos, staying at the hotel. Seems he's searching for a wagon full of mail-order brides due to arrive any day. Says he's looking for his niece, a girl named Glory. Heard she was traveling with a small group of women when he stopped at a trading post. Folks there remembered a pretty girl by that name, who bought a mirror, it seems. He's convinced she's the niece who knocked him cold and stole his gold. A mean fella, if you ask me. Little gal is in a heap of trouble if he catches up with her."

Jackson took off his hat and ran an agitated hand through his hair. "That's all we need."

The sheriff moved to the stove to pour himself a cup of coffee. "I insisted he let the law handle it, but he only wanted to know her whereabouts. No law against that."

"Does he know about Wyatt's little scheme?" Dylan asked.

"I didn't mention it." The sheriff tasted his coffee and grimaced. "That doesn't mean he won't get wind of it."

Jackson met Dylan's eyes. "All the more reason we need to ride out to Wyatt's right now."

"There's nothing we can do about it tonight," the sheriff announced with a tired sigh. "I trust everything will be straightened out in a few short weeks."

"We haven't got weeks!" Jackson snapped.

Dylan turned him around and pushed him back through the door. "I'll have a chat with him, Sheriff."

Outside, Jackson shook off Dylan's restraining hold.

"Look, McCall, if you're going to tell me to wait for the state boys to mosey down here, save your breath! Glory's in trouble, and I'm going after her. If I hadn't been outnumbered earlier, she'd be with me now."

"Glory? Ruth's up there too."

The two men faced off. Jackson's eyes steeled. "Look. There are six women up there who need our help. I don't intend to stand here and split hairs."

Shoving past the marshall, Jackson strode toward his horse.

"Wait a minute, hothead. You did the right thing—it would have been nuts to take on Wyatt and his two boys alone." Dylan blocked Jackson's path, motioning with a sideways nod to start walking. When they stepped into a deserted alley, he turned to face Jackson. "What you have here is a lawman willing to help you take those ladies into protective custody until the state investigators have this thing sorted out."

Jackson released the breath that he'd been holding. "I'd be much obliged."

Dylan clapped him on the shoulder. "Well, if Wyatt and his boys are as nasty as you say and Amos is on the prowl, we have a little short-range planning to do."

❧

"Didn't I tell you so?" Harper sat down on the hard bunk and crossed her arms, her dark eyes openly accusing. "Men are worthless, lying, sneaking . . . no-good . . . stinking, useless, vile—"

"Men," Lily finished.

Harper nodded succinctly.

The old bunkhouse was drafty, wind whistling through the cracks. A woodstove in the middle of the room gave off little heat in the icy mountain air. Wyatt didn't have to lock the door; the mountains and impending storm held the women prisoners.

Glory sighed. "Jackson isn't like that."

Harper snorted. "He's a man, ain't he?"

"He's not *that* kind of a man."

Harper sprang to her feet. "How can you defend him? Look what he's done to us." She snapped her finger. "Poof. He sold us out, Glory. Took the money and walked out the door. You saw him, same as us."

"I know it looks that way." Glory felt awful. It *did* look as if Jackson didn't care a whit about them, so he'd left her no choice but to suspect the worst. She turned her eyes on Ruth. "Do you think Jackson could really betray us?"

Ruth shook her head. "I would have never thought he would, but you saw what he did."

"I won't believe it," Mary whispered. The young woman lay on her cot, dark circles under her eyes, the high altitude making her breathing even more difficult. "I saw what he did, but I refuse to believe Jackson would desert us."

"Any man worth his salt wouldn't walk off and leave a woman in our position." Harper jerked her blanket over her shoulders. "We've been bought for hard labor, ladies. And I fell for Jackson's act—pretending to be oh so nice, pretending that he cared about us and that he'd protect us no matter what." She yanked the blanket closer to her neck. "He's just like any other man. Thinks of himself and doesn't give a hoot about others."

"Not all men are traitors," Lily contended. "I've met some very nice men who were thoughtful and considerate. Jackson was wonderful . . . until tonight."

Patience sneezed. Rummaging in her valise for a handkerchief, she said softly, "Rats. I'm coming down with the sniffles."

Harper eyed her imperiously. "Well, honey, if you do, don't expect Wyatt and his gentlemanly sons to bring you hot soup."

The girls shivered at the thought of Wyatt's repulsive sons, Luther and Jeb.

Patience had been unusually quiet, sitting through a supper of cold corn bread and water, and looking miserable. Glory glanced at the shivering girl. "What about you, Patience? Do you think Jackson will turn us over to Tom Wyatt without a fight?"

"Looks to me like he already has. I'm sorry, Glory. I know you believed in him; we all did. But maybe your trust, and ours, has been misplaced."

Mary started to cry, tears wetting her thin pillow. "If I can't work and pay back Mr. Wyatt for my journey, what will he do with me? I'm useless."

Glory crossed the short distance to her bunk and took the sobbing girl in her arms.

"Don't worry," Harper said gruffly. "I'll do your share of the work, and if Wyatt complains, I'll show him what for."

"I'll help too," Lily offered.

Patience sneezed again. "Me too."

"We'll all help, Mary." Glory held the girl tightly. "Dry your tears. Jackson won't let this happen to us."

Glory didn't feel nearly as confident as she sounded. She didn't know about Jackson. What *would* Wyatt do with a sickly girl? Would he sell her to some uncaring, thoughtless animal every bit as vile as he? Mary wouldn't last a week. . . .

Straightening, Glory lifted her chin. "I don't care what you say, Jackson won't do this to us. He . . . he has a plan. He's only pretending to go along with Wyatt because he was outnumbered. It would have been foolish for him to try to take on all three of them. Why, I bet this very minute he's arranging a rescue."

"Right." Harper rolled her eyes. "And I'm the Queen Mother."

Wind battered the bunkhouse; Glory huddled on Mary's cot, more scared than she'd been in her whole life. *Please, Jackson, don't do this to us. I love you.*

"We'll run away. We can do it," Lily whispered. "The door isn't locked; we can slip out when the others are asleep and—"

"We'd die, Lily!" Glory exclaimed. "We haven't any food or water. It looks like it's going to snow any minute. It's miles and miles back to Denver City." Glory glanced at Mary. "We can't leave shelter; the mountain roads are narrow and dangerous. It's pitch-black out there, and we have no lantern, barely adequate clothing—"

Lily leaned closer. "But you're used to the outdoors. You could lead us, Glory."

"I'm not that good, not nearly as good as Jackson."

The girls groaned.

"We can't count on him," Ruth said.

"When the storm's over," Harper began, "we sneak up on Wyatt and his no-good sons, and we knock them senseless—"

"We can't do that either, Harper," Glory moaned. She would like nothing better than to knock Wyatt and his boys senseless, but if that mission failed, then no telling what Wyatt would do. He might decide they were more trouble than they were worth and do away with the lot of them. Short of killing the three men, the plan was too risky, and she didn't want any part of killing.

"We should pray about this," Ruth murmured.

"We will, Ruth, but in case the Lord is tending other business right now, we'd be smart to help him out." Glory slipped off the cot and started to pace. "I know Jackson is bluffing. He's thinking of a plan to help us this minute."

No use mentioning that she didn't believe a word she was saying, but she had to be strong for the others.

Rolling her eyes, Harper pulled the blanket over her head.

Hope lit Ruth's eyes. "Do you think so, Glory? Do you really think so?"

Glory reached for Ruth's hand and squeezed it. She could believe what she was saying—she must. "I know so, Ruth. Now everyone listen to me. Sleep lightly, and keep a close ear out for any sound that might mean Jackson is trying to help us."

Lily lifted a brow. "Like what?"

"Like a peck on the window or the door opening softly."

"What if it's Wyatt and those awful sons of his?" Ruth shivered.

"If it's Wyatt and he tries anything funny, we'll fight him with anything we can get our hands on." Her eyes fixed on the iron poker lying next to the stove. "I'll use the poker. Lily, you hit him with your pillow. Ruth, take off your boots and knock the wadding out of him."

"I'll empty my valise," Patience offered. "It will make a weapon."

"Good."

"What about me?" Mary wheezed.

Glory's eyes swept the room.

"I know," Mary enthused. "I'll charge him from the back. I'm little and wiry, and I'll use my fingers as weapons to gouge his eyes out, if I must," she whispered.

"Perfect," Glory agreed, and the others murmured their support. Eyes pivoted to Harper.

Yanking the blanket off her face, she heaved a resigned sigh. "I'll take him from the front." Springing to her feet, she doubled both fists. "I'll make him wish he'd thought twice about lying to us."

"OK, we have a plan. Now, everyone buck up and have a little faith. Jackson won't let us down."

"And neither will the Lord," Ruth promised. "He might be off tending other business, but he still has an eye on all his children."

The girls knelt in prayer and joined hands. "Father," Lily whispered, "we need you to be looking right now. You are our hiding place; you will protect us from harm."

"Yes, Lord," Harper whispered. "You tell us not to worry about anything, but to pray about everything. You tell us to tell you what we need, and what we need right now, God, is for you to look after us."

Patience added softly, "You tell us not to be afraid, for you are with us. You are our God, and you will strengthen us. You will uphold us with your victorious right hand."

"You will keep in perfect peace all who trust you, whose thoughts are fixed on you, Father," Ruth reminded.

"You have loved us, even as your Father loved you," Glory said softly. "And God has given us his Spirit as proof that we live in him and he in us." Her heart overflowed with the joy of remembering the Scriptures.

"We feel your Spirit this hour. Protect us this night, our Father. For you are the only one who can," Mary prayed.

Squeezing hands, the girls extinguished the candle and climbed onto their hard cots, ready for battle.

Glory lay beside Ruth, listening to the first drops of cold rain hit the dirty windowpanes, rain that was destined to turn to heavy snow before morning. Glory tried to imagine how dark and cold a mine would be and finally gave up. Likely she'd find out soon enough.

"Glory?" Ruth whispered.

"Yes?"

"Do you really believe Jackson will come, or were you only trying to console the others?"

"I believe he will come, Ruth. Believe it with all my heart."

Ruth lay quietly for a moment. "Then I'll believe it too."

Stillness settled over the drafty bunkhouse. Only Mary's rattling cough broke the silence.

"Ruth?"

"Yes, Glory?"

"Do you really believe there is a God, and that he loves us and cares about us, died on the cross to save us and give us eternal life?"

"I believe there is, Glory. With all my heart, I believe there is."

Silence stretched between them. Rain pelted the windows, and the wind whistled through the cracks between the logs. The uncertainty of life never felt more certain.

"Ruth?"

"Yes?"

"I believe it too. With all my heart, I believe it."

Reaching across the small space, the two girls held hands in the darkness and waited.

Chapter Sixteen

In the middle of the night, the girls still lay wide awake in the Wyatt bunkhouse, their ears straining to hear every sound, listening to every gust of wind and their own rapid heartbeats. With every facet of her being, Glory willed Jackson to return before dawn to rescue them. She reviewed every memory, every thing she'd heard him say, every expression on his face, every action he'd taken. In none of those things could she see a man who would abandon them to a fate like this. Jackson Lincoln wouldn't—no, he couldn't—leave them behind, never to return.

Glory rose to toss another chunk of wood into the stove. There were precious few sticks remaining to last the night. She shivered inside her jacket and tightened her wool scarf around her neck. They had all agreed that Mary should have the only blanket. The poor girl's breathing was raspy, the cold night and unsettling hours taking their toll. Harper had handed it over willingly.

"Where do you suppose the others are?"

Glory turned to look at Lily. "Others?"

"The other kids who work the mine."

"Hidden away, probably. Wyatt wouldn't want—"

She stiffened, suddenly aware of a noise outside the single window of the bunkhouse. Her first thought was that Wyatt or his sons were returning to torment them. But that didn't make sense when they could simply open the door and walk in. Her heart leapt to her throat. To her, only one person could be outside that window.

"Did you hear something?" Ruth asked in a hoarse whisper.

"It's them," Harper said. "Get to your battle stations."

"Hold on." Glory eased away from the stove, careful not to make a sound. "It's Jackson. I told you he'd come back for us!"

"Not so fast, girl." Harper crouched beside her cot, whispering. "We don't know it's Jackson. Better get ready for a fight."

The girls scrambled out of their beds, but Glory rushed past on her way to the window. "No, no," she whispered, "stay quiet. We've got to help him."

She shoved back the rotting curtains and peered out, but the glass was so filthy and the night so dark she couldn't see anything. But her heart knew who was mere feet away. She could hear him grunting as he strained to lift the cumbersome window.

"It's OK, Jackson," she said in a low voice as she shoved at the window, trying to raise it. "I'll help you from inside."

She pushed up with all her might while he pushed from the outside. Suddenly, she heard a creaking and then a popping sound as the rusty nails gave way. The window slowly lifted from the sill, then suddenly slammed upward.

Glory sighed with relief, then gathered the shredded curtains and sprang aside to allow Jackson access. She could point him to the front door, but Wyatt and his sons might see him. The window was hidden from the back part of the house where Wyatt and his sons slept.

He landed inside with a thud, his heavy boots hitting the rotten floor planks in the thick darkness. Glory lunged forward to throw her arms around his neck. "You're here," she whispered. "I knew you'd come for me."

A man's harsh chuckle sent goose bumps down her spine. "Told you I'd find you."

"Jackson?" Glory whispered, praying that the darkness was playing tricks on her.

"Now don't tell me you don't recognize your favorite Uncle Amos."

Glory sprang back and would have fallen to the floor had Ruth not caught her. "Oh, no," Glory moaned.

"If I recollect, it was a dark night when you clobbered me and ran off with my gold." Amos's voice rumbled with rage. "Left me for dead, you did!"

Mary screamed.

"Making a habit of it, are ya?" Amos latched onto Glory's arm and jerked her upright. "Don't surprise me. Time you paid the piper, girlie. I want my gold. Now!"

Glory quaked with fear. There was nothing Amos wouldn't do to get Poppy's gold. "I'd give you the gold if I had it, Amos. You've got to believe me."

"I don't got to do nothing of the kind." He gave Glory a shove. "You give me that gold or I'll tear you apart."

Mary gasped, and then her wheezing intensified. She struggled for every breath now.

Amos stopped and turned in the darkness, homing in on the sound of Mary's raspy breathing. "Or I might grab me one of your friends. Is that what you want, Glory?" He had no trouble finding Mary. He fumbled in the dark until he reached her. With a jerk, he pulled the sickly girl from Harper's arms. Mary began to choke—wrenching sounds—as her fright shut off her air supply.

"No!" Glory fought her way through the inky blackness to Mary and tried to twist her free of his grip. "Let her go, Amos. You're hurting her!"

"I'll hurt her worse," he snarled. "Where's that gold, Glory?"

Patience and Lily started to sob; Ruth begged him to be merciful.

"Let her go, Amos," Glory pleaded. "She's sick. I'll take you to Poppy's gold. I have it hidden. We can make good time, just the two of us. We have to go now, before Wyatt and his sons hear the racket and come to investigate."

"No, Glory!" Ruth pleaded. "You can't go with him—"

"I'll take you, Amos," Glory repeated. "Now! But you have to let Mary stay here."

"If you're lying to me, I'll do away with the lot of 'em." He thrust Mary backwards onto the cot, his left hand closing around Glory's arm, pinching her tender flesh so hard it brought tears to her eyes.

Whirling, he dragged her to the window and hoisted her to the sill. With a wicked shove he sent her flying through the opening. She landed on the ground with a hard thump, and he chuckled with glee. "If you make a run for it, Miss Glory," he sang out on a high note, "I'll bring Miss Mary with me!"

"I'm not going anywhere, Amos," Glory returned.

He grunted with rage as he climbed through the window and landed on the ground in a heap. Struggling to his feet, he gave Glory a sound slap across her face. "That's a taste of what you'll get if you try anything.

I mean it. You try to run out on me again, and I'll come back here and take care of your little friends."

"I'll do whatever you say." Teeth chattering, Glory huddled against the icy wind. Snow had already begun to fall.

Snatching her arm, he ushered her to a stand of aspens, where a horse waited. He grabbed a fistful of her hair and then climbed into the saddle.

"Ow," she cried as he dragged her up behind him. She struck out at him. "That hurts!"

"Don't try anything funny, Glory. I mean it. Where did you put that gold?"

"In Denver City. I hid it before we came out here to Wyatt's."

"You better not be lying to me," he snarled as they set off at a trot.

Investigating the ruckus, Wyatt opened the door to the bunkhouse and held his lantern aloft. His nightshirt flapped in the howling wind. "What's going on out here?"

The women huddled close, sobbing and praying in the center of the room. They shrunk back as his spindly frame filled the open doorway. The only sounds were Mary's wheezing and the gusts of wind banging the door against the side of the building.

"I'm not a patient man!"

Ruth spoke up. "A man came in."

"What?" Wyatt roared, lifting the lantern higher. His long hair whipped in the wind.

"Through the window there. He took Glory, his niece. He's a horrible man. I think he means her harm. You could catch them if you leave now. They have about a quarter of an hour's start. I saw them heading into the woods—you could follow their tracks."

The other girls gasped.

"No," Lily exclaimed, "you can't send him after them."

Ruth turned to look at her. "It's the only way we can save Glory. This man is less of a danger to her than Amos. Remember, we're only worth something to Wyatt if we're alive. Glory's uncle will surely do away with her once he gets what he's after."

"Oh," Lily choked, burying her face in her hands to sob.

Wyatt strode to the open window and slammed it shut. "The next one who tries to escape will be shot, you hear me?"

"The dead could hear you," Jackson said, appearing in the open doorway with Dylan right behind him. Both men had pistols trained on Wyatt.

"*Jackson!*" Ruth sprang up to meet him. "Glory knew you would come. She lied to Amos, told him she'd hidden the money in Denver City. She sacrificed herself for Mary and us."

He strode into the room as Wyatt turned and extended his lantern to get a look at him.

"Are you hurt?" Jackson asked the girls as he moved toward them.

"No," Ruth said, "only scared."

"Get your things," Jackson said evenly. "You're coming with us."

"See here—" Wyatt stopped short when Jackson turned to face him.

"I don't want any trouble, Wyatt."

Dylan was standing watch at the door. "We've got company."

Outside, a man's voice filtered above the howling wind. "Daddy? It's Jeb. You want us to shoot 'em?"

"If these men step outside with the women, shoot 'em all," Wyatt yelled. He glanced at Jackson and grinned. "No trouble, wagon master. You're not going anywhere with anybody."

"OK, Pa," came the reply from the darkness outside.

Dylan, standing behind the door with his pistol aimed in the direction of the voices outside, spoke up, "Wyatt, shine your lantern this way. I have something you should see."

When Wyatt hesitantly complied, Dylan flashed the badge pinned to his jacket. "See this?"

"You the law?" Wyatt took a step back.

"Dylan McCall, U.S. marshall. I'm here to take these women into protective custody until investigators can check the legitimacy of your claim to them."

"Now hold on," Wyatt said, backing away now. "Why didn't you say so? You don't need to go stirring up a hornet's nest. We can work something out."

"Thought you might see it that way. Here's the deal. You call off your boys, and we leave peaceably. Nobody gets hurt. I can tell investigators how cooperative you were."

Wyatt grunted, then sighed heavily, took a deep breath, and raised his voice to shout, "Boys, change of plans! Put down your weapons, and let these two men and the women leave."

"Huh? You sure, Pa?"

"Do as I say," Wyatt roared.

Dylan motioned to Ruth, "Ladies, line up behind me and stay close. Jackson will follow behind."

Spreading her arms, Ruth quickly assembled the girls behind her. She stepped behind Dylan and took hold of his shirt. "We're with you," she murmured.

"Let's go." He stepped through the doorway, pistol held aloft. Quietly the group filed out with Dylan in the lead and Jackson protecting their flank. He grabbed Wyatt's lantern just before he slammed the door shut.

"What the—" Wyatt roared.

The group made a break for the nearest trees before Wyatt and his boys had a chance to change their minds.

Hurrying deeper into the woods, they could hear the shrill voices of Wyatt's boys. "Why you lettin' them take the women, Pa?"

"Because, you *fools,* there's more where they came from. Besides, more lawmen are on their way. Time we took to higher ground."

"We coulda shot those men, Pa!"

"If you lazy bums had rolled out of bed and come out here when I first called you," Wyatt bellowed, "we'd all been inside the bunkhouse, and those boys wouldn't have gotten the drop on me. But no, you don't listen to your pa!"

The ruckus faded as the small group scurried through the woods. They paused in an aspen grove, where Jackson bent to check two sets of footprints, one set large and one set small. He glanced up at Dylan. "Looks like this is where Amos left his horse."

Dylan nodded. "They can't be far. I'll go after them."

"You take the others and get them back to Denver City," Jackson said. "The wagon and teams are waiting about a mile down the road. I'll go after Glory, and we'll meet up by morning."

"Be careful," Dylan warned.

"I will. See to the girls' safety. The storm is about to break, and it's going to be a bad one." The two men shook hands and set off in different directions.

Within minutes, Jackson located a set of prints in the snow. Fresh, not over an hour old. As the sprinkle of falling snow grew heavier, Jackson urged his mare into a gallop. It looked like Amos was angling back toward the road. He had to catch him before the snow covered his tracks. Kicking his horse, he rode faster.

Rounding a bend half an hour later, Jackson spotted a light in the distance. He quickly dimmed his own lantern. Amos's horse was lunging up a hillside, while Amos awkwardly held his lantern aloft. The snow, combined with the awkward weight of Amos and his passenger, made it hard for the animal to keep his balance.

Jackson reined his mare to circle around, hoping to catch Amos by surprise.

When Amos's horse topped the next rise, Jackson put his heels to his mare, and she shot out of the trees in a blur of snow and wind. The wagon master turned his mare so she'd bump Amos's horse, and then he reached out and grabbed its bridle. Amos's lantern flew to the ground and smashed.

"Jump, Glory!" Jackson shouted, but she was already sliding off the animal's back.

Jackson glanced over his shoulder to be sure she was clear. Amos struck out, hitting him in the jaw. Jackson reeled and dropped his lantern but managed to keep his hold on the bridle. The two horses leapt side by side, brushing between the nearby aspen trees.

The trail narrowed; there was hardly enough room for one animal. Amos's knee collided with a tree trunk, and he pitched backward, losing his balance and falling heavily to the ground.

Jackson wheeled his horse around and galloped back. Dismounting, he kept an eye on Amos, who by now was raising one hand in the air. "Don't shoot," he hollered, bending forward to clutch his knee.

"Look out, Jackson!" Glory cried. "He's got a knife in his boot!"

Amos sprang, slashing wildly. Jackson instinctively raised his right hand to protect himself. Amos ripped his palm and wrist, tearing open glove and flesh.

Jackson swung his left fist and connected with Amos's jaw and sent him sprawling. Awkwardly, he drew his pistol out of his holster with his left hand. Amos rolled to his knees and crawled a few feet.

"Stop right there," Jackson warned, leveling the Colt.

"You won't get away with this," Amos snarled. He kept his eyes on the pistol in Jackson's hand. After a pause, he backed up a few feet and slid down a tree trunk and sat there, glaring.

Glory rushed to Jackson. He awkwardly put his left arm around her, pulling her close to his side. "Are you all right?"

"I'm fine. I knew you would come." She paused. "What about the girls?"

"Dylan has them. They're on their way to Denver City. We'll meet them by morning." He glanced up at the swirling snow. "Round up the horses. The storm is getting worse."

"You got it."

The two men stared at each other for a long moment in the silence of the falling snow.

"What are you going to do with me?" Amos snarled.

"Well, it comes down to this, Amos." Jackson leaned over to pick up the knife. His blood stained the mounting snow. "When we leave, we're taking your horse. I'll leave him tied about a mile down the road. Then you have a choice to make. You can give up the notion of taking the gold away from Glory, or you can continue to hunt her down and deal with me. In which case, you won't have a second chance. So you come after Glory again, and there'll be no mercy. Or you can walk to your horse, mount up, and ride on. You make the choice."

Amos glared up at him.

Jackson mounted his mare and pulled Glory up behind him. He fixed Amos with a solid stare. "May God have mercy on your soul."

Looping the reins of Amos's horse around his saddle horn, Jackson set the horses into motion.

Snow pelted their faces as Jackson galloped the horse back down the trail. Glory knew if the storm kept up, he wouldn't be able to see the road in another fifteen minutes.

"Will Amos come after us?" she shouted above the whistling wind.

"That's up to him!"

She knew Jackson had been fair enough to give him a choice; other men likely wouldn't have.

The wind shifted, and snow flecks turned to cottonball-size flakes. They approached an overhanging rock, and Jackson veered off to the side of the trail. Slipping out of the saddle, he tied Amos's horse to a low bush. He quickly remounted the mare, and they rode on.

"What about your hand?" she called in a worried voice a short time later. "It's bleeding!" It was a nasty wound. He was losing blood fast, and unless the gash was properly dressed, he could bleed to death. Jackson stopped the horse long enough for Glory to get down and scoop up a handful of snow and press it to his wound.

Blinding snow swirled as the horse and its riders pushed on through the mounting drifts. Conversation was impossible now. Glory clung to Jackson's waist, trying to summon faith like Ruth's.

God has his eyes on his children. Glory knew that accepting God's Word meant she had to believe that, no matter what, but she wondered if even Ruth could hold on to her faith tonight.

Clamping her eyes shut, she whispered between chattering teeth, *I believe, Lord. I just hope you're not off tending business elsewhere.*

Gradually, she felt changes taking place in Jackson's body. At first, they were small, barely perceptible: a relaxing of his muscles, an inability to answer her shouted questions. Then the changes became more pronounced. He slumped, weakened from the loss of blood. Her fingers rested in warm blood pooling on the saddle. Through the faint light reflected off the snow-covered ground, she detected the gaping wrist wound, and it looked bad.

"Jackson!" Fear choked her. If he lost consciousness, he would be too heavy for her to lift. "Jackson! Answer me!"

Stirring, he tightened his grip on the reins. "I'm all right."

But he wasn't all right; he was still bleeding. Worsening weather rapidly deteriorated into blizzard conditions. Wind shrieked through the boulders, and snow piled up on pine branches.

Reaching around his waist, she took the reins and pulled the horse to a stop.

"I'm all right," he protested. "Just got to find shelter before the storm gets any worse."

"You're in no shape to do anything." All the times she used to climb all over her mule, Molasses, gave her the courage to try a desperate move. She shifted her weight to one side, stood up in the stirrup, and swung out, easing her slight weight around his frame. Grunting, she climbed in front of him and landed just behind the saddle horn. She wrapped his arms around her waist and called over her shoulder, "Hang on."

Fumbling in her pocket, she pulled out a handkerchief. She twisted it into a rope and tied it around Jackson's hand. Gathering the reins, she tapped the mare with her heels and set off again.

Snow came down in heavy, wet sheets. Inching forward in the saddle, Glory strained to make out the road. She kept the mare to the far left and slowed her to a walk when they entered a narrow ledge. *Don't look down,* she chanted under her breath as the mare picked her footing through the narrow, rutted trail. *For heaven's sake, don't look down.* She didn't need a full moon to warn her of the two-hundred-foot drop-off on the right.

Reaching back, she grasped hold of Jackson, who was slumped over her shoulder now. "Hold on. I'll get us there." Wherever that might be. She had no idea where she was going or how to get there.

She couldn't feel her face. Frigid wind whipped around her head, and her lips were numb. She had to find shelter—but where? This mountainous terrain was so different from Missouri's gently rolling hills.

The mare cleared the narrow pass and plodded into a valley. Here, the snow whirled across the exposed land, piling to frightening depths.

Glory shook her head, trying to clear her vision. Jackson leaned on her shoulder, unconscious now. She could hear her own heartbeat in her ear. Everything began to blur; she was becoming disoriented.

Dear God, help me.

Reining the mare through another snowbank, she tried to think, but her mind was slow and unresponsive. Wind tore at her coat and seeped though her wool dress and leggings.

The horse stumbled and nearly went down. Flanking it hard and lifting the reins, she sent it surging back to its feet. At the same time, she fought to keep hold of Jackson.

We're going to die.

No! She wouldn't let Jackson die. She had to keep moving.

Ahead would be shelter somewhere: in a grove of aspens, or in a cave, maybe in an abandoned mine.

She couldn't see three feet in front of her. The mare thrashed about, trying to wade through the drifts, snorting with fear.

Suddenly, out of nowhere, a faint light appeared in the distance.

Bolting upright, Glory whispered to Jackson, "It's all right. Somebody's coming." Relief flooded her as the light bobbed closer.

Oh, thank you, God. Thank you for hearing my cries.

The light stopped in front of her. The stranger lifted the lantern to reveal his face. It looked like Poppy standing before her, moving the lantern slowly back and forth.

"Poppy?" she whispered. Grabbing hold of Jackson's hand, she tried to squeeze it, but her hand wouldn't close. "It's Poppy," she cried.

"Go back!" The figure waved the lantern in warning. "Go back, Glory. You're going to die if you don't."

"Go back where?" She twisted to look back over her shoulder at the swirling void. "Poppy, I can't go back!" Tears slipped from her eyes and rolled down her cheeks. The wetness froze in seconds. This couldn't be Poppy; Poppy was dead. Her mind was playing tricks on her. She turned to look again.

"Go back! Turn around!"

She obeyed. She turned the mare around, and when she looked back at the figure, he and the light had disappeared.

Leaning in the stirrups, she strained to locate him. "Poppy? Poppy!"

A howling wind caught in her throat and choked off her pleas.

Guiding the mare, she waded the animal back through the fresh tracks. She was losing her mind. Poppy was dead; Poppy wasn't here in Colorado in a blinding blizzard, holding a lantern and warning her to turn back.

The horse could barely clear the drifts. Snow swelled to the mare's belly and dragged against the stirrups.

The narrow ledge. She couldn't make it back over the tight pass. The snow was getting too deep. She wouldn't be able to keep far enough over, and they'd drop over the side.

She suddenly turned the mare, veering to a sharp left. The path tapered, then widened to a small pine grove. Slowing, Glory listened to the wind shrieking through the boughs. The pungent scent of pine mingled with the awful cold. She was so frozen the scene felt surreal, and she wondered if she was imagining it like she'd imagined Poppy and the light.

Holding tight to Jackson's gloved hand, she closed her eyes, barely able to think. *Are you going to let us die, Lord? I sure would appreciate it if you didn't.*

"Jackson," she whispered, tired now, so very tired. "This might not be a good time to tell you this, and I know you can't hear me anyway, but it's one of those things I'm fairly bursting to say. If I don't say it right now, I might never have the chance again."

Swallowing, she gathered her strength and her nerve. It was possible that they wouldn't make it through the night; that's why she had to tell him now.

"I love you," she whispered. "I know you don't want me to love you, but I love you anyway. I've loved you from the moment you found me sitting on the trail and offered me a ride. I loved you when you shouted and blustered at me; I loved you when you were kind, and I loved you when I couldn't get a bad word out of you."

His heartbeat was faint against her back.

"If I were as pretty as Lily or as smart as Ruth, I know that you would love me back. But I'm not. Don't suppose my looks would scare a man, but I don't have Patience's grace and beauty. You don't like my boyish ways, but Poppy raised me to take care of myself, and that's what I have to do. There's nothing wrong with a woman being able to take care of herself—you might even be grateful to me for saving our lives—if it turns out that I have."

Right now the prospect didn't look so good.

"What I'm trying to say is that someday, if we make it out of this, you will meet a woman you love as much as I love you right this moment, and I will envy her with all my heart. Hard as I've prayed about it, I'm still jealous when you pay attention to other women, not that you do that often, but sometimes you do. I'm sorry. I suspect we'd have to always deal with that . . . if you were to ever love me back."

A noise caught her attention. A soft, mewling sound. Opening her eyes, she looked around, trying to identify the source. Bear? Her heart accelerated, and her hand slowly searched for the rifle. What should she do? If she left the saddle, Jackson would slide off, and she wouldn't be able to lift him again. That would mean death for both of them.

Clucking softly, she eased the mare a step forward. If it was a bear, he had the advantage, but it couldn't be a bear. Bears were in their dens this time of year. Her hand closed tighter around the rifle, shifting it to the saddle horn. If she had disturbed a bear's winter sleep and he charged, she would shoot by sound and pray the bullet found its mark. She'd shot a black bear once, but it had been in broad daylight, and she'd had her wits about her. Unable to feel her fingers in her gloves, she wondered if she could squeeze the trigger.

Kneeing the mare another step, she waited, ear cocked to the wind. There it was again, louder. A snort. Heavy breathing.

Bring the rifle to your shoulder, Glory.

In slow motion she brought the Winchester into position. It was there—not twenty feet away on the right, in the bushes.

Why didn't it charge?

If it wasn't a bear, what was it?

The mare took another step.

Bushes rustled.

You can do this, Glory. It's either whatever is out there or us. Jackson can't help. You have to get Jackson's wound dressed . . . maybe he's already dead.

No! He's not dead; you can feel his breathing. He's weak, awful weak, but he's alive.

Fresh blood—the bear—the animal, it smells fresh blood.

Her heart thumped against her rib cage.

It was so close now; she could feel its presence, hear its ragged breathing.

The mare took yet another step.

A thrashing in the bushes. There it was. Dead right.

Straining to spot the enemy, Glory kneed the mare closer, positioning the rifle against her right shoulder. Jackson's weight mashed her against the saddle horn. Her shoulders shook from the weight of the gun, and she strained to hold the barrel level.

The bushes moved and against the ground's pristine backdrop, she finally saw it. An elk, with a four-by-four rack, wounded and hurting, lying on its side in the snow. Pain-glazed eyes stared up at her.

"Sorry, ole fella," Glory whispered. The animal had probably tangled with a mountain cat and lost. "I gotta do us both a favor." Taking careful aim, she willed a steady hand and slowly squeezed the trigger.

The explosion startled the horse. Rearing, it catapulted Glory, the rifle, and Jackson onto the ground. She landed with a thud in the softly packed snow. The Winchester went one way, and Jackson flew the other.

Glory lay for a moment, too tired and too cold to care anymore. "Jackson," she finally murmured after long moments. "I think the Lord is busy elsewhere." She paused, biting her bottom lip. "I'm real sorry, but I think we're going to die."

Searching the ground beside her with her right hand, she felt for him. "Jackson?"

Instead of Jackson's powerful build, she encountered something furry. Startled, she drew back. The elk. Struggling to her knees, she crawled to the dead animal. Breaking into sobs, she laid her head against the carcass and bawled with relief. *Thank you, God, thank you!*

Crawling back to the mare, she grabbed a stirrup, pulled her stiff body upright, and fumbled in the saddlebags for Jackson's skinning knife. *Jackson. Where was Jackson?*

She jerked the knife free, then dropped back to her knees and inched back to the elk. Within minutes, she'd cut through sternum, muscle, cartilage, and entered the stomach cavity. She worked methodically, scooping armfuls of entrails onto the ground. The knife sliced cleanly through hide, blessed substance that could save their lives.

"It's all right, Jackson. The Lord has sent us help," she called over her shoulder as she gutted the animal. "We're not going to die."

When the elk was field dressed, she crawled back to the mare, her hands blindly searching for Jackson. She found his unconscious form lying near the animal's hooves.

Struggling to her feet, she grasped him under his arms and pulled. Pulled.
Pulled.

Straining and pulling, she edged him only inches with each step. His weight resisted her slim frame and threatened to undo her.

Pausing.

Pulling.

Finally, she had him beside the carcass. Digging into the snow, she scraped a round ball into her hand, then pressed it against his wrist wound, praying that the cold would stop the bleeding until morning light. Summoning her last shred of strength, she rolled his still form inside the elk and crawled in beside him.

Lying spoonlike in the warm hollow space, Glory wrapped his arms around her waist and shoved, inching them farther back into the life-saving warmth before she, too, lost consciousness.

Chapter Seventeen

Ruth paced the mercantile porch, keeping an eye peeled on the edge of town. The soles of her boots scraped the planked floor as she strode back and forth, wringing her hands.

The mercantile door opened, and Dylan McCall came out. He paused when he saw her state, a slow grin spreading across his rugged features. Ruth saw him and turned to stare in the opposite direction.

Pulling the door closed behind him, Dylan joined her. "You still fretting? Jackson knows how to survive in the wilds."

She spared him the briefest of glances, then returned to her vigil. She'd been edgy and cranky all day, worrying herself to death about Glory and Jackson. *Lord, I trust you've held them in your care, but why don't they come?* "It's been a week. They should have been here by now."

The marshall calmly adjusted the brim of his hat. "Not necessarily. Snow could have held them up. We just got to Denver City a couple of days ago ourselves."

She paused to face him. Hands on hips, looking vexed, she spouted, "We started from the same place at the same time. Snow delayed our arrival a few days, but not a week. We're here; Jackson and Glory aren't. They could be lying out there dead, for all we know."

"Not exactly at the same time. Jackson took off in the opposite direction. No telling how far he rode before he caught up with Glory and Amos."

"If, *if* he caught up!" Dropping her hands, she resumed pacing.

Dylan pulled up a chair and sat down. He removed his hat and carefully settled it on his knee. His relaxed position clearly didn't set well with the serious brunette. Ruth shot him an annoyed look.

He lifted his palms defensively. "What? I'm just trying to stay calm."

"If you were any *calmer,* they'd be shoveling dirt in your face, Dylan McCall." She craned to see around the porch post. Where were they? *Lord, I can't stand the suspense a moment longer!*

"All right. I surrender. Stew till you lose your mind. I won't say another word." Dylan crossed one leg over the other, folded his arms, and stared at Ruth. The arrogant posture only angered her more, and she stared back. He lifted a brow. "Now I suppose you're going to tell me there's a law against a man sitting on a porch?"

"Can't you find someone else to annoy?"

He appeared to consider it and then shook his head. "No, I get my enjoyment stepping on *your* nerves."

"Oooph!" Ruth gathered up her skirt and moved to the far corner of the porch.

Grinning, Dylan took out a toothpick and stuck it between his lips, rolling it to the corner of his mouth. "Yes, sir, Ruth. I'm as calm as pudding."

Across the street, Lily, Patience, and Mary came out of the café. Harper lagged behind, talking to the owner, a small, frail lady who was raising a nine-year-old granddaughter.

"Did you hear the questions Harper was asking Mrs. Katsky?" Lily asked. "You'd almost think she was interested in buying the café."

"It would be a perfect job for her," Patience admitted. The three girls agreed there wasn't another woman on earth who could make a better apple pie.

"Her pot roasts cannot be beat," Mary confessed. "Only Harper can't buy a café. She doesn't have any money."

The girls smiled when they saw the pastor coming across the street. Smiling in turn, Arthur Siddons hurried to greet them.

"Hello, Pastor Siddons," Lily called.

"Hello, girls! Been searching all over for you!" The balding, plumpish sixty-year-old paused before them, his round face beaming.

Patience waited for him to catch his breath. "Was there something special you wanted, Pastor?"

"Yes, yes!" He took her hand, squeezing it firmly. "I've just come from a meeting. The church board wants me to extend an invitation to you ladies to remain here in Denver City for the winter."

Delighted smiles lit the women's faces. "That's wonderful, Pastor Siddons!" Patience sobered. "But how? We have no means of support—"

"We discussed that," Pastor conceded. "Tom Wyatt is a heinous man, and unfortunately we have no control over what he and his no-account boys do, but the folks of Denver City are good people. We want to extend our hospitality until spring. By then you ladies will have decided what you'll need to do, and the weather will be more cooperative." He pulled his collar up closer against the bitter wind. "Harry Rexell says he can use a hand at the mercantile, and Rosalee Edwards said she's going to need extra help at the millinery over the holidays. Imagine we can find enough work to keep you all busy until spring!"

"Oh, thank you!" Patience threw her arms around the older man's neck and hugged him.

Red-faced, the pastor stepped back, grinning lamely. "Oh my, it's our pleasure, miss. Having five pretty new faces in town won't hurt the feelings of our single men one bit. Five *eligible* ladies, I might add."

"Six," Mary reminded softly.

The girls looked at each other, sobering.

"Six, when Glory gets here."

Pastor Siddons nodded. "Your friends still haven't arrived?" He shook his head, making a clucking noise. "We can send a search party now that the weather's broken—"

"Thank you, Pastor. Marshall McCall insists that they're all right and will ride in any time. I'll talk to the marshall again, and we'll let you know what we decide."

"Good, good." Pastor Siddons rubbed his gloved hands together. "May I tell the church that you will stay? They can't wait to lend a Christian hand. Why, Old Mrs. Guffey already has all of you down for Christmas dinner at her house. She cooks a mighty fine turkey."

Patience glanced at Lily and Mary. The girls nodded happily. "And I'm sure Harper will be happy to stay. She might even find work at the café."

Pastor Siddons clamped a hand over his heart and nearly swooned. "Etta Katsky would be plumb tickled pink to find good help. She's trying to get by with her nine-year-old granddaughter waiting tables, but she's getting worn to a nubbin with all the extra work."

Mary stepped closer, extending her hand. "Thank you for all your kindness, Pastor Siddons. I don't know what we would have done without your help."

"You're welcome, Mary. And Doc says he wants to see you at his office this morning. Thinks he might have something for that cough."

Siddons walked on, calling a friendly greeting to a young couple coming across the street.

Patience, Lily, and Mary walked on, casting curious looks toward the mercantile.

"Poor Ruth. She hasn't slept a wink for the last week."

"She's terribly worried."

"We all are."

Patience frowned. "Don't know who she's more worried about, Jackson or Glory."

"Everyone's worried sick about both," Lily said. "What can be keeping them?" Silence overtook them since no one dared to speak of the dire possibilities.

Lily finally whispered under her breath. "Does it seem to you that Dylan is awfully interested in Ruth? They argue constantly, but I think they really like each other."

Mary and Patience spared a brief glance in the direction of the mercantile porch, and then looked straight ahead. A giggle escaped Mary.

"What's so funny?" Lily asked.

"Ruth and Dylan. She's so serious and he's so . . . not serious, unless he's doing his job. They would make a fine pair."

The thought of their contrasting natures resulted in a round of giggles.

Lily jabbed Patience's ribs. "Shhh, they'll hear us!"

"Can't help it," Patience gasped. "Wouldn't that be something? Ruth and Dylan married?"

Dylan shifted the toothpick to the other corner of his mouth. Leaning back in the chair, he watched Lily, Patience, and Mary walking on the opposite side of the street. Fine girls. They'd make some lucky men good wives one of these days.

"So, Ruth. What do you think about the price of corn?"

Ruth slowly turned around to look at him. "What?"

He lifted his brows. "What do you think about the price of corn?"

"I haven't an earthly idea what corn sells for these days."

"What about an unearthly one?"

She gave him a dirty look.

"None, huh." He removed the toothpick and stared at it.

"Why?"

"Why what?"

"Why do you want to know the price of *corn?*"

"I don't. Just trying to find a subject we can discuss without ruffling your feathers."

"Don't even try." Ruth turned back to watching the road. "And corn certainly won't do it."

"There's got to be something I can say that won't get your dander up—"

"Try 'I'll be leaving now, Ruth.' " She brushed past him, nearly toppling his chair, and he had to grab for the railing.

Springing to his feet, he spit the toothpick on the floor and yelled at her disappearing skirts. "Come on, Ruth! Hey, you want to get married? We get along so well; we would make a fine—where's your faith, woman?"

He ducked, grinning as an apple sailed over his head and hit the front window of the mercantile. Scowling, Harry Rexell burst out a second later, broom in hand.

Dylan turned and innocently pointed at Ruth.

Snatching her skirt in her hand, she stalked off to the other end of the wraparound porch.

Grinning, Dylan flipped Harry a coin. "For the lady's apple."

Pocketing the coin, Harry stared after Ruth sourly. "Well, tell her that around here, we prefer to eat 'em, not throw 'em at folks' windows."

The men turned at the sound of a horse galloping into town. Shouts went up as Patience, Lily, and Mary ran to meet the new arrivals.

Grinning from ear to ear, Glory slowed and walked the mare through the center of town with Jackson, bandaged hand and all, riding behind her.

"Where have you been?" Patience shouted, running beside the horse. Lily and Mary raced to keep up.

"Had a little trouble, but we're here now," Glory called back. Her eyes darted to Mary. "Don't run, Mary! You'll start coughing!"

Ruth raced around the corner, holding her skirts. Her eyes lit when she recognized the riders. "Glory! Jackson! Praise God you're all right!"

"Saw me an angel, Ruth!"

Ruth frowned. "You what?"

Glory beamed. "Saw me an angel! Looked a little like Poppy!"

A curious crowd started to gather. Patience, Lily, Mary, and Ruth pressed close as Glory dismounted and helped Jackson from the saddle.

"What's wrong? We were about to send a search party after you," Patience exclaimed.

Ruth enfolded Glory, and the two women hugged. "I was so scared something had happened," Ruth whispered.

"We got caught in the blizzard. Jackson was wounded and lost a lot of blood. We couldn't travel for a few days. I'm sorry if we worried you."

"What's this about an angel?"

Glory pressed her ear close to Ruth's. "Tell you all about it later on. Right now, Jackson needs attention."

They shared another brief embrace, and Ruth said softly, "Just so you're safe; that's all that matters."

Ruth turned her eyes on Jackson. "Are you all right?"

"Fine, Ruth." He glanced at Glory and smiled. "She took good care of me."

Glory flushed at the praise. "Shucks, anyone could do what I did. Used the snow and my hankie to stop the bleeding. The good Lord provided us an elk to keep us from freezing. When the storm passed, we set out and came to a cabin, where an old hermit who knew about herbs and such helped us."

Dylan joined the noisy reunion. He clapped Jackson on the back, relief evident in his eyes. "About to send the dogs out," he said.

Jackson smiled. "I was about to hope you would." The men exchanged a few brief words in private.

"Better have that hand looked at," someone in the crowd suggested. "Doc's in his office now."

The crowd cheered as Glory put her arm around Jackson to help support his weight and led him across the street.

"I can walk," he protested under his breath. "Stop mothering me."

"Plan to—just as soon as I know you're going to live," she whispered back. Leaning closer, she added, "Put too much effort in you to lose you now."

Grinning, he met her eyes and said quietly, "Lady, you couldn't lose me if you tried."

Dylan caught up with Ruth as she walked toward the café. "I'm waiting."

"For what? The price of corn? I told you, I don't know anything about corn."

"For an apology. I told you Jackson and Glory were all right."

Color dotted her cheeks. "Don't start with me, Dylan. For all you knew, they could have both been dead."

"But they weren't."

"They could have been!"

Grinning, he looked hurt. "Are we going to fight, or are you going to kiss me good-bye?"

Her footsteps faltered. Slowing, she turned to face him. Her features softened. "Are you leaving?"

Their eyes met and held. The teasing light was gone from his. "A wire came through about half an hour ago. I'm due in San Francisco in a few weeks. Now that Jackson and Glory are back safe, I have to move on."

Color drained from her face. "But the weather. It's so bad—"

Laying a finger across her lips, he said quietly, "Take care of yourself, Ruth."

Nodding, she caught his hand and held it for a moment, her eyes closed. "Be careful, Dylan McCall."

"You know me, Ruthie. I'm always careful."

She looked up, tears moistening her eyes. "No one calls me Ruthie unless they're given permission."

Leaning closer, he whispered against her ear, "That's my next project."

She swallowed back tears. "Will I ever see you again?"

Smiling, he took her hand, and they walked to his saddled horse standing in front of the livery. After swinging into the saddle, he finally released her hand. A cocky grin surfaced. "Why, Ruth, I could swear that's an invitation. Am I hearing things?"

Meeting his eyes, Ruth glowered. "Of course you are. Why would I ever want to see the likes of your no-good hide ever again?"

His features gradually turned serious. "I'll be back come spring. Will you be here?"

She lifted her chin saucily. "Guess you'll just have to come back and find out."

Throwing back his head, he laughed, his breath a frosty vapor in the cold mountain air. Turning his horse, he looked back over his shoulder and winked. "Did I mention I have two single brothers looking for wives?"

Her hands came to her hips. "And why should that matter to me?"

"Thought Patience and Lily might like to know. Chances are they'll be riding with me next spring. They're both even ornerier than me!" Nudging his horse, he rode out of town, his laughter still ringing.

Ruth turned and went into the mercantile, glancing over her shoulder.

But only once.

Two days later Glory and Jackson rode his horse up a narrow trail to the foothills. They tied the animal to a pine and swept the snow off a large flat rock to settle down and enjoy the view. The sun sparkled on the clear, wide stream and the mounds of white banks below. Pines hung heavy with new-fallen snow.

"Do you want to stay here with the other girls?" Jackson asked.

Glory sighed and shrugged. She'd been giving it a lot of thought. Patience and Mary had begged her to stay; Ruth had said she could make a new life in Denver City as well as anywhere else. Trouble was, there was only one thing she really wanted to do, and that wasn't possible.

"I do and I don't. I'll miss the girls something awful when I go, but I feel restless, like I haven't reached my destination. Does that make sense to you?"

He nodded. "To a man who's traveled most of his life, that makes sense."

"I suppose you'll go back to Missouri to lead another wagon train," she said wistfully.

"No, been thinking about giving that up." He grinned at her playfully. "I'm tired of cross-country travel. This last trip about did me in."

"You mean us women."

He frowned. "It's been real trying."

She could see he was teasing her, but there was some truth there, too. "I know I was a terrible burden to you."

"You exasperated me at times." His expression sobered. "But in all fairness, I learned a lot from you."

"From me?" she asked, amazed.

He nodded. "I watched you learn and grow, always with an open heart. It made me realize how little I had grown in the same amount of time."

"Not you. You know everything."

"I hardened my heart a long time ago. When a man does that, part of him stops growing."

"You mean . . . about your mother."

He nodded. "Being around women for all these months, seeing each of you dealing with your lives . . . I got to thinking that my mother couldn't have been much older than you girls when my father left. I could imagine her as she must have been then. She used to say I reminded her of my pa. No wonder she was cross with me. No surprise that raising a child without help made her bitter." He released his breath slowly. "Because of my time with you and the other women, I started to see my mother through the eyes of a grown man instead of those of a child."

Glory laid her hand on his arm. "You're not so bad, Jackson. We all get out of shape once in a while. The trouble starts when we refuse to do anything about it."

He smiled, dimples flashing. "About time I make peace with the past, learn to forgive, and move on. For too many years, I let it eat at me, almost destroy me. Figure one of the first things I'll do is visit Ma in Illinois, try to heal some old wounds."

She looked up at him in wonder, so proud she thought she might burst.

"Used to think all women were heartless, and then the Lord sent six young women into my life who taught me what it means to care about someone. Patience, Lily, Ruth, Mary, Harper—they had it tough, growing up. I'm ashamed to think of how good I had it."

She nodded. "Least you had a ma."

He nodded. "What happened to you didn't make you bitter. You, especially you—" his eyes softened—"faced everything with an open, willing heart."

She sat back, thinking. He was telling her his secrets. She had a few secrets of her own. "I have my faults. For months, I was torn watching you and Ruth together, wanting the respect that you gave her, wishing I could be as wise and confident as she is, knowing in my heart that she was the perfect woman for you—"

"Ruth? You still think—" He shook his head.

"You talked to her like she is your equal . . . you depended on her . . . anyone can see why you two would be good for each other."

He leaned over and tweaked her nose. "The reason I could share responsibilities with Ruth, the reason I could talk easily with her was because I had no romantic feelings for her. She was and is a trusted friend." He paused to smile. "And if I don't miss my guess, she's a little sweet on Dylan." He lifted his brows.

Glory shrugged. "Could be, but he sure makes her mad."

"Love's that way sometimes. The one who attracts you the most is the one who can get under your skin the worst."

Glory shook her head. "I wanted so much to be like Ruth. She was everything I wasn't—wise, serene, trusting in her belief in the Lord."

"Seems to me you're the spitting image of her right now."

She thought for a moment before answering. A light came into her eyes, and she nodded. "Yes, I suppose I am . . . more than I thought possible anyway. Guess all along I felt I wasn't good enough, been trying to earn God's love on my own. Then I decided I couldn't earn it at all; it's a gift. All I had to do was reach out and take it."

"Now you know what I mean about how you've grown."

She thought about that too, realizing that so many of her prayers had been answered, gradually, without her even noticing. She turned to look at him. "Well, if you aren't going to be a wagon master, what will you do?"

"I've been giving that some serious thought. After I go see my ma, I think I'll chase my dreams, do some things I've always thought I would do some day. I love the ocean, and there's a place in California I'd like to settle down, not far from Monterey Bay. I'd like to have a little farm there. You can ride on sandy beaches . . . watch the sea gulls." He reached out to brush a lock of hair off her cheek. "The sea is a sight you'd like."

She gazed back at him with wide, trusting eyes. "I've never seen the ocean."

"You could go with me." He met her gaze evenly. "We could be partners."

Her heart leapt at the thought. Partners? With him. "I have the money to buy a little spread. Poppy would approve of me using the gold for that. I could buy land . . . near you."

He shook his head. "I buy the land. You keep Poppy's gold. I was thinking more along the lines of you joining me, working the farm to-gether."

"Oh—" she paused to absorb that—"like partners."

"Partners."

Glory thought of what she'd read in the Bible, and she shook her head slowly. "I don't rightly think we could live on the same farm. It wouldn't be proper if . . . I mean . . ."

She was struggling, wanting to go anywhere with him, wanting to be with him, but needing it to be right. She wanted to be with Jackson more than with anyone else she'd ever known, but she'd tried to live with guilt before, and she didn't like it.

She knew herself better now, and she didn't want to start a new life with him that was wrong in the eyes of the Lord. That reminded her of the Bible that he had entrusted to her for the trip. It had served her well, and now he would be needing it back, since it appeared that they would be parting ways. "You'll be wanting your Bible back."

"I was getting around to that—"

"I haven't written your ma yet. Ruth says she'll help me, real soon—"

His fingers against her lips stopped her. "Pipe down. There's a few things about me that you should know."

She met his eyes, curious now. "Like what?"

"Well, for starters." Leaning closer, he kissed her softly on the mouth. He tasted of cold air and sunshine. "I think you're every bit as smart as Ruth, and in my opinion you're prettier than Patience."

Her mouth flew open. Why, she wondered, would he say that, unless . . . unless he'd heard what she'd said that night when she thought they would die, that night when she'd told him her deepest feelings. She looked up with questions in her eyes, and he nodded as his gaze softened. "You heard?" she asked. "I thought you were unconscious."

"I couldn't move, didn't have the strength to open my eyes, but, yes, I heard."

"Everything?" she asked in a tremulous whisper, realizing that if he had, he would have heard her say that she loved him.

"Everything that mattered to me."

"Oh." She sat back, stunned. He had known for days how she felt about him, and he hadn't run.

"I think you should know that I love you too."

"Honest?" Her eyes searched his to be sure he wasn't teasing, and what she saw was the warmth of love.

"I'm not prone to lying about a thing like that." He gathered her in his arms.

She closed her eyes, absorbing his words. He loved her, but did he love her the way she loved him? Did he feel sorry for her because she had no prospects? Was he wanting her to tag along . . . as a partner . . . the way they'd been on the long journey. Traveling partners? That wouldn't be enough, not anymore. She drew back in his arms. "Jackson,

I don't want you to feel obligated to look after me. I can go on, make a life for myself."

"Is that what you want?" His eyes looked accepting, but she saw hurt there as well.

"Don't take me wrong. Anyone would want to be partners with you. It's just that all my life I've lived on the kindness of others." She looked away at the distant mountain range. "Poppy found me and took me in. You and the girls found me and took me in. You see, I've always been a stray, found and later accepted, but never chosen. My continued existence has depended on the kindness of strangers. I don't mean to sound ungrateful." She studied his expression, looking for understanding, as her words began to falter. "It's . . . just that . . . I need to be chosen."

The tenderness in his eyes deepened. "What I'm hoping . . . what I'm asking is that you be my partner for life. Glory?"

"Yes?"

"I'm asking you to be my wife. If you want, I'll get down on my knees and beg, because my life wouldn't be the same without you."

"Marry you?" Her heart leapt with joy at the miracle of it. She thought Jackson would never marry, that he was dead set against it, and here he was, telling her that he loved her, asking her to marry him! Could it be that her silent prayer, her most cherished wish, was being answered? Her heart overflowed with joy. "Yes," she said in a rush, "Oh yes, Jackson—" She frowned. "Wait a minute. Honest-to-goodness marry you? Are you sure?"

He nodded. "Never more sure of anything in my life."

"Then, yes, Jackson Lincoln. I would be *proud* to marry you."

His mouth lowered to take hers, and she succumbed to the bliss of his kiss. Moments later, she gazed up at him, seeing all the love there she'd dreamed of seeing but feared she'd never have. It occurred to her that in all fairness there were things she should remind him of. She'd hate for him to later regret having chosen her.

"Don't forget that I'm not the best cook . . . and my sewing could be better, too." They exchanged a long, slow kiss.

"You're improving."

"I'm still impulsive, even when I try not to be."

"Oh, really," he chuckled, "like I hadn't noticed."

"Patience, Mary, Harper, Lily, and Ruth are staying here until spring—"

"Smart women, the weather being what it is." They exchanged another gratifying kiss. "I figure Dylan will be back for Ruth next spring," he whispered against her mouth.

"That's nice. Hopefully the others will meet someone they will fall in love with."

"They're all lovely girls. God has someone for each one of them."

She drew back momentarily. "Even Harper?"

He chuckled. "Most assuredly, Harper. And I can't wait to meet that man."

"You know what you're getting then," she said, snuggling back into his arms. It was more of a statement than a question.

He winked. "No, but since it's you, I'm willing to chance it."

She sighed, wrapping her arms around his waist, reminding herself that he'd had four months of daily contact with her, six hundred and eighty-five miles to observe her, plenty of time to get to know her faults, and still he'd *chosen* her for his wife.

"Thank you dear, sweet, heavenly Father," she murmured, "for loving me so much."

If you look for me in earnest, you will find me when you seek me.

A Note from the Author

Dear Reader,

As I write this letter, we are just three weeks away from spring. Outside my office window the birds are chirping, and the earth is starting to come alive. Oh, how I love spring and the promise of renewal!

Glory reminds me so much of myself in her childlike search for God. I accepted Christ as my Lord and Savior as a young girl, but each day is a new, exciting walk in his presence.

My mother's favorite song has a verse that says, "And he walks with me, and he talks with me, and he tells me I am his own." As I once did, Glory grows to realize that without those walks, her life would be as barren as the frozen winter ground. When I stare out my window at an awakening world, I thank God for the assurance that "he walks with me, and he talks with me, and he tells me I am his own." Jesus tells us in John 15:9, "I have loved you even as the Father has loved me" (NLT). His promise carries us through the long winter into a bright new spring.

Thank you so much for all of your letters of encouragement. They put a smile on my face and brighten my day. I never tire of hearing from you about the blessings God has brought into your life through Christian romance novels. I'm very excited about my first women's fiction novel due out in 2001. Please look for my other HeartQuest books, *With This Ring,* and the first three Brides of the West books: *Faith, June,* and *Hope.*

May God cradle you safely in the palm of his hand.

Lori Copeland

Ruth

LORI COPELAND

Brides of the West 1872

Romance fiction from
Tyndale House Publishers, Inc.
WHEATON, ILLINOIS

To three very special Christian young women
who will someday be brides:
Brittany King, Kelsey King,
and Bethany Chambers

Prologue

I've survived a lot of things, I'm right proud to say, for someone who grew up in the backwoods of Missouri and all her life thought the whole world consisted of Poppy's front yard and a one-room shack.

Glory sat back on the Siddonses' settee and tapped the tip of the pencil against her teeth. The parsonage hummed as women scurried about preparing for the afternoon celebration. Ruth said that it was important to record special days. Ruth was smart about such things—smart and sassy when the mood hit her. And today couldn't be more special: Glory was marrying Jackson Lincoln Montgomery.

She bent and hurriedly scratched out her story. . . .

When Poppy died, my life changed overnight. God's timing, Ruth says. Guess God thought it was about time for me to grow up, but to be honest I'd been real happy where he'd put me. I loved Poppy and the old cow and the few setting hens we had. Our mule, Molasses, died shortly after Poppy went to be with the Lord. The animal just laid down in the middle of the road and went wherever old mules go when they die. I felt empty then. The animals had kept me company after Poppy died.

My favorite memories are of those winter nights after the chores were done, the animals fed and bedded down. I loved those cold evenings by the fire when Poppy would spin yarns and play the old violin. Those were good times. No matter what you might believe, I know God had seen farther down the road than me, which was right good of him, since before I joined up with the wagon train and Jackson Montgomery I couldn't see beyond today and didn't know enough to come in out of the rain.

I learned many a new thing on the trail to Denver City. Some folks lie, like my Uncle Amos who tried to say the gold Poppy gave me was rightfully his. That was a big windy. The kind of lie you go to the burning place for telling.

Uncle Amos was mean and wouldn't know the truth if it spat on him. But some men are just plain despicable. Tom Wyatt is such a man. He tricked Jackson Montgomery into bringing a wagonload of mail-order brides clear from Westport, Missouri, to Denver City, Colorado. We were young orphaned women between the ages of fourteen and sixteen, who were expecting to have fine, strong, God-fearing husbands waiting for us. Instead, Patience, Harper, Ruth, Lily, Mary, and I found an evil, greedy disgrace of a man who wanted girls with strong backs and ample resilience to work the gold mines of Colorado. There was no matrimony-minded men awaiting us—only a gold mine and years of hard work. When wagon master Jackson Montgomery discovered the swindle, he helped us get away, with the aid of his friend Marshall McCall.

Anyways, everything turned out fine for me. Jackson Montgomery asked me to be his bride. If you'd hit me with a two-by-four and called me stupid I couldn't have been more surprised, what with me not knowing how to cook or sew or do any of those things Jackson deserves in a wife. 'Course, when he whispered in my ear that sewing and cooking was all right, but a man could live a lot longer on true love, well, I wasn't about to argue.

My only concern now is what will happen to Ruth, Patience, Harper, Lily, and Mary. The girls are like sisters to me; we're all one big family now. Winter's coming on and before the snow sets in, Jackson and I will leave for California, where we'll make our new home. The other girls can't leave because they have nowhere to go. They are approaching the age when the orphanage where they lived most of their lives will insist they find jobs and support themselves. Not a girl wants to go back to Westport. The kind pastor in Denver City, Arthur Siddons, and his wife had given them a home until spring, so they will be all right for a while.

I'm marrying Jackson today. This seventh day of November, eighteen hundred and seventy-three, is the happiest day of my life. Mary and Harper made my gown out of bleached muslin that the preacher's wife supplied. Simple but pretty, though it wouldn't matter to me if I wore duck feathers. I'll bet when Jackson sees me, he won't be able to take his eyes off me, nor will I take mine off him. He'll be dressed in black pants and a shirt with a string tie, and I bet he'll smell better than sunshine on a spring day. These past days, I have to say I've never seen him looking more handsome or seen love shining more clearly in his eyes—and that's saying a whole bunch.

Everyone is here for the ceremony—the girls and Marshall McCall, who joined up with us for the last fifty miles on the trail. Much to Ruth's dismay, the marshall is staying around for the ceremony, but he has to leave in the morning. He's been chasing an outlaw for over a year, and the trail's getting hotter.

Now, mind you, Dylan McCall isn't hard to look at either. He's almost as handsome as Jackson, but he carries a bucketful of stubbornness. Jackson can be ornery when it suits him, but Dylan can be charming and ornery at the same time—a dangerous combination in a man, Ruth says. She has all the learnin' in the bunch. Serious Ruth doesn't care for the cocky marshall, though the other girls titter, blush, and squeal at his harmless bantering.

Ruth and Dylan mix like wheat and hail. Ruth is serious, focused on the task. Unless I miss my guess, Dylan rides life lassoed to a cyclone. Those two can look at each other and have eye battles that make you duck for cover. Yet, it seems to me they do look at each other more often than they look at anyone else.

Ruth is every bit as ornery as Dylan, only she doesn't recognize it. I said to Jackson just yesterday, while snuggled in his powerful arms, that it would be pretty funny if Ruth and Dylan fell in love.

"Funny as stepping on a tack barefoot," Jackson murmured, and then he kissed me long and thoroughly.

I wasn't so sure he was right, though by then my thoughts weren't entirely focused on Ruth and Dylan. Jackson and I started out at odds with each other, too, and look where we landed—we're so much in love we can't talk without our tongues tying in a knot. It wouldn't surprise me if Ruth and Dylan discovered they have a lot more in common than mulish pride, and they've each got a wagonload of that. But as I wrapped my arms around my honey's neck and closed my eyes, happiness warmed me like a new Christmas blanket. In this new, exciting world God's allowed me, I believe most anything is possible.

Chapter One

On November 7, 1873, Denver City sat under a crystal blue dome. Ruth took a deep breath of crisp mountain air and fixed her gaze on the faultless sky. It was a truly remarkable day—beautiful in every way.

Sunshine warmed her shoulders as she listened to Glory and Jackson Montgomery repeat their marriage vows. Marrying outdoors was Jackson's idea. He was an outdoors man; he wanted to be as close to God as he and Glory could get when they became man and wife. The audible tremor this afternoon in the wagon master's otherwise strong voice amused Ruth, but she supposed the quiver was natural for a man accustomed to being on his own and about to commit the rest of his life to one woman.

Ruth cast a sideways glance at the man standing next to her. Marshall Dylan McCall stood stiff as a poker, his face expressionless as he witnessed the ceremony. What could he be thinking? The egotistical man was surely commiserating with Jackson, thinking that he was glad it was the wagon master and not he about to be saddled for life.

Well, no matter. She was not like some women she'd noticed, inexplicably drawn to the marshall. Besides, it must be God's will that she never marry. True, her head still reeled and her heart ached from the unexpected news she received from the doctor yesterday—news that she would never be able to bear children. Perhaps it was just as well that the mail-order bride thing hadn't worked out for her. Wouldn't her new husband have been dismayed to learn that Ruth had no uterus. "A rare defect," the doctor had said, "but it does happen sometimes."

Ruth lifted her chin and glanced again at the handsome marshall with eyes as blue as the color of today's sky. If it was God's will that she never marry, then she would accept it as another one of life's injustices that God allowed for his own purposes. Getting married and having children wasn't the have-all-or-end-all of life. At least not for her. She'd make a good life for herself, especially now that Tom Wyatt's spiteful trick had been discovered.

Ruth understood why a man needed a wife who could give birth to children, someone to give him strapping heirs to help with the work. Knowing this didn't lessen her desire to be loved. But then most men were like Glory's Uncle Amos. They made promises they never intended to keep and blamed other folks for their own shortcomings. The chances of her finding a man who would love her regardless of her barrenness were about as remote as her hitting the mother lode the local prospectors fantasized about. She had no such fantasies. Life was real, and sometimes hard, but it was the living of it in God's will that was important to Ruth, certainly not the finding of a husband.

With a mental sigh, Ruth shifted her gaze back to the happy couple. Glory was different. She loved Jackson and would give him a whole passel of kids. Ruth tried to imagine the feisty Glory as a mother. When the wagon train had first come across the homeless waif, they'd thought she was a boy—a young man *very* much in need of a good bath. It had taken several days for Glory to convince Lily, Patience, Harper, and Mary that Glory wasn't going to oblige. She was oblivious to her malodorous state, though how she missed them holding their noses Ruth would never know. The happy-go-lucky, will-o'-the-wisp Glory had no idea she wasn't socially fit. Finally the women took it upon themselves to throw her into the river, then determinedly waded in after her, wielding a bar of soap. Glory's squeals of outrage had not deterred them. When the boylike child had been scrubbed from head to toe, the transformation was amazing.

A smile hovered at the corners of Ruth's mouth. During those days on the trail Glory had become like a sister, and Ruth wished her nothing but happiness. Still, it was hard to imagine Glory married, nursing a child—Ruth's thoughts cut off and she forced down a tinge of remorse. She could accept God's will for her life; she really could.

The preacher concluded the ceremony. As Jackson swept his bride into his arms and kissed her breathless, the small crowd clapped and whistled. There wasn't a doubt in Ruth's mind that the two were made for each other, although for a brief and unreasonable time Ruth herself had suffered her own attraction to the handsome wagon master. She enjoyed Jackson's friendship, but Glory truly had his love and that was only right. Ruth felt not a twinge of regret about the match.

Everyone had helped to prepare the after-wedding festivities. Tables covered in lace tablecloths and adorned with bouquets of dried fall flowers had been set up in front of the church. A large wedding cake festooned with a tiny bride and groom stood amidst the decorations. An air of festivity blanketed Denver City as fiddlers tuned up.

Well-wishers descended on the happy couple as Ruth drifted away from the confusion. She'd be back to extend her best to the new Mr. and Mrs. Montgomery when things settled down a bit.

Oscar Fleming caught her eye, and she smiled back distantly. For the last few days the crusty widower had been on her trail. There had to be fifty years' difference in their ages if there was a day, but that hadn't stopped Oscar. He smiled, winked, and showed a set of brown teeth worn to the gum every time he could catch her attention.

Ruth stiffened as the old codger sprinted in her direction.

"Afternoon, Ruthie!" he called.

Ruth mustered a polite smile, her eyes darting to the marshall, who was watching the exchange with a self-satisfied grin. "Good afternoon, Oscar. Lovely ceremony." She tried to sidestep the old coot.

"Hit was, hit was." Grinning, he blocked her path. "Thought maybe I'd have me th' first dance."

"Oh," she said, her gaze swinging toward Patience and Mary, but they were both helping a group of women set food on the tables. They were too busy to pay heed to her silent plea for help.

Oscar held out his scrawny arms. "How 'bout it, Ruthie? You and me cut a jig?"

Jig, indeed. Ruth swallowed, drawing her wrap tighter as she tried to manufacture a plausible excuse. She glanced up when a hand wrapped around her left arm and Dylan McCall politely interrupted. "Now, Ruthie, I believe you promised *me* the first dance."

Though weak with relief, Ruth seethed. *Ruthie.* How dare he call her that! Still, it was a chance to escape. She stiffly accepted his proffered arm and mustered a friendly smile. Anything was better than dancing with the old miner. "Why, I believe I did, Marshall." She smiled her regrets to Oscar. "Will you excuse us?"

Oscar's grin deflated, his chin sinking down to his chest. "Maybe later?"

"Of course," she conceded. *Much, much later.*

As the couple strolled off, Ruth pinched Dylan. Hard.

Though he winced, the marshall kept a pleasant smile on his lips . . . and pinched her back.

"Ouch!" She jerked free of his grasp and flounced ahead, pretending to ignore him. The very *nerve* of Dylan McCall acting as her rescuer!

His masculine laugh only irritated her more. "Admit it, Ruthie," he called. "You welcomed the interruption!"

Ruth's face burned. "Not by the likes of you!"

He paused, chuckling as she marched to the punch bowl. She swooped up a cup, dunked it into the bowl, then quickly drank, dribbling red liquid down the front of her best dress in the process. She dropped the cup and swiped at her bodice, then felt punch oozing through her right slipper.

Her temper soared. It was Dylan's fault. He made her so mad she couldn't think straight. From the corner of her eye she saw Dylan politely tip his hat and ease into the crowd.

"Oooooph!" Ruth sank into a nearby chair, steam virtually rolling from the top of her head. How that man infuriated her. If only he weren't so handsome and charming at times as well. . . .

Forever. Whew. The vows the newlyweds had exchanged lingered in Dylan's mind as he threaded his way through the guests. He paused to speak to the ladies. Lily and Harper bloomed under his attention, but his mind was on the ceremony.

Forever. The word made a man break out in a cold sweat—at least a man who liked women but didn't care to tie himself down to any particular one, only one, for the rest of his life. Not unless he was planning to die tomorrow.

He'd been accused of breaking women's hearts, and he supposed he had broken his fair share. They could be as pretty as ice on a winter pond or ugly as a mud wasp, and he'd allow them a second glance. Dylan didn't judge a woman by the way she looked on the outside. He'd learned long ago that the outside didn't mean much. He'd told someone once that when he met the right woman he'd marry her, but deep down he knew he'd never see the day. There wasn't a *right* woman. Not for him. There were just . . . women. All softness and pretty curves, but inside they weren't worth a plug nickel. Sara Dunnigan had taught him that. Women were out to use men, use them up for their own purposes. Well, he had *his* own purposes, and they weren't to share with any woman.

The married women turned to watch him walk away; Lily and Harper tittered. Dylan neither welcomed nor resented the attention. A woman's naïve notice made him feel in control. He could always walk away, and he intended to always be able to do just that.

The receiving line had begun to thin as he approached the newly-weds. He shook hands with Jackson. "You're a lucky man."

The sincerity in his tone wasn't entirely contrived. Jackson *was* lucky. Glory was the one woman who could tame the wagon master, and Dylan wished them well. Jackson grinned down at his bride. If ever there was a happy man, Montgomery fit the bill today.

"It's your turn next, McCall!"

"Don't hold your breath, Montgomery."

Dylan leaned in and kissed the bride lightly on the cheek. Glory blushed, edging closer to Jackson. Beaming, Jackson drew her close.

"That's my girl. Beware of wolves in sheep's clothing."

Dylan lifted an eyebrow. "Me? A wolf?"

"The worst," Jackson confirmed with a sly wink. "Knew that about you right off."

The two men laughed.

The new Mrs. Montgomery frowned. "Jackson—"

Throwing the marshall a knowing wink, Jackson took his wife's arm and steered her toward another cluster of well-wishers.

Dylan milled about for a while, exchanging expected pleasantries and hoping he could leave soon. Events like this weren't his cup of tea. He spent the majority of his time alone, which he preferred. He was eager to get going to Utah. He would have left last week, but Jackson and Glory had talked him into attending the wedding. Jackson needed a best man, he said, and Dylan had reluctantly agreed, feeling torn between friendship and duty to his job.

Dylan spotted Ruth with Mayor Hopkins, her cheeks flushed, blue eyes aglow, thick, shiny, coal black hair hanging to her waist, laughing up at him. She'd never looked at Dylan that way . . . but then he supposed a woman like Ruth wouldn't. Men like him were loners. They had to be. Keeping the law was a dangerous business. Ruth, even with her independent streak a mile wide, would avoid a man like him, as well she should.

Dylan had stepped onto the sidewalk when Pastor Siddons threaded his way through the crowd toward him. "Marshall McCall! They'll be cutting the wedding cake soon. You won't want to miss that." The pastor beamed. "Etta Katsky makes the best pastries this side of paradise."

Smiling, the marshall acknowledged the invitation. The whole town was friendlier than a six-week-old pup. It was a good place for Ruth and the other girls to settle.

The two men stood side by side, watching the festivities. Arthur Siddons' pleasant face beamed. "Nothing like a wedding to make you feel like a young man again."

Dylan refused to comment. His gaze followed Ruth as she moved through the crowd. He'd never seen her smile like that, laugh like that, so happy and carefree.

Arthur looked up at him, a sly grin hovering at the corner of his mouth. "Right pretty sight, wouldn't you say?"

Dylan had to agree. "Ruth's a fine-looking woman. All the girls are."

The pastor nodded. "Mother was just saying how nice it is to have young blood in the town. Tom Wyatt and his boys are low-down pole-cats. The whole town's known that for years, but I have to say the devil was taken by surprise this time. Had it not been for you and Jackson, those six young women would be working the mines right now, without a hope for the future."

Dylan bristled at the thought. "The Wyatts ought to be strung up by their heels."

"Yes, many agree, but Wyatt's not done anything he can be legally prosecuted for. We know he promised the women husbands, but in a court of law he'd say the women, the orphanage, and Montgomery misunderstood. He would eventually set them free, once they worked off their debt to him. But considering the wages he'd pay, that would take a mighty long time. It isn't the first time he's used deceit to gain mine workers. Brought eight women out last year, and one by one they escaped. Found one this spring." The reverend shook his head. "Poor woman didn't make it."

A shadow crossed the marshall's features. "I thought once that Jackson and Glory had met the same fate."

"Yes, Jackson and Glory were fortunate to survive that blizzard." The pastor beamed. "Wouldn't have, without Glory's common sense."

"No." Dylan watched the laughing bride and groom. "She's quite a woman."

Arthur nodded. "Colorado's rough territory. A man can freeze to death in no time."

Sobering, the minister's gaze rested on Mary, who was smiling up at Mayor Hopkins. The couple seemed to be enjoying each other's company.

"Now, there's the one I worry about. The poor thing coughs until she chokes. Won't be many men who'd want to take on such a responsibility."

Dylan agreed. Mary's asthma would make it difficult for her to find a husband. He looked at Harper and Lily, who were busy setting out platters of golden brown fried chicken. Harper was so independent and quick-tongued it would take a strong man to handle her. Lily would do okay for herself, and Patience wouldn't have any trouble finding a husband. She was the looker of the bunch.

His gaze moved back to Ruth. She was now conversing with a tall, lanky man who looked to be somewhere in his late twenties. The couple made a striking pair. The young man's carrot-colored hair and mahogany eyes complemented Ruth's black tresses and wide blue eyes. But Ruth was going to be trouble for any man who took her on. She was as prickly as a porcupine—and as quick to raise her defenses. Made a man wonder what was inside her.

Not him, of course, but some man—some good man looking to settle down.

Patting his round belly, the pastor chuckled softly as he followed Dylan's gaze to the couple. "They make a fine-looking pair, don't they? Conner lost his wife a couple years back. Fine man, Conner Justice, so young to lose a mate. Lost Jenny in childbirth . . . baby was stillborn. His wife's death was mighty hard on him. Conner is only now coming back to community socials."

Dylan's gaze narrowed. It appeared to him that Conner Justice was recovering quite nicely. He was standing a bit too close to Ruth for manners. The sound of Ruth's lilting laughter floated to him, a sound he hadn't heard often. She was enjoying herself for the first time since he'd met her.

Well, good for Ruthie. Maybe Conner Justice needed a new challenge, and the saucy brunette would certainly provide him one.

The pastor patted his belly again. "Well, the bride and groom will be cutting the cake soon." He stuck his hand out to Dylan. "Guess you'll be moving on?"

"I have to be in Utah by the end of the month."

"Worst time of the year to travel."

"I'm used to it."

Dylan preferred to travel in better weather. But when he'd decided to help Jackson deliver the brides to Denver City, he knew he'd be delaying his trip to Utah and would probably face bad weather. It wouldn't be the first time he'd been inconvenienced, nor would it be the last.

"Take care of yourself," Pastor Siddons said.

Dylan smiled. His eyes involuntarily returned to Ruth and Conner, while the pastor wandered toward the cake table. Ruth looked like she was having a fine time.

"Well, I am, too," he told himself, but right now he couldn't have proved it.

Chapter Two

Shadows lengthened over the Rockies as the wedding guests danced and laughed the festive afternoon away. A grinning bride and groom, their faces flushed by wind and excitement, cut the wedding cake while the sun sank behind the mountaintops.

Crimson tinged Glory's cheeks as she smiled up at her husband and fed him the first bite. With good-natured humor, he fed her a piece; then one of the women invited the guests to step up and eat their fill.

Ruth felt herself being shuffled along with the crowd. Today's events had been magnificent—one of the best times she could remember. An aura of love surrounded the newlywed couple, and Ruth allowed the special feelings to seep through her pores. In her life, Ruth had known little love. When Edgar Norris, the only father she'd ever known, took her to the orphanage when his wife died, he'd left Ruth with a glowing promise that he would soon return. To a ten-year-old, *soon* meant "not very long." She remembered crying and holding on to his leg, begging him not to leave her. She didn't see how she could live without Paws— that's what she called Edgar—to greet her when she came home from school each day.

But Edgar Norris had lied to her.

He didn't come back; Ruth never saw the man again. Five years had gone by, and she didn't know if Edgar Norris was dead or alive. She made herself believe that she didn't care, but the Bible said she was to honor father and mother. Her real Mama and Papa died when she was

four, and she had been adopted by the Norrises. But she had no idea
how to honor a man who had deserted a child he'd promised to raise.

"What say, little missy? Is this our dance?"

Ruth froze when she recognized Oscar Fleming's feisty intonation.
Rats. She'd been on the lookout for Oscar all afternoon, terrified he
would seek her out. He'd tried to dance with every woman in attendance, including poor Mary, who had finally begged off and slumped
down in the nearest chair to catch her ragged breath.

Summoning a pleasant smile, Ruth whirled, confronting the nuisance. "Why, Mr. Fleming—here you are again."

The old man's eyes twinkled. He opened both scrawny arms and extended them wide. "What say? Saved the best for last?"

"Oh, Mr. Fleming, I know you must be worn-out—"

"Oscar! Call me Oscar, my beauty." He moved in closer. "They're
playing our song!"

Before Ruth could invent an excuse, Oscar swung her onto the platform and waltzed her around the wooden deck in a breakneck fashion.
The old prospector certainly had oomph!

Ruth hung on to the squatty miner as pins flew out of her hair and
landed beneath other dancers' feet. She flashed a smiling apology to
couples who slipped and stumbled when their feet encountered the
shiny hair fasteners. One man whirled to denounce her as he helped his
partner up from the dance floor.

"Hee, hee, hee," Oscar hooted as he cut between two jigging couples, nearly tripping them with his wild maneuverings. "I knew I'd
found me a ring-tailed molly!"

This ring-tailed molly was about to break her neck! Ruth, not accustomed to dancing, struggled to keep her slippers on her feet and her
tangled hair out of her eyes. She caught a brief glimpse of Patience, Lily,
Harper, and Mary on the sidelines, holding their hands over their
mouths, amusement flashing in their eyes. She managed to get off a
silent beseeching look before Oscar gave her a couple of swift turns and
then jumped in the air and clicked his heels.

"By gum, but you're a filly!"

Ruth lamely smiled, anxious for the dance to end. Instead, guitars
and banjos shifted into a slow waltz. It took Oscar a couple of beats to
make the physical adjustment. He jigged, then jagged, and then grasped
her so tightly she couldn't breathe. His breath was stale and his clothes
smelled of sweat. Ruth closed her eyes, praying for deliverance. She
opened them again, instinctively searching for Dylan. She found him

surrounded by a captive group of women as he leisurely ate a piece of wedding cake and exchanged friendly banter. Typical. Where was the courtly gentleman when she really needed him?

"You're one of them orphans Wyatt sent for, aren't you?"

Ruth's thoughts snapped back to Oscar, and her feet tried to keep time with his stomping boots. "Yes—I was on the Montgomery wagon train."

"Pity." The old fellow shook his head. "Wyatt's a known polecat around these parts. I could have told you him and his boys was up to no good." He swung her around, then propelled her roughly back into his arms—highly irregular for a waltz, as even Ruth knew.

"I like your name, Ruthie."

"Ruth," she corrected. "Nobody calls me Ruthie. My name is Ruth."

"Like in the Bible."

"Like in the Bible—only I'm not nearly as virtuous as that Ruth."

Oscar nodded as if that suited him. "You want to be a bride, do ya?"

Ruth felt heat shinny up the back of her neck. His foregone conclusion that she wanted to be married cheapened her forced decision. She hadn't *wanted* to be married; the orphanage had strongly advised her to agree to Wyatt's offer. She knew now that if a husband had awaited her in Denver City, the marriage would have been short-lived. Once the new groom learned that she was not able to conceive, he would have left for greener pastures. But she had no intention of confiding such personal information to Mr. Fleming. Now if only she could think of some way to abort this dance without hurting the old man's feelings.

"Do ya?"

"Do I what?" she asked sweetly, hoping to change the subject.

"Do you want to be a bride?"

"I suppose," she murmured, giving the expected response, though it wasn't entirely true.

"Well, hot diggity dog!"

Horrified, Ruth watched the prospector jump straight up in the air and click his heels again, then land on both knees in front of her on the wooden platform. He grasped her hand, his rheumy eyes peering intently into hers. The music started to fade and people stood rooted in place, all eyes focused on Oscar Fleming.

"Ruth . . ." Oscar paused and scratched his head. Then he brightened. ". . . whatever your last name is. Will you be my wife?" He grinned, flashing red gums.

A collective gasp came from the crowd. Ruth heard a drum beating in her ears and realized it was her heart. Harper's distinct giggle filtered through the beat.

Ruth's hand came up to her forehead as she tried to form a coherent sentence. Marry Oscar Fleming? A man old enough to be her grandfather! Her senses turned numb. No! She looked around, panic setting in. No!

But how could she tell Oscar no in front of all these people, people who were most likely his friends?

Her eyes darted for refuge, but there was none. Patience shook her head vehemently. Lily, Harper, and Mary all indicated the negative with their eyes.

Oscar peered up at Ruth hopefully.

"Oscar," she began, searching for strength and compassion. She didn't want to hurt the old prospector's feelings; he knew she had previously been receptive to marriage to a man she'd never met. What answer could she give that wouldn't wound the poor man's spirit yet leave no doubt of her refusal?

"I am very honored . . ."

"Hot doggedy!" Oscar bound to his feet and swept her up in his skinny arms, his face ecstatic. Ruth's eyes grew wide as he whirled her around and around. "I got me a *bride!*"

The crowd burst into a smattering of hesitant applause. With Oscar's declaration, Dylan McCall turned and set his cake plate on the table. A frown creased the corners of his blue eyes.

"No, Mr. Fleming!" Ruth protested when she realized the old miner had misunderstood. The band swung into an upbeat tune, and dancers flooded the platform to congratulate the newly betrothed couple.

"But I didn't . . ." Ruth protested with each congratulatory slap and sly wink Oscar received. Women stared in pity, and men grinned with an ill-concealed pride.

"Didn't think you had it in you, Oscar!"

"You old goat! Suppose we're going to be calling you 'Papa' before long!"

The crude remark brought a round of masculine guffaws that shook Ruth to her toes. She broke free of the crowd and ran toward the parsonage, holding a handkerchief to her mouth for fear she was going to be ill. Upon entering the Siddonses' foyer, she slammed the door behind her and took the stairs two at a time. Marry Oscar Fleming! She couldn't! She entered the upstairs bedroom and fell across the bed she shared with Patience and sobbed until exhaustion overcame her.

She dropped into a fitful sleep, her dreams filled with old prospectors spitting tobacco on clean kitchen floors. Oscar chasing her around the kitchen table, wearing a gummy grin, reaching for her . . . the stale smell of his breath . . .

Images floated in her dreams. Voices warned her: *Ruth, you can't marry that man, regardless of your desperate situation.*

"No," Ruth murmured, thrashing about on the bed. The thought of marrying a man nearly seventy years old was so dreadful that her head pounded and knots gripped her stomach. "I can't . . . please, God . . . I can't. . . ."

⌒

"Ruthie?"

Ruth stirred, opening her eyes. The room was pitch-dark, and she took a minute to gather her thoughts. Her eyes felt sore and swollen. Then the afternoon's events came rushing back—Oscar, the proposal, the old man's misunderstanding.

"Ruth?" A match flickered, then caught a wick. Candlelight penetrated the darkness. Mary, Harper, Patience, and Lily gathered close around the bed, their eyes solemn with worry.

Burying her face in the pillow, Ruth began to cry. Patience sat down on the side of the bed and held her hand. "Oh, Ruth. What are you going to do? Everyone thinks you're going to marry that old man."

Ruth bawled harder. What *was* she going to do? Did Oscar's misinterpretation constitute a promise? It couldn't—yet everyone knew the girls were orphans and in dire need of husbands. How could Ruth refuse a legitimate marriage proposal and not appear to be self-centered and ungrateful? Oscar's age didn't matter. He was so old that he couldn't possibly consummate the vows. . . . The image of the old man jumping up and clicking his heels together—the way he threaded in and out of the dancers like a man half his age—oh, goodness! She sobbed even harder.

"Now, now," Mary soothed. She sat down opposite Patience. Each girl patted Ruth's back soothingly. "It isn't that bad. Why, Mr. Fleming seems to be kind . . . and lively. *Very* lively for a man his age."

Harper nodded her head, her dark eyes troubled. "A little too lively, if you ask me."

Lily shot her a censuring look. "No one did ask you, Harper. And

Mr. Fleming can most likely provide Ruth a very good home," she added.

Ruth flung the pillow aside. "Then *you* marry him."

Lily drew back as if bitten by a rattlesnake.

Bolting upright on the bed, Ruth wiped her eyes and blew her nose on the handkerchief Patience pressed into her hand. "I *won't* marry that old man. I won't. Even if it means I have to work my fingers to the bone and maybe even starve to death. I won't marry Oscar Fleming."

Patience's hand closed tightly around Ruth's. "Don't say that, Ruth. This might very well be an answer to prayer. At least you'll have someone to care for you. The rest of us face very uncertain futures."

All four of the women nodded.

"It could be a blessing, Ruth." Lily stood behind, smoothing Ruth's back.

Ruth shook her head mutely. God wouldn't be so cruel. He had revealed his will for her life when the doctor told her she was missing a uterus and could never bear children. No children. She was trying to accept the doctor's words, but the knowledge still stung. Now? Marrying Oscar would give her a temporary home, but it would never give her love and children, the things she'd once wanted most in life. It would take a miracle from God to give her those things now, and at this moment her faith couldn't stretch far enough to believe she'd merit such favor.

"Oh, it might be fun," Patience encouraged. "Oscar could be like— like a dear grandfather. You could sew and cook and keep his house clean while he sat in the rocking chair in front of the window, drinking in the warm sunlight. . . ." Her words trailed as Ruth turned withering eyes on her.

Patience smiled lamely. "Look on the bright side—isn't that what Jackson told us?"

"There isn't a bright side, Patience." Ruth drew her knees up to her chest and rested her head on them. Lily gently tucked Ruth's skirts around her.

Harper humphed. "More like she'd get her exercise with the old coot chasing her round the house twenty-four hours a day."

The eyes of all five girls turned as round as boiled eggs. Silence shrouded the room.

Suddenly, Ruth threw her petticoats aside and straightened her hair.

"Where are you going?" Lily tried to restrain the determined woman as she got off the bed.

Shrugging Lily's hand aside, Ruth marched to the door. She hadn't wanted to resort to dire actions, but if ever there was a time for urgency, it was now. She couldn't let this ride another minute. She had to see Oscar and apologize for the misunderstanding and inform him she would not marry him. Then she would face Pastor Siddons and his wife, Minnie, in the morning and explain why she had turned down a perfectly good marriage proposal, further imposing upon them during the long winter, when the Siddonses already had four additional mouths to feed.

"You're not going anywhere." Ruth's four friends formed a physical barrier, blocking the bedroom door. "You have to at least promise to sleep on this and pray about it." Patience's eyes firmed. "In the light of morning you may discover that there could be a worse fate than marrying Oscar Fleming."

Ruth met the women's eyes stubbornly. She would rather have this out tonight and get it over with, but if they were going to be adamant about it, then so be it. Marching back to the bed, she dropped into it and yanked the covers over her head.

The candle went out. Silence fell over the crowded bedroom. Ruth felt the springs give as Mary crawled between the sheets on her side of the bed. Guilt gnawed at Ruth; she tossed and turned. The Siddonses had been kind enough to take all five women in until spring. By then other arrangements for Mary, Patience, Lily, Harper, and herself would have to be made. The good Lord knew the aging couple couldn't afford to feed five extra mouths. If Ruth wasn't so selfish, she'd marry Oscar. Maybe he would offer to look after Lily and Patience, or Mary and Harper. That would leave only two extra mouths for the Siddonses to feed during the long winter.

Patience had said to pray about it. Ruth tried . . . but images from her nightmares came back to her. Oscar chasing her around the house. . . . What if God wanted her to marry Oscar? She couldn't. She just *couldn't* marry that old prospector.

Cousin Milford. The name popped into Ruth's head. She hadn't thought of Milford in years. He was Edgar's youngest brother's son, and Edgar had always spoken highly of him. Milford lived in Wyoming—somewhere. Pear Branch, Wyoming, if she remembered correctly. Milford would be in his late twenties by now, probably married with a wife and children. If she could get to Pear Branch, Milford would take her in for the winter. She didn't know why she hadn't thought of him before!

Now, how could she get to Pear Branch with winter coming on? She had to use logic. The weather would be formidable, but with the proper clothing and a good horse she might make it. She had to think of a plan. . . .

She heard the hall clock chime two. Easing from beneath the warm sheets, she covered Mary more securely, then tiptoed to the door. A minute later she crept down the stairway, wincing at the telltale creaks. Pastor and his wife slept in the downstairs back bedroom.

Ruth fumbled in the darkness to pull on Mary's boots and the coat she'd left in the hallway. She slipped out the front door, closing it softly behind her. Moonlight lit a path on the ground. The sleepy town was quiet at this hour. The hotel where Dylan and the newlyweds were staying was dark as pitch when she approached.

She couldn't believe what she was about to do. But desperate straits called for desperate measures. Hadn't her biblical namesake done something similar with Boaz?

Ruth eased the establishment's front door open and crept to the registration desk, where a candle burned low. The old clerk sat back in a chair sound asleep, his snores falling in even cadence. Even wide awake, Mort Carol couldn't hear himself think, she'd been told. Turning the name register around, Ruth lifted the candle and located Dylan's name. Room 4. Glory and Jackson were in room 10.

The soles of Mary's thick boots clunked up the uncarpeted stairs. Holding the candle aloft, Ruth tiptoed down the hall and read door numbers. Two . . . three. Light snores resonated up and down the hallway. Mostly cattlemen stayed the night as they passed through on their way to deliver herds. This time of year the hotel was nearly empty.

Ruth paused at room 4 and knocked lightly. Holding her breath, she waited. Dylan McCall must sleep like a log. She'd have thought a marshall would sleep lighter, alert to unexpected trouble. So much for Mr. Know-It-All McCall's abilities—

She lifted her hand and knocked again. Suddenly, the door flew open, and Ruth found herself staring down the steel barrel of a very unfriendly looking Colt. She dropped the candle as her hands flew up to shield her face. "Don't shoot!"

She heard a masculine rumble that sounded very unpleasant—like an old bear awakened from hibernation—before she was physically yanked inside. After kicking the door shut, Dylan reached for his shirt. "What are *you* doing creeping around here in the middle of the night!" He jerked the shirt on, then lit a candle. His features looked sinister in the shadowy light. "Fool woman."

"Fool!" she mocked. "I could have burst in here and shot you dead if I'd wanted. You didn't hear my first knock."

"I heard it."

"You did not."

He glowered at her.

Ruth quickly decided she wasn't making any points with him, and that was her sole purpose for being here in the middle of the night. Pastor Siddons would faint if he knew she was visiting a man's hotel room at this hour. Brushing past the glowering marshall, she moved deeper into the room. "I have come to ask a favor."

"No."

"Just like that? No?"

Dylan calmly buttoned his shirt. "Maybe . . . if you come back in the morning."

She whirled to face him. "You're leaving in the morning, aren't you?"

He sat down on the side of the bed, running his hands through rings of tousled curls. The gesture reminded her of a young boy—a very good-looking, young, impatient lad.

"So?"

"I need your help."

He looked up. "My help." He laughed.

"Your help." Taking a deep breath, she clunked over to where he sat. "You have to take me with you in the morning."

For a moment he frowned; then the cad threw back his head and laughed harder. "In a pig's eye. I don't want to upset your fiancé."

Bravado crumbling, she knelt before him. "Please, Dylan. I can't marry Oscar Fleming—I can't. If I remain here in Denver City, I'll have no alternative."

His eyes hardened, and for a moment he reminded her of a spurned suitor. An illogical sense of elation filled Ruth, then dissipated just as quickly when she realized that the arrogant boar was only showing his usual insolence.

"Then why did you agree to marry the man?" His tone was flat and final.

"I *didn't* agree to marry him! Oscar misunderstood!"

"Misunderstood?" He *pffft*ed. "How does a man misunderstand yes from no?"

A hot blush crept up Ruth's neck. "I didn't exactly say no . . . I said, 'Oscar, I'm honored,' and he took it to mean yes."

Dylan stared at her. "'Oscar, I'm honored.' Hmm. Wonder how he mistook that for a yes."

"Honored *but,*" she argued. "I was going to say *but I can't marry you.* No! I was going to say a firm no."

"Then why didn't you? How hard is it to stop and say, 'No, you misunderstood'?"

Ruth knew he had a valid point. She should have stopped Oscar, but she was dumbfounded by the proposal, and the crowd was pushing around her, and Oscar was jumping up and down crowing like a proud rooster. She had bolted like a coward, leaving Oscar with the impression, no doubt, that she was suffering from a hefty dose of shyness and premarital jitters.

Desperate now, she grabbed both of Dylan's hands. "Look, I'll work my way. If you'll take me as far as Wyoming, I'll cook, wash your clothes, be your servant." Ouch! It galled her to say that, but she was a woman in dire straits.

"Take you with me?" he scoffed. "With winter setting in—take you to Wyoming? You are out of your mind."

" I'm not out of my mind; I'm desperate. Can't you see that?" She sprang up, her temper flaring. "You insensitive jackal! I can't stay here and marry Oscar Fleming. You *have* to take me with you—it's—it's the only gentlemanly thing to do!"

Maybe if she appealed to his chivalrous side. She knew he had one because she'd seen him turn on the charm with more than one unsuspecting woman. She was prepared to use anything in her arsenal— within reason—to make him relent and see the necessity.

"If I can get to Milford, he'll take me in!"

"Milford?"

"Milford—my cousin."

"You've never mentioned a Milford."

"So? I haven't mentioned a lot of things," she said. "Milford being one of them."

He laughed humorlessly. "Go back to the Siddonses and go to bed. There's no way I'm taking you with me, Ruth. It's too dangerous. And in case you haven't thought about it, your reputation would be ruined. A man and woman, unmarried, traveling alone together . . . "

The look he gave her implied she was as green as grass. Well, Mr.

Smart Aleck didn't know she'd already thought of that objection and had it covered.

"No one will ever know that I'm a woman."

"Yeah, right." Then the cad actually blew out the light and crawled back in bed. Ruth stood in the dark, fuming. How dare he. How *dare* he treat her like an unruly child!

"Let yourself out quietly," he mumbled beneath the covers. "There are people down the hall trying to sleep."

Ruth fumbled her way to the door. Why God let men like Dylan McCall inhabit the earth was beyond her. She lit a candle once she closed the door and stomped back down the stairs. She didn't bother to be quiet this time—someone could come in and carry off the hotel, and not a soul there would know.

She let herself out the front door, feeling like she was about to explode on the inside. How one man could get her so worked up and angry amazed her.

Her eyes focused on the water barrel as the heavy boots clunked down the steps. What an egotistical, self-inflated, pompous—! Her eyes lit on the bucket. Before she thought, she dipped a bucketful of water, then turned and let herself back into the hotel. The old clerk slept on as she pounded up the stairs again, lugging the heavy pail of water.

Liquid sloshed out, trailing a wet slick down the hallway. When she reached room 4, she paused to catch her breath. She wanted to have plenty of wind when he opened the door. Hefting the bucket waist high, she kicked at the door.

Dylan's gruff voice came through the wood. "Go home, Ruth, before I have to insult you."

Insult me, huh. She kicked harder. *Treat me like a child, will he?*

Voices from nearby rooms sounded. "Hey, what's going on out there?" "Whoever's kicking that door is gonna get his head knocked in!"

In a second the door flew open and an enraged Dylan appeared.

"You inconsiderate lout!" Taking a wide swing, she heaved the bucket of water, hitting him face first. Icy tendrils streamed from his hair. Staggering backward, he muttered an expletive under his breath as Ruth turned and ran.

The clunky boots were too big for her, and she had to squeeze her toes to the front of the leather to keep them on her feet. But she'd forgotten about the water slick. Her feet flew out from beneath her about the same time a large hand clasped around her collar.

Horrified, she felt herself being lifted into a pair of steel-banded arms. "Now, Dylan . . . remember, you're a man and I'm a woman. . . ."

"A hooligan," he corrected. He was drenched from head to foot, his clothes sticking to him.

She pounded his back as he hauled her, kicking and screaming, over his shoulder and headed toward the stairway. Doors opened and candle-light glowed. Sleepy-eyed guests gathered in the hallway to watch the fracas.

Mort Carol stirred behind the counter, licking his lips. His eyes flew wide open at the sight of the marshall carrying a young, screaming woman down the staircase. The back of Mort's chair smacked the floor as he bolted up. "Here now—what in tarnation is going on? Put that lit-tle lady down!"

Dylan carried Ruth out the door and down the porch stairs, and un-ceremoniously dumped her into the water barrel.

Ruth's indignant screams penetrated the late fall air as she hit the icy water. She surfaced, spitting water on him.

Pointing a stern finger at her, Dylan warned, "You're stepping on my last nerve, woman!"

Moments later Jackson appeared on the porch, wearing pants and his shirttail hanging out. "What in the—"

Dylan's gaze moved from the half-dressed bridegroom back to Ruth. She looked like a drowned rat. Her hair hung in tangled ropes, pieces of it clinging to her face; her dress drooped on her like a wet sack, but hot resentment burned in her eyes. He almost laughed.

"It's three o'clock in the morning!" Jackson bellowed. "Don't you two have anything better to do than have a water fight?"

Dylan noticed a crowd had gathered and now stood in various stages of nightclothes, gaping at them with wide eyes and not a few snickers. Pure fury rose in him. This stubborn, *irrational* woman had made a complete fool of him.

"Get away from that water barrel before you both freeze to death!" Jackson stepped off the porch and hauled Ruth out of the water. He propelled her toward the hotel lobby. "Show's over, folks. Get back to your beds, where sane people ought to be!"

Jackson stepped inside the lobby and motioned the dripping couple up the stairway. Mort preened his neck over the counter as he cleaned his glasses. "Do I need to get the law?"

"We *have* the law," Jackson called over his shoulder and then glanced at Dylan. "Although I'm sure the government wouldn't claim him at the moment." Wet leather boots creaked down the hallway as guests shrank back into the shadows. Doors shut—some softly, others with distinct slams.

Glory sat up in bed, clutching a blanket to her chest, as Jackson burst into their room with two nocturnal visitors dripping water. The new bride's eyes scanned Ruth's wet clothing.

Jackson sighed. "Honey, get Ruth some dry clothes before she catches her death. I can't think for her teeth chattering. Dylan, here. Put on a dry shirt."

Dylan would have refused the shirt Jackson tossed at him, but his fingers were turning blue and he couldn't feel his feet at all. Glory handed Ruth a dry garment, then held up a blanket for her to dress behind.

Dylan felt a twinge of guilt for disturbing the newlyweds. Well, Ruth had disturbed him too. She had *flooded* him, and he'd have to change clothes before he went back to sleep.

Jackson sat the warring couple in straight-back chairs. Dylan knew the groom was none too happy right now. Ruth sat meekly, her teeth still chattering. She looked as innocent as a choirboy.

"I don't know what got into you two, but I've got better things to do on my wedding night than referee for you and Ruth," Jackson grumbled.

Dylan wasn't sure himself what had gotten into him. Tossing a woman into a water barrel in the middle of the night wasn't something he would normally do, but this woman got under his skin. In more ways than one—none of which he cared to analyze. On the trail to Denver City he'd noticed she was the more educated of the young women and definitely the best cook. But the spitfire could make him angrier than anyone he'd ever known. Her stubbornness, her standoffish ways, had gotten to him.

Maybe that was what startled him tonight when she'd awakened him from a sound sleep and begged him to take her to Wyoming. Wyoming! Was she that desperate or just plain crazy? The old prospector proposing in front of half the town must have really shaken her.

Of course, he couldn't even think of taking her with him. Any day the deep snows would come, and Dylan would be lucky to survive the elements himself. He couldn't take on the responsibility of a woman even if he did see Ruth's point. What woman would take to the notion of marrying a man nearly five times her age? He cast a sideways glance at Ruth. Not this woman.

Jackson's hand came to his slim hips. "I thought you were leaving at sunup."

"I plan to." In just a few hours Dylan would ride out of here and out of Ruth's life. Maybe.

Jackson paced the floor, turning to cast looks over his shoulder. "Care to tell me what this is all about?"

"He—," Ruth began.

"She—," Dylan started.

"One at a time!"

Glory sat with her hands over her mouth. Dylan couldn't tell if she was appalled, amazed, or trying not to laugh.

"This crazy woman knocked on my door fifteen minutes ago and demanded that I take her with me to Wyoming!"

"I didn't *demand,*" Ruth retorted. "I asked."

"Sounded like demanding to me. Seems a prospector that's old enough to be her grandpa proposed to her tonight after you and Glory left—"

"Proposed?" Glory sat up on her knees. "Honest, Ruth? A man proposed to you? You're getting married?"

"Not really," Ruth said. "The prospector proposed, but I didn't accept."

"But Oscar still doesn't know that," Dylan said, shooting a cold look at Ruth.

Jackson focused on Ruth. "Ruth? Are you certain you don't want to think about this? I don't know the man, but I could do some checking—"

"No," Ruth stated flatly, "I will not marry that old man. I'm going to Wyoming instead and find my cousin Milford."

When Jackson frowned, Dylan added, "She says she remembers a cousin or something in Wyoming. This is the first I've heard of it."

Ruth's chin lifted. "There was no need."

"She says she'll do anything if I'd take her with me to find this 'cousin.'"

"Not *anything!*" Ruth snapped. "I said I'd cook and wash your clothes and that's more than sufficient payment. And I do have a cousin Milford in Wyoming."

"Wyoming's a big place. Do you have this man's address?"

She shrugged. "Not with me."

Dylan was a lawman, not a chaperone. Marshalling wasn't the safest profession, and he had to travel fast. A woman would slow him down. He ate out of a can most nights. A woman wanted dishes; all he had were two tin cups. He jumped into a stream to bathe when it was convenient and let cleanliness go when it wasn't. A woman had soaps and lotions and all sorts of pretty clothes and things. A woman—

Well, a woman on the trail wasn't his idea of heaven on earth. Not even a woman like Ruth. She'd done well enough in the wagon with the other women to help on the journey from Westport, but traveling on horseback was a different matter . . . a whole different matter.

Ruth looked over at Dylan and silently mouthed, "I would rather marry a goat than depend on you to take me anywhere."

He shrugged. "Then marry Oscar."

"Hold it." Jackson stopped Ruth's ready retort. "Ruth, even if Dylan was inclined to take you with him—"

"Which I'm not."

Jackson's mouth firmed as his eyes silently warned Dylan not to interrupt again. This whole thing was crazy. How had he gotten into this mess? All he'd done was agree to accompany Jackson's wagonload of mail-order brides to Denver City. He didn't deserve to be humiliated by this black-haired harridan.

"Even if he agreed," Jackson said, "the two of you can't travel alone together without being married. It wouldn't do. Are you willing to marry Dylan?"

"Not on my last breath!" Ruth exploded.

Dylan's incredulous laugh burst out. "Marry Ruth?" He wasn't the marrying kind. Lawmen and marriage didn't work. Besides, Ruth was religious like Sara Dunnigan. On the wagon trail he'd seen Ruth read her Bible frequently. She'd taught Glory to read, using the Bible. He'd had a bellyful of religious fanatics.

Oh, she was fun to rile. Every word he said ignited her fiery temper. But he wasn't about to *marry* for convenience. At his age, he didn't plan to marry for any reason. If he married that woman he'd never have a moment's peace.

"I won't marry her. I wouldn't take her to a barn burning, let alone Wyoming on some wild-goose chase looking for Cousin Milford. I have a job—remember? I'm late getting there as it is."

What sane woman would ask a lawman to take her hundreds of miles to a land she didn't know, to a person who probably didn't exist? Dylan had done his good deed when he offered to help Jackson on the trail.

"And I would rather walk barefoot through hot coals than marry him," Ruth stated, her chin lifting another notch.

"Then we're agreed."

Ruth whirled to face him. "Marshall McCall—you are the most—"

"Don't start again," Jackson warned, "or I'll dump you both back in the water barrel. Seems to me, there're only two solutions. Either you stay here, Ruth, and deal with Oscar—"

"Not on your life," she breathed.

"—or you marry Dylan."

"Not on your life," Dylan said. He crossed his arms.

Having observed all of this, Glory scooted closer to the edge of the bed. "What Dylan says is true, Ruth. Winter's coming on, and you can't travel alone with an unmarried man."

"I've already thought of that, Glory—"

"Forget it, ladies." Dylan pushed out of his chair. Damp curls were drying against his forehead. "Ruth has other choices. She doesn't have to marry Oscar. She can tell the old man no and remain with the Siddonses until spring. That was the original plan."

"I feel I can't impose on the pastor and his wife since I have received a marriage proposal," Ruth argued.

"Well, then I'd say you're in a heap of trouble, Ruthie." Dylan turned and walked toward the door, his boots squeaking with water.

Ruth crossed her arms and stared at the floor. "Fine. I wouldn't go with you now if the whole of Denver City was being swallowed by mountains."

Dylan tipped his head respectfully. "You and Oscar have a fine life together." He purposely grinned to rile her. "I can picture the happy bridegroom clicking his heels together in joy when the preacher says, 'I pronounce you man and wife.' Just be sure to keep him supplied with chewing tobacco with a spittoon by the door."

He ducked when a soggy boot sailed past his head and hit the door.

"Crazy woman," he muttered to himself as he opened the door and stalked back to his room. No way could she make the trip to Wyoming. Not in winter. She couldn't expect him to mollycoddle her. He had a job to perform and not an easy one at best. Having a woman along would be dangerous and foolhardy. Ruth needed to take care of her own problems. If that meant marrying Oscar, then so be it—though he did hate to see a young woman tie herself down to a man old enough to be . . . He switched the thought off. Nobody ever claimed life was easy or fair.

Ignoring the bitter taste the confrontation had left in his mouth, Dylan returned to his bed in hopes of getting some sleep before he had to ride out.

Chapter Three

M ary?"

Ruth gently shook the sleeping girl. Daylight would break in less than an hour, and she had to hurry. Shivering in her wet clothes, she shook Mary a little harder. She didn't want to wake the others—Mary would be the most likely one to help and the least likely to try to talk her out of what she was about to do. But Dylan McCall had left her no choice.

"Mary." Ruth grasped the young woman's shoulders more firmly.

Coughing, Mary stirred and opened her eyes sleepily. Ruth bent close to her ear and whispered, "Get up. You have to help me."

Predawn chill sheathed the bedroom. With chattering teeth, Ruth quickly reached for the towel on the washstand to dry her damp hair.

Mary's voice sounded raspy in the shadowy room. "Wha . . . what's wrong now?"

Ruth slid a sideways glance toward the three other sleeping women. Patience and Lily hadn't moved. Harper's head burrowed in her pillow, her back end protruding in the air beneath the heavy blankets.

"*Shsssh.*" Ruth bent to lay a finger over Mary's lips. She pressed closer, whispering. "I need your help. I asked Dylan McCall to take me to Wyoming and he refused. I have no other choice but to make him take me."

"Make him?" Mary struggled to sit up. She blinked. "You can't *make* the marshall do anything—" Harper stirred in the bed beside her.

Ruth slapped her hand across Mary's mouth and bent closer to her ear. "I'm going to trick him."

Mary coughed, the spasm racking her frail body. Ruth moved about the room as quietly as a church mouse. If the others heard and woke up, they'd try to talk her out of her plan. Mary would attempt to reason with her, but Mary would do what Ruth needed. Anxious to be about her plan, Ruth started to stuff personal articles into a knapsack.

Mary shivered as goose bumps popped out on her thin arms. Slipping out of bed, she wrapped a blanket around herself and watched Ruth's movements. "What plan? What are you talking about?"

"My plan to thwart that no-good scoundrel Dylan McCall and rescue myself from Oscar Fleming."

"Oh, Ruth!" Mary sank softly onto the side of the goose-down mattress. "You promised to think about Mr. Fleming's proposal."

"I have thought about it, Mary. I've thought of nothing else all night. I can't—I won't—marry Oscar."

Mary's eyes followed her movements. Ruth knew what she must have been thinking. Mary was an obedient person. If Oscar had asked Mary to marry him, she would have done so out of a sense of obligation to the Siddonses.

At one time Ruth was thought to have the most common sense of anyone in the group, but Tom Wyatt's deceit had changed that. She'd been gullible enough to fall for the man's deception. Dylan McCall was about to leave and alter Ruth's life irrevocably—that is, if she didn't do something to stop him.

Mary snuggled tighter in her blanket. "What are you going to do?"

"I'm going to follow Dylan when he rides out of town at daybreak."

"Follow him!"

"*Shhh!*" Ruth clamped a hand over Mary's mouth, her eyes darting to the sleeping women. "Just for a little way. Then, when it's too late for the marshall to turn around and bring me back, he'll be forced to let me ride with him."

"Are you nuts, girl?" Harper threw the covers aside and sprang to her feet. Ringlets of tight curly hair stood up like porcupine quills. "That man will hog-tie you and haul you back here like a sack of flour!"

"*Sssssssssssh!*"

Two more heads popped out from beneath the covers. "What are you *sssssssh*ing for?" Lily sat up, scratching her head. "Did you honestly think we could sleep through all this racket?" Beside her, Patience nodded.

"Sorry," Ruth mumbled. "But I don't have a lot of time." She continued throwing things into the sack.

Yawning, Patience peered out the window. "What time is it? It's still dark."

"It's late," Ruth said. *And getting later every moment.*

"What are you going to do if the marshall decides to ride on by himself?" Harper lit the candle on the nightstand, and the room came to light. "He could, you know. Don't seem like he's the type to let a woman trick him into anything."

"He wouldn't do that." Ruth paused. Would he? No, he wouldn't. Dylan was stubborn, but he wouldn't leave a woman in the Colorado wilderness alone and unprotected. She'd seen him be polite to other women—rarely to her, but she'd witnessed enough to know he wouldn't allow harm to befall any woman in his presence. And she planned to stick to him like honey.

"What are you going to do in Wyoming?" This came from Patience, who yawned in mid sentence.

"Find my cousin Milford. Actually, I suppose Milford is a step cousin—" Actually, Ruth didn't know how to think of Edgar Norris's kin. As relative? distant relative? Milford was the only hope she had right now, however distant he was. "Milford lives in Pear Branch, Wyoming—or he did ten years ago. The marshall has to go through Wyoming to get to Utah. All I have to do is trail along if he refuses to help me."

Ruth didn't fool herself; it would be most difficult to locate Milford after all these years, but she would work her way through the state until she found him. There was always the possibility that he had moved, but she doubted it. The Norris family were solid folk. Edgar had spoken often of his brother's youngest son who had made a name for himself in banking at a very early age. Once a Norris planted roots in fertile soil, that's where he stayed. Milford had written a few letters in the earlier years, but then the correspondence had ceased. Ruth figured he had married and filed the memory of his uncle's adopted daughter languishing away in a Missouri orphanage to a far corner of his mind.

"Oh, Ruth, I don't like this plan." Lily got out of bed and wrapped a robe tightly around her. "Dylan is going to be so angry when he discovers that you've followed him. It's almost winter—the weather will be dreadful soon. I know that you plan to follow him and eventually overtake him, but what if you lose sight of him out there in the mountains? You could, you know. Very easily."

The others nodded their heads in solemn agreement.

"You could die out there, with Dylan never even aware of your presence," added Harper.

"Not to mention that a single lady would never travel with an unmarried man," Patience put in. "Why, the stares you would encounter would ruin your name, Ruth. And you're going to hurt poor Oscar's feelings."

"What name?" Ruth pitched a man's shirt in the knapsack. She favored men's warm clothing over skirts and petticoats, and had worn them often on the trail from Westport to Denver City. All the girls had. "I have no name, no family to disgrace, and forgive me, Patience, but Oscar's feelings are the least of my problems. Nobody knows me, and furthermore it wouldn't matter if they did. I will never see my accusers again once I've ridden away." She stared at the pair of male britches in her hand. "Besides, no one will know I'm a woman. That's where I need your help."

The four women frowned and exchanged puzzled looks.

"I'll dress like a boy." She looked up to meet her friends' eyes. "I only have half an hour to get ready. I need men's clothing, boots, and a hat. And a warm coat and gloves." Ruth stared at the women, whose jaws were agape now. "Will you help me? I'm intent on doing this with or without your help."

Lily snapped out of her trance first. "Ruth, you don't know the dangers—weather, a woman on her own—why, you'll be traveling with a handsome, single man. It would be very easy to fall under Marshall McCall's spell—"

"Ha!" Ruth stuck a pair of heavy stockings in the sack. "That I can promise will never happen. The man is despicable—a heathen of the worst sort. He could be the last man left on earth and I would not be the least bit tempted."

As if she even cared about a man, period. Any man was safe with her. God had evidently preordained that she was to live her life alone—or perhaps with Milford and his family. She could help with Milford's children—be a governess. No, not a governess. She would become attached to the children and she couldn't afford that—not when she knew she'd never have children of her own.

"All the more reason for caution," Lily reminded. "If the marshall is really this awful—"

"Please." Ruth stopped what she was doing and turned to face the women with pained tolerance. She closed her eyes. "Please. You're the only family I have. If you don't help, then I'll have to do this myself, and there's so little time." She pleaded silently with each girl. If they didn't help . . .

Harper sighed. "I say you're nuts, but I'll help."

Mary slowly nodded. "I'll help—but it's against my better judgment. I love you, Ruth. I can't bear the thought of anything happening to you."

Ruth reached over to give Mary and Harper a hug.

"Count me in," Lily said. "Only I feel the same as Mary. This is crazy and dangerous, but I see you have your mind set."

"Coming all the way from Westport to Denver City was crazy and dangerous," Ruth argued. "We do what we have to do."

Patience joined the circle of hugs. "You know I would do anything for you, Ruth, but I'm still concerned about poor Oscar."

The girls burst into tears, hugging each other. When the moment passed, Ruth wiped her eyes. "Okay. Dylan will be leaving soon. I need those men's clothes. And a horse."

"Of course," Harper groused. "A horse. And me without a magic wand."

Patience had started to dress. "You leave the horse to me. I know where I can find one."

"I'll take care of the men's clothes," Harper volunteered. "We'll get some from Pastor Siddons. Me, Lily, and Patience will make him new pants and shirts—I don't know what we'll do about the coat and gloves. We'll find something."

"I'll gather enough food for a week—will that be enough?" Mary peered at Ruth.

"I'll make it last. In a week I should be able to reveal myself to Dylan."

"Whoooee," Harper grumbled. "That's gonna be a day of reckoning. And we're gonna have to be real careful or our stay in the pastor's house will be compromised."

Ruth knew the encounter wouldn't be pleasant, but she'd face that battle when it happened. "We'll be careful, and we won't take anything that we can't replace or that we haven't earned."

The girls flew into action. Patience and Lily went after the horse. They'd take one of Tom Wyatt's mares; the girls figured he owed them that. Harper gathered warm shirts and heavy pants, tiptoeing softly about the Siddonses' bedroom as the older couple snored, unaware of the subterfuge taking place under their roof.

"We'll pay you back, sir and ma'am," the black girl whispered as she eased out of the bedroom and closed the door. "It ain't like we're stealing or nuthin'—we're just borrowing in a pinch."

Pink was barely creasing the sky when the girls hefted a boyish-looking Ruth up into the saddle. Handing Ruth a sack of bread and cheese and a canteen of water, Mary smiled. "Be careful—our prayers go with you."

"Turn around and come back if you see this isn't going to work. Promise?" Lily grasped Ruth's hand tightly.

"Word of honor." Ruth returned the pressure. With a smile, Ruth whirled the mare and galloped off.

The women listened until the sound of hoofbeats disappeared into the mountainside. The sun broke through over the mountaintop, giving birth to a new day.

"This makes me as nervous as a long-tailed cat in a room full of rocking chairs," Harper breathed, wrapping herself tighter in a heavy shawl. Her breath came in frosty whiffs. "That girl's got David's courage."

"Yes," Patience murmured, "but this time I fear she's taken on more than a giant."

Ruth rode well to the rear of the marshall's path. Sheer elation fueled her, and she discovered a new world in the heady, brisk mountain air. The small mare was an easy ride, and she had no trouble keeping pace.

As brilliant warmth spread over the hillsides, she spotted a herd of elk feeding in a valley. The magnificent animals' young gathered close, but apparently they scented no threat as Ruth passed by on an upper ledge. Deer grazed in nearby thickets. Blue jays chattered noisily overhead. Her first day out was an adventure Ruth would never forget.

She tipped her face to the sun's rays and thanked God that she had escaped marriage to Oscar Fleming and that she would soon be reunited with family—albeit distant—she had gained the day two Sioux braves had dropped her at the orphanage after her parents died. She tried to picture Milford from the tintype the Norrises had kept on their parlor table. He'd always looked the bookish sort. His eyesight was poor, to the extent he'd worn glasses since an early age. His frail body didn't appear very manly, but he had a poet's heart, Mrs. Norris claimed. Not exactly the exciting sort of man to turn a woman's head, but a very good man.

Ruth would be glad to meet Milford for the first time, and she fervently hoped he would react kindly to her unexpected visit.

That night Ruth camped early, following the marshall's lead. She could see smoke from his campfire through towering bare aspens. She did not build a fire; though she craved the warmth, the risk of attention deterred her. She ate cold cheese and bread and drank water from the canteen. Then she opened her journal and while it was still light wrote:

> Day One
> It has been a most wondrous day, Lord. Thank you for keeping me safe thus far. I saw elk, deer, birds, and a wild turkey just before dusk. Dylan is unaware of my presence. The weather is mild for the eighth day of November; the sky is crystalline blue. I am tired but very happy as I write this.

Sighing, Ruth repacked the journal and rolled up into her sleeping bag to read the Bible by the last rays of light.

⌒

The wind picked up as Ruth saddled up and rode out of camp the next morning. She'd been awake since long before dawn. She didn't want to lag too far behind Dylan, and she wasn't sure what time he'd leave. So she'd played it safe, waking long before he would wake up. She waited until sunlight barely streaked the sky before she set out.

Within the hour she picked up fresh horse tracks. Smiling, she settled back in the leather saddle to enjoy the day. Animals seemed to be scarce today; by midmorning she spotted a lone hawk flying low to the ground. The wind blew harder and dark clouds skidded across a pewter-colored sky. By late morning she was clinging to the pommel, trying to hang on as a gale cut across mountain passes and howled like a banshee. Nothing fell from the threatening sky, but Ruth knew she would be fighting rain or snow before nightfall.

In the middle of the afternoon, Ruth stopped to water the horse and eat. Both of her arms felt like wet sponges from gripping the saddle horn. As she climbed back on the horse and tied herself in the saddle, she silently thanked Lily for the piece of rope she had thoughtfully included. Twice she'd considered turning around and going back, but then Oscar would pop into her mind. She couldn't go back—she couldn't fail. The wind would eventually die; then things would be better.

By nightfall, Ruth untied herself and fell out of the saddle onto the hard ground. Exhaustion seized her. A heavy rain fell. In the distance she spotted the soft curl of smoke coming from Dylan's campfire. Closing her eyes, she breathed in, certain she could smell roasting meat. Had they traveled far enough for her to reveal herself? Two days of moderate riding. Was that enough to delay Dylan from his duties—so much so that he wouldn't insist on taking her back to Denver City?

She didn't know; her reasoning was clouded. Best to wait one more day—to make certain. He would not waste three whole days to take her back. Teeth chattering, she ate cheese and bread, drank from the canteen, and then hurriedly opened her journal before light gave way. Huddled beneath a dripping pine, she scribbled:

> Today wasn't so good. The wind's been blowing so hard I could barely keep my hair attached to my head. Finally I tied myself in the saddle. Then it started to rain. I couldn't see my hand in front of my face. I held on and prayed the horse would follow the path by instinct.
>
> Dylan is still unaware that I'm following him. Am I doing the right thing? The weather will be better tomorrow—I'm told that weather changes fast in these parts. I have encountered no other traveler, but even if I did, I would be in no danger. Lily said I looked exactly like a boy with my denims and plaid shirt and my hair pulled up under my hat. I feel like a man tonight. Dirty, smelly like a plow horse. But the bother will be worth it when I see the look on Mr. Smart Aleck McCall's face when he realizes he's been tricked. Ha, ha. We'll see who has the last laugh.

Ruth shut the rain-smeared journal and huddled deeper into her wet coat. Her eyes followed the steady downpour. They'd just see who had the last laugh.

⌒

Ruth awoke to fog. Thick-as-pea-soup fog. Gray mist swirled around her like pieces of dirty lint. The air was so thick the mist on her face threatened to turn to a coating of ice. Her lips were cold and tight, and the air was so heavy it was like breathing water.

This morning Ruth couldn't tell up from down; only silence surrounded her. Even the sound of the mare's hooves was muffled.

Peering ahead in the hope of finding some clearing in the mist, Ruth urged the animal forward. She'd been able to stay a safe distance back from Dylan until now, but in order not to lose him she'd have to ride closer today. She had to hope he didn't look back over his shoulder or hear her horse. The fog would hinder him—he couldn't possibly see her, could he? And if he did, he'd think she was a fellow traveler.

Still, knowing the marshall's tendency to caution if he suspected anyone on his trail, he wouldn't leave the identity to speculation. U.S. marshalls were paid to be vigilant; he'd investigate. She would have to exercise caution, though common sense warned her to close the distance.

Ruth smothered a groan as she stretched her aching back in the hard saddle. Only a fool or a desperate imbecile would be out in this weather, and she and the marshall seemed to qualify on both counts. Shifting in the saddle, she flexed her numb toes in the tight boots and kept pushing forward.

The mountainous range was unfamiliar. There wasn't a clue, not a road marker, not a bent tree, nothing to guide her. Her only hope was Dylan. She needed to see him—even a speck of him—to make certain that she was riding in the right direction, but at the moment she could barely see her hand in front of her face.

Minutes seemed like hours. The mare carefully picked her way over the rocky terrain, clearly no more comfortable with walking blind than Ruth was. Leaning forward in the saddle, Ruth peered into the swirling haze until her eyes burned. Her muscles were so tense her whole body ached.

Was that faint sound ahead coming from Dylan's horse? The light pick of hoof against stone could have come from behind her as well as ahead. Fog made direction impossible to discern.

Suddenly the sound seemed right in front of her. Startled, Ruth reined in. She was too close! Dylan would hear her and turn back to investigate, and she'd be discovered! He'd take her back to Denver City and Oscar without a second thought. She recoiled at the idea. She had to be more careful. She'd never seen a man more determined to take a wife—to take *her* as his wife—than Oscar Fleming. Returning to Denver City and Oscar wasn't an option, no matter what uncertainties lay ahead.

Frightened as a snared rabbit, Ruth prodded the mare forward. Maybe she was foolish to think she could do this—foolish to think she was smart enough, cunning enough, strong enough to carry out this plan. She hadn't thought about fog so impenetrable she could neither hear nor see. She hadn't thought about there not being a clear trail. For all she knew she was going in circles. She blinked back tears.

Wyoming was north—of that she was certain—but with all the fog she couldn't tell north from east. She might as well be standing still for all the progress she was making. Tears stung her eyes. Why wouldn't the fog lift?

Fear was a hand at her throat. She couldn't breathe. Panic captured her. She was drowning—

Ruth halted the mare again and closed her eyes. "Get ahold of yourself," she repeated. "Don't panic. You never panic. Dear Lord, help me not to panic. Forgive me for being foolish. Show me the way. Please—I admit I've been a fool."

She nudged the horse forward, but the animal was as reluctant as she was to move. Only the fear of losing Dylan made her keep urging the horse along.

Ruth's fingers seemed frozen to the reins. Her legs ached and the pain in her lower back now extended to between her shoulder blades. She needed to get off this horse and walk around, gain some feeling back into her feet, ease the tension in her back and legs, but she was reluctant to lose time.

"Eat something," she murmured, refusing to surrender to the fear that threatened to paralyze her.

She reached down and fumbled for the saddlebag, then drew her hand back. The thought of food made her stomach roll. Nothing she could force down would promise to stay down until she knew she was safe, until she could pick up Dylan's trail again.

If she could find him again.

"Defeatist thoughts, Ruth. You can't stop now. You've come too far and you would never find your way back, even if you could face Oscar," she muttered to herself.

Cold seeped into every bone. If she didn't come across Dylan's trail soon, she was afraid she was going to freeze to death.

Suddenly she hit something big and solid—*smack!* The mare's high-pitched scream pierced the air. Before Ruth could control the reins, the horse reared, throwing her from the saddle. She somersaulted into the air and landed hard, the impact of solid ground jarring her teeth.

Dazed, she rolled over once before realizing she'd been catapulted into a pile of— She sniffed, her hand reaching out to probe the steaming, warm . . .

She clamped her eyes shut, gritting her teeth. *No! It couldn't be! This couldn't happen!* But there was no mistaking the stench. She groaned and would have flung herself down on the ground in exasperation except she was already flat on her back.

Manure. Fresh manure at that—clinging, stinking manure.

Manure meant cattle. Cattle and a manure pile meant a farm or ranch. Hope bloomed in Ruth's heart. God had heard her prayers! But why would a cow be in these wild parts? Unless . . .

Shrieking in frustration, Ruth bounded to her feet. Her screech made her already nervous mare bolt and gallop toward the swirling haze. Slamming her fists on her hips she yelled, "Well, if this isn't a fine howdy-do!" The animal disappeared, swallowed by the murky, gray mass.

Now what?

Flinging bits of manure off her clothing in all directions, Ruth tried to remain calm. But frustration gave way, and she screamed at the top of her lungs. She was on foot; her food, along with her blankets, was gone with the horse; and she was covered in manure!

What else could possibly happen?

She whirled when out of the fog she heard the last thing a woman in Ruth's predicament wanted to hear.

A thunderous masculine expletive that was anything but calm.

Chapter Four

Dylan had known that he was being followed an hour after he'd left Denver City. At first he thought it might be some of those pesky rebel Utes that plagued the territory. Then he figured it was more likely someone wanting to get the drop on him. He'd waited nearly three days for the confrontation and was beginning to wonder if he was imagining things.

Suddenly, in the fog, something ran into him. Dylan was thrown from his stallion. Quickly he braced for the intruder to make his move. Instead, a woman's screams pierced the air. Tense moments passed. Gun drawn, Dylan got up slowly and took a guarded step, then another into the swirling mist. His right boot encountered something slippery and mushy. Frowning, he took another step, and his feet suddenly flew out from under him. Airborne for a split second, he dropped his gun and landed on something squashy—and warm. The stench brought tears to his eyes.

Then the kicker happened—the upheaval of the day: he saw Ruth towering above him.

Ruth was following him? Mentally groaning, Dylan wondered why that surprised him.

Instantly he dived for her, trying to gain the advantage, but she was wiry and quick. He gained his footing first, but went down a second time in the slimy quagmire. Gagging from the smell, he shot back to his feet, driving for the gun.

Man and woman wallowed, rolling over and through the manure slick. Ruth broke free and crawled beyond his reach. Dylan rolled to the side, out of the path, his hand still searching for the Colt. Blood pumped from his nose.

Suddenly Ruth stood up and calmly put the gun to his temple. "Don't make a move, Mr. McCall, or I'll be forced to shoot you."

Muttering an oath, Dylan fell back when he realized that she meant it. She was desperate enough at this point to do anything.

Cold steel pressed against his temple. "Don't move a muscle or you're a dead man."

Her voice held enough conviction that Dylan decided not to test it. He'd learned long ago to pick his fights, and with a Colt positioned to blow his brains out of his nose, this wasn't one of them.

"Woman," he said calmly, "what is it going to take to get loose of you?" He couldn't see her now, but the firearm convinced him to play along. The fog would have to lift before he could gain the upper hand. Then what?

Throw her to the wolves? The idea appealed to his baser instinct—but then his nobler side kicked in.

"Get up slowly," Ruth ordered as she slid the menacing gun barrel to a site between his shoulder blades. He could turn and take her; her slight weight would be no match for his. But maybe he'd let events play out, see what she wanted—as if he didn't know. Play her by the rules of poker until he turned the tables on her.

He pushed slowly to his feet. "I suppose I have to put my hands over my head?"

She cleared her throat—a nervous habit. Oh, it was Ruth—Ruthie—all right. In her most irritating mode.

"That won't be necessary."

He pictured her chin lifting a notch. She was close enough now he could make out the wool shirt, faded denims, and battered hat. Who was she trying to impersonate? A man?

The adversaries stood for a moment, reeking of cow manure. After a while, Dylan tired of the wait. She'd make a poor cardplayer.

"Okay. Now what?" He squelched the urge to yell at her—to bring to her limited attention the idiocy of what she was doing. If she had the gun, Dylan couldn't be the protector. He swallowed back pride.

So she had been the one following him for three days. What did she think? That by following him, threatening to make him late for his appointment, she'd gain her way so he'd have no other choice but to take her to her cousin's place? Foolish woman. There was nothing to prevent him from wiring ahead to inform his boss, Kurt Vaning, he'd run into trouble and wouldn't be in Utah when expected. If he did that, though, the trail on Dreck Parson and his gang would turn cold, and he was getting too close to lose the outlaw now.

Ruth had him—on a spit and roasted like a Christmas goose. His gut seethed with resentment. He turned slowly to face her, irritably shoving the gun out of his face. Her gaze met his steely one in the swirling mist. "Now what?" he repeated.

"I don't know. I didn't expect to bump into you—literally—this soon," she admitted. " I'm thinking."

After a minute, he shifted his weight to one foot. "Can you think a little faster? I'd like to get out of these clothes." The smell of manure turned his stomach.

"Okay— don't rush me." She straightened, taking a deep breath. "As you might suspect, this is the first time I've ever tried to heist anyone."

"Heist." He grumbled under his breath. For two cents he'd forget common sense and take the Colt away from her. "Heist," he muttered. Why didn't she just say *ambush? bushwhack? buttonhole?*

Ruth took her own sweet time thinking about the situation. Eventually, she cleared her throat and explained. "I didn't want you to know I was following you—not for another day or two, but now that you do, you might as well know you're going to have to take me to Wyoming whether you like it or not."

"Oh yeah?" He shifted his weight to the other foot. "How do you figure that? I could leave your worthless hide out here and ride off." The idea was more than tempting—it lay in his brain like the thought of a steak dinner. "Someone might find you next spring. Then again—" he turned sinister now—"the buzzards would have picked your hide clean by then."

Her eyes bulged at the suggestion. She cleared her throat.

"But you won't because your conscience and duty as a U.S. marshall won't allow it, and if you turn around and take me back to Denver City, you'll be late for your appointment." She sent him a smug smile from beneath the brim of the tattered hat.

His eyes raked the man's clothing she wore. "You look ridiculous."

"Thank you. You don't look so spiffy yourself."

His hand self-consciously smoothed a bearded three-day growth. "What if I just took the gun away, shot you, and left you for the crows to eat? Seems to me that would take care of both problems."

Her eyes narrowed and she steadied the gun with both hands. "You can't do that. I won't let you." Her clasp tightened around the pearl handle.

He smiled diabolically. "Oh, but I could."

Inching closer, she pushed the barrel into the tip of his tender nose. "Just try it, mister."

He stared at her, teeth clenched. One swift move and she'd be flat on her back. But cool reasoning prevailed and made him hold off. He couldn't shoot her, could never gun down an innocent woman.

His sense of adventure began to override his annoyance. How far would she go? He'd bide his time and find a way to scare some sense into her. His features relaxed. "Okay, you got me. What now?"

Ruth jerked her head toward his waiting horse. "Reckon we'll have to ride double until we can find my mare."

"And if we don't find your horse?"

The tip of the gun mashed the end of his nose. "Then you walk."

"To Wyoming?" Again his temper flared. If she didn't move that gun she was a dead woman. His eyes skimmed her clothing a second time. "Why are you dressed like that?"

"If I'm dressed like a boy, no one will know that I'm a woman. My reputation won't be ruined, Mr. McCall. Not that I had one to uphold. Nobody knows me, and I'll never pass this way again. When I reach Milford and his family in Pear Branch, no one will be the wiser."

He shifted the gun barrel out of his face. "Saddle up. We have a long ride ahead of us."

She trained the pistol on his back as they walked toward the waiting animal. Dylan's horse shied as he reached for the reins. Dylan imagined the stallion wasn't fond of its own smell any better than he was. "But we should get out of these clothes first," he said.

"No time. Let's go." Ruth motioned for him to mount. Once he complied, she climbed up and slid on behind him, gun pressed to his ribs. He peevishly adjusted the barrel more to the left for comfort.

"You're not supposed to do that," she snapped. She rammed the gun back into place.

He moved it. "Do you want to lead?"

"I *could*."

"But you're *not*, so hold the gun in a more comfortable position."

She complied finally, grumbling under her breath about "remembering who was boss here."

He kicked the horse's flanks. Ruth yelled when her teeth slammed into her bottom lip. She grasped onto his coattail.

He calmly turned to peer at her over his shoulder. "Sorry—I thought you were in a hurry."

⌒

Ruth's mare was grazing on a hillside when they spotted her. The fog was thinner at this altitude. Dylan tied the mare to his bridle, and they rode on. Ruth insisted she ride behind him and hold the gun in place. Dylan knew the woman must be exhausted. Once or twice he'd felt her nod off, only to quickly straighten. By nightfall, his job should be easy pickings.

At the end of the long day, Dylan made camp and built a fire near a mountain stream. Though he could tell she hated the thought, Ruth suggested they take turns bathing. Clothes needed to be washed, and the manure stench had given them each a headache.

"You go first," Ruth ordered, her teeth chattering in the cold wind as they approached the water. Tall aspens lined the bank but provided little protection from the weather.

He feigned reserve. "Modest, Ruthie?"

Her reticence was apparent as she looked away. "Keep your clothes on. You'll have to wash them and yourself at the same time. Throw your coat onto the bank." The gun came up. "And don't try any monkey business!"

"Don't worry; this will be quick. I promise, Miss—" he paused— "what *is* your last name?"

"Priggish," Ruth answered.

Silence. Then, "You're kidding. Ruth Priggish?"

She lifted the gun another notch.

He grinned. "May I call you Priggy?"

"Just get yourself and your clothes washed quickly." She clamped her eyes shut. "And don't try anything. I'm not looking, but it will only take me a split second if you try anything."

She was smarter than he thought and pretty smug about it, Dylan conceded.

Muttering something that made her blush, Dylan stepped into the water and started to lather up.

⌒

While the marshall splashed and cursed his heritage, Ruth, and the icy water, Ruth moved deeper downstream, listening for his location. At the edge of the stream she removed her coat and scrubbed off all the manure she could. She did the same with Dylan's coat. She could hear him, apparently adjusted to the icy water now, singing at the top of his lungs. She couldn't help smiling at his antics.

In pants and shirt, she waded into the stream, biting down hard on her swollen lip to keep from screaming. Ducking beneath the water, she surfaced quickly, holding her breath she scrubbed her hair, body, and clothing free of manure stench.

Moments later she waded out. Her teeth chattered as she wrapped herself in a blanket she'd brought. She tiptoed back to the tree line.

"Can I come out now?" Dylan sang in a false contralto. "The big, bad marshall is freezing!" The fog was again so thick he was only a voice in the swirling mist.

"I left a blanket on the shoreline. You can wrap yourself in it. Properly!" she demanded. She heard him noisily wade out. There was a moment of silence before he appeared swathed head to foot in the blanket.

She herded him up next to the fire. They both sat there until their teeth stopped chattering. Then Dylan disappeared behind a thicket to change into dry clothes. Ruth did the same, keeping him in sight. He fashioned a makeshift clothesline from tree branches and hung their wet clothes near the campfire to dry. A few minutes later, Ruth smelled fresh coffee perking and fatback frying in a pan. Her stomach growled from hunger. Cheese and bread had been her only food for days. Would he offer to feed her? Well, she had the gun. . . .

Force proved to be unnecessary. He filled two tin plates with fatback and buttered toast. Handing her one of the plates, he turned and poured two tin mugs of steaming coffee.

Closing her eyes, Ruth bit into the meat, deciding she had never eaten anything that tasted so good. The rich, hot coffee trickled down her throat, warming her insides.

They sat beside the campfire, eating in silence. Ruth felt guilty for tricking the marshall this way. She'd be certain to ask God's forgiveness tonight in her prayers. Yet Dylan would be a free man when he dropped her off in Wyoming. Had she stayed and married Oscar Fleming she would have been indentured to the old prospector for the rest of her life—or at least the rest of his life. In that context, what she was doing didn't seem so ugly.

The hot coffee and warm meal began to take effect. Ruth's eyes drooped. She was so tired, so tense from holding the gun on Dylan all day, frightened to death he would physically take it away and leave her here in the mountains, alone. In the distance a mountain lion screeched. Was it waiting until she slept to pounce? No matter. Sleep was out of the question—she had to stay awake and watch Dylan.

Dylan unrolled their bedrolls close to the fire. Dumping the last of his coffee on the ground, he turned and threw a couple more logs on the fire. "It's time to turn in."

She shook her head. "I'm not going to sleep. You go ahead."

"You're going to stay awake all night?"

She nodded, taking another fortifying sip of the black coffee. "I've done it before."

One time she'd sat up two nights straight taking care of Mary. She'd dozed occasionally, but she had known the moment the girl's cough worsened. She glared at the big brute climbing into the thick warmth of his sleeping roll. Her eyes stole to her own bedroll. *Oh my . . . that does look tempting. A bath, warm food, warm blanket . . .*

She snapped back to alertness. "Just don't try anything. I'll be watching you every moment."

"Okay," he agreed. "Make sure I don't do anything to upset you." He pulled his bedroll up to his chin and turned his back toward Ruth.

Ha, ha, she thought. He was a clown too.

The campsite was quiet except for the fire popping and logs slipping lower into white ashes. Fog veiled the sky, so Ruth couldn't see the stars clearly. The night was as still as a corpse. Taking out her journal, she wrote about the day's events:

> Dear Lord,
> I wasn't very nice today. But as you know, I'm desperate. I've discovered desperation doesn't make you feel any better about doing something you shouldn't. It makes you feel worse.

A yawn made Ruth fumble for her coffee cup. The tin tipped, and the contents spilled out and seeped into the ground. Yawning again, she realized that she didn't have the energy to refill the mug.

Reaching for her Bible, she opened to the book of Isaiah. Words blurred as she tried to focus on reading about the potter and the clay. But tonight her mind wouldn't function—it refused to make the connection or find comfort in the passage.

Climbing into the comfort of her bedroll, she prayed for Mary, Patience, Lily, and Harper. She asked for kind husbands and gentle fathers for their children. Each girl was loyal and good . . . any man should be honored to marry any one of them. She prayed for Glory and Jackson. Then her mind turned toward the marshall. Now there was someone who definitely needed prayer. What, if anything, did he believe in?

Ruth yawned again, allowing her eyes to close momentarily.

Dylan's voice drifted to her. "Better go to sleep, Priggy. We have a long ride tomorrow."

"Don't call me Priggy—nobody has ever called me Priggy."

"Don't know why not. The name suits you."

She ignored the rather obvious affront.

"Better not go to sleep," he reminded sleepily. "I'll get the upper hand if you do."

"I won't, so stop wishing. I should think you would worry about your own welfare!"

"Well, you're right again. I am. I'm very concerned about this situation."

She rolled over into a more comfortable thinking position. Since she'd be up all night she might as well think through her plans. Wyoming was still a long way off. She yawned, patting her mouth gently.

"Never underestimate a determined woman," she reminded the marshall.

"So they tell me."

Midnight rolled around. Ruth could hardly keep her eyes open. The wind whistled and the warmth from the fire was nice.

She shoved the gun to the middle of her bedroll—close enough to grab but far enough to keep from accidentally blowing off a toe. She prayed for the Siddonses . . . and the nice people of Denver City . . . as she drifted off to sleep.

Ruth's eyes flew open. She lifted an arm to shield her gaze against bright sunshine.

Bolting upright in her bedroll, she blinked to clear the sleep away. Why, it must be nine—ten o'clock—by the sun's position. The fog had lifted. She lunged for the gun, searching, fumbling. Ripping the blanket aside, she crawled down into the roll, clear to the bottom, searching for the Colt. Instead of finding the expected steel, her fingers encountered a piece of paper that she ripped out and read in the sunlight.

Her heart sank as she deciphered Dylan's hastily scribbled message: "Miss Priggish. Never underestimate a man who has been royally suckered."

She crushed the maddening note in her hand, then threw it down and stepped on it. She couldn't think of a name bad enough for that lout.

"Well, at least he left my horse." Her eyes reassuringly located the mare and her saddle. "And my cheese and bread."

Relief flooded Ruth, followed quickly by irritation for falling so soundly asleep. She had no idea where she was—Dylan hadn't seen fit to share that information. She had no notion of how far they'd come or how far it was to the nearest settlement. The hard ground provided no tracks to follow, so Ruth had no idea which direction he had gone. Oh, she had a horse, bread, and cheese, but that was all . . . and the food wouldn't last forever.

Conscious of her vulnerability, she chewed on her bottom lip. She had no idea what to do now that she was truly alone. She buried her face in her hands. Now what? No matter what direction she looked there was only empty space broken by an occasional aspen grove. The purple snowcapped mountains in the distance were pretty to look at but offered no help for traveling, at least not for Ruth.

She'd never felt so alone, so hopeless. She had looked on the bright side at the orphanage, even on the trail to Denver City. But at those times there had been people around, friends who cared about her, depended on her. And on the trail, there had been Jackson, who knew where he was going.

Ruth blinked back tears and sat down. She stared at the mare. "Well, the marshall has left us in a fix," she muttered, still hoping to convince herself she was better off without him. Ruth felt a longing inside for Dylan—in spite of his orneriness—which she didn't care to identify. She straightened her shoulders. "You're a fool, Ruth." The man had refused to help her not once but twice. She didn't need to be clobbered over the head with a brick to know that he wanted no part of her.

Well, maybe she *did* need that brick. If she'd had any sense at all, she wouldn't be in this predicament.

She stared across the landscape. Now that the fog had lifted she could see how desolate the area was—wherever it was. A cloud of depression settled heavily over her. She sat with both hands covering her mouth, her eyes scanning the horizon on all sides. Nothing. Absolutely nothing. Just trees, rocks, and lonely mountain passes. Not even a rabbit whisker—let alone a human being—broke the empty expanse. Only the sound of the cold wind rattling dried grasses broke the silence.

The hard, cold truth seeped into her consciousness. She could die out here. Alone. No matter what direction she might go, chances were she wouldn't find a settlement. Hadn't someone said that was the reason outlaws went north, to avoid people and the law? The observation made sense now.

"We'll stay here," Ruth told the horse. She flicked an ear. "Maybe someone will come along. After all, Dylan was traveling this way. Surely it's a known path to somewhere." She wasn't sure that was a logical thought, but she wanted to believe it.

The mare was staked where Dylan had left her, foraging for what grass she could find. They had plenty of water—they wouldn't die of dehydration.

Ruth sat waiting, hoping, until her stomach reminded her she hadn't eaten since last night. The bread was dry and the cheese virtually tasteless, but she managed to force down the bland fare.

In late fall the evening grows dark early and quickly. At dusk a deer came out to forage and stopped to stare at her from a thicket. Ruth was grateful for that small acknowledgment of life besides herself. The animal eventually wandered off and she was alone again.

She ate the last of her bread, then drew one of the blankets about her shoulders to ward off chill. No one had come today. No one would come tomorrow. She was a fool to even hope so. If anyone had business that would bring him in this direction, he wouldn't travel this late in the year. Not unless he had to, and even an emergency would give the average man pause. The whimsical notion that another soul might pass this way held no merit.

She should have stayed in Denver City and put up with the humiliation of Oscar's public proposal and his following her around like a moon-eyed calf. The truth was a bitter pill to swallow. Marrying Oscar Fleming would have been better than this. Compromise would have been better than death, and right now death seemed likely, since she had no idea of how to get back to Denver City.

She sniffed. "Horse? Why did Dylan McCall have to be the first man I was attracted to and the man who obviously couldn't care less what happened to me?"

Ruth decided it was time to face the truth. This was just another incident in a long string of misfortunes. She kept hoping things would change, but they never did. Even if she could have located Milford, there was no guarantee he'd have helped her.

She lay back, staring at the sky—one she hadn't seen in days. "I was only four when my parents died of cholera, Horse. For some reason God spared my life. Mrs. Galeen, the orphanage mother, told me God had spared me for a reason, that he had a plan for my life."

Ruth glanced at the mare, who appeared to be listening. She smiled and continued. "I tried my best to believe that, but sometimes, particularly right now, the kindly woman's words are hard to accept. Still, God did spare me when the circumstances seemed hopeless. Mrs. Galeen told me that two Sioux braves found me crying in the wagon, my parents and two brothers dead of cholera. Instead of killing me, they took me to the orphanage. Mrs. Galeen saw them early one morning when she had risen to take care of Mary. One of the braves got off his horse, carefully cradling a wide-eyed, dirty-faced toddler, and set me, big as you please, on the orphanage steps. Then he pounded on the door and waited for Mrs. Galeen to recover from her initial fright and summon enough nerve to see what they wanted.

"Anyway, with limited vocabulary and using sign language the young man informed Mrs. Galeen of the deaths of my whole family. Then he quickly mounted his horse and the two braves disappeared before Mrs. Galeen could ask any questions.

"Mrs. Galeen named me Ruth—" Ruth peered at the mare. "Did you know that?" She lay back. Of course the horse couldn't have known that. Mrs. Galeen had named her after her favorite Bible character. Ruth had been adopted by Edgar and Beatrice Norris, a schoolteacher and his wife. She lived with them for several years, and they taught her to read, write, and figure her sums. But when Mrs. Norris died in childbirth, the grieving and distraught husband had returned ten-year-old Ruth to the orphanage.

Mrs. Galeen had been sympathetic to Edgar Norris's grief, but she disapproved of his choice not to keep Ruth with him when he returned East to his family. Edgar explained that he was unable to cope with a child, not even one whom he'd called his own for more than six years.

"It took me weeks to get past grieving myself," Ruth told the mare. "It was so hard to get over the death of the only real mother I'd ever known and what I then perceived in my childish mind as the betrayal by the only father I had. Mrs. Galeen, bless her kind soul, did everything possible to help me adjust. But I sought escape in books."

Ruth drew a deep sigh. "The orphanage was the fortunate recipient of any books abandoned by travelers, which afforded the shelter quite a good library of fiction, history, and the classics. I read everything and soon began reading to the younger children at bedtime, which allowed Mrs. Galeen extra time with the older ones."

Finally, Ruth grew to accept that she'd lost not only one set of parents but two. "Mrs. Galeen refused to let me blame God or anyone else for my misfortune. The time came when I accepted the Lord as my Savior and friend, not as someone who caused evil but allowed it for his own purposes.

"God allows events in our lives to take place in order to make us stronger in our faith—that's what Mrs. Galeen contends. In which case I ought to be really strong. One time I told her so. But Esther Galeen had only said, 'One day you'll need to be strong, and you'll have his strength to comfort you.'"

Well, Ruth thought as she drew the blanket snugly around her shoulders, *this must be that day*. She found no comfort in the prophecy. She was lost and alone . . . and it was Dylan McCall's fault. If he hadn't just gone off and left her—

Annoyance bloomed anew. What kind of man would just go off and leave a woman alone on an empty mountainside with no help? No one but a rotten, black-hearted, just plain mean kind of man. A man with *no* heart.

"And I wanted to be strong for that man," Ruth contended. "I wanted to be the shining light in his life, to prove—in spite of an occasional bout of temper and bullheadedness—that I walk in faith not in darkness. The marshall seemed to be struggling with a limited amount of trust in the Almighty. Mare, you notice that?"

But anger couldn't drive out her fear. The silence and the darkness began to close in, and tears slid from the corners of Ruth's eyes. She laid her head on the saddle and drew the second blanket close.

"Please help me, God," she murmured. "I know I'm foolish and do things and act when I should be asking your guidance. I'm sorry. Truly, truly sorry. But in your mercy, in your forgiveness, please send someone to get me out of this."

She must have fallen asleep, for when she next opened her eyes a hazy dawn surrounded her. Ruth slowly unwound from her blankets, groaning as her stiff muscles complained.

Distant thunder convinced her that she'd best take shelter from the approaching storm. Struggling with the weight of the saddle, Ruth managed to get the heavy leather over the horse that peered over her haunch with a pained expression, as if to ask what Ruth thought she was doing.

"I don't know," she muttered, tightening the cinch. "But I can't sit here and wallow in self-pity a moment longer."

By the time the mare was saddled, Ruth was trembling with exertion. She would have to find substantial food soon or she'd be too faint to ride. Urging the horse toward an outcropping of rocks, Ruth sought cover in a small cave. She squeezed the mare through the tight opening and thanked God for safety as the skies opened up in a torrential cloudburst.

She spotted the skunk the same instant it spotted her. Lifting its tail, it sprayed the area before Ruth could flee. She turned the mare, but it was too late. Throat choking, eyes burning, she clung to the saddle, barely able to hang on to the skittish horse.

"Oh!" she managed, gagging and blinking through tearing eyes.

The horse snorted repeatedly, trying to clear her nose of the suffocating stink. Ruth clung to the bridle and tried to breathe. Wind drove the falling rain back into the cave.

Easing the horse into the rain, Ruth galloped to an aspen, dismounted, unsaddled the mare, and looped the tether rope around a rock. Then she ran under an overhanging ledge. She sank to the ground and stared at the worsening downpour. She was tired, so weary her bones ached. She stank; her clothes reeked of varmint. Her stomach ached for hot food. She wanted a real bed, not blankets on the cold ground. She wanted someone to find her, to rescue her.

She stared at the falling rain, but she didn't cry. She was long past mere tears.

Her life couldn't possibly get any worse.

Chapter Five

Ruth clung miserably to the rock all night. When daylight broke harshly over the mountain range, she grudgingly opened her eyes to face a new day. Her bones felt frozen beneath the soggy ledge. The rain had stopped, but the air was damp and a chilly wind whistled through the gorge.

A noise caught her attention, and she glanced at the ridge below her. Eyes darting back and forth, she scanned the shelf. Undoubtedly there were all sorts of wildlife in these parts. She'd ridden by deer, elk . . . skunk. Her nostrils still stung from the unpleasant encounter. Late last night she'd moved farther away from the original experience and changed clothes, but the odor still lingered in the crisp mountain air.

She heard it again: a soft rustle—down below. She knew there were bears in Colorado—and mountain lions. Glory had skinned an elk once to save her and Jackson's lives when they were lost in an early blizzard.

Ruth waited, holding her breath, nervous now. *Imagination, Ruth. It's only your imagination. Out here you can imagine that you hear anything.*

She rolled to her feet and rubbed circulation into her arms. Fumbling with the knapsack, she removed the last of the cheese. Only enough rations to last the day. Then what? She didn't know what.

Crouched beneath the overhang, she ate her breakfast and pondered her actions. Actually, the marshall had every right to deny her demands, she decided. Marshall McCall had been thinking clearly. In the light of sanity Ruth realized that emotions had ruled her heart. A single man escorting a young lady across two territories would be disastrous to the lady's reputation and highly improper, however obscure Ruth considered her standing.

She took a bite of cheese.

Dylan was acting properly. It was she who had been demanding and difficult, and she would apologize if she ever crossed the marshall's path again.

Yet she wouldn't be here—stranded, alone, unprotected—if Dylan hadn't been so *infuriatingly* close-minded. Mulish pride it was. He'd behaved even more irresponsibly than Ruth—scoffing at her, playing her for a fool, biding his time until he could seize the advantage. Not to mention leaving her out here to die! She bit into the cheese again, yanking a hunk free with her teeth. A gentleman would never act as Dylan McCall had acted.

Remorse ate at her. Why had she fallen asleep and allowed him to escape? She was certain she had been watching the campfire flames lick at the burning wood, totally attentive.

She ripped off another bite of cheese.

Next thing she knew, Mr. McCall had fled like the rogue he was and left her with an embarrassing note—and egg on her face!

Springing to her feet, Ruth flung the last bit of cheese into the wind. Apologize to *him*? Never! Wild horses couldn't drag an apology out of her. If an act of contrition was in order, Marshall McCall should do the apologizing. She just ought to write the United States government and inform them exactly what kind of man they employed! And she would, the moment she could get her hands on suitable writing paper—not a page from a journal.

She started as a mountain lion suddenly appeared on the ridge below. The cat stood for a moment, green eyes assessing her. Then he lunged toward her, his sleek body sailing through the air.

With a high-pitched squeal, the mare bolted and scrambled over the rocky shelf. Ruth froze. She could feel her heart beating in her chest like a trapped sparrow.

The cat landed not twenty feet in front of her. It didn't move; nor did she. Eternity passed while beast and woman faced off.

Ruth's life flashed before her eyes. Early childhood—Papa bouncing her on his knee; Momma, beautiful Momma, thrashing about, pale and hot in the back of the wagon.

Years in the orphanage when she sat at the window and watched the road for any sign of Edgar Norris. He'd promised to come back; he'd said he needed her to help him begin a new life without Beatrice. But he'd ridden off. Ruth had waved and waved until she could no longer see the schoolteacher's slumped form in the saddle.

Other images raced by: the hot, dusty journey across Missouri and Kansas. Patience, Lily, Harper, Mary, and Glory—the only family she knew—laughing across the campfire as the girls cooked and washed dishes after the evening meal. Ruth didn't want to die—she didn't want to heap even more heartbreak on the girls—even if the women might never know her fate.

Ruth suddenly straightened, stretching taller than her five feet two inches. She was too young to die, but die she would before she'd run. She glared back at the cat, pasting her most determined look on her face.

Then as suddenly as he'd appeared, the animal turned and softly padded away. It took a moment for the act to register. Ruth dropped to her knees in relief and gratitude and burst into tears. But still, her resentment toward Dylan was so strong she felt faint.

After a while she harnessed her emotions. Picking up the knapsack and the saddle, she set off in search of the horse. The mare hadn't wandered far; she grazed in a small valley about a quarter mile from camp. Ruth threw the heavy saddle onto the ground and collapsed in a heap on the leather. Her arms ached from dragging the burdensome load, and her heartbeat had only now slowed to normal. However could she survive? She was a woman alone in the wilderness. A woman without a man's protection—curse that Dylan McCall's rotten hide.

Later she rose slowly and dampened the tip of her finger to test the wind. Should she ride back east, where she knew Oscar Fleming waited, or ride northwest, where her future was less certain?

She saddled the horse and turned northwest. As long as she kept her bearings and watched the sun, she should reach—what, Mexico? In a year? No, Mexico was south. Maybe she'd wander into Alaska—she had no idea where she was going, but she must keep going. She would have to work along the way, but she was capable of earning her keep. She knew how to cook, clean, sew—do whatever a new start required.

That night, as she warmed herself over a small campfire, Ruth decided God was taking care of her after all. She'd made it this far without any real harm. It was still possible she would find Cousin Milford. Then again, the effort might surely prove as futile as her demands on the marshall. Wyoming was a large territory. She hadn't had contact with

Milford since his last letter five years ago; he could be dead for all she knew. She had to stop this wishful thinking and concentrate on reality.

Turning a page in her journal she wrote:

> Dear God,
> Though I must try your patience, please forgive me. I know that you keep your promises and I unthinkingly break mine. Forgive me for my uncharitable feelings toward Dylan McCall. He must surely feel very proud of himself tonight. But his thoughts don't matter. You have protected me from harm as surely as you protected Daniel, who continued to worship you morning, noon, and night, even when King Darius sadly agreed to throw him to a pack of starving lions. I shall continue to worship you, too, and I give you praise and thanks. I am very tired tonight, but because of you, my hope remains intact.

The days started to blur. Ruth rode backcountry, wandering aimlessly at times. When the sun shone, she studied the cooling sphere, as its warmth grew more distant from the earth. Each rustle, each unexplained crackle, sent her hopes spiraling. Dylan. He had come back for her!

But when a squirrel or chipmunk scurried past, storing nuts for the winter, her spirits plummeted. She might never reach a town or a mining community. The prospect that she could very well die here among scented pines and industrious squirrels grew more probable with each passing hour.

Wind whispered through brittle branches. Each morning Ruth noticed evidence of fresh snowfall on distance peaks as she read her Bible. The air had a bitter bite now, yet she marveled at sights she'd never appreciated. Everywhere she looked she saw evidence of God's hand. Breathtaking land was dotted with pine stands so tall and thick that daylight couldn't penetrate the ground. Overhead the sky stretched wide, providing an endless canopy. When the sun shone, it glowed with a blinding radiance. Ruth had heard stories about miners going mad in the solitude, and she could understand why. Out here with no one but the horse for company, she was filled with loneliness deeper than she'd ever experienced. Other times, the solitude was her friend, and she communed closer with God than she'd ever thought possible.

Nights she camped earlier and earlier, eating what she could find—bitter berries or an occasional trout she managed to snag from an icy stream.

Nearing noon on the fourth day she came upon a sight that made her stop the horse dead in its tracks. An old mining road cut through a stand of pines. A canvas wagon pelted with arrows stood ablaze in the middle of the path. From her vantage point, she was able to make out two sprawled forms—men, she thought—lying beside the wreckage. Both dead, from the looks of it.

Shuddering, she eased the mare a safe distance around to pass. She said a silent prayer for the poor unfortunate souls. Indian attacks were less frequent now, but she'd heard that certain rebel bands still carried a deadly grudge. Fear rose like bile to the back of her throat when she realized the attack must have taken place not too long before she came upon the devastation. Her eyes scanned the area. Were the savages still around? Everything in her said, *Run! Don't go near the butchery!*

She swallowed back panic as the horse traveled slowly past the gruesome scene. Ruth's conscience nagged her. What sort of person refused to help a fellow human being? Though both men appeared lifeless, what if they weren't? What if a speck of breath remained and she rode past?

The poor souls are dead, Ruth. Don't be foolish. Ride on.

But one could be alive, and it wasn't as if she couldn't spare a moment. Maybe somewhere a distraught wife or anxious child prayed for a husband or father, and worried eyes scanned the horizon looking for him.

Pensively, she slowed the horse. She knew little about nursing, but she might hold the dying man's hand and pray with him until he drew his last breath.

Every instinct screamed for her to be rid of the obligation. Waves of apprehension rolled over her at the gory sight adjoining the flaming wagon. But words of Jesus rose unbidden to her mind: *"Inasmuch as ye have done it unto one of the least of these my brethren, ye have done it unto me."* The horse stopped and Ruth studied the situation. The savages could be lying in wait for yet another unsuspecting victim. *I'm afraid, Lord. I'm a woman alone,* she reminded him. *I don't have a gun.*

She listened for God's answer in the swaying pines.

What if one of the victims was alive? What if by a simple act of compassion she could save a life? Fear so thick she could taste it lay on her tongue. Then anger broke the surface. This was all Dylan's fault! How was the marshall going to feel if a prospector or some kind stranger found her arrow-riddled carcass picked clean by buzzards? Would he be so proud of his cowardly actions then?

And you, God. Why would you put me at the mercy of such a despicable man! Her bitterness smoldered, working her into an anxious state.

Clucking softly, she nudged the mare closer, aware that her hands were trembling. Well, why not? What hands wouldn't tremble at the sight before her? Even fearless Harper wouldn't think twice about kicking the horse into a gallop. Her eyes focused on the task, Ruth urged her skittish mare forward. *You can do this, Ruth.* Only a heathen would ignore the need. She could at least see if there was a breath of life left in either body. If both victims were dead, she'd set the horse into a gallop and never look back.

The sight before her strung her nerves tight. The only sound was the snap and crackle of the flames eating at the white canvas and Prussian blue wagon body. Whoever had committed this carnage was barbaric. Even the horses had been slaughtered, left lying in their tracks. Dread that she'd suffer the same fate warred with Ruth's sense of Christian duty. No. There was no reason for the savages who'd done this to come back, she told herself. Every living thing was dead, and the wagon would soon be reduced to ash. Whoever had committed this horrible deed had meant to leave no witnesses or anything of value behind.

Ruth girded up her courage and slid off the horse. Holding the reins tightly, she surveyed the scene carefully. Nothing. Not one sign of life in the motionless bodies that lay in the dust.

Her stomach pitched. So *much* blood. No one could survive after losing that much blood. One man lay faceup. An arrow jutted from his chest. No sign of life there. The second man lay facedown. She approached slowly, trying to determine if she could see even the hint of a rise and fall of his back to indicate life, hoping against hope that there was. Two long arrows protruded from his left shoulder.

Ruth whirled when she heard something above the roaring fire that was now making strong headway with the wagon canvas. A thin, high-pitched wail filtered through the hot inferno. What was that?

The cry came again, angry this time. Then it struck her. A baby! A *baby* was in that wagon!

Ruth dropped the reins and raced toward the fire. Heat radiated from the dancing flames, scorching her face. Black smoke stung her eyes, but she forced herself to rip away the back opening. The wagon was tall, and her gaze barely cleared the gate as she peered into the black pit. Flames had begun at the front of the wagon, but now burning scraps of canvas swirled upward over the frame and rained down to set fire to anything in their path.

A baby's cry came to her, weaker this time.

Concern for personal safety fled as Ruth stepped on a wheel spoke and heaved her slight weight into the burning wagon bed. The wail intensified—and then she saw it. A tiny hand waving above a makeshift bed secured against one side of the conveyance.

Horror filled Ruth. *Hurry. Hurry!*

Swallowing back dread, she fought her way through thick smoke. *Hurry! Hurry!* Coughing, her lungs burning, she refused to acknowledge the licking flames. The child's cough and strangled screams tore at her heart.

She snatched up the infant and the blankets around it, and stumbled her way blindly back through the wagon. Bits of burning canvas filled the air, burning holes in her shirt, but Ruth ignored the pain and clutched the screaming infant to her chest. With one hand grasping the wagon frame, she hurled a leg over the tailgate. In her haste, her foot caught and she sprawled out of the wagon, but she kept a firm hold on the child. Her breath was knocked out in a whoosh, and for a moment everything turned black. She staggered to her knees, then to her feet, and ran away from the wagon, now fully engulfed in flames. Ruth sprawled back to the ground and groaned audibly, now acutely aware of burns on her shoulders, arms, and hands. But she'd made it out alive, and the baby was safe.

The baby snuffed and grasped Ruth's hair with its tiny hands. Balancing the infant on her lap, Ruth drew back the blanket.

A round, smoke-smudged face dominated by large brown eyes peered up at her. Tears formed dirty rivulets down its cheeks, and its pug nose was running. Absently, Ruth wiped the moisture with a corner of the blanket.

Serious dark eyes studied Ruth, and then a short stub of a thumb popped into a rosebud mouth. A thatch of straight, black-as-coal hair fell over the rounded forehead.

"Oh my," Ruth murmured.

The baby looked to be about six or seven months old. Just big enough to sit up alone and perhaps begin to crawl. Ruth studied the little chubby hands, the fingers wrapped around her thumb. Perfect little nails and smoke-smudged, brown skin.

"Why, you're an Indian baby," Ruth whispered. "What were two grown men and an Indian baby doing out here alone?" The gruesome discovery didn't make sense, but Ruth was so exhausted she could hardly think. What were they doing here? Unless . . . unless the two men had stolen the baby. But why? Why would two men steal an infant? That didn't make any sense. Still, here were two white men, probably both dead, and an Indian baby. Had the Indians followed and massacred the thieves? But if that was the case, why didn't the Indians take the baby with them? Nothing made sense here, but the fact remained that an infant survived, and the child was now her responsibility.

Ruth sighed, gazing down at the child, whose eyes were beginning to droop with sleepiness. Behind them, flames destroyed the wagon. "What am I going to do with you?"

The baby peered up at her as if to say, "I thought you might know."

Something twisted inside Ruth. A baby. Knowing she could never have children of her own, Ruth had carefully pushed all thoughts of a baby to a dark corner of her mind and safely locked the door. God didn't intend for her to have children, nor a young husband. . . . The two naturally went together.

But she wouldn't think about that—not now. If she didn't think about it, then it wouldn't hurt. *You cannot care about this baby; it isn't your child. It belongs to someone else. Don't care about it; don't get attached to it. Just take care of it until you can get it to someone.*

Her eyes searched the area. Now what to do? What to do about those two men? Could she just leave them out here like this? She had nothing with which to dig graves. She could say a few words over them, but that was all she could do.

Immediately a host of new problems presented themselves. Food. The baby was probably hungry, and she had no food or milk to feed it. She could barely feed herself. Shelter. Ruth struggled with a flooding sense of urgency to leave the scene of massacre as quickly as possible. Refusing to acknowledge minor burns that now were quite painful, Ruth made her tired mind think logically. What should she do first?

Holding the baby close, she turned back to survey the scene. The wagon was nearly gone. Even as she stared, the wagon bed burned through and fell to the ground, taking the remainder of the canvas with it as the wheels fell inward. Soon all that would be left were ashes the wind would blow away.

What had two men been doing with a baby? Would anyone miss the thieves? Was someone nearby waiting for their return? Was this baby's mother frantically pacing a tent and wringing her hands in despair? Or had the mother died during a battle and that's why these men had the child? There were a thousand questions and no answers.

Ruth drew a deep breath as she studied the two men—one obviously dead, the other surely—

No. Ruth felt brief hope. No. The one lying on his face had moved, hadn't he? She shook the notion away. Maybe she only *wished* he had moved. Then she wouldn't be alone. His bloodstained shirt was a stark reminder that no one could survive such grave injuries. She stared harder. But there it was again . . . the slight, almost imperceptible movement that meant . . . he was alive?

Ruth carefully set the baby aside and stood up, her eyes fixed on the wounded man. She wondered what, if anything, she should do. She possessed no experience with such dreadful wounds. A few times she had helped Mrs. Galeen dress a cut finger or bandage a scrape, but certainly nothing this serious. Two arrows stuck out of the stranger's left shoulder blade. Blood pooled near his waist. Perhaps he wouldn't welcome her help; perhaps she should just leave and allow the poor creature to die in peace.

A man who would steal a child could hardly be worth saving, but the Good Book said that each man was a creation of God and therefore worthy of attention. So this man was actually, in a way, a lost brother. Must she lay claim to him? Jesus' story of the Good Samaritan came to her mind. But the Samaritan had an inn to take the man to; Ruth didn't even know where she was.

She edged forward, hands clenched at her side. She didn't have herbs or healing tonics. She couldn't supply blood. But she could pray with the poor soul—that she could do. Jesus promised the thief on the cross, when the miscreant petitioned the Lord for salvation, that that very day he would be in heaven.

The baby started to cry—a reedy, pitiful appeal. Ruth shushed the child under her breath. "Quiet, baby. *Shush.*"

Overhead a mountain jay circled, its shrill cry blending with the baby's. Wind whistled through the passes and a threatening sky lowered.

Cautiously approaching the inert man, Ruth knelt in the dirt and laid her hand on his back, wincing as her hand encountered warm, sticky, life-sustaining blood. Her heart went out to the stranger though she knew he must surely be evil. But life was precious—too precious to waste in pursuit of wickedness. She said a silent prayer for his soul.

At her touch, he moaned and she sharply drew back. So he *was* alive!

She sat back on her heels and thought, trying not to look at him. The sight made her squeamish, and she couldn't afford to faint now. The arrows had to come out. Her stomach heaved at the mere thought of what that would entail. He needed to be rolled to his back, and that wasn't possible with the arrows still protruding. If he lived—and that was optimistic thinking at this point—it would be more merciful to remove the weapons while he was unconscious.

Stripping out of her coat, she laid it aside and rolled up her sleeves. The baby fretted, needing attention.

"I'll be there in a moment," she said, her eyes fixed on the task ahead. Bracing a boot on the injured man's back, she leaned over and pulled, jerking the first arrow out cleanly.

Sweat pooled on her forehead as she took a step back to view her work. A tiny stream of blood seeped out of the open wound. Not bad—he wouldn't bleed to death—at least not from that particular wound.

Biting her lower lip, she braced her boot on the man's right shoulder, then grasped the second arrow in both hands and yanked. The stubborn projectile had imbedded deep. She got a firmer grip and pulled, gritting her teeth as the flint tip refused to budge. Tightening the hold on the arrow's shaft, she strained, pulling now with all her might.

A scream rent the air as the man drifted close to consciousness.

Sweat rolled from Ruth's hairline. She bit her lip and pulled harder, the man's pain barely penetrating her numb senses. The baby started to wail louder. Ruth felt like crying herself, but she couldn't let up now. She tensed, pulling, ignoring the man's screams of agony.

"Come on," she pleaded, then tightened her hold again and pulled with all her strength. Sweat dripped into her eyes now. Only adrenaline kept her focused. The baby's howls fused with the injured man's voice. On the fifth try, the stubborn arrow gave way, propelling Ruth backwards. She landed hard on her backside, her teeth slamming into her upper lip. She tasted blood. Her head was spinning.

The arrow rested in her hand, its pointed head still attached to the shaft. This was good, she knew. She wouldn't have to dig any part of the arrow out—she doubted the man could survive such torture.

Getting to her feet, she returned to the sprawled form and bent close, trying to detect life. Surprisingly, his back rose and fell laboriously. The second gaping wound pumped like a geyser. She ripped a strip off his shirttail and carefully packed the most severe wound, oblivious to her burns. It wasn't an ideal bandage, but she'd done all she could to try and save his life.

Confident she'd done all that she could do, she stepped to the other man and checked for a pulse. The unshaven man looked old enough to be her grandfather, his faded blue eyes staring up at her sightlessly.

"May God have mercy on your soul," she whispered before closing his lids. Straining, she lifted the limp body to strip off his jacket.

Ruth returned to the squalling infant and tried to quiet it. The child alternately sucked its fist and screamed, thin arms thrashing the air. The baby was hungry. Responsibility felt like a wad of cotton in the back of Ruth's throat. How would she feed a child? She had no cow—nothing. The wagon had been reduced to smoldering rubble, its contents destroyed.

She picked up the child and walked, jiggling it up and down. Her mind raced. She was suddenly responsible for two lives, and she had no idea how to help either one. The injured man remained facedown in the dirt, as still as lake water. And the baby had worked itself into a hysterical fervor.

Lifting her face toward the sky, she called out, "What do I do? Help me!"

When no answer came readily, Ruth took the child and sat down on a rock. Gently prying the baby's mouth open, she probed for teeth. Her heart sank when she encountered two rows of smooth pink gums. Well, so much for berries and fish. Her eyes scanned the area. Black smoke was boiling up from the charred, boatlike remains of the wagon. She got up and scavenged through smoldering debris, searching for anything usable. How had the men fed the baby? Perhaps they hadn't meant to feed it.

Horror made her catch her breath. What if they'd intended to do the child harm? let the poor thing starve to death as some sort of horrible reprisal? She shook the ugly thoughts away. *Concentrate, Ruth. You have to find food for the child.*

Hope surfaced as a new thought beset her. Maybe the men planned to take the child to a nearby community. If so, the town couldn't be far. Relief flooded her and she carefully held the baby, taking care not to cradle it. If both men died, she'd take the baby and ride to the nearest town—settlement—whatever.

Returning to the sprawled form, she bent down and peered at his bloodstained back. She could detect only the faintest rise and fall now, but he was still clinging to life.

Her eyes fell on his boots and she frowned. They looked vaguely familiar—but she supposed all men's boots were similar. These looked new and made of expensive leather.

Her thoughts turned to the job ahead. She wasn't strong enough to bury either man by herself, and it wouldn't seem fitting to bury one and not the other. She would be forced to leave both victims and pray that a stronger stranger would take pity and bury them before the vultures had their day.

Laying the baby on the ground, she turned and took the younger man's shoulder and gently tugged, trying to roll him to his back. He was so large his deadweight was impossible for her mismatched strength.

Straddling his shoulder blades, she grasped his right arm and strained, managing to get his lifeless form rocking. She got a firmer grip and rocked until she managed to flip him to his side. She gave him a final heave, and he flopped over on his back. Task accomplished, she paused to take a deep breath and assure the baby she was nearly finished. "Maybe God will even provide a cow along the way," she encouraged.

She turned, gearing up to put a face to the injured man, when her jaw dropped. For a moment she forgot to breathe. Lying before her, bleeding to death, was none other than Marshall Dylan McCall!

Her breath caught in a short gasp before she fell to her knees and began ripping the hem of her shirt into narrow strips. Dylan! *Dear God, don't let Dylan die!*

The smoking water barrel from the wagon still contained a few precious drops. Ruth dashed the cloth strips into the dampness and rushed back to Dylan.

Rolling the law officer to his side, she packed the damp cloths in the worst wound, all the while incoherently praying that her pitiful effort would be enough.

As she watched life drain out of the impossibly stubborn Marshall McCall, her thoughts screamed for answers. *What* was the marshall doing with an Indian baby and a man old enough to be his grandfather? If the thought of Dylan's dying wasn't enough, the realization that she might never know the answer to this crazy puzzle was almost as unsettling.

Chapter Six

An exhausted Ruth studied Dylan, who hadn't moved in over two hours. Only through God's grace had she managed to drag him away from the carnage to the small fire she'd built.

Darkness closed around the woman, injured man, and child. Fifty yards away the smoking rubble burned low. She'd gathered enough firewood to last the night, then dragged the older man's body farther away—far enough that she could no longer see him.

Over and over Ruth mashed bits of dry berries into the little girl's gums, but she only spat the bitter fare out and cried harder. "I know it isn't milk, but you have to cooperate," Ruth cried in frustration. "We're both making sacrifices here." She'd been at this process for over an hour, and she was crying as hard as the baby. She couldn't get enough of the sustenance into the child to ease her hunger.

She got up and walked the baby around the fire, jiggling, jostling. For the first time in her life she was actually thankful that God had spared her from motherhood. She definitely would have been an abject failure! As darkness fell, a cold chill settled over the campsite. She took the coat from the dead man and laid it over Dylan. She was cold; the baby was chilled and crying. She sat down, staring at the campsite. She would have sworn hell had more flames—but then she'd been wrong about other things, too.

In the wee hours of morning, Ruth couldn't take the child's agony any longer. She decided to try nursing her. She had no idea if she could sustain the infant until she could find a source of food, but she was down to her last option. The child hungrily suckled. Ruth's eyes smarted at the infant's vigor. Nursing hurt! After a while, she settled back, listening to the blissful silence. Whatever fluids the child was getting, the effort had worked, for now.

Ruth rested against a rock and closed her eyes as exhaustion overcame her. Dylan couldn't die—the idea was simply too horrific. Though their wills clashed, she didn't wish him harm. The thought of his dying almost stopped her heart. She was afraid, so terribly afraid to check his reedy pulse. She had no idea what he was doing out here with a baby and an old man, but he must have had his reasons. Jackson thought highly of the marshall; Dylan must possess some redeeming features. Instantly his smile came to mind, his teasing voice, the way he'd helped protect the wagon train of girls on the trail . . . . Just because he got under her skin was no reason not to see the good in this man.

Her gaze turned back to check on the sleeping man, and she felt something inside her soften. This insane, intense notion that strong men—particularly men like Edgar Norris and Dylan McCall—would take care of women wore on her. She didn't like the direction her thoughts were taking. She felt almost pity for the marshall . . . perhaps it was just deep compassion.

She gazed down at the now sleeping baby warmly cuddled against her bosom and fought back a burgeoning wave of pride. She had to be careful about this; the baby was an unwanted responsibility, just like Dylan. She couldn't let herself fall in love with the black-haired cherub.

The sound of wind first penetrated Dylan's awareness. The wind was rising, howling through the passes. Recoiling from the feverish pain in his left shoulder, he realized he was lying in the dirt. What was he doing on the ground? His brain refused to function and when it did he was ambushed by images—the wagon, the old man. Comanches. And then came the pain. Searing, blinding pain.

He lay with his eyes closed, listening. Where was he? He heard the wind—and a woman's soft murmur . . . sounds, not words. Who? What?

Summoning the courage, he slowly opened his eyes and saw sky. It was early morning and he was cold—very cold. There was a blanket—no, a man's coat—over him. Then he saw her.

Ruth.

Ruth sat across the fire, bent over something small she held in her arms. He blinked to clear the haze from his sight. A tiny hand—a baby. Ruth was holding an infant.

She glanced up and saw him, and relief momentarily crossed her face. "You're awake," she said softly. She laid the infant on the ground and moved around the fire to kneel beside him. Her touch was gentle, almost caring, as she lightly brushed the backs of her fingers along his forehead.

"Your fever isn't as high. Would you like a drink of water?"

His throat was a hot, dry bed of pain. He nodded.

She reached for the canteen and took off the lid. "Is the pain bad? I'm sorry, I don't have anything to treat the injuries—I tried."

"Water," he whispered.

"I know. Here. Drink." She lifted his head and allowed only tiny bursts of relief to fill his parched throat. "Careful. You haven't had anything to drink or eat in a while. Slowly . . . slowly," she encouraged. He hungrily lapped at the moisture trickling into his mouth.

"I found a spring yesterday—there, over that rise," she said, pointing to the east.

He laid his head back, warring with the threat of losing consciousness again.

"There," Ruth said in a hushed voice, "you should feel better now. You may have more in a few minutes." She twisted the lid back on the canteen and set the container aside. Bending close, she adjusted the coat more tightly against his neck. He watched her movements, wanting to ask why . . . when . . . but pain stole the effort.

It was dark when he opened his eyes again. Ruth was holding a baby. How and why was Ruth with a baby? His thoughts refused to come together.

"How did you get here?" he croaked.

She jumped, apparently startled by his voice. When she recovered, she modestly turned so that her back was to him. "I could ask you the same thing. I saw smoke and found you and another man full of arrows and the wagon on fire. How did you happen to be here?"

Words refused to form. It hurt to speak. Finally, he found his voice. "I . . . heard the confusion . . . made my way closer. Comanches . . . had the old man surrounded. He was under . . . wagon, behind the wheel, . . . holding them off with a rifle. I started shooting from . . . behind a rise. I surprised them, but . . . too many. By the time I worked . . . close, they overrode us." His fevered eyes moved to the bundle she was holding. "Where . . . did you get . . . baby?"

Surprise marked her features. "Here. It was in the wagon. Those savages set the wagon on fire with the baby inside it."

He closed his eyes briefly. "I didn't know. I didn't know there was a baby."

The blanket fell away from the infant's head. Black hair, shiny as a crow's wing, registered with his dulled senses.

Ruth changed the infant's diaper, fastening at the baby's hips the strips of cloth she'd made from the dead man's shirt. She spoke in soothing tones as the infant protested the cold intrusion.

Dylan closed his eyes, pushing pain away. Sometimes he clung to consciousness by a thread; other times he felt almost clearheaded.

In one lucid moment, he looked at Ruth again. Her hair was in tangles; her clothes had holes burned in them. She looked very different from the girl he'd met on the way to Denver City—older, more tired. Very different from the scared girl he'd backtracked and kept an eye on for the past several days. This Ruth was different from the spitfire he'd left on the trail; this Ruth was tender, warm, and caring.

Though he'd been so blindingly furious at her, he hadn't ridden far before he realized he couldn't leave her alone. He'd circled back each morning to make sure she was traveling in the right direction. She had piqued his exasperation even more by staying put the first day. She'd delayed him so long he wondered if he'd ever reach his destination. She'd stall, but then the determination that drove Ruth Priggish marched out like ants at a church picnic, and she was off again. He'd made sure he was riding far enough ahead that she couldn't detect him. He wanted her to stew in her own gravy—make her think that she was lost and alone and had no way out. Her reckless behavior warranted a few anxious days, but he'd known all along he'd be the one to see her safely to Wyoming—on his terms.

Now here they both were: Dylan with two holes in his shoulder; Ruth sitting there in a charred shirt and scorched trousers, nursing a Comanche baby. He closed his eyes and wished that he had the strength to ask how she'd fallen into this one, but he didn't. Maybe later . . .

The answer was sure to confuse him.

Dylan next woke to find the fire blazing and Ruth bustling about the campsite, talking to the baby. Somehow he had lived through another night. Because of Ruth's prayers? He doubted it.

His smothered groan drew Ruth's attention, and she quickly set the child back on its blanket and returned to his side. "Would you like more water? I know you must be hungry. So am I. When you feel well enough to keep an eye on the baby, I'll search for food." Her eye fell on the rifle. "Perhaps I can shoot something . . ." She tipped the canteen to his dry lips. "I'm sorry I can do so little, but I have nothing to work with."

"Is the baby all right?" Dylan asked between drops.

"As well as she can be under the circumstances." Ruth cocked her head to one side in query. "We need to find a town, to find suitable food for her."

He weakly pushed the water aside. "Sulphur Springs . . . we can't be too far."

Her face brightened. "There's a town nearby?"

"Not nearby, but within fifteen, twenty miles." He shifted and then closed his eyes as the world spun. "Three—maybe four days' ride."

She got up and threw another stick on the fire. "You should be happy I came along. Otherwise, you'd be dead."

"You're lucky you're not dead as well."

Comanches were a fierce lot, and the band that attacked the wagon had been bent on destruction. Dylan's blood ran cold when he thought of Ruth and the child unprotected. He was as weak as a newborn—there was nothing he could do to help her or the baby in his present condition.

"I hope you've . . . consulted your God . . . about our state."

Ruth glanced over as she picked up the baby. "He knows our state."

"Yeah?" Dylan closed his eyes, trying to picture a man big enough to manage the universe and have time left over to care about his predicament. His sense of logic fell short.

⌒

As Ruth spent the next day searching for berries and nuts in the Colorado wilds to feed her newfound family, she couldn't help but think about Thanksgiving. She wondered if Patience, Mary, Harper, and Lily had thought about her as they gathered around the Siddonses' bountiful harvest table to return thanks.

Ruth concentrated on what she could give thanks for. Though it was approaching the end of November, the weather was holding . . . Dylan and the baby were still alive, and . . . and there was the hope that God had not abandoned them. That's all she could think of.

She made frequent trips to the spring to carry water back to camp.

Despite Ruth's best efforts to produce some kind of nourishment for the child, she cried endlessly.

Dylan grew stronger, but when Ruth plopped the baby next to him later that morning, doubt filled his eyes.

"You watch her while I hunt for food."

Without waiting for an answer, she walked away, praying the baby wouldn't need anything while she was gone. But she had to get away from both the man and the child. She'd grown to care about the baby, and that wouldn't do. She couldn't care about her—or Dylan. When the marshall gained sufficient strength to travel, they would move on to Sulphur Springs. There Ruth would turn the child over to the sheriff, who would find a suitable home for her. A good home. Some place where the little girl would have a mother and a father, and grow up graceful and lovely.

Ruth marched toward the thicket with the rifle under her arm. She wasn't going to nurse the child today; she was going to shoot something and cook it. Later she returned with a small bird and a lighter attitude. She would survive—with God's help and Dylan's gun.

Ruth awoke early the next morning. The feel of snow was in the air. She looked over at Dylan; he was getting up slowly, testing his strength. He looked stronger today.

"We have to move on," he said.

She set the baby aside and went to him. "Yes, we do. We need food. Real food. What little I provide for the baby isn't enough." She frowned. "But are you ready—are you capable of traveling this soon?"

"If Mary can do what she does, I can match her." Dylan's smile at the mention of Mary's name caused a twist of jealousy inside Ruth. Why, Dylan McCall had a soft spot for Mary!

"I'm not sure how far Sulphur Springs is," he admitted. "But the weather isn't going to hold any longer—we have to get you and the baby to shelter soon."

Ruth already knew time was now of the essence. Each day got colder and more miserable. They could easily freeze to death in this climate if hunger didn't take them first. Not to mention Dylan's injuries.

"I haven't seen any sign of human life for over two weeks," she conceded. "Other than you and the baby."

"Houses are few and far between up here. It's not likely we'll see anyone."

Her heart fell. What were they going to do?

"Sulphur Springs is a mining community—almost defunct now. I rode through about a year ago, and the veins were drying up. A few families should still be around, though. If I remember right, the community's less than twenty miles from here." He turned to study the sun. "To the west. If we start now, we should make it in a few days."

"If your strength is able to hold out." With pity, Ruth watched the baby try to pick up a dry leaf. After the first few days of nearly inconsolable crying, she was mostly quiet now. Probably getting weak. She needed food, milk. Ruth's hunger was never satisfied, and Dylan needed better fare in order to gain his strength. The few wild game she'd managed to kill hardly sustained them. They were in trouble—real trouble. Moving on was their only hope.

The baby deserved to grow up and have a good life. Ruth deserved . . . well, nothing, actually. She was fortunate God had let her come this far. "Then let's get started," Ruth said.

They only had Ruth's mare, and Dylan would have to ride. The stench of dead horses filled the air, but Ruth knew she had to get Dylan's saddlebag off his horse to take with them.

Working with grim determination, she stripped the saddle off, tugging at the cinch until the belly strap came loose. They couldn't take the saddle with them, but she could hide it somewhere so at some point he might be able to come back for it. A good saddle was nothing to be sneezed at even if it was government issue.

Once she had both saddlebags and bedrolls on her horse, Ruth helped Dylan to his feet. Pain etched his craggy features, and she silently applauded his bravery. They had to move. Dylan knew it; she knew it, but knowing it didn't make his injuries any less painful.

Dylan slumped in the saddle, his face pale, his mouth thin with pain. Ruth carried the baby, whose eyes were wide with question. She wished she could set her on the horse in front of Dylan, but he was too weak to balance her. If she had a sling or a carrying board . . . but she had neither. Maybe given another day she could depend on Dylan not to lose consciousness and fall off the horse or on the baby. Then he could help.

When Ruth had her charges prepared to travel, she drew a deep breath and tucked a warm blanket around Dylan's waist. "West, did you say?"

"Head straight toward those mountains," he grunted. He held on to the saddle horn.

"Okay." Ruth straightened her shoulders and set off. She held the baby in one arm and led the horse, praying with every step. *You must be with us, Lord. How else would we have made it this far?*

What a sight they must be. A seriously wounded U.S. marshall, who might at any moment die from his injuries. A baby, who needed to be fed and cared for. A young woman, who felt grimy and whose clothes were full of burn holes, suffering from still-painful burns on her shoulders, arms, and hands. Ruth realized she must look at least as bad as Dylan. What she wouldn't give for a bath, hot food, and clean clothes. She was sick of pants and boots and half-raw meat.

Sulphur Springs meant new hope. The Comanches had stripped nearly everything of value from the wagon and from the two men, so the travelers were penniless. All they had left was Dylan's badge, which might convince a merchant to advance them credit, should they reach the community. Ruth's mind examined all the possibilities as she mechanically put one foot in front of the other. A town. She put her mind to imagining a town over the next rise.

But by late afternoon she was just hoping for shelter. Somewhere—anywhere—warm where she could rest her aching feet. Snow had started to fall, making travel even more laborious. Head bent, Dylan gripped the saddle horn, speaking only when spoken to.

Ruth wondered if her life would end this day—here, on a snowy, windswept mountainside. *Ironic*, she thought as she trudged through a narrow pass. If her life was over this day, wasn't it odd that God had chosen to let her die with a man she could easily love under different circumstances and a baby she could deeply love if she allowed herself—two precious fundamentals she was most certain never to achieve in life?

Odd? Or was it God? she wondered with overpowering gratitude. Just when she thought she knew what God was up to, he proved her wrong once again.

A day later, Dylan motioned for Ruth to mount the horse in front of him. By now she looked tired enough to drop, and she was limping. She didn't argue. Two adults and a baby on the horse was a tight fit, but Dylan figured there was little choice. "The mare can carry us," he told her.

He cut the animal off the traveled path to save distance and rode through thicket until Ruth complained that the brambles were cutting her legs. The thick trousers did little to protect her from the prickly briars. Her disguise was adequate; only the most discerning traveler would notice that she was a woman. Dylan alone knew that feminine beauty lay beneath the wool and denim. Had he been half the man he was a week ago, the lady might be in trouble. . . . He must be getting better.

The baby's cries were weaker this morning. He had to find a cow or goat, and soon. Despite Ruth's efforts to feed the baby, it didn't look as if she could nourish her herself. Sulphur Springs was still a few days' ride away. Would they make it through the endless miles of trees and falling snow?

With each jounce in the saddle, Dylan sensed the wounds in his shoulder give way. He'd lost a lot of blood. He felt the warm stickiness seep through his shirt fabric.

He was late for his appointment with Kurt Vaning, but surely his boss would know he had a good excuse. Trouble was common in these parts this time of the year. Kurt wouldn't start to worry for a few weeks if Dylan still didn't show up, but the assignment would go to another marshall. That Dylan resented. He'd been on Dreck Parson's trail for months. He wanted to be the one to haul the outlaw in for justice. Now that wasn't going to happen.

"The baby is so hungry," Ruth said. The three fit in the saddle snugly: woman, man, child—and supplies. Dylan felt uncomfortable with the close proximity. Despite his earlier assurance to Ruth, he doubted the animal could take the load for much longer.

"The first thing we do when we reach Sulphur Springs is get you to a doctor," Ruth said.

"The first thing we do is get the baby milk."

"Fine. I'll get the milk while you see a doctor." Worry tinged her voice as the sharp wind caught it and flung the words over her shoulder.

"What about you?" Dylan asked.

"What about me? I'm fine."

"No, you're not fine. I see the way you favor your shoulders—you have some burns, don't you?"

"Nothing serious," she contended. "Nothing worth even mentioning."

Dylan bet otherwise. If she had climbed around in a burning wagon searching for the child, the wounds had to be more than minor. But she had not complained once.

"We'll both see the doctor in Sulphur Springs," he said.

"If it's a small community they might not have one."

"They'll have someone who can help." He cut the mare back to the path, which was deepening with snow.

He'd see a doctor about his wounds and make sure Ruth and the baby were okay. They'd rest up a few days, ask around about couples interested in taking a child. He'd have to send a wire to Kurt . . . then what? What would he do with Ruth? Take her with him? Over his best judgment, he'd gotten close to the pretty nursemaid the past few days. The strange bond hammered a dent in his plans to leave her and ride on once he was stronger.

He cleared his throat. "Be on the lookout for a cow or goat."

They were all hungry. Ruth hadn't complained, but he knew she hadn't eaten a decent meal in more than a week. Only what she could run down, pick, or accidentally kill with his rifle. But she wasn't a whiner. That both surprised and relieved him. If she'd been a complainer on top of a nuisance, he would have ridden over the first cliff.

He felt her nod in agreement as she shifted the baby in her arms. He noticed that she never held the infant close. She kept the little girl at bay, almost as if she feared intimacy. A slow smile started at the corners of his mouth. He couldn't imagine this strong-willed woman fearing the devil himself. But a tiny baby had her on edge. Why? Didn't most women take to mothering?

Toward dusk, Ruth and Dylan dismounted and walked. Dylan offered to carry the crying baby, but Ruth refused. "You can't carry a child."

She walked ahead, breaking a path for him, her flushed features marked with grit. When they spotted a cow grazing on the side of the road, they stopped and stared. Some farmer had a fence down, and the last of the fall grass poking up near the roadside had proved too tempting.

Their breaths came in foggy vapors. "Am I dreaming?" Ruth murmured.

"If you are, I am too." Dylan noticed the cow's bag, tight with milk.

The cow lifted her head and met their stunned eyes as she chewed her cud.

"I'll get her," Ruth said without moving her lips.

"I'll get her," he insisted. He wasn't an invalid, though he was close.

Before the matter was settled, Ruth handed him the baby and slowly approached the cow. "Here, Bossie."

"Bossie?" Dylan shook his head. "Now you've insulted her."

"What's wrong with the name Bossie? I knew a lovely woman named Bossie who brought fresh vegetables to the orphanage every week during the summer." Ruth crept toward the cow.

The animal mooed, startling the baby, who started crying.

Ruth approached the animal cautiously. At least she had enough sense to know that if the cow bolted, they wouldn't see it again. She walked slowly, speaking softly under her breath.

"Good Bossie. Good girl. We just need to borrow a little milk—you have lots to spare, don't you?" She peered around the cow's fat sides, eyeing the bulging treasure. "Well, look at that. You sure do. How about that—and I suppose a nice cow like yourself wouldn't have strong objections to sharing a quart or two—would you? Thank you, I thought not. You're very kind."

Dylan frowned, focusing on Bossie's udder, swollen with rich, creamy, life-giving substance. "Go easy," he warned.

Ruth turned to look at him. "Do I look like I want to scare her?"

"Just go easy—don't make her bolt."

She eased close enough to reach out and hook her arms around the cow's neck. For a moment Dylan wondered if Ruth planned to ride it to the ground. The animal seemed tame enough. She chewed content-edly, bawling occasionally as if trying to carry on a conversation with the strange-looking creature who had her by the collar.

"Give me your hat," Ruth called over her shoulder.

Dylan carefully shifted the baby into his left arm and removed his hat. Ruth took it, and seconds later she knelt and buried her face in Bossie's side, her fingers probing for teats. "Do you just pull these things?"

"You've never milked a cow?"

She shook her head. "You will discover, Mr. McCall, I have not done a whole lot of things."

Dylan slowly walked over and handed her the baby. "I'll milk."

She stepped back and within minutes the crown of his hat overflowed with warm, foamy milk. Ruth surveyed the bounty, grinning. "How do we get it down the baby?"

"Tear a piece of fabric from your shirt—" Dylan frowned when he noticed the already-tattered sleeve hem as she quickly shimmied out of her coat.

In seconds Dylan had fashioned a makeshift bottle by tying a knot in one end of the material and pouring warm milk into the fabric. "It's not the cleanest, but it will have to do."

He put the end of the fabric into the baby's mouth and squeezed. The baby gulped hungrily. The milk seeped out almost as fast as Ruth poured it in. It took over half an hour to get enough milk down the child to fill her hungry stomach. For the first time in days, the child curled into a tight ball and fell sound asleep in Ruth's arms.

A proud Dylan and Ruth looked on, their faces glowing.

Dylan spoke first. "She's kind of cute, isn't she?"

Ruth quickly looked away. "I . . . I hadn't noticed."

That night when Ruth took off her boots Dylan's eyes fixed on her bleeding feet. Large, angry blisters covered her toes and heels. He felt a flash of anger. "Why didn't you say something?"

She looked up to meet his eyes. When she looked at him that way something inside him moved—something he didn't like. "Would it have made a difference? We have no choice but to walk."

He got up slowly, favoring his wounds, and got a knife out of his saddlebag. "You could have ridden."

"And let you walk?" Her chin lifted with stubborn pride. "I'm capable of holding my own. I don't plan to be any trouble—I only want to reach Wyoming and my cousin Milford."

He returned to the fire and picked up her left boot and cut the toe out. She gasped. "What are you doing? That's my only shoe, and it's snowing!"

"Those are your only toes and heels," he reminded her, severing the toe from the right boot. "Put on more socks." He repeated the procedure on the heels of both boots. Ruth watched, her eyes set in horror.

He set the boots close to the fire, then carefully dropped back down on his sleeping roll. "Tomorrow you ride."

Jaw agape, Ruth's eyes moved from her butchered boots to Dylan on the other side of the fire. Closing her mouth, her eyes narrowed and she handed him the sleeping infant.

Without another word, he tipped the milk-soaked brim of his hat over his face, drew the sleeping baby closer in his arms, and promptly went to sleep.

Chapter Seven

After they milked the cow and fed the baby again, Dylan began to tie the cow to the horse to take it with them.

"What are you doing?" Ruth asked.

"Taking the cow; what does it look like?"

"We can't," Ruth said, chin jutting out. "We don't know whose it is. We can't take it without permission. Stealing isn't going to help the situation."

"Dying is going to improve it?"

"Dying would not be the worst thing that could happen—though I'm not ready to go yet," she admitted. "God will provide food for us and the baby without us stealing."

Dylan ignored Ruth's optimism and made her and the baby ride while he walked this morning. He was in no mood for an argument after grudgingly leaving Bossie behind. His strength was waning; he could feel his limited energy stretched to the limits. Each night he took off his blood-soaked shirt and Ruth washed it and hung it over the fire to dry. Though she said nothing, the unspoken fear he saw in her eyes disturbed him. She was afraid he would die and leave her and the child out here alone. The same fear hampered his concentration.

"If anything happens to me," he told her as he walked the mare up an incline, "you head straight northwest. Sulphur Springs is that direction—I'm not sure how far, but I know it's there. Someone will help you and the baby."

Ruth fixed her eyes straight ahead, her chin set with determination. "Nothing's going to happen to you. I've already talked to the Lord about your condition."

"Yeah, well . . ." He absently rubbed his burning shoulder. "I hope he feels better about the situation than I do."

"He's given me no reason to be discouraged at this point." She locked gazes with him. "Do you know him?"

Dylan shook his head. Did he know God? They'd never officially met—not the God Sara Dunnigan had claimed to know. "I never talk religion or politics, especially with a woman or on an empty stomach."

Ruth's small teeth worried her bottom lip. She was pretty when she was upset; yet he grudgingly admired her for holding her tongue when he knew she wanted to spout off. Her concerns were warranted, but he saw no reason to give them new light. Either they made it or they didn't. He hoped for the best but mentally prepared for the worst. They couldn't make it long in this kind of weather. They either ran into help soon or . . . the *or* bothered him the most.

He wasn't ready to die yet either—he had a lot of living to do. And he wasn't as sure about the hereafter as Ruth professed to be—but then he didn't read the Bible like Ruth did. Dylan didn't depend on God to look after him; he figured God gave him the brains and experience to take care of himself. Though he had to admit, in his current straits, he sure could use a little extra help. . . .

Later that morning, Ruth sat up straighter and pointed. A nanny goat was grazing in the ditch, oblivious to the travelers. When the animal spotted the horse and couple, it bolted. Its thin, reedy voice shattered the silence. *Blaaaaa. Blaaaaaaaaaaa.*

Dylan was closest to the fence line. Automatic reflex sent him spiraling through a deep snowbank in pursuit. Ruth clamped her hands over her mouth as man and goat burst through the thicket. Dylan heard Ruth yelling to "come back!" her voice edgy as he pursued the life-giving source. But all he could think about was milk for the baby. And silence from the infant's constant crying—peace and quiet.

Yet Ruth's fear registered as he felt his wounds tear open; only pure desperation kept him going. The pesky animal darted in and out, disoriented by the chase. It spun and dashed back toward the road. Dylan slipped on icy grass, then regained his footing and lunged. The animal slid through the thicket and bounded back up the snowbank.

Dylan was hot on the trail now. With a flying leap, he managed to snag the nanny by the left back leg and hold on. The goat went down, bleating desperately. Dylan reeled the creature in, fell across the animal, and pinned its bleating carcass to the ground.

Ruth was off the horse in a split second, running toward him with the crying infant in her arms. "You *fool!*" she accused, dropping to her knees in the snow beside the sprawled marshall. Anxious tears filled her eyes as he looked up and gave her a goofy grin.

"Got more milk," he announced. And then he promptly passed out.

Ruth was bent over a book when Dylan opened his eyes. Firelight shed a rosy glow on her pretty features as she intently scribbled in her book. He'd give a month's pay to see what she'd written. The baby lay next to her, sleeping soundly. He averted his head slightly to focus on the goat firmly secured to a low branch near a stream of running water. How had she gotten him, the goat, and the baby here?

"It wasn't easy," she said as though she had read his thoughts. Closing the journal, she set it aside and came around the fire to kneel beside him. He was in his bedroll, his bloody shirt washed and draped on a stick hanging near the fire.

"I put a rope around the goat's neck and tied it to a tree," she said as she tucked the blanket closer around him. "I dragged you here—by the way, you could stand to lose a few pounds—but the packed snow helped. Then I put the baby in your arms and went back for the goat, which has a worse disposition than I have."

He grimaced. He knew he'd lost so much blood he was reaching the critical stage. "Impossible."

She shook her head before her features sobered. "You scare me like that again, and I'll have to beat you."

Was that real worry he saw in her eyes? The thought brought a warm, irrational sentiment. Ruthie was worried about him—really *worried* about him. He wasn't sure if that was good or if it only complicated the situation, but he liked the feeling. For the moment, he decided he liked it more than he resented it. It had been a long time since anyone had worried or cared about him. He'd forgotten how first-rate that could make a man feel.

Struggling to sit up, his effort failed, and he dropped weakly back to the bedroll. "How long have I been out?"

"Most of the afternoon." She rose and turned to stir the contents of something bubbling over the fire in a makeshift pot. The scented air set off an ache in his empty stomach.

"What are you cooking?"

"I found oatmeal in your saddlebag, and I mixed it with goat's milk. The fare would taste better with sugar or honey, but it isn't bad now."

She dipped a small amount of the bubbling mixture into a tin cup and knelt to spoon-feed him. "Rather good, actually," he affirmed. The oatmeal was steaming hot so she spooned slowly.

Dylan took the nourishment, his eyes meeting Ruth's. She was a far cry from Sara, the coldhearted female who had raised him. Sara was so full of religion it ran out of her pores and tainted everything it touched. He'd hated Sara Dunnigan and everything she represented until the welcomed day she was lowered into her grave. Dylan figured every religious woman possessed Sara's hostility, her narrow-minded views, and her judgmental nature.

Until he met Ruth.

Ruth puzzled him. She claimed to know the same Lord Sara had touted to serve. But that wasn't possible; the two higher powers were direct opposites. The God Ruth believed in seemed to care about individuals. Sara's Lord was a mean tyrant who demanded ritualistic worship. Sara had taken glee in those going to hell; Ruth seemed to care genuinely about others' souls and the threat of eternal damnation. Which woman was right?

Which woman served the true divine being, if there was a God? Something basic in Dylan wanted to lean toward Ruth's belief—that whoever had created him watched over him. But a man's thoughts didn't often consider how he'd gotten here—only why.

During his years with Sara after his parents died, he had thrown his head back and yelled the question, trying to prove to himself that no one was up there listening. And to his knowledge, nobody was up there. Nobody had cared about him; nobody had come to save him from "Sister Sara's" wrath. Once, when he was very young, he'd caught the woman praying out loud, lying facedown on the floor, arms extended, petitioning the Lord to give her strength to raise the awful burden he'd sent upon her. Dylan didn't know what a "burden" was at the time— only that he was one and Sara hated him.

He shook the thought to one side as he swallowed one last bite of oatmeal and moved the spoon aside. "Can you get the map out of my saddlebag?"

Ruth nodded, wiping his mouth gently. He gave her a don't-do-that look as she got up and headed for his saddlebag.

Over firelight, they bent their heads close, and he showed her the exact spot on the map marked Sulphur Springs.

"It looks to be still some distance away," Ruth said softly.

"At least another eight miles, best I can figure." He realized they hadn't come as far as he'd hoped.

He saw her eyes darken at the news, but she kept a stiff upper lip. "Then we're practically there."

For the first time, Dylan realized he wasn't going to rise to the occasion. He'd lost so much blood that he could no longer walk. The baby still lay in his arms, satiated with goat's milk for now, but how long would that last? As long as Ruth could hold on to the goat, they would have nourishment for the baby. But their survival was up to Ruth now—a young woman, a girl who had never been in rough country or even knew how to shoot a gun properly. Some higher power had to be watching over her.

Yeah—and there must be an all-knowing, all-caring God looking after him too. *McCall, get your head screwed on properly.*

Mentally groaning, he dropped his head back to the bedroll. The baby sighed and snuggled deeper into his warmth. If Ruth's God was listening, Dylan told him he'd better have a plan, because at this point Dylan had run out of options.

In the gray, still dawn, the small group hit the trail early. Ruth studied the map, nodding as Dylan pointed out the way.

"Stay to the road. The ruts will be deep, but we'll have better footing," he said.

The baby lay in Dylan's arms, contented now. Ruth walked, leading the mare with the marshall and the infant riding.

Taking charge gave her a sense of belonging—of being needed. It wasn't often that a man like Dylan needed anything or anyone, and she was proud to serve. The goat trailed, balking occasionally as the mare dragged the tenacious milk source through mounting snowdrifts. Cotton-ball-size flakes swirled around Ruth's face as she trudged on, holding the collar of her coat over her mouth. Icicles formed on her eyelashes. Hard as she tried to be optimistic, her spirits began to sag.

Her burns had scabbed over but they itched now. Her clothing was in tatters. She didn't think she would ever be able to get a comb through her hair. Her feet hurt so badly she wanted to cry. Every step was agony, pain radiating from toe to knee. Even with the toes and heels cut out of her boots, the blisters were still raw and bleeding. The toes of her socks were stiff and wet—it wouldn't be long before she lost feeling. She actually looked forward to the numbness that would surely come after walking long hours in the snow. She could make it until then. She had to. At least the baby was fine, tucked in a snug pouch inside Dylan's coat lining, cocooned in the warmth of his body.

She alternated between praying that they would find someone to take the child soon and begging the Lord to let the baby remain with her for a while longer. Death didn't seem so frightening; at times she resolved to meet her fate without regret. Dying was merely a transition—not one she welcomed, but neither did she fear it.

She wanted Dylan and the baby to live, though. No matter how hard she'd tried not to—and she had tried her very hardest—she was starting to love both the child and the marshall. Maternal feelings were seeping out of every pore, and she didn't know how much longer she could bear the feeling. What if she were to slip and allow Dylan the briefest glimpse into her thoughts? Would he think she had lost her mind? He clearly wasn't a man destined for marriage, not to a woman so clearly his opposite. Then there was the matter of their difference in faith. She didn't know where he stood in terms of belief in God, but his answer to her question about God offered little encouragement. No way could she let herself fall any further in love with the marshall.

Conversation had now ceased. They were too weary to attempt to converse above the icy wind that snatched their words and flung them away. At dusk they dropped onto the ground, and she dealt with the child who was too tired, too cold, and too hungry to do much more than whimper. Ruth knew the same could be said about her and Dylan—they were too tired to exist. They lay down without a simple good night and fell into an exhausted sleep.

At dawn, they got up and continued on. Ruth laboriously put one foot in front of the other and climbed each rise. She could hear Dylan's labored breathing as he rode the horse and carried the baby. At times she was forced to rest her hands on her knees for support. At the top of each hill she stopped to catch her breath.

Suddenly she saw what looked like a trail below them. Recent wheel tracks showed in the snow-packed ruts. She yelled back at Dylan. "Is that what I think it is?"

Dylan opened his eyes and focused on the scene below. Snow had tapered into swirling, barely perceptible flakes. "It's a road." His mouth thinned. "I don't know—could be the one to Sulphur Springs, Ruth. Maybe not."

Elation filled her, and tears brimmed in her eyes. She would take the chance. Grabbing the mare's reins, she started down the incline, stumbling, falling twice before she reached the road. Her mind whirled. Food, shelter. Tonight they would sleep in a warm room and have hot food and coffee in their bellies.

Her eyes searched the distance for signs of life—anything that moved. Panic crowded her throat. What if this wasn't the road? What if nobody lived for miles around? What if the miners had all gone and Sulphur Springs was nothing more than a deserted camp now? But the tracks indicated recent passage.

Please, God. Let someone come to help us. We're going to die out here if you don't help us.

"Do you hear that?" Dylan's voice rose over the wind.

Ruth stopped in her tracks and listened carefully. "Is that a wagon?" she whispered. It sounded like wagon wheels churning through packed snow. There it was—the unmistakable creak. Turning wheels . . .

Before her eyes a wagon pulled by a team topped a rise in the road. Tears blinded her now, and she bit back a smile. It *was* a wagon! *Thank you, God.*

Dylan lifted his fingers weakly to his lips and gave a shrill whistle. The sound ricocheted over the snowy mountainsides. When the male figure in the wagon spotted the travelers, he stood up, gaping in surprise. "Helllooo!" the stranger called.

"Helllooo!" Ruth called back. She cupped her hands to her mouth. "Can you help us?"

The buckboard rattled closer, and Ruth turned back to grin at Dylan. "It's okay—we made it! Hold on . . . in a very short while we'll have food and a warm fire . . ." Her voice trailed off as she viewed the marshall's ashen features. Help had come none too soon—but it had come and Ruth was grateful.

The buckboard rattled to a stop and the man set the brake. He stared at the frozen strangers. "Surprised to see travelers on a mornin' like this—what are you doing out in this weather?" The grisly-looking old man was bundled in heavy buffalo robes; a fur hat sat atop his head.

Ruth drew back, intuition warning her not to move closer.

"Coming from Denver City," Dylan told him. "Ran into some Indian trouble some miles back."

"Indians, you say?" The old man's eyes narrowed. "Trouble's been scarce lately." His gaze swept the mangy travelers. Ruth imagined they looked more like a couple of scarecrows than human beings.

"We're trying to reach Sulphur Springs." Ruth edged forward.

The man nodded. "Town's still five . . . six miles away," he said, gesturing over his shoulder with his thumb in the direction he'd come.

Dylan shifted in the saddle. "We're without food, and we've traveled by foot and mare for days. Can you help us? We need shelter for the night, a hot meal, food for the child."

The man peered at them. "Got a baby there, I see."

"Yes. The child needs shelter," Ruth said.

The man, who looked to be in his sixties, eyed the couple. Ruth wasn't sure he was buying their story. Finally he reached for the reins. "Well, climb aboard. Name's Nehemiah Ford. The missus and I have a place not too far from here. Got some cattle, some horses, do a little farmin'. You can stay the night. I reckon the missus can rustle up some grub for ya and the babe."

"Thank you, God," Ruth breathed aloud.

Dylan nodded. "Name's Dylan McCall, and this is Ruth."

" 'Pears you're Christian folk," the man said, staring at Ruth's trousers. She thought an explanation of why she was dressed like a boy might be in order, but then the response wouldn't help the cause. Some things were best left a mystery.

"Yes, sir, we're Christian," Ruth said, noting that Dylan neither agreed nor disagreed. Perhaps he was making some progress spiritually.

The marshall dismounted and helped Ruth into the wagon bed. He handed her the baby, then secured the horse and goat and climbed in himself. The wagon was piled high with supplies—two fifty-pound sacks of flour, two of sugar, cans of sorghum, other canned goods, as well as sacks of corn that would probably do for both horses and chickens, if the old man was indeed a farmer, Ruth thought. Somehow nothing rang true about Nehemiah Ford.

"Hi-up," Nehemiah called to the team, slapping their rumps with the reins.

The wagon lurched forward, and Ruth and Dylan leaned gratefully back against the sacks and rested.

The buckboard rattled as it plowed through the deep snow. Ruth closed her eyes, exhausted. When Dylan nudged her shoulder, she opened her eyes to the welcome sight of a tightly constructed cabin with smoke curling from the chimney. Her gaze followed to the right side of the house to another structure, quite clearly serving as a barn with a small corral beside it. The corral was empty, but a dozen or so chickens pecked in the snowy barnyard. Ruth's mouth watered. Fried chicken. Or maybe even an egg or two.

Nehemiah Ford drew the wagon to a halt and set the brake. The front door opened and a short, heavyset woman appeared, wiping her hands on a cloth. Her dark eyes landed suspiciously on her husband's two passengers.

Nehemiah jumped down from the wagon seat and looped the reins over the brake handle. "Got company," he announced. Then he spoke Indian, something Ruth didn't understand. Ruth slid from the wagon bed, wincing when her tender feet touched ground. The baby awoke in a fretful mood. She was so hungry, Ruth thought. She spotted a lone cow standing near the fence line and breathed a sigh of relief. It looked to have sufficient milk.

The woman stood back from the door as Dylan handed the baby to Ruth; they trooped in and gravitated to the fire. Nehemiah hung his hat on a peg by the door and went immediately to the stove to pour a cup of coffee from a huge black pot.

"This here's my wife, Ulele. She's full-blooded Cherokee. She don't speak much English, only 'sit' and 'go' and a few other phrases." He took a sip of the scalding coffee, his gaze on Ruth. "You look plum tuckered out. Why don't you give the baby to Ulele? She'll take care of the young'un whilst you catch yore breath."

Ruth was reluctant to surrender the child to a stranger, but if the old woman could help, she would be grateful.

The woman pointed to a chair by the fire. "Sit." The guttural command was low, but the authority coming from the woman with thickened features was unmistakable.

Ruth and Dylan sat at the table before the fire. Ulele held the child in the crook of her arm, her velvet-brown eyes evaluating the infant. The two looked as if they belonged together, each dark-skinned, each with coal black hair and a prominent nose. The baby seemed fascinated by the woman and immediately quieted down. Chubby hands reached out to touch the woman's face, patting it with exploring hands that were grimy from travel.

"Gonna see to the team," Nehemiah said. "Ulele will get ya somethin' to eat. Real lucky I came along. Ordinarily, I buy supplies in the early fall. But I been feelin' poorly and couldn't get to town until yesterday."

"Can I help?" Dylan slowly moved from the fire.

The old man's eyes noted his condition. "Not this time. Looks to me like yore in bad shape."

Dylan sank gratefully back into the chair. "I'll be fine once I get warm."

Ruth's heart broke as she watched Dylan's valiant effort at normalcy. It would take more than a simple fire to help him. "He was injured almost two weeks ago now—gravely injured. We haven't had the necessary medicine to treat his wounds," she explained.

"Well, the missus can help. Woman, git yore healing herbs—this man needs help once he's et and got the chill outta his bones."

Ulele wordlessly shuffled off to the bedroom, carrying the baby on her hip.

"Whilst she's getting her herbs, I'll stow the supplies and get the horses in the barn." With that, the old man went back outside and started hauling in sacks of flour to store against the back wall before he drove the wagon to the barn.

Ulele returned with a small wooden box and set it on the hearth. While Ruth watched, the stout woman, still holding the baby, put bowls and cups on the table and dipped brown beans and some kind of meat from a kettle on the stove.

Ruth's stomach cramped from lack of food. She wasn't able to wait for the food to cool. She snatched up a bowl and eagerly spooned beans into her mouth.

Ulele filled a fourth bowl, then sat at the end of the table opposite Ruth. She picked a piece of meat out of the dish and chewed it. Then, before Ruth's astounded gaze, she removed the piece from her mouth and popped it between the child's lips.

Ruth's stomach heaved as Dylan leaned over and whispered, "That's how squaws feed their infants, chewing the food first so the child can swallow it."

"But—"

His warning look made her clamp her lips together. *Simple milk would have done.*

Ruth couldn't bear to watch the woman feed the starving infant. Maybe it was common practice for Indian mothers to chew the food prior to feeding, but she couldn't imagine that it was healthy, even if the baby seemed to accept it. Though she'd been famished earlier, Ruth couldn't eat the food in front of her. But she noticed Dylan had no problem. When he had cleaned his bowl she nudged hers toward him.

He glanced up, concern darkening his face. "You've got to eat."

"I can't right now," she murmured. She averted her eyes as Ulele spat beans into the child's mouth.

In a short while Nehemiah returned from the barn and sat down across from Dylan. Ignoring his wife, the man quickly devoured his meal, like a hog emptying a trough, not even noticing its content.

"What are your plans?" He studied Dylan as he pushed back a few minutes later.

Dylan drained the last of his coffee and set the mug back on the table. "I'm a U.S. marshall. I was on my way to Utah when I ran into trouble." He glanced at Ruth. "We're trying to reach Sulphur Springs, where I can wire my boss and inform him that I'll be late for my assignment, and I hope, get credit for clothes and supplies. Right now we're at a bit of a disadvantage. We have no money and only one horse."

Ruth held her breath while the old man appraised Dylan. Would knowing that Dylan was a marshall make the man more likely to help? She knew that sometimes men who were running from the law came to this desolate area to make homes and were never heard from again, and this old man and his wife were strange. Both looked as if they could be running from anything, or was it only her imagination running amok again? Ruth couldn't be sure. Lately, she couldn't think straight. At least these people had been kind enough to take two frozen strangers and a baby into their home.

"A marshall, huh?"

"Yes, sir."

After a while, Nehemiah leaned back and said quietly, "Well, I got a proposition for you, Marshall. I got some work to be done around here before winter sets in. Don't look like I'm gonna get it done myself. Say you work for me a few days, earn a couple of horses, some supplies—even a bit of cash money? Maybe a week or so, depending on how fast you work." He glanced at Ruth. "My woman here, she can use an extra hand, and yore wife looks like she could stand some help with the baby."

Ruth held her breath. Should they tell the Fords how they came to have an Indian baby? She wasn't sure how much they could trust these two peculiar people, though it seemed they must.

Dylan glanced at her, his ready answer evident in his eyes. It appeared the good Lord had just laid a miracle at their doorstep—the perfect solution to their problem. With the weather so bad, they couldn't move on—at least Ruth hoped the Fords wouldn't expect them to leave until the storm broke.

But Dylan couldn't work; he could barely hold his head up, so Ruth was surprised at the old man's offer. "You're not well enough to work," she reminded the marshall softly.

Dylan glanced at the Fords, then back at her. Lowering his voice, he said calmly, " I'm sure Mr. Ford understands my condition, but I can work some, Ruth. A good night's rest, solid food—I'll be better in the morning." His eyes silently urged her. "So will you. Your feet are raw. You can't go another step. Think of the baby—we're lucky she's made it this far without enough milk or warm clothing. We'll be better off here for the time being."

Ruth knew he was right, though she was still leery of the terms. The offer seemed odd—couldn't the old man see that Dylan was in no condition for physical labor?

Dylan's jaw firmed. "I don't see that we've got any other choice. We either stay here a few days or we start walking again. We can't walk a mile, much less another five, to reach Sulphur Springs."

"Shame you didn't come along earlier," Nehemiah observed. "You coulda rode into town with me, but I won't be going back 'til spring now."

Of course Dylan was right; he always thought more clearly than she did. But Ruth still didn't like the circumstances. Yet, the child was warm and had something other than milk in her tummy—albeit nause-atingly so—and she wasn't crying so much.

"All right," Ruth reluctantly agreed. "But I still don't know how you're going to be of much help to Nehemiah." She would try to do more than her share to help Ulele as a trade-off.

"I'll do what has to be done. We don't have a choice," Dylan said.

Admiration swelled within Ruth for the marshall's continuing con-cern for her and for the baby. He'd never once grumbled about taking care of the infant, though he had to wonder why she wasn't tending to the child more. Still, he hadn't asked. He'd kept pushing on when she knew he was too weak to walk and in terrible pain. Dylan McCall was, she had to admit, a man of true grit.

"We'll stay," she agreed. Not that she'd ever had any real say in the matter. The set look on Dylan's face told her he was only being polite; they would stay no matter what she felt.

"We'll be glad to work for you," Dylan told Nehemiah.

The old man nodded. "We'll start at daylight then. You two can put your bedrolls over there in the corner."

The accommodations weren't the best, but at least the weary travelers were inside and warm. Ruth managed to eat a piece of buttered bread with her coffee so her stomach didn't growl. Her eyes were growing heavy when Ulele motioned toward her feet.

"Go," she said.

Ruth didn't understand.

"I think she wants you to take off your boots," Dylan said.

"Why?"

"The missus is good with herbs and such," Nehemiah said. "She can do something for those feet of yours, as well as for Dylan's back."

Ruth was still apprehensive. Dylan bent and began unlacing her boots.

She drew back. "I can do that."

"Don't look," he advised her. Ruth met his gaze and realized that her feet were in worse condition than she thought.

She gritted her teeth and closed her eyes against the pain as Dylan gently worked off each boot. Her stockings were worn through, her broken blisters raw and bleeding.

Ulele shook her head when she saw the damage.

Dylan's face clouded and he swore under his breath.

"Don't," Ruth whispered, stifling back a groan. "I can just imagine what your shoulder looks like now."

Ulele brought a small tub with warm water and motioned for Ruth to immerse her feet. Ruth couldn't hold back the moan this time as she very gingerly put her toes into the pan.

While Ruth soaked her feet, Ulele motioned for Dylan to remove his shirt. Ruth winced as he pulled the fabric loose from the wounds that were raw and puffy. Tonight it looked like infection had set in again; from Ulele's grunt the woman agreed.

The stern Cherokee mixed a batch of vile-smelling herbs, forming a poultice, which she applied to Dylan's shoulder. He hissed in a breath, and then relaxed after a few minutes. Ruth wished that she could be the one to administer the care but she didn't intercede. Her sudden envy puzzled her.

"Feels good," Dylan conceded, smiling at Ulele.

"The herbs draw out the poison," Nehemiah said. "The missus is a fair hand at doctorin'."

A few minutes later Ulele threw down a clean rag and indicated that Ruth was to put her feet on it. She then handed Ruth a small tin of some kind of foul-smelling cream.

"Smells like polecat," Nehemiah conceded, "but it's good for raw skin."

Ruth carefully dried her feet and applied the cream. After she'd warmed the salve in her hand it was easier to spread on the sores. Within a few minutes the wounds didn't hurt so much. Whatever Ulele put in the concoction seemed to be working. She sent the old woman a smile of appreciation.

That night, bedded down on the opposite side of the room from Dylan, Ruth listened to Nehemiah's snores rolling from the bedroom. She stared at the glow of the banked fire in the stove. Ulele had taken to the baby, so Ruth was momentarily free of the responsibility. She wasn't sure how she felt about that. While she didn't want to become attached to the child, she missed her. She missed the cute smile and the way she clasped onto her finger and held tight. Ulele had taken a drawer from a dresser that stood in a corner and made the baby a makeshift bed, where the child was now sleeping peacefully with a full stomach.

"What are you thinking about?" Dylan whispered.

"About how different this is from last night," she whispered back. "How is your shoulder feeling?"

"Better. Whatever that old woman put in the poultice, it seems to be working. How are your feet?"

"Better as well." She hesitated to voice her thought. Deep down she felt guilty for sometimes, in her lowest moments the past few days, secretly blaming God for letting them get into such a life-threatening situation, though part of her knew it was their own fault. "Dylan?"

"Yes?"

"I . . . wanted to take care of your wounds myself, but I didn't want to ask Ulele."

It was quiet from his corner, then, "You did?"

"Yes. Would . . . would you have minded?" She held her breath, praying that he wouldn't.

"No, I wouldn't have minded."

She smiled. "Then I will tomorrow."

The fire popped as she grew drowsy. The heat felt wonderful. She could hear the howling wind battering the thick front door. "God was good to lead us to Nehemiah," she murmured.

Dylan was silent and Ruth wondered if he agreed. Certainly he must—they were sleeping by a warm fire; the baby had milk and food in her tummy. Ruth's feet were better; Ulele had given Dylan something in a glass to make him sleep better. Perhaps his silence indicated the herb had worked and he was resting comfortably. She closed her eyes, praying it was so. For so long she had watched his agony.

Turning on her side, she tried to see his face, but the room was dark. "Dylan?"

"Yes?" he said quietly.

"Oh . . . I thought you were asleep."

"Not yet."

"You're so quiet." She bit her lower lip. "You do agree that we're better off tonight, don't you? Nehemiah and Ulele are sort of like our own personal angels." Everyone had angels; the Good Book said so.

"Angels?" He chuckled and for the first time in a long while he sounded like the old Marshall McCall. "Go to sleep, Ruth."

Snuggling deeper into her bedroll, Ruth closed her eyes. He could be such a riddle: one moment all tender, a complete gentleman, compassionate to her and the baby's needs. The next moment he could be as mysterious as God's workings.

Right now, the chuckle didn't reassure her.

Chapter Eight

Ulele Ford was a dictator.

Ruth was firmly convinced the woman was a tyrant as she cleaned the old shack from top to bottom. She scrubbed floors down on her knees. Since she'd been here she'd hauled heavy water buckets up from the creek, cooked three meals a day, and washed the old couple's clothes in the icy stream. The whole while Ulele sat in the rocker and talked gibberish to the baby.

On the second afternoon Ruth caught the Indian staring at her.

"What?" she asked, attempting a genial smile. Though she treated Ruth as nothing more than a servant, Ulele, with her strange herbs and tonics, had most likely saved Dylan's life. Ruth tried to summon gratitude, but mostly she rued the day she and Dylan had accepted the old couple's help. Ruth was accustomed to hard work, but the labor the old woman forced on her was nothing short of a crime. And Nehemiah worked Dylan like a plow horse.

The squaw shook her head, which Ruth had come to recognize meant that the woman was in no mood to communicate. Ruth understood little of what the Cherokee woman said, though Ulele made her work instructions very clear.

"Clean!"

"Wash!"

"Cook!"

"Sit."

Nehemiah seemed proud that his wife's vocabulary was broadening. Ruth preferred the "sit" and "go" commands.

It was no wonder the woman was a domineering bully. The way Nehemiah treated his wife was shameful. He ordered her around in quick curt sentences, much as he would one of the old hounds lying on the front stoop. The woman did as he ordered and never offered a single rebuke. Ruth would flash a cold stare at the evil man as she dished piping hot stew into bowls. There was no need to speak to a woman in that tone—no need at all.

Tonight Dylan was sitting by the fire, his head drooped from exhaustion. Ruth laid Ulele's mending aside and got up to pour a fresh cup of coffee.

Dylan briefly smiled his gratitude when she closed his hand around the steaming cup. The fire burned low; outside, a cold wind whistled across snow-packed ground.

"Must you leave so early each morning?" she asked softly. She cast a glance at Ulele, who was preoccupied with the baby. Snores rolled from the old man's mouth as he slept by the fire, his pungent stocking feet propped on a wooden chair.

Dylan shook his head. At night it seemed to Ruth that his pain was unbearable. He nodded toward the sleeping tormentor. "He insists we start before sunup."

Dylan rose at three-thirty and left the house with Nehemiah a short time later. Ruth made sure he had a warm breakfast of oatmeal and thick slices of toasted bread spread with honey, but the marshall ate very little these days. Night covered the land when the two men returned. Dylan said little about his work, but Ruth knew by their scant conversations over supper that he was doing hard physical labor: cutting wood, setting fence posts, working long hours behind the heavy anvil Nehemiah kept in the barn. Her heart ached for the marshall, but there was nothing she could say or do to lighten his load. When she tried to broach the subject, he'd cut her off and remind her they had to have food and protection for the baby.

Bending close to his ear, she rested her hands on his corded arms and pleaded in a throaty whisper, "We don't have to do this. We can leave."

He closed his eyes. "We need the money, Ruth."

Anger rose up and nearly strangled her. Why did he *have* to be so pigheaded! Nehemiah Ford was killing him. Couldn't he see that?

"Not that badly," she argued. Her eyes darted to Ulele. She had quit playing with the baby and was staring at Ruth. How much did Ulele understand? Sometimes Ruth thought she understood nothing, but at other times she wondered if the cunning female knew more than she let on.

Dropping her voice even lower, Ruth pressed her mouth next to Dylan's ear. "We walked for days without food or shelter. We can do it again. We'll take the goat—the baby will have milk. We can make it." She pressed closer. "Please, Dylan."

Being this near to him set off a strange lightness in the bottom of her stomach. The smell of soap, water, and herbs rose from the poultices. She couldn't bear to watch the way Nehemiah worked a man in Dylan's condition. The punishment was cruel and uncalled for. Yes, they were at the mercy of strangers, but no mercy had been shown them. She feared if they didn't leave here soon the old man would work Dylan to death.

"No," Dylan snapped. "It's only for a few days. I can make it—I have to make it." He set his jaw. As if that settled the matter, he got up and went to his bedroll on his side of the room.

Chewing her bottom lip, Ruth sat down and resumed the mending. Her back ached and her eyes blurred from the blue mist that continually hung in the cabin. Her clothes and hair smelled of pungent wood, and she longed for a hot bath. Was that possible? She'd spotted an old washtub hanging on the back of the house. Obviously, by the way the Fords smelled, the tub wasn't used often. Putting the mending aside, Ruth ran her hand through her hair and scratched. If she only had a brush . . .

She glanced at the Indian woman. "Ulele?"

The woman pretended not to have heard.

"Ulele?"

Ulele grunted.

"Is it all right if I heat water in the morning and take a bath?"

Ulele picked up the baby and shuffled into the bedroom, yanking the thin curtain closed behind her. Ruth resented the fact that the old woman insisted that the baby sleep in the Fords' room. It wasn't fair. Ruth wanted the child with her; she was the infant's caretaker, not Ulele.

Sighing, she scratched her head furiously. She didn't care what Ulele thought; in the morning, after the men left, she was taking a bath.

The next day Ruth washed under Ulele's watchful eye. The old woman eyed the tub suspiciously when Ruth dragged the wooden bathing apparatus in and set it by the stove, while heavy pots of water bubbled on top. Ruth imagined the device was foreign to Ulele.

Ruth felt like a new person once she'd scrubbed away weeks of grime. Afterward, she bathed the baby, laughing when the infant cooed and splashed water in her face. She glanced up to see the Indian's face turn as dark as a July storm cloud. She knew the woman wondered what Ruth and Dylan were doing with an Indian child, but Ruth made no effort to explain their situation. It would only sound worse if the Fords knew that she and Dylan were traveling alone, unmarried. Dylan had been the perfect gentleman, but the Fords couldn't know that.

After the baths, Ruth stood by the fire and dried her and the infant's hair. The baby cuddled affectionately against her bosom, and Ruth felt a rush of maternal pride that rattled her to the very core. She couldn't do this—she couldn't lay claim to the child—or to Dylan. Both were only temporary passersby in her life—ones she hadn't asked for and couldn't allow herself to love. Their paths would part in Sulphur Springs. She would have to find a home for the baby and then her life would be . . . what?

Empty. Empty and unfulfilled. Ruth wondered why the thought bothered her now. She'd never had anyone, and she thought she'd accepted the future she felt God gave her.

But deep down, she knew the reason: she was starting to depend on the arrogant marshall—to look to him for security. The baby was . . . well, who could resist a baby?

That afternoon she wrote in her journal:

> Dear God,
> I am so confused. Sometimes I get so angry at Dylan and his refusal to listen to me—then at other times . . .

She stared at the terse paragraph and wondered what she had been about to confide. Whatever it was, the desire now escaped her. Closing the book, she went to start supper.

When Dylan came in that night he threw her a look that had her on edge during supper. Was he finally ready to call it quits, to leave these terrible people? She fervently prayed that what she'd glimpsed in his eyes was an end to his patience, silently hoping that he had decided that all the money in the world wasn't worth what they were going through.

After supper, Dylan sat by the fire and played with the baby. Ruth smiled when she heard him singing her a lullaby in a soft, resonant baritone. He was very good with children; he would make some lucky child a fine papa some day. He could be tender when the situation warranted, compassionate yet firm when needed.

Ruth wondered why she couldn't openly react to the child as easily. She felt guilty if she laughed when the baby laughed, embarrassed if she spent too much time with her. Once Ulele had sternly scolded her—at least Ruth assumed it was scolding—when the old woman caught Ruth carrying the infant under her arm like a sack of potatoes. She had quickly confiscated the child and demonstrated the proper way to hold a baby: gently, cradled against Ulele's huge chest.

For the rest of that day, Ruth had carefully toted the baby around like a piece of glass until her back hurt something dreadful. Being a mother was hard work; she supposed that's why the Lord had decided she wasn't up to the job.

The next morning Ruth hauled a basketful of dirty clothes to the stream. A thin sun warmed the frozen ground, so she'd convinced Ulele that the baby needed fresh air.

Before Ruth washed and rinsed heavy shirts and pants, she fastened the baby's papoose board to a low-hanging branch where Ruth could watch her. Kneeling beside the rushing water, she stared at the happy child, resisting the urge to grin back. The infant was incredibly charming with her shiny black hair and smiling eyes. As Ruth busily scrubbed a shirt against a rock, she found herself humming the same lullaby Dylan had sung the night before. She sang the song, repeating verses when she heard the baby's soft, cooing response. So the child had an ear for music—that wasn't uncommon.

Ruth remembered when Mrs. Galeen had sung to her sometimes at the orphanage, fanciful songs of butterflies, stardust, and angels. Tears filled her eyes and she swiped them away, blaming the moisture on the cold wind. Where were the baby's mother and father? Somewhere not so far away? Or were they dead? Ruth had no way to identify or return the baby to her people. Dylan hadn't known that a child even existed until she had told him. So many questions would never be answered now, with the death of the old man in the wagon. Was he a kind grandfather—a distant relative, perhaps—or just a plain thief?

Ruth dried the last dish later that night and then carried the supper scraps to the dogs huddled beside the back step. Dylan got up from the fire and followed her outside on the pretext of gathering wood.

Ruth bent against the sharp wind as she edged closer to meet him. "What was that look about last night?"

He leaned down, picking up a couple of sticks of dry oak. "You're right. We have to leave. The sooner the better."

She shut her eyes with relief, silently thanking God that Dylan had come to his senses. "When?"

He glanced toward the back door. "I'll talk to Nehemiah in the morning. We'll be short some of the pay I'd hoped for, but I can find work when we get to Sulphur Springs."

Ruth nodded, eager to be on their way. She could stretch a penny into a gold coin if she had to. Anything to escape the Fords' house and Ulele's suffocating authority. "Ulele isn't going to be happy about us leaving. She's gotten very attached to the baby."

A muscle worked tightly in Dylan's jaw. "I suppose if we were taking the baby's needs into account, we'd leave her here. Ulele would raise the little girl, and the baby would be reared in her own heritage."

"Never!" Ruth said hotly. "I would *never* leave a child in this stifling household." She wrapped her arms tightly around her middle. Nehemiah was a cold and heartless brute. He'd rarely if ever given the child a second glance. Ulele would raise the child, but not with the tenderness and consideration the little girl deserved. True, Ulele seemed fond of the child. But Ruth shuddered to think about Nehemiah's influence. If he treated the little girl anything like he treated his wife . . . no, Ruth would die before she'd leave without the infant. Once they were in Sulphur Springs she would search for a respectable couple who would raise her with love and reverence for the Lord. If she wasn't mistaken, that was relief she saw on Dylan's face. He didn't want to abandon the child any more than she did.

"You know I'm right," she whispered. "The Fords are miserable people. You've built fences, trimmed and notched the logs for a chicken house. You've done more work for Nehemiah than he's done himself this year, and you know it. He's taking advantage of you; they're taking advantage of us. We can't leave the baby with people like them."

"But we need money and supplies to get to Wyoming, Ruth."

"I understand and I admire you for thinking of the baby's and my welfare, but we have to leave now, before you collapse."

The rationale seemed to reach him. He nodded briefly again. "All right, tomorrow we leave as soon as I've collected my pay from Ford."

They stood in silence, contemplating the next move.

She glanced at him. "Do we know how to get to Sulphur Springs from here?"

"We follow the road. One, two days, depending on how fast we travel. We'll take it easy. Your feet are beginning to heal. Maybe Ulele will let you have another pair of socks—"

"And maybe Nehemiah will let you have another shirt."

"Maybe."

Their eyes met in the cold moonlight. *Then again, maybe not,* their gazes acknowledged.

Ruth impulsively stood on her tiptoes and gave him a brief kiss on the mouth before she turned and hurried back into the house. She didn't want to arouse the Fords' suspicions, but she was excited about the plan, even though a few days ago they had been in grave danger of freezing to death. In her heart, she knew leaving was the right choice. They would make it; they had made it farther on less and managed. The three were hearty survivors.

Later, she cleaned and dressed Dylan's wounds by the firelight. Ulele's poultices were doing the job; the angry swelling looked less aggressive tonight.

"I'll take the herbs with me," she whispered. "You'll still need to see a doctor once we reach Sulphur Springs."

Dylan caught her hand. Gazing at her with amusement, he teased, "What was that all about?"

"What?" she asked. She could feel heat creep up her neck when she realized what she'd done earlier. Had she lost her mind? Kissing Marshall McCall, of all things!

Why, she had barely noticed the simple gesture of appreciation, and that's all the kiss had meant. Had he taken that *peck* for a real kiss? Apparently he had.

"That wasn't a kiss," she denied. "I was merely expressing a moment of simple gratitude." She summoned the courage to meet his smiling eyes. "*Stop* that, Marshall McCall. You know it was a harmless peck— nothing more."

His grin widened.

"*Stop* that," she demanded again. She got up and carried the pan of water outside. Her whole body felt aflame from his personal scrutiny!

Early the next morning, Ruth quietly ate breakfast as Dylan and Nehemiah discussed the day's work. Dylan was expected to dig a trench alongside the house where the hogs could wallow this spring—as if anyone would want hogs next to their house—even if the marshall could stick a shovel in frozen ground. Yet Ulele didn't dispute her husband. She fed the baby breakfast, seeming to ignore the conversation. The men left the house soon after, and Ulele went to milk the cow, taking the baby with her.

The moment the back door closed, Ruth started to gather their meager belongings. She packed herbs and clean bandages, a fresh loaf of bread and cold meat left from breakfast. She took two warm blankets from the closet, figuring Nehemiah could deduct the cost from Dylan's wages.

Then she sat down in the silent kitchen, listening to the ticking mantel clock. By now Dylan would have told Nehemiah that they were leaving and the old man was settling up.

While Ulele's poultices had drawn the infection out of the arrow wounds, the physical labor he was doing from dawn to dusk prevented the wounds from healing. Nearly every day they had reopened and were bleeding when he returned to the cabin. Yet every evening when they sat down to dinner, Dylan had asked Ruth how her day had gone, how her feet were healing. Ruth tried not to complain, especially when the marshall was working so hard, but his sympathetic glances told her he knew how worn out she was every night. If Nehemiah was a slave driver, Ulele was not far behind.

Ruth got up to peer out of the kitchen window. Dylan had been gone a long time—long enough to tell Nehemiah and be back.

She returned to the table and sat down. Ulele would be upset when she heard that they were taking the baby, and Ruth wasn't sure how Nehemiah or Ulele would react. Well, she decided, she and Dylan would have to take a firm stance. They'd brought the child here; they would take her when they left.

Ruth wasn't exactly sure how to handle the situation, but she felt that kindness would go further than being brutal about the situation. She would have to find the right words. Though she could hardly stand to be around Ulele, she couldn't be mean about taking the baby. Ulele had no children of her own, and Ruth could understand how she'd fallen in love with the little girl. After all, she'd had to fight the same feeling herself. She might loathe Ulele, but she couldn't deliberately be cruel. The old Indian had a terrible life with Nehemiah. Not only was she isolated from human community, but from the way Nehemiah spoke to his wife, Ruth suspected he wasn't strong in sentimentality. Ulele kept a close eye on her husband when he was in the cabin; Ruth had a hunch that he might have been physically abusive as well. Those suspicions only strengthened Ruth's resolve to be kind.

She got up and looked out of the window again. Was Dylan negotiating for a second horse? She could hardly bear to think about walking a mile—much less five or six—if that was the remaining distance to Sulphur Springs. They couldn't depend on Nehemiah to have told them the truth. She'd learned that much from her experience in the past few days.

She bit her bottom lip, her worry increasing. Dylan had been gone too long. Something was wrong.

Ulele returned to the cabin with the baby. At Ulele's direction, Ruth started to scrub down the walls while the old woman entertained the baby.

The lye soap ate into her hands and water ran down her arms, wetting the front of the shirt Ulele had loaned her. Ruth could hear the baby cooing in response to the woman's native tongue. She wished she could understand what Ulele was saying. Ruth scrubbed harder. Where was Dylan? They needed to be on their way before the day was over.

Just before sundown Ruth saw the marshall coming toward the cabin. By now Ruth was sick with worry. Nehemiah must have stopped off to take care of something in the barn because she didn't see him immediately, which was unusual. Dylan's strides were measured, his shoulders stiff. His posture told Ruth that her suspicions were right: all was not well. The fact that he hadn't come back this morning was troubling enough. Had the marshall changed his mind and consented to stay the day and leave tomorrow morning?

Ulele was busy with the baby so Ruth picked up the water bucket and slipped out the door to meet the marshall at the edge of the water barrel. His face was pale and his eyes sunken with shadows as he began to wash up. Was it pain or fury that burned like hot coals in his blue eyes?

Ruth shivered as the icy wind whipped around the edge of the cabin. The sky was pewter gray with the lowering clouds. Snow clouds? She prayed that another storm wasn't brewing. "Did you talk to Nehemiah?"

"Yes." The marshall's voice was clipped and concise.

"What did he say?"

Dylan took a deep breath, and a flash of pain marred his features. Ruth felt so bad for him she almost reached out to touch him.

Standing back, she allowed him a moment to recover. "What happened?" she asked.

"He laughed."

Ruth blinked in surprise. "Laughed? He *laughed?* Why?"

"He said we shouldn't be so easily fooled next time."

Ruth didn't understand. "Fooled? What did he mean?"

"He meant he tricked us. We're getting nothing. We've worked for *nothing,* Ruth."

"For nothing?" she echoed. The words refused to register. They had toiled for five days of relentless labor. For nothing?

"You mean you've worked so hard that you've nearly killed yourself, for nothing? He's giving us *nothing?*"

"That's what I said." Fury tinted Dylan's cheeks, and his hands, now calloused and red from labor, made fists at his sides.

Ruth whirled and pretended to dip water as he splashed his face and dried it with a towel. Ruth could hardly believe that anyone—even Nehemiah—could be so deceitful. Dylan had worked from sunup to sundown, working through the fever of infection, hardly able to stand, and Nehemiah was refusing to pay him? He had apparently delighted in his little game, duping them into doing his work when he never intended to pay up. She'd never known anyone so dishonest—except the Wyatts. What was wrong with people out here? Were they all out for personal gain at the expense of anyone and everyone?

"I wanted to kill him, Ruth. For the first time in my life I wanted to shoot a man down in cold blood and leave him lying in the snow," Dylan admitted through gritted teeth.

"You should have." Ruth knew the words were uncharitable, callous and cold, but at the moment she couldn't feel anything but hatred for Nehemiah Ford.

"I didn't have a gun." Dylan stared at the horizon, which was fast disappearing as night approached. "The horse and goat are ours, and I'd say he owes us supplies. I've already taken what we're owed."

Ruth wanted to wring her hands, but instead she kept calm. Bursts of temper had gotten her here in the first place. "I think you're right. We made a bargain and Nehemiah reneged. He agreed to the terms. That's a bargain, whether Nehemiah Ford chooses to honor his words or not."

Dylan met her gaze. "Let's get out of here."

Ruth nodded in agreement. She picked up the bucket of water; Dylan started off for the barn.

The baby was on the floor playing while Ulele stirred a pot of beans on the stove. Ruth set the bucket of water in its usual place behind the stove, pretending all was normal. When the old woman turned her head, Ruth quickly scooped up the two bedrolls, but when she turned for the child she found herself staring down a double-barreled shotgun.

Ruth's blood froze.

The Cherokee woman held the wide-eyed infant in the crook of one arm. In the other arm she steadied the shotgun. The baby looked at Ruth curiously, clearly happy and healthy after a few days of care and nourishing food. Ulele had taken good care of the child, but the baby wasn't hers to keep.

Swallowing her fear, Ruth remained where she was. Would the old woman really shoot her? The shotgun would rip her in two. She had to be brave. Dylan was just outside the door. She had to measure up.

God, help me, she prayed.

"We're leaving," she said, though she knew the woman didn't understand a word. "Give me the baby." She held out her hands, demanding the infant.

Ulele shook her head no.

Ruth nodded yes, keeping her eyes glued to the gun. "Yes," she ordered, still holding out her hands.

Ulele shook her head. No. The woman refused to relinquish the child, and the shotgun never wavered.

Ruth felt her bottom lip quiver. Suddenly she was angry. Fighting mad. How dare this woman think she had a right to keep this child! Nehemiah and Ulele Ford were mean, deceitful heathens. Nehemiah had noted her Christianity when she'd thanked God for Nehemiah's appearance on the trail, but not once had he offered a prayer before meals or at bedtime. Not once had either Ford said thank you for anything. And now Nehemiah thought he could keep them here by force? By not giving them the horse and supplies they earned? And Ulele thought she could steal this child by holding Ruth at gunpoint?

I don't think so, Ruth decided. Ulele motioned Ruth toward the door with the barrel of the shotgun. Bracing herself for a fight, Ruth lunged for the gun, catching the Indian woman off guard. Ruth grabbed hold of the gun barrel, shoving it toward the ceiling, but Ulele wasn't letting go. While she held on to the gun barrel, Ruth tried to take the baby from Ulele, but the woman was older, taller, and stronger.

All Ruth could do was hold on and fight to gain control while protecting the child. "No," Ruth grunted with effort, "you're not keeping *her.*"

Ulele responded with a guttural word. The baby was howling now.

Suddenly a masculine hand swooped down and grabbed the gun, yanking it out of both Ruth's and Ulele's grip. Before Ruth knew what had happened, Dylan shouldered Ulele aside and snatched the baby out of her arms. Shoving the child at Ruth, he snatched up the two bedrolls, grabbed her hand, and dragged her out of the cabin.

Hand in hand, they sprinted for the waiting horse, on which Dylan had managed to load meager supplies. He hoisted Ruth and the baby atop of the animal and then sprang onto the mare behind them.

"Keep low," Dylan shouted, shoving Ruth down. He covered her and the baby with his body while he held the reins.

A bullet whizzed over their heads, and Ruth buried her face in the smell of leather. She clung tightly to the baby, who was wailing. Glancing beneath Dylan's arm, she saw Ulele standing in the doorway, her hands over her face, the old farmer running a few steps before stopping to fire again. Ruth closed her eyes and concentrated on holding on. They rode at full gallop as far as the horse could safely go carrying double weight.

Finally Dylan drew the animal to a standstill beneath a bare aspen and slid off. He helped Ruth down. "Are you okay?"

"Scared half to death, but I'm fine." Ruth gazed down at the baby, straightening her blankets so they covered her shoulders.

Dylan grinned. "Was that a fight I just witnessed between two women over one baby?"

Ruth's chin raised a notch. "She wasn't keeping this child." She wouldn't admit that she would have fought a whole tribe of Indians before she'd see this baby fall into the wrong hands. A hundred years would pass before she'd openly acknowledge that she cared for this tiny life—cared so much it hurt.

Part of Ruth wanted the small girl so badly she couldn't stand it, but another, stronger, part of her knew she would never be her mother. The baby needed a home with two parents; that was only fair for the child.

As Ruth gazed at the child in her arms, love nearly suffocated her. "Maybe I should have let Ulele keep her," she backtracked. "After all, she is an Indian baby."

Then why had she fought to keep the child? She should have grabbed the bedrolls and run, and not put the baby in danger again.

Well, she'd done it for Dylan, she told herself.

Dylan had taken to the child; she could see it in his smile, though it did seem odd. He was a marshall, a man accustomed to being alone. He liked his solitary life. He'd said so not once but many times. But she'd watched him holding the child, talking to her every night. While the baby slept she'd caught him smoothing down the thatch of black hair that persisted in standing straight up. She'd seen him cup that tiny head with his large hand . . . and she had ached with the knowledge that his hard heart was softening toward the child but not so much toward her.

"Ulele wasn't going to let me have her. I knew you'd be upset if I didn't get her."

"Me? Upset?" He looked incredulous. Then he laughed. Hooted, in fact.

The baby started to howl, and Ruth shoved her toward Dylan. He automatically took her, staring at Ruth with puzzlement.

Ruth wouldn't look at either of them. "She likes you better," she said. Her heart ached because she knew it was true. And the knowledge hurt.

Chapter Nine

The man should be horsewhipped," Dylan observed as they ate bread and cold meat over a small fire that night.

Ruth agreed, wondering how anyone got to be that mean; it would surely take work and the devil's help. How many other unsuspecting travelers had the Fords ensnared?

Ruth steadied the marshall's cup as she poured coffee. Dylan's hands were trembling—a sure sign of his rage. When a person's hand trembled from anger, there would be a price to pay.

Ruth knew the consequences of anger. Lately, hadn't she let flashes of emotion overrule good sense more often than not? She hated the feeling of not being in control; she'd prided herself on using good judgment, relying on the Lord, but lately she'd failed miserably. The rigid set of Dylan's jaw reminded her of her own short fuse. But who wouldn't be angry? Nehemiah Ford was an evil man, so evil Ruth doubted the devil would lay claim to his own.

Once when Ruth was small, there'd been a man who tried to take advantage of Mrs. Galeen's goodness. Ruth had been young, barely able to remember the incident. Mrs. Galeen had paid the worker to help pick apples in the small orchard behind the orphanage. They had agreed on a full day's work—sunup to sundown. Shortly after noon break, Mrs. Galeen had caught the young man snoozing beneath a low, spreading branch ripe with fruit. Ruth could still recall the woman's reaction. She'd whacked the boy smartly on the bottom of his thin boots. When he'd jumped up in surprise, she'd paid him for the work he'd done and escorted him off the property in a dead run.

The woman had been demanding but fair and compassionate. Character traits Nehemiah Ford wouldn't have recognized.

"Men like Ford should be strung up by their heels," Dylan said. "Shot like a rabid animal."

Ruth released a breath of relief. It was good to know that he was angrier with the Fords than with her. "Well—" she turned to pick up a clean bandage—"maybe not shot. The Good Book says an eye for an eye, but I've never quite understood how far a person could actually go without receiving God's disapproval."

She'd never shot anything but necessary food—and she wouldn't— except she would be mighty tempted right now if Nehemiah Ford caught up with them.

Dylan took a drink from the cup, eyeing her. When he continued to stare, Ruth looked up. "What?"

"You actually believe in the Lord and this Good Book, don't you?"

Ruth gaped at him. "You don't?"

Though in her mind she'd accused the marshall of being a heathen more than once, she supposed she didn't really believe he was. He'd had the tenacity to keep going, to protect her and the baby as best he could under the circumstances. A lesser man might have rid himself of the problem long ago. She didn't know if she could have done all that without the Lord's help, so she had begun to wonder if maybe Dylan was starting to trust more than he knew. He didn't speak coarsely—at least not as much lately—and never the way Nehemiah had gone on, taking the Lord's name in vain with every breath. Though Dylan sometimes made her so angry she couldn't see straight and his stubbornness drove her to distraction, she had to admire his tenacity.

Dylan looked away from the fire. "Never had an occasion to believe in anyone other than myself."

Sorrow twisted in Ruth, deep and hurtful. She hated the way she was softening toward this man. Ruth might not be alive at all if it weren't for this wonderful man. He was a good man. Yet something in Dylan's childhood must have stifled his ability to believe. Some bitterness from his past seemed to haunt him.

Dylan had functioned under incredible odds. Only through God's grace had he managed to travel with his injuries, yet he couldn't seem to see that. The five days at the Fords' place had been torturous.

Dylan was still in no condition to travel. Neither was she; it wouldn't take much to start her feet bleeding again. Could they possibly make it the five or six miles to Sulphur Springs?

Ruth didn't see how the marshall could hold up or how they could feed the baby. They'd left in such a hurry, they'd forgotten the goat. They needed help, and needed it badly.

She walked to the brook and wet a cloth, then returned to clean and apply poultices to Dylan's shoulder. Anything placed on the raw flesh made him wince, but this was necessary. The marshall endured the treatment twice daily only by gritting his jaw and turning his head away. It hurt her to hurt him.

"I don't know why you won't let me give you something for the pain." On the second night at the Fords', she'd given him some of the sleeping weed from the store that Ulele kept. When Dylan first drank it, his mood had improved, but in a strange way. His eyes would go wide and soon he would think that he saw spiders running up the wall. The first time it happened, Ruth jumped up and grabbed a shoe, her gaze searching for the offensive bug. But there had been no spiders. Dylan was out of his mind. His hallucinations had lasted for hours until she had given up. She threw the shoe in a corner and let him rave.

After two doses, he had refused any more of the medicine. "I don't want any more of that locoweed!"

He winced now as she applied the herbs. Their eyes met over the firelight. Tonight she found it impossible to break the look, and her touch lingered far too long to be polite. The baby slept nearby, warm beside the fire. "I'm sorry you're hurt," she said. "I feel very responsible."

"Responsible?" His gaze softened. "You had nothing to do with me riding to the old man's defense. When I topped a rise and saw Indians attacking the wagon I acted out of instinct—I should have realized I was outnumbered. If anyone's to blame, it's me."

She wound a clean bandage around his shoulder. Such a nice shoulder—broad and heavily corded. The past few days he'd lost more weight, but he was still a large, well-muscled man.

"I should thank you, Ruth. I doubt that I would be alive tonight if you hadn't stopped to help."

She smiled. "It was nothing—I would have done it for anyone."

Truth be known, she didn't want to examine too closely what she'd done. If she had known it was Dylan lying near death, would she have passed on without a single backward glance? She didn't want to think so, but at the time she well might have. She was ever so grateful that she hadn't let her fear override kindness. She was glad she'd been able to pull Dylan back from the jaws of death. He was, after all, a decent man.

Perhaps if they had met under different circumstances . . .

But they *had* met under different circumstances—on the wagon train—and Ruth well recalled the marshall's arrogance, the endless teasing when she came into his sights. Yet tonight Dylan McCall was nothing like that man. He was soft-spoken, respectful and, yes, humble. She didn't know how to react to this new man. She was more comfortable with the ornery side of Marshall McCall.

At any rate, she no longer felt animosity toward him, just empathy— for his wounds, for the fact that he had been saddled with a woman and baby so he couldn't carry out his duties. But his trials would be over in a few days, God willing, and hers would have just begun.

"Penny for your thoughts?"

She glanced up. Could her feelings possibly show on her face? "Oh, they wouldn't be worth a penny."

"They might. Are you worried?"

She shook her head. "I'm not worried about me, only about you and the baby."

"I told you I'd help you find a home for the baby when we reach Sulphur Springs."

"I know. It's just that I feel so overwhelmed by the task. I want the child to have a good home, to be raised by Christian parents. What if we make a mistake and give her to the wrong family?" She glanced at the baby, who dozed beside Dylan. The child needed care and love— most of all love.

Tonight's feeding had been an ordeal. Without the goat's milk, Ruth had been forced to chew the baby's food for her. The primitive food chain was unpleasant and sickened Ruth, but the child accepted the fare without protest.

"Tomorrow we'll find another cow or goat," Dylan promised. Was he a mind reader? No, he wouldn't still be with her if he could read her mind.

"It isn't that." She set the roll of bandages and herbs aside and helped him struggle back into his shirt. "I know the baby and I are keeping you from your work."

He shook his head. "I'll wire my boss when we reach Sulphur Springs and explain what happened. There won't be a problem."

"You need to see a doctor before you do anything else."

He grinned, buttoning the shirt. "Yes, Mama. And I'd suggest that you send a wire to your cousin Milford so he will be expecting you."

She dropped her gaze and grinned. He could be as charming as an old-maid aunt when he wanted. "I might very well do that, smarty."

And she would, *if* she had any inkling of how to contact Milford. Regardless, she had made up her mind that she was no longer going to be a burden to the marshall. When Dylan left Sulphur Springs without her, it would be with her blessing and prayers.

They turned in for the night. Her bedroll was on the opposite side of the fire, but when she lay down she met Dylan's gaze. They looked at each other for a long time. Love stirred inside Ruth; she pushed it down. It was only natural under these circumstances to feel gratitude and yes, even a smidgen of affection for her protector. Dylan had not wanted the job, certainly never asked for it, but he was fulfilling the role admirably. If she was foolishly falling in love with him, it wasn't his fault.

The fire burned low. Overhead a cloudy sky stripped the night of any light. Dylan's eyes closed with fatigue, and he cradled the baby to his chest protectively. Ruth smiled. How she envied that child . . .

Rolling to her back, she closed her eyes. *Don't think that way, Ruth. You're getting soft.* She opened her eyes when she heard Dylan singing now—a soft lullaby—Irish, wasn't it? Ruth had heard the song before but didn't know where. Perhaps from her father's lips.

" 'Oh Danny boy, the pipes, the pipes are calling

From glen to glen, and down the mountain side . . . ' "

Melancholy stole over her as she listened to the rich baritone softening the darkness. Her thoughts turned to the only family she knew now: Patience, Mary, Lily, Harper. What were they doing tonight? Was Mary's asthma worse? Would Mary ever find a man to love her—to adore her the way Jackson cherished Glory? Would any of the women be that blessed?

The other girls must be worried sick about Ruth, fearing the worst. She'd been gone almost a month and hadn't written.

She flipped back to her side, stuffing her fist into her mouth to mute her crying. If she hadn't been so willful, so stubborn, she would be with them tonight, in a warm bed or sitting at Pastor Siddons's table, or at Oscar Fleming's. Should she have married the old prospector? The thought still rendered her numb, but maybe God had intended her to marry Oscar. Oscar would be well past the years of wanting children. . . . Perhaps Oscar had been God's way of providing for Ruth, given her barrenness. She didn't want to cheat any man by marrying him and not being able to give him children. God had set her path, but in her self-centeredness she had failed to be obedient to his will, instead running off to Wyoming to build her life. Now she was paying the consequences of her folly.

She would never love another man like she loved the marshall. Hard as she tried to put dreams of a family away, sometimes the hope sprang up to strangle her.

Closing her eyes, she prayed silently. *I will do whatever you want, Lord; only you must show me the way. I am truly blind and cannot see which direction to take at this point. I don't know why I'm here with Marshall McCall and a motherless baby, but I will do my best to find a home for this child and make Marshall McCall's life a little easier—with your grace.*

For some reason God had appointed her—what?—surrogate mother and marshall caretaker? Seemed an unusual responsibility to be given to her, but she didn't question the Father's will. She would function wherever he put her.

She drifted off to the sound of Dylan's singing.

The first ray of light drew Ruth awake and she lay, listening and waiting, reluctant to face what a new day would bring. She could hear the baby cooing as Dylan talked to her. How was it he could relate so well to an infant but triggered her temper so easily? She couldn't understand that. They could walk together for hours, each seeming to know when the other was tired and needed to rest, always anticipating what the other was thinking. Then Dylan would tease her about marrying Oscar, about her ridiculous decision to follow him, or about her temper, and she would boil over. There was just something about him—

"Do you intend to lie there all day?"

Like now.

"No. But I didn't fancy rising before sunup."

"It's dawn and we're burning daylight."

She sat up and looked at him, holding the baby. "She needs milk."

"And I'm fresh out," Dylan returned, his blue eyes mocking her.

"Grump."

"Let's get moving."

Sometimes he acted like he was running from her as hard as she was running from Oscar.

They rode slowly this morning, sparing the mare since it was carrying double. Ruth sat behind Dylan, who held the baby against his good shoulder. She was careful to avoid touching the marshall's back, to allow the herbs to do their work. Besides, she didn't want to touch him any more than necessary because . . . well, just because.

The baby's serious dark eyes peered at her over his shoulder, and Ruth wished Dylan would change the baby's position. Guilt still nagged her over the decision to bring the child. But as soon as she thought of Ulele and Nehemiah, she praised God that she'd had the nerve to fight. Surely when they reached Sulphur Springs there would be a family eager to take her.

"Well, well," Dylan said, startling Ruth out of her reverie. "God does provide."

Ruth peered around his shoulder. In the middle of the trail was a cow standing there as if waiting for them to happen along. Ruth could hardly believe her eyes. "Do you think it's . . . tame?"

Dylan's shoulders shook with laughter. "Tame?"

"Yes," she said, stung. "I don't fancy getting kicked from here to kingdom come." She'd been lucky; the other cow had been gentle.

"Guess one of us will have to find out. Should we flip a coin?"

He was teasing her again, laughing at her when she was entirely serious. Well, it was up to him to figure out how to catch this one.

Ruth slid off the horse. Dylan dismounted, too, and handed her the baby. Then he took the rope from the saddle and uncoiled it, keeping the horse between him and the cow. The object in question continued to stare at them, chewing contentedly. Ruth was astounded. Was it just going to stand there while Dylan roped and milked it? Somehow she didn't think so. Finally Dylan stepped back into the saddle.

"What are you doing?" Ruth asked, wondering if he'd changed his mind and decided to ride on. He probably wasn't eager to reopen the wounds a fourth time—or was it the fifth time by now?

"I'm going to rope a cow," he said.

He urged the horse forward, moving parallel to the cow. He began to gently twirl the rope above his head. Ruth watched curiously. He did seem to know what he was doing. When he was within three or so yards of the cow, Dylan sent the rope flying with a flick of his wrist. The cow stood quietly as the noose settled around its withers and the horse planted its hooves in the sod. For about three seconds the cow and the horse looked at one another, and then the cow decided she'd had enough of the game.

With a toss of her head, she attempted to rid herself of the rope. She failed. The mare had, at some point, been a good cow pony, because she stood her ground, keeping the rope taut between her and the cow.

"Good job," Dylan said, patting the animal's neck.

"Now what?" Ruth asked.

"Now we're going to see if that cow has some milk for our baby."

Our baby. His words hit her like a sandstorm. No. She wouldn't even entertain the thought. Dylan's words signified a slip of the tongue—nothing more.

Dylan got off the horse and cautiously followed the rope toward the cow. He spoke gently. Ruth couldn't hear the words, but the cow watched him warily. In a few minutes he was able to rub the beast's nose and apparently convince her that he was harmless. He ran a hand down her side, then knelt gingerly beside her. He tested the udder, then gently squeezed a teat.

"We have milk," he announced softly. "Bring me a canteen."

Taking a cue from him, Ruth moved slowly and quietly, hoping the baby wouldn't choose the next few minutes for a screaming fit. Grace was with them. She handed Dylan two canteens and backed away.

Before long the marshall had filled both containers with milk. When he removed the rope from the cow's neck, he patted her and thanked her for cooperating.

"Well, that wasn't too difficult," he announced, returning to Ruth. "Let's have breakfast."

The baby drank from the canteen greedily. Dylan offered Ruth the first drink from the second canteen. She'd never drunk milk fresh from the cow before, and the warm taste was different. Not distasteful, but different.

"You've milked a few cows in your life."

"Raised on a farm," he said.

She wondered where he'd been raised, and how, but it didn't seem a subject he wanted to open so she left it. There was a lot about Dylan McCall she didn't know, and it seemed, a lot more he wasn't willing to share. At least not with her.

Dylan stood up and stretched. "We'd best move on. I don't want to take a chance on Nehemiah catching up. He's crazy enough to try and snatch the baby and shoot us in the process."

"You think he'd come after us?" Ruth's eyes searched the road they traveled.

"I don't know what that old man might do," Dylan replied, a remnant of his former anger still evident in his tone. "And I don't want to know."

At noon they fed the baby from the canteen again. She cooperated and soon dropped off to sleep in Dylan's arms.

At midafternoon, when Ruth was about to close her eyes from need of sleep, Dylan's soft voice woke her. "Well, well, look at this."

Ruth peered around his shoulder. A wagon drawn by a team of bays was coming toward them. She could see a heavyset woman at the reins. Dylan halted the mare just off the trail, and the woman stopped the wagon beside them. Four children, ranging in age, Ruth guessed, from around ten to four years, peered up at her. Their faces were smudged, as if they'd eaten candy before their ride, their eyes wide with question as they looked up at Dylan.

"Afternoon," Dylan greeted.

"Mama," the youngest whined.

"You hush," the mother admonished.

"But, Mama—"

The woman reached around the three others and thumped the boy on the head. His eyes immediately smarted with tears. Ruth's heart went out to the child as she wondered what the little boy had wanted.

"Mama, Davy needs to—"

"Didn't I tell you all to *shut* yore pie hole?"

The youngest child sniffed and swiped his sleeve across his runny nose. The woman turned back to focus on Ruth and Dylan. "What are you two doing out here in the middle of nowhere?"

The woman wore a much-washed blue dress with a round collar. A wool cape hung on her shoulders, and she wore a broad-brimmed bonnet. Her face was rosy from the cold air. The children's clothes looked worn and wrinkled, as if they'd traveled some distance since the morning, and none of them wore a coat that fit properly. Thin arms stuck out of threadbare sleeves, and not one had a coat buttoned up.

Dylan addressed the woman. "We're going to Sulphur Springs. I understand it's not too many more miles."

"Just three or four. Just came from there. Heading to my folks' place," the woman said. "Marge Donaldson's my name."

"Dylan McCall. This is Ruth."

Mrs. Donaldson nodded. "Pleased to meet you."

"Mama, Davy—"

The woman elbowed the oldest child back into his seat.

"Where'd you come from?" another child queried.

"Joshua, you just sit back there and shut up—"

Ruth studied the woman's strong face. She saw a woman worn down from hard work and too many mouths to feed, but she took a chance. "We have a baby who needs a home." The words slipped out before Ruth could stop them. Surprise crossed the woman's face.

"Let's see him."

Dylan glanced at Ruth over his shoulder, and then held the sleeping baby up for the woman's perusal. "It's a her."

Marge frowned. "That's an Indian baby. Where'd you come by it?"

"Her—she's a her, and I rescued her from a burning wagon after an Indian attack," Ruth explained.

The woman's frown turned into a scowl. "The red heathens didn't take the kid with them?"

"I don't believe they knew the child was there," Ruth said shortly.

"Well, well. Ain't that somethin'." Mrs. Donaldson's eyes ran over God's perfect creation like she was inspecting rancid meat. And with just about the same emotion.

"Mama—"

"Sharon, I told you to sit down and be quiet!" She smacked the little girl hard and shoved her back into her seat in the corner of the wagon, where one of her brothers quickly moved to shield her.

Ruth wondered if the children ever wished they could disappear. She'd been raised without parents, along with the other children at the orphanage, except for the time she'd lived with the Norrises. She'd been spared this kind of treatment.

"So yore lookin' for a home for the baby?"

Ruth glanced at Dylan.

"Well, I'd surely be willin' to take her. My husband took off a while back and I'm alone, 'cept for th' kids. Got a homestead not too far from here, cattle to take care of, garden in the summer. Need all th' help I can get. Not too many people out here, ya know, so I got to raise my own help. 'Course, it'll be some time before that one can be anything but a burden, but—"

"Mama, there ain't—"

"You *sit* down, Jacob, and keep yore mouth shut!"

Taking the baby from Dylan, Ruth drew her protectively to her chest. "Ride on," she whispered to Dylan under her breath.

"Don't you have any hands on your place?" Dylan asked.

"Got one. Once in a while some man hidin' from th' law will come through, work for food and a place to sleep. I give him a bunk, and he does a few chores until he up and leaves." She shrugged. "Generally, they don't stay long."

"Go," Ruth murmured, giving Dylan a stern look. "Now. She isn't the one."

Clearing his throat, Dylan said kindly, "Well, I think we'll ride on into Sulphur Springs."

The woman seemed unfazed by his dismissal.

"Suit yourself—"

"Mama—"

"Jacob, if I have to tell you young'uns to hush one more time," the woman threatened, turning to catch the ear of the offending youngster and twisting it until the child yowled.

Ruth winced.

Marge looked back. "Say, bet you two could use some grub."

"No," Ruth said, glancing up at Dylan. He wagged an eyebrow.

Marge Donaldson turned on the wagon seat and yelled at one of the middle kids. "Boy! You hand me up four ta five of those turnips back there. Where's yore manners?"

Jacob, his ear fiery red, his eyes brimming with tears an eight-year-old would hate, Ruth guessed, turned and handed the vegetables to his mother.

"Here. Ain't much, but it's somethin' to fill yore belly."

"Thank you," Dylan said, leaning down to take the vegetables, which he handed to Ruth.

"You take care now," Marge advised, then slapped the reins over the rumps of the team.

"Mama!"

"You *hush!*"

As the wagon rattled down the road, Ruth could still hear the children complaining and Marge Donaldson still advising each to "shut up."

"Oh my," Ruth breathed, hugging the baby tightly.

"Wonder why her husband left?" Dylan said, turning to grin at Ruth.

Ruth stifled a giggle. She felt sorry for the children and wished she could do something to make their lot in life better, but she knew that was impossible. At least she and Dylan hadn't given her the baby to raise and abuse.

"Well, looks like we have our supper," Dylan said, eyeing the turnips.

"Praise the Lord," Ruth agreed, feeling good that God had left the baby in her care a while longer.

It wouldn't be forever, she knew. She accepted that . . . didn't she?

Chapter Ten

The long day had sapped Dylan's strength. As Ruth walked, he clung to the baby and to the saddle, careful not to show Ruth his growing feebleness as shadows began to lengthen.

Ruth had carried more than her share lately, and most of their problems were due to him. If he could live that fateful day over when he'd decided to ride to the old man's rescue. . . . In all likelihood, however, he would make the same decision again, to go in with guns blazing, and that would be all right, but only if Ruth weren't drawn into the fiasco.

He closed his eyes, grimacing when he thought about dying out there beside that wagon, alone, without ever knowing Ruth, really knowing her. He'd have missed discovering that her stubbornness was part of her strength, her ability to focus on an end result without being distracted by her own pain. She cared for the baby, cared for her without complaint. She'd determined to go somewhere new, to begin a new life—whether in Wyoming or elsewhere—and that's what she would do in spite of this major setback. The baby and Dylan were only minor detours in her mind.

While he could appreciate that focus, it bothered him as well. He found himself wanting to distract her, wanting her to think about him in ways other than a responsibility—an unwanted one to boot.

But who took care of Ruth? She was the one who had taken on the job of teaching Glory to read and write, to bathe like a cultured young woman, and to acquire manners. Ruth had worried over Mary's poor health and sat up with her for company and comfort when Mary's coughs wracked her slight frame.

But who took care of Ruth?

And why did Dylan find himself wanting things to be different right now? Why was he angry because he was injured and couldn't properly protect Ruth? He wanted to carry the burden of worry and the weight of protection for her and the child. Worry grated on him; she'd had to be the stronger one, even when she had her own problems.

The mental exercise kept his mind off the fact that it was taking four times as long to make the trek to Sulphur Springs as it should have, and that his back felt like a hot poker had caught him between the shoulder blades.

Ruth.

What awaited her once they reached town, found someone to take the baby, and he went on his way? He knew he'd been more hindrance than help, but what would she do without him? What would *he* do without Ruth? The fact that they were together had made the circumstances more tolerable—at least to him.

Then was in the future. Right now Ruth was barely able to put one foot in front of the other. Though it was early, they both needed rest. The baby started to fret.

"Looks like a good place to camp."

Ruth swayed on her feet. "So soon?" She blinked, holding her hand to her head.

"Are you all right?" The question was stupid; she was obviously far from being all right.

"I'm fine," Ruth insisted as she took the baby from him. "But I'm grateful we've stopped early today." She gave him a thankful smile.

"Well, you need to thank the Lord special tonight. We have something to eat." Dylan patted his pockets, which bulged with the turnips Mrs. Donaldson had given them.

"Good idea. Maybe we can both thank him."

The suggestion made Dylan uncomfortable, but he saw her point. The Lord—or whoever—had had plenty of chances to do them in, but for some reason decided not to. It had to be because of Ruth's influence, because he still couldn't bring himself to trust in anyone but Dylan McCall. If he let himself down, he had no one to blame but himself. If Ruth's Lord let him down—well, he'd been let down in that way before, and he might not take kindly to the situation now.

Ruth helped him drag the saddle off the horse and wipe the animal down with dry grass before staking her out to graze for the night. The winter spring trickling into a small pool provided sufficient water. After starting a fire, Dylan dipped water into their single pot and peeled the turnips with his pocketknife, while Ruth changed the baby's diaper. He set the pot on the edge of the campfire to boil.

"We should be in Sulphur Springs no later than late tomorrow afternoon, I'd guess."

"Good," Ruth murmured. She lay back against a tree and closed her eyes. The dark circles under her eyes troubled Dylan. She needed a comfortable place to sleep, decent boots, and a hot meal. How had he allowed the situation to get so far out of hand? He should have turned around the moment he'd realized that she was following him and had taken her back to Denver City. If he had, none of this would have happened. He'd have missed the old man and the Indian attack by a good two days, and he wouldn't be here, huddled around a tiny campfire, helpless as a turtle on its back.

But as Sara Dunnigan used to say: If wishes were pickles and *buts* were bread, you'd have a fine sandwich but nothing else.

Ruth got up and unrolled her bed, then collapsed on it in a heap, staring glassy-eyed up at the threatening sky. "I pray we can make it before the weather breaks."

Dylan turned a skeptical eye on the lowering clouds blocking a weak sun. They held snow, and plenty of it. They would be walking knee-deep in the white stuff by the time they reached Sulphur Springs, but he didn't bother to tell Ruth. She had her hands full with the baby tonight. The child seemed fussier than usual although she'd drunk her fill of milk.

As the turnips bubbled over the fire, Ruth roused herself enough to dress his wounds. He saw the hollow look in her eyes and wondered if she was getting sick. That's all they'd need—for both to be incapacitated and leave the baby vulnerable. He set his teeth, sheer will forcing him to remain alert. Wounds that had shown promise of healing yesterday had broken open today and seeped green pus tonight. Ruth shook her head, her eyes solemn as she cleaned the infection and applied the last of the herbs. Her eyes met his, and he wished that he could erase the fear he saw in their depths.

"It's not good, is it?" He asked the obvious.

"No," she whispered.

"One more day," he promised, answering her mute question. "I'll see a doctor when we get to Sulphur Springs."

She nodded, tying off the clean strip of bleached muslin. Ulele had been smart enough to know that the wound must be kept clean, yet all the herbs in the world weren't going to heal these wounds. They'd had such poor care at the first, then had reopened too many times to heal properly. A doctor would have to lance and cauterize the wounds before healing could set in.

Dylan mutely shook his head. Despite his best efforts, disaster had struck. And it would strike again if he didn't do something to prevent it. Sulphur Springs was only a day away. Yet could they make it?

He had never felt so helpless in his life. How he wished that he believed in Ruth's God—had her peaceful assurances that someone besides herself controlled the situation.

They ate the turnips, each huddled separately in a blanket. The baby fell asleep shortly after dark. Ruth tucked her in, using one of Dylan's blankets to protect her in spite of the dropping temperature. She would stay warm in her wool cocoon.

The wind howled, bending towering aspens, rattling their branches like dry bones. The clouds continually lowered and the constant wind spit random flakes into the air. Dylan watched Ruth refuse to acknowledge the worsening conditions. She moved as if she were sleepwalking, until he told her to roll up in the bedroll to get warm.

Every bone in the marshall's body ached tonight. He closed his eyes, willing the pain to ease. It was an old trick he'd learned from a friend. The Kiowa Indian was a scout for an army fort where Dylan had stayed from time to time early in his career. The brave had taught Dylan survival skills, including how to endure pain. Tonight those skills failed him. He'd never been more exhausted or felt more useless. Though he was bone weary, sleep failed to come.

In its place he thought about Ruth and the baby, responsibilities he couldn't shirk despite the growing weakness of his body. For the first time he tasted defeat, and he didn't like the flavor.

He opened his eyes to stare at the sleeping infant cradled in his arms. Long, dark eyelashes feathered across her nut brown skin. Tendrils of black shiny hair framed the little girl's face. This was what fatherhood must be like—staring at the miracle you created with the woman you loved. Dylan had never thought much about being a father; that would come years down the road, if ever. He'd never seriously considered being a parent, taking on a responsibility he couldn't walk away from. But here was responsibility nestled in his arms like a purring kitten. The surprise was, he didn't mind, nor did he mind having Ruth around. Most women got on his nerves with their silly giggles and flighty nature, but Ruth was neither silly nor flighty. Independent as a hog on ice, granted. Set in her ways but not fickle.

The admission amused him.

When had he come to that realization? When had he begun to forget she was a nuisance and start looking forward to her nippy responses, that sudden glow in her cheeks when she knew she'd pushed him too far or had embarrassed herself?

He'd never met a woman he wanted to marry, and he'd met his share of females. Attractions had come along, but it had been surprisingly easy to ride away when the time came to leave.

He glanced across the fire and studied Ruth's form huddled against the cold wind. He'd always walked away easily . . . until she'd happened along. This woman wasn't going to be easy to ride away from—but he would. When it came right down to it, women were all alike—actors, deceivers. He'd learned that from a master. Sara Dunnigan had fooled the world—at least her world. She'd burned with religious fervor, thumping her Bible and predicting the imminent end of the world and telling him he'd better repent of his sins. Every Sunday morning Sara and Dylan were in their place on the hard wooden church pew. Second pew from the front, where the preacher would be sure to see them and know righteous Sara was doing her Christian duty by the child God had put upon her.

The preacher—Dylan couldn't remember the name but he saw the face every night in his boyish nightmares—was a pulpit pounder. Sweat rolled from his temples and his booming voice lifted the rafters when he proclaimed that sinners were going to burn in a pit of fire.

One morning, the man had taken off his coat and beat the pulpit with the homespun fabric, his voice bellowing off the walls. Dylan couldn't have been more than six or seven at the time. Overcome with terror, he suddenly sprang to his feet and hopped up on the pew. He looked at Sara and declared in a voice loud enough to be heard over the brimstone, "Let's go, Sara! That man is angry!"

Sara yanked him by the ear and set him down in the pew. "You sit!" she hissed. "God will punish you for this."

He'd sat for the next hour and a half, cowering and crying, confused and angry. How could God love him and want to hurt him at the same time? Suppose he could punish him. Suppose there was a hell. Dylan didn't know how it all worked, but it sounded terrifying.

When they got home that afternoon, Sara had switched his legs and back with a willow branch until red welts formed. With every strike Sara had reminded him that God was angry, that he didn't like smart-mouthed boys, that God had given him to Sara to teach him righteousness, and she would do her Christian duty by him even if it meant humiliation in front of her neighbors.

That was the day Dylan decided he didn't put much faith in God, couldn't love a God that meted out such harsh judgment on a boy who couldn't understand him or his ways. Dylan's feelings hadn't changed over the years. He'd endured the horsewhippings and verbal abuse, but Sara Dunnigan couldn't beat religion into him. He swore that someday he would be on his own, and he'd never answer to another person. Sara's God would have no say over him.

If there was a God who had made women like Sara Dunnigan, Dylan didn't want anything to do with him, no matter what Ruth said about the deity she believed in.

Ruth's sleepy voice drifted to him across the fire. "Penny for your thoughts."

He stirred, uncomfortable. Had he voiced resentment aloud? "I thought you were asleep."

"I am . . . sort of." She sighed, snuggling deeper into the bag. "You were looking so serious. What were you thinking?"

He closed his eyes. "Nothing." He didn't usually think much about his past, but all this stuff with Ruth and the baby had set him off.

Ruth persisted. "You were thinking something. I could see it. Are you worried?"

"Only a fool wouldn't be."

"That's true," she whispered. "But God will see us through."

"God." He shifted, pulling the blanket tighter. He stared at minuscule flakes whipping the air. Conditions could be worse and he figured "God" was about to prove it. "Don't you ever get angry about Norris taking you back to the orphanage?"

A log snapped in the campfire, sending sparks shooting up like a shower of red stars. He thought Ruth wasn't going to answer the question.

"Anger doesn't do anyone any good. It's taken me a while to get that through my stubborn head, but I finally realized anger only hurts the person experiencing it."

Dylan smiled, thinking of the day he'd first met her. A real spitfire, all explosion and bluster. Had that been only weeks ago? Impossible. It seemed she had been in his life always, and yet the past few days he had started to experience something inside him he thought had died. Hope. The first stirrings of real feeling.

He didn't trust the emotion. He didn't want it; he liked his life. He liked answering only to himself, worrying only about himself and today.

"Tell me about your childhood," she said quietly.

He rolled to his stomach, careful not to disturb the baby. His childhood. Now there was a black page in history.

"Didn't have one."

She laughed softly. "Everyone had one whether they liked it or not. I gather you didn't like yours?"

He thought about the answer, fully aware she wasn't going to give up. She'd find another way to ask the same question.

"I liked part of it. The part when Grandma was alive."

She flipped over and met his gaze across the fire. "You had a good grandma?"

"The best." A smile formed at the corners of his mouth. "Ma and Pa died in a wagon accident coming west. Grandma took me in and raised me until I was six." He hesitated, memories starting to compete with the pain in his shoulder. "The Indian wars were going on then, and a band of renegades rode onto the farm one day. They were hungry and Grandma took them in and fed them. That was her way. She'd take the food off her own plate and give it to a stranger. She sent me to the barn to gather eggs. When I came back, the savages had cut her throat and were sacking up food. I dropped the egg basket and ran as hard as I could. They came after me, but I hid in an old root cellar on a neighbor's property. Sara Dunnigan's root cellar." He laughed humorlessly. "Sara had gone to church that morning or the renegades would have killed her too."

Cynicism seeped into his tone. "Pity that her life was spared. Sara found me the next day still huddled in the cellar. She took me to raise because there wasn't anyone else to do it. She was alone, set in her ways."

Dylan paused, aware he had just told Ruth more than he'd ever told another human being. There was something about her that drew the truth from him, truth that he never intended anyone to know.

"Did she mistreat you?"

He stared up into the black sky, scenes flashing through his mind like a succession of painted pictures: A redfaced Sara with a belt in her hand. Sara making him roll out of bed long before daybreak to hoe and plant, milk the cow, then work in the cornfield under a blazing sun. Sara yelling, threatening, berating him morning, noon, and night until her voice rang in his head like a drumbeat.

"I hated her." He heard Ruth's small gasp and realized that this was the first time he'd ever spoken about it out loud. He hated Sara, simple as that. Nothing about the feeling fazed him; he'd lived with hate for so many years, he'd hardened himself against the sentiment and what it could do to a man. He was content to let the emotion fester and taint his life without ridding himself of the pain. He would never rid himself of the memory of Sara Dunnigan.

"I spent my childhood figuring how to get away from her. When I was fifteen, I escaped and never looked back."

"Oh, my goodness."

Ruth's tone held pity. He didn't want pity. Yet he couldn't keep from telling Ruth more about the evil woman draped in "Christian love and duty." He'd heard her brag to others about her own generosity and goodness of heart—about how she'd taken in the McCall boy, fed and clothed him, "though goodness knows I'm just living hand to mouth myself," she'd say. Given him a pallet and a place at her table was all she'd done, and she'd done that grudgingly. She'd never shown one ounce of love or compassion toward him. He grew up with a willow switch at his backside and the guilt that he was a burden Sara felt forced to bear. With Sara and her friends as examples, God-fearing women had come to mean one thing to Dylan: hypocrisy.

After spilling his bitterness over Sara Dunnigan, Dylan fell silent. He thought of how different Ruth was. In getting to know Ruth, he witnessed a strong faith of a seemingly different stripe. . . .

He mentally shook the thought away. Ruth had tricked him. She wasn't Sara, but she had lied to him. She'd tried to bend him to her will, just like Sara did. Ruth was a contradiction within herself. One part of her was giving and kind, another part as manipulative as Sara had ever been. Well, he'd been fooled by women before, but not lately. Ruth would need more accomplished wiles than he'd seen so far if she intended to coerce him into doing anything he didn't want to do.

Beware, Dylan. Women are still all alike even though the one on the other side of the fire stirs a longing in you that you never knew you had.

"It's late." He shifted to his opposite side. They lay in the darkness with only the popping fire breaking the strained silence. He wondered what she was thinking. He wished he'd never mentioned Sara or his past. Now Ruth would be trying to pry information from him, and there was nothing more to tell. She seemed to think that sharing information was important, like the girls on the wagon train had done with each other. Ruth had prodded Glory until she learned all about Uncle Amos and the gold and how Poppy had died. Glory had embraced Ruth's friendship and caring like a hungry pup, and she'd become a part of the "family" of women.

But Dylan wasn't part of the family; he wasn't part of any family. He was a loner, and that's how he wanted to keep it. He wasn't going to be swayed by Ruth's plight, even though he suspected her childhood couldn't have been any better than his.

"I'm sorry, but I want you to know that I care about you. In a friendly way, of course." She had spoken so softly he wasn't sure she'd spoken at all or if his imagination was working overtime.

"Dylan, did you hear me?"

He closed his eyes. "Go to sleep, Ruth. This snow is going to come down hard by morning, and the walk will take more energy."

"But I am sorry, Dylan. I'm sorry that a woman like Sara gives religion a black eye. Most likely she believed that she was doing the right thing, but obviously she didn't know the God I worship. He is a God of love and certainly a God to be feared and respected. But he chastens as a loving father, not a vindictive tyrant. Some read the Good Book and try to accept the Word, but deep down they're not willing to let God's Spirit abide in them.

"I make no excuses for Sara. What she did to a vulnerable young boy is inexcusable, but that rests on her soul. My concern is why you let evil continue to ruin your life. Sara will be held accountable and have to face her mistakes. You are responsible for your own errors."

Preachy women drove Dylan crazy. "No sermons." He'd had enough of those to last a lifetime. Empty words meant nothing. "I'm going to sleep now, Ruth. You can stay up and talk all night if you want."

"The Lord loves you, Dylan. You can fight the knowledge all you want. Whether you accept it or not, it won't change how he feels about you."

"Good night, Ruth."

"Good night, hardhead."

Ruth stared into the fire, thinking how differently life had treated both of them and how differently they looked at life as a result. Dylan absorbed the hurt and let it isolate him from everything and everyone around him. He had built steel barriers around his heart, afraid to let himself care about anyone or anything other than his job. For a moment—just a moment—Ruth let herself resent the woman who'd done this to Dylan. He was a fine man, but a man who couldn't give of himself for fear of being hurt; and that woman, in her zealousness, had taught him hate without realizing it.

Ruth tried to imagine fifteen-year-old Dylan going out into the world to make his own way. She wondered what he'd done between that age and when he'd become a marshall. Had anyone cared about him? Had he ever allowed anyone to get close? Her heart ached for the marshall, for the blessings he'd missed by daily living with bitterness toward Sara Dunnigan—and mistrust toward women in general. He had to put aside that bitterness and accept that not all who professed to follow God knew the truth of his love. Truth is precious, enlightening, and enriching. Truth in the heart crowds out hate and bitterness. *And ye shall know the truth, and the truth shall make you free.*

She'd experienced that freedom. When Edgar Norris had taken her back to the orphanage, she'd hated him for abandoning her. She'd railed against the unfairness of losing parents not once but twice. She'd blamed God for forgetting about her. But Mrs. Galeen had refused to let her wallow in self-pity or blame God. For a long time Ruth had refused to accept the guardian's insistence that God had a plan for her life and all she needed to do was let him unfold it before her. Over time, by giving of herself to others, Ruth had learned to let go of her bitterness and count her blessings. Dylan had not had anyone in his life to encourage him, to teach him God's ways. As a result, he saw only what he'd lost.

"I always wanted parents," she whispered. She knew Dylan heard, but would he answer? "Someone to take care of me." In the firelight, she saw his face was still set with bitterness even though his eyes were shut.

"When my parents died, that was bad. But I was found by two kind Indians who knew of the orphanage. They didn't take me to their people, where my future wouldn't have been certain. They took me to the orphanage, which was a good thing.

"Then Edgar and Beatrice Norris came to the orphanage, seeking a child. They were both teachers. I went to live with them, and I remember them fondly. Beatrice was so pretty." Ruth turned on her side, her thoughts going back many years. "The Norrises taught me to read and write and to appreciate books. That was a blessing. But Beatrice died and Edgar was so grief stricken that . . . well, he couldn't stay at the school that held so many memories of her."

"But you hated him for taking you back to the orphanage." Dylan's voice intruded on her musings.

"I did," she admitted. "For a while, but then I saw that I was needed at the orphanage. I helped take care of the little ones, read to them, taught them their letters and numbers, helped them with their lessons when they started school."

"So you made yourself believe that his abandoning you was a good thing."

Ruth observed him in the firelight. "Yes, I suppose I did. But it was better than hating him. Hate hurts only the one hating, not the one it's directed toward. It's a waste of effort."

She could see he was skeptical.

"I don't suppose you could put a good spin on old Oscar's proposal?"

Ruth had to grin. "No, I can't quite get around that one. But I do have to wonder what God wanted me to do about Oscar. Maybe he wanted me to marry the old prospector, and I refused to obey. If so, I will be the loser, not God."

Pessimism was apparent in the marshall's tone. "Why would God want you to marry a man old enough to be your grandpa, an old coot that chews and might take a bath twice a year?"

Ruth suppressed a shiver. "I don't know. I didn't bother to ask God, and that was wrong."

"I don't know about a God who would want to give a pretty young woman to an old codger," Dylan said. "That seems a little unfair—not only to the woman but to the man."

"There could be a reason," Ruth contended. "After all, I'm not someone who will probably ever have a family."

"Why not?"

"I . . . I can't have children." She whispered the words, saying them aloud for the first time. "A man wants a family—children—and I can't give a husband children."

Dylan didn't answer for a long time. Ruth was certain his reaction was what any man's would be—aversion. An unexpected sadness, a sense of having lost something special, flooded her, and she blinked back tears. Why had she told the marshall something so personal? She felt like a complete fool.

"If a man's in the market for kids, then you may have a point. But if a man's looking for someone to spend his life with, then the problem shouldn't get in the way."

Ruth blinked with surprise. How like Dylan to put something so painful so simply. She swallowed back a cry of gratitude. "You . . . you really think so?"

"I know so. Most men want to find the right woman, not a broodmare."

A light popped on inside her that she didn't recognize—a kind of blossoming of hope. "Well, guess you would know, you being a man."

"Go to sleep, Ruth. Tomorrow is a long day of walking."

"You're right." But she would sleep better tonight knowing that not all men would find her condition appalling. Why, maybe someday, through God's grace, the Lord would reveal such a man to her.

She snuggled into her blankets and closed her eyes. Then they popped open wide. Maybe God already had, and it was Dylan!

She couldn't let nagging doubt override her earlier joy. If Dylan was right and not all men looked at a woman with the idea of producing children, then perhaps she had a chance of marrying one day, having a home of her own. . . . She wouldn't allow herself to think about Dylan, to wish—

No. Better go to sleep and keep such nonsense where it belonged: in the wishful-thinking drawer.

"Ruth?"

She turned, sitting up halfway. "Yes?"

"How do you know your last name is Priggish if you were orphaned at a young age?"

"My father's Bible. The Indian braves brought it with them. My father's name was written in the front: *Harold Priggish.* I don't know my mother's name."

Chapter Eleven

Dylan opened his eyes to the sight of snow coming down in blowing sheets. The baby reached out to capture a flake and giggled. Her dark brown eyes shone like a child's on Christmas morning as Dylan handed her to Ruth. A large snowflake lit on the end of the baby's nose, and she looked cross-eyed at the marvel.

Dylan grinned. "She's real cute, isn't she?" Carefully feeding the coals dry leaves, then twigs that he'd dug out from beneath the snow, he soon had a fair fire going.

"The cutest." Ruth touched her nose to the child's. "The very cutest."

"We need something hot in our bellies. I'll warm the milk for the baby."

"All right."

Dylan turned to glance over his shoulder when she didn't move. "Ruth, we've got to get moving."

She drew the baby close, hugging her tightly. "What if I can't? I can barely feel my feet this morning."

Dylan felt his stomach twist with fear. What would he do if she couldn't walk? He squatted in front of her. "We can't give up now. We're going to make it to Sulphur Springs by nightfall."

As he searched her face, he could see that she struggled to believe him. He suddenly wished he had the time or energy to shave. He scratched the prickly growth of beard and realized why he'd never grown a beard before. It itched.

"I'll boil some coffee. That'll make you feel better," he said.

"Do we have any left?"

"Enough for breakfast." He broke ice at the water's edge and filled a coffeepot with water, and then tossed in the last of the grounds and set it on the fire.

Ruth drew her blankets closer to the warmth and changed the baby's wet clothes, hurrying since she was putting up a fuss about the cold air on her skin. Afterward, she fed the baby half the milk that was left in the canteen. Dylan and Ruth drank their coffee in silence while Ruth jiggled the fussy baby.

As gray dawn broke over the mountains, they mounted up, knowing the horse was about played out and needed a good meal and dry shelter as much as they did.

The early morning passed without a single word between them. Ruth tried to pacify the baby. When the little girl finally fell asleep, Dylan could feel Ruth relax against his back.

Midmorning, a speck materialized in the distance. The rocky terrain had leveled to better footing. A small wagon with two figures on the driver's seat appeared. As they neared, Dylan saw a man and a woman dressed in dark clothing. The woman sat close to the man, eyeing the approaching horse with wide, apprehensive eyes.

"Hallo there," the young man called, drawing the wagon to a halt. "Didn't expect to see anyone out here in the storm."

"Neither did we," Dylan confessed. Ruth's free arm tightened around his waist with silent warning. They'd met Nehemiah Ford this same way and look where it had gotten them. Dylan discreetly loosened her grip before inquiring, "How far to Sulphur Springs?"

"Oh, just a couple miles. Should get there this afternoon, but the snow will slow you down if it gets any heavier."

"We plan to make it," Dylan assured him.

"We're gettin' ourselves to home before it sets in for the night," the young man said. He stood up to peer at the bundle Ruth carried. "What's that you got there? A baby?"

Dylan glanced over his shoulder at Ruth. This couple was young—sturdy. The woman looked thin, but kind enough. The child was cold and hungry; she needed solid food, a warm bed, care—care he and Ruth were not able to give. If they didn't reach Sulphur Springs soon, the child would sicken, perhaps die. His uncertainties reflected in Ruth's eyes. Could this couple be the answer to the baby's needs? Would they be willing to love and care for her, give her the things a child needed to grow strong and healthy?

"Is that an Indian baby?"

"Yes," Dylan confirmed.

The man sat back down, suspicion blooming in his eyes. "Where'd you come up with an Indian baby?"

"Found her in a burning wagon."

Dylan didn't think the couple needed to know the particulars of how they'd come in possession of the little girl. He looked at Ruth again and wondered what she thought. Prospective parents? But they didn't know anything about this couple—they could be fugitives from the law for all Dylan knew. The man had shifty eyes. . . .

And on closer inspection, the woman looked frail—in no condition to care for a small baby. Where were the couple's children? Home, unattended, while their ma and pa rode about the countryside on a snowy day? That was highly unusual—folks out in a snowstorm when they should be home looking after the family—

Ruth broke into Dylan's thoughts when she gently nudged him to ride on.

"We'd better be on our way if we're going to make town before dusk," Dylan said.

"Good luck to you then." The man slapped the reins against the horse's rump and with a wave moved on past.

"I didn't like them," Ruth said quietly. "I think they would have traded the baby or passed her on to someone else as soon as we were out of sight because she's Indian."

"I didn't trust them either."

Dylan urged the horse through deepening snowdrifts as they continued their journey. At noon Ruth fed the baby the last of the milk. Dylan recognized her feeling of helplessness because her face mirrored his own. As each hour passed without a sign of the settlement, he grew more troubled. Snow swirled around them, thicker than before, and Dylan began to seriously doubt that they'd make town before they froze to death. Death was a real possibility, he knew. This was a foolish journey and he was the chief fool.

"Are we going to make it?" Ruth's question was quietly spoken, which gave her fear more weight.

"I don't even know if we're going the right direction anymore," he admitted.

"Oh, God, help us. You're our only hope," Ruth breathed.

Dylan set his jaw. Only Ruth's God knew where they were or if they would make it. For the first time in his life, he couldn't depend on his own conviction and abilities to carry them through a dangerous situation. For the first time since he was fifteen years old he was thinking—hoping—that God was there, that he had his eye on them. Dylan wondered if he was losing his mind, thinking about God and asking for his help. Still, with his head bent into the blowing snow, he silently asked that for Ruth's sake, God might spare her and the innocent child. What happened to him didn't matter; what happened to Ruth and the baby mattered a lot.

If you're there, help her, Lord, because I can't.

Toward dusk, Dylan was certain that Ruth's Lord was as fickle as Sara Dunnigan's. Both he and Ruth had lost feeling in their hands and feet. Ruth's face would be frostbitten if they remained outside a half hour longer.

Look, God, if you're going to show your hand, do it now. I don't ask anything for myself. I deserve my own fate, but it's not fair to let the woman and child die—

Dylan's thoughts broke off abruptly when he spotted a light in the distance. The glow was dim, but it was a light. Sulphur Springs. They had made it! "There it is," he shouted to Ruth above the howling wind. "There's the town!"

Her feeble grip tightened on his shoulder. "Thank you, Father."

Yeah, Dylan thought as he urged the horse through a drift. *Much obliged. I owe you one.* For the first time in his life, something warm stirred inside him, and he didn't have a name for it.

⁓

Ruth stretched out on a feather mattress, exhaustion invading every limb. Transfixed, she stared at the ceiling, reliving the sheer bliss of soaking in warm water up to her neck. She'd sat in the porcelain tub in the bathroom at the end of the hall for over an hour—until feeling returned to her hands and feet.

Dear God, thank you for your grace, she murmured, for she knew full well that it was only his grace that had brought them this far.

Outside the boardinghouse window, snow continued to fall heavily, mounting on branches and porch railings. Wind howled through alleyways, battering storefronts on Main Street.

At first Ruth had thought she was hallucinating when she'd spotted the outcropping that appeared to be in the middle of the road. The horse was laboring heavily under their weight as they plowed through deepening snow. Once she had suggested that they get off and give the horse a rest, but Dylan had said that was a sure way to die. So they kept moving. The mare had earned a dry stall and the dinner of sweet prairie hay she was now enjoying.

Ruth had resolutely prepared to die in the blizzard. Dylan had taken the baby from her and cuddled the infant inside his coat, grief visible on his frozen features. Ruth had heard his halting prayer for help become a litany. When she'd recognized that he was praying, pure elation filled her. Then fear, the likes of which she'd never known, took over. If Dylan was scared, that meant her mounting anxiety wasn't groundless.

Yet she had refused to give in to panic. Dylan had made the long trip from Colorado to Wyoming more than once, he'd reminded her. But never in winter, and never with an infant and a woman to look after. Or a grave wound in his shoulder. As wind shrieked and snow blew in random bursts, they had pushed on.

Ruth sighed, closing her eyes. She was safe in a warm bed now, wearing one of Annabelle's long, flannel nightgowns that smelled of soap and had been warmed on the woodstove. Images of snow still whirled through her head as she recalled entering Sulphur Springs.

The first building they'd seen happened to be the livery stable. They'd pounded on the wide doors until they roused someone. The door eventually opened, and a small round man with a long white beard and twinkling blue eyes appeared. "Why, he looks like Santa Claus," Ruth had marveled. Eyes widened below the white bushy brows, the friendly man ushered in the nearly frozen strangers. Later Tom Ferry, the town blacksmith, bundled up tightly against the blowing storm, had walked the shivering travelers to the boardinghouse.

Sulphur Springs didn't have such an establishment until last year, proprietor Niles Seaton had explained. Two years ago the town was chosen by Welborne & Sutton Stage Lines as an overnight way station—provided the Seatons turned their residence into a boardinghouse. The town council liked the idea of the stage coming through town, so Niles and his wife, Annabelle, had done a little remodeling and created this right nice place for weary travelers. Folks would spend the night in a spacious bedroom, and the next morning Annabelle Seaton would send them on their way with a hot meal and a friendly smile.

Mrs. Seaton was a solemn woman who had stoically gone about heating water for the weary guests. She mixed oatmeal in a pan of warm milk and fed the baby. The thin, spry woman had offered little in the way of chatty conversation, but Ruth was ever so grateful for the woman's hospitality. Both Niles and Annabelle saw to the guests' immediate needs and never asked about their circumstances other than to offer them comfortable rooms. Neither Ruth nor Dylan had explained why two rooms were necessary; Ruth guessed she should do that in the morning when she was thinking more clearly.

Ruth settled into the bed, drinking in the smell of clean linens. Pot roast and rich brown gravy filled her stomach. She felt so drowsy she could hardly stay awake long enough to properly thank God for sparing them. She remembered how Annabelle had insisted that she and Dylan have a hot meal, a warm bath, and go right to bed.

"I'm too weary to argue," Ruth said. "Thank you . . . thank you so much."

Annabelle nodded. "I'll lay out towels and soap."

Over Dylan's protest, Ruth had insisted that he bathe, be cared for, and put to bed first. That he allowed her to win the argument attested to his grave condition.

The town didn't have a doctor, but at Niles's request Tom Ferry went to fetch a Mrs. Fallaby to look after Dylan's injuries. Gert Fallaby had breezed into the room on a gust of cold air, her hearty laugh filling the boardinghouse. After she examined Dylan's wounds, she clicked her tongue and shook her head, then cleaned the aggravated wounds and applied a vile-smelling salve. Ignoring Dylan's skeptical looks, Gert made him open his mouth, and she administered a large teaspoon of laudanum for his pain.

Twisting the cap back on the bottle, she grinned. "That ought to hold you a spell."

"I hope it's nothing like Ulele's locoweed," Dylan muttered.

Gert only smiled. "Let's just say you won't be feelin' much of anything until morning."

Ruth was so thankful Dylan would spend a night free of pain. So thankful. . . . Now he was resting comfortably down the hall from her room. She gratefully pressed both feet against the hot-water bottle Annabelle had thoughtfully placed beneath the covers and thought she'd never be cold again.

Her thoughts started to blur . . . screeching wind, blowing snow . . . anxiety deeply etched on Dylan's wind-chapped features. She knew most of his concern had been for the baby, yet the thought that he might, deep down, harbor a tiny speck of concern for her wasn't entirely impossible. Since leaving the Fords' he'd been kind and tolerant, barking at her far less than before. She opened her eyes and looked at the little girl sleeping next to her. She seemed none the worse for wear, now that she was warm, dry, and fed. *Thank you, God.*

Sighing, Ruth slid deeper into the goose-down mattress and smiled. For the briefest of moments, she pretended that God had made a rare mistake. She *should* have babies and a loving husband. She *should* love someone here on earth she could truly trust—trust to protect and care for her. Someone like Dylan. Someone like this precious child.

Her lids grew heavier. Annabelle had brought clean clothes for the baby, explaining they were outfits her grandchild had outgrown. Ruth had once more been moved to tears as she'd dressed the child in the flannel gown and crocheted booties. Compared to Ulele, Annabelle was an angel—albeit not a very talkative one.

Ruth was unable to keep her eyes open. Sleet pinged against the windowpane, peppering the glass. They could have been out there in the storm. They could have frozen to death on the outskirts of Sulphur Springs.

Yet she was very much alive, lying here beside the baby. Dylan was sleeping two doors down. Her heart overflowed with gratitude; she hardly knew how to thank God. Dylan wasn't in pain, the baby was safe, her belly was full, she was clean, and she was sleeping in a wonderfully warm bed tonight.

For the moment, life was good. *No, Lord,* she amended. *Good* was such an inadequate word that it seemed close to a complaint, and she didn't have a thing in the world to complain about.

Life was perfect. The words of a psalm floated into her head as Ruth drifted off to sleep: *"Bless the Lord, O my soul: and all that is within me, bless his holy name. Bless the Lord, O my soul, and forget not all his benefits."*

⌒

Ruth didn't stir until well after sunup. She woke to the sound of the baby cooing at her own fingers. Ruth pushed back the mound of covers and bent over the baby snuggled against her. The infant stared up at her with affectionate, dark eyes. Giggling and kicking, she happily thrashed her arms when Ruth stroked her brown cheek with the back of her finger.

"Yes, you just think you're a big girl, don't you?" Ruth cooed. She tickled the baby's tummy. "Yes, you are; yes, you *are.* You're a cutie."

She caught herself up short. A hot flush crept up her neck when she realized she was acting like a silly goose. For heaven's sake! Shaking her head, Ruth rolled out of bed and yelped when her bare feet hit the icy floor. The baby giggled, waving her fists.

"You think that's funny, huh?" Ruth tickled the little girl's tummy. "Well, maybe I'll just put your feet on the icy floor!" In a moment she had the baby laughing out loud. Her uninhibited giggles made Ruth laugh. A knock sounded at the door. She jerked upright at the sound of Dylan's voice.

"Ruth?"

Ruth hesitated. "Yes?"

"Is the baby all right? What's going on in there?"

"We're both fine. Why?" He'd heard! He'd heard her making a fool of herself! The flush grew hotter.

"Breakfast is on the table."

Clearing her throat, Ruth kept her tone neutral. "I'll be right down."

She dressed and entered the kitchen fifteen minutes later. She avoided Dylan's amused gaze and walked to the stove to spoon up a bowl of oatmeal for the baby. Dylan was dressed in clean clothing, freshly shaven, and looking incredibly handsome for a man who had spent the last weeks fighting off death. Annabelle and Niles were nowhere in sight this morning.

Dylan poured two cups of strong black coffee. "Sleep well?"

Ruth nodded, afraid to look at him. He'd be likely to ask what all the laughing had been about, and she didn't want to explain.

"Very well. And you?" She perched the baby on her lap and began feeding her small spoonfuls of oatmeal, resisting the urge to giggle out loud at the sweet smacking sounds she made after each bite.

"I didn't know a thing until this morning." He moved his right arm, then his left, working the stiffness in his shoulder loose. He focused on the little girl. "Did she sleep all night?"

"She never woke once, and she slept late this morning."

Dylan grinned. "That's good. Cream?"

Ruth nodded. Cream. Such luxury! "And two sugars, please."

Dylan ladled sugar, then poured cream into her coffee and set the cup in front of her. "I was talking to Mr. Seaton earlier. The storm has shut everything down, but he says Ed French can use me a week or so at the mercantile to build new shelves. They need to be able to stock more for the winter, though folks say it looks to be a mild one. Since we're not going anywhere until the passes clear, I thought I'd take the opportunity to make up for the money we lost with the Fords, before we move on."

Ruth looked up. "Are you able?" She thought he might be the only one leaving.

He shrugged. "The wound is healing." He grinned as he spread thick molasses on a biscuit. When a drop slipped onto his finger, he leaned forward to let the baby lick it off. His grin widened when she giggled and wiggled two chubby fingers to signal she wanted more.

Ruth grinned too. "I think that's a very sound idea." She took a sip of coffee, still refusing to meet his eyes, though she did glance at him quickly. "Very noble of you." Could that be relief she saw in his eyes?

"We'll stay until the weather breaks—those passes are snow blocked now. Meanwhile we'll ask around and maybe come up with a home for the child."

She broke into another smile. "That sounds good to me." She kept the smile in place even though her mind rebelled at the thought of ever walking away from the child. Could she do it? She *had* to do it. She had no way to care for this child. She needed a mother and a father, a couple with the wherewithal to rear a child.

"Dylan," she said softly, gazing at the little girl in her lap.

"Yes?"

"Could we name her?" She looked up, and her next words tumbled out. "I mean, most folks would expect a baby this old to have a name, and we can't keep calling her 'her' and 'child' and 'baby'."

Dylan concentrated on his coffee. "I'm sure she has a name, Ruth."

"Probably, but we don't know what it is, and she's too young to tell us." Warming to the idea, Ruth covered his hand with hers. The simple touch sent ripples of warmth up her arm. "Please, Dylan. Let's name her."

The idea seemed to set with him. He smiled and looked at their hands. "What do you have in mind?"

"Rose," she announced. "Look—her mouth is like a tiny little rosebud."

Dylan peered at the child. "Rose? That's sort of frilly, isn't it? What about Maude? There's a good, solid woman's name."

Ruth shook her head pensively. "She doesn't look like a Maude."

"Really?" Dylan studied the baby. "Well, maybe not . . ."

"Rose. Rose Priggish McCall."

Doubt crossed the marshall's features. "McCall?"

"Why not? Rose—for her. Priggish—my last name. And McCall—

your last name. Whoever takes her will change her name anyway." Ruth lifted the little girl above her head, the playful action resulting in a cackling drool. "Hello, Miss Rose Priggish McCall. Now you have a name just like the rest of us. In dat *sweet?*" She glanced up, embarrassed. "Isn't that nice?" she amended in an adult tone.

"Yeah," Dylan agreed, "dat's *weal* sweet. Yesitis, yesitis," he teased. Tickling the baby's tummy, he stepped back and admired his namesake. "What do you know? I'm a daddy."

Ruth grinned smugly. *Yeah,* she thought. *And for a short time, I am a mommy.*

The snow tapered off by late afternoon. Ruth pulled the lacy parlor curtain back and looked out the front window. She counted twenty-five long, thin icicles hanging from the roof. It was still cold as a banker's heart and that made the hospitality of Niles and Annabelle even more welcome. She didn't know when she'd been more comfortable, and the warm bath yesterday made her want a second one soon.

How strange that the long trek into Colorado had awakened in her the realization that simple, everyday things like feeling clean and warm constituted a luxury when one had been without them for a period.

Annabelle bustled into the kitchen carrying a load of linens. She smiled when she saw Ruth. "You got a fine family, Ruth—a real nice husband. Most men wouldn't function with the marshall's injuries. But he's over at the mercantile doing what he can."

Ruth nodded absently. "He's a strong man."

Annabelle stored the sheets in a side drawer of a bureau and closed the door. "Been married long?"

Ruth went silent. She couldn't lie to the woman; the Seatons had been too good to them, and besides, she wasn't going to ever lie again. Lying didn't pay; goodness knows she'd learned that, if nothing else.

"We're not married, Mrs. Seaton."

The woman turned, censure mirroring in her eyes.

Ruth hastened to explain the situation and ended by saying, "The marshall is escorting me to Wyoming, where I hope to locate a distant cousin. Mr. McCall has been the embodiment of a gentleman, although at times I've been quite a trial to put up with, I'm sure."

Annabelle nodded. "Don't surprise me. I can read a man like a book, and I was telling Niles this morning that Dylan McCall is a fine soul." She paused behind Ruth's chair to rest her hands on the young woman's shoulders. "Don't let him get away, honey. If you're lucky enough to find a man like McCall in your lifetime, don't play coy."

Ruth smiled sadly. "He doesn't love me, Mrs. Seaton. He's deeply fond of the baby and he protects me with his life, but he isn't a man looking to settle down. Not now and most certainly not with a willful, foolish girl who tricked him into taking her to Wyoming, who nearly cost him his life."

Annabelle's clasp tightened. "Don't know about the willful part—you'll have to answer that—but I'd say there's nothing foolish about you, my dear. Otherwise, you wouldn't be here. It takes a hearty soul to survive in these mountains, and it looks like you and the marshall have pulled it off." Annabelle left the room, bustling toward the stairway.

Ruth was sitting at the kitchen table drinking a cup of hot tea when the back door opened and Dylan came in. He stamped his feet and wiped his boots on the woven rug inside the door. "Hi."

"Hi."

"Sent my boss a telegram." He winced as he shrugged out of his coat. "Told him where we are." He poured himself a cup of coffee from the pot on the stove.

"Is he angry with you?"

Dylan shrugged and sat down opposite her. "No. Kurt wired me back immediately. He says he knows travel is dangerous right now, but Dreck Parson's leaving a trail a mile wide. If I don't get to Utah soon, though, I'm going to be too far behind him to catch him." His features sobered. "I don't know if I can let that happen, Ruth."

She leaned closer, her eyes shadowed with concern. "Of course not—we'll leave immediately."

He reached out to cover her hand with his large one. The contact sent an electrical current through her—like lightning on a hot summer day. "I'm torn. I've worked hard on the Parson case, and I don't want to lose Dreck. But I don't want to endanger you or Rose any further. Can you understand?"

She nodded. "We made it this far, Dylan. I'm not afraid."

Her concern was much larger than physical danger: Dylan's inability to accept and trust the Lord. She could never marry a man and be un-equally yoked. Of course marriage was the last thing on Dylan's mind, but the idea had started to crouch in the back of hers—like a hungry lion. How could she walk away from this man? Yet how could she fall in love with a nonbeliever?

"I think you should stay here. You'd be safe—and so would Rose."

Ruth shook her head. "I've already asked. Mrs. Seaton says there isn't any work for me in town—that even the residents are having a hard time keeping food on the table. If I stayed, the baby and I would surely be a burden—and I'm not willing to impose like that."

"But the weather, Ruth. It's not safe. We almost died yesterday. I can't put you and Rose in danger again."

She closed her eyes. *Lord, what on earth do I do? There's nothing for me in Sulphur Springs. How can I just let Dylan walk away?*

After a few moments, Dylan said quietly, "I asked around and found out there's another town not too far from here that's bigger and more prosperous because there's gold there. Perhaps you can find work in Deer Lick. And a home for Rose. We can set off as soon as the weather clears and we're strong enough to travel. I don't see any other way, Ruth."

Ruth nodded mutely. As usual, God wasn't giving her more than the next step of the way. "The weather will break—you'll see. And if I can't find work in the next town . . . I might just follow you all the way to Wyoming, Marshall McCall."

Dylan grinned. "I just can't seem to get rid of you, can I?" They gazed at each other for a moment. What was that she saw in his eyes?

Dylan broke contact and glanced over her shoulder. "Where's Rose?"

"Asleep." Ruth stretched like a lazy cat. "I wanted to just sit and enjoy a cup of tea. Is that silly?"

He smiled, and it hit her anew how wonderful he really was. Dylan McCall was an attractive man, even with his flaws. He was stubborn and single-minded, but he could be caring too. He had made sure nothing happened to her on the trail even though she thought she was alone. The whole time, Dylan had her in his scope much like God kept her in his sights. That suggested a man who cared, whether he wanted to admit it or not.

"No, that's not silly," he said. "But I'm concerned about you, if you travel on with me any farther. We have a chance to end this right now with your reputation still intact."

She bit her lower lip. "We both know that nothing indecent is going on. I'll dress like a boy again. We can go into town separately." Her gaze met his. "I can't stay here, Dylan. I don't know whether God has something for me in Deer Lick or in Wyoming, but I do know I want to move on with you. Please, Dylan."

Dylan sighed. "I know you, Ruth. If you have a mind to follow me,

I wouldn't be able to stop you. I don't think I can take the strain." He grinned. "All right. We'll set off in a day or two, as soon as we're rested up."

She nodded and changed the subject. "Did you have Mrs. Fallaby look at your injuries again?"

"Not yet. I was over at the mercantile. I'll start on the shelves soon."

"Be careful—"

"—you still have infection," he finished for her. He took a drink of scalding coffee. "If you're set on worrying, worry about yourself. How are those feet?"

She glanced down at her toes encased in the soft slippers Annabelle Seaton had supplied. The blisters were better—much better now that she could stay off her feet. "They'll be as good as new in a few days. And you're the sickest." She reached to lay the back of her fingers against his face. "I would wager that you've got a fever right now."

He seemed comfortable with her touch. Embarrassed, she felt her cheeks warm. What was she thinking? He could take care of himself, except that she wanted to take care of him so badly it hurt. But the marshall wouldn't want that. He was a solitary man; he'd made that clear.

Ruth got up from the table and busied herself at the counter. "Perhaps before we go we can ask around and see who can take . . . who would want Rose." Giving an Indian baby away wouldn't be easy. There was a lot of prejudice in the world.

"I mentioned that to Annabelle. She said she would ask around. There's a specific couple who might be interested in taking her," Dylan informed her.

"Oh," Ruth said faintly. *It's the right thing,* she told herself. *The only fair solution for what's best for Rose.*

When the door opened again, ushering in another burst of cold air, they both looked up.

"Well, well, you two look better," Niles boomed.

After he unwound his bright red muffler, he pulled off his gloves and jammed them into his coat pocket. He shrugged out of his coat and hung it on a peg.

"It's amazing what a good night's sleep and a bath will do for a man," Dylan said.

"Saw Gert a minute ago. Said for you to come on down and let her look at those arrow wounds again."

Dylan got up and set his cup in the sink, then began putting on his

143

coat. Noting the difficulty he was having, Ruth went over and helped him, though the marshall looked a little self-conscious about needing help.

"Want me to go with you?" Ruth offered.

"No," he said, "you stay with Rose."

"Oh, th' missus said she'd already talked to the Carsons about taking Rose. They thought they might like to consider it," Niles said.

"Oh," Ruth managed, "that's good. Your wife hadn't mentioned the Carsons earlier—I'll talk to Mrs. Seaton about it later. She said she was going to the church."

"Yes, decorating for a wedding, you know. Nice young couple. Known them all their lives."

Apparently Annabelle Seaton was a pillar of the community in spite of her quietness. Of course, it wasn't every day three frozen strangers materialized out of a snowstorm. This morning Annabelle was as friendly as Ruth could have asked.

"Yes, she told me," Ruth said to Niles.

She felt distracted, as if she couldn't concentrate properly, and she didn't know why. Rose needed a home. A real home. And if Annabelle had found a good family, well, that was good.

Dylan opened the door. "I'll be back later."

"Yes," Ruth said absently. "Have Gert make sure you have no infection."

He gave her a tolerant grin. "I'll do that."

As the door closed, Ruth heard Rose start to awaken. She hurried out of the kitchen to see about her. Annabelle had pulled out a spare drawer to make a bed for the baby and promised to look for a more appropriate crib today. Ruth was afraid Rose would crawl out of the cramped space.

Rose had a wet diaper, so Ruth quickly changed her, grateful that Annabelle had provided the luxury of diapers. She hugged Rose close, enjoying the baby's clean scent. Her heart ached. Rose needed parents—real parents—but Ruth was going to miss holding her little body close.

"I bet you'd like some milk," she murmured.

Since they'd reached Sulphur Springs, Rose wanted to eat all the time.

"Making up for all those weeks when you had so little, are you?" Ruth said softly. She laughed when Rose gurgled happily, but guilt assailed her. When they moved on, would the baby go hungry again—

and cold? Ruth sat at the kitchen table, holding the cup, avoiding Rose's efforts to grab it. Soon the little girl settled down and drank the milk.

"Oh, Ruth," Annabelle said as she came in later, her cheeks rosy. "I forgot to tell you. I found a couple who might like to have Rose."

Ruth knew she should be elated, but she just felt empty.

"The Carsons. Henry and Clara have no children. They're about . . . well . . . forty, perhaps. It's so hard to tell," Annabelle finished, reaching to brush a work-worn hand across Rose's hair. "I don't think I've ever seen a child who enjoyed milk so much," she said. "It's good to see her contented."

Nodding, Ruth ignored the moisture suddenly filling her eyes. "Tell me about the Carsons."

"Oh, they're fine, churchgoing people. Wanted children for years but none seem to come along. Henry breaks horses for a living. There's a real need out here, you know. In fact, they've got a bunch of horses in the corrals right now. Got some for sale," Annabelle said.

Once Annabelle warmed up she was actually rather chatty.

"What is Mrs. Carson like?" Ruth asked.

"Well . . . Clara's a hard woman to get to know." Annabelle poked up the kitchen fire in preparation for the evening meal.

"Why is that?"

"She's very quiet—and very neat and orderly. Hardly says a word. But she's a fine woman. Henry's quiet as well. They have a peaceful home, I think. They live just outside of town. A small house, but there's room for a baby. Would you like to go talk to them tomorrow afternoon?"

Ruth didn't, but there was no way around it. Rose needed a home and the Carsons sounded ideal. "That would be fine. If the snow has cleared enough."

The concession tasted sour. Her heart twisted at the thought of going. But she'd made a commitment to find a good home for Rose, and she would do it.

"They're not far out. We'll be all right in the buggy. If not, we can wait a day or so."

Ruth played with Rose while Annabelle prepared supper. When Rose discovered the joy of playing with a ring off a pickle jar, Ruth sat her on a blanket on the kitchen floor where she would be warm, so Ruth could help Annabelle cook.

By the time the meal was ready, Dylan had returned, looking a little pale.

Ruth helped him off with his coat. "Are you all right? What did Gert say?"

"I'm fine—"

"I'll go ask her myself," Ruth warned.

Dylan appeared uneasy, as if he wasn't used to someone worrying about him. "There's some infection, but she poked around and said she didn't think it needed to be lanced. Gave me something for pain."

"Let me see what she gave you." Ruth stood in front of him and extended her hand.

Dylan reluctantly surrendered the brown bottle. Ruth sniffed at the contents and wrinkled her nose. "How much of this are you supposed to take?"

"A teaspoon three times a day, if I can get the stuff down. Smells like rotting garbage."

Ruth sniffed the vial. "Have you taken any yet?"

"Gert made me choke down a teaspoon of the medicine—it's strong enough to drop a buffalo." He sat down in the nearest chair. "Would you get me a cup of coffee, Ruth? If you're not too busy."

Concern filled Ruth. His request for her to get his coffee must mean he felt worse than he'd ever admit. "Are you sure that's all Gert said?"

"That's all she said." Dylan looked at Annabelle. "Chicken sure smells good, Mrs. Seaton."

"Going to make some gravy to go with it," Annabelle promised.

"I may have died and gone to heaven."

Dylan's grin set the woman atwitter. Ruth hid a smile by turning away. Dylan had not lost his charm. It still oozed from every pore. Even Annabelle had fallen under his spell.

Ruth met his eyes solemnly. "Mrs. Seaton said she's found a family who might be willing to give Rose a home."

"Oh?" Something flickered in his gaze—Ruth wasn't sure if she saw relief or disappointment. "Are you going to talk to them?"

"Tomorrow afternoon."

Dylan studied her for a long moment. "What if they're a good family for her?"

"Then—then Rose will have a family."

Ruth picked up the baby and put her into the wooden high chair that Annabelle had brought down from her attic.

As if he'd received a silent call, Niles strolled into the kitchen as his wife set the food on the table. Ruth spooned potatoes and gravy for

Rose, letting the mixture cool while Niles and Annabelle came to the table.

"Offer a blessing, Father," said Annabelle.

Niles had a voice that could carry halfway across town, and when he prayed he made sure every word was heard. Ruth caught Dylan's eye as she bowed her head and hid a smile. Niles liked to hear his own voice, but he was truly a man of God and she liked to hear him pray.

They enjoyed a fine meal of fried chicken, mashed potatoes with gravy, and the last of the green beans from Annabelle's garden. The conversation flowed as if it were any other day. But for Ruth it was anything but normal. By tomorrow night Rose could belong to a couple of strangers.

After lunch the next day Ruth and Annabelle climbed into the buggy and tucked thick robes around themselves. Dylan had insisted on going with them despite Ruth's urging him to stay and rest.

"Not on your life," he'd proclaimed as he put on his coat. And so the threesome set off to talk to Henry and Clara Carson.

The Carson place was, as Annabelle said, not far outside of town. The house was surrounded by corrals, many of which held five to eight horses each. No doubt Mr. Carson was a prosperous horse wrangler. The dwelling itself was small, with a porch across the front. Rosebushes, now winter-dead, had been trimmed back, but their branches still poked out of the snow.

Annabelle, Ruth, and Dylan had barely stepped out of the buggy when the front door opened and a tall, pretty woman stepped onto the porch. She was wearing a blue-flowered dress with a rounded collar and a white apron covering the front. She looked like a perfect mother for Rose, but Ruth couldn't conjure up one smidgen of happiness about it.

She swallowed hard and summoned up a pleasant smile as she walked toward the porch. Her only hope now was that Clara kept house like a gutter rat.

Chapter Twelve

Clara, this is Ruth and Dylan, and the little one is Rose," Annabelle introduced. Ruth hugged the baby protectively as Dylan took Ruth's arm and steadied her.

Clara Carson looked nervous. She clasped her hands in front of her and smiled. "Come in."

Ruth followed the others into the house, taking in every detail. The front room was neat and smelled clean. *Rats,* Ruth thought.

A Christmas tree adorned with white candles stood by the fireplace. Brown, braided rugs, faded by many washings, covered the floor. Heavy curtains hung at the windows, blocking out winter's feeble light. Crocheted doilies graced the backs of three chairs, books were neatly and evenly stacked on a small table, and a framed picture hung on the wall. Ruth thought it was a landscape but the colors were so dark she couldn't tell.

Ruth let the baby's blanket fall away and removed the small pink crocheted hat Annabelle had found among some baby things she'd packed away.

The woman took a step backwards, her eyes noting the child's heritage. Her features twisted.

Dylan squeezed Ruth's arm reassuringly. If it had not been for his presence she couldn't have done this. She looked at him, and a silent, compassionate message passed between man and woman . . . father and mother.

"As I mentioned, Clara, this is a tragic circumstance," Annabelle began as the four were comfortably seated in the immaculate room. "This baby was found in a burning wagon, with the only man who might know whom she belongs to dead from Indian arrows. Ruth rescued the child and has been caring for her ever since. But the baby needs a good home, and Ruth and Dylan are not in the position to keep the child." Ruth noted how skillfully Annabelle skirted the truth.

"The mister and me are God-fearing folks," Mrs. Carson said in a strangely flat voice.

"I've assured Ruth of that."

Rose reached toward a glass dish that sat on a lamp table.

"That's not for play," Clara warned.

Ruth distracted the baby by jiggling the jar ring she'd brought with her. "Sorry."

Clara leaned forward, cautiously touching the child. "She's a pretty little thing—even if she is one of those savages."

Ruth caught back a sharp retort.

Clara looked up and met Ruth's eyes. "The mister and I have need for children what with all the work to be done around here, but the good Lord has not seen fit to send any until now."

Rose reached out and latched onto Clara's hand. The woman smiled, tears shimmering in her eyes. Rose brought the hand to her mouth, and Clara paled as drool pooled in her hand. Gently prying the tiny fist loose, she reached for a crisp handkerchief and lightly blotted her hand. "My, they are messy, aren't they?" She smiled.

Ruth glanced at Dylan. Messy. Yes, Rose could be very messy.

"May I get anyone coffee? tea?" Clara asked.

The three guests declined.

"Would you like to hold her?" Ruth hesitantly lifted the baby and held her toward Clara. For a moment the woman looked as if she didn't know what was expected of her. "Oh . . . I don't think that's necessary." She patted her stiffly starched apron. "I have my Sunday best on this afternoon . . . the mister thought it appropriate. Perhaps later . . ."

Nodding, Ruth lowered Rose back into her lap.

Dylan spoke up. "Will your husband be along shortly?"

Clara shook her head. "No, he leaves family things to me. He's a very busy man, you know. He has little time for outside interests." She smiled again.

Ruth lifted her eyes sourly. Rose was *not* an "outside interest." This was a child they were talking about, not a hobby. As far as Ruth was concerned the interview was over.

Dylan stood up, twisting the brim of his hat. "We'll not keep you, Mrs. Carson. Ruth and I will give this some thought."

Surprise crossed the woman's face, and she slowly stood up, carefully straightening her blouse collar. "You're leaving so soon?"

"We need to get back to town," Annabelle explained. "Looks like it could snow again anytime."

Clara nodded. "You will let me know when you might want to bring the child here? I'll need a few days' preparation. . . ."

"We'll let you know what we decide," Ruth managed. "I want to pray about this."

"Certainly prayer is called for," Annabelle agreed.

Ruth held Rose close as they made the silent trip back to town. As Dylan and Ruth got out of the wagon, Annabelle laid her hand on Ruth's arm.

"You weren't satisfied with Mrs. Carson?"

Ruth felt a thrill when Dylan pulled her and Rose protectively against his side. A muscle worked in his jaw. "No, but Ruth will pray about it."

Annabelle gave him a curious look. "Of course. Only God knows what he has planned for this little one."

Niles Seaton was leaving as they approached the boardinghouse. "Old Mrs. Brown is feeling poorly. Thought I'd stop by to see if there's anything she needs from the mercantile. How did the visit with the Carsons go?"

"Why don't I walk with you to Mrs. Brown's?" Annabelle looped her arm through her husband's. "We can talk later, Ruth."

"Yes, thank you for taking us to meet Mrs. Carson."

Dylan took Ruth's elbow and steered her toward the door. "What did you really think of Mrs. Carson?"

"She's not getting my child."

"*Your* child?"

Ruth whirled to face him. "Dylan, she wouldn't even hold Rose or talk to her. Her only concern was that silly glass dish. She was . . . cold, Dylan. And she called Rose a savage." Ruth stiffened her chin. "Clara Carson is the savage."

"Annabelle seemed to think the Carsons are good people."

"I'm sure they'd do all the right things. The house was nice. Clean. Mrs. Carson appeared to be affluent and well mannered. But that doesn't make a parent." Ruth rested her hand on the crop of black hair. "A baby needs someone to get down on the floor and play with, Dylan. Even I know that. I can't let Rose go there." She pleaded silently for him to understand.

Dylan met her gaze for a long moment. "Then she won't go there."

As simple as that? She wouldn't go? Relief flooded Ruth. She drew a shaky breath. "Then she won't go." When she met Dylan's smile, she thought her heart would burst right out of her chest. *Then she won't go.*

The next afternoon Niles delivered a note to the Carsons informing them that the child would remain with Ruth and Dylan for now.

Sunshine glinted on the crusted snow so brightly it made Ruth squint. She took a cleansing breath of air, turning her face to the warm rays. They were on the trail again. They'd started out not long after sunup.

Niles and Annabelle had stood on the front porch of the boarding-house and waved them off. Ruth had to laugh when she thought of how Rose had melted Annabelle's heart. The night they'd arrived, Annabelle had been woken from a sound sleep and seemed distant, but oh how she had warmed to Rose and Ruth and Dylan while they were there. Why, by the time they left the woman was practically conversational.

A part of Ruth regretted leaving Sulphur Springs. But another part, the bigger part, felt a rightness about being with Dylan and Rose. There was hope for her future, wherever she ended up. Hadn't she just read Jeremiah 29:11? "For I know the thoughts that I think toward you, saith the Lord, thoughts of peace, and not of evil, to give you an expected end." She clung to the hope that God would do good things for them, and that God would lead her to her expected end—a new life, either in Deer Lick or in Wyoming. Perhaps she could find a job in Deer Lick that would allow her to support Rose. . . .

Dylan had agreed that when they reached Deer Lick, he would see a doctor about his wounds. If the doctor said he needed more time for them to heal, he would stay, even though she knew he was eager to move on and not lose Dreck Parson. What if there was nothing for her in Deer Lick? Well, she'd just have to go on to Wyoming with Dylan after all. How long had he said it would take to reach Wyoming? Two or three weeks, depending on weather. It could take two months.

Ruth smiled. Thanks to Ed French and the new shelves Dylan had built in his mercantile, Dylan had a few dollars in his pocket, and the saddlebags bulged with enough food to last them well into the next territory. They had two fresh horses, a cow for fresh milk for Rose, and a pocketful of dreams. At least she had dreams. Dreams that someday a man like Marshall McCall would fall in love with her and she— She stopped the thought. Whether they reached Deer Lick or Wyoming, she would just be plain Ruth again. Ruth the orphan. Ruth, the woman who was destined to spend the rest of her life alone.

Oh, God, why did you allow me to experience the joy of motherhood—of loving one man so much that I don't think I will be able to exist when he leaves me? It would have been so much better for me to have never met Dylan, never known the joy of little Rose.

Was it possible she had misunderstood God's direction? Her pulse hammered at the idea. Yes, it was possible . . . but not likely. Once they reached Deer Lick, once they found a suitable home for Rose . . .

Then she must concentrate on building a new life, the one she'd hoped to find in Denver City. Those days seemed so long ago, though it had only been a few weeks. She glanced at the baby nestled in Dylan's coat, wisps of dark hair peeping out from under her wool cap. Already her arms ached to hold her . . . to hold the man who carried her.

She angrily shook the notion away. She had never held Dylan, not in the truest sense. Never close to her heart, whispering all the hidden longings bursting inside her.

"Cold?"

Ruth jerked at the sound of the marshall's voice. Shaking her head, she took a firmer grip on the reins of her horse and rode ahead a short distance. She needed to put distance between herself and this man she had come to cherish. *You're daydreaming, Ruth. Of all people, you should know better than to daydream.*

By midafternoon they were approaching the small community of Shadow Brook when Ruth spotted a small gathering ahead. Men on horseback. She peered in the distance, wondering if bandits had waylaid some innocent traveler. She set her jaw. They were not stopping this time. She reined up abruptly and allowed Dylan to catch up.

He rode up beside her and asked, "What's going on?"

"I don't know. Look—ahead." Eight figures gathered in a tight circle. Ruth noticed a corral to the left—with a horse standing by the railing.

Dylan leaned over and handed Rose to her. "You and the baby stay here. I'll find out what's going on."

Fear shot through Ruth. "Dylan! Remember what happened the last time you rode to a stranger's aid!"

"Yeah." He glanced at Rose. "The best thing that's ever happened to either one of us." Her protest fell on deaf ears as Dylan kicked his mare into a gallop.

The snow had thinned to almost nothing as they had ridden west, and Ruth was grateful. It certainly made the trip easier. She grew almost ill every time she thought about how close to death they'd come before reaching Sulphur Springs. Dylan couldn't take another setback. She watched cautiously as he rode off, her heart offering a wordless prayer for protection.

The circle of men opened as the marshall approached. He reined in and the men talked. The wind was slight and voices didn't carry. Ruth wished she knew what was happening, prayed that it wasn't more trouble.

Finally, Dylan motioned for her to join them. Clucking her tongue, she nudged the horse forward. As she rode toward the group, she saw Dylan shaking hands with one man, glancing toward the horse in the pen. Well, at least the strangers were friendly.

Reining in, she smiled as Dylan made the introductions. Pointing to Ruth, he said, "This is . . . Jim, and the baby's name is Rose."

Ruth still wore trousers and boots as well as two layers of flannel shirts because they were warmer and it was easier to ride astride in pants. By now she was accustomed to receiving odd looks, but it still made her slightly uncomfortable. The cowboys acknowledged the greeting by ducking their heads, their gaze sweeping over her and the child. Rose and a bulky coat hid Ruth's telltale curves from the men's views.

Dylan grinned at her. "They're having a contest."

Lowering her voice the best she could, Ruth repeated, "A contest?" She turned and looked at the horse prancing nervously in the corral, his low whinnies edgy. When she looked back, Dylan met her gaze. "They've invited me to join in."

An alarm went off inside her. "What kind of contest?"

He motioned toward the waiting stallion. "A riding contest."

Her eyes darted to the corral, then back to Dylan. "Riding what?"

"That horse there. Bert." He nodded toward the spirited animal. "Fifty dollars to the man who can ride him the longest."

Ruth's jaw dropped. "Dylan—"

The marshall quickly took her mare by the reins and pulled her aside. Out of earshot, he pleaded with her. "I can double our money, Ruth. I can ride that horse longer than any man here."

Ruth was aghast. Gamble? She didn't hold with gambling—the Good Book clearly advised against it!

"How could you think of such a thing?" she demanded. "We have enough money to last us to Wyoming if we're frugal. Besides, you're a sick man! Your wounds have barely begun to heal!" she hissed, staring over his shoulder at the horse in question. Why, riding a bucking stallion would be suicide for him. "What is wrong with you? I thought you had better sense—I will not allow you to kill yourself or squander money on a horse!"

She looked at the prancing stallion. He was lively for an animal bearing the innocuous name of Bert. Bert. He wanted to ride a horse named Bert. True, it would be easy money, but clearly against God's instructions.

Dylan's eyes narrowed. "Since when do you make my decisions?"

She met his gaze stringently. "Since you clearly lost your mind."

"I can ride that stallion, Ruth." His stance softened. "Okay, look. I won't wager the money—I'll put the cow up for entry fee." He stepped closer, his eyes shifting to the waiting men. "Shadow Brook is only a half mile or so away. Even if I lose the cow—which I won't—we'll make it there this afternoon and I'll buy you another cow."

"No." She looked away. "You're not wagering the cow or the money. Rose needs her milk, and I won't risk you losing the cow on some silly man thing. I forbid it."

Dylan's jaw firmed. "You're not going to make me look like a henpecked husband— I'm riding that horse."

"You are not! And I couldn't make you look like a henpecked husband because I look like a boy, Dylan, and even if I didn't, we're not even—" She caught herself and lowered her voice when the men turned to gawk in their direction. "You're not riding that horse. Now let's go."

"You're right. We're not married." Throwing her a defiant look, he turned and rode back to the men. "Gentlemen," he announced—loud enough for the dead to hear, Ruth noticed—"I'd be honored to take your money if you'll accept the cow as entry fee."

Ruth fumed; she was mad enough to spit nails. How could he! How could he do this to her and the baby? Just when he showed signs of thawing, the conceited worm threw her a curve hard enough to flatten her.

"Okay," she yelled, "have your own selfish way! Go ahead, kill yourself and starve poor Rose to death! See if I care!"

The marshall shot her a withering look. The men shuffled their boots, looking to Dylan for explanation. He met their puzzled gazes. "When do we ride?"

"Be a couple of hours yet," one of the men said, glancing at Ruth. "We're waitin' for Hank Grisham to show up."

The marshall nodded. "I'll be ready." He turned his mount and rejoined Ruth.

Ruth gritted her teeth. If the man wanted to kill himself, there was obviously nothing she could do. *I told you not to get your hopes up, Ruth. Dylan McCall cares nothing for you or the baby. Hasn't he just proved it?*

Dylan was checking the cinch on his saddle, purposely ignoring her, which stirred her temper even more. Was he being stubborn or was it a man's pride? She didn't have the right to order him around, and this was his stubborn way of showing her that he answered to no one—most certainly not a woman.

Oh, Sara Dunnigan, if you were alive I could cheerfully wring your cold-hearted neck, Ruth stewed. *You've made the man distrust all women, when in truth only one woman has betrayed him. You.*

Ruth knew she shouldn't have pushed him. But somehow, someway, she had to stop Dylan from killing himself to prove to her he was his own man. Straightening in her saddle, she turned to face the marshall, who was stoically going about his business. "Dylan," she called sweetly.

He glared at her.

"If you're going to do this, could we go into town first? The baby will be hungry soon, and I'd like to feed her some warm mush. Might as well get a room for the night, if there's a hotel or boardinghouse." She left the "because you lost the cow" go unsaid.

He shrugged his agreement. Leaving the cow behind, they rode to Shadow Brook, which could hardly be called a town. The main street was a rutted track. Half a dozen cow ponies were tied to hitching rails in front of a mercantile, and another building stood farther down. The travelers stopped at the general store, and Dylan went inside to ask about a place to stay the night. He learned that there was a boardinghouse located just behind the saloon.

The establishment was smaller than the Seatons', but it looked nice enough. When Ruth and Dylan approached, the owner, Jess Clark, was just leaving to go care for his sick brother.

"If you don't mind fending for yourselves," he said, "you're welcome to stay the night. You being a U.S. marshall," he told Dylan, "I trust you not to run off with the family silver."

Dylan laughed as they went inside. "We'll need two rooms—the baby's crying keeps me up at night."

The clerk barely raised a brow, but Ruth kicked Dylan in the shin for the ridiculous explanation.

They paid for a night's lodging and chose rooms on the first floor, handy to the bathing room and kitchen. Jess Clark had let the fire in the woodstove burn down to coals. Ruth poked the flames alive and fed the fire kindling as she plotted how to keep Dylan from killing himself on that horse.

When a rosy flame burned, she bit her lower lip and prepared to do battle. Dylan was going to be awfully mad at her, but he was going to be awfully alive when this was over.

Dylan sat at the table playing with Rose, who was settled contentedly on a soft blanket on the floor. Ruth laid her hand lightly on his broad shoulder as she paused beside his chair. She meant the touch to be warm and comforting, though still he tensed. "Dylan."

He eyed her suspiciously. "What?"

"If you insist on doing this, please let me clean your wounds and apply fresh bandages. I'll bind the injuries tightly so they won't break open again."

She looked at him pleadingly, using all of her feminine wiles. She didn't feel good about tricking him, but she loved him enough to do anything to keep him alive. If those wounds broke open again, he might not be so fortunate this time. Didn't the marshall realize his mortality? Or was he so intent on besting her that he was blind to danger?

"Please?"

"Gert said I was healing okay. I don't need new bandages."

"For me?" she insisted. "I would feel better if I knew the wounds weren't likely to break open."

He didn't want to appease her; that was evident when resentment flared in his eyes. But maybe the part she'd hoped existed—the tiny part of him that was finding it increasingly hard to ignore her—finally made him consent.

"All right."

She released a pent-up breath. "Thank you. And why don't we have a cup of coffee before you ride? Something hot would make us both feel better."

He shrugged.

The smell of fresh-perked coffee saturated the air as Ruth cleaned and rebandaged his wounds. She worked quickly, her nimble fingers now familiar with the task. Dylan sat stoically, refusing to confront her. When she finished, she got two mugs from the cabinet and poured coffee. As she handed him a cup, she suddenly turned toward the baby, who was happily chewing on her fist.

"Oh . . . I think she's choking, Dylan!"

When Dylan turned his full attention to Rose, Ruth reached in her pocket and withdrew the bottle of laudanum and dumped a healthy dose into Dylan's cup. She hurried to screw the cap on and shoved the bottle back in her pocket before the marshall turned around.

"She wasn't choking."

"Honest? Sorry."

She picked up her cup and took a sip, eyeing him over the rim. He watched the baby a few moments before he took his first sip. He grimaced. "This is the worst coffee I ever tasted."

Ruth shrugged. "I've had better, but at least it's hot. Dylan, why don't you go lay down a minute? I'll wash these cups and feed Rose."

"I'll take the saddlebags to my room."

"Thank you."

Ruth prayed that the laudanum would take effect quickly. She'd given him enough to fell an elephant, and even though he hadn't finished his coffee, she hoped it would do the trick. She heard him leave the house, then return. When she didn't hear him come back down the hall, she waited several more minutes, then tiptoed to the door of his room.

Listening outside, she heard his soft snores and grinned. Success. In a flash she darted into her room, tucked her long dark hair beneath her hat, and ran back to the kitchen to check on Rose. She might be as foolish as Dylan, but she was healthy—at least for now. She was saving the marshall's life, she told herself.

Bert would throw her in two seconds. She was light, and if the fall didn't break her neck she could withstand the impact. She'd been thrown by a horse before and had learned how to fall. But Dylan, she knew, would try to win—and that meant he could die. This way, they'd lose the cow for sure. But they had enough money to buy another one, and no amount of money could replace Dylan McCall.

She pulled on Dylan's gloves, eyeing the sleepy baby. She'd have to take Rose with her and ask one of the men to watch her while she rode. They would find the situation curious, but she was good at bluffing. At least she'd had lots of practice along those lines over the last few weeks.

"Come on, Rose. Let's go save Daddy." She picked her up, then went to make sure Dylan was all right. He was out cold, breathing evenly, stretched out across the bed as if he'd fallen over asleep. She hoped she hadn't given him too much laudanum, but enough to keep him down for at least a couple of hours.

This was her first opportunity to study him. He was always on the move, except for the days he'd been unconscious after the attack. But then she'd been afraid to look for fear he was dying, and she'd had the baby to care for as well. But now, oh my. Dark lashes against tan skin, the faint shadow of beard, defined cheekbones and square jaw . . . she sighed. She was risking her neck to keep him alive for another woman. She frowned.

Soon he'd be an angry man. *Furious* wouldn't describe what he'd be when he woke up and found that she'd tricked him. But he'd be alive and thanking her when he cooled off.

At the last minute, she decided to take his boots. She set Rose down on the floor. Straddling Dylan's unconscious form, she tugged, finally dislodging the left boot, then the right. She tucked the boots under one arm and hurried out of the room with Rose, closing the door behind her.

When she reached the corral, the cowboys were gathered to watch the stallion try to rid himself of his first rider. Ruth was careful to carry Rose the way a man would, letting her head bob like an apple in a barrel. She carried Dylan's boots tucked beneath her right arm.

Hank must have showed up, because nine men turned to watch Ruth approach. She dropped the boots and shifted the baby to her right hip, then turned and spit in the snow. The spittle wasn't enough to make a blotch, but it made a convincing show. Swiping her hand across her mouth, she said gruffly, "Me and the marshall decided I'd best do the competin'."

The men cast a glance at the boots and then back toward town as if they expected to see the marshall approaching.

Ruth eyed them harshly. "Any problem with that? The cow's still up for grabs."

The men shrugged. "No problem," they chorused.

"Guess not."

"Suits me."

"Care to keep an eye on the young'un whilst I ride?" She hawked up another wad and spat on the ground, gagging. Whew. That tasted awful! Why on earth did men find it necessary to do that all the time?

The men grumbled under their breath. Finally one agreed. "I'll keep an eye on the kid."

The cowboys turned back to the corral, where the rider was picking himself up from the ground. Over to one side Bert snorted and pawed the frozen ground. Ruth kept both eyes on the horse, swallowing against a dry throat.

Lord, have mercy on my soul. How did that horse come by his name?

She stood by, jiggling the baby as the second man prepared to ride. Grasping the stallion by the mane, he swung up as two men tried to control the angry beast until the rider was set. At his signal, they let go and bolted for the fence.

The stallion gave a couple of spirited bucks with a twist and sent the rider flying over its head. The cowpoke sprawled in the snow, looking dazed.

Contestant number three mounted a few minutes later.

One by one Ruth watched Bert pitch each rider in record time. She cringed, turning away as the fourth rider flew past her over the fence, taking out a row of oak pickets. He raised out of the snow, trying to shake off the blow. A front tooth hung by its root.

"Hey, kid," someone yelled at Ruth. "You're next!"

Ruth swallowed and handed the baby to the man standing next to her. She ran her tongue lightly over her front teeth, praying she could keep most of them.

"I can do all things through Christ which strengtheneth me." She prayed silently as she dragged her feet toward the four-legged keg of dynamite. *"The Lord is my shepherd; I shall not want. He maketh me to lie down in green pastures: he . . . he . . ."*

The stallion turned a jaundiced eye in her direction, seeming to smirk, as if he was amused at the idea that she'd even think of getting on him. He looked meaner than Satan himself.

Approaching the animal, Ruth caught her breath and tried to hoist herself onto the broad back. It took three men to hold the horse now. Bert snorted, his eyes wild. After several minutes of her feet flailing the air and failing to get a leg up, someone took pity and hefted her onto the brute's back.

For a moment the stallion stilled. Taking a deep breath, Ruth dug her hands into the mane to get a firm grip. Then she waited.

The men stepped back, freeing the horse.

The stallion stood meek as a lamb.

She flashed a lame grin. What was wrong here? Praise God! The Lord had seen her point and he was assisting—

Suddenly the horse lunged, jarring Ruth's teeth. Horse and rider shot out into the middle of the corral. Bert jumped straight up, as if someone had lit dynamite under him, and landed stiff-legged. Ruth's brain ricocheted against the top of her head. Bert, all twelve hundred pounds of him, jumped again, humping his back and twisting in midair. Ruth slid to one side but by some miracle managed to right herself when the horse went the opposite direction on the next jump. She saw stars, then planets shattering around her. Stark terror of being pounded into the ground beneath Bert's hooves was all that kept her hanging on to his mane.

On the next buck she lost her grip. A wicked spiral of the stallion's back sent Ruth sailing though the air, straight toward a water barrel. She crashed into its side, splitting the timber wide open. Icy water gushed everywhere, and she landed in the snow face first.

The last coherent sounds Ruth heard were the men hesitantly, but politely, clapping.

⟶

Silence. Dylan heard nothing. Why was there no sound? For weeks now the first sound he'd heard every morning was either the baby or Ruth.

His eyes popped open. He didn't recognize where he was at first and then remembered they were in Shadow Brook. A boardinghouse. He rolled over, wincing when his shoulder reminded him he wasn't healed yet.

He groaned.

His head felt like it was stuffed with cotton, his mouth dry. When he sat up, he couldn't focus. He blinked, trying to clear his head. He tried to stand, but his legs and arms didn't feel a part of his body. He stumbled and nearly fell face first into the braided rug. Holding on to the bedpost, he managed to remain upright but felt on a tilt. What was wrong?

Drugged. Someone had slipped him something!

Ruth. What had she done to him this time?

Hearing a commotion outside, he looked out the window to see a number of cowboys hightailing it out of town . . . toward the corral. Now, why did instinct tell him that whatever was going on involved Ruth?

His mind began to clear. Jamming his hat on his head, he took a step toward the door before realizing he was in his socks. His boots were nowhere in sight. He'd had them on when he—

Ruth. She'd taken his boots. If she thought that would stop him she had another think coming. If she thought she could talk the cowboys out of holding the cow as collateral for his bet, or use his injuries as a reason for letting him out of the competition . . .

The more he thought about her embarrassing him, the madder he got. Thankful that he hadn't stabled the horses yet, Dylan mounted and galloped toward the corral, intent on stopping Ruth before she made a fool of him.

As he neared the corral he heard yells and calls. His horse skidded to a halt and Dylan slid off, dropping the reins. The sound of men's laughter and hooting filled the charged air.

Walking gingerly across the snow-packed ground, Dylan gravitated toward the noise. Something told him that the answers to why he'd been drugged—and where his boots were—were there. The closer he got to the melee the more certain he was of it.

He reached the corral in time to see Ruth fly through the air and into the water barrel tied to the corner fence. He winced when he heard the dull thud of her body hitting wood and bouncing off like a rag doll, her black hair flying when her hat flew off.

Two men jumped off the fence and ran to divert the still-bucking bronco, while two other hands grabbed Ruth's arms and dragged her outside the fence.

Rage cleared the last of the fog from Dylan's mind. Rage and cold fear—fear like he'd never experienced before. Had the woman lost her mind?

Ignoring his stocking feet, he jumped the fence and sprinted across the corral in the direction they'd dragged Ruth. She lay unconscious, her head cushioned by her crushed hat. A cowpoke bent over her, patting her cheek in an attempt to bring her around.

"You okay, girlie?"

Dylan jerked the man away from Ruth and dropped to his knees to pull her into his arms. Feelings he'd never had before washed over him. Warmth. A need to protect. A need to love.

Too late. Ruth was dead. Crazy, stubborn, misguided Ruth. Ruth, who'd rescued Rose from fire but had tried her best not to love her. Ruth, who had stubbornly followed him across a territory with the idea of finding some distant cousin. Ruth, who had bullied him, saved his life, stood beside him, cared for him. Ruth. His Ruth.

Closing his eyes, he rocked, tenderly cradling her close to his chest, her coal black hair spilling over his arm.

"I'm sure sorry," one of the cowhands said. "We had no idea she was a woman. Then when we realized she was a girl dressed like a boy—"

Dylan looked up at him. "Couldn't you tell she was a woman? How could you miss it?"

"Well, we didn't know at first," another put in, "but then when we did it was too late to stop her."

"You let her ride that horse anyway?"

"She was determined," another said.

"We didn't think she'd get hurt," the first added.

Dylan bit out, "You should have known she wasn't an experienced rider. The bet was for *me* to ride!"

The men looked at each other. "We just thought . . . well . . . we thought we'd play a little trick on her, 'cause she dressed like a man, tried to fool us—"

"She wanted to keep me from losing the cow," Dylan said softly, "and keep me from killing myse f."

He continued to rock Ruth gently, his mind filled with memories. Memories of this woman on the wagon train taking care of the other girls, reading her Bible, teaching Glory to read and write, trying to persuade Glory to take a bath. Ruth laughing in the firelight, sunlight tingeing her hair.

He saw a spirited Ruth determined to follow him though she hadn't a clue how to survive on the trail. But she *had* survived. Ruth, who wouldn't hold the baby more than she had to, but still found a gutsy way to keep her alive those first few days. A furious Ruth facing an irate Ulele and then jumping on a horse and making a run for it, clinging to him like she'd never let him go.

Never let him go.

But she had let him go. Why? Perhaps she *did* love him. Had she taken his wounds because she loved him?

Tears stung his eyes and he held her closer, the pain of loss nearly suffocating him. He'd never wanted to care. Not about her. Not about anyone. He'd pushed her away because she got to him. Made him hope for things that were impossible. He'd been ornery and rude to her, made her think he'd ridden off and left her to fend for herself in an unforgiving land, but she'd stood her ground all the way. He'd been surprised by her determination, shamed by her willingness to take on the responsibility of a homeless child. She was a good mother, once she got used to the idea. Then she'd taken to it like a bee took to honey.

She'd pulled those arrows out of his shoulder when a weaker woman would have fainted. She had refused to let him die. She had found water, worked day and night to bring down his fever. When he was sharp with her, unreasonable, she'd stood up to him and gave back as much as he dished out. He'd never met a woman like her.

He loved her.

The power of that revelation hit him in the middle of his chest like a sledgehammer. He'd never thought love would find him, never wanted it to. But love had attacked him in the guise of this good-to-the-bone woman. He'd been a fool to tell himself he could leave her, that he could live without her or the baby. They were a family—an unusual one, but a family nonetheless.

Suddenly the cowhand's admission registered. They'd known she was a woman and yet they'd set her on that bronco. A bronco that had never been ridden and, from the looks of at least three limping cowboys, hadn't been yet.

Dylan gently put Ruth aside before his rage clicked in. He stood up and lashed out with his fist, which landed solidly on the nearest cowboy's jaw. The man rocked back on his heels, his knees buckling before he recovered and threw a solid punch into Dylan's belly.

The two men rolled on the snowy ground, going after each other with a flurry of fists and shouts as the other men formed a circle and cheered their chosen opponent. The melee gathered steam as the cowhands joined in. Fists flew as they all waded into the brawl, yelling and shouting.

Chapter Thirteen

Ruth slowly gained consciousness, aware first of a piercing pain in her left side, followed closely by a whole new host of aches and pains throughout her body. Then she became aware of men yelling. Yelling loudly. The noise was deafening, causing her head to pound even more. She wanted them to stop. Someone had to make them stop!

She tried to move, but she couldn't. She tried taking a deep breath, but a sharp pain near the base of her skull rendered her helpless. She lay back again. Then she remembered.

Bert. The bronco—the ornery horse had thrown her. *Rats.* There went Rose's milk.

She'd warned Dylan against betting the cow; she'd warned him that this would happen. But would he listen? Noooo. He had to enter this silly contest. It didn't matter that he was barely able to remain upright on a tame horse, much less a bronco that nobody could ride.

Ruth opened her eyes. Blur. She was blind!

No. That was sky. Blue sky. She relaxed and her eyes focused. She realized she was in the middle of a free-for-all. Snow and fists were flying everywhere. Grunts of pain and fury filled the air. Blood. Men's feet flew out from under them like broken stilts. The group was going crazy.

Then she saw him.

Dylan. Smack-dab in the middle of the whole mess! Well, if he hurt himself it served him right!

Then she saw Rose. The cowhand still held the baby, but Rose's head was bobbing like a cork as the man egged on one of the fighters. Rose was clapping and laughing at every blow Dylan landed, as if she was cheering him on. Ruth sat up gingerly, amazed.

Then it occurred to her. Bert. That bronco had never been ridden, had tossed several experienced cowboys straight into the ground, and yet she'd been put on him. They tricked her! No wonder the cowpokes had snickered when she hadn't been able to muster enough leverage to mount without help. They had known she was a woman—why, they probably made side bets on how far the bronco would throw her!

Did Dylan know? A slow, warm fuzziness crept over Ruth. Somehow she knew that he did know, and that was what had sparked the brawl. He was fighting for her—the woman he swore he'd throw to the wolves without a second thought. Her insides turned to mush and tears filled her eyes. He loved her; the big buffoon was fighting for her and the baby—the family they'd created.

Happiness puddled from the corners of her eyes as she watched the marshall down one cowboy, then another. She loved this crazy man, this man who'd been so afraid to care about her. She loved him heart and soul, and loved the baby as much, maybe even more, though she didn't see how that was possible. Love was love, and she had enough to supply both Rose and Dylan for the rest of her life.

Now she had a choice. Would she admit her love, stay and help him fight, or get up and walk away from it all? Walk away from the baby, away from Dylan? She could ride until she found a town that had work for her; she could earn enough money to return to Denver City. She could do that.

Then she remembered a Scripture verse she had read this morning before they set out on the trail. It was from Jeremiah 18. God told Jeremiah to go to the potter's house. As Jeremiah watched him work on a clay vessel, it "marred in the hand of the potter: so he made it again another vessel, as seemed good to the potter to make it."

The words struck her because one day in Sulphur Springs she'd encountered an old Indian inside the livery. He'd been working there in the warm barn, forming pots from the earth, his hands making a beautiful vessel out of a shapeless lump. The old man's face was weathered and lined with age, his eyes ageless. Ruth had stood watching him, commenting on his skill.

In broken English he'd told Ruth that people were like his pots.

Some were already baked—set in their ways, inflexible, hard. "They miss out on a lot of good in life," he'd said.

But then he picked up a lump of unformed clay and began to mold it into a pretty shape. "Some are like this clay, ready to become something useful. They go through the fire and come out of the oven beautiful."

She'd held a pot in her hands, almost sad that it could no longer be molded. One of the pots had a bump along the bottom edge, a bump that would be there until the pot was broken. A flaw. The pot had a flaw, like all people.

She had a flaw too. Many of them, actually. The Jeremiah verse gave her hope that perhaps God could still mold her life into something useful, even though she was marred. Perhaps she could be useful, despite the flaws.

But not if she was already "baked," already set in her ideas of what God was doing in her life. She'd assumed that because she could never have children, a husband and family were out of the picture. She'd hardened her heart against the possibility. But was she being so headstrong in her prior notions that she was blind to God's taking her in a new direction? Was it possible that God was now bringing love into her life—and a child—and that she had been too much of a "baked pot" to recognize the gift?

So, Ruthie, what are you going to do about it? Are you going to set aside those old beliefs and open yourself to a new direction? Or are you going to walk away with your old thoughts and patterns and miss out on the blessings God stands ready to give you?

Of course, there was still one barrier left before she could give her heart to Dylan. Unless they were spiritually matched, she couldn't think of a life with him. Could she trust God right now, even if she had no idea of the outcome?

One thing she knew: she hadn't come this far to see some cowboy destroy this man she loved. Holding her aching side, Ruth pushed herself up and managed to roll to her knees. She squinted against the sea of brawling fists, searching for a weapon. A shovel leaned against the corral railing.

Shoving herself to her feet, she stumbled through the fighting cowboys and grabbed the shovel. A moment later she was in the middle of the chaos, her screaming pain forgotten, fighting alongside Dylan.

When Dylan spotted her, his mouth fell open as he stared in amazement and relief before he ducked a roundhouse by another cowboy. "I thought you were—," he yelled.

"Dead?" Ruth smacked the shovel against a cowpoke's head, knocking him out cold. "You're not that lucky, McCall!"

Grinning widely, Dylan hooked his arm around Ruth's waist and pulled her to him for a long, thorough kiss while the battle raged around them. When their lips parted, he smiled down at her. "You're some woman, Ruth Priggish."

"You're some man, Marshall McCall." They both ducked swinging fists and reentered the fray.

A man knocked Dylan down. As he crawled out from between the legs of two fighting cowpokes, he called out, "Hey, Ruthie?"

"Yes?" She took a wide swing and clunked a man over the head.

"Been meaning to ask you something."

"Can't it wait?" She dodged an oncoming fist, bringing her weapon squarely down on the man's hand. The cowpoke yelped and backed off.

"Don't think so—at the rate we're going we're not likely to live to a ripe old age." Dylan swung a hard left.

"Yeah." She brought the shovel down, nearly tripping over her feet. At the rate they were going, life was mighty risky. "You're right. What's the question?"

"Want to get married?" he asked, shoving aside a windmilling cowboy with a left hook.

Her eyebrows shot up.

"Later," he added, felling another attacker.

"Later?" She swung the shovel and leveled a cowboy, who went down like a shot.

"Not too much later—say, later this evening?"

She bit down on her lower lip and hauled off and let another man have it. She had some serious thinking and praying to do, but "later" sounded good to her.

⌣

"How's that rib, cowboy?" Dylan smiled as they rested on their horses before the last descent into Shadow Brook. Rose lay contentedly in Dylan's arms.

Ruth gingerly touched her aching side. The doctor had bandaged the cracked rib at the horse corral and shook his head over the angry dark blue bruises, which proved to be plentiful. Bert had done a job on Ruth Priggish.

"I'm fine, Mr. McCall." She flashed a merry smile. "Never better in my life."

Dylan sobered. "I still can't believe you'd love me enough to risk your life for me."

"It wasn't entirely unselfish. If something happened to you, what would happen to me and the baby?" She leaned closer to touch his sleeve. "Love isn't that difficult to understand, Dylan. Sacrificial love is mystifying, but maybe that's because it comes from God. God's love for you, Dylan McCall, knows no bounds. Is it so impossible for you to accept such perfect love? A love that's true and born of grace and compassion, not the twisted form Sara practiced."

He sat very quiet, his eyes focused on the town ahead. She didn't know if her words had reached him; she could only pray that the Holy Spirit had finally found an open door.

"God did the same for you, Dylan. He gave his only Son to die for you. And for me."

"The years have hardened me, Ruth. Until you came along I spent my life scoffing at God. It was easier to convince myself that he was the outlaw and not Sara." His eyes sobered. "If the Lord will have me, I'll do my best to honor him—start making him first consideration in my life."

"Oh, Dylan!" She leaned over and threw her arms around his neck and showered his face with kisses. The horses shied, but Ruth held on tightly. "It's shoutin' time in heaven! When you invite God into your heart, he will remain with you forever. Forever, Dylan."

Leaning back, Dylan blew out his cheeks before he offered a brief, tentative smile. "Forever. That's pretty overwhelming."

"But true." She kissed him soundly on the mouth. When she would have pulled back, he pulled her closer and lengthened the embrace.

Later, he confessed, "I accept the Lord and his salvation, Ruth, but I still have much to learn."

"I know . . . but you will learn, Dylan. You will learn." Filled with the Holy Spirit, Dylan would grow in faith and forevermore walk in the light of the truth. How could anyone want more?

"All right, then." She picked up the reins, grinning.

"All right what?"

"All right. I'll marry you." *Thank you, God, for leading this wonderful man into your fold. Help us both, Lord, to grow and trust in your Word.*

Maneuvering his horse closer again, Dylan bent from the saddle and kissed her. "Then why are we wasting time sitting here? Let's go find a preacher."

"Not much call for rooms in the winter," Jess Clark repeated as he handed Dylan the keys to their rooms. He grinned when he heard they were hoping to get married yet that evening.

"Don't see a problem with matrimony. The missus and I were hitched forty-three years before I lost her five years ago."

"Thank you so much," Ruth said. "I . . . could I order a hot bath?"

"Is it possible to get hot water for two baths?" Dylan asked.

"Sure thing. Just give me an hour."

Ruth took in her spacious bedroom with a huge triple window facing south. Snow fell outside in a heavy blanket, but warmth from the woodstove had begun to seep into her chilled bones. Favoring her left side, she pulled back the lace curtains to look outside. The world was beginning to look like a fairyland.

Mr. Clark was warming kettles of water for their baths, and Rose was sleeping on the bed that was covered with a colorful Double Wedding Ring quilt. The friendly room contained a comfortable, overstuffed gingham chair and massive, dark cherry furniture: a dresser, chest of drawers, a cheval mirror and a washstand with a pretty porcelain bowl and pitcher.

Ruth stared at her image. It was the first time in weeks that she'd seen her whole self in a mirror, and she winced. Long days on the trail had dulled her hair; it felt like straw. Wind and rain had left her skin tough as cowhide, and she hadn't been careful enough about wearing a hat in the blinding sun. Traces of tan rimmed her eyes and reddened her cheeks. She wanted to be beautiful for Dylan, especially today, their wedding day. But instead, she looked like a tired, bruised scarecrow.

Later Ruth joined Dylan in the parlor to wait for their baths. Dylan wrapped his arms around Ruth's waist. His gaze met hers. "You've never looked prettier," he whispered.

"I look awful—my skin—"

He caught her hand and brought it to his lips, lightly kissing her fingertips. "You're a beautiful woman, Ruth."

She closed her eyes, relishing the warmth of his breath on her hand. How was it possible to know such happiness? such contentment? Six weeks ago she would have said it wasn't possible, not for Ruth Priggish, but she'd been mistaken.

As he held her hand tightly, Dylan's kisses explored her neckline. She leaned back, allowing him further access to the graceful curve. The baby slept soundly upstairs; snow fell gently outside the large windows.

"Dylan?"

"Hmmm?"

"How long will we stay in Shadow Brook?"

She wasn't sure of his plans; the marriage proposal had come so suddenly. Did he regret the impulsive moment, or had he clearly thought the proposition through? She prayed for the latter.

"We're in no hurry to leave."

She snuggled closer against his warmth. "I'm going to be generous and allow you to retract the proposal. I know everything was so hectic, and you thought I was dead."

His grip tightened. "A jury couldn't make me take it back." Turning her gently to face him, he smiled, his eyes openly adoring her. "I love you, Ruth. I've waited all my life for you to come along. I didn't know that day I joined the wagon train that you were the one, but somewhere along the way I got a pretty good hunch." He kissed her again and, to Ruth, the world was suddenly as perfect as God intended.

His gaze darkened with desire. "You can have the first bath."

"All right." She touched his features lovingly, wanting to memorize the character lines she saw. He had a strong face, gentle yet resolute; eyes as blue as an October sky. The dark growth of beard would soon vanish, and the clean-shaven marshall would be handsome enough to break any woman's heart. Ruth surmised that Dylan McCall had broken more than his share of hearts. She felt a prick of jealousy when she thought of other women and her man. Funny how possessive of the marshall she'd become practically overnight.

"And—" he kissed her earlobe—"then we get married. I paid Mr. Clark to send for the preacher."

Ruth threw her arms around his neck. Her slight weight impacted his, and they staggered back into an overstuffed chair. Ruth held her left side, wincing in pain as she giggled. She showered his prickly face with kisses.

Chuckling, he caught her face between his hands and stilled her long enough to catch his breath. "I have never proposed to you properly."

"That's all right. You did ask—" He usually ordered her to do things, which would have been all right in this instance.

"But not properly." Sitting her upright, he sank to his knee beside the chair and caught her hand. Gazing into her eyes, he asked softly, "Will you spend the rest of your life with me, Ruth Priggish? Will you be the mother of my children—"

Her pulse quickened and she stopped him. "Dylan—"

"Let me fin—"

She brought her left hand to cover his mouth. The air had suddenly gone out of the room. In her blissful state she had forgotten to remind him of her condition. Her heart ached. Once he remembered, he would surely take back the proposal, and she couldn't blame him. "I can't . . ."

"You can't?" Disbelief flickered across his features. "You can't marry me?"

She shook her head, tears spurting to her eyes. "I can't be the mother of your children. Remember? I told you—that night we were talking about our childhoods? I thought you understood."

Her heart was breaking. Holding her side, she got up and walked to the window. As she stared out, she sorted her words, wondering why she had let herself get so excited. Why hadn't she even thought that perhaps he had not understood the seriousness of her condition that night under the stars, when they had shared their deepest secrets? They would have Rose, but Dylan would desire a son and eventually other children. And she wouldn't be able to provide him heirs. Oh, God, why hadn't she made sure he understood sooner?

He remained on one knee, viewing her tolerantly. "You're going to have to be a little more specific, Ruth."

Ruth bit her lower lip, trying to stem her rising tears. "I wasn't born like other women, Dylan. I'm physically unable to bear children. . . ." Hot tears rolled from the corners of her eyes. "I'm so sorry—I should have been more specific but . . ." She licked away salty wetness. "It's my fault . . . I'm so sorry."

He came to her, turning her and taking her tenderly into his arms. She closed her eyes and relished the moment, probably the last time he'd hold her like this. If he ever held her again it would be out of pity, and she couldn't bear that. They clung to each other while her tears dampened his shoulder. It seemed like hours before she found her voice again.

"I know it matters . . ."

His voice was as soft and gentle as she'd come to expect these last few days. "Well, sure it matters, but probably more to you than to me, Ruth." Holding her away from him, his eyes searched hers. "Until I met you I didn't think I'd ever have a wife and children. I know how

172

badly you want to be a mother, Ruth, but we have Rose. I'm sorry that you want more—"

"Me?" She reached out to trace the curve of his chin with her fore-finger. "It isn't me I'm concerned about—it's you."

The light of everlasting love shone from the depths of his eyes. "I love you, Ruth. That's all that matters. Mothers aren't born—I know that from living with Sara Dunnigan. You're a mother at heart. That's what counts. You thought you'd never have children, but God put one right in your lap. You just didn't realize it."

She smiled up at him, almost unable to believe how God had blessed her with this man. Oh, there were still wounds, wounds Sara Dunnigan had caused. Emotional scars like Dylan's didn't heal overnight, but there'd been a good start. With love and God's grace, Ruth felt she could help the process along. She'd love him so fully, so completely, that he wouldn't have time to think about the past; he would only look forward to the future—a future with her and Rose.

"So you're not so mad at God anymore?" She kissed his cheek softly.

"I'm not mad. You have shown me that Sara Dunnigan did not wor-ship a God of love, the God you know . . . the God who must have been watching over us all along the way. I'm hoping you can show me how to know more about your God . . . no, my God too, now. I'm willing to learn. Right now, though, the road looks pretty steep."

She caught his hand. "Not with both of us walking."

"Oh, Ruth." He kissed her. "I have a lot to learn if you're willing to teach me and be patient—"

"I would be ever so glad to help you get to know our Savior and heavenly Father." She moved back to nestle in the crook of his arm. "God willing, we're going to have a good life together, Dylan."

"No doubt," he whispered, stroking her hair. "And about those babies you can't have—well, we can adopt more children if that's what you want. Then there will be grandchildren and great-grandchildren . . . "

She didn't let him finish. She turned and kissed him, murmuring her love. "I love you, Dylan McCall. I love you so deeply it hurts."

Lifting her gently off her feet, he swung her around, holding her tightly. The excruciating pain in her left rib was well worth the price. "I thought after we got married this evening, we'd stay around here a few days, then ride back to Denver City."

Ruth's smile faded as he set her back on her feet. "Denver City?"

"Well, seeing as how we've traveled no more than thirty miles since we left and winter's set in, I thought with your cracked rib, Christmas coming on, and my being so late anyway, we'd go back to Denver City for the winter. I'll have to let Dreck Parson go and trust that another marshall will bring him to justice. Anyway, after all the excitement, I could stand a little recovery time." He grinned wryly. "You can spend the next couple of months with Patience, Lily, Harper, and Mary and get adjusted to having a husband and baby before we move on." He kissed her again. "Maybe you should write to your cousin Milford and tell him you won't be coming."

"I never told—oh, you!" she said, swatting him lightly when she realized he was teasing. She shrugged, looping her arms around his neck. "Finding Milford would have been a long shot anyway."

"I'd say—but thank God you chose to bluff it out and follow me."

She drew back and peered up at him hopefully. "You truly do thank God?"

He smiled, holding her tightly. "You're a hard woman to please, you know that?"

He did trust God, though; Ruth could feel it, and it erased the last vestiges of doubt that this new path was the one God wanted for her.

That night in Jess Clark's parlor, while snow fell outside the windows, Marshall Dylan McCall and Ruth Priggish exchanged marriage vows. Jess witnessed the ceremony with a smile and a dutiful shower of rice.

The fee: one bucket of milk from the cow Ruth and Dylan hadn't lost after all.

Epilogue

Dylan, Ruth, and Rose McCall rode into Denver City three days before Christmas in a stagecoach, in relatively luxurious fashion considering the way they'd left.

The treat was a gift from Jess Clark, who claimed that he made investments in the future—young folks' futures. In this particular case, Ruth and Dylan McCall's shining future.

"You kids be happy—that will make my speculation one of the soundest I've ever made," the good man had said as he put the new family in the coach and shut the door.

"I'll send the money as soon as I collect my pay," Dylan had promised.

"No need. Send it, don't send it. I'll simply pass the money along to some other struggling stranger."

The world needed more Jess Clarks, Ruth decided.

"Whoa, there!" the driver yelled, sawing back on the reins, drawing the coach to a snow-fogged stop in front of the stage office.

"Den-ver Ci-ty!" he yelled, wrapping the reins around the brake handle. "Everybody out!"

Dylan glanced at his new bride. "Ready?"

"Sure am," Ruth said, smiling up at the handsome marshall. Her husband. She'd never been more ready or happier in her life. All her dreams had come true. She had a wonderful husband—a man who cherished her, a man who had proven his love and whose smile restored her faith in miracles.

175

And she had a baby.

A charming, captivating little brown-eyed child whose laughter was the light of her life. Each time Ruth held her sleeping daughter she experienced God's love afresh; when the baby reached for her she felt complete. She'd changed. She'd become pliable. She'd become a usable pot, even with her flaws.

Dylan climbed from the coach and reached for the baby. Settling Rose on his hip, he reached for Ruth. He smiled up at her as sun broke through the clouds.

"Ruth!"

"Harper!" Ruth stepped down from the coach and threw herself into the black girl's waiting arms.

"I can't believe it! What are you doing here?" Harper exclaimed. "We thought by now you'd be in Wyoming!"

Ruth laughed, taking the baby from Dylan. "I'm bringing my family to meet my folks."

Harper's puzzled gaze traveled from Ruth to Dylan to the baby. "I'm not even going to ask. Not before I get the others. Then we want to hear the whole story." She shook her head, her black eyes sparkling. "I know it's got to be a good one."

"It is." Ruth laughed. "It *surely* is."

Dylan retrieved the small bag. "How are you, Harper?"

"Fine, just fine, Marshall." Harper glanced at Ruth. "How are you?"

"Never better." Dylan adjusted the brim of his hat and winked at Ruth. "I'll get a room at the hotel," he said. "I need to send Kurt a telegram as soon as we're settled."

Harper tripped behind as the couple walked toward the hotel, Marshall McCall proudly showing off his baby girl and his new wife. Ruth knew Harper was fairly bubbling over with curiosity about how she and the obstinate marshall had gotten together, and where the Indian child fit into the picture.

"I'm getting the others," Harper announced, "then we'll have tea and you can tell us everything. *Everything,*" she emphasized. Her eyes traveled to the good-looking marshall and she repeated, *"Everything,* Ruth."

"I'm hungry," Dylan said. "And I'd bet this one would like something to eat." He tapped Rose's nose with the tip of his finger and she giggled.

"We'll be in the café," Ruth told Harper.

Harper dashed off and Ruth grinned up at Dylan. "Hope nobody gets in her way."

"She'll mow them down if they do."

They settled at a table and studied the one-page menu. They'd barely ordered before Mary, Patience, Harper, and Lily burst through the doorway, their faces animated with excitement.

They all spoke at once, but somehow Ruth managed to tell the story of her trek into Colorado Territory, the baby's rescue, Dylan's injuries, Ulele and Nehemiah Ford's deceit, their escapades trying to find a home for baby Rose, and finally how they had managed, through it all, to fall in love and get married.

"Married! You got *married* without us?" Patience demanded.

"I didn't plan on getting married," Ruth said softly. She reached over and took her husband's hand. "But this handsome man simply swept me off my feet."

"Oh, you two." Mary chuckled. "I am so *happy* to hear the news, but Ruth, Oscar was rather put out by the way you up and disappeared." She took Ruth's other hand and held it.

"I'm sorry," Ruth said, feeling sorry for the old prospector in spite of her aversion to his smell and manners. She squeezed Mary's hand. "What's been happening here? Tell me everything."

"Well, nothing like what's happened to you, but we've been doing quite well," Lily said.

"Harper and I take in sewing," Mary said softly. "Denver City is growing so fast that Rosalee Edwards can't handle it all. Why, just the other day two wagon trains pulled into town and decided to stay the winter. The families might even remain when spring arrives. Families get settled and sometimes, Pastor Siddons said, they like it so well here that they don't want to move on." She shrugged. "That's good for the sewing business. Plus, the cowboys can't even sew on a button, and there are a lot of cowboys around here— ranchers and the hands who work for them."

Ruth grinned. " I'm so happy for you." Everything seemed to be working out splendidly.

"I'm working on a wedding dress right now. It is so beautiful," Mary enthused. "The wedding is going to be quite an event."

"Surely is," Harper added. "The bride comes from the Hawthorn family, who has been involved in a feud with the groom's parents, the McLanes, for over a year. The fathers hate each other and the mothers won't speak. It's real shameful the way those two sides carry on—why, they even designated certain days to come to town for supplies. The

Hawthorns come on Thursdays, the McLanes on Fridays. Both sides decided that shortly after the feud broke out."

Dylan bit into a piece of cherry pie. "What are the families arguing about?"

Mary shrugged. "Water rights—what else?"

"I bet Ben's folks don't even know what his intended looks like," Lily surmised. "Last time the McLanes saw Lenore Hawthorn was five years ago." Lily shrugged. "The young couple met at a church social. The parents don't go to the church socials, but this time they let their children attend. Ever since then Ben and Lenore have been meeting secretly, refusing to let their parents interfere with true love. They're so happy together, but the shine's taken off the engagement since both sets of parents vehemently object to the love match."

Harper nodded. "They both really love one another—you can just tell. It's very romantic."

The match didn't sound romantic to Ruth. It sounded like trouble waiting to happen, and she'd witnessed enough trouble to last her a lifetime.

Patience joined the discussion. "The dress is so beautiful, Ruth. Lenore will be a gorgeous bride, but I don't know how she and Ben are going to carry this wedding off with their folks so dead set against it."

Mary looked sad. "Lenore's folks won't even let her come to town to try on the dress—Patience has been helping me, modeling the dress so I can mark hems, fit the bodice. She's about the same size as Lenore, or I'd never get the dress done in time. They're getting married on the thirty-first . . . New Year's Eve. Lenore's grandmother is paying to have the dress made, or poor Lenore would have to get married in a regular gown."

"If you'll excuse me, ladies, I need to send a wire." Dylan leaned over and kissed Ruth. "The Good Book mentions something about gossip, doesn't it?" He winked.

The girls reserved further comments until the café door closed behind the marshall's back.

Mary slid to the front of her chair. "How long are you going to stay?"

"Until my rib heals and the worst of the weather is over." Ruth sighed. "Maybe two months or longer, Dylan promised. Then we're off to Utah."

Mary clapped her hands. "Wonderful. We'll get to spoil this precious baby." Mary reached for Rose, and the baby happily made the transfer.

178

Several days later the girls had caught up on all the news. The town had surprised Ruth and Dylan with a bridal shower two days after Christmas. The Siddonses hosted the festive event at the church.

"I am overwhelmed by your generosity," Ruth told the women in attendance with a grateful smile. Mounds of unwrapped household gifts piled around her chair. "I have never felt so loved."

The next morning, Ruth visited Mary and Harper's sewing room—a small cubicle at the back of the mercantile. When Ruth entered the establishment, Patience, wearing Lenore's wedding dress, turned from her perch on a stool, while Mary knelt at her feet, fastening Irish lace along the hem and train.

Harper, Lily, and Ruth sat near a cheery fire, admiring Mary's handiwork.

"It's so beautiful," Ruth praised. "Mary, you have such a talent."

The young woman blushed. "I've really enjoyed designing the dress."

The women turned abruptly as the back door suddenly burst open and a masked man entered the store. He stood for a moment, beady eyes surveying the situation.

Ruth gasped, reaching for baby Rose, who played at her feet.

"Nobody move, ladies."

The women did as they were told. Mary coughed, and the man leveled the gun at her. "I said *quiet!*"

Patience stepped off the stool, wide-eyed. "What do you want?"

The outlaw motioned for her to step forward.

Patience's hand flew to her chest. "Me?"

"You. Get over here."

When Patience obeyed, he hooked his arm around her waist and dragged her out the front door.

Ruth and the other women sat frozen in place, shock paralyzing them as Patience's screams echoed up the street.

Recovering first, Ruth raced outside in time to see the bandit riding away, Patience imprisoned on the saddle in front of him. Ruth started running for the sheriff's office, bumping smack into Dylan when he stepped out of the telegraph office.

"Whoa." He reached out and caught her. "Where's the fire?"

"Patience. *Man,*" Ruth panted, pointing down the street. "Took her."

The marshall whirled. "Calm down. Catch your breath. Someone took Patience?"

"We were . . . in the shop. Mary was pinning . . . hem on Lenore Hawthorn's wedding dress—bride's parents forbid her to try it on . . . so Patience was wearing it. A man burst into the mercantile . . . and grabbed her. They went that direction." She pointed west of town.

"You go back with the girls. I'll get the sheriff, get a posse together." Dylan kissed Ruth soundly. "We'll find her. Don't worry."

Tears filled Ruth's eyes. "Oh, Dylan, be careful."

His hand brushed her hair. "I'm always careful."

They had come too far to lose each other now!

Late that night the posse returned to town without Patience. A deputy and Dylan met Ruth and the other women gathered outside the mercantile.

"You didn't find her?" Ruth wrung her hands at the sight of the two men's solemn faces.

Dylan shook his head. "Not a trace of her. We'll have to wait until someone contacts us—see why the man took Patience, and what he wants."

Ruth walked into his arms. "I'm so afraid for her."

Dylan held her tightly. "I know, and I'd do anything to bring her back." He spoke over Ruth's head to the assembled women. "Any idea why someone would want to kidnap Patience?"

"We've discussed that all afternoon." Ruth stepped out of his embrace and wiped her eyes.

"And we can't come up with any reason," Harper reported.

"She's not had a problem with anyone? Didn't turn away from a suitor?" the deputy asked.

"No," Lily protested. "Conner Justice has called on her a few times, but there's been no problem."

Sheriff Jay Longer rode up just then and climbed out of the saddle. "Just been talking to some of my men. You said Patience was wearing Lenore Hawthorn's wedding dress, right?"

Ruth nodded. "Yes."

The young man frowned. "Well, there's our answer. There's been bad blood between the Hawthorns and McLanes all year. Ben and Lenore's wedding has set them off again—I'd bet a dollar to a doughnut the kidnapper is from the groom's side."

Mary feebly lifted a hand to her forehead. "Oh, dear goodness. The outlaw mistook Patience for Lenore?"

The sheriff nodded. "That'd be my guess. What about you, Marshall?"

Dylan nodded. "It would seem that way."

The women murmured their distress.

Ruth's eyes grew wide. "What will he do when he discovers he's got the wrong person?"

Dylan drew her back to him. "I don't know, honey."

"But, why?" Mary argued. "Why would anyone snatch a bride? What do they plan to do with Lenore—Patience?"

The sheriff and marshall exchanged grave looks.

"Let's not panic," Dylan said. "Maybe when they find out they got the wrong woman, they'll bring Patience back."

Ruth and Dylan trailed the sheriff and deputy to the sheriff's office while Lily watched Rose. Dylan told her Jay Longer had been sheriff in Denver City for three years and was considered an effective lawman. "You're not to worry," he ordered.

"Jay, we've got a problem," Dylan said as the three men stepped inside the sheriff's office.

"Well, like you said, let's not panic until we see if he brings her back."

"And if he doesn't?"

Jay took off his Stetson and hung it over a peg. The sheriff was maybe a year or two older than Dylan, powerfully built, ruggedly handsome, Ruth noticed. "That's not good," Jay said.

Perched on the side of a battered desk, Dylan put his arm around Ruth. He said softly. "Don't worry, Ruthie; we'll find her."

Closing her eyes, Ruth tried to take comfort in her husband's assuring words. The past weeks had been so hectic—she'd hoped their lives would settle down, but apparently peace wasn't to be. Someone had taken Patience in place of Lenore Hawthorn, someone with a grudge.

Lord, please watch over Patience, Ruth silently prayed as she succumbed to the warmth of her husband's embrace.

There just seemed to be *no* end to trouble in Denver City.

A Note from the Author

Dear Reader,

When I first began the Brides of the West series I thought I would tell only the Kallahan sisters' story: Faith, June, and Hope. Then Glory came along, and she opened a whole new realm of possibilities. Ruth, Patience, Harper, Lily, and Mary were created—and as you see, the Brides of the West just keep involving themselves in the most unlikely knee-slapping escapades. As the Brides of the West continue, I hope you will see something of yourself and your own life in the stories of Ruth or Patience or any of the other courageous young women. My prayer is that this fun-loving fiction containing simple truths will minister to you, my reader, and put a song in your heart and a smile on your face.

The most exciting thing for me about life (other than opening my eyes to each new day God has given me) is the element of the unknown. Can you imagine being a young woman and having to travel hundreds, sometimes thousands, of miles to marry a man you never even met? Sounds strange, doesn't it, since we live in a world of instant communication, fast cars, and even speedier courtships. Sometimes it only takes one date to make us say, *"Uh-uh! This is not the man I'm going to spend my life with!"*

I met Lance in high school, and we married at the very tender ages of 17 and 19. This June we will celebrate four decades together, and I praise God for sending such an amazing man into my life—and I found him right here in Missouri! I didn't have to endure heat, rutted roads, lack of water, poor tintypes, or pesky flies! Lance lived within a mile of my parents' house. He has brought love and stability into my life—bolstered and upheld my faith, and been the source of my strength here on earth.

Ah—patience, beautiful Christian young women. "Mr. Right" is out there, and God will reveal him in due time if you pray and ask for guidance in seeking the man God has for you. "Charm is deceptive, and beauty does not last; but a woman who fears the Lord will be greatly praised" cautions Proverbs 31:30.

Marriage—true and lasting love—is one of God's greatest gifts. My prayer for you today is that in God's perfect timing you will find the man of your hopes and dreams.

In his name,
Lori

Lori Copeland

Patience

LORI COPELAND

Brides of the West 1872

Romance fiction from
Tyndale House Publishers, Inc.
WHEATON, ILLINOIS

HeartQuest is a registered trademark of Tyndale House Publishers, Inc.

Edited by Kathryn S. Olson

Designed by Zandrah Maguigad

ISBN 0-7394-4129-9

Printed in the United States of America

To Barbara Warren.
Every author needs a helping hand,
and Barbara supplies me with knowledge,
encouragement,
and much-needed spiritual uplifting.
Thank you, friend.

Chapter One

Patience Smith might have been surprised to know that her life had just changed dramatically. Sheriff Jay Longer didn't realize his had changed at the same instant.

Swinging a long leg over the saddle, the sheriff of Denver City, Colorado, climbed aboard his mare. His eye caught Dylan McCall hugging his wife on Main Street, right in broad daylight. And in front of the sheriff's office, too. He frowned. Was that any way to uphold the dignity of law enforcement?

A moment later Jay rode up to the waiting couple, sliding out of the saddle before the mare came to a stop.

Ruth McCall whirled to face him, her pretty face a mix of warring emotions. "We were in the shop. Mary was pinning the hem on Lenore Hawthorn's wedding dress—the bride's parents forbid her to try it on, so Patience was modeling it. A man burst into Mary's millinery and grabbed Patience. They went off in that direction!" She pointed west. "Go!"

"Honey, slow down," her husband warned. "I don't want you upset."

Tears brimmed Ruth's eyelids. "You have to *do* something, Sheriff!"

Jay frowned. Deliver him from newlyweds and estrogen-produced hysterics. All that sweet talk between the marshall and his bride should take place in the privacy of their home, not in the presence of people who might find it scratchy to watch. Of course, time was, when he still had Nelly, he might have been as love-struck as Dylan, but he'd have had enough sense of propriety to keep it to himself.

1

Sure, he would.

If he had Nelly back, he'd get down on his knees right out there in the middle of the street and tell her all the things he wished he'd said when he had the chance.

Jay casually straightened the brim on his Stetson. "She was wearing Lenore Hawthorn's wedding dress when she was abducted?"

Ruth nodded, tears rolling down her cheeks. "She was standing in for Lenore for the final gown fitting."

Jay glanced at Dylan, then back to Ruth. "Well, there's our answer. There's been bad blood between the Hawthorns and the McLanes for years. Ben and Lenore's wedding has set them off again—my guess is that the culprit has a connection with the groom's family."

With the Hawthorn/McLane wedding scheduled to take place tomorrow night, Jay figured that had to be the circumstance. Old man McLane was a crusty old reprobate, and he'd sworn to stop the nuptials between his oldest son and Hawthorn's youngest daughter. Apparently he'd found a way to interfere.

Ruth lifted a shaky hand to her forehead. "Sakes alive. The kidnapper mistook Patience for Lenore?"

Jay nodded. "That'd be my guess. What about you, Marshall?"

Dylan agreed. "That's the way I have it figured."

Denver City bustled in the background. An hour from now it would be dark, and a posse would find it impossible to track the young woman. Jay would have to set out alone and follow the trail until it got cold—or until he found Patience Smith.

"But *why?*" Ruth argued. "Why would anyone snatch a bride? What do they want with Lenore—Patience?"

The sheriff and the marshall exchanged sobering looks before Jay finally admitted, "Well now, that's hard to say." Could be a million explanations, but only one thing mattered. What would the kidnapper do with the girl once he discovered his mistake?

"Let's not panic," Dylan said. "When Patience tells the man that he's got the wrong woman, he'll probably turn her loose."

Whirling, Ruth bolted back into Mary's millinery shop in tears, and Dylan approached the sheriff.

"We've got a problem," the marshall said.

"Could be—then again, he might have realized his mistake instantly and let her go at the edge of town."

"Maybe—but if he didn't?"

Jay took off his Stetson and wiped his forehead. "Then you're right—we have a real problem."

Dylan stood by while Jay slid a Winchester Model 1873 into the hand-tooled rifle scabbard tied to his saddle. A cold wind buffeted the men's sturdy frames. Tomorrow night 1873 would be ushered out with parties and noisy celebrations, but Jay wouldn't be part of the festivities.

Dylan ran a hand across his face. "I still think I should be the one to go after her. Those girls and Ruth—they're like family to each other."

Longer busied himself checking cinches and stirrups. He knew Dylan had brought the girls all the way from Missouri to be mail-order brides, an arrangement that hadn't worked out. The orphaned young women were as close as sisters, so Dylan's bride's tears were understandable. "You're newly married, and you're the marshall. I'm single, the sheriff, and the crime was committed in my county."

Not that Jay wanted to go after this particular orphan. He'd had more than one disagreeable run-in with Patience Smith, the last occurring a couple days ago. She'd burst into his office carrying a bird with a broken wing and asked if he knew anything about setting bones. He'd calmly pointed out he was town sheriff, not town vet. He'd eyed the critter that scattered droppings on the office floor.

She'd eyed him back sternly, then asked if he was coldhearted.

He had to admit that he was—had been for a long time. And he wasn't in the bird-fixing business.

She'd left with the bird in hand, and the last he'd seen of her she was crossing the street, head held high, determination evident in her squared shoulders and stiff back.

Dylan's voice broke into Jay's musings. "The kidnapping took place in my town."

Jay sighed, knowing how stubborn McCall could be. "Look, let's not argue. I'm going after her, and I'm going to bring her home. That's my job; it's what I get paid for."

Conceding, Dylan stepped back. "I'll look after the town while you're gone. That much I can do."

Nodding, Jay gathered the reins between his gloves and mounted. "Finding her—finding anyone—in these mountains isn't going to be a cakewalk." The sheriff settled his hat more firmly on his head. He'd be lucky if he survived the search this time of year. January wasn't for the fainthearted. But he had another reason for going, one he wasn't going to mention. The wire he'd received today crackled in his shirt pocket. He knew what it said by heart. His gambling debts had caught up with him. The people he owed were coming to collect, and he didn't have the money to pay. If he wasn't here, there wouldn't be much they could do, and if he could buy enough time, maybe he would recoup his losses. And then again, maybe he wouldn't.

Turning the horse, he rode out of town due west. Somewhere out there a young woman was in danger, and as sheriff, it was his responsibility to rescue her.

He could only hope that Patience Smith was as tenacious with her kidnapper as she'd proven to be with him.

Patience decided that getting rid of trouble was like sacking fog. You grasped, fumbled, and blocked, but it kept coming. She shivered. The late-afternoon air was cold as granite, and she was wearing little more than lace and tulle.

She wanted off this horse, and even more, she needed to make sense of what had just happened. She glanced sideways at the man who held her on his horse and wondered about his intelligence. How could anyone mistake her for Lenore Hawthorn? Lenore had blonde hair, angular features, and blue eyes. Patience had brunette hair, a round face, and dark brown eyes.

The swarthy man's hold tightened. "Stop squirming, Lenore!"

"I'm not Lenore!"

"Yeah, yeah. That's what they all say." He set his spurs deeper into the mare.

"But I'm not Lenore!" Patience yelled.

"Shaddup!"

She swallowed back her mounting hysteria. The outlaw gripped her tighter around the middle and galloped around a curve. This mistake had something to do with the ongoing feud between the Hawthorns and the McLanes, she was sure. Hatred between the two families ran as deep as still water, and she feared there was no telling what fate awaited her if this man thought she was Amos Hawthorn's daughter. The families' insane feud had been going on for decades.

She frowned when she thought of Mary, Lily, Harper, and Ruth. The girls had all looked thunderstruck when this man had burst into the sewing shop and seized her. If the situation wasn't so grave, she'd laugh; but right now all she could do was cling to the horse and pray she'd survive the frantic ride.

The scoundrel was dirty and his rancid breath repulsed her. Where was he taking her? How soon would he accept the fact that she wasn't the intended bride? And then what? Would he dispose of her before she could convince him that he'd made a terrible mistake?

Relief suddenly flooded her. *Dylan.* Ruth's husband—or maybe the own sheriff, Jay Longer—would come after her. The bigheaded sheriff and she mixed like oil and water, but right now she wasn't particular about her rescuer. Considering their simmering animosity toward one another, she wondered if he'd even bother to come after her—but Dylan would make him. His job would make him. With his piercing blue eyes and hair as red as a Colorado sunset, Sheriff Longer was a hard man to understand. But whether he liked her or not, the tough-minded sheriff would not let this brigand get away with kidnapping a woman from his territory.

She clung to that belief as the horse's shod hoofs pounded the frozen ground. Wind stung her face and cold seeped through her bones. She had no protection from the wintry elements—no coat, only the lace sleeves of Lenore's wedding dress to protect her from the icy wind.

Suddenly, as if the hand of God swooped down and smote the enemy, the horse stumbled and pitched forward, throwing Patience and her captor over the animal's head. Patience went airborne. Seconds later she slammed into the frozen ground.

Lying motionless, she struggled to catch her breath, and then, dazed, she sat up in a feeble attempt to regain her bearings. She was alive! The horse lay prostrate on top of the kidnapper. She wished she felt compassion, an urge to offer assistance to the poor, unfortunate villain, but relief flooded her. She was free! The man must surely be dead, or very close to death; she didn't have the strength to even budge the horse to look.

Rolling slowly to her feet, Patience groaned. She tentatively tested her weight on one foot and then the other, and discovered that she could walk. Which she did, as fast as her injury would allow, grasping the hem of the fragile gown, trying to protect the sheer material from the rough trail.

Limping over the frozen ground, she sucked in deep drafts, the cold air stinging her lungs. Where was she? She had no idea; she wasn't familiar with the region. From the time Dylan had brought the five mail-order brides to Denver City, she hadn't ventured far from the outskirts of town. Her eyes searched the barren, snow-swept land, and she shuffled faster. She'd heard talk of prospectors in the area, how fiercely the men vied with each other for gold. Hysteria now threatened to overtake her as she realized she would freeze to death if she didn't find shelter soon. Her teeth chattered and her breath came in ragged gulps. *Walk, Patience. Walk like your life depends on it.*

Heartsick, Patience realized that in these circumstances, it actually did.

A blast of winter wind buffeted the sheriff, and he huddled deeper into the sheepskin-lined coat. The girl had only a thin, silk wedding gown to protect her from the cold. If he didn't find her soon . . .

Jay rode slowly, leaning from the saddle to search for tracks, but the frozen ground made tracking difficult. He didn't stand the chance of a snowball in a skillet of finding her, but he set his jaw in determination.

And then he spotted the dead horse. Dismounting and hanging on to the reins, he approached the carcass. His mare was skittish, and he had no desire to be stranded out here on foot. This was unfriendly country. If a man didn't freeze to death, he stood a good chance of running into a belligerent miner defending his claim.

Jay examined the animal, noticing a boot half hidden beneath the horse's body. When he had satisfied himself that Patience wasn't there, he mounted again. He had no shovel; he couldn't bury the miscreant. Animals would take care of what he couldn't. He nudged his horse and rode off slowly. Supposing the woman was still a captive, for it was possible the dead horse and victim had nothing to do with Patience Smith.

Then again, there was nothing to suggest that he *wasn't* the kidnapper, and when the horse stumbled she'd gotten away. If that were the case, where would she have gone? Running the questions through his mind, Jay came up with the same answer to both: most likely to one of the mining camps dotting these mountains or an isolated shaft, which would make finding her even more difficult.

He had been in these parts long enough to know that he couldn't go riding into camp dressed like a lawman. That would tip off the kidnappers that he was on their trail if she was still being held somewhere. He studied the rugged landscape, weighing his options. As far as he could see, there was only one choice open to him. Miners were a rugged lot, suspicious of strangers, so he'd ride into the closest town and get himself a shovel and a gold pan. Going undercover wasn't his style, but he was going to hit those camps disguised as a miner.

Chapter Two

Bitter cold air burned Patience's lungs. She had lost dexterity in her fingers a long time ago. She clung weakly to the hope that someone was looking for her—if she could only hold on, *someone* would find her any moment. She had wandered for hours. When darkness fell, she had curled inside a fallen log and wrapped herself in pine branches and dead leaves. She had survived the elements—but barely.

When she opened her eyes this morning, she realized that she had so many things she wanted to do—climb a tall mountain, eat a store-bought cake, make an edible blackberry cobbler. And if the good Lord was willing, find some way to make life easier for Mary, Harper, and Lily. Being single and alone out here in a man's world wasn't easy. She needed to find work, something that would pay better than clerking in a store or teaching school. If she lived.

Ahead, nothing moved. She was surrounded by icy nothingness. She walked on, the hem of Lenore's Irish lace gown dragging the uneven ground. Her hands felt like two blocks of wood. She crossed her arms over her chest in a feeble attempt to warm her fingers; her breath made heavy vaporous gasps. It seemed days since she had put on Lenore's lovely dress, standing motionless while Mary pinned the silken fabric. No other garment was as pretty as a wedding dress, but if she didn't find real shelter soon, this one could very well become her shroud.

The sun, a huge globe of pale, polar yellow, broke through a ragged veil of clouds, washing the landscape with a cold, clear light. Patience plunged ahead, aimlessly walking. Moving. She had to keep moving.

"Oh, God, help me. I need you!" she called out.

The words hung in the frozen air. She stumbled over unseen roots, having lost the road long ago. Brittle branches of winter-bound shrubs lashed her face. The wind brought tears to her eyes, which froze on her eyelashes. Shelter. She had to find shelter.

"God? Where are you? Can't you hear me?" He had always been near; Patience had always felt his presence, but not today. Not now. She felt completely, utterly on her own. She longed to lie down under a rocky overhang, out of the wind, just for a moment, but she pushed the thought away. To stop meant death.

When she did find signs of habitation, she almost missed them—a battered bucket, a small pile of mine tailings. She jerked to a halt, staring at a hole in the side of the mountain. A big hole covered with boards, but with a wooden door set in the entrance. A mine?

She paused before a shabby sign, the weatherworn letters almost too faded to read. Dropping to her hands and knees, she tried to make out the lettering burned into the old board staked to the ground. "Mul . . . Mle . . . Mule Head." Her breath pushed between frozen lips, and she repeated the crude markings. "Mule Head?"

She sat back on her knees, staring at the deserted site. "Mule Head," she repeated. "What's a mule head?"

Bitter cold seeped into her bones, and her joints felt like raw meat. Shadows played across the weather-beaten boards nailed above the entrance to the big hole, highlighting the sturdy door.

Getting to her feet, Patience dusted off her hands. "Well, it isn't exactly what I'd hoped for, God, but the name of the shelter isn't important. Thank you."

Her head pounded and her stomach knotted with hunger. She desperately needed warmth and sustenance.

Wind shrieked through the mountain pass. She rattled, then banged on the heavy door. What if no one was here? Was this a deserted mine shaft? She pushed hard on the door and stepped back when it slowly swung open on creaking hinges.

Sunlight stretched higher in the New Year's Eve sky. Her eyes anxiously searched beyond the dim light, into a seemingly endless black void. "Hello!" she called, forcing the greeting from frozen vocal cords. Her eyes roamed the shadows.

There were bears out here—big ones—and she'd spotted herds of gigantic elk with big horns earlier this morning. She recalled that Ruth had almost died in a snowstorm. She'd shot an elk and gutted it, then crawled inside, pulling Dylan McCall in behind her. Had she failed to take those drastic steps, the newly married couple wouldn't be alive today.

Drawing a deep breath, Patience resolved to be as strong as Ruth. But she wasn't as strong as Ruth. She was a coward. She didn't have a gun—no way to protect herself from wild animals.

Teeth chattering, she studied the odd-looking construction. Some hundred feet from the main shaft someone had tunneled into a steep hill face, fashioning a dark earth chamber about eight by ten feet. A six-by-four, crudely built wooden door secured the hole.

Her breath caught and she refused to accept the absurdity of the situation. Kidnapped, and now at the weather's mercy. No. God was here; he was always with her. The thought assuaged any immediate concerns.

Stepping up on a flat, granite boulder that served as a step, she tried to see into the dimly lit dugout, but the effort proved useless. Her vision cleared, and she could barely make out the interior. In one corner someone had piled pine and juniper boughs. Two or three chunks of old tree bole were scattered about for tables. Close to the entrance, a crudely built fireplace with a small bed of coals dominated the west wall. Fire. Warmth.

She shook her head, refusing to believe her eyes. Did she risk entering and perhaps encountering something worse than kidnappers? What choice did she have? A few more moments in the cold and that would be a moot point.

Her gaze centered on the primitive lodging; she took a deep breath and stepped inside. *Wood. Please God, let there be firewood.*

She inched forward, shuffling, one step, then another. She stumbled and fell; her hands touched cloth. An arm!

Scrambling to her feet, she fought back a scream, but a shriek escaped anyway. She had fallen over a body—*a lifeless body.* There could be no mistaking the rigidity of those limbs. She backed up, moving deeper into the darkness.

A rustling sound from behind her sent her scrabbling for something to use for protection. Her hand closed around a short stick she recognized as a chunk of firewood. Not much use against a bear or a mountain lion. She gripped the club in both hands, straining to see in the fading light of the dying coals.

Something moved in the shadows, and Patience swallowed, caught between what was hiding in that corner and the dead man's body. She fought back a hysterical giggle. Between the frying pan and the fire.

Did that make sense?

Her eyes adjusted to the light, and now she could see that the figure trying to struggle upright was human, a small human.

A child.

She dropped the stick of wood, staring at the ragged boy who slowly rose on unsteady feet. "Who are you?" Patience asked.

The answer came in a thin voice. "Wilson. I'm Wilson."

Jay rode into Fiddle Creek with his badge in his pocket. As far as the residents were concerned, he was just another miner. He'd had a time finding clothes to match his new identity. For most of his life, when he could afford it, he'd dressed well, but today he wore pants with a hole in the knee, a shirt with a couple of buttons missing, and a hat he wouldn't have put on a scarecrow. It wasn't much consolation to see that he looked like most of the people he met.

A tinhorn gambler, resplendent in gray broadcloth with a beaver hat, strode down the boardwalk, looking for a game. For a minute, Jay was tempted. See if his luck had changed . . .

But duty came first. He had to find the Smith woman. And a thankless task it would probably be. *She talks to birds! I ask you, what normal woman with any common sense would talk to a bird?*

Headstrong, too. He'd seen that. Stubborn as a cross-eyed mule. Well, it wasn't any skin off his nose. He wasn't looking for another woman, except in the line of duty. He'd had Nelly. All other women paled in comparison. No. Face it; he was a one-woman man. His woman had died.

He entered the mercantile, closing the door behind him. "Morning."

"Morning," the man behind the counter replied. "Help you?"

"Looking for a shovel and a gold pan. Some ornery critter stole mine."

"There's a lot of it going on," the clerk agreed, placing the items on the counter. "Anything else?"

"Got any licorice candy?" He had a sweet tooth.

"Yep." The clerk added the candy to the pile. "Don't I know you?"

"Don't think so."

"Seems to me like you used to do some prospecting over around Cutter's Gulch way. Jay something, ain't it?"

"Jay Longer. You've got a good memory. That's been a spell."

"Well, some have it, some don't. I never forget a face."

Jay paid for his purchases and left. Rum luck, hitting someone who knew him right off the bat. It had been a long time since he had prospected in this area. Never found any windfall. When it came to mining he was a jinx.

He stopped at Tillie's Café for breakfast. The hot coffee tasted good going down his throat. He was cold and tired, and he wanted a hot bath and a soft bed. He'd spent a long morning working his way through small mining camps scattered through the mountains. This afternoon he'd check out Fiddle Creek. If Patience wasn't here . . . he shook the thought away. She could be dead for all he knew—some grizzly could have gotten her or another hungry predator. He ran a hand over thick face stubble and hoped he didn't run into too many other people he used to know. They'd wonder about Nelly, and he didn't want to talk about her. It still hurt to say her name.

Patience eased closer to the small boy. "Are you all right?"

"No, I don't think I am." The child spoke with an English accent, like a drummer who had come to the store where she worked one day, peddling notions. "I'm feeling puny."

She stepped closer, reaching out to feel his forehead. Her hands tingled with warmth. "You're running a fever. Is there a lantern—a candle I can light?" She had forgotten how cold and hungry she was in the terror of the moment, but now it came flooding back. She was alone in an abandoned dugout with a dead body and a sick child.

The boy's voice came back to her. "Yes, but I don't know where."

Lord, forgive me for thinking this, but we sure have different notions of what might be considered help.

She fumbled, locating a basket of pine knots, and held one to the coals until it caught fire. Now she could see more clearly. A crude cot had been built along the wall where the boy was. He slumped down, pulling a ragged quilt around his thin shoulders. A shelf held tin plates and cups and a few containers of what she guessed to be sugar, flour, and cornmeal. She hoped there was coffee.

The boy stared at her with fever-dimmed eyes. "Are you real? I haven't imagined you?"

"I'm real enough. But we can go into that later. Right now, I'm going to build up this fire and fix something to eat. You lie down and cover up. I don't want you to get chilled." Speaking of chilled, her hands and feet were thawing, sending a hundred tiny prickles through her wind-frozen flesh.

She knelt before the fireplace, making a pile of wood shavings and twigs, covering it with small pieces of dead branches, blowing on the tiny flame until it caught. As soon as the fire was strong enough, she added larger pieces of wood, fanning until the sticks caught and the flames roared up the chimney. Warmth beat against her face, her hands, and body, wrapping her in a blanket of hot air. She knelt there until her joints loosened and her teeth stopped chattering. Aware that she had to do something about the dead person in the room, she rose and discreetly covered the body with a blanket.

Next, she rummaged through the meager store of supplies, finding a chunk of salt pork. Soon the smell of meat sizzling in an iron skillet filled the small space. While the meat cooked, she mixed cornmeal, baking powder, salt, and water, which she poured into a second skillet and pushed close to the fire. That done, she hunted for and found a can of coffee, filled the pot with water and grounds, and soon the fragrance of freshly brewed coffee filled the shelter.

Now to get the boy close to the fire, where he could get warm. She helped him to his feet, letting him lean against her until she had him settled in an old rocking chair.

"There. You'll be all right now." She tucked the faded quilt around him, wishing she had some willow-bark tea to break the fever.

He bent closer to the flames, teeth rattling. "I still . . . think . . . I'm dreaming. Do you have a name?"

"I don't believe anyone ever called me a dream before. My name's Patience."

"Patience." He tried it out. "It's a strange name."

Well, *Wilson* wasn't all that great either, but she was too polite to say so. "My friends think it's a strange name for me. Patience isn't necessarily one of my virtues."

Stubborn, maybe. Patient? Never. She glanced anxiously toward the body on the floor. "Who's that?"

A spasm of emotion she took to be grief twisted the child's face. "He's the old prospector. He took me in when I had no place to go, and when he got sick I tried to help him, but he died."

The boy's forlorn face touched her heart. She wanted to take him in her arms and comfort him, but they were strangers. He would reject her efforts. Moving closer to the fire, she forked slices of meat onto the plates and sifted flour into the grease in the skillet, letting it brown. When it met her satisfaction, she stirred in water from the bucket sitting next to the door. Not as good as milk gravy, but it would be hot and, with the corn bread, filling.

When the gravy thickened, she filled the plates with food and poured the coffee into tin cups. Wilson reached for his plate, but she stopped him. "First we thank God for this food."

"Why? He didn't fix it."

"Don't you believe it. When I was stumbling around on the mountain, thinking I was going to freeze to death, God was leading me straight to this place where there was shelter, fire, and food. He sent me here to help both of us, and we're going to thank him."

Wilson stared at her with a skeptic's eye. "Perhaps so, but the prospector bought that food. He paid for it with gold he found panning in that creek out there. It didn't come from God."

Gold? Creek? The words caught her attention. A creek meant water. Water to drink, a necessity. And gold? Maybe she could manage to find enough gold to pay her way back home, if she ever found out exactly where she was.

"Wilson, you listen to me." She leaned closer, clasping his hands, noticing they were rough and chapped. "Everything in this world belongs to God. He allows us to use it. He gave that prospector the strength to pan for that gold. He led me here to be with you, and he's going to take care of us. Never doubt it. Now bow your head because we're going to thank him for all he's done for us."

The boy started eating the moment she finished saying amen. He ate with the desperation born of hunger. How long had he been here alone with a dead man? She placed another slice of meat on his plate. He needed it more than she did.

"How old are you, Wilson?"

He thought for a moment. "Eight—I think."

"Where are your parents?"

"They're dead. The cholera killed them. The prospector found us, and he helped me bury them. He took care of me until he got sick."

The picture was all too clear. Wilson had no one now. Eight years old and alone. Sometimes the world was a sad place. Patience knew what it meant to be alone. She was an orphan too. Before she had come to Denver City with the other mail-order brides, she had lived in an orphanage.

"Is there a town nearby?" She had to let the others know she was safe; Mary would be worried sick about her.

"Fiddle Creek. About a forty-five-minute walk from here."

She made a bed for Wilson in front of the fireplace, thinking he would be warmer there. Once she'd made him comfortable, she added another log to the fire, carefully banking it with ashes. If she was lucky they should have coals in the morning.

Rolled in her own blanket, she sat on the hearth, staring at the smoldering coals, grateful for shelter, for food and warmth. God had brought her here and she praised him for it, but with the blessing had come a new responsibility.

Wilson lay curled close to the fire, looking younger than his years. She studied the sleeping child's feverish face. Any plans she made would have to include him. The two of them were bound together, fighting for their lives in this formidable wilderness.

For all of her brave words, she felt alone.

Resting her head on her knees, she silently called for help. Tears wet the bedraggled cloth of Lenore's wedding gown. She wanted to go home.

Stretching out on the hard ground, Jay rolled tighter into his blanket. Stars hung low in the sky, and a crescent moon barely illuminated the landscape. He'd forgotten how peaceful it was out here. Maybe if he spent more time out of doors, enjoying creation, he would spend less time at the gaming tables. He'd been a fool to keep playing when he was losing, but he had kept telling himself the next hand would be the winner. Well, the winning hand never came.

His thoughts turned to Patience. Where was she tonight? She wasn't in Fiddle Creek. He'd searched a couple more nearby camps, asking discreet questions, but no one had seen her. It was like she had vanished into thin air. But he'd keep looking. He'd stumble over information sooner or later. He couldn't help wondering what she was going through if she was still alive. She was a little thing, just the right size to fit in the curve of a man's arm. The way Nelly used to.

He pushed the thought away. Nelly was gone, and he wasn't interested in Patience Smith. She was a job. Find her and take her home. That's all he had to do. Nevertheless, he found himself thinking of her out there in a flimsy wedding gown. She would have found shelter by now or she wouldn't be alive. This country was rough on women. He shifted to a more comfortable position and closed his eyes.

Yet sleep wouldn't come. Images of a young woman dressed in a wedding gown kept him awake. Tempted as he was to quit, he couldn't. She was out there somewhere, and it was his responsibility to find her—dead or alive.

Chapter Three

Patience bent nearer the fire and tried to soak up its paltry warmth. The flames had burned low, letting the frigid air seep back in.

"I'm *so* c-cold." Wilson huddled beneath a blanket, teeth chattering. His fever had broken sometime during the night, and he looked more alert.

"I know you are." She bit her lower lip, wondering how long they could survive the elements. One lone log remained, and she had hoarded it the past hour. After much internal debate, she'd taken off Lenore's gown and put on a pair of wool pants and a shirt that were hanging on a peg. The old prospector's clothing swallowed her frame, but the warmth overrode any fashion concerns.

She knew by now the moon had slid behind the tallest mountain and darkness blanketed the mine. She stirred up the fire, seeking the coals' meager warmth. Come morning she had to find more firewood. They must have heat to survive. She didn't know what time it was. The prospector didn't appear to have had a clock, and she didn't feel up to stepping outside to check the sky. How would they know when it was light outside if they were buried in the depths of the earth?

Her joints were stiff and sore from her wild ride, the fall from the horse, and the stumbling around in an attempt to find this place. Sleeping on a stone hearth trying to stay warm hadn't helped matters. She had an ungrateful thought, quickly squelched, that it would have been nice if God had led her to a house with a comfortable bed. She immediately felt ashamed. God had promised to take care of her needs, not her wants. She had needed shelter, food, and warmth. He had supplied all three. Wilson had needs too. If God had sent her to care for him, who was she to complain?

"Where did you come from, P?"

She looked up. "What did you call me?"

"P. I like it better than Patience."

She suppressed a grin. "And what's wrong with Patience?"

His eyes twinkled with mischief. "Possibly nothing, but it seems a bit pretentious."

She laughed. "Perhaps you're right. Regarding where I came from, I was kidnapped."

His eyes grew wide. "Really?"

She nodded. "Really. There was an accident, and the kidnapper and his horse were killed. I wandered around in the cold until I found this place."

Wilson's features sobered. "Why were you wearing a wedding dress? Did you get married?"

"Oh, no." She smiled, wishing she had, but she hadn't met her intended yet. She explained the circumstances, and the boy nodded.

"What are you going to do now?"

"I don't know. Try to find my way back to Denver City, I guess. Whatever I do, I'll take you with me. I wouldn't leave you behind."

Wilson picked up the poker and stirred the fire, making the flames come to life. The dancing light threw the planes of his face into sharp relief. Patience picked out the clean-cut features, the shock of carrot orange hair, which was almost as bright as the flames. Put him into better clothing, put a little meat on his bones, and he'd be a good-looking boy, she realized. He had nice manners too. Someone had done a fine job of raising him. And educated. All those big words, like *pretentious*.

Now he looked at her, his expression grave. "You can stay here and run the mine."

"Mine?" She had forgotten about the mine. How could she forget something like that? "What kind of mine? Productive or played out?"

"Oh, there's gold all right. The old prospector worked it a little every day, even though the mine's haunted. Some days he got a fair amount of gold."

Patience gasped. *"Gold?* There's really *gold* here?" Her face fell. "We can't work the mine; it isn't ours."

"We can claim it. Nobody knows the old prospector's dead. It's ours for the taking."

"Ours?" She eyed him doubtfully. "And what do you mean, the mine's haunted?" She didn't believe in ghosts.

"Gamey O'Keefe. His spirit lives in the Mule Head, but the old prospector paid him no heed. He worked the mine anyway."

"Did the old prospector ever see the ghost?" She'd put this to rest right now.

"I don't know, but it's haunted all right. I've never seen anything either, but I've heard things."

"Well, when we see the ghost, we'll worry about it. Until then, I prefer to believe he's just a superstition." Patience pursed her lips thoughtfully. "And we could . . . honestly claim the mine?"

"Sure—it's ours for the taking. I can't claim it for myself because I'm only a child. No one would take me seriously. But you could claim it in both of our names. You'll have to do it quick because there's a lot of unscrupulous people around who'd love to get their hands on this piece of property."

She could tell from Wilson's earnest expression that he wasn't sure if she would include him in the venture, and she hastened to assure him, "I wouldn't leave you out."

But still, the idea of running a mine was overwhelming. There was so much she didn't know. Excitement flickered through her, in much the same way as the slow flames flickered around the heavy firewood.

Gold! Think of all she could do with the money from the mine. Why, God had turned a scary situation into a blessing. With a gold mine, she and Mary and Lily and Harper would never have to worry about their welfare again. And it was a worry. They couldn't stay at the parsonage in Denver City forever.

She could buy a house, and the four of them could make a home. Wilson too. He had to be included in this. Mary was sickly with asthma. They could take care of her. And Harper was black. There weren't many opportunities for black women. Blacks were treated unfairly even though the war to free them had been fought years ago.

Suddenly she wasn't scared anymore. She should have known God would take care of them. With gold from the mine, the people she cared about the most would be secure. Instead of worrying about a bleak future, they would have plenty. She smiled, looking forward to the exciting and productive months that lay ahead. She would find a crew to work the mine. The diggings would pay their salaries. She would take care of Wilson—and notify Mary, Lily, and Harper of her whereabouts as soon as she found out for sure just where she was. Why, the kidnapping had been a blessing all along! She had to pinch herself. Gold!

She owned a *gold mine!*

Or she would, just as soon as she could get to an assayer's office and stake out her claim.

Wilson interrupted her plans. "What are you thinking about? Dreaming of being rich?"

"No. Well, yes, I suppose. I was just thinking of what we would be able to do with our earnings."

"My guess is we won't be doing much. You'll never get a crew to work here."

She stared at him. "Why ever not?"

"I watched the old prospector try to get men. They won't come. They're superstitious, and they think it's a bad-luck mine."

She laughed in relief. Bad luck? Superstitious nonsense. "They must have other reasons. He probably didn't know how to approach them— or more likely, he didn't have any business savvy. There are people like that. You can always find someone who needs a job. I'll find men to work the mine, and I'll make us rich in the process."

She closed her mind to Wilson's doubting smile.

Hefting a canvas knapsack over her shoulder, Patience started off before sunup the next morning, with Wilson in tow, to claim the mine.

Cutthroat, Randy Doddler, Shirttail Diggin's, Bloody Run, Bladdersville, Gouge Eye, Humbug Creek, Red Dog, Tenderfoot Gulch, Lost Horse Gulch, Gulch of Gold, Mad Mule Gulch—there were a hundred and one gulches where her mine could have been.

And the closest town to Mule Head was Fiddle Creek.

What struck Patience when they entered town was that nearly every man wore a beard. Not one man in a hundred had a clean-shaven face. Some looked to have cut a swatch of hair from around their mouths so they could feed themselves more easily, but in general all the males looked alike: flannel shirts, heavy boots, trousers saturated with muck, and long, matted hair.

Stepping over ankle-deep ruts to cross the street, she stared at the large assemblage of masculinity. She jerked Wilson out of the path of a careening wagon. They had walked for forty-five minutes to reach the small mining community, but the weather had held. Frozen ground had not impeded their journey.

The town itself was an eye-opener. Tucked at the base of a foothill, the camp appeared on the surface to have no civilized refinements. A vast sea of tents sprawled at the base of the mountain, interspersed with crudely assembled buildings that looked to have been thrown together with rampageous zeal. Wagons were lined up, people living out of the back of them.

Traffic had no right-of-way, with many conveyances traveling right down the middle of the street. Patience yanked Wilson from the path of another careening wagon. Rude. The citizens of Fiddle Creek were downright rude!

The stench coming from the livery stable was crippling. Manure from hundreds of horses and oxen that freighted up and down the main street was piled high.

A round of six shots erupted from one of the nearby saloons, and patrons scrambled out of windows and doors in search of cover.

Gripping Wilson's hand tightly, Patience forged her way down the crowded sidewalk in search of the land office. Her eyes watered from the blend of odors of livery stable, chicken feathers, grimy cats and dogs, and unwashed humanity.

Wilson, wearing his Sunday best, made a face when his shoes made a loud clunking sound with each step. "I'm not going to like it here," he predicted. Pinching his nose between his thumb and forefinger, he hurried to keep up with her. "It smells as bad as the old prospector's socks in late August!"

"It'll be fine," Patience soothed, more concerned over how she was going to find the assayer's office than the odors around her. She must also send word to her friends in Denver City that she was well and happy, and that she had a gold mine!

Coming down the middle of the street was a small funeral procession. The bereaved walked hand in hand, grim-faced. Some wept openly. Stepping aside to allow the mourners to pass, Patience restrained Wilson, waiting while the small cortege stopped in front of a modest-looking house with an open grave beside it. A couple of sturdy-looking chaps gently lowered the casket into the ground.

The minister, a tall, sparingly built man with ruddy cheeks and a receding hairline, opened his worn Bible, and addressed the people. "Brethren, it is a sorrowful occasion that unites us this day. In this most solemn of hours we gather to pay our final respects to Sister Oates—let us pray!"

The minister's powerful voice washed over Patience. She nudged Wilson, and they bowed their heads with the mourners.

"Heavenly Father, we ask that you look down on Sister Oates's family and her precious loved ones. Grant them the peace that passeth all understanding—"

With her head still bowed, Patience snuck glances at the crowd through lowered lashes. She noticed that one of the mourners began to examine the dirt he was kneeling on as the preacher droned on.

"He's not bowing his head," Wilson whispered.

"Shhh."

"Sister Oates was a kind and obedient servant, Lord! Those she leaves behind will take comfort in knowing that at this very hour she walks hand in hand with loved ones who have gone before her."

The mourner began to edge his way to the mound of fresh dirt piled high beside the grave, passing the word to the fellow next to him. *Gold!*

The preacher shot him a disapproving stare but continued. "Ashes to ashes, dust to dust . . ."

Whispers of "gold!" gained momentum throughout the crowd. First one man and then another started to paw the earth. The preacher, setting his Bible aside, gazed thunderstruck at the ground, then shouted. "Gold! You're all dismissed!" Dropping to his knees, the man of the cloth clawed the dirt, the solemnity of the moment shattered.

Shaking his head, Wilson watched the spectacle taking place. "It bears repeating. I'm not going to like it here."

Grasping him firmly by the hand, Patience crossed the street, glancing over her shoulders to watch the greedy frenzy. The casket was dragged out of the grave and moved to a different spot to allow for more digging.

To her dismay, she learned the wire line between Fiddle Creek and Denver City was down due to heavy snows. She could not send a wire informing her friends of her whereabouts.

"When will the line be fixed?"

The man behind the counter shoved his green eyeshade back and glared at her. "When will the line be fixed?" he mimicked. "If I've heard that question once, I've heard it a hundred times. I'll tell you, I ain't got no crystal ball, and the good Lord don't let me in on no secrets. So I don't know *when* it's gonna be fixed."

"Well, goodness, there's no cause to shout." Surely this was the rudest place she'd ever been. She left the telegraph office, intent on laying claim to the mine and getting home before dark. She'd wire Denver City the next time she came to town.

"Oh, dear," she murmured when she finally spotted the assayer's office a few minutes later and saw that the line was backed up clear to the street.

"It's going to take forever, isn't it?" Wilson said nasally, still holding his nose from the stench.

"A while, I'm afraid."

Taking her place at the back of the line, Patience looked around her, dismayed to see the recorder's office was every bit as chaotic as the streets. Yet she had no other choice but to wait. She had to claim the mine before greedy speculators beat her to it.

For more than two hours they stood in line, wedged between smelly old men who shouted and pushed and shoved and said awful things to each other.

Recalling the earlier conversation with Wilson who said that most men worked for the larger mining companies, she leaned forward to shout above the din to the man standing in front of her.

"What's going on?"

"New strike—big one, over near Poverty Flats!"

"Gold?" she asked hopefully.

"Silver."

As Patience's part of the line edged nearer the building's entrance, she heard male voices raised in a circuslike atmosphere. Timidly, she opened the door and stepped inside. A sea of men's faces turned to stare, then continued on with their conversations.

Around two o'clock her head began to pound. She glanced down when she felt Wilson yanking on the hem of her jacket.

"I'm hungry."

"It won't be much longer." She patted his head consolingly. It had been hours since they'd eaten a meager fare of cold bread and salt pork, but if she stepped out of line she'd lose her place and have to start over again.

"I'm tired, and my shoes are too tight," he complained. He sagged against her, visibly weary from the long journey and the extended wait. Patience was starting to wonder if she was doing the right thing. What if the mine *was* worthless? What if it yielded so little gold she would be forced to return to Denver City empty-handed? She couldn't bear the thought of coming so close to an answer for her and the other orphans and losing out. They depended on her, and she had promised God she'd always take care of them. This mine would help her keep that promise.

Here, in a strange town, with even stranger-looking men flanking her on all sides, doubts assailed her. If anything were to happen to either Wilson or her, there would be nowhere to turn for help. Loved ones in Denver City were worrying themselves into a stew—how was she going to let them know that she was okay?

A scuffle broke out and two hefty-looking men hauled the ruffians outside. She tensed when she overheard two men ahead of her talking.

"Silas Tucker will grab any unoccupied mines around here; you can bet on that."

"Tucker's a leech," the second man sneered. "Wouldn't be the first time he jumped a claim."

Patience moved Wilson closer. For over an hour she had been aware of a scruffy individual two places in line ahead of her. He was, without exception, the most tattered and torn man she had ever seen. He was a caricature of an old miner—unkempt red hair, filthy beard, the rim of his old brown hat disgraceful. What had once been a flannel shirt now hung in ragged scraps, covering most of his soiled trousers.

Her eyes meandered to his boots and found that they had more holes than leather. The man stood head and shoulders taller than the other miners.

"Look, Wilson," she whispered. "There's a man with hair the same color as yours."

Wilson's face screwed with disgust.

"Except yours is cleaner," she added.

"P!"

She patted his shoulder. "Much, much cleaner."

The man suddenly turned, his eyes nailing Patience.

With a hushed catch in his throat, Wilson stepped back.

For a moment Patience couldn't breathe. The stranger's arresting clear blue gaze captured hers. Caught off guard, color flooded her face, and she realized he knew she had been staring at him. For a moment she thought she recognized him; then she quickly dismissed the idea. She couldn't know him—she didn't know anyone in Fiddle Creek.

Yet recognition briefly flashed in his eyes, and he suddenly smiled. He was about to doff his hat when he must have thought better of it. Instead, he graciously bowed from his waist. "The boy is weary. Would you like to take my place in line?" His hand indicated their chaotic surroundings. "It won't help much, but some."

Moving Wilson protectively closer, Patience summoned her most charitable smile. "No, thank you. We'll wait our turn."

Conceding with a gracious nod, the man turned back to continue the wait.

The hands on the clock crept from three to four. Wilson reeled with fatigue, clinging to Patience's trousers like a wet blanket.

"Are we *any* closer?" he asked. She heard his stomach rumble conspicuously.

The line moved at a snail's pace. Men's voices rose and fell with anticipation and anger. The room was so hot Patience could hardly breathe. Loosening the top button of her collar, she took deep breaths, directing an evil eye to the man who kept dumping coal into the corner stove. It was hot enough to cure meat in the room, but the man didn't seem to notice. Every half hour, he stepped up and fed the black monstrosity another bucket of coal.

Patience had worked her way to within five places of the assayer's desk when she suddenly felt light-headed. Fighting the weakness that threatened to overcome her, she squeezed Wilson's hand tighter.

Wilson's glasses tilted askew as he sagged against her, catnapping.

Minutes ticked by. Sweat trickled down the small of Patience's back. Bringing her handkerchief to her forehead, she blotted perspiration, willing her eyes to focus. *Only four more,* she told herself. Then she could seek a breath of clean, blessedly cool air.

She was third in line when her knees buckled. With a whimper of despair, she was overcome with blackness.

Chapter Four

Patience felt herself being lifted, carried out the door. The cold air hit her like a blow. She gasped, reason returning slowly. She could hear Wilson calling her.

"P! Wake up, P! What's wrong with her?"

A deep rumbling voice answered him. "Got too warm, probably. It was hotter than July in there."

Patience opened her eyes to find herself lying on the ground, her rescuer kneeling beside her.

"Are you feeling better now?"

"Yes, thank you," she said, grateful for his help and recognizing the scruffy miner who had offered her his place in the line. He bore a striking resemblance to Sheriff Longer. . . . "It was so hot in there." She hoped her smile was properly apologetic to make up for her earlier exclusion. The miner had been exceedingly kind. "I'm sorry you lost your place in line."

He shrugged. "It doesn't matter." He studied her features intensely. "What about you?"

Sighing, Patience got up and readjusted her old hat. "I have to claim my mine tonight."

The man's eyes skimmed her trousers. "It's getting late," he said. "And the boy's hungry. Can't you wait until morning? The lines are usually not so long then."

"I can't." Patience took Wilson's hand, trying to comfort him. He was bone weary, and neither of them could go much longer without eating. "I have to get back in line."

"It will be dark soon."

For a moment Patience was tempted to tell the man he was being intrusive. She knew it was foolish to encourage conversation with a stranger—much less one so disreputable-looking. Yet he had been kind enough to help her. . . .

Sighing, she noticed that the shadows were lengthening. Soon it would be pitch-black. "I'm afraid I have to get back into line."

Studious blue eyes assessed her, and he dropped his voice. "Is someone watching you?"

She frowned, glancing around her. "No . . . why?"

"Just pretend we're discussing a claim," he advised.

She smiled at him lamely.

He glanced at the crowd in front of the assayer's office, then back at her. "Where is your mine?"

Loosening the buttons of the worn coat, she searched for a way to get rid of him. "Not far—Mule Head. Have you heard of it?" Getting a closer look at his hands, Patience was surprised to see they were strong and tanned. Why, he wasn't nearly as old as she'd first thought. No one to take care of him properly and hard living, she suspected when she studied his features beneath the scrubby beard.

He nodded. "I know where it is."

Relief flooded her. Maybe he knew something—something she should know. "Is it a good mine?"

"Depends on what you call good. It's haunted."

So, he'd heard the speculation. She supposed the ghost was common speculation around here.

She stood shivering in the mountain air, holding tightly to Wilson's hand. "I'm afraid rumors regarding the Mule Head have been greatly exaggerated." She paused when she saw him staring at her in an odd, almost embarrassing way. She touched her hair self-consciously, aware of her manly attire. "Is something wrong?" She was quite certain she didn't look her best—maybe her hairpins had come loose.

He glanced over his shoulder again, then back to her. "Are you all right?"

"All right?" She frowned. "I'm fine. Why?" For heaven's sake—why was he so worried about her health? The room was too hot—that's why she fainted.

Stepping closer, he lowered his tone. "It's me." He lifted the brim of his hat to allow her closer inspection. She stared at the red beard and ruddy complexion. Nothing. Whoever "me" was, she didn't know him.

Her frown deepened. Oh, dear. He was peculiar. A hundred men in the vicinity, and she attracted the addled one.

"Me." His tone turned a little sharp. "Take my arm and walk slowly away from the area. Once we're clear, I have a horse waiting. You don't need to be afraid."

She nodded blankly. Oh, *dear*. "Wilson," she called brightly. "Time to get back into line—"

The man reached out and grasped her by the forearm, suddenly propelling her in the opposite direction.

"Excuse me!" she bellowed, trying to jerk free of his steel-banded hold. Why the man was more than addled—he was deranged!

"P!" Wilson called, running to catch up. The miner threaded Patience through the teeming crowd.

"Let go of me this instant!" She managed to break the man's grip, incensed that no one was coming to her defense. What kind of men were these rowdies?

"Stop it! You're causing a scene." He latched onto her arm again and purposely marched her in the direction of the livery.

"*You* stop it!" She was making a scene big enough to alert anyone to her situation—but nobody seemed to notice. Men and women went about their business with barely a glance at the growing fracas.

"I'm trying to get us out of here without a fight," he muttered. "Will you please cooperate? You're just plain lucky I doubled back through Fiddle Creek today, or I would have missed you completely."

He didn't make a lick of sense. "Why would anyone fight over us?" She stumbled over her own feet and had to steady her balance on his arm.

He glared at her, shooting furtive glances over his shoulder. "Are your captors nearby?"

"Captors—?" Patience suddenly stopped in midtrack. Now she knew why he bore such an uncanny resemblance to Jay Longer. He *was* the sheriff of Denver City! He was her rescuer! But why was he dressed so—awful?

She voiced her shock. "Why are you dressed so awful?"

He glared at her. "I'm in disguise."

"Oh." Well, she should have figured that out. Of course he wouldn't ride into one of these rowdy mining towns with a tin badge on his chest. He was infuriatingly contrary but not stupid.

29

"Sheriff Longer, isn't it?"

He quieted her with a dour look. "I'm *trying* to get us out of here in one piece."

She drew herself up straighter, eyes narrowed. "How very kind of you to come after me. There is no captor—the horse stumbled and landed on the kidnapper and I got away." She frowned. "Didn't you find the horse carcass and the man's body?"

"I found it, but I thought maybe the culprit was part of a gang and they still had you. I've been trailing you for days."

"Well, how nice," she said, and then straightened her hat. Turning to a wide-eyed Wilson, she said, "Wilson, Mr. Longer is Denver City's sheriff. He's been looking for me."

Wilson refused to warm to the stranger. "Hello," he mumbled.

Briefly Patience filled Jay in on the past days' events, the death of the old prospector, the mine, and Wilson's role in the strange circumstances. She said she was here to claim Mule Head and that she planned to stay for however long it took to get the mine producing gold. "Mary, Lily, and Harper will never have to worry another day about their future," she finished.

Longer took off his hat and swatted the brim on his dusty thigh, apparently unconcerned whether the material would hold together. Annoyance lined his weary features. "Denver City is twenty-eight miles from here; I know these parts as well as I know the back of my hand. Mule Head is worthless, Miss Smith—"

"Call me Patience." She didn't know why she was so charitable, but they couldn't keep calling each other by their last names.

He conceded, "Okay. Your mine is haunted, Patience Smith. You won't get one man to work it—let alone a crew of men."

Her face fell. "That's just plain not true. The part about the mine being haunted is silly rumor. I don't believe in ghosts."

"Neither do I, but the majority of folks around here do, and that's your problem. You best forget about staking a claim and come back to Denver City with me. Your friends are worried about you."

Patience could feel her dream crumbling, and she struggled to hang on. That mine was the only future she had. Go back to Denver City—to an uncertain life? His advice wasn't fair—not fair at all! She could find men to work the mine; she knew she could. The sheriff gave up too easily.

Stiffening her resolve, she turned and reached for Wilson's hand. "I'm sorry, Sheriff Longer; I don't want to be rude—" *like you,* she wanted to add but didn't—"and I truly appreciate your coming all this way to rescue me, but I don't need rescuing. I'm going to claim the Mule Head and work it, because it will give us a chance to have a future—a future we would not have otherwise."

With a curt nod in the sheriff's direction, she stepped back into line.

Women! Jay watched her flounce off. Stubborn, ornery . . . wouldn't listen to a blessed thing. A woman didn't have any business running a mine. Some men believed women were bad luck in a mine. If you asked him, women were bad luck, period.

Take this one. He had been looking for her in one mining camp after another, sleeping on the ground, spending restless nights, and then when he did find her, she brushed him off. Didn't want to go home. Going to work the mine and get rich.

Not at the Mule Head, she wasn't. He knew that mine. Knew most of the mines in this area. Had worked some. Even if she managed to file the claim—and she was just bullheaded enough to do that—she'd never find a crew. He wondered where she'd picked up the boy. Spunky kid. He'd tried to protect her when she'd passed out.

Jay chuckled. Funny little guy. Doubled up his fists and started swinging. Jay had held him at arm's length and let him whale away until he'd run down. But he'd tried; he had to give him that.

He watched Patience and the boy inch along in line. They'd be a while yet. Probably getting hungry. Well, he could do something about that. Satisfied they weren't in any immediate danger, he sauntered off, searching for food.

Sheriff Longer was leaning insolently against the surveyor's office, arms crossed, when Patience emerged two hours later. Darkness cloaked the mining town. Lanterns glowed brightly in the cold mountain air.

When the sheriff fell into step beside them, Patience ignored him. She had filed her claim, and he wasn't going to talk her out of working it. Nobody was going to talk her into giving up. Too much depended on it. The other three and Wilson. Four people who needed the security the mine would give. She couldn't fail.

He didn't argue. They walked to the edge of the town in stony silence. Once he reached into his pocket and took out two warm biscuits

31

stuffed with fat sausage slices, and handed one to Wilson and one to her. Wilson tore into the food like a ravenous animal.

She ate hers more slowly, savoring the first warm thing in her belly all day.

"You're walking back to the mine tonight?" His voice broke the strained silence.

"I don't have a choice." She swallowed a bit of biscuit and meat. "I have no money for a room—even if a room were available." She hated to admit her immediate disadvantage, but there it was; she was flat broke and she had to go back to the mine.

"You're not going alone."

"I came alone—at least, Wilson and I came alone, and we had no trouble."

"You walked daylight hours, didn't you?"

She had to admit that she had. And that she was terrified to walk in the dark. So many ravines and gulches. One misplaced step and . . . she closed her mind to the dangers. She had responsibilities now—as Wilson's self-appointed guardian, she had to put on a brave face.

"You'd be better off waiting until morning," Longer said shortly.

"We'll walk a ways and then rest until dawn."

His eyes accessed her trousers and wool coat. "You'll freeze before dawn."

She didn't break pace. "I've survived overnight in a wedding gown, sir—besides, I brought extra clothing." She wasn't that green. The old prospector owned quite a few clothes, and she'd packed every one of them in the bag—and extra food and water, hidden along the trail.

"These mountains are treacherous if you don't know them."

A smile filled her eyes when she heard the hesitation softening his deep baritone. "But you do know them, don't you?" She wasn't sure why, but she knew he would help her. She wasn't foolish. For all she knew he could be dangerous *and* contrary under that scruffy façade; yet she sensed that he wasn't. His outward appearance was a well-executed ploy, but his eyes gave him away. Patience saw a sense of nobility in them.

"You do know the mountains?" she repeated softly.

A muscle flexed in his bearded cheek. "I know them."

"Then I'm sure we could not ask for more capable assistance." Her pleas formed a soft vapor in the cold night air.

Glancing at the boy, he said quietly, "We'll need lanterns."

"I don't have money to buy one," she reminded him.

"Wait here . . . and wrap that scarf in your pocket around your neck. The temperature is dropping."

Patience took Wilson's hand, found a large rock, and sat down to await the sheriff's return. She couldn't be rude, and he had agreed to walk them back to the mine—sort of. When he returned to Denver City he could assure the others of her well-being and explain why she hadn't come back with him.

So she'd wait—and accept the sheriff's kind offer of help—if it killed her.

Jay returned half an hour later carrying two lanterns, canteens, and more biscuits and sausage. "I've decided to leave my horse at the livery. I don't want to take a chance of the animal breaking a leg. We'll walk up the mountain."

Wilson asked for seconds on the biscuits and sausage, stuffing the steaming fare into his mouth. They started off. The moon rose higher. Wilson walked beside Jay now, apparently satisfied he was more friend than foe.

Jay glanced at the top of the boy's head. Good kid, but an odd little duck. "What's your name, son?"

Wilson swallowed, panting to keep up with Jay's long strides. "Wil . . . son."

"Wilson?"

He nodded, running to stay alongside.

"You good with your fists, Wilson?"

"Not very . . . but with a name like Wilson, I should be, huh?"

Jay let his lips curve in a hint of a smile. "Is that an English accent I hear?"

"Yes, sir. My parents were traveling from England when they died of the cholera. I escaped the disease. The old prospector found me three days after they died—I was hungry and quite a pitiful sight, I understand. I don't know if my name's Wilson—but that's what the prospector called me."

Jay shook his head. Rough break, but a common enough story in these parts. Life could be tough on kids.

"What was the prospector's name?"

"Prospector. Sometimes Mr. Old Prospector. Me and you have the same color hair; you notice that?"

"I noticed."

"I could almost be your boy, couldn't I?"

The sheriff's face hardened. "I don't have a boy."

"Well if you *did,*" Wilson insisted, "I could be him."

Not in a million years. Jay kept his eyes fixed straight ahead. His boy was lying in a six-by-three-foot mound next to his mother.

Chapter Five

It got dark early. That was what Jay hated about the mountains. He didn't mind the cold when he came to Colorado years ago, but he hated it now. Mexico—that climate suited him. Hot winds and long, sultry nights with strumming guitars.

Leaving Patience and Wilson in the dugout, he picked his way back down the mountain, trying to erase the boy's face from his mind. Wilson. Odd little fellow. Reminded him in a strange way of Brice. His son. He'd have been about the same age as Wilson. Seemed like when Jay had lost Nelly and his boy to the fever, he'd sort of lost himself too. Took a long time to come to grips with their dying. He'd wake up in the night and feel the horrible, twisting pain of knowing he'd never see them again—not on this side of heaven, anyway.

He'd been so proud of his boy, had looked forward to teaching him how to shoot a gun and saddle a horse. To be a man. A good man, the kind who would do right, a man who would be honest, clean, trustworthy. The kind of man he wanted to be but couldn't quite muster after Nelly died. He'd planned to teach Brice to fish and ride and hunt, too. Oh, he'd had plans for that boy. Big plans. And then the fever had swept their home, and he'd buried those plans with his wife and son.

Jay had lost something else that day: his trust in God. How could a loving God take Nelly and Brice and leave him behind with nothing but broken dreams and a black, blinding despair that had almost destroyed him? Oh, he still believed there was a God—you couldn't live in these mountains and not see his handiwork—but he didn't believe that God cared about people.

He'd learned the truth that day, standing beside an open grave and listening to the wind wailing through the pines and the preacher droning on about God's love. The truth came to him, driving through his grief, hardening his heart until it was like a lump of stone inside him.

God didn't care.

If God had any love or compassion for Jay Longer, he wouldn't have taken Brice and Nelly.

That was the truth, and you couldn't get around it.

He'd learned to hide the pain and push away the memories, but this boy Wilson had brought it all back. Jay realized now that he'd made a habit of avoiding young boys, afraid of letting himself get too close. Afraid to revive old hurts.

He'd tried to reason with his wife, pleaded with her to let him take her to the doctor when the fever overtook her and the boy, but she didn't believe in medicine. Had some foolish notion that trusting in doctors showed a lack of faith in God.

Nelly came from a religious family, probably the most religious people he'd ever known. Lived by a set list of rules. Sometimes he'd wondered whose rules—theirs or God's? Mostly he couldn't find their rules in his Bible, and he'd searched. But they believed in them and lived by them.

Nelly had gone to an old herb woman who'd mixed up some kind of potion for her to drink. According to Nelly, it was all right to take the potion because herbs were natural medicine. He couldn't see it himself. Sure, herbs could be powerful medicine sometimes, but so could store-bought medicine. Seemed to him if God could use an old herb-doctoring woman, he could use a regular doctor. But Nelly had followed her beliefs and she'd taken her potion and she died. And Brice had died with her.

Nelly had been real stubborn. Just like Patience Smith. And now Patience had this fool notion of working the mine. No one could do a thing with her. Get a notion in her head and you couldn't budge it, and dreaming of gold was a powerful notion.

Since he'd been in Colorado Jay had seen more stupidity than he could shake a stick at. Some of it his. Yeah, he'd followed the gold dream, but not anymore. When it came to mines, he was a jinx. Still, it was amazing how some people responded to the mention of gold.

The boy looked downright scared. Couldn't blame him. The Mule Head should scare anyone in their right mind.

But the two would be all right overnight. The dugout was dry, and he'd made sure they had plenty of wood before he left. Come morning, Patience would start the process of hiring a crew, and she'd find out what she was up against. She wouldn't stick around long after that.

Jay would bide his time. Let her learn the hard way. He could force her to go back to Denver City with him, sling her across his horse and haul her back, but she had a temper. He'd seen plenty of flashes of it. Twenty-eight miles would seem like a hundred-mile ride with a spitfire like that. He remembered a piece of Scripture from the book of Proverbs: "It is better to dwell in a corner of the housetop, than with a brawling woman in a wide house." Solomon had, what—about six or seven hundred wives? Jay bet the old king knew a lot about brawling women.

He was on the right track. Let Miss Patience Smith see what she was up against, and she'd beg him to take her back to Denver City.

He tried to think of more pleasant things as he walked, but he couldn't get Patience's face out of his mind. Odd, since he hadn't thought about a woman since Nelly's death. Not for any length of time. Seemed like he couldn't get interested in a female after Nelly; he'd just drawn into a shell and stayed there. Nelly had been so sweet and so pretty, so eager to please him in everything except where her beliefs were concerned. And in the end, her beliefs had killed her.

They'd married young, sort of growing up together. Life had been good then. When Brice was born, Jay had held the two of them in his arms, his heart filled to bursting with love.

Maybe they'd have died anyway, even if he'd gotten them to a doctor. No way of knowing. If only Nelly had loved him enough to listen, to forget the rules for once, to trust him enough to seek medical help.

He suddenly lost his footing, stumbling.

Quickly righting himself, he concentrated on the trail. *Watch it, Jay; you can't fall and break your neck. . . .*

Who'd care? he thought, laughing outright now.

Sure, Jenny would be upset, but she'd get over it. His kid sister didn't know where he was, let alone worry about him. Hadn't kept track of him for years. She was in Phoenix being a dutiful wife to her husband, good old reliable Joe. Together they had respectfully produced three strapping heirs in less than four years. Pop was probably real proud of them.

"And he'd consider me a flat-out disgrace," he acknowledged.

Loose rocks gave way beneath his heavy boot as he edged the steep incline. If he fell and broke every bone in his body, there'd only be one man who'd care.

That, of course, would be Mooney Backus, the man who held his gambling debts.

How much did he owe Mooney now? Twenty-five hundred dollars. A small fortune—one he didn't have. Sheriff's pay didn't cover his former insanity, the years following Nelly's death.

Years ago—when he'd believed in a caring God—he'd have been worried about owing a man money and then suddenly finding himself unable to meet his debt. Yes sir, there'd been a time when he'd have stayed up nights trying to figure out how to repay the money.

And gambling would have been the last thing on his mind. But when God stepped out of Jay's life—the day God took Nelly and Brice—Jay's responsible thoughts ceased.

Back then he'd been honorable. Honorable and full of himself.

But no use crying over spilled milk. He had no one but himself to blame for his problems; he could easily have become a town doctor. Pa was a physician, and by the time Jay turned sixteen he'd helped deliver half the babies in the territory and even helped Pa when he cut out bullets and sewed up men's faces. If doctoring hadn't suited him, he could have married Mary Porter. Mary's pa wasn't exactly a pauper. The old man would have given him fifty acres of prime farmland—no, more like two hundred and fifty—in order to spare his daughter the agony of spinsterhood. But that wasn't what he'd done.

No sirree, not Jay Longer. Not the brash twenty-year-old who had life all figured out. He'd married his true love, pretty Nelly Briscoe, whose family lived on a neighboring farm, and like so many other misguided fools, the two had started out for Colorado to claim their fortune. He'd sunk every last penny he had in a gold mine that had produced nothing.

Absolutely nothing.

Not particularly bright of him, but when a man had gold fever he wasn't thinking straight.

From the day James Wilson Marshall discovered the first gold nugget in a ditch that channeled water from river to sawmill, gold had enriched and ruined men's lives. That afternoon of January 4, 1848, forty-five miles east of Sutter's Fort in Sacramento Valley, changed the course of history.

And put a fair-sized dent in Jay's life.

But that was neither here nor there. Pop had given up on Jay's ever taking over his doctor practice; Mary had been spared spinsterhood when she married the depot clerk, Pete Wiler; and any day now, Jay would be dead.

Mooney Backus wasn't long on patience. He'd been after Jay to pay off his debt for over two years now. Jay was running out of excuses and was tired of avoiding Backus's thugs, Red and Luther.

He laughed, wondering what the good folks of Denver City would say when they found out their sheriff was a wanted man. Not by the law but by something more deadly.

Four days ago, Backus had delivered an ultimatum by wire. Jay had exactly two weeks to come up with five hundred dollars. Which had a lot to do with why he wasn't in a hurry to get back to Denver City. If Mooney wanted him, he'd find him, but no sense making it easy for him.

Jay caught himself again as his boot slid in the loose dirt, the rocks spilling down the precipitous incline. The trail started to blur. Shaking his head, he tried to focus on the path. Cold seeped through his senses, and the moon barely shed enough light to walk by. He'd stayed at the mine longer than he should have, stacking wood and making sure the girl and kid were settled. There was a hundred-foot drop on either side of him. One slip, and he'd save Mooney the trouble of coming after him.

Concentrating now, he slowed his pace. The wind whipped his frayed coat. His hand came up to hold his battered hat in place. A lone coyote howled at the moon. He rather liked this disguise, might even keep it to throw Backus's men off his trail.

One moment he was walking, and the next he felt himself hurtling down the mountainside. Panic-stricken, he tried to catch himself, but he was too far gone. He tumbled end over end, arms and legs flailing wildly.

Bile came up in his throat and he choked, hitting the ground hard. Sliding, he snatched for a handhold, his life flashing before him. Miraculously, one of his hands snagged something and latched on.

Silence closed around him. He lay, afraid to move a muscle, panting, praying that whatever he held on to would continue to support his weight.

A coyote yelped, its cries fading into emptiness.

Using his free hand, Jay slowly felt around, determining that he was on the edge of a mine shaft or maybe a deep precipice. His scraped and bleeding fingers explored the uneven ground. Sweat beaded his forehead. He touched the small outcropping of rock he was lying on.

He was afraid to risk even the slight movement needed to yell. Besides, no one would hear him. Not here on this remote mountainside.

Flat on his back, he watched a cloud drift across the moon, temporarily obscuring it. Snowflakes started to swirl. A cold wind buffeted the hillside.

Jay lay motionless, his eyes fixed on the sky. Nothing he did lately worked out.

"P, I *am* thankful for food, but I don't like turnips," Wilson reminded Patience the next morning. "Especially not for breakfast!"

No longer than they'd been together, Wilson had decided he liked P. Liked the way she smiled—and she was kind. She didn't yell or cry or act like a baby even though he knew she was scared.

Animals prowled the mine site, growling with hunger. Once last night, Wilson had heard something big lumbering around outside—a bear, he suspected. A big out-of-sorts grizzly. It sniffed around for a long time. Patience heard it—he knew she heard it—but she pretended to be asleep, although he could see the blanket quivering over her slim frame.

He didn't blame her. The boards the old prospector had nailed over the mine entrance and the heavy door over the dugout kept out most four-legged intruders, but a grizzly would be hard to stop.

"Turnips are good for you—and we can be thankful that the old prospector laid up plenty of store for the long winter."

This morning she'd discovered the small root cellar adjacent to the mine, stocked full of potatoes, turnips, beans, butter, and salt pork— "enough to see a small army through the hard months," she'd exclaimed. You'd have thought she'd hit the mother lode the way she carried on. She got more excited when she discovered the old cow. Even tried her hand at milking and did as well, or maybe better, than the old prospector had done. It looked like she was settling in for a long spell. Probably he shouldn't have suggested working the mine. She had the fever now, and it would be hard to discourage her.

Sighing, Wilson quietly set to work eating.

Patience let her mind pleasantly drift, and she contemplated all the things they could do now that she owned a gold mine! Wilson needed shoes, and she needed a new dress—maybe even two! And, oh, what she could do for Mary. She could rent—no, *buy*—larger quarters for the millinery, and for Harper she could buy Mrs. Katskey's café so the grandma could devote all her time to raising her young grandson. Harper would have income for the rest of her life.

Then she would buy a big house—big enough for Mary and Harper and Lily and her and Wilson to live in comfortably. Oh, it would be so grand—they would be a family, a real family, with Thanksgiving dinners and plum pudding and lots of oranges and peppermint-stick candy at Christmastime.

The mine's proceeds would mean that an exceptionally bright young boy could attend college and have all the things his parents would have wanted for him. The orphanage had supplied life's necessities for her, as long as she was young, but the headmistress made it clear that once Patience reached adulthood she was expected to provide for herself. Well, she had tried her hand at becoming a mail-order bride. That had fizzled, but God had given her another chance.

Wilson reached for his glass of milk. "Will we live here in the dugout?"

"We'll have to—I'll have to oversee the mine." She'd managed to stake a claim to the Mule Head before news of the prospector's death reached other materialistic would-be miners. Maybe they could build a cabin. She didn't fancy living underground like some burrowing animal.

Wilson peered back at her through his bottle-thick spectacles. "Mining is hard work, P—"

She didn't mind the shortened name, but she'd reminded him that she shouldn't be so lenient since she was his elder. Nodding, she took a bite of potato. "We'll hire strong men to do the work. At least eight or ten."

The boy sighed. "The old prospector said that wasn't possible. All the men in this area have jobs, and besides, they're afraid to come near Mule Head."

"Nonsense. You're talking about the ghost again, aren't you?"

"How do you know it's nonsense? Just because you've never seen a ghost doesn't mean they don't exist."

She stared at him. "I asked you once before. Have you ever seen the ghost?"

He squirmed, turning red in the face. "I'm not saying what I've seen, but I do believe it might be a mistake to be overly confident. Whether you believe in ghosts or not, the men do. They won't want to disturb a 'haint,' as they call it, and they might not want to work for a woman."

Patience glared at Wilson. "It was your idea to claim the mine. Why are you trying to discourage me now?"

"I've had time to think, and I do believe we might be taking on more than we can handle."

She sighed in exasperation. "So I should let someone else have the mine? Do you really think I'm going to do that? Stop coming up with reasons why this won't work. We've claimed this mine, and we're going to work it, and we're going to be rich. I already know what I'm going to do with the money."

This wasn't just about her. It was a chance to do something for others. Jay Longer couldn't see that, but he was a rigid, arrogant . . . ole goat. God would help her help Mary, Harper, and Lily. After all, he'd brought her here.

Wilson sighed. "I've never thought it wise to spend money you haven't received yet. We have a long way to go before we see any monetary compensation."

Patience sent him a reprimanding glance. "Wilson, where *did* you learn those big words?" He was eight going on forty. She didn't know where all that wisdom came from, but at times he seemed the adult, not her.

Wilson shrugged. "I have a flair for English."

Grinning, she reached over and tousled his flamboyant thatch of carrot-colored hair. In many ways he *could* be Jay Longer's son, not only in looks but in stubborn persistence. "With all that money we'll even be able to buy you some new glasses."

"That would be nice. The old prospector didn't have money to be throwing around. He said I was lucky to have any." He stabbed a turnip with his fork and stared at it. "Can I have a dog now? The old prospector strictly forbade pets. He said they ate too much, and barked and left stuff in the yard he was always stepping in."

"Sure, but no more than one—too many mouths to feed."

Taking a bite of bread, he frowned. "I wouldn't be counting my nuggets yet if I were you."

Her brows lifted. "And why not? We own our own gold mine."

"Well, I don't know," he contended patiently. "I'm only eight, but I sense we're in over our heads here. I realize you don't want to hear about that, but who will do the work? I'm telling you, the old prospector couldn't find anyone to help him."

"But I can get help. Once I set my head to something, I usually achieve the end result. At the orphanage, if anyone wanted anything done, they'd come to me."

Wilson's eyes returned to his plate. "You can be so naïve, dear friend."

They continued eating breakfast, letting the subject drop momentarily. Finally Patience looked up again. "Are you really suggesting that we desert the mine? that I go back to Denver City?"

"How old are you?"

"It isn't proper to ask a lady's age."

"I'm sorry. How much do you weigh?"

She'd sooner tell her age. "Wilson!"

"What funds have you set aside for your welfare?"

"Well, none . . ." Her words wavered when she saw him shaking his head. "I lived in an orphanage before coming to Denver City, where I was supposed . . . to be . . . a mail-order bride." She paused, worrying her teeth on her lower lip.

"Homeless and broke." When she was about to argue, Wilson continued. "I'm homeless and broke too, and I'm only eight years old. It's nothing to be ashamed of—just a small nuisance."

She slid to the front of her chair. "Don't you see? Our situations make it even more imperative that we work the mine. We don't have any other choice. I can take you back to Denver City with me, but to what? I don't have a home—Mary, Lily, Harper and I are living with Pastor Siddons and his wife, and the house is fairly bursting at the seams. Listen, Wilson—" her eyes pleaded for understanding—"maybe the Lord will shine on us and we'll unearth a vein of silver. That's even better than gold, isn't it?"

"Silver would be better, but a good gold vein is capable of producing a handsome profit," Wilson mused.

Patience leaned in closer. "Then let's do it. Let's ask the Lord to bless our efforts, and let's do it."

"Most assuredly." He slid a piece of turnip into his mouth, momentarily gagging. He continued. "There are still a few small problems."

"What?"

"You don't know how to mine, I'm too little, and Gamey's ghost won't let anyone in the mine."

Smiling, Patience continued eating. "There is no ghost, and there's enough gold here to make our wildest dreams come true."

Taking a drink of milk, Wilson sighed. "Logic isn't your strong suit, is it?"

The first warming rays of the morning sun woke Jay. He flexed his feet, feeling like one solid block of ice. Turning his head, he gauged the width of the ledge on which he lay. It protruded maybe six inches past his body. He shuddered. Lucky for him he had landed here. Now he had to do what he could to get out of this fix.

He reached up and grasped an outcropping of rock, carefully pulling himself to a sitting position. His body ached from various bruises and scrapes, and he felt stiff from the cold. Tilting his head back, he squinted up, relieved to find that the top of the ledge was only about nine or ten feet above his head. He was a good six feet tall. If he could find hand-holds, he could possibly get out of here.

Easing to his feet, he avoided looking down. By standing on his tip-toes and reaching up as far as possible, he managed to grip a small ledge. Inch by inch he pulled himself upward, scrabbling for toeholds. He tried not to think of the stabbing pain in his shoulders and the way the rocks scraped his hands raw. A few more inches and his groping hands caught a tree root. He tested its strength, not sure if it would hold his weight, but it held firm.

His head crested the top of the ledge. He grabbed a slender bush, hauling himself up. His shoulders were over the rim, now his waist. He scrambled forward on his belly until he lay full length on top of a smooth boulder. Sun warmed his shoulders and he breathed deeply, knowing he would live.

After a few moments, he got to his feet, stumbling a little in his haste to get off this mountain and find shelter and warmth. As he strode down the trail, he tried to ignore the thoughts that troubled his mind.

All through that long, lonely night, when he wasn't sure if he'd live or die, it wasn't Nelly's face that had filled his dreams. It had been the stubborn, irritating image of Patience Smith.

Get a grip, man. Give the lady enough rope and she'll hang herself.

The thought wasn't all that disagreeable. Yet it was, and for the life of him, Jay couldn't understand why. Until Patience was kidnapped, his life had been going smoothly; no problems—other than bad debts. He kept to himself and encouraged others to do the same. He'd eaten steak and potatoes, slept on clean sheets, and propped his feet in front of a roaring fire every night. He resented having to chase a mulish woman over the hillsides. Resented the dickens out of her.

If that was the case, why did he have to remind himself three times a day that what he was doing was a job, pure and simple? Patience Smith didn't factor into the picture.

Actually, this woman was more trouble than she was worth, and the sooner she got this get-rich notion out of her head, the quicker he'd be back home in his own bed.

Well . . . he grinned. Maybe he'd just hurry Miss Smith's reasoning process along a little bit. The thought of steak and potatoes and a warm bed was powerful motivation for a man who hated the cold.

Not to mention the dark.

Chapter Six

Before the sun topped the ragged summit on the crisp January morning, Patience stepped out of the dugout and took a deep breath of mountain air. Confronted with magnificent beauty, she clasped her hands in awe of Colorado's snow-covered peaks silhouetted against a flawless blue sky. Icy tendrils hung in long, glistening blades off craggy ledges.

Searching for the proper term to describe such breathtaking beauty, she found none. Yellow pines, Douglas firs, and blue spruces covered the mountainsides. Just below the timberline, hardy bristlecone pines, gnarled by the constant winds, dotted the land. And the aspens—their magnificent trunks were resplendent beneath a layer of fresh snow.

On the lower slopes, mule deer browsed on nuts and lichens. Elk and bighorn sheep leapt among the crags at higher elevation.

How could she describe such splendor—such grandeur— when she told Mary, Lily, Harper, and Ruth about her adventure? How could she find the words to define the simplicity—the marvelous beauty that God had made? The troubles they had experienced had drawn them together until they were as close as sisters. They were the family she'd never had. When the mine began producing, Patience was going to bring the three single women here and let them experience the sights for themselves.

Sighing, she breathed deeply of the pine-scented air. Her friends would be so worried about her. She'd go into Fiddle Creek today and try again to wire them or ask around and see if perhaps someone planned to travel to Denver City soon. She thought of the mine she now owned. *Lord, I'm not greedy. Really, I'm not. It's just that we need that gold.* It was difficult to be a single woman out here, or anywhere for that matter. There weren't many jobs available. If she could get this mine producing, none of them would ever have to worry again.

She sighed. She'd claimed her mine over two days ago—but Jay hadn't returned.

Worry nagged her. Had he gone back to Denver City without her? Would that audacious man just *ride off* like that without saying good-bye? She was conscious of a flash of disappointment. Flustered, she tried to ignore the emotion. Why should she care what Jay Longer did? He was nothing to her. Wasn't likely to ever be important in her life. Sure, he was a big healthy specimen of manhood. Nice to look at too—or would be, if you cleaned him up and put some decent clothes on him.

They'd gone nose to nose in Denver City, and thinking back, Patience remembered that he had a very nice nose. A very manly nose indeed, but he'd always been aloof, not talking much or paying her any attention. She realized now that she—along with every other single woman in town—had been miffed at his conspicuous lack of interest.

He was obstinate too. Trying to take her away from Fiddle Creek by discouraging her efforts—although she tried to tell him she could get a crew. This was her only chance to make a future for herself, and she had a lot of people depending on her.

She kicked a rock out of her way, hoping he hadn't left the area yet. She hated to admit it, but she liked him. Was even a little attracted to him, although she wouldn't ever want him to know it. She was hoping he would help her hire a crew before he returned to Denver City.

Hands on hips, she focused on the mine's boarded entrance, determined not to be beaten by her circumstances. Sure, there were problems she hadn't considered, but problems were meant to be solved, weren't they? And the ghost? The Good Book said not to acknowledge superstitions.

Sitting down on the stoop, she sighed. Surrounded by God's glorious work, Patience found it hard to be pessimistic about the future.

The Mule Head wasn't that bad. Why, in the time it took to say, "What am I doing here?" she'd have the mine operating at full speed.

Ghost or no ghost, the men in Fiddle Creek would welcome new employment opportunities. The big companies couldn't offer the caring, family-oriented workplace she intended to give her crew. Wilson's college nest egg would be growing—

Feathers! Who was she kidding? The living conditions were de-plorable. Vile, dirty, cold, horrible . . . and lonely. So very lonely.

She'd be lucky to hire a monkey crew if the Mule Head's reputation was as bad as Jay seemed to think it was.

Patience got up, went into the dugout, and closed the door. Rubbing the goose bumps on her arms, she hurried to the fire.

"Wilson!" She eyed the tuft of russet sticking out from beneath the blanket. She swung a pot of water over the flame to boil. "Rise and shine! We have a lot to do today!"

"Freezin'," Wilson complained in a muffled voice from under his covers.

"Get up, slug bug! Sun's up!"

A jumbled thatch of reddish hair poked out of the blanket, followed by a pair of disgruntled eyes. "I'm stiff as a poker."

"We'll have to do something about that draft," she agreed.

"Draft!" Wilson exclaimed. "It's more like a cyclone whistling be-neath the door." Throwing the blanket aside, he stared at his feet. "I'm crippled," he announced.

"No, you're not," Patience assured him cheerily. "Your feet are just cold." She stirred oats into the pot of boiling water. "The circulation will return once you're up and around. Hurry now—we have a crew to hire!"

Wilson watched her as she fixed breakfast. "Are you going into town today?"

"I thought we would." Her first visit to Fiddle Creek had been fo-cused on filing a claim. Now she was anxious for any tidbit of informa-tion, however small, regarding the mining town. For instance, did they have a school? She'd been thinking that if she was going to work the mine, Wilson would need proper schooling. He also needed to be with children his own age. He'd probably been with adults most of his life, and he needed youthful, carefree days. The good Lord knew Wilson had seen few of those.

Besides, she would be too busy working to teach him. She had to set up a household, hire a crew—oh! There were so many things to be done!

Breakfast finished, she went outside again to check the weather. It had snowed last night. The door opened behind her and a tousle-headed Wilson stepped out, snuggling deeper into a fur-lined coat. He squinted against the sun's glare on the fresh snow.

"If you're planning to hire a crew, most of the bigger mining companies have taken over. In order to have their families with them, the men settle for an hourly wage now."

Patience's brows lifted. "Then we'll pay our crew hourly."

The boy shook his head. "I've been thinking, P. The old prospector thought silver was more profitable."

"Silver?"

He nodded, shuffling through knee-deep snow to reach her. He stopped, took a big sniff, and then wiped his nose on his coat sleeve.

She frowned. "Don't wipe your nose on your sleeve, Wilson."

"But it's dripping."

Patience remembered that he had mentioned silver earlier. But gold! Now gold was always gold and surely profitable.

It was still fairly early when Patience and Wilson walked down the mountain. Approaching town, she searched for any sign of Jay, but he wasn't around. Yet she couldn't make herself believe that he'd actually left her and Wilson here alone. He was pouting; wasn't that what men did when they didn't get their way? She bet Jay Longer was a big pouter. Her attention was diverted by the schoolhouse. She hadn't noticed the building the day she claimed the Mule Head.

"There's the schoolhouse."

Wilson shrugged his shoulders. "I've never been interested in academics. The old prospector said I had enough schooling to use words no one could understand. I didn't need any more."

Patience was aghast. Not need schooling? Of course he needed to go to school. She realized that she could probably be considered Wilson's guardian. At any rate, she had taken on the responsibility of looking after him, and if she had anything to say about it he would go to school. Even at the orphanage, she had received an education.

"Of course you need to go to school. We'll check into it this morning."

"P, I don't want to go to school! I want to stay with you."

"Wilson, you need schooling. How do you expect to get ahead in the world without it? You'll always be at a disadvantage with people who are more educated."

Wilson screwed up his face in outrage. "I've been told I'm exceptionally smart for my age. I don't think many eight-year-old boys could outthink me."

"Probably not, but you won't be eight years old forever, and all of those people who are sitting in school and learning from books will soon know more than you do. Knowledge is power, Wilson. Never forget that. Besides, the Bible says we are to study to show ourselves approved."

Wilson peered at her over the tops of his spectacles. "I do believe God was referring to studying his Word, not arithmetic."

The schoolhouse was a one-room affair of plain boards weathered to a soft gray. Patience noticed Wilson eyeing the building with distaste.

He looked up at her. "This is a waste of time. Someday I'll be grown, and then no one will make me do anything I don't want to do."

He followed Patience up the steps and inside. Nine pairs of eyes stared at him. He stared back. Patience stiffened with irritation. Look at him. He'd already decided the other students wouldn't like him and he wouldn't like them. He shuffled a little closer to the door, and she took a tighter grip on his collar, thinking he was probably considering making a run for it.

The young teacher with plain features introduced herself, greeted them warmly, and had the children bid Wilson a hearty welcome. He mumbled a reply.

The schoolroom was dimly lit and drafty. Twelve student desks, the teacher's platform, a blackboard, and a large potbellied stove crowded the interior. Along the back of the room, heavy coats, knit hats, and warm mittens haphazardly hung on pegs. Nine pairs of children's galoshes and one pair of adult's formed muddy puddles along the wall.

Miss Perkins smiled. "We're just about to work on our geography, Wilson. Please take a seat."

"Geography," Wilson whispered to Patience, "my *worst* subject!"

"You're welcome to stay and visit the class this morning," Miss Perkins invited Patience.

"Thank you," she said. "I can't, but I will another day."

"*Psst.* Four eyes—over here!" a big kid in the third row jeered.

Placing her hands on Wilson's shoulders, Patience gently steered him to a seat close to the blackboard.

"Can you see clearly from here?"

Removing his glasses, Wilson wiped a film of steam off the lenses with the handkerchief Patience had stuck in his pocket earlier. Hooking the earpieces back over his ears, he squinted up at the blackboard. "I can see."

"Good." Patience squeezed his shoulder reassuringly. "I'll be back to

51

walk you home." Leaning closer to his ear, she whispered, "Don't be nervous; the first day is always the hardest."

Wilson nodded, his eyes glued to the colorful world map covering the blackboard.

"Geography," he muttered. "And on my first day too."

The first person Patience saw after leaving the school was Sheriff Jay Longer, leaning against the front of the mercantile and looking more disreputable than ever. Her heart threatened to pound out of her chest.

He tipped his hat. "Morning, Miss Smith."

Swallowing the monstrous lump suddenly blocking her airway, she said, "Mr. Longer."

"This your first trip to town after filing your claim?"

"Yes, it is." *And none of your business.*

"Planning to hire a crew?"

"Yes, I am." She tilted her chin, meeting his eyes. "That's exactly what I'm going to do."

"You're not going to have any luck." He grinned. "Might as well give it up now and come back to Denver City with me."

The palms of her hands itched to wipe that grin off his insolent face. What right did he have to interfere? "I appreciate your staying around to look after me, but as you can see, I don't need your help. Why don't you go back where you belong and leave me alone?"

He straightened, towering over her. "Number one: I'm not staying around to look after you. I'm just not in any hurry to leave town. Number two: I'll go back when you're ready to go with me. I told Dylan and your friends I'd bring you back, and that's exactly what I plan to do."

"*You* plan? What about *my* plans? Aren't they important?"

"Not to me. Go ahead and try to hire a crew. See how much luck you have, and when you fall on your face, look me up."

She drew herself up to her full height, blistering him with a look she hoped he'd not soon forget. "That day will never come. I'll go back to Denver City when I'm ready, and I won't need your help getting there."

He calmly adjusted his hat back on his head. "All right. I'll leave you alone. You go your way and I'll go mine."

She firmed her lips. "That's fine with me."

He bowed mockingly from the waist. "Me too."

"Fine."

"Fine."

He strode away and she glared after him. *Ill-mannered bore.* Who did he think he was? She was so tired of men pushing her around. First Tom Wyatt and now Jay Longer. She had one more reason to make the mine pay. If she could strike it rich, she would never have to put up with an arrogant, insolent man again.

"Your best bet's to post the work notice on that thar board, lady."

Patience thanked the elderly prospector and walked on. She tacked her notice on the public-information board. She had carefully compiled the handbill while Wilson ate his breakfast. It read:

> Wanted: Men willing to work for competitive wage. Must be honest and hardworking. Age no factor. Dinner provided. Contact Patience Smith, proprietor of the Mule Head.

She stood in front of a nearby saloon, waiting for takers. Returning to the board at 11:26 A.M., she rewrote:

> Wanted: Anyone willing to work. Wage negotiable. Two square meals a day. Contact Patience Smith (woman standing in front of the saloon), proprietor of the Mule Head.
> P.S. Thank you.

Men came and went, pausing in front of the board long enough to read the advertisement. One or two glanced in her direction. Several laughed. One even snorted.

But not one approached her about the job.

At 1:43 P.M. she marched back to the board and scrawled:

> Hello? Anybody out there? I am willing to pay above-average wages, expect you to work no more than forty hours a week, and promise to provide three delicious meat-based meals a day.
> What more do you want?
> Patience (the woman who's been standing in front of the saloon for hours now!), proprietor of the Mule Head.

By 2:35 P.M. sheer desperation set in. Pacing back and forth, Patience observed Fiddle Creek's male population with mounting resentment. What was wrong with these people? There had been no fewer than two hundred men who had read that handbill and walked away. Family men—men she suspected could certainly use the money.

She had been as generous as projected funds allowed. She wasn't made of gold. What more did they want?

"Might as well save your energy. Ain't nothin' you're offerin' likely to entice 'em, miss."

Patience glanced over to see the elderly prospector who'd spoken to her earlier sitting on the sidewalk steps, whittling. Jay leaned against the hitching post, passing the time of day.

"Is *everyone* employed?" she asked. "Doesn't *anyone* in this town need a job?"

"Nope." The old man leaned forward and spat. Wiping tobacco juice on his coat sleeve, his eyes returned to the small deer he was carving. His crippled hands worked the wood slowly and lovingly. The carved figure was intricately fashioned with delicate details.

Stepping around Jay, Patience came over to sit beside the man. She watched him work for a moment before she spoke. "That's very nice. Have you been carving long?"

The old man spit another reddish stream. Wiping his mouth on his sleeve, he nodded. "Pert near all my life."

"You're very good at it." She'd never seen an image so lifelike. The doe's supplicating eyes immediately drew her in.

"He sells his work," Jay observed.

Patience lifted her eyes coolly.

"Ain't no one gonna work your mine," the prospector predicted.

Patience's thoughts unwillingly returned to the problem at hand. "The men can't *all* have jobs."

"Nope, lot of 'em looking for work. But they don't wanna work for you."

What was wrong with her? she wondered. She hadn't been in town long enough to make enemies.

The old man held the carving out to study it. "Well, it ain't *you* exactly. It's the mine."

"Mule Head?"

"Yep. Gamey O'Keefe won't let no one come near it."

"Oh—Gamey O'Keefe. I should have known." She glanced at Jay.

He held up his hands in protest. "I didn't say anything."

"He didn't say a thing," the miner confirmed. "Didn't need to. Gamey's ghost is living in your mine."

"Oh, that's nonsense. You mean to tell me that grown men would actually refuse to work for me because they think the mine is haunted?"

"Yep." He spat again.

"Feathers."

He looked, frowning. "What's that?"

"What's what?"

"That thar *feathers*. You a cussin' woman?"

"That's *her* way of cussin'." Jay grinned.

"Oh, my . . . no," Patience stammered. She could feel her face burn and she wanted to throttle Jay Longer for telling tales. If *feathers* was offensive, she hadn't been told. "I wasn't being vulgar. *Feathers* means nonsense, empty talk . . . you know."

"No, cain't say as I do. Never heared the term before. Thought feathers were something you found on a bird or duck." He smiled. "Rumor has it that you come from Denver City. They talk like that over there?"

"Well, some do—but I don't think *feathers* is especially prevalent." The orphanage housekeeper favored the term, and Patience had latched onto it. She eyed Jay, who seemed to be enjoying her discomfiture. The big brute.

"Yeah? Well, it's a new one on me," the miner confessed.

Patience watched while he painstakingly shaped the carved animal's hind leg with a knife blade.

Drawing her knees to her chest, Patience rested her chin, watching the men come and go, their incredulous laughter getting on her nerves. The old prospector's clothes she was wearing were three sizes too big for her, and she had to roll up the coat sleeves to use her hands. "Do you believe in ghosts?"

"Ain't never seed one, but I allow they could be some."

"Well, apparently everyone around here thinks there are." She sighed. "I have a problem."

"Yep, guess you do."

"I'd say," Jay added.

Patience shot Jay a warning look that said *You're not in on this conversation, mister.*

"What should I do?"

The old miner looked thoughtful. "Hard to say. Rumor also has it you have to work the mine. You need the money, bad."

Patience snorted. *Rumors* certainly spread fast in these parts.

"Heared tell thar's some Chinymen over at Silver Plume. They might help ya."

"How far is Silver Plume?"

"Oh . . . day, day-and-a-half ride from here."

"A *hard* day-and-a-half ride," Jay confirmed.

A day-and-a-half ride! Patience didn't own a horse, and she couldn't leave Wilson alone.

The old miner seemed to read her thoughts. "I got a jenny. She ain't pretty, but she'll get you there."

"It isn't that—I don't care what the animal looks like. It's the small boy I'm looking after. I can't leave him unattended."

"Wilson? The boy's old enough to take care of himself, ain't he?"

"Do you know him?"

"Seed him around with the old prospector."

"Wilson is sensible, but I wouldn't leave him alone," Patience said. She noticed Sheriff Longer didn't come to her rescue. Well, good. She wouldn't have accepted his insincere help anyway.

"Well, ole Widow Noosemen will help you out." The old miner held the carving out for final inspection. "She'll look after the boy till you git back."

"I can't pay her anything for her services."

Handing Patience the carving, the old man smiled. "That's all right. Widow Noosemen's service ain't worth nothing, but she'll see to the boy."

⟜

"Ole Widow Noosemen," Wilson groaned. He and Patience walked up the mountain late that afternoon. "She smells funny!"

"I'll only be gone four days, Wilson. That old miner Chappy Hellerman told me there are some Chinamen in Silver Plume who might be willing to work. I've already spoken to Widow Noosemen, and she has agreed to let you stay with her until I get back."

"But, P—"

"No *but*s, Wilson." Patience hated to disappoint him but there was no other way. "Widow Noosemen is very nice, and I'm grateful for her kindness." The widow did reek of snuff, but she adamantly refused Patience's eventual offer of money, saying it was her Christian duty to help out. "You know I've tried everything I know to hire workers, but no one wants to work for me. Maybe if I go far enough away, I'll find *someone* who's never heard of the Mule Head."

Wilson huffed and puffed, climbing higher. "How you gonna get there? Walk?"

"No, Chappy has graciously offered to let me borrow his mule."

"Aw, rats."

"I'm sorry; that's how it is. I'll be back as soon as I can. With any luck, we'll have our crew, and maybe some nice Chinaman will even teach you to speak Chinese."

"Aw, rats. What about Jay? Can't I stay with him?"

"Absolutely not! And don't ever mention his name to me again."

"You mad at him?"

Patience bit her lower lip, deciding if she couldn't say anything nice about the sheriff she wouldn't say anything at all. So she kept quiet.

As they trudged up the incline, Wilson bombarded her with all the logical arguments against staying with Widow Noosemen he could think of: someone might steal him, he might get hurt, he could fall off the mountain and no one would ever find him, an elk could eat him, he could lose his glasses and never see again, Widow Noosemen could beat him.

But in the end, Patience held her ground. First light tomorrow morning she was going to Silver Plume, and Wilson had to stay with Widow Noosemen.

Things would have been a whole lot simpler if Sheriff Longer wasn't deliberately making her situation harder. It wouldn't *hurt* him to watch Wilson, and it sure wouldn't kill him to help her hire a crew. He had seen they had plenty of firewood and fresh water, and she had thanked him for that. But then he just left her alone. She wouldn't have thought it of him. A knight in shining armor he wasn't.

She stifled a grin. A knight in shabby clothes, maybe. She'd never seen a man so raggedy. His shirt would surely come apart if you washed it. Still, there was something solid about him. But if he hoped to soften her up by leaving her alone, he was wasting his time. She owned this mine, and she planned to work it if she had to do it all herself.

Jay watched Patience and Wilson leave town and start their ascent up the mountainside. He'd kept an eye on her all day. A rough miner's camp wasn't any place for a pretty woman like Patience Smith.

Pretty, *aggravating* woman like Patience Smith. Seemed every time she failed, she just dug her heels in a little deeper. Now she was going to try her luck in Silver Plume. If he had any sense, he'd go on back to

Denver City and let her fish or cut bait. But somehow he couldn't do it. It wasn't in him to leave a woman in a dangerous situation, and the Mule Head was no place for a woman. He'd just saddle his horse and follow her to Silver Plume.

But she'd never know it.

Chapter Seven

Who'd ever have believed news could travel so fast! Even the Chinese had gotten wind of Gamey's ghost. Week two flew by, and Patience still didn't have a crew. Jay Longer was still hanging around, goading her to go back to Denver City. Well, she wouldn't. Not as long as there was a breath of hope to get the mine up and working—albeit the breath was getting a mite ragged.

Brave words, and she tried to believe them, but she was getting discouraged. Worse, sometimes she got so downhearted she even cried, and she wasn't a crying woman. She'd always been the type to pull up her socks and go on. "Crying won't mend no britches," the matron at the orphanage used to say, but it seemed like Patience just couldn't help it.

At first she had been so excited thinking about how she could take care of her friends back in Denver City. She'd even made plans for Wilson, wanting to help him get a good education, more than he could receive in a mining camp. She had been so certain that God had led her to the Mule Head, but now she had doubts. How could she work a mine if she couldn't even get a crew?

She tried to keep Wilson from knowing how discouraged she got, but she knew he noticed sometimes how red and swollen her eyes were after she had cried at night when he was supposed to be asleep. Well, she'd have to think of something. Somehow there had to be a way to get a crew together. If God wanted her to work the mine, he would lead her to a solution.

Lifting an egg out of the skillet, Patience called Wilson again. "Hurry up! Breakfast is getting cold!" She sliced bread and her mind raced with a new plan.

Women. That's where she'd go. Fiddle Creek women enjoyed an uncommon amount of independence. Miners, it seemed, were starved for the fairer sex, so women were revered and seldom hampered by propriety.

The town ladies were mostly shopkeepers' wives who enjoyed certain refinements within their own social realm. They might welcome a break in their monotonous routine. After all, a woman could mine gold just as easily as a man. Patience would just go to the women, explain the problem, and offer to pay them a man's wage to help her.

Of course, they wouldn't be able to work the mine forever, but they could at least get the work started. They had little else to occupy their time but a few frivolous activities that Patience had prudently avoided by saying her obligations to the mine prevented her from joining in the fun.

During her recent journey to Silver Plume she'd witnessed an incident that left her both amused and sad. A woman's bonnet had been found lying in the middle of the road. No one seemed to know how it got there, but it caused quite a stir among the miners. Three or four of them had nabbed the saucy little hat with its ribbons, bows, and laces and erected it on a maypole in the center of town.

Their shenanigans turned into a near riot. The other men, looking for an hour of diversion from the cold streams and damp mines, poured into camp to join in the fun.

The bearded, booted roughnecks were so hungry for female companionship they staged an impromptu dance around the bonnet, joking and laughing as they took turns dancing with the lovely "Miss Bonnet."

Patience had watched the good-natured fiasco, wondering if Jay Longer was as eager for female companionship. Her thoughts surprised her, and she wondered why she'd thought them in the first place.

She'd seen Jay in Silver Plume, but he'd steered clear of her. Now, what had he been doing in Silver Plume the same day she was there? Drawing her knees to her chest, she grinned, admitting that with a little cleaning up the handsome sheriff of Denver City would be downright interesting. She had never seen eyes so remarkably blue or hair more fiery red or a chest so broad and manly.

She couldn't imagine why he kept himself so distant and—unhappy. He looked to be in excellent health—too thin, perhaps, but a few good meals would remedy that. He had no zest about him, no anticipation for life. He was a man with no purpose other than to drag her kicking and screaming back to Denver City.

Wilson's voice jerked her back to the present. "Couldn't we wait until it warms up?" he complained, decidedly disgruntled about being pulled from his bed before daylight.

"Just eat. We have to hurry."

He cracked one eye in the direction of the door. "It isn't even day yet, is it?"

"Just barely. Now hurry and eat, grouch."

Directly after breakfast, they set off. "You'll be a little early for school, but I want to be the first one at the mercantile this morning," she explained. They descended the narrow trail. She didn't want to miss talking to a single woman. The moment the school bell rang, the mothers would head for the store to exchange the latest gossip. This morning she planned to be there waiting for them.

"I don't like school, Patience. Nobody likes me," Wilson complained, his feet hurrying to keep up with her. "The girls talk mean to me, and the boys call me Four Eyes and Bat Boy."

"Bat Boy?"

"Yeah, 'cause I'm blind as a bat. Butch Miller tried to make me eat bugs yesterday."

"Why?"

" 'Cause that's what bats eat, P."

"The moment we start making money we're going to get new glasses for you," she promised. He needed stronger lenses—these lenses were barely adequate. Yesterday he'd bumped into the door and bloodied his nose, and she knew it was because he couldn't see clearly.

"Why do I even have to go to school? You could teach me at home."

"I have a gold mine to run."

"No, you don't. You're trying to get someone to run it for you. Once you do, then you can teach me at home, *hmm,* P? Then I won't have to put up with Butch Miller anymore."

"I can't do that, Wilson. Money will be extremely tight, and I'll have to work no matter who I get to run the mine." She gave him a quick hug. "Besides, it'll do you good to be around children your own age. You'll make friends. The others will warm to you."

"They won't. They're mean. Butch Miller took my sandwich yesterday and threw it down the privy hole. I was hungry all day."

"Did you tell Miss Perkins?"

He looked aghast. "No! Butch would've creamed me!"

Oh, Patience wished she knew how to fight! She would teach Wilson how to hold his own against bullies like Butch Miller! She caught herself, knowing that the Good Book said to turn the other cheek—but there were some folks you had to allow for, and it sounded like Butch was one of them.

"If Butch Miller takes your sandwich today, you tell Miss Perkins, you hear?"

Wilson sighed. "I can't."

"Well, for heaven's sake, why not?"

"'Cause he'll just take my apple too."

After depositing Wilson on the school steps, Patience went straight to the mercantile, hurrying up the steps so lost in thought that she slammed into Sheriff Longer, almost knocking herself off balance. She grabbed at him instinctively.

His arms went around her, breaking her fall. He grinned down at her. "You in a hurry this morning?"

She was all too aware of his nearness. When he made no effort to release her, she placed her hands on his chest and pushed him away. "I'm sorry. I should have been watching where I was going."

"Don't apologize. It's always a pleasure running into you."

She flushed, remembering the way she had clutched at him. "I thought you would've gone back to Denver City. You do still have a job there, don't you?"

He shrugged. "I'd be in Denver City right now if you weren't so bullheaded.

She stiffened. "I am merely taking care of business."

"And it doesn't concern me?"

"That's right."

His expression softened. "Look, Miss Smith, you've done your best, but it isn't going to work. You aren't going to find a crew. Give it up and go home. You're fighting a losing battle."

She looked up at him, near tears. "You don't understand. I can't quit. You're a man. You can't know what it's like to be alone with no money, no job, no home. Well, that's what it's like for me and for Mary, Lily, and Harper, and for Wilson too. That mine is our only chance. I have to make it pay."

She pushed past him and entered the mercantile.

Jay stared after her. Now why did she have to go and get womanly on him? He could handle it as long as she was as prickly as a hedgehog cactus, but he'd seen tears in her eyes, and now he felt like a heel. He walked off with a sinking feeling that he was going to hang around Fiddle Creek and the Mule Head a little longer.

Using the money Jay had left her, Patience bought a half pound of sugar, three apples, half a pound of tea, and a spool of white thread before the women started to arrive.

The more she thought about her new plan, the more she warmed to it. Women working in the Mule Head. Not only would they enjoy the added income, they could also take pride in the fact that they were lending a sister a helping hand, and she doubted few, if any, believed in ghosts.

One by one the women came into the store, their conversations ranging from diaper rash to peach butter. When the most recent gossip, innuendoes, and rumors were adequately *ooh*ed and *ahh*ed over, they started to browse.

Patience approached each one singly, striking up a friendly conversation. "Hello! My name is Patience."

"I don't know anybody."

Patience blinked. "Pardon?"

"I don't know anybody to work your mine."

"Oh—well, thank you." Patience moved to the dry-goods table, still looking over her shoulder. "Hello! My name is—"

The woman sorting through the bolts of calico never looked up. "Patience."

"Yes." Patience smiled. "I'm the new owner of—"

"Mule Head."

"Yes, that's right, and I'm—"

"Looking for a crew."

"Yes—do you—"

"Know anyone who'll work for you?" The woman laughed. "No."

"Nice talking to you."

63

⌒

"Hello, my name is Patience."

"So nice to meet you."

"Have you ever considered a job outside the home? The pay is good, and it can be arranged for you to be home when school lets out."

"I have a job: five kids and a lazy husband."

"Yes, but haven't you ever wanted to stretch? Do something on your own?"

"No. Never."

"Nice visiting with you."

⌒

"I'm Patience Smith—"

The young mother turned and smiled. "I know, dear. Welcome to Fiddle Creek."

"Thank you. I was wondering if you could possibly help me?"

The young woman's smile never lost its vigor. "I'm afraid not."

Patience frowned. "You don't know what I want."

Lifting a spool of ribbon, the woman waved to the clerk. "I'll take two yards of the lavender, Edgar!" She flicked a glance over her shoulder. "Nice talking to you."

"The same, I'm sure." Patience moved on.

⌒

"Think about it. The pay is excellent, and I'll arrange to have you home before your family even realizes you're gone. You don't believe those silly ghost stories, do you?"

"Certainly not!"

"That's what I thought. The moment I saw you, I said to myself, *Patience, this is an intelligent, hardworking woman whom you would be honored to call an employee.*"

"Well, thank you. I certainly would try to be."

Patience's smile lifted. "Then you'll help?"

The lady gave her an affronted glare. "Do I look like I've lost my wits?"

Snatching up a tin of peaches, Patience moved on.

⌒

Coming out of the store several minutes later, Patience blew her bangs out of her eyes and sighed.

Jay leaned against a hitching post, whittling. She shot him a disdainful glance and walked past him, her chin in the air. She could hear the thud of his boots following her. Why wouldn't he go away and leave her alone?

"No luck?"

She stopped and turned to face him. "You know what kind of luck I had. It turned out just the way you said it would. I guess that makes you happy?"

He frowned. "Not exactly."

She stared at him. "What does that mean?"

"I admire someone who doesn't have enough sense to give up, but you're fighting a losing battle. These people have a thing about the Mule Head. You'll never get anyone to work there."

She stepped closer, looking up at him. "You could help me if you would."

He shook his head. "No, ma'am. I'm not a miner. I'm a lawman."

"Then go back to Denver City and do your job."

"Right now my job is taking you back where you belong."

"I belong here." Her eyes locked with his, challenging him. "If you'll help me hire a crew, I'll cut you in on the profits."

He removed his hat and slapped it against his thigh. "What is it about *no* that I'm not conveying to you?"

His eyes, electric blue, burned into her. His hair glowed in the sunlight. She fought an urge to brush her fingers through it. What was she thinking? This . . . oaf infuriated her!

She gripped her hands behind her back. "I'm staying. Go on back to Denver City. You found me; that's all you were supposed to do. Tell my friends I'm all right, and I'll come when my business here is finished."

He opened his mouth, closed it, clapped his hat back on his head, turned, and walked away.

Patience stared after him, feeling suddenly lost and alone. She looked up to see Chappy sitting on the porch steps, whittling.

"Hire a crew?"

"No." She glanced in the storefront resentfully. "They must all think I'm a fool."

"Well—" the white-haired prospector calmly inspected the hummingbird he was carving—"I wouldn't feel too bad. I could have told you they wouldn't be interested. Women are considered bad luck in a mine."

"I've heard." She crossed the wooden planks and sat down beside him.

"Known men to set fire to a mine if a woman's been in it."

"Why, that's mad."

"Might be, but folks up here are a mite set in their ways."

"Well, I guess it doesn't matter." Patience leaned back, soaking up the sun. She didn't have the slightest idea what plan four was. "The women didn't want to work anyway."

"Got their hands full taking care of the family."

"Seems that way."

He chuckled. "Don't know much 'bout miners, do you, sissy? Or men?"

"Nothing," Patience admitted.

"Well," he said, a foxy note creeping into his voice now, "you ought to learn. A pretty little thing like you will be wanting to take a husband someday. Might need to know what he'll be looking for."

"And what might that be?" Patience asked, not really interested. From what she could tell, the only prerequisite a woman needed to catch a man around here was that she was breathing.

"Well now, the Frenchies think it's got something to do with a woman's legs."

"A woman's legs."

"Yep, the dark-haired girl with a large leg will get fat at thirty and lie in bed reading novels until noon."

Patience looked back at him, sneering.

"The brunette with the slender limbs, now she'll worry a man's heart out with jealousy."

Patience's gaze moved to her wool trousers.

Chappy examined the bird's progress. "Now, the olive-skinned maid with a pretty rounded leg is sure to make a man happy. The blonde woman with big legs will degenerate by thirty-five into nothing more than a pair of ankles double their natural size and afflicted with rheumatism. The fair-haired woman will get up at the crack of dawn to scold the servants and gossip over tea."

"So, a man wants the olive-skinned maid?"

"No, the light, rosy girl with a sturdy, muscular, well-turned leg is the one men want. But if he's lucky enough to find a red-haired little gal with a large limb he'd better pop the question quick as he can." The old man's eyes twinkled with devilment.

"What about a redheaded man? Do the same rules apply to him?"

"You know any redheaded men?"

"Maybe," she answered evasively.

There were only two in camp: Jay Longer and seventy-year-old Webb Henson.

"The short lady should have a slender limb, and the tall lady should possess an ample one." He handed Patience the finished bird. "Think you can remember that?"

She nodded. Of course she could remember that, but she couldn't for the life of herself see that the observations held any credibility.

She walked back to the mine, fighting tears. At least no one could see if she cried way out here. She wouldn't give them the satisfaction of knowing she felt like giving up.

And there was Wilson. He'd been brought up right, you could tell that. His parents must have been good people. But the old prospector probably hadn't been a proper influence on the boy, and he was exposed to a rough element in the mining camp. A boy needed a man's influence, a godly man's influence. Although where she'd find that kind of man in Fiddle Creek, she couldn't imagine.

Her thoughts turned to red-haired Jay Longer. He seemed like a good enough man, but godly? Not that she could see, but then prayer could work miracles. She might pray for him; surely God would understand she wasn't asking anything for herself, although he was surely a decent man. She climbed toward the mine, with her thoughts of the sheriff for company.

Chapter Eight

P had a problem. Wilson wasn't supposed to know it, but he did.

He might be only eight years old, but he had a big mind. Almost old—really old—adultlike sometimes.

And his adultlike mind told him Patience had a problem.

She'd done a good job hiding it, but she didn't fool him. He saw how red and swollen her eyes were every morning. And she blew her nose a lot lately. She kept saying she was coming down with a cold, but if that were so, she'd already have gotten sick.

No, Patience couldn't fool Wilson; she was worried. Worried sick because she couldn't get anyone to work that ole mine—and Jay Longer wasn't very friendly. Wilson suspected P would like for the sheriff to be friendlier.

She'd gone everywhere there was to go, done everything there was to do, talked to anyone who would listen, but nobody wanted to work for her. Nobody liked ghosts. Some didn't believe there was such a thing, but others only shook their heads and said they didn't want to take a chance on running into Gamey if he was in the mine.

Wilson walked to school with a heavy heart. P said it was okay for him to walk by himself this morning. He appreciated that. He liked it when she treated him like an adult. She did most times, except lately, when she couldn't think of anything but ghosts. And maybe the sher- iff—only she got mad when he mentioned that man. Called him pigheaded and . . . something else. He couldn't remember what, but he didn't think Jay would like it.

Wilson didn't know if he believed in ghosts.

Maybe he did; he wasn't sure.

Patience wouldn't be having such a hard time getting workers if it wasn't for the rumor. If he were a man and P asked him to work in the mine, he'd do it—whether he believed in ghosts or not—because P was nice. And even better than that, there were some things a man just ought to do.

Swinging his dinner pail, Wilson made his way down the mountain. He bet that sheriff would work in the mine. He didn't know why P hadn't asked him to.

Hunching deeper into the coat lining, Wilson pretended he was smoking a cigarette. The crisp, cold air formed a perfect vapor for his favorite make-believe game. He played it every day when no one was looking. When he grew up, he was going to smoke for real. Smoke and cuss and spit tobacco and look mean, because that's what men did, only P would never let him. She said a boy wasn't to live that way, that God frowned on smoking and cussing and spitting tobacco and looking mean—well, she hadn't said anything about looking mean, but if God didn't like the other things, he probably didn't like anyone looking or acting mean.

Exhaling, inhaling, exhaling, inhaling, out, in, out, in. Wilson watched the air take on fascinating shapes. It was easy to play like he was smoking because it was freezing cold. Colder than kraut—though he didn't know why he was thinking about kraut. He hated the stinky stuff.

His foot struck something and he stumbled, nearly pitching face first into a snowbank. He caught himself in the nick of time.

His face brightened when he spotted the sheriff coming up the hill, walking toward him.

"Jay!" he called, happy to see a familiar face. He hadn't seen the sheriff in a long time. "What're ya doing?"

When Jay didn't answer, Wilson veered off the path to visit.

Jay watched Wilson trotting toward him. He looked closer to see if Patience was with him, but she wasn't.

Irritating brat. Look at him—scrawny, red hair; wearing bottle-thick glasses that make him look like a hoot owl.

"Hey, Jay? You got a minute to talk?"

"I guess so." Not that he wanted to talk to the boy. He didn't; he was just killing time until Patience came to her senses. Once that happened, he, the girl, and the child would be on their way back to Denver City in the blink of an eye.

"Why haven't you been back to see us? P misses you."

Nosy kid. "I don't have time for visiting. Got things to do."

"Like what?"

Jay glared at him. Someone needed to teach this boy some manners. It wasn't polite to ask questions like that. Besides, he couldn't think of an answer. He'd not been all that busy, but that was his business. He had a reason for not going back to the mine. That stubborn woman would have him working for her if he wasn't careful.

"I don't have to discuss my affairs with you."

Wilson cocked his head to one side, appearing to think about this. "No, I suppose not. Are you doing something you don't want anyone to know about?"

Jay bit back the word he wanted to say. "No, I'm not doing anything I need to hide. Didn't anyone ever tell you not to ask questions?"

"Yes, all the time. But how will I learn anything if I don't ask?"

"You're liable to learn more than you want to know if you do."

"I don't see how that would be possible," Wilson said, after giving the matter some consideration. "I'd think it would be difficult to learn too much about anything."

Jay smothered a sigh. What could you do with a boy like this? You couldn't talk to him, for sure. Hard to talk to someone who had an answer for anything you said. Kid acted odd too. Hard to tell if he was all there or just being obnoxious.

He was going to be a handful when he grew up. A mining camp was no place for him. Patience meant well, and someone had to see to Wilson's needs, but the boy wanted a man's influence. A man's firm hand. But he wasn't that man.

Apparently aware of Wilson's close scrutiny, Jay growled. "Shouldn't you be somewhere, kid?"

"I'm walking to school by myself this morning. P said I could."

"You better hurry along—you're going to be late."

"It doesn't matter. I only go because P makes me. I hate school."

When the sheriff didn't answer, Wilson continued. "Want to know why I hate school? Because the kids don't like me."

"Have you done something to make them not like you?"

"No, honest." He hadn't done anything—not that he could remember. He sure hadn't thrown Butch's sandwich anywhere.

"Yeah, well, that happens. Don't worry about it; it'll work itself out." Jay pulled the collar of his wool coat tighter. "You better run along."

"The girls talk mean to me, and Butch Miller steals my sandwich every day."

"And you let him?"

Wilson made a *humph* sound. "I can't *stop* him."

Rubbing his shoulder, Jay looked away. Sunlight danced off the heavy layer of early morning hoarfrost.

Wilson suddenly thought about P and all the trouble she'd been having. Why, he bet she had forgotten to ask Jay to help her run the mine! Excited now, he realized how he could make P happy! He'd take Jay home with him; that's what he'd do. He'd surprise the smile right off P!

Wilson sized up the sheriff's muscular frame and decided he was *strong*. Strong as a bull. Fit as a fiddle. Tight as a drum, and all that other stuff people always said. He'd make a good gold miner.

He could mine a bunch of gold and then P wouldn't cry herself to sleep; she wouldn't cry anymore, period, because the sheriff would be around every day and she would like that.

Wilson wasn't a fool. He knew he'd have to be pretty crafty to trick Jay into coming home with him. The man would be a good worker, all right, but it seemed like he didn't like work. He frowned a lot—and he got mad sometimes, though Wilson could tell Jay tried to hide his anger as much as he could.

Wilson noticed that the night he'd brought him and P up to the mine. Maybe that's why P forgot to ask him to help her: she knew he was a testy sort.

Jay was probably a little uninspired because P wouldn't go back to Denver City with him. Even Wilson knew that men preferred the women to mind.

Well, he'd just have to fool Jay into going home with him. Once he was there, P would see that he was strong, and she'd remember that she hadn't asked *everyone* to work the mine: she hadn't asked the sheriff. She was good about talking people into doing things they didn't want to do. She called it tact, but Wilson called it plain ole browbeating.

But Wilson liked his idea a whole lot and decided to follow through with it. "Jay?"

The sheriff looked up. "Yes?"

"I'm not feeling so good." Wilson clutched his stomach. "I'd better not go to school today."

Jay frowned. "What's wrong with you?"

"My stomach hurts."

"Well, go back home."

"Okay." Wilson made it sound like he didn't want to go home but he guessed, since Jay said it, he ought to obey. "You'd better walk me home, huh, Jay?"

Wincing, Jay glanced down at him. "You know the way back."

A ray of sun glinted off the rim of Wilson's glasses. "I'm feeling kind of dizzy. I can't see straight." He held his head for effect.

Jay shifted to the opposite foot. "You'll be all right— it's not far."

Grabbing his middle, Wilson bent double. "Noooo, I think you're going to have to walk with me, Jay, because I'm *real* sick."

"Wilson—"

"*Really* sick, Jay. Honest."

Jay shifted his stance, annoyed.

"Yeah—please don't tell P!" It was a white lie; the old prospector had said only the black ones counted.

"You have to come with me. P'll be mad if anything bad happens to me."

"Look, kid, I didn't take you to raise."

Wilson peered up at him. "You don't want me to walk home by myself, really sick, do you?"

Actually, Wilson didn't think Jay cared one way or the other, but he was beginning to suspect he didn't have a choice. *If I'm sick, he'll have to walk me home.*

"All right, let's get it over with."

Wilson's face lit up. "You'll do it? You'll walk home with me?"

"I said I would. Let's go."

"Okay. Just a minute." Wilson motioned for him to lean over.

Eyeing him warily, Jay refused to comply. "What?"

"Lean over."

"Lean over? Why?"

"Just lean over."

Jay hesitantly bent over.

Wilson set to work sprucing him up. "Do you have a comb?"

"A comb?" One eye cracked open. "Do I look like I have a comb?"

No, he sure didn't look like he had a comb. He didn't look like he'd ever *seen* a comb. "Never mind, I'll use my fingers." That's what P did.

Wilson carefully fluffed Jay's hair and knocked the crumbs out of his scraggly beard. He had to get the sheriff more presentable or P wouldn't hire him. She didn't like messiness, especially bad messiness.

Knocking dust and twigs off the back of Jay's coat, Wilson took his handkerchief out of his pocket, spit on it, and was about to wash Jay's face when a big hand with curly red hair on the knuckles stopped him. "Don't even think about it."

The sheriff could've used a full bath, but Wilson knew he wasn't smart enough to fool him into that. He'd just have to make sure Jay stood downwind of P.

When Wilson finished, Jay didn't look any better. He could've used a lot more attention, but this would have to do.

The sheriff returned his critical look impassively. "What are you doing?"

Wilson shrugged. "Nothing."

"Obviously you're trying to accomplish something."

"No, I'm not." He grinned. "Wanna stay for dinner? P cooks turnips real good." If he stayed for dinner that'd give P more time to remember to ask him to help her work the mine, plus the two of them just might take to each other.

"I'm not staying for dinner."

"Well, you can think about it."

"I'm taking you to the mine; then I'm leaving. You don't look sick to me."

"What does sick look like?" If he knew, Wilson could fake a lot sicker, but for now he'd have to just look puny. "Okay." Turning, he walked off, casting a sly look over his shoulder to make sure Jay followed.

Patience stood in front of the mine, watching Jay and Wilson approach. They stopped before her, and it only took one look to see that Wilson was up to something. She just didn't know what.

Jay nodded. "Miss Smith."

"Mr. Longer." She could be just as polite as he was.

"The boy's sick. I brought him home."

"Really?" She looked at Wilson, who was winking frantically. She hid a grin. Sneaky little kid. All right. She'd play along. "Thank you for bringing him. It was very nice of you. It will be lunchtime soon. I can whip something up in a jiffy. Won't you join us?"

Jay wouldn't look at her. "No, I'd better be running along."

"There's peach cobbler for dessert."

He looked at her, a curious expression in his eyes. "I don't get much home cooking."

"Then we'd be really happy to have you join us." She turned and went back inside before he had a chance to refuse.

Jay entered behind Wilson, apparently uncomfortable with the situation. Patience busied herself throwing together a hearty dinner, letting Wilson play host. Thank goodness she had fried a chicken last night and saved the leftovers for today.

When everything was ready, she motioned for them to take their seats. Jay started to reach for a biscuit, but she stopped him. "First we say the blessing."

"Oh, sure." He bowed his head, flushing.

Patience folded her hands. "We thank you, dear Lord, for this food we're about to eat and for all of your blessings. Thank you for sending Sheriff Longer to be with us. Lead him to do what is best for all of us. And bless our work in the mine, Lord, and we'll give you the praise. Amen."

No harm in giving the Lord some suggestions.

Wilson echoed "amen," and Jay followed, sounding reluctant. His eyes were accusing when he looked at Patience, but she merely put on a sweet, innocent smile. Sweet was always good.

Jay thawed perceptibly under the influence of cold fried chicken, biscuits and gravy, and two helpings of peach cobbler. By the time they finished eating, he was laughing and teasing Wilson. His manner toward her was a combination of suspicion and deference.

She did her best to be charming. He only pokered up once when she asked for advice about opening the mine, but she tried to look like a helpless, admiring female, although it almost choked her to do so, and he relaxed.

He went outside with Wilson while she cleared the table and fixed the rest of the chicken for him to take home with him, although she could certainly have used it herself. As she tidied up, she hummed a satisfied little tune. Jay Longer would help them; she could feel it in her bones.

That Wilson was positively a genius.

Chapter Nine

Toward dark, Patience rinsed the last supper dish and laid it aside. With a tired sigh, she recalled how the sheriff had eaten like a hired hand—a very underfed hired hand. His tall frame could use a few extra pounds—the kind a family man carried with pride. It was a treat to cook for someone other than herself and Wilson.

Of course she had seen right through Wilson's ploy. It had taken very little persuasion for her to talk the sheriff into staying for dinner. After dinner, Wilson's usual robust health returned, and he pressured his new friend into a game of stickball.

Stickball turned into mumblety-peg. The sheriff showed Wilson how to hold the knife just right, so that with a flick of the wrist he could stick the blade into the ground. Watching from the dugout doorway, arms crossed, Patience decided she hadn't known how many different ways a knife could be thrown.

Later in the day she looked out to see the tops of two red heads, one big and one small, disappearing over the hill. Seemed the fish were biting.

She grinned, grateful Jay was spending time with the child. Wilson needed a man's influence—and Jay, it appeared, needed a small boy's adoration.

Late in the afternoon, the two had returned toting an impressive string of trout, which she rolled in cornmeal and fried for supper. It had turned out to be quite an extraordinary day.

Jay Longer was anything but ordinary. Normally she would have
thought twice about taking up with someone who cared so little about
his personal appearance, but Jay had been different in Denver City.
Always clean shaven and his clothes freshly laundered and neatly
pressed. During both dinner and supper he proved to be an interesting
conversationalist, and his table manners were impeccable.

She wasn't entirely certain yet of the role he'd play in her life, but she
knew he had one.

One really did have to wonder what lay beneath Jay's defensive fa-
cade. It might be interesting to find out. There hadn't been much opportunity for getting acquainted with men at the orphanage, so one
might say she was inexperienced. She'd seen enough of male behavior at
Fiddle Creek and Denver City to suspect there was more to Sheriff Jay
Longer than he chose to reveal.

The way he got along with Wilson seemed to be more than just an
adult spending time with a child. He *enjoyed* playing games with the boy,
and the sight of the two of them wandering off to go fishing had been
downright heartwarming. Judging by the looks on their faces when they
returned, she had felt that just being together had filled a need in each
of them.

And what about her? She had needs too. She had watched Glory and
Ruth fall in love and get married, wondering if she would ever find
someone with whom to build a life. Sitting at the table with Jay, listening to him talk and watching him tease Wilson, had revived those feelings. No matter how many times she tried to pretend she wasn't
interested in Jay Longer, she couldn't deny the truth. She was attracted
to the man. He would ride away someday, back to Denver City, and she
would miss him. Too much.

She would have liked for him to stay and visit longer, but he seemed
uncomfortable with the notion. The moment he swallowed the last bite
of fish, he had bolted for the door like a jackrabbit.

Hastily downing the last of his milk, Wilson ran after him, explaining
over his shoulder that the sheriff was going to teach him how to tie
trout lures. He had returned alone at dark, tired but happy.

Maybe Jay would find her more interesting if she had something important to talk about or if she wasn't so stubborn and agreed to go back
to Denver City. He was a man who honored his word, and he'd promised Dylan to bring her home safely. Well, she would eventually return
to Denver City, and the girls would sit up all night talking about their
newfound fortune. That thought alone kept her going, because every-

thing else about the situation appeared hopeless. No crew; no gold. She had to find help—and quickly—or circumstances would force her to abandon the mine. She couldn't bear to even think about that.

Emptying the dishpan, she wished she had a book to read. Always after supper at the orphanage she read—stories about Calamity Jane, Deadwood Dick, and Kit Carson. When she tired of dime novels she'd pretend to be Meg in *Little Women* by Louisa May Alcott.

She loved them all.

Untying her apron, she laid it aside, then knelt beside Wilson's pallet. He was fast asleep, exhausted from his busy day. Lifting a stockinged foot, she gently tucked it beneath the blanket.

Gazing down on his cherubic features, Patience was once again overcome by doubts. Was she doing the right thing? Colorado, for all its beauty, was a harsh land. Maybe too harsh for a child. They had been here over three weeks, and she had yet to find one man or woman willing to work for her. Emotions surrounding the mine shaft ran high and were coupled with deep-seated suspicion. It was useless to try to persuade the residents of Fiddle Creek there were no such things as ghosts. Years of skepticism and unexplainable events surrounding the mine had convinced them otherwise.

Last night she had found the old prospector's Bible under the cot and read to Wilson. Hoping to dispel any notions about ghosts, she had pointed out that ghosts, as we call them, were not mentioned in the Bible, probably because God knows they don't exist.

She read to him about Jesus on the cross, hanging between two thieves. Taking advantage of the chance to do a little teaching, she brought out the fact that one thief mocked Christ. The second thief believed in him and asked to be remembered when Jesus came into his kingdom.

Although she had read the printed words many times, they still had the power to thrill her: "Today shalt thou be with me in paradise."

"You see, Wilson, God has prepared a place for our spirits to go when we die. We can't interfere with God's plans and decide we'd rather stay on earth and hang around where we used to live, having fun scaring people.

"Gamey's spirit went to either heaven or hell when he died. He didn't have the opportunity to stay in the mine. We aren't given that choice. God created us, and he is in control, in this life and the life to come."

Wilson had looked serious, reflecting on what she said. "I guess that has to be right. The Good Book doesn't lie."

"No, it doesn't. We can trust what it says." She had closed the book, relieved that at least she had provided sound principle for her decision to stay.

But Wilson, with his inquisitive mind, had had another question. "What about all the strange things that happen in the mine? How do you explain them, P?"

Patience had no explanation for the strange goings-on Wilson had related: cold gusts of air coming from nowhere, strange lights seen in the shaft, falling rock endangering the lives of anyone who ventured deep into the tunnel. Nothing unusual had happened the few times she'd ventured into the shaft—no odd cave-ins or peculiar lights or bizarre singing—none of the various incidents people claimed had happened.

Restless now, she moved to the door for a breath of fresh air. A full moon bathed the mountain. Loneliness gripped her. She had been alone few times in her life. The orphanage had always been full and rowdy; then on the long journey out west she didn't have a private moment.

Leaning against the doorsill, Patience thought about Missouri and the life she'd left behind. She had been content there—comfortable. And she'd thought that by coming to Colorado she would become a wife and eventually a mother. Now, here she was in the Rockies, the sole caretaker of a small boy—friends miles and miles away. If she couldn't find anyone to work the mine, what good would it do for her to stay? She couldn't work it herself. She knew nothing about mining.

Her mind drifted to the other girls, and she was consumed with guilt. Mary had to be worried sick, and the others just plain worried. She'd tried to send them word, but the telegraph line was still down. It took forever to get anything done out here. Men would rather seek their fortunes in the mines than work at anything so mundane as repairing telegraph lines. Mail service was erratic, taking weeks to deliver, if it got through at all. For the moment, there was no way to let them know she was all right or to tell them about her quest to prosper them all.

A twig snapped and Patience's hand flew to her heart.

A deep voice came to her from the shadows. "Didn't I tell you to keep your door shut at night?"

"Sheriff?" She shaded her eyes against the bright lantern rays. "I thought you had gone."

"Sorry, didn't mean to alarm you." Jay stepped from the shadows, removing his hat. "The name's Jay."

Calling him by his first name didn't feel quite right, but maybe in time she could get used to it. *Sheriff* did seem awfully formal. Opening the door wider, she smiled. "Would you like to come in and warm yourself by the fire?"

"No, thanks. I just wanted to make sure Wilson was all right."

Now why was he making up excuses? He had to know Wilson had pulled a fast one on them. The boy was no more sick than she was, but the funny way her pulse leapt at the sound of the sheriff's familiar voice made her realize she didn't care why he was still there. She was just glad that he was.

She nodded. "He's fine—doesn't seem to have a trace of whatever was ailing him on the way to school this morning."

"He's okay, then. Figured I might have worn him out this afternoon."

"Oh . . . yes." She smiled, meeting his cool direct gaze. "He's sound asleep."

An awkward silence hung between them.

Why, the man was lonely! She smiled, reaching for a wrap hanging on a peg next to the doorway. "He was asleep two minutes after his head hit his pillow." Stepping outside, she closed the door, settling the woolen shawl around her shoulders. They casually fell into step. "I'm glad you decided to come back."

"It got dark on me—I decided to bed down close to the mine."

They walked for a while, she mindful of his company, he mindful of hers.

Twisting the brim of his hat in his hands, the sheriff appeared to be searching for a mutual topic. "Nice night. Not so cold," he ventured.

Pulling her shawl closer, Patience gazed at the overhead star-studded canopy. "You think so? I haven't been warm since I got here."

"It doesn't get cold in Missouri?"

She grinned. "Oh, yes—it gets cold in Missouri. Ever been there?"

"No." He glanced up to study the sky. "I've heard that it's pretty, though."

"Very pretty—especially in the fall. The leaves turn magnificent reds and ambers and golds. In the spring, bright green grass carpets the hillsides, and yellow jonquils and forsythia pop out. Summers are hot and humid with savage thunderstorms, but then fall rolls around again and you forget all the things you don't like about Missouri weather. Suddenly you find yourself thanking the good Lord for seeing you through another year."

The edge was gone from the silence now; she liked that.

"I wanted to tell you . . . you're a good cook," Jay said. "Haven't tasted fish that good in a long time."

She felt her cheeks grow hot even though the wind was brittle. "Just plain old fish and corn bread. Nothing special."

He touched her elbow, directing her around an outcropping of rock shooting up through the uneven ground. She decided she liked his gentle pressure on her arm—manly, persuasive, without being intrusive.

"Been here long?" she asked.

Jay shrugged. "Few years."

"I assume gold brought you here?"

"No." He smiled, his tone lighter now. "Actually, it was a train, but I came in search of gold."

"Oh." She laughed, relieved to discover he had a sense of humor. At times she would have guessed otherwise.

A cloud shadowed the moon, and the wind picked up. She drew closer into the wrap, wondering why she'd left a warm fire to walk a rocky ground with a man who opposed her at every turn.

"Warm enough?"

"Fine, thank you. And you?"

"Fine." His eyes skimmed the dark clouds. "Snow before morning."

"It seems it snows every night."

The conversation started to lapse.

"You're sure you're not too cold? We can go back," Jay offered.

"Really, I'm fine. Thank you."

"The 'quarters' warm enough?"

She laughed, recognizing the tongue-in-cheek tone. "Well, actually, there's a crack at the bottom of the door big enough to throw a moose under. We're losing a lot of heat."

"I'll take a look at it tomorrow. Meanwhile, stuff a blanket in it."

"In the door?"

"In the crack."

"Oh . . . thanks. I will."

They walked to the edge of a precipice and stood staring across the snow-covered landscape. Ragged summits draped with snow jutted upward in the light of the passing moon.

"So, you're doing okay?"

"Sheriff—"

"Name's Jay."

She glanced up at him. "Do you really want me to call you Jay?"

"That's my name."

They stood for a few minutes more, their breath making frosty air vapors. She wondered how much longer it would be before the sheriff ordered her back to Denver City. Had news of her failure to hire a suitable mine crew exasperated him? Would he now demand that she go back? She supposed he reasonably could; she had failed—that was pretty common knowledge. Without the mine's proceeds she couldn't hold out any longer. The old prospector had laid in a good supply of food, but firewood was running low, and she couldn't seem to chop enough to keep up with the demand. And there was still plenty of winter left on this remote mountaintop.

"You were saying?" Jay prompted.

What had she been saying?

"I asked if you were doing okay, and you said—"

"About to say I was, but that isn't the truth," Patience admitted. She didn't know how he'd feel about her confiding in him, but she had to talk to someone. Even an enemy was better than no one.

"Something wrong?"

"I can't find anyone to work the mine; but then, you know that, don't you?"

To his credit, his tone held a note of humility. "I don't stick my nose in other people's business, Miss Smith."

"If I have to call you Jay, you have to call me Patience. Smith's just a name they gave me at the orphanage. I didn't know my last name. None of us did, except Mary; her last name is Everly."

His expression softened. "Does it bother you, not knowing your last name or who your folks were?"

"Some," she admitted. "I'd like to have known my parents, but then, I guess who you are isn't as important as what you are. I try to live in such a way that no matter who my folks were, they wouldn't be ashamed of me." He looked stricken. She had touched a nerve somewhere. Best leave the subject. "Please, call me Patience."

That would be hard for him, she knew. *Patience* was too personal, and the last thing he wanted was to get too personal. She had known that from the moment she'd set eyes on him.

"You do know why no one will help me, don't you?" she asked.

"I know why." His gaze fixed on a distant point, and she could see his jaw firm.

She sighed. "Well, you did warn me the mine was haunted."

"That I did."

"But you also said you didn't believe in ghosts."

"I don't, but everyone else does. That's the problem."

Gazing at the mountain, she said softly, "I'm in trouble, Jay. I've been everywhere, tried everything, and I can't find one single person willing to work for me. You know what happened in Silver Plume. The Chinamen just laughed at me. Even they had heard of the Mule Head."

A wry smile touched the corners of his mouth.

"Then I got this bright idea to ask the townswomen to work in the mine."

His grin widened, and she figured he'd heard about that too.

"They thought I was crazy. I didn't know women were considered bad luck in a mine." Sighing, she leaned back, staring at the moon darting in and out of clouds. "Guess I shouldn't be burdening you, but I don't know who else to talk to—Wilson's tired of hearing about my problems. The old prospector's food supply won't last forever. I have to get that mine operating."

When he didn't respond, she glanced sideways, silently praying that he wasn't laughing at her. That would greatly upset her. "What would you do?" she asked.

"Me?" He laughed. "You're asking the wrong person."

She cocked a brow in disbelief. Since when was he shy about offering his opinion? He'd been pretty verbal before—now she really needed some common sense. "You've worked in mines, haven't you?"

"I've staked claim to several, but as you can see, my success has been limited."

"Perhaps you're too modest."

"Perhaps I've been skunked one too many times."

"But you know a lot about mining."

"Not a lot."

"But some—you know what needs to be done."

He looked away. "I know enough to recognize when it has me whipped."

"Feathers—nonsense," she amended quickly. Their eyes met briefly in the moonlight. "You're not the kind of man who gives up easily. You've nearly driven me *crazy* ordering me back to Denver City. I cannot imagine that something like a little old mine would intimidate you."

"No disrespect intended, but you couldn't know that."

"I am an excellent judge of character."

He found that amusing. "Trust me. You're wrong about this one."

"Why don't you work the mine for me?" He was strong, capable, and knew about mining. "I'll hire you to run the mine. You can operate it any way you see fit."

"I'm afraid not. I am gainfully employed—sheriff of Denver City. That's my home and I like it that way."

She had seen no indication that he had a permanent home—here or in Denver City. He seemed more like a man who hung his hat on a different peg every night.

"I could make you rich."

"Rich," he scoffed. "That notion's for fools and dreamers. Not interested. I appreciate the offer and I regret your circumstances, but I'd be of no use to you." He pulled his threadbare jacket closer around him. "We need to go; wind's coming up stronger."

Patience turned to face him. "I beg you to reconsider. You must have come here with a dream. Apparently, that dream hasn't worked out. I'm offering you a second chance."

He looked down at her, and for one crazy moment she saw something akin to anticipation flash in his eyes; then it faded just as quickly.

"Another chance, Jay Longer, to realize your dream." She pointed to the mine. "Right now, the Mule Head's got me whipped. I'm asking—no, I'm *begging*—you for help. You don't believe in ghosts. You said so yourself. So that shouldn't stop you. Work the mine for me. Half of whatever gold it yields will be yours."

"Miss Smith . . ."

She lifted her hand. "My name is Patience, and I mean every word of what I've said. If you'll supervise the work, half of whatever the mine yields is yours."

He turned away. "I don't want your money."

"It wouldn't matter if you did." She took his chin and turned his face back to meet hers. "I'm desperate. See? My only hope to offer Mary, Lily, and Harper a future is buried in that shaft. The *only chance* Wilson and I have is that mine."

"The mine could be *worthless*. Most likely is," he argued. *"Will be,* I can assure you, if I work it."

"Maybe, maybe not. We won't know until we try. Think about it: more gold than you've ever dreamed about. Another chance. A fresh start. A probability to realize your dream."

For a moment, hope flickered in his eyes.

"If you can't find anyone to work the mine, what makes you think I can? I haven't got the best record in this area. Other miners have seen me fail—not once, but several times. No one would take me seriously even if I attempt to run a crew."

Patience was relying on instinct now, but instinct told her she was on solid ground. "Because you're a man who doesn't want to give up his dream, and I believe in you."

"Believe in me?" he jeered. "Why would you believe in me? I've done nothing to deserve your confidence. Sorry, I can't help you." He turned and started to walk away.

"Say you'll think about it," she called, refusing to give up. He could do it. She knew he could.

"Sure, I'll give it some thought."

"And you'll let me know?"

Lifting his hand aimlessly, he dismissed her. "Sure, sure, I'll let you know."

Chapter Ten

Snow drifted from the sky in thick, wet flakes, piling up onto the crude building Fiddle Creek called a hotel. The primitive structure, which sat on a hillside overlooking a deep ravine, was joined side by side, sharing a common wall with the other buildings. Elegant it wasn't.

Jay's rented room was about the size of a clothes closet with one dirty window. A rough bedstead made of planks dominated the small space. A mattress and pillow stuffed with dried meadow grass discharged a rustling sound when lain upon. An old blanket, a washstand with a chipped bowl and a fragment of a mirror above it, and a bar of claybank soap topped off the dismal setting.

Crawling off the bed, he reeled to the washstand. Fumbling for the tin pitcher, he dumped the contents over his head. Shuddering, he threw back his hair in an effort to minimize the icy jolt. Grabbing a towel, he buried his face in the cloth, trying to block out the morning light.

Catching his image in the mirror, he bent closer. A stranger stared back at him. Long dirty hair, matted beard, bags beneath his eyes. Not a pretty sight. Maybe it was time for the disguise to go. He hadn't seen Mooney's thugs around in a while.

For no particular reason Patience came to mind. If things had turned out differently he might have fallen for a woman like her. She was pretty, smart, spirited. There wasn't a woman in Fiddle Creek who could hold a candle to her.

She had spunk. He used to like that. Nelly had spunk . . . and warmth and compassion. He'd seen the way Patience fought to assemble a crew. Even watched her become the laughingstock of Fiddle Creek. He'd turned his back on the unkind remarks, closed his ears when they ridiculed her perseverance, but he still admired her. Maybe a little too much.

A smile creased the corners of his mouth. What a pair the two of them would make. She refused to give up; he gave up too easily.

Pounding sounded at the door. Spinning around, he dropped the towel.

"Open up, Longer! We know you're in there!"

Mooney's thugs. Red and Luther. They'd caught up with him.

Snatching his trousers off the hook, Jay hopped on one foot, trying to get them on, his eyes searching for his boots.

"Longer!" The racket got louder. "Open up!"

Jay dropped to his knees, frantically searching under the bed. Where were his boots?

Grabbing his shirt off the chair, he yanked it on, all the while gravitating toward the window, hoping it wasn't far to the ground.

Lifting the window sash, he managed to throw a leg over the sill before the door splintered in half. Two beefy characters rushed into the room, snaring him by the shoulder before he could jump.

"Not so fast, Sheriff!"

They spun him around and a fist slammed into his stomach, then another. Red backhanded him across the face. His bottom lip split, and he tasted blood.

A well-aimed kick found its mark, sending him sailing across the warped floor. Yanked back to his feet, he felt a meaty knuckle connect with his nose. A swift knee smashed to his groin, followed by a right hook to his chin.

A left, then another fast right, and the floor came up to meet him. Sprawled flat on his back, Jay stared up at the double images floating above him.

"Mooney's gettin' impatient," a gravelly voice reminded.

"Yeah, he wants his money."

A boot smashed into Jay's rib cage, knocking the wind out of him. Rolling to his side, he teetered on the brink of unconsciousness.

"It ain't nice not to own up to your debts."

"Yeah, it ain't nice, Sheriff. How many times you got to be told that?"

A sharp blow to Jay's back sent an excruciating pain spiraling up his left shoulder.

"This is your last warning. Either pay up, or you're a dead man."

Turning, the two thugs stalked out of the room, slamming what was left of the door behind them.

Shifting to his back, Jay squeezed his nostrils to stem the stream of blood gushing from his nose. He lay for a moment, trying to clear his head.

As his vision gradually returned, he spotted his boots, crammed upside down on the bedposts. *Nice,* he thought. *Now I find them.*

Patience answered the knock at the dugout door later that morning to discover the sheriff, hat in hand, standing there. For a moment she didn't recognize the stranger before her. He was cleanly shaven, freshly bathed, his hair fresh cut, and he was wearing a new red flannel undershirt under a blue woolen shirt, jeans tucked into new leather boots, and a brand-new hat. Only the color of his hair remained the same—fiery red.

Jay Longer had transformed himself back into one fine-looking, respectable-appearing man. The conversion nearly took Patience's breath away.

He also had a humdinger of a shiner, a deep slash across his right cheekbone, and a wad of cotton stuck up his right nostril.

"Morning, P."

"What in the world happened to you?" Taking his arm, she pulled him into the dugout and shoved him into a chair. Grabbing a dish towel, she wet the end and went to work cleaning away the remnants of blood circling his cuts.

He seemed awkward with her sympathetic clucking. His thoughts were as transparent as his wounds. It was bad enough she had to see him this way. It was bad enough he had to show up here at all, and he sure didn't like her making a big fuss about it.

She stepped back, planting her hands on her hips, frowning. "Have you been fighting?"

"No, ma'am, I haven't been fighting. Unfortunately, I never threw a punch."

Taking the towel out of her hand, he laid it aside. "Patience, I've come here to say something, and I'd appreciate it if you let me get it said."

Relaxing, she waited. "All right."

"This is no place for a good-looking, single woman. It isn't safe. I'm surprised you haven't had trouble before now."

Good-looking? He thought she was good-looking? Or was he just saying that to sweeten her up and bring her round to his way of thinking?

She scowled at him. "Save your breath. I'm not leaving."

Jay sighed. "Please don't be like that."

"Like what? Don't you talk down to me."

"I'm not talking down; I'm talking sense. You can't get a crew. These people are too superstitious to go down in that shaft. It's not going to happen. You may be sitting on a fortune in gold, but it won't do you any good if you can't get at it."

"But I can get the gold if you'll help me."

"Would you just listen? This is no place for either of us. Give it up, P. Let's go back to Denver City. We'll take Wilson with us. If you insist on staying here, you'll just cause grief for both of you."

Patience sank down in a chair and stared at him, willing him to understand. "I can't leave. It's not that I want the money for myself. I have too many others depending on me. Lily isn't robust. She's not able to do heavy work. Harper's black, and you know what that means. People treat her like she's not a real person with feelings and needs. There's no future for her. Mary is sickly, and Ruth and Glory are married, so I guess you wouldn't say they're dependent on me, but I'd help them if I could, and now there's Wilson."

Jay shook his head in frustration. "You're not leaving, are you?"

"That's what I said. I can't."

"You won't."

"I guess it means the same thing. Either way, I'm staying."

He sighed gustily. "All right. I'll make a deal with you. I'll give you two weeks to see if we can find a crew."

"We? You'll help me?"

"For two weeks only. If we don't get a crew by then, you'll go back to Denver City with no argument. Agreed?"

She pursed her lips, staring at him. Two weeks wasn't a lot of time. Still, it was more than she had expected. She held out her hand. "Agreed."

God would help them; she knew he would. He wouldn't have

brought her this far to abandon her now. She had no idea where they would find a crew. If they didn't, she would have to keep her part of the agreement and go back to Denver City. In her heart, she refused to think of that possibility.

"Then you will work the mine for me?"

"I'll run the crew for you."

"Oh, thank you so much!" He still had to find a crew willing to confront Gamey O'Keefe's legend. Until the mail got started regularly, by the time she could get a letter to the others, she'd probably be on her way home with a trunk full of gold.

"Run the crew," he stressed. "I don't intend to work in the mine. And you have to know, Patience. I lost my faith five years ago. God doesn't figure into my life anymore, so don't be spouting things like 'God will take care of us' or 'God is good; he'll provide,' because he doesn't provide and he's got a strange way of showing his goodness. I don't want you to cram religion down my throat. Do we understand each other?"

He had been deeply hurt, she realized. And he blamed God. But he hadn't said that he didn't believe in God. Somewhere in his tortured mind he must still have a seed of trust, or else why would he say, *"He's got a strange way of showing his goodness"*? To admit that meant he still believed in God. And if that was the case, Jay needed healing, not censure.

"Do we have an understanding about your faith?" he asked.

She nodded, thinking they really didn't, but she needed him on any terms. "What about a crew?"

He looked away, his gaze rather sheepish, she thought. "I know where I can put one together."

"I've asked everyone," she warned. "I even borrowed Chappy's mule and rode to Silver Plume, but to no avail."

"I know all about that, but there's one place you haven't tried. There's a female work camp over near Piety Hill. I think I can arrange to have the convicts work the mine."

"Women? Women are bad luck in a mine." If she'd heard that once she'd heard it a hundred times in the last week. Gamey's perceived ghost *and* women would be a dicey match.

He gave her a long-suffering look. "You really think our luck can get any worse?"

She frowned. He had a point. "Who do you have in mind?"

"Moses Malone. She and several other women were working a worthless claim over at Piety Hill before they were arrested for murder.

Rumor has it they shot a couple of prospectors and jumped their claim. But they say they didn't do it."

Patience swallowed, aware her eyes were as wide as doorjambs.

"I can't say for certain, but I think I can pull strings and get the women released to my custody during the day. If you don't have any objections, I'll talk to the warden this morning and see what I can arrange."

"Objections? Of course I don't have any objections."

Murder. Moses Malone and her cohorts may have shot two miners. Was she that desperate?

The answer came more swiftly than her opposition. She'd do anything to secure the others' future. If that meant hiring cutthroat murderers to mine the gold—as long as Jay oversaw the operation—then she was going to count blessings instead of doubts. "How soon do you think the women can start?"

"I'll have to see if I can pull this off first." He stood up, looking as though he had something more to say.

She met his direct gaze. "What?"

"You should know . . . Moses and her crew are tough cookies."

Patience stood and gripped the edge of the table for support. "I suspected as much. Other than murder, how bad does it get?"

"You name it. They're no church choir."

Women convicts. How reckless was she? Pretty much that reckless.

"Will I be endangering Wilson?" She wouldn't jeopardize Wilson's safety for any amount of gold.

"The women are loners. They'll keep to themselves."

"Do they know about the mine?"

"About the ghost?"

"Yes . . . him." Gamey O'Keefe.

"I don't know anyone around these parts who doesn't," he conceded.

Sighing, Patience lifted her hand to her temple. It was sink-or-swim time, eat or be eaten. She'd stake her life on the fact that there was no ghost, but would anyone else? "I'm desperate. Do whatever it takes to get them."

He nodded. "This brings me to the next question. What can you afford to pay?"

"Nothing at the moment, but I'll match any wage around once the mine is producing." If there was no gold, she was sunk. Wilson said the old prospector buried his diggings in a coffee can. She had already dug up half the hillside, and she hadn't found anything but the bones of a dead animal. She had a mental image of herself lying faceup, brains in a puddle beside her, when the disgruntled convicts rode off with empty saddlebags. Shuddering, she shook the thought away.

"Not good enough," he stated.

"Well . . ." She started to pace the tight quarters, anxious now. "I don't know. What can I offer?"

"That depends on your funds."

"Nonexistent. I had a paltry amount saved over the past few weeks when I helped Mary and Harper in the millinery, but as you're aware, I left town rather unexpectedly and didn't have an opportunity to pack." She wasn't being facetious, merely truthful. "I'm counting on that mine to contain a lot of gold."

He shook his head. "Fools. Men and women are fools when it comes to gold. What happens if that hole is nothing but a dry vein?"

"I'll face that when it happens," she said. "I'm willing to put my trust in God, Jay. Some folks believe in ghosts; I believe nothing coincidental happens to those who trust their life to God."

He pointed at her sternly.

She changed the subject, aware she had already violated their agreement. "What about you? You can't keep walking to the mine every morning. It's at least a forty-five-minute walk each way, and we'll work daybreak to sundown."

"There's a miner's shack half a mile from here. It isn't fancy, but I can bunk in there."

Walking to the door, he opened it. "You know we're going to have to hit the mother lode."

She nodded. "I'm praying—" she stopped—"I think we will." Otherwise she was as good as on her way back to Denver City.

He returned her gaze. He appeared competent and self-assured—a far cry from his former self. What had happened to Jay Longer? A miracle? He said he didn't believe in miracles, but maybe God had jerked a knot in his backside. A big ole painful knot.

"Jay?"

"Yes?"

"What made you change your mind?" He'd been so adamant about not taking the job—insistent that she return to Denver City. He was still sheriff—still negligent in his obligation to take her back, with or without her consent.

"I need the money."

She knew it took a good deal of courage for him to admit that, though she'd rather that she was the reason he was staying. Smiling, she said quietly, "Then I guess you'll want to get started right away."

Nodding, he turned to leave when she added, "I want you to know I don't care why. I'm just glad you're doing it."

He looked up, his gaze meeting hers. "Don't be; I'm no bargain."

She hoped something deeper than a smile shone in her eyes now. "Isn't that for me to decide?"

Chapter Eleven

But, Patience! It's only a chicken! He won't eat much!"

"Wilson, take the rope off that chicken's neck and turn him loose immediately!"

"You *said* I could have a pet," Wilson reminded sullenly.

"One pet, Wilson, not an entire zoo." Balancing the wash basket on her hip, Patience sidestepped a raccoon, a squirrel, two rabbits, a stray hound dog with its ribs showing, and a rooster. The child had tied ropes around the animals' necks and staked them to the ground in front of the dugout.

Wilson was suddenly adamant about acquiring yet another pet. "He lays eggs!"

"He does not lay eggs."

Wilson bent over to examine his latest acquisition. Straightening, he called back expectantly. "He can wake us up!"

"Turn that rooster loose." Jamming a clothespin in her mouth, Patience marched to the line to hang the wash out to freeze-dry. All she needed was another mouth to feed—even if it was a chicken's!

She realized she was on edge this morning. Jay had been gone for over twenty-four hours. He said he'd be back by dark, and she stayed up long into last night, waiting to hear if he'd hired a crew. She wanted to believe he was a man of his word, prayed that he would come back, yet doubts colored her faith.

Why should he be concerned about her and Wilson? He was a full-grown man, and he probably didn't want to be bothered with an eight-year-old boy and a headstrong young woman.

Her heart told her that, and yet she'd lain awake most of the night listening for his footsteps. Toward dawn she accepted that he wasn't coming.

The rooster set up a terrible squawk, and Wilson slipped the rope off his neck and set him free. Feathers fogged the air and the bird ran around in circles, flapping its wings and screeching. In a burst of energy, it charged Wilson, sending him shrieking toward the dugout.

The remaining animals scrambled for cover, but their tiny legs jerked from under them as the ropes around their necks yanked them to a screeching halt.

"You're going to get spurred!" Patience called out. Wilson raced headlong around a bush hounded by a reddish white blur.

At the height of the ruckus Jay arrived, followed by a group of women, all carrying picks, axes, and shovels.

With an exclamation of relief, Patience dropped the wet shirt she was about to hang back into the basket and ran to meet him. She was so relieved to see him that it took concerted willpower to keep from flinging herself headlong into his arms. She deliberately slowed her steps. The odd assortment of humanity approached.

"Hi," Patience greeted him.

Jay swept off his hat. "Morning."

Wilson rounded the bush again, the rooster bearing down on him hard.

"The trip over to Piety Hill took longer than expected," Jay apologized. "And it wasn't easy to talk the warden into our plan."

She smiled gratefully and said, "I'm glad you're back." Her eyes switched to the women, and she swallowed. A church choir they certainly weren't.

"Patience Smith, Moses Malone," Jay introduced.

Patience recoiled. She faced the rawboned Indian woman who looked mean enough to fist fight a weasel. Dressed in men's boots, faded overalls, and a heavy bearskin coat, Moses Malone's squat, two-hundred-pound, five-foot-plus frame was intimidating.

Moses' eyes coldly skimmed Patience. "Heard you're looking for someone to work your mine." Her voice was whiskey-deep, her hair cut with a butcher knife. The uninspired salt-and-pepper locks hung in dirty strings below the flaps of a dingy, yellow wool hat. Her features were ageless. She could have been thirty or sixty.

"Yes," Patience said, unhappy about the sudden squeak in her voice. "I understand you might be interested?"

Moses' eyes roamed over to the small shaft. "Might. For a price. A third of the profits."

Patience's gaze shot to Jay. "A third?"

"A quarter," he corrected. "That was the agreed amount."

Patience's mind was busy trying to add and subtract. Half to Jay, a quarter to Moses . . . that left a quarter for Patience and Wilson. Not exactly the fortune she'd envisioned, but enough, if the mine proved generous.

Moses locked eyes with Jay in a silent duel. After a while she turned and said over her shoulder, "A quarter of the profits."

The women, having exchanged a series of harsh looks, nodded.

A quarter of the profits. They'd gone for it. Patience released a breath she hadn't realized she was holding.

Moses turned back to address Patience. "You know about me and my crew?"

"Yes . . . somewhat."

"Couple of prostitutes, bank robber, an ax murderer. And I'm just plain mean," Moses said.

Patience nodded. Definitely not your typical mining crew.

"Got any problem with that?"

"No—" Patience swallowed— "ma'am."

"Longer says we work for him."

Patience glanced at Jay. "He's the boss."

Wilson rounded the bush a third time, flinging his arms and screeching.

The convict threw him a practical glance. "The boy has a rooster after him."

"I know. One or the other will eventually give in." Patience grinned. "How soon can you start?"

"Tomorrow."

"Thank you—tomorrow it is." Money would be coming in now; Patience thought her troubles were over. "I'll have breakfast waiting."

"We fix our own breakfast." Moses' gaze drifted again to the mine.

Holding her breath, Patience wondered if she knew about the ghost.

"We use our own equipment."

That was good, since Patience didn't have any. "All right."

Eyes still fixed on the Mule Head, Moses pledged, "If there's gold in there, we'll get it."

Patience didn't doubt that. This woman was downright scary.

When Wilson raced toward him, Jay reached over and plucked him up by the collar, and the rooster shot past.

At daybreak the next morning Patience's crew arrived. The women convicts looked like fifty miles of bad road.

When Patience asked to be introduced to the other women, Moses told her they were there to do a job, not to socialize. Names didn't matter. Folks called them shady ladies, and Patience could do the same if names were important to her.

Armed with their picks, axes, shovels, and lanterns, the women went to work. Day one passed without incident. At dusk the women came out of the mine and snaked their way back down the mountain, trailing Jay, who had stood guard over the mine entrance all day.

Neither Patience nor Wilson was allowed inside the mine; they could tote water and Jay would ferry it to the workers. When the women emerged, black-faced from the mine, Wilson was allowed to visit with them briefly but Jay kept him in sight.

Patience watched the strange assemblage go, wondering how the day had gone, but she wasn't brave enough to ask. If *they* encountered the likes of Gamey O'Keefe, *he* would have been the one to vacate the mine.

After they left for the day she ventured into the mine, curious as to what they were doing. She walked cautiously over the rough ground, lifting the lantern high to help her avoid rubble. Fresh pick marks showed where the women had worked. She shuddered, thinking of spending all day in this dark and damp place. Although she searched the walls diligently, no golden gleam caught her eye.

Suddenly a low moan came from nowhere and everywhere, swelling in intensity. Patience backed up, moving as fast as she dared toward the exit. The sound ebbed around her, bouncing off the walls, and then died away.

She stumbled out of the mine, trembling so hard she almost dropped the lantern. Sinking down on a nearby boulder, she thought about what she had heard. She didn't believe in ghosts, but a few more experiences like that and she might start to.

Day two dawned. The women returned. After a short meeting, Jay dispersed them into the mine. His gaze touched Patience's briefly before he turned and walked away. As far as she knew, he entered the mine only to dole out water.

She sensed he avoided contact with her, and she wondered if he disliked her faith or her optimism. Both seemed to disturb him. Was he playing games with her— letting the mine prove her wrong? Was he hoping for defeat—for a dry vein—so he could take her back to Denver City without a quarrel? She'd done everything she knew to make him feel comfortable around her. She'd cooked food and put it in his saddlebag so he would find it at the end of day.

She'd racked her brain trying to come up with interesting things to talk about and, although she still wore the old prospector's clothing, she tried to be clean and well groomed, but at times she wondered if the fine-looking sheriff even noticed.

Day three came and went.

Day four.

Jay showed up each morning to issue the women their orders. By sundown he disappeared again, and Patience and Wilson spent another cold night huddled before the fire. Not one word was mentioned about gold. Not one single word.

Sighing, she shook out a rug, praying that gold would soon be found. Jay Longer—and Denver City—were beginning to look good to her.

During week two, placer deposits, small hollows in the streams near the dugout, began to show up. Gold dust, flakes, and nuggets were found scattered throughout the sand and gravel downstream of the Mule Head.

"That's encouraging, isn't it?" Patience exclaimed when Jay told her the news that evening.

"It's going to take a lot more than flakes and dust to meet the payroll," he warned.

"Still, it's encouraging." She smiled expectantly. "Maybe we're getting somewhere."

"Maybe, but the old-timers say the easiest way to find gold is to get a burro and turn it loose."

Taking three browned loaves of bread out of the oven, she set them on the table to cool. "A burro?" She laughed. That's all she needed, another animal to feed.

"Laugh if you want, but there's been many a prospector who's hit pay dirt because of his donkey."

"Now what could a donkey possibly have to do with finding gold?"

Jay took off his hat. "Whiplash Johnson tells the story about how his donkey got away from him one afternoon. When he finally caught up with it, the animal was standing next to an outcrop of gold."

"Jay," she chided, wondering if he really believed such exaggerated claims.

"Go ahead, laugh. Spineless Jake Henshaw swears his mules ran away, and when he found them they had taken shelter from a storm behind an outcrop of black rock. While Jake waited for the storm to blow over, he got to looking around, and what do you think he found?"

"Gold."

"Not right away. He chipped a few samples out of the rock and talked a friend of his into having them assayed. Know a lot of men who've found water, gold, and silver with a dowsing rod."

She gestured to the simmering pot of stew she'd just taken off the stove. "Stay to supper? There's plenty."

"Thanks, not tonight."

"There's fresh butter," she tempted. It would be so nice to have adult company at the table tonight. Wilson sometimes thought and talked like an adult, but he was still an eight-year-old. Although Jay had already taken the shady ladies downhill, he had come back to work awhile longer.

"No, I need to be going."

Patience wasn't going to let him see her disappointment. "Maybe next time."

He nodded. "Maybe next time."

You will stay next time, she added under her breath as the door closed behind him.

⌒

"Apple pie?" she called from the doorway the following night.

Jay glanced up. He'd taken to honing knives while he stood watch over the women convicts.

"It's just coming out of the oven!"

"Don't much care for apples," he called back. "They give me the hiccups."

She frowned. *Peaches next time.*

⌒

"Biscuits and rabbit?" She stood in the doorway the next evening, shading her eyes against a fading sun.

Jay glanced up from his work. "Fried?"

"Boiled—with dumplings."

"Like my meat fried. Much obliged, though."

Sighing, she closed the door.

"Hot biscuits and honey!" she sang out the next night.

Getting to his feet, Jay dusted the dirt off his pants. "Give me a few minutes to wash up."

"Take as long as you like!" She burst into song and closed the door with her backside. "Wilson, pick up your shoes! We're having company for supper."

Chapter Twelve

Thanks to a late January storm that night, the snow was so deep the women couldn't make it up the incline, but they were back the following morning. Mining the Mule Head was exasperatingly slow. Only a few small nuggets came out of the shaft—hardly worth counting.

"Boy, this is hard work, huh, Jay?" Wilson, standing behind a crouching Jay, rested his elbows on the sheriff's shoulders while Jay checked the day's work.

"Pretty hard," Jay agreed absently. He tightened his grip on the knife handle and shifted a blade.

"Wilson," Patience reached to pull him off Jay's back. "You come back to the dugout with me and let Jay work."

Jay gave her a smile. "He's all right. Go bake those apple pies."

"Are you sure?" she asked. "I know he can be inquisitive—"

"He's fine."

Smiling, Patience patted the boy's shoulder, then turned and walked off.

Wilson settled more comfortably against Jay's back. "You smell better'n you used to."

"Thank you."

"You don't stink or nothin'."

"I appreciate that."

"And you look better. I didn't like your beard."

"Well, I guess I needed a change." He looked at Wilson briefly. "You could talk the leg off a table—anyone ever tell you that?"

Wilson nodded and went back to the subject. "Your face is cleaner this way," he explained. Shifting his stance, he squinted thoughtfully. "Jay?"

"Yes?"

"If a word is misspelled in the dictionary, how would we ever know?"

"I'm . . . not sure."

"Well, then—" Wilson frowned, thinking—"why do they call it 'after dark' when it's really 'after light'?"

Jay turned to look at him. "Shouldn't you be taking care of your animals?"

He shook his head. "And why do we wash bath towels? Aren't we clean when we use them?"

"You'll have to ask Patience." Jay stepped farther into the mine, holding a lantern aloft.

Wilson trailed behind. "What're you doing now?"

"Cleaning a crevice."

"Why?"

"Because a little piece of gold might have been overlooked."

"Gold?"

"Yeah."

"We found gold already?"

"Not in any quantity yet."

"But soon, huh, Jay?"

"I hope so."

"How much gold is in the crevice?"

"I don't know if there's any, but we clean them once we've worked an area. It's called coyoting."

"Coyoting?"

"Yeah, coyoting."

"That's a funny name."

"Yeah."

"How come?"

"How come what?"

"How come they call it coyoting?"

"I don't know. They just do."

"Who calls it that? Moses?"

"Moses, and other miners."

"How come?"

Jay paused, cocking an ear to the wind. "Listen, I think Patience's calling you."

"Uh-uh. You *said* I could stay and keep you company—long as I don't ask a bunch of questions."

"I said that?"

Wilson viewed Jay charitably through his thick lenses. "Aw, you're just teasing again, huh, Jay?"

"Yeah, only teasing, Wilson."

Wilson followed the tall sheriff deeper into the shaft.

"How come you're in the mine this afternoon? You don't like to come into the mine, huh, Jay?"

"I'll only be here a few minutes." Wilson could already hear the sheriff's breathing quicken. The sheriff didn't like the mine, Wilson knew that, but he didn't know why. P said it was because he'd worked his own mines for five years and had gotten real discouraged when he didn't hit gold.

"You afraid of the ghost?"

"No, Wilson, I'm not afraid of the ghost. I don't believe in ghosts, and you shouldn't either. Ask Patience to read you what the Good Book says about the supernatural."

"She already did." Wilson felt a sense of relief. He really liked Jay, and he wanted Jay to like God more. "You believe in God, huh, Jay? Everybody with a lick of sense believes in God because what's the alternative? If you don't believe in God and you die and then there is a God, then—"

"Haven't you got something else to do?"

"Oh." Wilson caught himself. He was talking too much. Jay didn't like a lot of kid racket. He'd said so—lots of times.

"Are you sure Patience isn't calling you?"

Wilson listened for a moment. "No, she's not. Honest. Where's Moses?" Wilson had taken an instant liking to the convict. Although Patience forbade him to get in anyone's way, Wilson still managed to sneak in a daily visit when the women came out of the mine. Moses told him stupid jokes, like what do you get if you cross a dog with a chicken? Pooched eggs. Or, why are skunks always arguing? Because they like to raise a stink.

Moses was funny—and nice, even sharing part of a fish with him for lunch one day. She didn't cook it, but Wilson ate it anyway because he didn't want to hurt her feelings. But, boy, he'd spat and spat and spat on the way back to the dugout.

He didn't like them other convicts much because they never talked to him. Just Moses was nice.

"Moses went home," Jay said.

"How come?"

Holding the lantern higher, Jay inspected a heavy beam. "Because it's time for her to go home. Didn't you see me walking the women down the hill?"

"No." Wilson shook his head. Switching subjects abruptly, he launched into a review of his day. "Thursday Matthews almost ate lunch with me at school today, but she changed her mind and said she was going to eat with Prudy Walker, but *maybe* she would eat with me on Monday, or maybe on Friday. She'd have to think about it."

"Well, maybe she will," Jay mused.

Wilson sighed. "Who knows? Women are a mystery to me. She thinks I talk too much."

"Can't imagine that." Jay swung a heavy rope onto a rock ledge.

"Do you think P's a mystery?" Wilson could tell Jay a thing or two about P—like how she cooked all the things the sheriff liked most, and only baked pies Jay liked, and how she was always opening the dugout door to see if she could spot Jay. She'd always say she was checking the weather, but Wilson knew the weather didn't change that often—just Jay's whereabouts.

"P thinks I talk too much too." He didn't think Jay was listening to him. The sheriff's breathing was more pronounced now—like he could hardly breathe and he was real nervous or something.

"Did you know my parents died when I was a little boy? The old prospector found me, and since he didn't know anything else to do, he brought me home with him."

"You told me that, Wilson. I'm sorry."

"You've worried about that, huh?"

Jay shot him a tired look.

"Oh, it's all right. I'm not sad anymore. P says Mama and Papa are up in heaven, singing with the angels and walking on streets of gold. That's nothing to be sad about, huh, Jay? P says they're real happy, and we shouldn't wish them back. That would be selfish of us."

"She's usually right, kid."

Wilson cocked his head cagily. "You think P's pretty?"

Slipping the blade of his knife inside a crack, Jay pried a piece of quartz loose. "She's okay."

"She can cook good, huh?" He'd seen the way Jay enjoyed her meals, and the funny way he looked at her when she wasn't looking back. Outright stared at her twice, he'd noticed. He didn't think Jay was supposed to be looking at her that way, all warm and soft—the way the cat looked at a bowl of cream—but there was still a lot Wilson didn't know about men and women. Just a whole lot.

A smile lifted the corners of Jay's mouth. "She's a good cook."

A thump at the back of the mine suddenly diverted Jay's attention. Halting the discussion, he cocked an ear, listening.

"What?" Wilson whispered. "You hear something?"

"Shhh," the sheriff warned, listening intently now.

A low rumble centered at the back of the mine. Dirt and loose rock showered down through the cracks of uneven timbers.

Wilson coughed. "What's happening, Jay?"

"Come on, son." Taking the boy's hand, Jay started propelling him toward the shaft opening.

"What's wrong? Is it the ghost?"

"Keep walking, Wilson." Glancing over his shoulder, Jay moved the child swiftly back through the mine. Bedrock showered down on them, hindering their progress. The ground vibrated, and walls started to crumble.

"Run, Wilson!"

Breaking into a sprint, Jay impelled Wilson toward the mine entrance. A loud roar followed on their heels as they burst clear of the shaft.

A thunderous explosion rocked the ground, and dirt and rock came crashing down. Dust obliterated the fading twilight. The entrance to the mine was sealed shut.

Clasping Wilson tightly to him, Jay seemed shaken by the unexpected onslaught of destruction.

Swallowing hard, Wilson squeaked, "We must've made Gamey O'Keefe mad."

Jay snapped. "It was a cave-in—a cave-in, Wilson. Nothing more."

For a moment Wilson stood transfixed, afraid to move a muscle. When he couldn't stand the silence anymore he finally said, "Hey, Jay?"

"Yes?"

"Knock, knock."

"Is this another one of your silly jokes?"

He nodded, eyes fixed to the sifting dust still pouring out of the hole. "Ahab."

"Ahab who?"

"Ahab to go home now."

Jay stared at the obstructed mine. Like he'd said, it was just a cave-in, all it could be, but what had caused it? The timbers were sturdy; he'd checked them himself. That noise had sounded like an explosion, but how could anyone set off an explosion inside a mine without blowing themselves up with it?

The timing was suspect too. After the women had gone home. Of course, he was in the mine with the kid, but no one knew that. He didn't want to think someone deliberately blew up the mine, but he wasn't convinced the cave-in was natural. There was one other alternative he didn't want to think about.

Gamey O'Keefe's ghost.

Chapter Thirteen

Patience finally knew what hades was like; she'd lived five weeks in it.

"Why?" she agonized. She stood beside a pale-faced Jay, viewing the latest catastrophe.

"It just happened, P!" Wilson was still visibly upset over the experience. "Jay and I were just talking, and all of a sudden we heard this funny noise and Jay said, 'Run, Wilson!' and I did!"

Patience looked at Jay expectantly.

He shrugged. "I don't know what happened. The timbers were shored up properly. I checked them myself." Kneeling before the pile of rubble, he examined it for color.

Patience closed her eyes, heartsick. It would take *days* to get the mine running again. "Now, what?"

Jay's eyes firmed with resolution. "We dig."

It took all of them—shady ladies, Patience, and Jay—working twelve-hour shifts to extricate the rubble from the mine entrance. The front section of the tunnel had collapsed, and after days of digging, they managed to clear the biggest part of rubble away from the opening.

It was challenging, backbreaking labor. The women swung picks, axes, and hammers, sweating like men in the cold temperatures.

Even Wilson did his part when he got home from school, lugging heavy buckets of water from the stream to slake their thirst.

Jay labored steadily, working alongside the women, giving orders when needed, a strong back where necessary.

Patience wasn't surprised by his quiet leadership. It was just one more facet of him that intrigued her.

She had a growing need to prove her own worth, but by the end of the week, she realized she was no match for his strength.

He discovered her late one evening sitting outside the dugout, trying to conceal her emotions. "What's wrong?" Concern filled his voice, and he knelt beside her. "Are you sick?"

"No, of course not. I just needed a few moments alone, that's all." With all the activity and confusion lately, heaven knew she'd had little of that.

"Are you sure?"

She shook her head, smiling. "I'm fine, honest."

"Wilson sick?" Jay turned to peer over his shoulder, where the boy was forcing worms down his latest acquisition, a blackbird with an injured wing.

"No, Wilson is fine. We're both fine," she insisted. "I just wanted to be alone."

"What then?" he asked, exasperation filling his demand.

Sighing, she turned her hands over, revealing the huge watery blisters covering her palms.

"Blisters?"

She nodded. "I don't know what to do for them."

Reaching out, he gently took both her hands in his. "Why didn't you say something sooner?"

She gazed back, biting her lower lip to keep it from trembling. "I've . . . never had . . . blisters."

"Well, you do now." He smiled at her, and she immediately felt better. She hadn't known he knew how to smile. The realization did wonders for her flagging enthusiasm. She suddenly missed Mary, and Harper and Lily even more. They would have tended her injuries, sat and talked for hours, sipped tea, and encouraged her with Scripture. Why was she holding so tightly to what increasingly looked like a worthless pipe dream?

"Where's the old prospector's salve?"

"I didn't find any."

Bending, he lifted her into his arms and calmly carried her down to the stream.

Wilson, sitting on his heels, looked up and saw Jay disappearing over the hill carrying P. Dropping a grub, he sat up straighter. "Hey! What's the matter with P?"

"She's got blisters!"

"Oh." Sinking back to his heels, he crammed another worm into the bird's mouth. "Blisters. I get 'em all the time."

Kneeling beside the stream, Jay dipped Patience's palms into the icy runoff. The crystal-clear liquid bubbled and danced musically over the jagged rocks. Leaving her momentarily, he returned carrying a tin of salve Moses kept in a leather rucksack.

Liberally coating her palms with the thick ointment, he gently bandaged them with a layer of clean, white cloth.

Patience watched him tend her wounds, gently as he would a child's. Something akin to love stirred within her heart.

When he was through, he continued to hold her hands cupped in his. "Better?"

Nodding, she smiled, embarrassed he'd had to take care of her again. First fainting at the survey office—now blisters. He undoubtedly thought she was a world-class weakling. "I'll bet you think I'm something—crying over some silly blisters."

He put the lid on the salve tin and stuck it back into the sack. "You'll need to change the bandages twice a day."

Patience was determined to hide her swelling frustration with him. The moment he sensed he was getting too close, he retreated into a shell. Was it just her, or women in general, that frightened him?

"Will you be working the mine tomorrow?" she asked. Now that the entrance was passable again, there was a lot of work to be done.

"Moses can handle it."

"I suppose. But because of all the delays, I thought you might be working with her."

She thought it was strange that Jay rarely entered the mine. He did so only at the end of the day, and only long enough to review the women's work.

"That's Moses' job."

She squirmed to look at him. "Yes, but if you were working too, it would go faster."

They had already lost a week, and she couldn't imagine what he did with the rest of his time. He vowed that he didn't believe in ghosts, but something kept him out of the mine.

"I agreed to run the crew for you," he said. "You agreed to the terms."

"Well, feathers! What's wrong with going into the mine?"

"I don't want to. Moses and her crew can bring the diggings out, and I'll work the sluice boxes—day and night, if necessary, but I'm not going into the mine any more than I have to. I've had my fill of mines, Patience. Five long years of wasting time digging for gold, and I'm not doing it again."

"Of all people, Jay Longer, you would be the last person I'd think of being a quitter," she fussed. "Whoever heard of a foreman of a mining crew refusing to enter the mine?"

He turned away, seemingly unaffected by her scorn. Apparently she could think whatever she liked. He'd agreed to oversee the mine, not to work it.

"A quitter!" Patience taunted in a surprising spurt of annoyance. "Quitter, quitter, quitter!" She was going to replace his apathy with enthusiasm if it killed her!

Springing to their feet, they butted noses.

"You're calling *me* a *quitter?*"

"Yeah, a big one."

His eyes glittered dangerously.

Hers flashed in resentment. "You don't scare me, Jay."

"I could if I tried."

"Truth is, you are a scaredy-cat." Their gazes locked in a poisonous duel.

"You don't know what you're talking about."

"Then tell me why you won't go into the mine," she goaded.

"Because I won't. That's all you need to know."

"No, it isn't. I want to know why you won't go in there. You are afraid of ghosts, aren't you?"

"I am not."

"Yes, you are!"

They were shouting now.

"One of us has to be in there," she reasoned. "We can't let Moses do all the work."

"That's why she has a crew."

"I'm hurting, Jay. I can't hold out much longer without paying the crew, and I haven't found enough gold to meet the payroll. Work will go faster if you're in there helping. That's what I'm paying you for."

"No," he contended. "You are paying me to run the crew."

She had a fit of stubbornness. "Then I'll just have to try to help—get in everybody's way, because I don't know anything about gold mining!"

Bending from the waist, he politely gestured for her to be his guest. She whirled, her anger exploding. "You *are* a sissy."

"Think whatever you like."

He was about to walk off when she reached out and latched on to his coattail. "All right," she relented. Her gaze shifted to the mine—she was beginning to hate the thing. It was a curse! "I'll help, but you have to give us more guidance. You know gold mining inside and out, Jay. What are you not telling us?"

His tone was gentler now. "I've told you all I know. Gold mining is a gamble, Patience. You win some and lose most of the others. Give up this idea you're going to get rich. Let me take you back to Denver City, where you can enroll Wilson in school and get on with raising the child. This mine is never going to produce anything."

The time for honesty was at hand; Patience knew it, yet she continued to fight the inevitable. "There is more to your story. Tell me why—if you truly don't believe in the supernatural—*why* are you being so stubborn?"

Stripping his hat off, he beat the dust from it, his face a stained mask. "Jay?"

"All right! I'm claustrophobic."

She gasped. Terminally ill. She knew it. The first man she was ever interested in, and he was dying.

"Oh, Jay . . . how long . . . ?"

A muscle flexed tightly in his jaw. "Four and a half years."

Four and a half years. So little time left for a man who was still young and vital.

"I'm so sorry," she murmured, prepared to do anything to make what time he had left bearable. "When did you find out?"

He glanced up. "Four and a half years ago. At first I didn't know what was happening. Every time I went into a mine I felt like I was suffocating."

"Oh," she soothed. *A horrible lung disease.*

"One day it got so bad I blacked out. My partner hauled me in to see a doctor, and that's when I learned the truth."

Her heart ached. *Consumption.* "It must have been dreadful."

"No. Embarrassing."

She gazed back at him, longing to cradle him in her arms. God love him; he was so brave—so sensitive. He was dying, and *he* was embarrassed.

Meeting her stricken gaze, he suddenly frowned. "Patience?"

"Yes?"

"Do you know what *claustrophobic* means?"

Patience felt faint. She needed to be strong in his hour of need, but she was hampered by a delicate constitution. "No," she admitted hesitantly, hoping he wouldn't find it necessary to go into detail.

"It means a fear of tight places. It's a relatively new term in medicine. I was fortunate enough to be diagnosed by a young doctor who had recently completed his training in Boston and knew of the latest medical advances."

Nodding in total understanding, she sighed benevolently. That would make the grave even more dreadful.

Cupping her chin in his hand, he said, "I am not dying. I *faint* when I'm in a mine because I have a fear of being closed in."

It took a moment for his words to register. When they did, Patience was giddy with relief. *"That's* what's wrong with you? You're afraid of tight places?"

He looked away. "Isn't that enough?"

"Well, all you had to do was say so," she chided. "Then you're *really* not afraid of ghosts?"

"Afraid of Gamey O'Keefe?" He laughed. "No."

"While we're on the subject, who *is* this Gamey O'Keefe?" She'd heard the name until she was sick of it, and yet she hadn't the faintest idea who he was.

Jay's gaze pivoted to the shaft. "A long time ago Gamey and Ardis Johnson both laid claim to the Mule Head. Seems Gamey stole the mine from Ardis while Ardis was gone into town for supplies and . . . other pursuits."

"Other pursuits?"

He looked away. "Other pursuits."

"Oh," she said, getting it.

"The story goes, O'Keefe was trying to bluff Ardis and the sheriff off the property when he blew himself up."

"How did he do that?"

"The stories vary, but apparently it was a blunder on O'Keefe's part. Some say he never intended to kill himself, only to trick Ardis."

"But if Gamey was dead, the mine would have returned to Ardis."

"It did, but from that day on, no one has been able to work it. Legend has it, O'Keefe's spirit lives in the mine and isn't about to let anyone near his gold."

114

Patience laughed. "That's absurd. And now Gamey is supposedly in the mine, aimlessly roaming around?"

"Worse. The legend is that he's locked in the Mule Head forever."

She glanced back to the mine. "I don't believe a word of it."

"Others do."

She crossed her arms, thinking of the agony she'd gone through to hire a crew. "People can't conceive that this 'ghost' has been blown out of proportion—that it's only silly folklore that's been passed from one miner to another. No one's thought to question whether or not it's just a figment of someone's highly active imagination?"

"It looks that way."

"Feathers."

His brows rose a notch.

"Rubbish," she amended. Turning away, she muttered, "Fiddle Creek men are a disgrace." She glanced over her shoulder protectively. "Present company excluded."

Scooping up the leather rucksack, Jay followed her up the hill.

"How do you figure?"

"They've left a bunch of *women* to do their work."

Chapter Fourteen

Patience lingered in the door of the dugout and watched the activity going on at the mine. Wilson spent most of his afternoons hanging around in the way, and even though she scolded him and so did Jay, he was so fascinated with the work and with Jay he couldn't stay away. His assortment of animals was growing too. Where on earth did the boy find all of his pets and how did he catch them?

She hadn't been back to Fiddle Creek lately. Seemed as if she had so much to do here, and like Wilson, she didn't want to be away for very long. She thought of Mary, Lily, and Harper and felt guilty. She should make a greater effort to send word to them, maybe find someone going to Denver City who could carry a message, but it seemed that the longer she stayed away, the more remote her old life became. Right now, she was content to see Jay every day, cook for him and for Wilson, and look forward to the times they spent together talking. They were sort of like a family—a real family, something she knew little about.

She knew her way of thinking was dangerous. Jay Longer wasn't interested in her that way. He was just being friendly, and as he had made clear, he was only working the mine because he needed money. Her needs were secondary. She had learned a lot about mining since they had started working the Mule Head. Of course there was a lot she didn't know, but she was gaining in knowledge every day.

Jay said the Mule Head was a lode mine. Once the diggings were brought out they were scooped into long flumes and sent to the bottom of the mountain. There they were washed in sluice boxes—long troughs, sometimes in several sections, from fifty to one hundred feet long, designed so water could run through them. Riffle boxes, which had false bottoms with cleats to arrest the flow of water and mud, were used to let the gold and heavier particles sink into the shallow boxes. Most of the equipment was in good condition from the old prospector's time, and Jay had repaired the rest.

It was excruciating, backbreaking work, but Moses Malone and her crew didn't seem hindered by their gender. Two of the women stood beside the sluice boxes with hoes and shovels, keeping the dirt stirred up. The residue washed down the trough. Two more women shoveled in material at the head of the sluice, while yet another pair hauled dirt from the mine in wheelbarrows.

Patience ceased trying to help; she only got in the way. But she could cook, toting large pails of food and piping hot loaves of fresh-baked bread to the mine daily. To vary the menu, she fried pans of rice with tomatoes, onions, and chili powder; baked pans of beans flavored with salt pork and thick, rich molasses; made crusty brown peach pies from canned peaches, and piping hot skillets of cinnamon-fried apples. She stayed busy trying to find something new to add to the menu—not that it was appreciated as far as she could tell.

The shady ladies consumed the meals without comment.

Patience wandered over to where she could sit on a boulder and look at the grandeur of the mountains. She'd never seen anything so beautiful. A couple of the women pushed a wheelbarrow of dirt out to be processed. Again she thought of the dark interior of the mine. If Tom Wyatt had had his way, she would be working in his mine right now, with no hope of escape. So would Harper and Lily. Mary might not have survived the rigors of digging for gold. Patience lifted her face to the sky, watching an eagle riding the air currents, thankful she was free to sit in the sun and enjoy God's creation.

Wilson came to join her. "P?"

"Yes, Wilson?"

"I've been going to school for some time now. Do I have to keep on with it?"

"Of course you do. Why?"

"Well, it seems like you and Jay could teach me all I need to know. Jay's real smart, P; don't you think so?"

"He's smart enough." So where was he going with this?

"I've been thinking. I don't believe I want to go to college. I want to be a lawman like Jay. He gets to do lots of exciting things."

"Like working in a mine? Do you think he finds that exciting?"

"Well, maybe not that, but he gets to carry a gun and hunt for bad men, and I don't think you need much book learning for that."

"What's the real reason you don't want to go to school?"

"I don't like being inside all day. The old prospector never made me stay inside. I could do anything I wanted to do, and he never complained."

"It isn't good for us to do just what we want to do. Life is mostly made up of doing what we *don't* want to do."

Wilson thought about this, his face screwed up in concentration. "That doesn't seem fair to me. You like Jay, don't you, P?"

"Of course I do; he's a good friend."

"Friend, huh? I was hoping for more than that." He seemed disappointed.

"Friendship, Wilson. Leave it at that."

"All right, if you say so." He sighed and picked up a broken branch to use for a walking stick. "Well, I guess I'll go explore for a while."

Patience watched him walk away, probably looking for a pretty rock or another animal he could claim for a pet. She thought about his last question. Yes, indeed, she *did* like Jay Longer. Maybe more than she should. But that wasn't anything she could admit to Wilson, because she was fairly sure Jay didn't care that much for her.

The next day was Sunday, and the women didn't work. Jay hadn't shown up either. Patience and Wilson sat on rocks in the sun, dressed in heavy coats, having an early morning worship service. The silence seemed almost unnatural after the daily clatter of mining activity.

Patience read slowly and with reverence: " 'I will lift up mine eyes unto the hills, from whence cometh my help. My help cometh from the Lord, which made heaven and earth.' Isn't that beautiful, Wilson? The psalmist never saw our mountains, but somehow he knows how we feel about them. God's creation is so wonderful."

"Did God make these mountains?"

"Yes, he did."

Wilson pointed to a small pinecone. "Did he make that cone?"

"Yes, that too."

"He does good work, doesn't he?"

"He does very good work. And he made us, in his own image."

"And he made Selmore and all of the other animals all different. God's so amazing, P. Sometimes it just takes my breath away to think about it."

"Mine too, Wilson. He's truly an amazing God."

They sat in silence for a few minutes, before Patience closed her Bible. "What do you want to do today? We can take a walk down the other side of the mountain, or go fishing, or I can make a pan of cinnamon rolls and we'll just be lazy the entire day."

Wilson didn't appear to be listening. "Someone's coming. Maybe it's Jay."

He ran toward the trailhead, coming to an abrupt stop when two burly, unkempt men came into view. Wilson backed slowly toward Patience.

She got to her feet, conscious of the isolation of this spot and her own inability to protect herself and Wilson against intruders. The old prospector's gun was in the dugout, but she had no idea how to use it.

"Howdy, ma'am," the one with the dirty blond beard said, revealing teeth stained brown with tobacco juice. "Jay Longer here?"

"No, he isn't here." She was furious at the way her voice trembled.

The one with brown hair and beard, wearing a grimy tan shirt, narrowed his eyes at her. "We was told he hangs out here."

Patience stiffened. *Hangs out here?* How dare they speak to her like that? "Neither Jay Longer nor anyone else *hangs out* here." Her hand shot out to clamp over Wilson's mouth, just as he started to speak. She didn't like the looks of these men. Whatever they wanted with Jay, they'd get no help from her.

The blond grinned. "If you see him, pass on a message: Red and Luther's looking for him. We got some unfinished business to take care of."

"If I see him, I'll tell him." Anger held her voice steady. "Good day, gentlemen."

The brown-haired one, Luther, nodded. "We'll be back. Maybe stay and visit a little while next time." His eyes skimmed her with disrespect.

After another look around the clearing, they turned and strode back down the trail. Patience, her knees gone weak, collapsed on the boulder, sighing in relief.

Wilson stood beside her, his eyes wide. "What did they want with Jay?"

"I don't know, but I don't think they were friends of his."

"Do you think they'll come back?"

"I hope not."

Wilson stood a little taller. "Don't you be afraid, P. I won't let them hurt you."

She was touched by his evident sincerity. "Thank you, Wilson. I appreciate that."

But if they ever did come back, she needed a plan of action. She had felt too helpless in this encounter. It was foolish to think she and Wilson could fight off two thugs like Red and Luther, but they might have to make the attempt. She needed to find something to use for a weapon.

Patience glanced up that afternoon when Jay came into the dugout. She smiled, relieved that he seemed to be more comfortable with her lately. He stayed for every meal now.

"Hi!"

"Hi."

"Seen any ghosts today?" It was getting to be a standing joke between them.

"Nary a one."

She hadn't told him about her experience in the mine. She wasn't sure she ever would. The passage of time had dimmed the fear she had felt. Probably it had been the wind howling through the old mine shaft. The wind could play tricks on you. She wasn't going to tell him about Red and Luther either. After thinking about it, she had decided they might be passing through and wouldn't come back, and she didn't want to say or do anything to make Jay leave.

"Finding any gold?" she asked.

"Nothing to get excited about."

Jay poured water into the wash pan and scrubbed up for supper. "Something smells good." He scooped water with his hands and flushed the grime from his face.

"Slumgullion," she verified. *Poor man's hash,* the orphanage cook used to say.

"It would be nice to have some fresh meat," she mused. They'd had very little the past few weeks. Just a few rabbits and a deer roast someone had given her last time she was in Fiddle Creek. Fresh vegetables were unheard of, and fruit was scarce as hen's teeth, unless you were fortunate enough to get a few cans of peaches in Fiddle Creek. She gave thanks every day for the old prospector's foresight. She couldn't believe how much food he'd managed to stockpile. Next summer she was going to plant a garden, a big one, and can everything she raised.

Jay blindly fumbled around the washstand, and she slapped a towel in his hand. Lifting his head, he smiled. "Thanks. I'll see if I can scare up some for you."

She smiled, happy to see the way his face had filled out lately. "Fresh venison or a plump, wild turkey would be delicious."

Taking the lid off the skillet, she stirred the hash. "I was just thinking how grateful I am that the mine isn't in Dawson City. Have you heard what's going on over there?"

"They say things are pretty crazy." He pulled out a keg and sat down. She took a pan of bread out of the oven and sliced it.

Jay seemed to deliberately turn his eyes in the other direction.

Setting the bread on the table, she brushed a lock of stray hair from her eyes. "You know what I heard the last time I was in town?"

"What did you hear?"

"I heard that picks and shovels are going for twenty-five dollars apiece in Dawson City. Nails, ten dollars a pound; flour, seventy-five dollars a sack; a can of tomatoes, eight dollars. Salt's worth its weight in gold, and eggs are two dollars apiece. Can you imagine?" She wouldn't be able to survive a day!

"They say the miners are paying the prices. Chappy Hellerman was telling me the hay is running five hundred dollars a bale nowadays."

"How is Chappy?" She hadn't seen the old prospector around the last time she went into town.

"He's staked a claim over near Cherry Creek. Word has it he's found a few good-size nuggets."

When she handed him a slice of warm bread, their hands touched. Her gaze fixed on his. "There's blackberry jam if you like."

"Thanks. I'll wait until you make biscuits again."

Her eyes seemed hesitant to move on, her breathing imperceptibly more shallow. "Guess I should call Wilson. Supper's getting cold."

"He's just outside the door. I had to cut the rope on the skunk. Wilson was upset, but if his luck ran out, you wouldn't be able to live with the smell that close to the dugout."

"You did the right thing. I've told him as much." It was a miracle the skunk hadn't turned on them already.

Don't you dare look the other way, her eyes admonished. *Is your lack of interest because I'm a burden to you? Not only did I defy your order to return to*

Denver City, but I have a small boy to raise. Do you dislike children? Are you afraid of responsibility?

Then again, maybe it isn't indifference I see in your eyes, only idle curiosity.

"Butter?" she asked.

Jay looked away first. "Thanks."

The door flew open, and Wilson burst in on a draft of cold air, dragging a lynx on a leash. "Hey, guys, look what I just found!"

Patience and Jay bolted toward the door, scrambling over each other in their haste to clear the room.

Overturned kegs and the pan of bread clattered to the floor as they darted through the open doorway.

Chapter Fifteen

Don't *ever* do that again!" Patience, still shaking from the encounter, scolded Wilson. "You're going to get somebody killed!"

"But P, he's not very big! He wouldn't hurt nobody—and now you've gone and let Jay scare the cat off with a gun. It's not fair! You said I could have a pet, but then you get all excited when I try to bring one home."

"It was a *lynx*, Wilson. A wild animal. He has to hunt for food. When he grows up, he doesn't know that you're not his supper."

"I could train him. He likes me a lot! When he grows up, he won't be mean, honest. I'll teach him to be nice!"

"You can't keep him."

"Well, *feathers*," Wilson said disgustedly.

Patience gasped. "Wilson!"

"What?"

"Where have you heard such language!"

Wilson peered up at her. "You say *feathers* all the time."

"Well, don't say it again. And while we're on the subject, young man, your attitude is terrible lately!"

"Butch says worse things. He says really bad words when he throws my sandwich down the privy. He says, 'Say good-bye to your behind because it's going down the privy next'!"

"Wilson! Stop that this instant!"

"Privy is bad *too? Nothing* suits you lately!"

Patience started off in a mad huff toward the door. "Get into the house. I'm washing your mouth out with soap."

"Soap!" Wilson wailed.

"Yes, soap!"

"I won't say *feathers* again, I promise!"

"I know you won't, young man!"

Wilson whooped and kicked and yelled when she caught him by the ear and marched him straight into the dugout.

Feathers, indeed!

They were sitting at the supper table the following night when Wilson swore again. Patience's fork clattered to her plate. She glared at the child, her pupils large.

Silence seized the room.

Jay lowered his head, staring at his plate.

". . . please?" Wilson added when the air started to palpitate.

"What did I tell you about using that kind of language?"

Wilson tried to think. *What* language? He'd asked for the beans! "What's wrong with saying—"

"Wilson!"

"That's what Butch calls them."

Shoving back from the table, Patience motioned him to the sink.

"What? What'd I say *now*?" The boy's pleading gaze shot to Jay.

Jay refused to look up.

Latching onto Wilson's ear, Patience hauled him to the sink, verbally castigating Butch Miller every step of the way. "You're turning into a common, foulmouthed hooligan!"

Patience opened the door and looked out to see the frost-frozen ground glittering under a full moon. Plagued by remorse, she stared at the small figure swathed in a heavy blanket sitting on the log, his revered pets gathered about him for support.

Emotion formed a tight knot in her throat. She was such a failure. "But Lord, I'm trying to be a good influence," she whispered, consumed by the need to talk to someone who understood. Anyone.

Maybe she was too young to raise Wilson properly. She didn't know the first thing about nurturing a child; that was all too apparent. In the past, she had relied on Mary's and Ruth's insight; now there was no one but herself to lean on. And her wisdom was running on empty.

Settling a coat around her shoulders, she stepped outside the dugout and closed the door.

Moonlight lit her pathway as she strolled to the log. When she approached Wilson, she was met with a frostier reception than the cool February night.

Undeterred, she sat down, nodding hello to the pets. A raccoon stared back with inquisitive eyes.

One by one she acknowledged the other animals' presence. "Hello, Edgar, Pudding, Jellybean, and of course a good evening to you, Selmore." She sat for a moment, enjoying the night.

Wilson refused to look at her.

After a while, she reached over and pulled him onto her lap. He was getting awfully big for such an action, but he wasn't too big yet.

He set up an indignant protest but she held him firmly to her until he gradually relaxed. They gazed at a sky ablaze with stars. Just the two of them, the way it had been for a while now.

"Bet you can't find a big fat cow."

Studying the sky, Wilson solemnly pointed to a cluster of odd-shaped clouds. The orphanage cook had played the nonsensical game with the girls from the time they were infants. The frivolous diversion never failed to win a smile or mend an unintentional slight.

"Bet you can't find a skinny pig."

Patience's eyes searched the sky studiously. "How skinny?"

"Real skinny."

After a while, she pointed to a configuration of stars just to the left of the Milky Way. "There, the scrawniest pig in the whole universe."

"No, it isn't."

"Yes, it is."

"Bet you can't find a fish wearing a hat."

"What kind of hat?"

"A *miner's* hat."

"Too easy." She pointed out a clump of stars to the right of the moon. "Right there, plain as day. A silly-looking fish wearing an even sillier-looking miner's hat."

"The kind Moses wears?"

"Even sillier."

Giggling, they played the game a while longer. The moon climbed higher in the winter sky.

Wilson snuggled deeper into her warmth. "I'm going to try and do better. I'll never say *feathers* or that other word and *beans* again." Sadness touched his voice now. "I miss the old prospector."

Resting her chin on the top of his head, Patience hugged him tightly. "I know, Wilson. I miss my friends in Denver City too."

"Sometimes it's hard to remember what the prospector looked like," he admitted. "I think real hard about him, but sometimes I just can't see him."

"Maybe if you didn't think so hard, you might see him."

"What *did* he look like, Patience?"

Patience recalled the old man. "Well, he was about medium height, sort of skinny, with white hair and a beard. His hands showed he'd worked outside." She thought hard. "His nose was a little bit crooked."

"I remember that," Wilson exclaimed. "He broke it when he slipped and fell and hit his nose with his shovel."

"He must have been a good man," Patience said.

"Yes, he was," Wilson agreed. "I don't know what would have happened to me if he hadn't taken me in. I was so scared when he died, but then you came and it was all right again."

"God sent me, Wilson. He knew we needed each other."

"He always knows, doesn't he, P?"

"Yes, Wilson, God always knows."

They sat for a moment, recalling happier times.

"Wilson, I'm sorry I've been so hard on you lately."

He sighed. "I don't mean to say bad things."

"I know you don't. You know the Good Book tells us not to take the Lord's name in vain."

"*Feathers* is taking the Lord's name in vain?"

"No, but it is a mild form of cursing, and we shouldn't do it. I know I'm guilty of saying *feathers* myself when it would be better to just say yes or no. I think we'll both have to work on watching our language more carefully."

Wilson was immediately repentant. "I'm sorry. Butch says bad words all the time."

"Well, maybe no one has told Butch that he shouldn't. The Lord says we are in the world but not of it, and that means we are to be especially aware of what we say and do."

"But sometimes we mess up, huh, P?"

"Many, many times, but that should only make us try harder to be the very best that we can be."

Wilson thought about that for a while. "Jay messes up sometimes."

"Yes," Patience whispered conspiratorially. "Sometimes he does. Real bad."

"But he's getting better. He's nicer now than he used to be; why, he even shaved off his beard so's he wouldn't get snot in it anymore."

"Wilson, there you go again. Your language is slipping."

"Well, that's what *he* said."

She laughed, hugging him. "Well, I agree he is getting much better than when we first saw him at the land office."

"You knew him before, huh?"

"Just barely." Patience knew *of* him—had seen the handsome sheriff in Denver City a few times, even tangled with him on occasion, but he'd always kept to himself.

"Maybe he just needs someone to take care of him, huh?"

"Yes," she said softly. "Maybe he does."

"He's a real good worker."

She felt good about the work even though Jay contended mining was a waste of time. Any day now they would hit pay dirt, and then he'd know he'd been wrong. She shivered, thinking about the looks on the other girls' faces when she handed them each a sack of gold. She felt encouraged at the rate of progress. And there hadn't been a breath of whisper about any ghosts. She had proven that the rumors were just silly superstition that had abounded for over thirty years.

"Very good worker," she admitted. "We're lucky to have Jay helping us."

"Why doesn't he like to go into the mine?"

"Because he has something called claustrophobia, which means he's uncomfortable in closed places."

Neither spoke for a moment.

"How 'bout we ask him to marry us?" Wilson suggested.

Patience blinked. "Marry us?"

"Yeah. You like Jay, don't you?"

"Yes," she admitted. "I like him a lot." She liked him more than a lot, and every day the attraction grew. But he didn't seem to notice that she existed except for the day he had bandaged her blistered hands. At times he seemed almost afraid of her—afraid to look at her or talk to her.

"Well, I think he likes you too, so why don't we just keep him? He doesn't have a home, except that old deserted miner's shack. I bet he'd like for us to marry him."

"Well, I'd like to think he'd like that, but I don't think he would."

"Why not?"

"I think he's used to living alone. I think he likes it better that way."

"Want me to ask him if he likes us or not?"

"No! Under no circumstances are you to ask him that, Wilson."

"Why not? He always answers whatever I ask him. He's real good about that." His face brightened. "I'll even ask him if he wants to marry us, how about that?"

Scooping him off her lap, she hastily stood up. "It's late. You need to be in bed."

She helped him gather his pets, and together they herded the animals back to the dugout.

Ask Jay to marry them. Patience blanched at the thought—but she couldn't say the idea was entirely objectionable.

Jay had left to take the shady ladies home, and Patience was surveying the plot where she planned to plant a garden come spring, poking at the frozen ground with an old hoe she'd found. Produce she could raise would help with expenses and be better than anything available in Fiddle Creek. And she wanted a supply of stuff for the root cellar. Maybe a good variety of root vegetables. Like Wilson, she wasn't all that fond of turnips, but they beat nothing. Squash, onions, carrots, potatoes, even late cabbage would keep for some time. A well-stocked root cellar was like money in the bank.

Wilson came running. "P! Those men are back."

She turned around in time to see Red and Luther approaching. She waited, gripping the hoe in front of her like a gun. "What do you want?"

"Now, is that any way to treat company?" Red asked. "We might get the idea you're not glad to see us." He winked at Luther.

Luther moved a little closer. "Where's Jay Longer?"

"I don't know where he is." Which was the truth. He was somewhere between here and wherever he left the shady ladies, but she had no way of knowing where, and she had no intention of telling these thugs anything.

"Don't give me that," Red snarled. "You know where he is, all right, and you're going to tell us."

Patience noticed Wilson approaching with his most recent pet in his arms. A magnificent black-backed rooster with golden head and neck feathers and a tail of rich bronze. His large comb was a deep scarlet.

The men ignored the boy, concentrating their attention on Patience. Red spat a stream of amber juice, which missed her foot by two inches. "Stop giving us the runaround. We're here to see Longer. If you tell us where he is, you won't get hurt."

"You're threatening me?" Patience didn't try to keep the scorn out of her voice. "I have nothing to say to you."

"All right," Luther said. "You had your chance. What happens next is your own fault."

When he took two steps toward her, she jabbed the hoe handle hard into his midsection. He bent double, holding his stomach, and she slapped him across the back with the wooden handle.

Wilson flung the squawking, scratching rooster straight at Red's head. The man tried to ward off the angry bird, which only infuriated it more. Luther, still doubled over, tried to scurry toward the trailhead, with Patience behind him, whacking him across the seat of the pants with every step. The rooster flogged Red, jumping high in an attempt to spur him. The two men fled down the trail with Wilson hurling pinecones after them.

The rooster strutted back, crowing lustily. Patience held out her hand to Wilson. "Shake, partner."

Wilson placed his hand in hers. "We make a good team, don't you think?"

"A very good team."

"Do you think they'll come back?"

"I doubt it. Their kind only fight people they think can't fight back. They got more than they anticipated here."

And if they did come back, she would be ready for them.

Patience hefted the kettle of hot water and added it to the wash pan. She was still trembling inside from the unpleasant encounter, but she had to wash her hair. The cloud of brunette locks now fell below her waist in heavy waves. It had been over a week since the last good scrubbing, and if she hurried she would have time to wash it before Jay got back for supper. The dirt kicked up by the mine kept her constantly scratching her scalp. Colorado in winter wasn't the ideal time for hair washing, but she couldn't stand it any longer. Occasionally Missouri would have a nice spell during the winter, and that's when the girls really bathed and groomed themselves. Otherwise, they washed from a pan of hot water and simply brushed dust out of their hair.

She worked up a good lather, then rinsed it well, her mind still troubled by the two strangers. What had those two men wanted with Jay? It could be for no good—that was certain. She would die before she'd let them know that Sheriff Longer was here. Blinded by soap and water, she groped for a towel. She thought she had placed one within easy reach before starting the worrisome project.

Someone placed the towel in her hand, and she dried her face. "Thanks, Wilson."

"I'm not Wilson."

She lowered the towel to see Jay grinning at her mischievously. "Oh, I thought you were taking the shady ladies home."

"I did. I'm back."

"Yes, I see." She toweled her hair, thinking how awful she must look with her hair wet and hanging down her back. Taking a seat in front of the fire, she began to brush the tangles out with long flowing strokes. Jay watched, his intense blue eyes centered on her.

"Did the work go well today?"

"For a change. No problems so far."

"Find any gold?" She fell back on the old joke.

"As a matter of fact, we did find a small vein."

"Really?" She stopped brushing in her excitement. "That's good, isn't it?"

"As far as it goes. Big enough to keep us going for a while, but not good enough to help much."

"But it's a start." She refused to be disillusioned.

He didn't answer and she searched for a new topic of conversation.

"Your hair is pretty hanging loose like that."

She looked at him in surprise. "You think so?"

"Yeah. Bible says a woman's hair is her crowning glory. Not hard to understand when you see it hanging down like a waterfall. Been a long time since I've seen a woman dry her hair."

She'd heard rumors that the sheriff had once been married, so she figured he was talking about his wife. For a moment she was disappointed, but then she realized she wouldn't want him to forget the woman he had loved. A man like Jay Longer had room in his heart to love again. Her brush strokes became more sensuous as she relaxed in the warmth of the fire and the inner glow caused by the tender expression in his eyes.

"Do you ever miss Denver City?" he asked.

"No. I miss Mary and Harper and Lily, but I don't miss the city. I've learned to love the solitude of these mountains. I'd hate to have to move back to town."

"Me too." He leaned back, staring lazily at the fire. "I used to hate it here, too different from Phoenix. But now I've changed my mind. I'd like to build a cabin in this spot and sit and enjoy the scenery until I'm too old to see any more. It would be hard to live any place else, but few women would want that kind of life, I guess."

"Oh, I don't know," she said. "I guess it would depend on the woman."

He leaned forward, "What about you, Patience? Are you the kind of woman who'd prefer a cabin to a mansion? What about that gold we're looking for?"

"That gold isn't just for me. It's for the people I care about. I want to make life better for them. I'm not a mansion person, Jay. I've never had a real home, so this dugout is paradise to me." She could see in his eyes that he wanted to say something, but the door burst open, and he jerked back in his chair.

Wilson entered, carrying his rooster. "Supper ready? Say, P, how come you're just sitting there with your hair down? What are you doing?"

Patience sprang to her feet. "I'll fix supper."

Wilson sat down in the chair she had just vacated. "When did you get back, Jay? I wanted you to show me how to make a peashooter like Butch has. The next time he pops me, I'm going to pop him back."

Jay frowned. "Anyone ever mention your timing stinks?"

Wilson looked bewildered. "What? What did I do now?"

Chapter Sixteen

Bellyache. Bad." Moses stood in front of Jay early the next morning, looking sick as a dog.

"All of you?"

The Indian nodded. "Bad whiskey."

How had the women gotten liquor? he wondered. He had hoped to wind up the week on a promising note. So far, Mule Head was yielding only enough gold to get by.

"Loaded cart in mine."

"You left a cart in the mine?"

She nodded.

"Can't you bring it out?"

Paling, Moses grabbed her seat. "Go now." Turning, she trekked off, doing the green-apple quickstep.

Dropping the wild turkey he'd just shot, Jay glanced at the mine entrance. The women had left a loaded cart in there. If they were too sick to work, that meant he had to go in after it or cause even further delay. He broke out in a cold sweat just thinking about it.

"Turkey!" Patience rejoiced when he deposited the bird on her doorstep a few moments later.

"It's been hanging around the shaft. I thought it would look better on your table."

"I'd say!" Picking up the bird, she held it up for inspection. "Nice and plump! We'll have him for supper." She looked up, grinning. "I'll even make dumplings."

Jay smiled. "I'll be looking forward to that."

"Not half as much as I will," she teased, enjoying the way he immediately colored.

Settling his hat jauntily back on his head, he started off for the mine. Patience called after him, "Where're the shady ladies today?"

"Sick."

"All of them?"

"All of them," he confirmed grimly.

Wilson came out of the dugout carrying his dinner pail. He frowned when he spotted the limp turkey dangling from Patience's right hand.

"Uh-uh," she *tsk*ed before he could set up a loud protest. "Turkeys are not put upon this earth as pets. They're meant . . . for other purposes."

Wilson's eyes flew to Selmore, who was still safely tied to a tree.

"With the exception of Selmore," she allowed. Leaning forward, she tapped her cheek. "Big kiss."

Grumbling, Wilson gave her the perfunctory peck. With a sympathetic look toward the deceased bird, he stepped toward the trail, whispering to Selmore, "I hope it wasn't anybody you knew."

Jay paused at the mine entrance, trying to see inside the dark hole. The narrow chamber stretched relentlessly down the tight corridor.

Undoubtedly, the cart was sitting at the point farthest from the entry.

Kneeling, he lit the lantern, trying to control the tremor in his hand. This was insane. All he had to do was go in, find the cart, and push it out. He wouldn't be in the mine for more than a few minutes. He was used to that from checking the ladies' work each day. How much harder could this be?

Straightening, he took off his hat, wiped the sweat from his forehead with his shirtsleeve, and put the hat on again. Why was he doing this? Retrieving abandoned carts wasn't his job. He could think of only one reason why he would go into that pit: Patience and the boy. They needed the day's diggings.

When he left Denver City, determined to rescue Patience from the kidnapper, he had no intention of becoming attracted to her. Just do the job he got paid to do. Now he looked forward to seeing her every day. He'd never thought anyone could take the place of Nelly and Brice, and no one ever could. They'd always have a special place in his heart. But Patience and Wilson were beginning to fill a void he'd thought could never be filled again.

Taking a deep breath, he picked up the lantern and entered the shaft. A damp, musty smell met his nose, and he hesitated at the entrance. The cart was nowhere in sight. Great. That meant he'd have to venture in farther.

Edging deeper into the tunnel, he raised the lantern wick, flooding the shaft with light. The temperature was cooler in here. Lantern glare played along the walls, exposing shored-up timbers and overhead leakage. Water stood in shallow puddles on the mud floor.

Rounding a corner, Jay lifted the beam higher. The familiar tightening in his lungs warned him that in a few minutes he would be struggling for breath. Light flickered off the walls, and his leaden feet picked up the tempo. Where was that cart?

Following a left fork, he moved through the tunnel, his breathing strained now. Rounding a third bend, panic nabbed him. This was much deeper than he wanted to go. The walls closed in and his lungs battled for air. Rationality fought with phobia, but as usual fear won out.

Whirling, he started to run. Had to get out—now! Gasping for breath, his left foot tangled with his right and the lantern went flying. Diving headfirst, he managed to grab it just before it smashed to the ground.

Struggling unevenly back to his feet, Jay leaned against the wall, sweating in earnest now.

"Heh, heh, heh."

Jay's head shot up. "What?"

"Some days it jest don't pay a man to git outta bed, does it, buddy boy?"

Cocking an ear, Jay peered into the darkness, hearing nothing but the sound of his ragged breathing.

"Tee, heh, heh, heh."

He crooked his head from side to side, trying to find the source of the sound. "What?"

"Some days it jest don't pay a man to git outta bed, does it, buddy boy? Tee, heh, heh, heh."

"Who's there?" Lifting the lantern, Jay's eyes searched the darkness. Light played along the cracks and crevices, revealing nothing. Someone snickered—he heard it.

Snort, snort, snigger, chortle. "Tee, heh, heh!"

Jerking the lantern back, Jay ran the beam along the walls more purposefully. "Who's there? You're trespassing on private property!"

"I know. Mine."

Nailing the beam in the direction of the voice, Jay hit pay dirt. What he saw made his blood curdle.

Perched on a ledge, a man, small of stature and sporting a long white beard, lifted five fingers and waved at him.

Stunned, Jay's heart pumped faster. Lowering the lantern, he tried to think. It had to be his imagination. This was not the ghost of Gamey O'Keefe. Couldn't be . . .

Waiting a moment, he lifted the light again, moving it back to the perch.

Grinning, the figure on the ledge devilishly wiggled five fingers at him. He cocked his head. "Yo? Hello?"

Lowering the light, Jay wiped at sweat running down his sideburns. He'd lost his mind; claustrophobia had turned to delirium. He was deranged, loco. Gone nuts.

"Yes, you see what you see, buddy boy. It's me. Shine that light over here. I want to get down, and my eyes ain't the best."

While Jay searched for his voice, the man bellowed. "Hey! You deaf? I said shine that light over here!"

The light shot up and over. The man hopped down off the ledge. "Thank ya. That's better."

Aghast, Jay watched the little old miner walking toward him.

"Gamey O'Keefe here. How ya doin'?"

Mesmerized, Jay reached out to shake hands when Gamey quickly drew back. "Wouldn't do that if I was you." He looked sheepish. "The hand's still a mite hot from the blast."

Putting his palm at the small of his back, Gamey stretched. "Rheumatism kickin' up on me again." He glanced back to Jay. "What's th' matter, boy? Cat got your tongue?"

"Who *are* you?" Jay whispered. "And what are you doing in the mine without a light?"

The old man grinned again. Slapping his hands on his knees, he leaned forward. "Who do you think I am?" He bent closer. "I'll give ya a clue. *Boo.*"

Jay edged backward, speechless. The ghost. The ghost of Gamey O'Keefe. But it couldn't be Gamey—he was dead.

"Now, now, buddy boy—you ain't scairt of me, are you? Ain't you the one who's been blowin' off 'bout not believin' in ghosts? Eh? That was you, wasn't it, buddy boy?"

"Gamey O'Keefe," Jay murmured, unable to believe his eyes.

Gamey bowed modestly. "In the flesh—oops—guess that ain't exactly the truth." He suddenly straightened. "Say, where's them ugly women today? That one they call Moses? Whooeee! That woman's so ugly, when she was born the doctor slapped her mother!"

Dumbfounded, Jay stared back. "Does Moses know about you?"

"Well, now." Gamey doffed his hat and mindfully scratched his head. "I reckon she does—don't everybody?"

"Then she's seen you?" Relief flooded the sheriff; he wasn't the only one losing his mind.

"Who, Moses?"

"Yes."

"No, she ain't seen me. I ain't gonna show myself to nobody but you, buddy boy."

"The name is not buddy boy."

"Oh, I know that, *Jay.*" He put more emphasis on the name than Jay thought necessary. "But that's what I'm gonna call you."

Why me? Jay agonized. He didn't want this responsibility, and he sure didn't need more aggravation! Why hadn't he ridden off for Denver City and left Patience here to deal with her mine and her . . . ghosts. No. He didn't believe in ghosts. Whoever this was, he was a living, breathing human being. Question was: what was he doing in the Mule Head?

Gamey hefted himself back onto the ledge and got comfortable. "I haven't showed myself to nary a soul since the accident. Been real ornery—causing all sorts of trouble with cave-ins and whatnots, but haven't showed myself to nobody." He laughed. "Not until today." A devilish twinkle lit his rheumy eyes. "Now, why do you suppose that is?"

Jay was powerless to say, but he didn't believe a word this man was saying.

"Say, buddy boy, you're not breathin' so hard. Ya feelin' better?"

Jay realized his breathing had stabilized. When Gamey appeared, the phobia had receded.

"That classtrefabio stuff? What is that?" Gamey asked.

"How do you know about that?"

Gamey shrugged. "I know everything."

Jay inched backward farther, convinced he was imagining the encounter. It wasn't happening. The phobia was doing bizarre things to his mind. There was no ghost. Gamey O'Keefe had been dead for thirty-six years. Folks in these parts knew of him, and someone had put this man up to pretending to be the ghost.

"You leavin'?"

Jay refused to answer. If he responded, he acknowledged his insanity. If he kept quiet, there was still hope he could shake it off. He continued backing up, one foot, then the other, round the first corner, one boot behind the other, then another, then another.

The man's voice pursued him down the corridor. "What's yore hurry? It gets lonely in here."

Jay rounded the last corner, and he turned and broke into a sprint.

Patience was working in the kitchen, humming softly to herself. She'd cook a supper tonight like Jay Longer had never tasted before. The turkey was young and plump, just right for good eating. She wanted something special for a sweet. Maybe peach upside-down cake. He'd like that.

She'd make good dumplings too. Take flour, baking powder, and salt, add milk, and drop them in the boiling broth and keep the lid on tight until they were done. No soggy dumplings for Patience Smith. The cook at the orphanage had taught her to create a masterpiece that would rival thistledown and taste a whole lot better.

She paused in her work, thinking how much better her life had become since meeting Jay. He had seemed so aloof back in Denver City and when she first met him here, but now he was almost nice. Most of the time.

She gasped. What was wrong with her? She had gone to Fiddle Creek last week and had plumb forgot to see if the telegraph lines had been fixed. She still hadn't gotten word to Mary, Lily, and Harper that she was all right.

"There you are! I was worried about you."

Late that afternoon, Jay glanced up to find Patience coming toward him. Shoveling more dirt into the sluice box, he continued working.

Pausing beside the cart, she shaded her eyes against the sun.

Jay had discarded his coat, and now worked in shirtsleeves.

For a moment Patience could only stare at him. Ridges of taut mus-

140

cles glistened beneath his shirt, open at the neck. She had seen appealing men, but she was certain there could be none more remarkable than this one.

The thought shamelessly intrigued her.

When Jay looked at her, she quickly looked away.

"Did you need something?"

"I've lost Wilson."

Lowering the shovel, he repeated, "You've lost Wilson."

She smiled. "Not permanently, but I haven't seen him in a while."

His eyes skimmed the area. "I'm sure he's around somewhere."

"Have you seen him lately?"

Plunging the shovel back into the dirt, he dumped another scoop into the box. "He was here for a few minutes after school."

Patience studied the sun, wrinkles creasing the folds of her eyes. "That was hours ago. The sun will set soon."

"He'll be along."

"Could you see if you can find him? The turkey's ready to come out of the oven."

"All right. I'll drop what I'm doing and look for Wilson."

Patience decided to ignore the note of acrimony in his tone. "Thank you. Supper'll be ready soon."

Once he got a taste of her turkey and dumplings his mood would improve considerably.

Chapter Seventeen

Jay plunged through the underbrush searching for Wilson. No telling where he might be. Ran around like a rabbit most of the time. The boy needed responsibilities, needed a father to help him grow into a man, but it wasn't his job and it wasn't going to be.

He'd already allowed Wilson to get closer than he ever intended. He and Patience both. He had to stop this invading relationship before it went any further. No point in starting something you didn't intend to finish.

"Wilson!"

Where was that boy? Never seen anything like him. Out of one thing and into another. Give the kid his due. Once Patience straightened him out, he never pulled the same trick twice, which wasn't much consolation, considering he apparently had an unending supply of new ideas he hadn't tried yet.

Jay approached the mine with a knot in his stomach. He'd looked everywhere else, everywhere he knew to look.

Wilson had been told a hundred times to stay away from the shaft; he prayed this wasn't the time he'd decided to test his mettle.

"Wilson!" *Wilson, Wilson, Wilson . . .* Jay's voice echoed back from the mine.

"Wilson!" *Bless that boy's hide. Where is he?*

Stepping closer to the entrance, the sheriff admitted this had been the longest day of his life. This was the third time today he had been forced

143

to go into the mine. He wasn't sure he could do it again. The last time had been bad enough. Going back into that mine to get the loaded cart had taken all the nerve he had. Particularly after seeing that old miner who claimed to be Gamey O'Keefe.

He'd had to bring out the cart for his own sake. He couldn't live with the knowledge that he was a coward. Worse, he would never be able to face Patience again. Afraid of a so-called ghost. Now that he'd recovered from his first reaction, he was a lot more skeptical of Mr. Gamey O'Keefe. There could very well be another opening to the Mule Head, which would allow someone to come and go at will.

He didn't like that thought.

"Wilson!"

Jay's voice echoed back on a cold wind.

He didn't know why, but he knew the boy was in there. Simple knowledge that it wasn't his day sealed it. If anything happened to Wilson, Patience would be heartbroken. That thought alone made up his mind, because he didn't want to think that he cared about the child. He couldn't afford to care. Everyone he'd ever cared about had been taken from him.

Lighting the lantern, he entered the shaft. "Wilson? You in here, son?"

Overhead, timbers creaked. He mechanically set one foot in front of the other. *Gamey could arrange for one of his cave-ins*, he thought. Having met the outlandish ghost, he couldn't deny that he was eccentric enough to wreak havoc—

What am I thinking? I didn't meet the ghost! The encounter was a figment of my imagination! But in here, alone with his own fears for company, it was a lot easier to believe.

His footsteps wavered, and his ears picked up the sound of dripping water. *Plink, plink, plink.*

"Wilson, can you hear me?"

Maybe the boy *wasn't* in here. Premonition had led Jay astray more than once. Relief flooded him. There was no telling where that boy was—

"In here, Jay."

Jay's heart sank when Wilson's muffled voice reached him. Turning, his gaze searched the jagged crevices. "Wilson?"

"In here, Jay."

Running the light over the uneven clefts, Jay tried to determine where the voice was coming from. The boy was close. He could hear him clearly.

"Where are you?"

"In here."

Swinging the light around, Jay checked the passageway jutting to the right. A bat darted up, disappearing between two ragged clefts. "Wilson, what are you doing in there?" Wherever *there* was.

"Just sittin' here."

Jay followed the sound, holding the lantern aloft. It was here he had encountered Gamey earlier. His eyes warily searched the blackness. "Come out, Wilson. Patience's waiting supper for us."

"I can't come out, Jay."

Jay muttered under his breath. He wasn't in the mood for games. Dampness seeped through his coat. His hands trembled and his breathing grew more labored. "Wilson, get out here! P's looking for you."

"I *can't,* Jay!"

Jay swung around and the light pinpointed a small chamber opening. "Wilson?"

Wilson's voice came from inside the chamber. "Jay, why do you keep saying 'Wilson'?"

"Why don't you stop asking questions and get out here?" He was losing patience with this kid.

Dropping to his knees, Jay crawled through water to get to the chamber. He realized why he wasn't overly fond of children lately. They were too much trouble. Women were interruptions, and children were too much trouble, and he had way too much of both in his life.

"Wilson, how did you get in there?"

"Crawled in. It was easy."

"Well, crawl out. That should be double easy."

"Uh-uh."

"Come on, Wilson." Poking his head through the chamber opening, Jay rammed his nose straight into something hairy.

Warm and hairy.

Springing backward, he swiped at his nose, jarred by the putrid smell.

"Jay?" Wilson called.

"Wilson, what do you have in there with you?"

"A bear."

A bear! There was a *bear* in there! "Wilson, get out!"

"I can't; the bear's sitting in front of the door."

Jay racked his brain. *Wilson is trapped in a chamber with a bear. What kind of bear? Big? Small?* Did it matter? It was a bear.

A bear, a boy, a tight chamber.

"Wilson, listen. Now, don't panic." He glanced around for something to distract the animal. How did a bear get in there? The opening was barely big enough for a child to squeeze through.

The kid was trapped in there with a bear, and it was up to him to do something about it. For an instant he remembered Brice, his own son. Would he have hesitated if that had been Brice trapped by a bear? No, he would have taken this place apart rock by rock. He couldn't do less for Wilson. He hadn't wanted to let Wilson become important to him—or Patience either, for that matter—but it seemed like the heart had a way of ignoring what the mind knew was best. That thought scared him more than the bear.

"Wilson?"

"Yeah?"

"Did you hear what I said?"

"Yeah. 'Don't panic.'"

"Stay calm."

"I have to go to the outhouse. I have to go bad, Jay."

"You'll have to hold on—do you know anything about bears?"

"No, sir. I come from England, and I don't think they have bears over there. Leastways, none I've ever seen. But they might, 'cause I probably didn't see much of England after I was born."

"What's the bear look like?"

"Like he's real aggravated."

Black, cinnamon? Mama bear, cub? Jay knew his luck wouldn't let it be a cub. "What color is he?"

"Mmm, well, kind of black . . . no, maybe reddish brown . . . no, well . . . I don't know. My glasses are fogged up."

"Hold on, Wilson. I'm going to have to find a way to get the bear out of there."

Wilson's voice came back, urgent now. "You'd better hurry, Jay, 'cause I have to go to the bathroom real bad!"

Jay ran out of the shaft, returning a few minutes later carrying a pickax. "Wilson?"

"Are you hurrying?"

"I'm hurrying. Now listen. Where's the bear now?"

"Same place. Sitting in front of the door."

"He's just sitting there?"

"Yeah. Staring at me."

Jay's gaze skimmed the cramped area, trying to think of a way to lure the bear out of the chamber. He needed bait. "Wilson?"

"Yeah?"

"I'm going back to the dugout. Don't move. I mean it—*don't move a muscle* until I get back! Don't do anything to antagonize the bear. Hear me?"

"I have to *go,* Jay, real *bad!*"

"I'll be back in five minutes, Wilson. Five minutes." Whirling, Jay sprang into action.

Racing back through the shaft, he dashed to the dugout. Patience glanced up, smiling when he blasted through the door.

"Hi. The turkey turned out beautifully—" She gasped as he jerked the bird off the platter and whirled and sprinted off with it.

"No time to explain!" he shouted and disappeared out the door again.

"Jay Longer! Have you lost your mind?" Stamping her foot, she marched to the door and slammed it behind him. "Beans for supper *again!*"

Dashing back to the mine, Jay tore down the narrow passageway, juggling the hot turkey with both hands. "Wilson!"

He could hear crying coming from the chamber now. "Wilson!" Jay shouted, panic-stricken. "What's wrong?"

The bear let out a death-defying roar that ricocheted off the walls.

"Wilson!"

"What?"

"Are you hurt?"

The sobbing increased, more intense now.

"Are you *hurt?*" Had the bear attacked him? Sweat beaded Jay's forehead and rolled down his face.

Wilson mumbled something Jay couldn't make out and cried harder.

Jay glanced around helplessly. Ghosts, bossy women, and bawling kids. He couldn't take much more.

Desperate now, he tore into the meat, laying a trail of turkey away from the chamber. If the bear took the bait, the meat would lead it out of the mine.

"Better spread it thick, buddy boy. That's a *big* bear in there. *Tee, hee, hee, hee.*"

Jay closed his eyes. *Not again.*

Looking up, he saw Gamey sitting on an overhead ledge, swinging his stubby legs in a carefree manner. Lifting his hand, the old miner wiggled five fingers, waving at him.

Ignoring the apparition, Jay tore off a drumstick and crawled through water to the chamber entrance.

"Okay, Wilson, I'm back. Everything's going to be all right. Where's the bear now?"

"Sittin'—" *sniff, sniff*—"in—" *sniff*—"front of the door."

"Okay. I'm going to try and lure him out."

"He won't come out," Gamey predicted in a whisper. "You'll have to have a bigger turkey than that."

"He'll come out."

"No, he won't."

"Yes, he will."

"Who you talkin' to, Jay?"

"Bet ya he won't."

"Just shut up! Okay?"

"Okay," Wilson called back, pained.

"I'm . . . not talking to you, Wilson. I'm talking to . . . someone else."

Wilson couldn't hear Gamey in the chamber. "I don't hear anybody else. Are you okay, Jay?"

Placing his index and middle finger in the center of his tongue, Jay whistled loudly and beat on the chamber, trying to get the bear's attention.

"Ain't no use. I put him in there, and he ain't comin' out," Gamey taunted. He got to his feet, dancing a lighthearted jig.

Jay thought his exhibition disgusting. "You'd do that to a child? That's pretty low, isn't it?"

"Shore! I'm bad!"

Jay turned away. "You're more than bad; you're rotten to the core."

"I'm sorry, Jay!" Wilson sobbed harder. "I don't know why you're talking mean to me—"

The ploy worked. Roaring, the bear dropped to all fours. Gamey jumped up and down, having a whale of a time at Jay's expense.

"Here you go, boy. Come and get it." Jay fanned the tantalizing drumstick aroma into the chamber.

Growling, the bear sniffed, slapping out with his paw.

"Right here, boy." Shoving the steaming meat into the hole, Jay fanned it around, scenting the air.

"Right here, boy," Gamey mimicked, clapping his hands with glee.

"He's gonna tear yore head off, buddy boy! Yore gonna be blowin' yore nose out yore ear!"

The bear slapped out again, catching the back of Jay's hand with its claws. Blood spurted. Swiftly retracting the decoy, Jay held the meat on the ground within the bear's reach.

Roaring again, the bear sniffed around the chamber entrance to capture the scent.

"That's it, boy. Come and get it," Jay coaxed.

"That's it, boy," Gamey heckled. "Come and eat Jay up!"

"Shut up!" Jay blazed, sick of Gamey's interference.

"I didn't say anything, Jay, honest!" Wilson agonized from the chamber. "I'm being quiet as a church mouse except when you talk to me!"

"See what you're doing," Jay snapped. "The kid thinks I'm talking to him!"

"I don't care."

Jay heard the bear suddenly drop on his belly, trying to tunnel his way to the smell.

"He's coming out, Jay!"

"Better run, buddy boy. The bear's comin' after ya! *Heh, heh, heh."*

Jay continued to wave the drumstick, keeping it within easy smelling distance.

The bear squirmed, maneuvering his thick body through the tight opening. Gradually a head emerged, then hairy shoulders. The animal's back legs slid free. Jay tossed the drumstick into the passageway and jumped into a crevice, nearly tripping over the old miner.

Gamey bristled. "Hey! Watch it thar, buddy boy! You caught my bunion!"

The bear quickly located the meat and devoured it. Lifting his head, he roared, his nose sniffing the air. Loping forward, he found another chunk of meat, gobbled it down, and loped on.

Jay watched, hoping the animal's appetite held.

The animal's fleshy backside waddled down the tunnel, and Jay quickly dropped to his knees and crawled into the small cavern.

Wilson was huddled in a far corner, crying.

"It's okay, Wilson. He's gone."

Lunging into Jay's arms, Wilson clung to his neck. His frail body trembled. Jay held him tightly. "It's all right, son. You're safe now." He was getting a soft spot for this kid—and he knew it.

When the boy's terror subsided, Jay removed Wilson's glasses and wiped the dirt off them. Hooking the wire earpieces around the child's ears, he positioned the glasses back on his nose. His heart wrenched at the boy's tearstained face. "It's all right. You're okay, and that's all that matters."

Wilson swiped his sleeve across his nose and sniffled again. "Jay."

"Yeah?"

"P's going to be real mad at me."

"That's okay. I'll explain it to her, and she'll be so glad to see you're safe that she won't say a word."

Wilson looked glum. "Yes, she will. P knows lots of words, and seems like I must have heard most of them."

Jay grinned. "I've heard a few of them myself."

Wilson sniffed the air. "What did you feed that bear?"

"P's turkey."

Wilson stared at him, wide-eyed. "You did?"

"Yeah. She's probably going to have something to say to both of us."

Wilson frowned. "You scared?"

"Sure. She's hard to handle when she really gets going."

Wilson bit his lip. "I'll tell her you saved my life. That might help."

Jay smoothed Wilson's hair back off his face. "Why did you crawl in here? I've told you repeatedly to stay out of the mine."

"I was looking for gold for P. Guess that was kinda stupid, huh?"

"No one made you come in here? No one put the bear in here with you?"

Wilson shook his head. "He was already in here when I crawled through the hole. Pretty stupid, huh, Jay?"

"Not stupid, but what you did was dangerous. I don't want you in here alone."

"I won't do it again if you don't want me to." Wilson blinked back tears. "Hey, look. Your hand's bleeding!"

"It's okay. The bear just grazed me a little."

Wilson gazed up at him imploringly. "P needs the gold real bad. That's the only reason I was looking," he explained.

"Next time you want to look for gold, you come and get me and we'll look together."

"Okay."

"It's dangerous in here. You could get hurt."

"Okay. I'll come and get you."

"It's for your own good, you know."

"Yeah, I know. I'll come and get you next time. I don't mind."

Wilson's teeth chattered, and Jay took off his coat and wrapped it around the boy. "I wish P didn't have to know."

"Well, I grabbed that hot turkey off the table and ran out with it. How do you expect me to explain that if I don't tell the truth?"

Wilson giggled. "I'll bet she was surprised."

Jay grinned. "I think you could say that." He ruffled Wilson's hair. "If you're ready, I guess we'd better go face the music."

Wilson emerged from the chamber and paused to wait for Jay.

The sheriff crawled out behind him, keeping a close eye out for the bear. He got to his feet and winked at the boy. "Can you imagine what would have happened if one of the women had run into that bear?"

Wilson laughed. "They'd be upset, all right. Screaming and carrying on!"

"Well, everyone but Moses. If she'd run into that bear, we'd probably be having bear stew. That's one tough lady."

"I like her," Wilson said. "She talks to me."

"She does grow on you," Jay said. He knocked mud off his knees. "I'm hungry. How about you?"

"Yeah, starving!"

"Let's see if we can sweet-talk that pretty P out of some dumplings."

"Yeah, and turkey!"

Jay patted his head. "No, just dumplings."

Wilson grinned. "Oh yeah . . . I remember."

They walked in silence for a minute, and then Wilson said, "Jay?"

"Yes?"

"I know what I want to be when I grow up."

"What's that, Wilson?"

"I want to be a lawman, just like you."

Jay stopped in his tracks, staring down at the boy. "What did you say?"

"I want to be just like you when I grow up."

Jay swallowed. He wasn't any role model for a kid. "Wilson, I'm not all that good. You can do better than me."

Wilson's face turned solemn. "You are *too* good. And you're nice. Is it hard being a lawman?"

"It can be." He was at a loss to know what to say.

"You have to be brave?"

"The good ones are, but look at me. I'm scared of Patience."

Wilson squinted his eyes in thought, "Well, that's different. P can be very strong-willed."

Jay laughed. "I believe that's called stubborn."

Wilson slipped his hand into Jay's, and the two walked hand in hand away from the mine. "Say, Jay, I about forgot."

"What's that, Wilson?"

"P wants me to ask you something."

"Oh? What's that?"

"She wants to know if you'll marry her."

Chapter Eighteen

Marry me?" Patience flushed a deep scarlet. "Did he *say* that?"

Jay casually ladled beans into individual tin bowls. "I just wondered if you had a specific date in mind."

Patience might have been mortified at Wilson's audacity if she hadn't recognized the teasing note in the sheriff's voice. "I don't know what's gotten into that child!"

Carrying the bowls to the table, Jay smiled. "Naturally, I warned him I wasn't interested in matrimony." He looked up, his smile bordering on deviousness now. "Not until more gold was coming out of the mine."

Blushing to her roots now, Patience poured coffee, longing for a deep hole to crawl into. She couldn't believe Wilson had repeated their conversation when she had specifically warned him not to!

Taking their seats at the table, they bowed their heads, and Patience asked the blessing. "Dear Lord, thank you for this food, and especially for Jay's and Wilson's safety. Amen."

Reaching for the bowl of dumplings, Jay spooned a helping onto his plate. "Where was Wilson going in such a hurry?"

"When there wasn't any turkey, he ate three biscuits, gulped down a glass of milk, and ran out to assure Selmore his kinfolk did not die in vain. In fact, he told me he was going to tell Selmore that his kin was a hero."

Jay chuckled. "The boy earned my respect today. Most kids faced with that situation would have panicked."

Patience smiled. "He's a strong little boy. Look at all he's been through, losing his parents, losing the old prospector who befriended him. He was sick when I found him. After he recovered, he admitted he didn't know what would happen to him after the prospector died, but then I came along."

"I guess that was the best thing that could have happened to him."

She flushed with pleasure. "Oh, I expect someone in Fiddle Creek would have taken him in."

"I wouldn't bet on it. Folks out here are doing well to take care of their own without taking in every motherless child that comes along. I'm not saying someone wouldn't have fed him and given him a place to sleep, but he wouldn't have the love he has here."

She looked at him in surprise. Who would have thought he'd understand? "I do love him. He's rather special."

"He is that."

Leaning back in his chair, Jay watched Patience work. He had said she was the best thing to happen to Wilson. What he had no intention of saying was that she was the best thing to happen to him too. He'd miss her when he moved on. But he wasn't the man for a decent, God-fearing woman like Patience Smith.

He thought of what Wilson had said, about wanting to grow up to be just like him. Remembered the hero worship shining in his eyes. Sure, he had just saved the kid from a bear, but that didn't account for all of the boy's reaction. Jay knew love when he saw it. The kid loved him, a worn-out lawman with no dreams, no future, and a gambling debt hanging over his head. He needed to think about moving on. The thought depressed him.

He considered whether to tell Patience about the ghost—if there really was a ghost, which he didn't believe by a long shot. There was too much of the flesh and blood about this Gamey O'Keefe. He never got close enough to find out for sure, but for Jay's money, the man looked too sturdy to be a spirit. From all he'd heard, ghosts were supposed to be a mite frail, just a "ghost of themselves," so to speak.

He smiled at his own humor but sobered almost immediately. Was someone trying to run Patience away so they could claim the mine? Well, he was a sheriff, and investigating was part of the job. He'd do a little nosing around in Fiddle Creek. If there was something going on, he'd find out what, and he'd put a stop to it.

Resting her elbows on the table, Patience laced her fingers together and gazed at Jay. Each day brought a new awareness of him.

She knew the way he walked, the way the corners of his eyes crinkled when he laughed, the sound of his now-familiar voice. Just having him near, sitting across the table from her, seemed so right. She hadn't missed the way he looked at her either . . . and could it be possible that he liked what he saw? Shivers assailed her.

"Thank you."

"For distracting the bear?" He shrugged. "Anyone would have done the same."

"No, for being you."

Avoiding her gaze, he handed her the bowl of dumplings. "Can't say I've heard that recently."

Setting the bowl aside, she said, "Then I'll say it again. Thank you for being you, Jay. Why do you find it so hard to accept a compliment?" She could see he was uncomfortable with the subject.

He slathered butter on a steaming biscuit. "You have a lot to learn about men."

"Such as?"

"Such as, men don't want compliments."

Her brows lifted. "They don't?"

"This one doesn't."

"Nonsense. Everybody likes compliments." She didn't know one person who didn't.

"I don't." He took a bite of beans.

"Really down on yourself, huh?" Picking up the bowl of dumplings, she spooned a helping onto her plate.

"I'm not down on myself, and I wish you would quit implying that I am. From the moment we met, your eyes have accused me of being indifferent. What right do you have to accuse me of anything? I'm doing my job, minding my own business. That should be enough for anyone."

"You are indifferent to me."

"I am not."

"Yes, you are."

Lowering his spoon, he leveled his gaze at her.

Edging forward in her chair, she stared right back. "You *are*."

Jamming his spoon into the beans, he took another bite.

She wasn't going to let him avoid the subject this time. He was quite proficient at hiding his feelings. "Tell me why you don't like yourself."

"Eat your supper."

"I'm eating." She slid a spoonful of beans into her mouth, studying him. She was in a feisty mood tonight. "I know," she ventured. "You hate yourself because of your red hair."

Glancing up, he caught her grinning.

"That's it, isn't it? Rather be dead than red on the head."

Shaking his head, he reached for a second biscuit.

"Yes, you hate your red hair. That's clearly the reason you're so down on yourself." She picked up her cup and took a sip of coffee. "You're downright embarrassed because of it. No one in your family other than old, fat Aunt Fanny has red hair, and you had to take after her." She smothered a giggle, loving the way she could frustrate him so easily.

The man patiently spread butter on a biscuit, appearing not the least frustrated. "I don't have an old, fat Aunt Fanny. My mother had red hair. My sister Jenny has red hair. And the color of *my* hair has nothing to do with my character. It so happens that I like red hair."

"Mmmm, me too," she mused. She hadn't been all that fond of it before meeting Jay Longer, but now it was a favorite with her.

His features sobered. "Wilson told me about your mother and father."

Patience nodded. "I'm told they were killed by a band of renegade Indians. Someone found me and took me to the orphanage." She met his eyes across the table. "What about your parents?"

She knew so little about the man she loved. And she did love Jay Longer. Each day brought a clearer—if not understanding, then complete acceptance, of that love. He didn't love her. Goodness, he was terrified of her. But he would love her someday. He would someday.

"Mother's dead. Pop's alive."

"Any brothers and sisters other than Jenny with the red hair?"

"No, only Jenny. She's married, with children of her own."

"Living where?"

"Phoenix."

"Phoenix?" She racked her brain trying to recall American geography. "Where is Phoenix?"

"Arizona Territory."

"You lived in Arizona? Isn't that the place with all the cactus?"

He nodded. "I lived in Phoenix most of my life."

"Why did you leave?"

He shrugged. "I was young, wanted something different."

"So you came to Colorado? Then what?"

He stared at his plate, and she thought he wasn't going to answer. She waited, her eyes daring him to remain silent. Finally he spoke, slowly at first, then picking up speed.

"I got married. We had a boy, and then both Nelly and the child got sick. You wonder why I don't have any faith in God—I'll tell you why. Nelly had strong ideas because of her religion. Wouldn't have a doctor. She died. Brice too. I lost them both. God took them. He could have let them get well; Nelly believed he would. She prayed about it, but he let them die. I lost my faith in God the day I lost my wife and son. It changed me. After Nelly, I knew I'd never love another woman, and I knew I'd never trust God again."

He took a drink of coffee, lost in memory now. "After I lost Nelly and Brice, I wandered around for a while, settled in Denver City, and took the sheriff's job. Got involved in gambling. Right now, Mooney Backus is hunting me to collect a debt I can't pay. That's the only reason I've stayed to help run the mine. I need the money."

Patience felt like he'd thrown cold water in her face. She'd been feeling sorry, wanting to take him in her arms and comfort him for his loss, only to learn he hadn't stayed because of her. He didn't care a thing about her. Why keep hoping for romance when obviously the man didn't have a romantic bone in his body?

Once a personal note was injected, he changed the subject. "There's a square dance in Fiddle Creek tomorrow night."

"Really?" After what he'd told her she wasn't in the mood for a party. To him she was nothing more than a way to pay off a gambling debt. The thought hurt—not that he'd ever given her any indication he was romantically interested in her.

"You should go," he observed. "A young lady like you needs a social life."

Toying with her food, she wondered how he could tell her that he would never love another woman then callously ask her to attend a square dance with him. She shook her head, then casually observed, "It's too cold to make the long walk."

"Would you pass the salt?"

She absently handed him the shaker. "So the square dances are respectable?"

"Far as I know they are."

Patience wondered. She had seen men dancing with each other in Silver Plume. She had also heard stories about Fiddle Creek men and how they made such a spectacle dancing with one another, half drunk and shamelessly disorderly during their Saturday night forays. She didn't want to go to a square dance with anyone other than Jay.

Have you no pride? He just said he wasn't interested in other women. Still, if he asked, what would it hurt to go? Enjoy his company for the evening?

He handed the saltshaker back. "I'll watch Wilson if you like."

She glanced up. "What?"

"I'm not doing anything. I'll watch Wilson for you." When she glared at him, he clarified the offer. "While you go to the square dance."

Shoving back from the table, she stood up, her hackles rising. "You're not going?"

"Me?" He laughed. "I hate to square-dance."

"Then why did you ask me to go?"

"I didn't *ask* you to go; I merely said you should go."

"Oh, really?"

He looked back mulishly. "Really."

Picking up the bowl of dumplings, she heaved its contents at him. Dough and gravy hit him, sending him reeling backward on the stool. He wiped his eyes, nearly blinded, but he could see well enough to catch the gleam in her eyes. He cringed instinctively, halfway expecting to have the beans hurled at him too. She glared at him for a moment, then turned on her heel. Marching to the door, she jerked it open and slammed it shut on her way out.

A minute or two passed before the door opened again, and Patience stuck her head around the corner. "You're not coming after me?"

He brushed dumplings off the front of his shirt. "Not on your life." What kind of fool did she think he was?

She slammed the door again.

~

When a knock came at the door the following evening, Patience laid her sewing aside.

"Want me to let Jay in?" Wilson asked.

"Yes, and if he wants to talk to me, tell him I'm busy."

Wilson's eyes appraised the cramped quarters. "Won't he know I'm lying?"

Crawling into her cot, Patience jerked the blanket over her head.

Setting Jellybean aside, Wilson went to open the door. "Patience's busy," he relayed.

Looking inside the dugout, Jay's eyes traveled to the conspicuous hump in the middle of the cot. "I want to talk to her."

"She's busy," Wilson repeated.

"Doing what?"

His eyes gestured toward the cot. "She's real busy, Jay. She can't talk right now."

Stepping around the boy, Jay closed the door, holding his index finger to his lips. Tiptoeing to the cot, he lifted the corner of the blanket to reveal Patience's head.

She stared up at him.

"You look busy."

"I'm asleep," she murmured.

"I can see that, and I hate to bother you, but the square dance starts at eight. It's seven-thirty now, and it's a forty-five-minute walk to Fiddle Creek."

"So?" She jerked the cover back over her head.

He lifted the corner again, and his gaze ran lazily over her. Goose bumps raced down her spine. "I had that coming, but let's not argue. Let's go to the square dance."

"No."

"Are you going to wear what you have on, or would you like to change?"

"Please go, P." Wilson held Jellybean in his arms, his face a mask of concern. "It'd be fun."

Nodding, Jay dropped the cover back into place. "Wilson, tell P I'll wait outside."

"What about me?"

"Guess you'd better get your dancing shoes on. We're going dancing."

"Oh, boy!" Wilson dropped Jellybean and ran to grab his coat.

Jay and Patience lagged behind Wilson. The boy carried the lantern despite a full moon overhead lighting the trail.

"You look mighty fetching tonight," Jay admitted, helping Patience descend a slippery slope.

She knew he was only being nice. If only she had a pretty dress and

159

shoes to wear—anything other than the prospector's clothes. "I feel very foolish about throwing those dumplings at you."

"Why? I like dumplings."

Grinning shyly, she refused to look at him. "To eat—not to wear."

"Well, I was being insensitive. Forgive me?"

Her smile widened. "You're forgiven."

Without thinking, she slipped her hand into his. His warmth was reassuring. He might vow to never love another woman, but that didn't mean *she* couldn't love *him*. Secretly, down deep in her heart, where no one would ever know.

The square dance had already begun when they arrived. The chandeliers above the dance hall burned brightly.

Wilson spotted a few of his classmates sitting together on the sidelines and reluctantly went to join them.

Offering Patience his arm, Jay led her to the floor, where the musicians were just beginning a new set of square dancing.

The caller went to work.

"Allemande left with the old left hand
Honey by the right, then the right and left grand!"

Bowing to one another, Patience took Jay's hand, and he twirled her gracefully around. They moved across the room, passing each other twice before joining the other couples in a square.

"Side couple turn their ladies;
Ladies turn side couples.
Gentlemen turn side couples,
All hands round, back again.
Pass on through and a do-si-do
Like a chicken in the bread pan a-pickin' out dough!"

Laughing breathlessly, Patience collapsed into Jay's arms at the end of the third square.

Several men approached Patience, asking her if she would do them the honor of dancing the last dance with them. She refused graciously, waiting for Jay to ask her.

He gripped her hand. "Let's sit this one out. All right?"

She nodded, relieved.

He led her to a remote corner and then brought her a cup of punch.

"Hello, belle of the ball," he teased, fondly smiling down at her. The fabric of his shirt made his eyes look as blue as a field of cornflowers.

"Thank you for bringing me tonight." She gazed up at him, cheeks flushed, eyes sparkling. "I'm having a wonderful time."

"Wilson seems to be enjoying himself. He and his school friends have emptied the punch bowl twice."

She laughed, thinking about the expert way he had guided her through the complicated square-dance formations. "Sheriff Longer, you're good! Do you dance often?"

He smiled. "Only when I have to."

She feigned amazement. "Other women have thrown dumplings in your face?"

"I'm afraid they've thrown more than dumplings," he confessed, "but none have had your charming persuasion. Besides, you make very good dumplings."

Wrinkling her nose, she made a face.

The music slowed, the fiddle sang sweetly. She hummed along, re-membering the words. "I love this song," she confessed. "Do you know it?"

"I've heard it."

Softly, she began to sing, "I dream of Jeanie with the light brown hair," only she substituted *Jay* for *Jeanie,* and *red* for *light brown* hair. Her gaze locked with his, willing him not to look away.

In soft, whispery tones, she sang the words for his ears only, in a voice pure and sweet as a nightingale's. Others around them faded away, and they were in a world of their own.

That moment something changed between them. Patience could never be sure exactly what, but something changed. They both were aware of it.

After the dance, Jay walked Patience and Wilson home. Wilson, yawn-ing, promptly said good night and slipped inside. Jay said good night, then turned to walk back to his shack. Suddenly he spun around. "Patience?"

She looked up expectantly. "Yes?"

"I was wondering . . ." He hesitated.

"Yes?"

"If it wouldn't offend you, I'd like to kiss you good night."

"It wouldn't offend me," she returned softly. "Actually, I've been hoping you would."

"You were?"

She nodded, smiling.

They stood for a moment, neither one certain of what to do next.

"Should I come to you?" she asked hesitantly.

"Oh . . . no, of course not. I'll come to you." Approaching her, he tried to position himself properly.

With darting, chickenlike neck gestures, they hemmed and hawed around a few moments, struggling to come to a meeting of the lips.

When it finally happened, Patience felt a stab of disappointment. She'd not seen stars—or skyrockets. Nothing at all like that romantic novel she'd read.

"See you in the morning," Jay murmured.

"Yes." She smiled, trying to hide her frustration. Was it her? Surely he could do better than that. "See you in the morning."

Chapter Nineteen

Moderation now seemed to be a thing of the past. Jay drove the shady ladies with a passion, working them long after the sun went down over the mountaintop. He suddenly had a will to live—and if he was to survive the gambling debt, he had to make the mine pay off.

Only a minimal amount of gold was coming out, but Jay knew there was more, much more, buried deep within that black, abysmal creation called the Mule Head. Otherwise, whoever was trying to scare Patience away wouldn't be setting up residence in the mine.

Once or twice, he thought of telling her about his encounters with the "ghost," but he never did. She didn't need to know; the old man hadn't shown himself to anyone but Jay—and wasn't likely to. Jay figured the less Patience knew about the strange goings-on, the better.

Unexpected floods, unexplainable fires, collapsing timbers, strange noises, and obnoxious belching sounds occurred in the mine on a routine basis now, but the shady ladies didn't seem to mind.

Jay was determined to get to the bottom of this mystery without alarming Patience and Wilson. If the mother lode was in the Mule Head, he was going to unearth it. He had taken the job to save his own neck; now he'd made up his mind to save Patience's also.

Moses approached him as he worked outside the mine one afternoon. "Man at assay office say no weigh gold for two weeks."

"Tell him we have to have it sooner."

"Told him." She shook her head no.

Jay paused, resting on the handle of his shovel. There wasn't another assay office around for thirty miles. Consequently, the one in Fiddle Creek was running behind.

Lifting his hat, he wiped the sweat off his forehead. If he had a choice, he'd do business elsewhere. Sage Whitaker was an ill-tempered old coot. Area miners were having to wait weeks to get their ore assessed, but Jay couldn't wait weeks. Already the ladies were starting to complain about low wages.

Smiling, Jay winked at the sober-faced woman, knowing she could arm wrestle a man out of his hide if she was pushed. "Why don't you see if you can get Sage to cut us some slack?"

Moses returned his look stoically. "Diplomacy?"

He hadn't realized she knew the word. Her English was broken at best. "You know what *diplomacy* means?"

She nodded. "Boy teach me: Be nice until I find big rock."

He chuckled. Wilson. "Unless we can find another assayer, we're going to have to get along with Sage."

Moses trekked off, apparently to see what she could do about the situation.

Tossing a shovelful of dirt into the sluice box, Jay wondered what sort of man would take Moses on. Most miners were so hungry for female companionship they'd marry anything in a skirt. "That Moses would be a handful." He spoke the thought out loud.

"Not for me, buddy boy. I'd take her on in a minute."

Gamey reclined on a nearby rock, arms scissored behind his head, lazily soaking up the sunshine.

Jay hadn't heard him approach. "That might be a mistake," Jay pointed out. "She could whip you without breaking a sweat."

"You got your own problems, buddy boy. Especially in view of what you've been thinking about that Patience woman lately. Better leave now, afore you suddenly find yourself tied down to a woman and an eight-year-old boy."

Jay shot him a cross look. "How do you know what I'm thinking?"

"Been watching you. Ain't hard to tell when a man's got a woman on his mind."

Jay was getting used to the old man's observations and sudden visits. They were daily now—and annoying. He switched the topic back to Moses. "Thought you said Moses was ugly."

"Oh, she is. Ugleeeeee. But she's got possibilities," Gamey allowed.

"Winters get mighty nippy up here. That woman's bulk could provide some powerful warmth to a man."

"Winters shouldn't bother you," Jay goaded. "You're dead."

The old man sat up. "Don't believe that I'm dead?"

Jay threw another shovelful of ore into the sluice box. "You're about as dead as I am. What do you want? The mine? Or are you working for someone—someone who thinks I'm stupid enough to believe in ghosts?"

The intruder shifted positions. "You ever been in love, buddy boy?"

"Might have."

"Don't try to tell me you haven't, 'cause I know you have. Her name was Nelly, and she had your boy, Brice."

Jay froze, anger overflowing him. Whoever was trying to claim-jump the Mule Head had done his homework. Considering he and Nelly had lived in these parts while he was mining, it wouldn't be any trouble to learn about his past, but he didn't like anyone digging around in things he'd rather not have to talk about.

Guarding his tongue, Jay said quietly, "Well, guess that saves me the trouble of telling you." Taking his shovel, he moved on downstream. "Someone's coached you real well, haven't they? But everything you're saying could have been learned in Fiddle Creek. So who's paying you to go to all this trouble?"

Gamey tagged along behind him, ignoring the question. "Some other little gal got yore heart now, eh?"

"Not that I'm aware of."

"Liar."

"I said, *not that I'm aware of.*"

' And I said, *liar.*"

"Okay, so you tell me who has my heart now." Jay felt like a fool discussing the subject.

"Patience. You're sweet on her—but not sweet enough. If you was, you'd take her back to Denver City where she could be with them other orphans. I ain't ever gonna let her alone, ya know. She won't bring any gold outta this mine." Smiling, he winked. "You can bet on it." Trailing behind, Gamey aggravated Jay. "Cute little bugger. Shame she got mixed up in this mine."

"She deserves better," Jay agreed.

"Who?" Gamey baited. "Go ahead, say her name. You ain't got no secrets from me."

Jay refused to be drawn back into the conversation.

"Sweet on her, are ya?"

"No," Jay denied.

"Are too."

"I'm not."

"Big liar."

"I *admire* her," Jay conceded. "That doesn't make me sweet on her."
Patience wasn't like most women. She accepted people for what they
were, and with the exception of the time she flung a bowl of dumplings
in his face, she was usually even-tempered.

And if he felt different than he was saying, well, it was no one's business but his.

"Even had a good time at the square dance, huh, buddy boy?"

"Good enough to suit me."

"But?"

"The last thing Patience needs is a man like me in her life."

"Cain't agree. You ain't no blue-ribbon prize, I'll grant ya, but she
could do worse."

"Look, do you mind if we just drop the subject?"

The old man shrugged. "What else we got to do?"

"*I* have work to do."

But pretty soon Gamey was heckling again. "Like to hitch up with
her, wouldn't ya?"

Jay didn't bother to answer. He'd learned the less he said the quicker
Gamey would tire of badgering him and leave—go wherever he was
camped out for the charade.

"Oh, you'd like to all right, but you've got this idea yore not good
enough for her."

"You talk too much. Go away. You're wasting your time here. Go
tell whoever you're working for that it isn't going to work. This mine
belongs to Patience and the boy."

"You ain't so bad," Gamey said. "You ain't necessarily anyone I'd
choose for *my* daughter, if I had kids, but you've been behavin' yoreself
lately. Quit gambling, haven't ya?"

"You tell me."

"You have—mighty hard habit to shake, but you did it. Guess you
got real ashamed of yoreself and realized yore ma would be real disappointed to see how you'd turned out. It's hard for a man to get away
from the way he was raised. Now ya need to get Backus off yore back."

Jay whirled, temper flaring. "How do you know about Backus?"

"His thugs, Red and Luther, been lookin' everywhere for you—bound to find ya real soon, if I was to tell 'em what I know."

Plunging the shovel back into a cart, Jay wondered exactly how much the old coot did know about him. So Red and Luther were nosing around town. He hadn't seen them since he'd left the hotel and moved into the miner's shack. He'd hoped they had given up and gone back to Denver City, but no such luck.

"You don't like me knowing yore business, do ya? Ghosts can go anywhere they want to without being seen. I can find out anything I want."

"Way I heard it, you were supposed to be locked in the mine forever. Gamey O'Keefe couldn't go wandering around like you are now."

Gamey looked startled. "Eh! Where did ya hear that?"

"Around. If you know so much about me, then you should know that I don't like you or anyone else butting into my business."

"I know *that!* I'm jest tryin' to tell you, you ain't as hopeless as ya think."

Jay's laugh rang with irony. "I'm the epitome of success."

"Shoot, no, you ain't that neither, but you've had a run of bad luck. So what? You want to talk bad luck?"

The old miner raised his hat and scratched his head. "I was sixty-two years old when I blowed myself up. *Sixty-two,* and not a penny to my name, but I ain't never considered myself worthless. Why, I'd worked one hopeless claim after the other—seen the elephant a hundred times, but always had the gumption to keep going. Gamey O'Keefe give up? Not on yore life. Drank too much, yes; 'ssociated with women too much, yes; got discouraged, yes; complained a lot, yes. But give up? Never entered my mind. I've lived through winters so cold I've seen horses froze solid standin' up, and the horns on cattle freeze and burst off from the pith. I suffered through summers so hot you'd swear you was in hades. I've witnessed fires sweep entire towns and lay 'em out in ashes. I've seen grown men cry when everything they'd worked for went up in a sheet of flames or their claim didn't pan out.

"Shoot, buddy boy, gettin' what you want out of life takes a powerful lot of effort. Nothin' worth havin' ever comes easy. Jest 'cause you lost yore wife and boy, couldn't make a mine pay off—because you found out you couldn't work 'cause of that phobia thing—why, that's sissy stuff. Stop beatin' yoreself up. If that's all life's got to throw yore way, consider yoreself lucky."

At his age, probably most of what he'd said had a grain of truth, except for that part about blowing himself up, Jay figured. "For a man who claims to have blown himself to pieces, you seem to be well preserved. I'm guessing your job is to scare me off; if that's the case, you're doing the opposite. Why boost my morale?"

"I don't know." Gamey scratched his beard. "Shore as shootin' I don't know—maybe I'm startin' to like ya, buddy boy."

"Then why are you trying to scare me and Patience out of the Mule Head?"

The old man stiffened. "Didn't say that, did I?"

"You didn't have to. Now clear out of here and don't come back."

Gamey scoffed. "Too hard on yoreself. Ain't dead yet, are ya? Never met a man who didn't have somethin' to learn and wasn't the better for learnin' it."

Jay considered his prospects. Come spring, he would turn thirty. Thirty, flat broke, with the future of a salmon spawning upstream. He had nothing to offer a woman. Patience was intelligent and pretty. Though she didn't know it, she could have her pick of eligible suitors. What did she need with a broken-spirited man like him?

"Look at it this way: you were decent enough to help her," Gamey reminded him. "You cain't be all bad."

Jay laughed caustically. "She didn't have a whole lot of choices now, did she? There wasn't anywhere else for her to turn."

Gamey dipped his hands in the stream, letting water trickle through his fingers. "There ya go again, selling yourself short, buddy boy. Now take my gold—which you won't—but for right now, we'll pretend you will. You're convinced that with enough time you're going to find that gold, ain't ya?"

"I'll sure be doing my best."

"Won't find it."

"I'll keep looking."

"Ya lookin' for Patience's sake, or do ya want it to save yore hide from Mooney?"

"You tell me."

"Well, at first it was the latter, but now yore tiltin' more to the former."

"That just goes to prove you *don't* know everything."

Smiling, Gamey gradually began to fall behind. "Ya still got a powerful lot to learn about women, buddy boy."

"Yeah," Jay conceded. "But not from you." When he looked again, the miner was gone, disappeared over a ridge.

Jay leaned on his shovel, thinking about the little man who seemed to know so much about him. Someone had coached him well. Question was, who? He'd never talked much about Nelly and the boy. Some things lay too close to the bone for general conversation, but he guessed it was no secret. People in these mountains were interested in each other. With no newspapers and the hit-or-miss mail service, they didn't have anything else to do. So they talked. Not hard to find out anything about someone if you wanted to bad enough.

Mooney Backus, now, he'd probably been rampaging around, blowing off steam. Him or those goons he employed. Bragging about what they'd do to him. But this so-called ghost, he wasn't working for Mooney. Whoever had hired him to pull this scam had brains, something notably lacking in Backus.

Why didn't this Gamey, or whoever he was, show himself to anyone else? to Patience? Seems like a woman would be easy prey. He must have a reason to appear to Jay only when no one else was around. It didn't matter, except that it looked like whoever was behind this wanted to run him off more than he did Patience.

Jay paused in the act of lifting a shovelful of dirt. Maybe he was on to something. Whoever wanted the Mule Head knew Patience couldn't work the mine by herself. Get rid of Jay, and she would have to leave. The unknown claim jumper could move in and take over.

He whistled through his teeth. Shrewd. Except it wasn't going to work. What kind of no-account varmint would he be to walk out on Patience and Wilson?

Jay Longer didn't run.

Two nights later Jay knocked on Patience's door. She unhooked the latch and opened it, surprised to see him up so late. She supposed he'd been asleep for hours.

"Did I wake you?" he whispered.

"No, I can't sleep." Opening the door wider, she allowed him entrance.

"Is it too late?"

"No," she whispered. "I'm grateful for the company."

He stepped inside the dugout, closing the door quietly behind him. Wilson was asleep on his pallet before the fire, his arm gently curved around a kitten.

Moving to the fireplace, Patience slid the coffeepot over the flame.

Her hair was loose tonight, a dark auburn cloud swinging below her waist. "What are you doing up so late?" she whispered.

"Had something on my mind; I couldn't sleep either."

Seating herself at the table with Jay, she gazed at him. "Is something bothering you?"

"Patience, there's something you ought to know. At first I thought I'd keep it from you, but you should know. There's someone in the mine who's pretending to be Gamey O'Keefe."

He couldn't keep the information from her any longer. The old miner was getting reckless. Today he'd initiated two minor cave-ins, one trapping the shady ladies for over two hours before Jay could dig them out. Moses was furious. She and the other women were getting tired of the hassles.

Patience's jaw dropped. "You've seen the ghost?"

"There is no ghost," he confirmed. "My guess is that someone is trying to steal the mine, and they've hired an old miner to be the ghost of Gamey O'Keefe. In the process they've learned a lot about me." Jay gave her a level look. "The man is human flesh and blood. He roams wherever he wants and shows up unexpectedly to throw me off."

Patience stood up, returning to the fire. Pouring two cups of coffee, she inquired softly, "Someone is trying to steal the mine?"

"You shouldn't be surprised. Man is greedy, and the Mule Head is rumored to have the mother lode, whether it does or not."

Carrying the tin cups to the table, she set them down. Ladling two heaping teaspoons of sugar into hers, she cautiously reached out and laid her hand over his. "Jay, we've been working hard lately. Why don't we take the afternoon off tomorrow? I'll fix a picnic, and we'll find a nice place to eat in the sunshine." She smiled encouragingly. "Doesn't that sound nice? The shady ladies can surely do without us for one afternoon."

Shoving back from the table, he stood up. "Sorry I bothered you."

"Jay—" Springing up, she hurried around the table, realizing she had hurt his feelings. "I'm sorry. . . . It's just, well . . . an odd story. Moses hasn't said a word about seeing anyone. Are you sure it's a man?"

Jay's eyes turned grave. "I see him every day, Patience. I talk to him. He wants to scare you off."

Her features softened. "Jay . . . if you say you see him, then I believe you. It just seems strange . . ."

He'd been working too hard. His claustrophobia must be bothering him. Did the condition have side effects that might cause him to see things?

"You don't believe me, do you?" His expression was as blank as a tin-horn gambler's running a bluff.

No, she didn't believe him, but she couldn't let him see that. "I believe you think you see him—," she began.

He interrupted her, his eyes bright with anger. "Don't try to con me, Patience. I know what I saw."

"I'm not trying to con you," she stammered. "I didn't mean—"

He changed the subject. "I'm going into Fiddle Creek tomorrow morning."

She blinked. "Why? What about the women?"

"They won't work the mine tomorrow; we need fuses and a few other supplies."

"But Jay—"

Before she could answer, he left, slamming the door behind him.

She sank down in a chair, her thoughts troubled. She shouldn't have let him see that she doubted him, but what else could he expect? Her shoulders slumped in despair. She'd depended on Jay, and now he was seeing little men in the mine. . . . She had to help him.

But how? This was something she had no experience with. What if Jay turned violent? What would the shady ladies do? She visualized her crew. Well, led by Moses Malone, they'd probably beat him to a pulp. No man would be a match for that bunch.

She'd heard a sound in the mine today, but after thinking it over, she knew what it was. These mountain winds could blow fiercely sometimes. She'd heard it moaning through the trees. But hearing the wind was different from seeing and talking to someone who wasn't there.

Patience took a deep breath and straightened her shoulders. Tomorrow she would insist that Jay rest, and she'd cook him a good lunch. Suddenly the gold didn't seem so important compared to Jay.

He'd be all right. He had to be.

Chapter Twenty

The next afternoon Jay sent the shady ladies into the mine before taking a gold pan and wandering upstream. He needed some time alone. Might do a little panning for nuggets.

Patience had stood in the door of the dugout watching, but he ignored her. She didn't believe him. Well, that was fine with him.

Thought he was crazy, huh? He'd show her. He'd show them all. Mooney Backus and his thugs, that little runt who called himself a ghost, and Patience. Particularly Patience. Somehow, even though Jay admitted he wasn't good enough for her, he'd expected her to trust him.

He swirled the pan, letting loose gravel wash out while the heavier flakes of gold settled on the bottom. Picking out the scattering of flakes and a couple of nuggets, he dropped them into a drawstring tobacco pouch he'd gotten from an old-timer in Fiddle Creek.

He felt lower than a snake's belly today. For two cents, he'd pack up and leave. Or he would if it weren't for Mooney Backus. He sighed. He was honest enough to admit that Mooney wasn't the only reason he stayed. There were Patience and Wilson. He'd never intended to let it go this far. Although he wouldn't admit it to Gamey, the day seemed a little brighter when he could see Patience and hear her voice. But he'd never let her know how he felt. Couldn't. She was a fine woman, and she deserved better than he could give her.

And some low-down varmint was trying to steal her mine.

In a sudden burst of temper, he picked up a rock and slung it at a pine tree.

He heard snickering and glanced up to see Gamey perched on a limb of a neighboring cottonwood tree, watching him pan for gold.

"You don't seem to be in a good mood this afternoon. I'd guess you let it slip out, didn't ya? Jest couldn't stand it. Bet you had to tell her about me."

"You can relax; she didn't believe me."

"Well, now—" Gamey squinted and scratched his mangy beard— "that's a real shame. For you—not for me."

"Get out of here, Gamey."

"No, not until I help ya."

"You can't help me."

The little man eased carefully down from an overhead branch, dropping to his feet in front of Jay. "Yep, buddy boy, you've got me pegged dead center. I've done told you: no one but you is gonna see me, and no one—not even Moses, though goodness knows I've got an itchy feelin' for that woman—is gonna get their hands on my gold."

Slamming his gold pan to the ground, Jay lit on it with both feet. Trouncing on it, he jumped up and down, venting his pent-up frustrations. Up and down, up and down, he stomped the pan, mangling the tin and fouling the air with a string of epithets that made Butch Miller sound like a choirboy.

He'd had it! Cave-ins, floods, egotistical ghosts, Mooney Backus threatening to kill him, Patience thinking he was seeing things, Patience and the gold, Patience and the boy, Patience, Patience, Patience!

"Leave me alone! You hear me? I don't want to ever see your face around here again! Torment someone else! *You hear me? I've had it with you and your nutty ways!*"

Hammering the pan with the heel of his boot, Jay viciously ground it into the gravel bank. Rage burned out of control. He pounded the tin with the heel of his boot, cursing the day he was born.

When a shadow crossed the ground, he glanced up. Standing beside the stream, Patience had witnessed his fit of temper. Her baffled gaze shifted from his boots to the throbbing vein in his neck to his anger-splotched face.

Regaining his composure, he paused, his hiked foot in midair. "Yes?"

She murmured, "Supper's ready."

Giving the tin one last brutal stomp, he refused to look at her. "Okay."

She continued to stare at him as if there were something more that needed to be said. But he wouldn't meet her stupefied gaze.

"I'll be along in a minute."

"Are you all right?"

"Fine. Never better. First-rate."

She walked away, turning back to look over her shoulder, frowning.

Muttering under his breath, Jay gave the mangled gold pan a swift kick, sending it skittering into the stream, and followed her up the hill.

Supper was a tense affair with Jay eating in silence. He still looked angry, but there was something about him that broke her heart. He seemed shamefaced, as if her seeing him pitch that violent tantrum bothered him. Well, it bothered her too.

What had come over him? Jumping up and down and cursing that way. If Wilson had been anywhere within hearing distance—and he probably was—he'd no doubt learned several new words. She'd have to stock up on soap.

What really bothered her was the way Jay had been shouting at someone but there was no one there.

She cut a wedge of dried-apple pie and set it in front of him. "More coffee?"

"Yes, thanks."

She sat down across from him, watching him eat. "Is there anything you want to talk about?"

He raised his eyes and looked at her briefly before shifting his attention back to his pie. "We already talked."

"I see. Anything you want to add?"

"Nope. Subject closed."

He finished his pie and left, and she conquered the desire to throw his plate at the door he had slammed behind him. A reluctant smile curved her lips. Well, she knew what it was to be provoked. Hadn't she flung a pot of dumplings at his head just a few nights ago? So something had provoked Jay. Who and what? She'd made a mistake last night when he'd confided in her about Gamey. Now she had to regain his confidence.

Patience left Wilson trying to braid the cat's tail while she stole a few minutes alone with Jay the following night.

The scene yesterday at the stream still bothered her. Jay was behaving so strangely lately. Even so, he continued to stand by her when it seemed they were fighting a losing battle. Any day now, she expected Moses and the shady ladies to walk out. There was barely enough gold coming out of the mine to pay them a paltry sum at the end of a long week. And the constant interruptions were more than annoying—they were dangerous. Patience was beginning to think they were an indication of something more sinister than just plain bad luck. And now Jay thought he was seeing the ghost.

She made her way across the mountain, shivering in the night wind. If she went to him, he couldn't walk away; he had no place to go. She should never have let him see she didn't believe him. Tonight she would try to regain lost ground. If he didn't trust her, she couldn't help him. Jay needed her, and she had to be there for him.

Pausing in front of Jay's shack, she called softly, "Are you awake?"

A moment later the door opened and he appeared in the doorway. In the background she saw a rosy fire in the fireplace. He frowned when he saw her huddled against the biting wind. "Something wrong?"

"Can I come in?"

Standing aside, he allowed her to enter.

Hurrying to the fire, she undid her scarf, permitting her hair to fall unrestricted around her shoulders.

She'd seen the way he had looked at her the other night when her hair was down. The decision to wear it loose tonight had seemed good at the time, but now she had her doubts, considering the way he stared at her, like a thirsty man seeing a stream of fresh water.

Something inside her stirred, responding to the look in his eyes. He was older than she was, and she had an idea what he was thinking: that he was too old for her with nothing to offer a woman. Somehow, she had to change his mind.

Jay broke the silence. "Where's Wilson?"

"Braiding Jellybean's tail."

"How can he do that?"

She shrugged. "Not easily, but it keeps him occupied. How was your trip to Fiddle Creek?"

He busied himself stacking dishes. "Routine."

She wondered what the unexpected trip was really about; she found a box of fuses in the cellar when she'd gone for another jar of pickles, so obviously he hadn't been completely honest about his reason for going.

Had he been in Fiddle Creek asking questions? trying to gain solid evidence that someone was trying to jump her claim?

Lifting her hands to the fire, she warmed her fingers. "It's so cold. Jay, I worry about you here, alone in this drafty shack."

He stooped and put another stick of wood on the fire. "I'm thinking it's time I went back to Denver City."

"Why? We need you here."

He shrugged. "I should have left sooner, but I thought you'd give up and see reason. I don't know, P; seems like I have to get away, regain my perspective."

"Are you leaving because of me?" She almost whispered the words.

"That's part of it. Seems like everything I do these days is because of you."

Patience caught her breath. She'd never been alone with a man like this. What would Lily and Mary and Harper and Ruth say? She could just imagine. He stepped closer to the fire, and she turned to face him, aware of the isolation of the cabin. She shouldn't have come. What had she been thinking?

Suddenly—she didn't know how—she was in his arms and he was holding her close. She knew she should pull away, but somehow she couldn't make the effort to move.

"This is crazy," he murmured, but he didn't try to break the embrace. Stroking her hair gently, he said softly, "I was thinking about the look on your face today when you found me at the stream."

She held him tightly, feeling a spurt of alarm. "Jay, what was that all about? Everyone loses their temper at times, but the incident today was more than a simple fit of anger."

"Gamey O'Keefe."

"Jay," she complained, "we're not going to start that again!"

"All right, don't believe me," he said, apparently willing to let it go for now. "What brings you out this time of night?"

Sighing, she rested her head on his shoulder, absently fingering the woolen fabric of his shirt. She felt surreal, as if being in his arms was a dream—one she didn't want to awaken from. "If it's true, why can't I see him? After all, I own the mine. If he wants to frighten someone, why not frighten me?"

She didn't want to talk about the ghost, but Jay seemed determined to have his say. He lowered his face in her hair, whispering, "Maybe he doesn't like to provoke beautiful women."

Her eyes drifted closed, relishing his nearness. It felt so right to be in his arms—*he* was so right for her. Why couldn't he see that? "Does he say why he appears only to you?"

"Of course not; he wants me to believe that he's a ghost, but I don't. What I believe is that he's been sent here to convince me that someone will never let us work the mine. Once you leave, they'll move in and stake a claim."

She held him tightly, wanting desperately to believe him, even though the thought of someone trying to trick her out of the mine was distressing. If this . . . *man* truly did exist, her future looked dim indeed.

She'd had enough talk of the mine and ghosts for tonight. The gold was important, but she had something else on her mind. Tilting her head back, she looked deeply into his eyes. "Do you ever think of me?"

He shifted. "What kind of question is that? We were talking about ghosts."

"But we're not now. We're talking about you . . . and me. . . ." She smiled up at him. "Do you ever think of me?" Some days she thought of nothing but him.

"I'm thinking of you right now."

"Then you feel the attraction too?" She was both relieved and frightened by the revelation. If he felt the same magnetic pull that continually drew her, there might be hope. . . .

"Yes, I feel it," he admitted. His voice dropped to a low, husky timbre. "I don't want this to happen, Patience. I'm wrong for you."

"Why are you so afraid of your feelings?" she asked. She wasn't afraid of hers. She raced to embrace them.

"I don't want to fall in love again, Patience. I have nothing to offer a woman."

She gazed up at him, aware of how hard he was fighting the way he felt. "Don't you think that's for the woman to decide?"

"No, it's what I've decided, and I don't want to complicate matters between me and you. You're young, beautiful, alive. You need a man who will match your spirit, not an ex-gambler who can't pay off his debt."

"I've found that man."

"You're young and impressionable, Patience. You know nothing about me."

"Then tell me about you, Jay Longer. What are these thoughts you find so frightening?"

"They're foolish thoughts, and I'm a fool for thinking them."

"There's nothing foolish about you," she assured him.

He hesitated, and then said softly, "At night, before I drift off, I find myself wondering why you like sweet potatoes so much—or questioning your love affair with pickle sandwiches."

Laughing, she contentedly nestled deeper against the solid wall of his chest. He smelled of woodsmoke and mountain air. "I was expecting to hear something a little more romantic."

"That wasn't romantic enough?"

"No. Try again."

"I'm not very good with romance." He held her closer. "What do you want me to say?"

"Tell me what's in your heart."

"I can't . . . not now, Patience. Maybe never—"

She laid her finger across his lips. "Then tell me the sort of things a man might say to a woman when he loves her so much he can think of nothing else."

His mouth moved to the nape of her neck, lingering hesitantly. "If I were to say such things, let alone think them, I would be twice a fool," he confessed.

Eyes drifting shut, Patience held him close. The fire crackled, swathing them in a warm cocoon. "Then tell me what is in your heart."

"I wonder how you make your hair smell so good, or why your eyes turn the color of warm honey when you smile," he whispered. His breath fell softly upon her ear.

"Hey! There you are!"

Wilson's voice jerked them back to sanity. Patience had not heard the door open.

The boy stood in the doorway, holding his cat. "What're you doing?"

Springing apart, Patience tidied her hair, disappointed, but knowing the interruption was for the best. What must Jay Longer think of her, throwing herself at him like this? Her cheeks flamed. "It's late." She hurriedly tied the scarf around her hair. "I have to go."

Brushing past Jay, Patience pointed Wilson back out the doorway. "What are you doing out at this hour of the night?"

On the way back to the dugout Patience walked so fast Wilson struggled to keep up.

"P?"

"What?"

"Are you mad at me?"

"No, of course not. What makes you think so?"

"The way you're walking, like Moses when she's working on a temper fit."

Patience stopped so abruptly, Wilson bumped into her. "I do not walk like Moses."

"Well, when she's upset about something, she steps out fast, like that. You upset about something, P?"

"No, Wilson. I am not upset about anything."

She had behaved in a way she would have trouble explaining to her friends back in Denver City. Going to a man's cabin this time of night with her hair down and throwing herself at him like a common hussy. She could only pray the others would never learn of her bold behavior. And then to have Wilson walk in on them . . .

She walked slower now, letting Wilson keep up with her.

"P?"

"Yes?"

"Did Jay decide to marry us?"

"He didn't say anything about it."

Wilson sighed. "Well, I wish he'd hurry up. Then he could move in with us instead of staying in that cabin."

Patience's face burned. "I'm not sure he wants us."

Wilson stopped dead still. "Not want us? Of course he does. I'll talk to him."

Patience stopped, goaded beyond endurance. "You listen to me, Wilson. If you ever talk to Jay Longer again about marrying me, I'll . . . I'll . . ."

"You'll what?" he asked, interested.

"I don't know, but I'll think of something."

They walked on in silence, with Patience remembering the natural feel of Jay's arms around her. Whether he admitted it or not, they belonged together. Somehow *she* had to convince him of that. Not Wilson.

Chapter Twenty-One

Early the next morning, on his way to fetch Moses and the shady ladies, Jay decided to drop by Fiddle Creek and see if the old whittler Chappy was around.

The air was fragrant with the scent of pines, the sky a pearl gray, the scattering of fluffy clouds touched with peach glow from the searching rays of the as-yet-unseen sun. Jay paused to enjoy the scene. Seemed like he had learned to appreciate the mountains. The cold didn't bother him the way it used to.

He thought of Patience, the way she had felt in his arms last night, the scent of her hair. The man who won her would be lucky. He turned his face resolutely toward Fiddle Creek. He'd give all he owned if he could be the one. Realizing the turn of his thoughts, he laughed bitterly.

All he owned? A horse and saddle? Not much to offer a woman. A rich man he wasn't, and unlikely to become one. One thing he could do for her: find out who was behind the problems at the mine.

He rounded a stand of scrub pine and jerked to a halt. Down the trail a ways stood the "ghost" of the Mule Head in earnest conversation with a tall, burly man with a bushy black beard and clothes as disreputable as Jay's had been when he was in disguise.

Jay was too far away to hear what they were saying, but the big man was doing most of the talking. Gamey's ghost didn't seem all that happy, and Jay got the impression they might be disagreeing about something.

The two men separated and Jay felt torn, but he decided to follow the bigger man. The old miner was probably going back to the mine, using a different entrance than the main one by the dugout. But Jay lost the man he was following because he didn't want to get close enough to be seen.

In Fiddle Creek he bought two cups of coffee and carried them outside to where Chappy had already taken his post outside the mercantile.

"Thankee." Chappy took the hot coffee. "What brings you to town so early?"

"Wanted to talk to you."

Chappy's expression didn't change. "About what?"

"About a man—tall, broad shoulders, black beard, wears an old battered hat and a shirt that used to be blue and gray, far as I can tell."

Chappy took a drink of coffee. "Silas Tucker."

"What do you know about him?"

"Worst claim jumper in these parts. Supposed to have a nose for gold. Thinks there's a mother lode in the Mule Head."

"Mother lode?"

"Yep. Don't know if it's so or not, but Tucker thinks it is."

Jay nodded. "Tell me about a little old miner who is pretending to be the ghost of Gamey O'Keefe."

Chappy grinned reluctantly. "Frank Innis. Tucker's paying him to be the ghost. Promised him a cut of the gold if he can run the woman off. Frank ain't up to working much anymore. Was a good one in his day, but got stove-up in a cave-in a few years back. You've seen him?"

"Yeah, but no one else has."

Chappy turned serious. "Frank's all right. He may work for Tucker, but he's solid."

"Trying to take a mine away from a woman doesn't seem too solid to me."

Chappy shook his head. "A man will do funny things when he's hungry enough, but give Frank a chance. He'll do what he thinks is right."

Jay didn't argue, but he had his doubts. At least he'd gotten what he came for. "Thanks, Chappy." He held out his hand. "Appreciate it." He took a couple of steps away and turned back. "How come you didn't tell me all this before?"

Chappy smiled. "You never asked."

On his way out of town Jay saw Silas Tucker talking to a bunch of men. Working his way around behind the livery stable so he could get closer, he listened in growing anger as Tucker outlined the plan to scare Patience into leaving.

He looked up at the sun. Getting late. He still had to collect Moses and her crew, but now he knew what he was up against. He'd put a spoke in their plans if it was possible. Silas Tucker and Frank Innis weren't going to cheat Patience. He wouldn't let them.

He knew the truth now. This so-called ghost was Frank Innis. Just like he suspected, Gamey O'Keefe was dead and gone or never even existed. The problems with the mine were human problems.

But the man pretending to be Gamey's ghost hadn't caught on yet. He showed up the next day right on schedule, as if he had been waiting for Jay to come. "I know where that gold is. Know exactly—could take ya there in a minute, but I won't."

Jay grunted, ignoring the man as he set a charge.

"Has anyone ever told you that you're bullheaded?"

Jay shot him a penetrating glance. "Give it up."

"Never." He rolled his eyes and studied the roof of the shaft. "It's my mine, ya know."

"I believe you've mentioned that, Frank."

Disbelief crossed the man's face. He sat up halfway, eyeing Jay. "Frank?"

Turning, Jay smiled. "Frank Innis, isn't it?"

The miner's eyes narrowed. "Don't know what yore talkin' about. Name's Gamey O'Keefe."

Leaning on the shovel handle, Jay surveyed the imposter coldly. "That's not what some say. Some say you and Silas Tucker are in cahoots. You're working for Silas to scare Patience—and me—out of this mine. Rumor is, Tucker's promised you a hefty cut if you stick around long enough to get the job done."

The old man paled. "You're talkin' crazy. I never heard of Tucker—I've been dead over thirty years."

"You're about as dead as I am." Jay picked up a pick and rammed it into the shale wall. "How much gold do you suppose is in the Mule Head?"

"In the Mule Head?"

"How much gold is in here?"

The miner squinted up at him. "Is this here a trick question?"

"Just curious. How much gold is actually in the mine?"

"A lot. The mother lode. Pay dirt. Tons."

"And you know where it is."

"Exactly."

"How would you know that, Frank?"

"I've always known where the gold is—know just where to find it, but someone else always owned the claim. You know any reason why I should tell someone else how to find my gold?"

Jay eyed him in speculation. At least he had stopped claiming to be a ghost for the present. Probably because finding out that Jay knew his real name had shocked him into admitting the truth.

"I'm betting you and Tucker would own the claim right now if you'd known the old prospector had died."

"She got a bill of sale? Ya know if it's held under purchase it has to be under a bill of sale and 'certified by two distinguished persons, honorable folks, as to the genuineness of the signature and the consideration given.'"

"She's got all she needs. Are you saying you and Tucker could find 'two honorable folks' to sign anything for you? Doesn't seem likely to me."

Frank looked offended. "This mine can't be more'n a hunnert square feet, and a 'jury of five persons shall decide any question arisin' under the previous article.'"

"You memorized it all, didn't you? Why—since you don't have a mine? Or did you think the information might come in handy in claim jumping?"

"And last but not least, 'soon as there is enough water for workin' a claim, *five days' absence* from said claim, except in case of sickness, accident, or reasonable excuse shall forfeit the property.'"

"So if you can scare Patience into leaving for more than five days, you and Tucker are home free. That your game? What if Patience offered to cut you in on the profits? Give you more than Tucker ever dreamed of giving you?"

The old man didn't flinch. "Cain't negotiate if I don't know who or what yore talkin' about."

Jay shook his head. The old coot was loyal—he'd give him that. "What good is the gold if nobody can have it?"

"Ain't worth a ball of spit," Frank conceded.

"It could make some people's lives a lot easier," Jay said, thinking of Patience, Wilson, and the girls in Denver City. They desperately needed the money. Patience couldn't last much more than a week at the rate they were going—Moses and the women were getting antsy about missed pay.

"Nobody ever made my life easy." The little man started backing up, stepping deeper into the shaft.

"Give it some thought," Jay called. "Do something nice for once—*Frank.*"

"Honest, Patience! I *heard* him! He was talking to somebody, but when I asked him who he was talking to, he said, 'Nobody, and stop asking so many questions, Wilson!' Then he walked off real mad-like."

Patience ladled stew onto Wilson's plate, finding it increasingly difficult to defend Jay's odd behavior. She had caught him on several occasions mumbling, talking out loud, arguing with thin air. And his ongoing obsession about Gamey O'Keefe was getting serious. Perhaps she should insist he see a doctor next time one passed through Fiddle Creek.

"Maybe he was talking to himself—people do sometimes," she offered.

"They talk *bad* to themselves?"

"Sometimes," she acknowledged. "Has Jay been talking bad in front of you?"

Wilson nodded. "Real bad—but he didn't know I heard him."

Patience frowned. "Where were you?"

"I wasn't hiding or anything," Wilson upheld. "I was just sitting on a ledge eating a biscuit when I heard him start yelling and cussing, waving his shovel in the air and saying, 'Get away, you—' "

Patience whirled on him sternly.

"I didn't say it!"

"You'd better not!"

"Well, *he* said it, anyway." Wilson halfheartedly drew a trail through his stew. "He couldn't have meant for *me* to get away because he didn't know I was even there, and he's never called me that, no matter how mad he gets."

"Where were you when you heard this?"

"Sitting on a ledge—" Wilson stopped.

Patience's hand shot to her hip. "In the *mine?*"

Developing an unusual preoccupation with his meal, Wilson started spooning stew, cramming his mouth so full an answer would be rude.

"Wilson, you are to stay *out* of the mine."

He stared back at her, cheeks round as a chipmunk's.

"The women are blasting in there now, and it's extremely dangerous!"

Nodding, he chewed emphatically.

Unfolding her napkin, she sighed. "In regard to Jay's odd behavior, I wouldn't worry. He has a lot on his mind lately—and we have not said grace yet. Will you bless the food, please?"

Swallowing, Wilson bowed his head and scrunched his eyes tightly shut. "Please help us, God. We're in big trouble."

Patience slid him a sideways glance.

"And thank you for this good, nutritious stew. Even though we don't have any meat, carrots and onions are better than beans any day. Amen."

"Amen," Patience echoed.

Wilson reached for his spoon. "We're not doing so well, huh, Patience? Moses is shouting a lot lately because of all the accidents."

The third cave-in in a week happened early this morning, and the women had lost another day's work clearing the shaft. Patience thought she must have the worst luck in the world. Unless . . .

She shook Jay's strange wanderings away. "No, I'm afraid we're not, Wilson."

The boy's features turned solemn. "Do we have to go to Denver City?"

"It's possible. We have no money, and we're not mining enough gold to pay wages. I'm going to be honest; we're down to needing a miracle, Wilson."

"But I don't want to go to Denver City. I like it here."

"I know. I don't want to go either, but we have to do what's best for your welfare." She leaned closer. "I can't take care of you here, Wilson. Not unless the mine starts producing."

"If we go to Denver City, can I take my animals?"

She shook her head, swallowing around the knot suddenly forming at the back of her throat. "I'm sorry—your animals wouldn't be happy there, Wilson. This is their home."

Tears formed in the young boy's eyes. "What'll happen to Jay? He's ours now. He doesn't have anybody, and we love him."

Sighing, Patience pushed her plate aside. "I don't know about Jay." She wished she did. Oh, he'd go back to Denver City—that's where his job was—but she wasn't sure she'd see much of him after that. He'd retreat into an impenetrable shell and—

"Why is he acting so *nutty?*"

"Wilson, can I tell you something?" He suddenly seemed like the old, wise-beyond-his-years Wilson in whom she'd always been able to confide, and right now she badly needed a confidant.

"Certainly. May I have more stew, please?"

The ghost isn't a ghost at all, just like we've always known. His name is Frank Innis, and he works for a man by the name of Silas Tucker."

"Frank Innis, Silas Tucker," she murmured, trying to speak calmly. "That's interesting. . . ."

"Chappy says they're trying to convince you and everyone else the mine is haunted so you'll give it up."

"But, Jay, everyone in Fiddle Creek *already* thinks the mine is haunted. That's why they won't work here. If they know it's a scam, then they'll change their minds and come work for us after all."

"No. No, they won't, Patience. That's the problem. I'm the only one who has seen the ghost of Gamey O'Keefe. He doesn't show up in town. I just happened to see 'Gamey' and Tucker meeting down the mountain a ways, and since I'd seen Frank pretending to be Gamey, I went on into town and dug into Tucker's background."

"And what did you find out?" Humor him. That's all she could do.

"I learned he has a sidekick named Frank Innis, who fits the description of the man I'd seen in the mine, and the sidekick hasn't been around for a while. I overheard Tucker bragging that after you give up, he knows how to rid the mine of the ghost. That's what he's planning. Something to fool people into believing he's gotten rid of Gamey O'Keefe. It will work too. Can't you see that?"

Patience watched him, sure he believed what he was saying but unable to accept the strange tale herself. "Why does he just appear to you, Jay? I'm the one he's trying to scare off. Why doesn't he show himself to me?"

"They've got that all figured out. Get rid of me, and you won't have a crew. Without a crew, you'll have to give up. And if no one else sees him, then, when I try to tell the truth, I won't be able to get anyone to believe me. They'll think I'm seeing things; Gamey's ghost has got to me."

That was so close to what she was thinking, it startled her into letting him see her doubt. She tried to recover, but he'd caught her expression.

He drew back, the excitement dying from his eyes. "See? Even you don't believe me. You think I'm losing my mind."

"I didn't say that."

"You didn't have to. It's there in your face for me to see. You don't believe I've seen him, do you?"

"Of course, if you say so." She knew he wouldn't be convinced by the weakness of her response and tried desperately to think of something to restore his pride, but he moved away from her.

"All right, that does it. I want you to go back to Denver City until I can get the mine producing. Take the boy with you. I'll expose those two thieves and hire a crew, but I want you out of the way in case things get rough."

She shook her head. "I'll not leave you alone. If you're right on this, why would you expect me to run? It's my mine too, and my future that's at stake. I'm not leaving."

"Patience—"

"I'm *not leaving.*"

He sprang to his feet. "Of all the stubborn, hardheaded women . . ."

She stood up also, facing him. "Calling me names won't help. Are you going to *make* me go back?"

He stared at her, his expression frustrated. "I can't *make* you do anything you don't want to do, but you owe it to the boy to put his welfare first."

"I *am* putting his welfare first. That's exactly what I'm doing, and you know it. How dare you talk to me like that!"

That was why she clung to the mine in the first place—for Wilson and the others. She hadn't been this stubborn and endured so much for self-interest. The Mule Head was their only hope for a bright future—for all of them.

"I know that look on your face," Jay fumed. "You're digging your heels in, as stubborn as a mule. Too contrary to admit you're wrong."

"I'm not wrong." Patience's temper flared, hotter than a pine-knot torch. "The gold is there. I can't just walk away from it."

"Maybe you can't, but I can." Jay's face flushed with sudden rage. "I've had enough. Why should I stay here, working my fingers to the bone, when you have the faith of . . . of . . ."

"I'm *trying* to believe you," Patience said, making an effort to curb her temper. "But be fair. No one but you has seen that man."

He threw up his hands. "Have it your way. There is no Frank Innis or Silas Tucker. I'm a raving lunatic, and you can run the mine by yourself. Well, be my guest, honey. I've had enough."

He stalked off, leaving her to stare after him. She should have hung on to her temper. Should never have crossed him. What if he had been telling the truth, and she had refused to believe him? What would she do if he didn't come back?

Patience opened the dugout door and looked out. Jay hadn't come to supper tonight, although she had cooked his favorite: panfried catfish that Wilson had caught in the cool sparkling waters of the little creek.

Closing the door, she cleared away the remains of the meal and washed the dishes. After Wilson lay sleeping in front of the fire, she sat in the old rocking chair, staring into the flames, reliving their argument. What would she do for a crew? If Jay wasn't here to guard the women, they wouldn't be allowed to work.

Why had she let him walk away? It felt like he had ripped her heart out and taken it with him. What would she do if he never came back? She had grown so used to having him around, had looked forward to seeing him every day.

She sat before the fire until the flames burned low and the creeping cold drove her to her bed. Wrapped in a blanket, she lay staring into the smoldering coals, seeing Jay Longer in the flickering shadows, until she cried herself to sleep.

Chapter Twenty-Two

Patience waited at the mine entrance before sunup with a lump of lead for a heart. Would he come? Wilson was outside, feeding his animals, completely oblivious to the storm raging inside her.

She watched the trail, ears straining to hear the approach of the shady ladies. When she first heard them coming, she couldn't believe her ears. They plodded up the trail, Moses in the lead, Jay trailing along behind. Patience sank down on a nearby boulder, her knees too weak to support her.

He glanced at her and then looked away. Moses and the other women walked past her into the mine.

Patience waited until Jay stopped in front of her, not smiling. She wet her lips. "You came back."

"Yeah."

"I was afraid you wouldn't."

"If I had any sense, I'd be halfway to Denver City by now."

"I'm glad you stayed. I'm sorry. I shouldn't have doubted you."

He looked away. "I have to get to work."

She watched him walk away, but the sun shone in her world again. She'd fix him a good dinner. If the way to a man's heart was through his stomach, Jay Longer wouldn't know what hit him.

"Please, God," she breathed, "don't let anything else go wrong."

Later that morning, a fracas broke out in front of the mine, bringing Patience running. Wilson left his beloved animals to join the uproar. The shady ladies milled around, making more noise than a flock of hens. One convict, looking more groggy than usual, staggered around in circles, muttering something about wanting to take a pickax handle to that ghost.

Moses stood, arms akimbo, dark brows drawn together, lips set in a bitter line. As Patience joined them, she glared in her direction. "We quit!"

"Quit? You can't quit, Moses!"

"*Quit.*" Moses sported an angry bruise between her eyes.

This morning's incident was the last straw. Someone had rigged the women's picks so that when they swung them the heads flew off and hit them squarely between the eyes. One of the ladies had been knocked cold and hadn't come around for a full ten minutes.

"I know it's hard to work with all these accidents, but if you'll be patient just a little longer—" Patience looked to Jay for support.

He looked the other way, stubbornness etched on his stoic features.

The shady ladies picked up their shovels and walked off with Moses, mumbling something about there not being enough gold in Colorado to put up with this.

Patience watched them leave, realizing what it meant. There wasn't a man, woman, or child left willing to work the Mule Head.

Trying not to cry, she turned to Jay. "Shouldn't you walk them to the prison camp?"

"I'll follow them back. Are you all right?"

Dropping her face to her hands, Patience whirled and ran to the dugout. She sank down at the kitchen table, letting the tears flow. How could he ask her if she was all right? He had stood there and said nothing as the women walked away. Didn't he *care* they had no other help to work the mine?

Where are you, God? He'd promised to be there in time of need. Why didn't he do something about all of these accidents? She raised her head, wiping away tears. They couldn't all be accidents. Not *all* of the pick heads coming loose at once. One, maybe, but not all of them at the same time. Jay was so sure someone was trying to drive them away. Had he been right all along?

Her heart hardened with resolve. No one was going to drive her away from what was rightfully hers. She would fight as long as she had breath.

Forgetting the convicts, Jay pitched the shovel aside and angrily strode toward the mine, with no thought of his phobia. For the first time in a long time, rage blinded him. He didn't care about the gold. Mooney Backus could do whatever he wanted to him, but without the gold Patience was sunk. She wasn't chasing luxury; she was fighting for survival. And he was going to fight Frank Innis to the death, if that's what it took.

Snatching up the lantern, he entered the mine, shouting, "Frank! Show yourself!"

A bat darted up and away, vanishing into the darkness.

"Frank!"

Frank . . . Frank . . . Frank echoed back.

Moving deeper into the shaft, Jay's eyes searched the darkness. "Enough's enough!"

Overhead, timbers snapped and splintered down. Jumping aside, Jay avoided the flying debris.

"Cut it out, Frank! For once in your life fight like a man!"

Water rushed through the mine. Grasping the wall, Jay struggled to keep his balance. A whirlpool swirled around his thighs. The shaft plunged into darkness as the lantern fell from his hand and the current swiftly carried it away.

He could feel his lungs closing. Struggling for breath, he held tight to the sides of the ledge. "If you want to fight someone, fight me. Let Patience have the gold. You've lived your life—she's young, got most of her life ahead of her. She needs the means to take care of the boy and three other women who don't have a chance in this world without that gold. This plan of yours and Tucker's won't work. I'll personally dog you for the rest of my life, Frank. That's a promise!"

An explosion rocked the mine, splintering rock and pitching timbers through the air.

The thought hit him: He was going to die. This was how his life would end, alone in a black hole. He should have enough sense to be afraid, but he wasn't. Blackness closed around him, filling his senses, squeezing the life from his lungs.

Walls collapsed and buckled.

Racked by coughing spasms, Jay clung to the wall. Dust fouled the air, and a thick grit filled his mouth and stung his eyes. The air supply in the narrow chamber dwindled. "You're evil, Frank," he choked out. "You can kill me, but you won't kill her spirit. She'll stay and fight . . ."

A sheet of fire burst overhead. Angry flames licked across the ceiling, searing the timbers.

Strangling, Jay struggled for breath. And for life. Plowing through the rising water, he blindly felt his way back through the shaft. He didn't want to die. The realization hit him hard. If he died, Patience would have no one.

She needed him.

And he needed her.

He didn't want to die. The revelation was exhilarating and sobering. The meaning of life, which he had forgotten, suddenly came back. Wallowing in self-pity was for cowards. It took guts to stand up and fight back.

The ground vibrated beneath his feet. He inched along the shaft wall and edged toward the entrance.

Timbers shattered; dirt and shale hurled through the air. The tunnel became a living, roaring nightmare.

Stumbling out of the shaft, he fell to the ground, gasping for breath, only seconds before the mine entrance violently collapsed shut.

Patience raced for the mine, heart in her throat, when she heard the roar of an explosion. A big explosion. Much bigger than Jay or the shady ladies ever set off. Dust and rocks blasted through the mouth of the mine. The crash of falling debris boomed like cannon fire.

Wilson, white-faced, came running. "Jay! Where's Jay?"

Patience saw him lying facedown a few feet from the shaft. She and Wilson caught him by the arms, pulling him away from the mine as another explosion rocked the earth.

"Wilson, bring water. Hurry."

She knelt beside Jay, her fingers groping for a pulse. *Dear God, let him be all right.*

Jay felt a cool cloth on his face. P was softly calling his name. She tenderly dabbed the wet cloth back and forth over his battered face.

"Jay . . . please . . . wake up. Please . . . Jay."

Cracking one eye open, he scowled. "What for?"

With a sob of relief, Patience dropped her head to his chest, hugging him tightly around the waist. "I thought you were dead."

He struggled to sit up, massaging the knot on the back of his head. "I thought I was too."

She lifted the hem of her apron and wiped fresh tears, then glared at him. "You scared the life out of me!"

Getting to his feet slowly, he knocked the dust off his denims, grimly surveying the blocked entrance to the mine. "I can assure you, this wasn't my idea."

"Oh, Jay!" She turned to survey the damage. "Not *again!*"

Reaching for his hat, he dusted it off before settling it back on his head. "Are you convinced now that we're fighting a losing battle?"

Whirling, she grasped the front of his shirt, catching him off balance. "We *can't* let those evil, claim-jumping thugs beat us!"

Gently loosening her hands, he said quietly, "They already have, Patience. Face it."

Her face crumbled. "But what will I do? I have no money—nothing for Wilson . . ."

His eyes softened. "Patience, it's over. Moses just quit and took her crew with her. We've dug that shaft out too many times to do it again. We don't have enough funds to buy fuses and dynamite, and we couldn't hire another crew if our lives depended on it."

She gazed back at him, defeat shadowing her eyes. "Wilson's and my life do depend on it."

"No, they don't." Taking her by the shoulders, he made her look at him. "I'm not a quitter, but I know when I'm beat. You and I sure can't dig that shaft out again. We're beat. Men like Frank Innis and Silas Tucker are never going to let anyone get that gold."

"But—"

"No *buts*. You're not going to talk me out of this. I'm taking you back to Denver City. You don't belong here. You deserve to sleep in a warm bed, take decent baths, and go to sleep with a full belly every night. You need pretty clothes and proper suitors." His eyes gentled. "You need a husband, Patience—one who can give you all you deserve."

"But the gold would pay off your gambling debts."

A muscle flexed in his shadowed jaw. "We don't have the gold; we never will."

Meeting his eyes, she bit back tears. "What about us?" He tried to look away but she wouldn't let him. "What about *us?* You can't deny there's something between us—something incredibly special, Jay. You can't just walk away from me and Wilson—"

Pain shot through him. Five years dropped away, and he was losing the one he loved again. "There is no *us,* Patience. I thought you understood that."

"No," she whispered. "I didn't understand that."

He gently broke the embrace. "I worked your mine. That's all I promised."

"Yes," she said brokenly, "that is all you promised."

The hurt he saw in her eyes cut him deeper than any knife could, but he wasn't the man for her. She deserved more than a loser unable to pay his gambling debts, a man who would be hounded or shot, depending on how much he could come up with.

Tears rolled down her cheeks.

"Don't start that," he warned. "We gave it our best shot, and we lost. I have to see if Moses and the other women made it back to the prison. It's my obligation. If they decided to run, that's also my obligation."

"And I'm *not* your obligation." Before he could answer she whirled and walked off.

He watched her climb the hill to the dugout, her small frame buffeted by the cold wind, and he wanted to stop her, hold her, kiss her until the hurt left her. But he knew he couldn't. Right now she felt wounded and betrayed, but someday she would understand what he'd just done. She would realize that he loved her enough to set her free.

Hot tears formed in his eyes, and he self-consciously wiped at the moisture, mentally castigating his weakness.

Someday, she'd thank him.

The thought didn't cheer him the way it should. He didn't want her thanks. He wanted her beside him, in his arms. He could close his eyes and smell the sweet wildflower fragrance of her hair, see the way her eyes sparked with laughter.

He stumbled over a loose rock, almost falling. She only thought she loved him. Sheltered by life in the orphanage, she had no experience with the relationship between a man and a woman. She'd find someone her own age. Someone who could give her the kind of life she deserved.

The thought almost choked him. He couldn't bear thinking about

Patience in another man's arms. How could he walk away? But for her sake, he had no choice.

She would go back to Denver City and make a life. He'd see her from a distance—but he'd keep that distance. That was the problem now; he'd let down his guard.

But never again. *Never* again.

Chapter Twenty-Three

What time is it?"

"Ten minutes later than the last time you asked." Chappy held the miniature hummingbird he was carving up to the light. Thick clouds formed a low-hanging, pewter-colored ridge in the west. "You got it bad, haven't you, son?"

Perched on the hitching rail, Jay watched loaded wagons moving up and down the street. Oh, he had it bad, all right. Once his anger cooled, he realized that he couldn't walk away; Patience and Wilson were his life now. He'd given himself quite a talking-to back at the mine, but the walk down the mountain had done a lot to clear his thinking.

Yes, he was too old for her, and no, he wasn't good enough—probably never would be—but he loved her, and he wasn't going to let any other man have her. He'd let down his guard, but God had turned that into a blessing. All his doubts and insecurities had hardened into resolve. Patience belonged to him, and he wasn't planning to give her up.

Trouble was, he didn't know how to tell her. *How do you tell a woman that you've fallen in love with her against every determination not to, and that you're not a prize catch for any woman, but that you'll gladly spend the rest of your life taking care of her and the boy—if she'll have you?*

He'd work night and day to pay off his gambling debt and get his life back in order—if she would forgive him for the way he had acted. And if God would forgive him for the last five years of bitterness and blaming his ills on everybody but the man responsible for his misery: Jay Longer. All he had to do was ask.

His blood raced with expectancy when he thought of Patience. He missed her: the touch of her hand, her smile, the sound of her voice. A foreign feeling, to be sure, but one he couldn't deny.

"Gonna marry her?"

"If she'll have me."

"Unless I miss my bet, she will." Wood chips from Chappy's knife flew to a scattered pile at his feet. "You never talked much about yourself. Where'd you say you come from?"

"Phoenix."

"Phoenix, huh?" Chappy paused, brushing the shavings off his lap. "Suppose you got family there?"

"Some. Sister, father."

"Mother?"

"She died in '59."

"Sorry to hear it. Your pa in good health?"

"I haven't seen my father in a while, but I suspect that he's in good health for a man his age."

Jay thought about the long hours Gordon Longer worked, delivering babies, treating dyspepsia with doses of bismuth, rheumatism with bicarbonate of soda laced with lemon juice. He had apprenticed four years by his father's side before marrying Nelly. His life had turned out different from what anyone expected.

"Suppose you'll be going back someday?"

"No—don't ever plan to." Jay's eyes skimmed the ragged, snow-covered Rockies, and he knew he would never go back. He loved this land; loved the way the sun kissed the mountain slopes, the wildflowers that bloomed in the high meadows, the clear streams, and the abundant wildlife. The rugged pioneers who had settled here were good people for the most part. He was proud to be one of them. Together, he and P could make a good life for Wilson. He wasn't sure about kids of his own—the thought of Brice still hurt—but Wilson needed a father. "Colorado is home now."

Smiling, Chappy turned the carving over in his hands, critically examining his work. "What d'you think the woman will do now? Heard the Mule Head sealed tighter than a tick this morning. Crew walked off—left the woman empty-handed."

"I'll open it again." Jay had been doing a lot of thinking the past few hours. Odds were against them, but if Patience wanted to reopen the mine, he was going to hire another crew, even if he had to go to Denver City to do it. Right now, he had to work up the nerve to face her. She couldn't be too happy with him at the moment.

Chappy's voice broke into his thoughts. "You talked to Frank yet?"

"Yeah. I've talked to Frank, but I've got a few more things to say to him. He almost killed me."

Chappy glanced up. "Doubt if he knew you were in the mine. He'd have thought you were taking the women home."

"Patience or the boy could have been inside. He should have thought of that. Don't try to make me change my mind about Frank Innis. If it weren't for Innis and Tucker, Patience would own the mother lode right now. You know that—don't you?"

"You hear all kinds of rumors about mother lodes in these parts. Ninety percent of the time it's just speculation."

"Frank admitted it's there. He and Tucker wouldn't be trying to steal the Mule Head if it was a dry hole."

Chappy glanced up a second time. "You gonna let them get away with it?"

Jay eyed him. "What do you think?"

The old miner laughed, flashing a gold tooth in the cold air. "Didn't think you would be a man to set by and watch a woman being swindled."

The two men sat in comfortable silence.

"It's close to three, isn't it?"

Chappy consulted his watch. "Yep, a few minutes afore three."

Eventually, Jay got up, pulled his collar closer in the rising wind, and ambled off.

Rubbing the carving between his hands, Chappy watched him go.

Jay set out for the Mule Head an hour before dark. He'd concocted a speech—not necessarily a persuasive one, but one he hoped Patience would accept:

"Patience, I'm sorry. We'll reopen the shaft. I'll go as far as I need to go to hire a new crew. I'll throw Innis out of the mine—and oh, by the way, I love you, and I want to marry you if you'll have me. We can raise Wilson together, here in the foothills. . . ."

The discourse ran over and over in his mind. What if she refused him? What if she insisted on going back to Denver City and marrying the likes of Conner Justice? The man was town mayor, well established, and well thought of in the community. Lost his wife and child a few years back. P deserved a man like Justice. But Jay wasn't in a giving mood. He would work hard to be a husband she deserved; he would make her proud. And he would take care of Mary and Lily and Harper—he'd never let them be in want of anything, if only Patience would have him.

The brief afternoon's separation had been a revelation for him. For someone who thought he didn't need anyone, he'd discovered he needed her.

Content for the first time in a long while, he whistled. Brisk, pine-scented air filled his nostrils. The sky, overcast and dreary, failed to make a dent in his mood. Pewter-colored clouds promised snow by nightfall, but he knew by that time he'd be with Patience and Wilson, hopefully sitting before the fire, eating popcorn, being a family.

Family.

That sounded so good. He closed his eyes, walking on. *Forgive me, God. I've put you out of my life the last five years, and I'm asking for forgiveness. I've been blind to how good you've been to me. For a long time I couldn't think about anything but Nelly and Brice. I couldn't get past that black hole that kept me imprisoned, but today you've given me back a reason to live.*

Near the mining camp's outskirts, the sun momentarily streaked through the clouds, touching the frozen earth with pale, icy fingers. Savoring the knowledge that Patience and Wilson waited a mile or so up the mountain, he trekked on.

Up ahead, he spotted Edgar Miller's outhouse. The small building with a half-moon notched in the door was active this afternoon. Edgar himself emerged, fastening his suspenders on his way back to his shack.

Jay drew closer and frowned, spotting one of Mooney Backus's thugs walking up ahead. The ruffian had caught up with him again.

Slackening his pace, Jay let the man get well ahead, figuring he'd just as soon not inflame an already volatile situation.

Suddenly veering off the road, the thug made a beeline for the outhouse, loosening his suspenders on the run. He wouldn't miss three hundred pounds by much, so he'd be a tight fit for the small quarters, but when nature called, she sometimes shouted.

The door swung shut behind him with a slam.

Ordinarily, Jay would have left well enough alone. But this wasn't an ordinary day or an ordinary opportunity. This particular thug—along with another—had beaten him to a bloody pulp, and Jay wanted retribution.

Glancing around the deserted area, he noted he was the only one on the road. Pausing in front of the door, Jay grinned. Revenge was sweet. Bracing his shoulder against the door, he mustered all his strength and shoved. The outhouse toppled backward amid a flurry of the man's startled oaths.

Whirling, Jay broke into a sprint. Jay didn't plan to be within a country mile when the thug crawled out.

He'd covered half of that country mile before his pace started to moderate. Trotting along, he threw his head back, laughing out loud. He imagined the look on Red's face when the structure went down. Confident the man would never know who or what hit him, Jay relished the brief victory.

All at once three hundred pounds—give or take a few ounces—slammed into him from the back, felling him like gunshot. Jay's eyes stung from the putrid smell. The thug's clothes reeked.

Anger flushed the man's fleshy cheeks. His nostrils engaged, retracted, fury boiling over in his eyes. He pinned the sheriff to the ground. "I'm gonna break your neck, Longer!"

Jay struggled to break the headlock, but wasn't having much luck. The guy had one hundred pounds on him.

Then he saw it coming. Planting his knee in the middle of Jay's chest, the thug drew back, murder in his eyes. A belated thought crossed Jay's mind: *You should have toppled the outhouse on its* door, *lunatic!* It was his last coherent thought before Red knocked him cold.

Snow began falling shortly before dusk. Pacing the banks of the stream, Patience tried to blow feeling back into her hands. Her eyes anxiously searched the trail. Where was Jay? He'd been gone for hours now. Was he not coming back? The thought both frightened and angered her. How could he just walk off and leave her and Wilson to fight for the mine alone? Was he completely heartless?

Her mind sought to justify his absence: Maybe Moses and the other women had run off—failed to return to the prison. Of course they would run if they smelled freedom. Jay had to go after them—the women were his responsibility.

While she assumed he was still in the vicinity of Fiddle Creek, that didn't necessarily mean that he was.

Wilson, huddled on a fallen log, was losing heart. They had been waiting since early afternoon. Now his hands and feet were trembling with cold. Teeth chattering, he voiced Patience's worse misgiving. "Maybe he isn't coming."

Her tone was more caustic than she intended. "Don't say that. He's coming." She'd thought he wasn't coming this morning, but he had showed up. He'd come tonight.

Her eyes stubbornly returned to the trail. He wouldn't walk away and never come back. He might have shortcomings, but he wasn't cruel. Nothing would convince her of that. There was a reason he hadn't come back—she had to believe that. If only she waited long enough, he would come.

Another hour passed. Snow blanketed bare tree branches. Wind whistled through pines that were taking on spring finery.

Periodically, Patience's gaze returned to the trail. Wilson's followed. Yet no matter how long and hard they looked, Jay's comfortable, familiar figure failed to appear.

"Are we gonna stay here forever?" Wilson finally asked.

Patience continued to pace. Her feet had lost feeling fifteen minutes ago. Where could he be? In her heart she believed he would never betray her welfare, yet what could possibly delay him this long?

A new thought hit her. Had he fallen off the mountainside—broken a leg or hip?

Another hour passed, then another. Wilson's lips were starting to turn blue. Sinking down beside him, Patience stared blindly at the falling snow. It was so late. They couldn't wait much longer.

"We better go now, huh, P? It's dark, and we still have to walk back to the dugout."

Patience's eyes yielded to the trail, as she desperately prayed that Jay would appear, but she had to conclude he wasn't coming. Getting up from the log, she ignored the pain in her icy limbs.

"Are we going now?"

She stared at the trail. Empty. "We can go now."

Wilson's eyes darted to the deserted road, his voice strained with emotion. "He really isn't coming, is he?"

"No." Patience stiffened her resolve. She needed to be strong for Wilson, but she was crying inconsolably on the inside. "He isn't coming."

"Well, maybe a bear got him or something. There're a lot of them around, you know."

They started walking.

"Maybe he's at the dugout instead. That's it, P! I bet he's at the dugout right now, waiting for us! I bet he's waited all afternoon, wondering where we are."

When Patience looked at him she saw that the child's glasses were frosted over.

He peered back at her. "Don't you think?"

"Perhaps, Wilson . . . perhaps."

Their footsteps left deep tracks in the snow. They labored to walk. Bitterly cold wind howled about, snow blinding them now.

Wilson suddenly started crying. Softly at first, then deep sobs. Patience knew he'd tried to be brave for her sake, but his love for Jay overwhelmed him.

But Jay didn't love them. He didn't care that they had sat in the cold, waiting all afternoon for him.

"Shush," Patience said quietly, blinded by her own tears. She was suddenly tired, so awfully tired.

Jay slowly came around, aware of sounds. Logs whispering and popping in the fireplace, a ticking clock, the metallic chink of a spoon scraping across the bottom of a kettle, a cat lapping cream from a saucer, the faint brush of slippered feet against a wooden floor.

Smells permeated his thick fog: woodsmoke, a subtle detection of lye soap coming from the woolen blanket, meat sizzling in a skillet.

Ensnared in a murky haze, he struggled to orient his thoughts, but his mind refused to serve him. A fire raged in his gut. The smallest motion caused excruciating pain.

Breaking into a cold sweat, he started shaking, his feverish body burning up beneath the heavy blanket. He threw the cover aside and struggled to sit up. His head swam, and blackness momentarily encased him.

Hands penetrated the darkness, bearing a cool cloth. He moaned and allowed himself to be lowered back to bed. Even the small act of kindness brought a cry of anguish from his swollen lips.

He stilled the faceless hands, trying to speak. "Patience . . . ," he murmured.

A dipper of water touched his parched lips and he drank thirstily. Water spilled over, splashing onto his bare chest. Each point the droplets touched brought more torment.

"Patience," he whispered hoarsely. "Patience . . . need to get to the Mule Head."

When he'd drunk his fill, his head was gently lowered back to the pillow. A pungent smell filled his nostrils, and he cried out again. Hands that had once been benevolent became instruments of anguish.

Jay prayed for death, but the pain continued.

"Patience . . . Patience . . ." Hands restrained him; he struggled to sit up. He had to get to her; she would be waiting for him. "Have to go . . . Patience . . ."

He fought consciousness; the hands ministered to his body. The pain was unspeakable.

When the ordeal finally ended, he was lying in a pool of sweat. Once again he was gently turned, the damp cloth cooling his heated body. The sheet beneath him was whisked away and replaced with a soft, dry one.

"Have to get word to Patience," he mumbled, praying that the angel of mercy would understand. Patience was waiting for him; if he didn't come, would she leave?

The angel didn't understand. A woman's voice penetrated his fog. "You have been severely injured. Don't move." Unrelenting hands pressed him back into the mattress.

Groaning, he lapsed back into unconsciousness.

Chapter Twenty-Four

The covered wagon pulled into Denver City and stopped in front of the parsonage. The hefty driver jumped down and hurried to help Patience down. Wilson tumbled from his perch on the back of the wagon and stood beside her, staring at the hustle and bustle of town.

He reached out to take her hand. "I don't like it here, P."

"You will, Wilson. Give it a chance." She took the satchel the driver lifted down and handed the second one to Wilson. "How much do I owe you?"

"Nothing at all, ma'am. It was a pleasure to have you along. You take care now, hear?"

He climbed back into the wagon seat and slapped reins on the horses' rumps, driving away.

Patience sighed. Well, here she was, but it wasn't the homecoming she had dreamed about. She looked down at the old prospector's trousers, wondering what the others would think of the way she was dressed.

The front door opened and Mary ran down the walk, followed by Lily and Harper.

"Patience! Oh, Patience!"

She was hugged, laughed and cried over, and pushed and pulled up the walk. At the porch steps she remembered Wilson and turned back to find him standing at the gate, looking lost.

Patience hurried back to take his hand. "Come, Wilson. We're home."

"Home?" He peered up at her through his bottle-thick glasses. "It doesn't feel like home, P."

"It will." She tugged at his hand. "Come on. Trust me; it will get better."

He followed, pulling back slightly.

Mary stooped down to his level. "I'm Mary. Who are you?"

"Wilson."

"Well, Wilson, this is Lily and Harper. We're glad to meet you."

Harper reached for the satchel he carried. "I made sugar cookies today. Got a batch cooling. You like cookies, Wilson?"

Wilson nodded. "I suppose . . . if I have to."

Patience followed the women into the parsonage, gazing around at her old home, which looked familiar but strange in some way, as if she didn't belong here anymore. She felt hemmed in, missing the space and majesty of the mountains. Even the air smelled different.

Pastor Siddons and his wife welcomed her back and gladly accepted Wilson. She had never doubted their generosity, but just the same, she didn't want to be here.

That night she lay awake in the room she shared with Mary, staring at the wall as her tears soaked the pillow. Where was Jay? He hadn't come back to Denver City. That was the first thing she'd asked. Was he all right? How could he just walk away and leave her and Wilson?

God? Are you there? Be with him, and, O God, help me. How can I give him up? Let me see him one more time.

A week later Patience pulled an apple pie out of the oven and placed it on the table to cool. The Siddonses were so good, but she and Wilson were an added burden. She knew the good pastor and his wife would never complain about two more mouths to feed, any more than feeding Mary, Harper, and Lily, but there had to be a limit to the number of people who could live in this small house.

Patience turned away to look out the kitchen window. She'd had such dreams, planning to bring them bags of gold, showing them how she could take care of them. Maybe that had been her problem. She had been so wrapped up in *her* plans, *her* wants—*her*—so sure that was where God was leading her, but had she ever bothered to ask *him* to show her what *he* wanted? Maybe the problems at the mine were a judgment on her.

If she had left with Jay when he had wanted her to, they would both be back in Denver City. Now she was here alone with no idea where he was or how to find him. Instead of being rich and successful the way she had planned, she was a failure.

A failure at money, and a worse failure at love.

Lenore Hawthorn's wedding had taken place on the thirty-first of December as planned. She'd worn a simple gown instead of the lovely creation Patience was wearing when she had been kidnapped. The bride's and groom's families were still feuding.

Patience sighed. She missed Jay. Last night Mary had heard her crying and slipped over into her bed to comfort her. The two had held each other; Mary had cried too, confiding that she was so sickly and her asthma was such a burden she was sure no man would want to marry her, which made Patience feel even worse that the mine hadn't worked out. She'd had such plans.

Wilson entered the kitchen, interrupting her thoughts. "I'm worried about my animals. Are you sure they're all right?"

"Chappy promised to take care of them until we come back."

"Are we ever going back?"

"Maybe someday." Probably not, but she couldn't tell Wilson that. Without Jay she couldn't fight Silas Tucker and Frank Innis. She couldn't hire a crew. With Jay's help she might have been able to hang on, but alone she didn't have a chance. And by now someone else had probably jumped the claim. They had no place to go back to.

"P?"

"Yes, Wilson?"

"I miss Jay."

"So do I."

"I thought he'd come after us. Doesn't he love us anymore?"

The boy was getting upset. Since they'd left the mine he'd been confused and unhappy.

Patience untied her apron. "Tell you what. How would you like to visit Jay's office? He won't be there, but you might like to see it anyway."

"I'd like it better if he was there."

"Oh, Wilson. He'll come back someday. We just have to wait." She took his hand. "Come on; let's go see that office."

The trip to the office was a partial success. Wilson had liked seeing where a real sheriff worked, and she could see him imagining Jay sitting behind the desk, but walking back to the parsonage, he seemed downcast.

When they entered the kitchen, he noticed the empty pie dish before she did.

"Somebody ate all the apple pie!" he exclaimed. "Every last crumb!"

"I'll make another one, Wilson."

"When? You're busy all the time. Since we've come back you're always busy cooking and cleaning." Patience could see that he was getting worked up again. "I *hate* it here! I hate not having Jellybean and Selmore. I hate Jay. I hate Denver City. I want to go back to the Mule Head."

"I'll make another pie shortly," Patience said calmly, aware that Wilson's outbursts were due to grief. He missed Jay. He was not adjusting well to his new surroundings.

Nor was she. Tossing for hours at night, she found sleep impossible. She yearned for Jay. Mornings she was drained of emotion.

Harper called her a thousand fools for falling in love with a lawman, but deep down she didn't regret one moment. Her biggest concern was for Jay. Was he ill? Did he need her? Were his nights as unbearable as hers?

Picking up a handful of dirty dishes, Patience pushed through the swinging door, Wilson's voice following her.

"I hate school! I hate towns! I hate my teacher! I hate this kitchen, I hate this house, I hate this table, I hate these dishes, I hate this butter dish, I hate . . ."

Mary wasn't feeling well, so she changed rooms with Lily for the night. Patience helped her get settled into the small room at the rear of the house, while Lily moved her things into the room Mary had shared with Patience.

The household quieted down for the night. Wilson had been upset, angry, wanting to go back to the Mule Head and his animals. She couldn't blame him because she felt the same way.

Now, with Lily sleeping, Patience sat on the side of her bed, holding Jay's shirt. She had laundered it for him, but he never returned and she couldn't bear to leave it behind. Her fingers caressed the worn material, remembering his face, the way he smiled, the light in his eyes when he looked at her.

"Yes, you may, and I'm very proud of you. Your language has improved considerably."

"I'm working on my behavior," he divulged. "And I'm trying to teach Butch the proper way to express himself without making Teacher blush." He took a swallow of milk. "I'm embarrassed for him sometimes, but he just won't learn."

"Where are that boy's parents?" Patience mused, more rhetorically than not.

"Miss Perkins says she thinks he's being raised by wolves." He looked up from his plate. "Could that happen?"

"No. Miss Perkins was only teasing."

"Oh." He took another sip of milk, carefully wiping the white mustache rimming his upper lip. "What did you want to tell me?"

"You have to promise not to say anything to anyone about this."

"Who would I tell? Hardly anybody ever tells me anything."

"I sure don't want you telling Jay."

Wilson quickly took another drink of milk.

"Jay says he's seen Gamey O'Keefe." She absently ladled carrots and onions onto Wilson's plate, watching his reaction.

He peered back at her questioningly.

"The ghost—Jay says he's seen the ghost," Patience repeated, hoping he would think the notion ridiculous.

"Did he like him?"

"Wilson! That's insane. There's no such thing as a ghost!"

"Who said?"

"Everybody *says.*"

"Not everyone. I heard Moses and the other women talking, and they believe there's a ghost—though they've never seen him. But Moses said they're getting tired of him causing all these cave-ins and stuff."

"When did they say that?"

"Today." His eyes lowered back to his plate. "When I . . . *wasn't* in the mine."

Her heart sank. If Moses walked out, she was doomed. She'd have no other choice but to return empty-handed to Denver City. Then what? She couldn't impose on Pastor Siddons and his wife much longer, and neither could the other single women.

"I'm so confused. I don't know what to believe. The number of accidents and cave-ins is unusual. How much bad luck can one person have?"

"Jay said he saw the ghost, didn't he?" Wilson spoke as though the matter were settled.

"He says he has, and on more than one occasion."

Wilson nodded gravely. "Maybe Jay just needs someone to love him, huh, P? Then he won't be seeing ghosts."

She smiled. "Maybe so." She could love him. Very easily, if he would permit it. She had walked away from him that night in his cabin, but she couldn't stop thinking about him.

"We love him, don't we?"

Patience looked away. "Your stew's getting cold."

"But we do love him, huh? I won't tell him if you don't want me to. Honest."

"Yes, we love him," she conceded.

"A lot."

She nodded, fighting back tears, and started to clear the table. "A whole lot."

"Wilson and I are worried about you."

Jay glanced up when Patience kneeled beside him the next morning. Icy water bubbled in the stream.

"He overheard you yesterday—you have to be more careful. Granted, everyone talks to themselves on occasion but—"

"He overheard me what?"

"Talking to yourself."

He turned to face her, carefully placing the gold pan on the bank. "I wasn't talking to myself."

"He heard you."

"He heard me talking to Frank Innis, the so-called ghost of the gold mine." He got to his feet, pulling her up off the cold ground.

She shivered. Seemed like it was colder here close to the creek.

He motioned toward a ledge of rock, waiting to speak until she was seated. "Listen, Patience. I went into town yesterday and asked some questions. What I found out was more or less what I had expected."

She watched him, wanting to believe. He seemed so earnest. . . . He sat down beside her, and she fought an urge to reach out and smooth back his hair, the way she did Wilson's sometimes. Her heart ached for him. He'd worked so hard. Too hard. Maybe there *was* a curse on the mine and it was making Jay sick.

"Hear me out—I'm not losing my mind. I know what's going on.

Chapter Twenty-Five

Late one afternoon Jay found himself walking up to the mine shaft. The gray, overcast day with miniature flakes of blowing snow peppering the air only deepened the growing ache in his heart.

He walked slowly, not completely recovered from his injuries. After being beaten half to death by Mooney's goon, someone had found him and delivered him to the town midwife and self-styled nurse. She'd taken care of him, bringing him back to life by her sheer bullheaded refusal to give up. He owed her a lot.

But sometimes he wished she hadn't bothered. Patience was gone, believing he had abandoned her. How could he go back to Denver City and face her, broke and with a tale of not being able to come to her because of his injuries? Why would she believe him?

He walked the familiar path, fighting memories at every turn. Pausing at the top of the hill, he stared down on the mine. Snow drifted deep around the dugout, obstructing the doorway. The irrational thought that he should clear it away crossed his mind.

He squinted, trying to remember, and the scene began to take shape in his mind: Smoke curled from the dugout's old smokestack; Selmore was staked outside the door, and Jellybean pawed the air at a passing bug.

He watched, transfixed, when Patience stepped out the door, her laughter carrying on the icy air. Pausing at the clothesline, she waved up at him, her eyes bright with mischief. The gentle breeze caught her hair and tossed it like a kite on a windy day.

She waved again, calling his name.

Hesitantly lifting his hand, he smiled, waving back.

Blowing him a kiss, she started to hang wash. The musical strains of "Jeanie with the Light Brown Hair" floated across the barren countryside. He could hear the soft refrain she had half sung, half whispered to him at the square dance . . . how long ago was it? It could have been a million years. Or maybe it all had been a dream.

He stood on the hilltop for over an hour, oblivious to the wind and the cold.

On his third outing, he took along a shovel. This time, when he reached the top of the hill, he continued down the steep incline.

It was over a mile to the mine. Today he wore snowshoes, so walking came easier. But by the time he reached the dugout, his strength was sapped.

Resting for a spell, he sat on the log, trying to invoke Patience's image again. This time his imagination refused to cooperate. How long had it been since he'd last seen her? Three, four weeks. He couldn't remember.

After he'd rested, he got up and started to slowly shovel snow away from the dugout door.

"Better save yore strength, buddy boy."

Closing his eyes, Jay wondered why Frank was sticking around. Hadn't Patience deserted the mine? If so, Tucker had moved in, to be sure.

"Surprised ta see me? It's not like I have places to go, things to do."

Frank was up to his same old rhetoric, but with a different tone. He didn't sound as ornery or as pleased with himself. He emerged from nowhere and paused in front of the dugout. "Missed you, buddy boy."

Jay ignored him. Frank had what he wanted; Jay wasn't going to congratulate him on his good fortune.

The old man leaned against the dugout. "Pert near got yoreself killed. Gonna have to be more careful."

"I'll concede that I'm just plain stupid. Since you didn't finish me off that day in the mine, I thought I'd let one of Mooney's thugs have a shot at it."

"Now, buddy boy, I didn't *hurt* ya, did I? I was jest makin' a point."

Jay shoveled snow aside, ignoring him.

"Mad at me, ain't ya?"

"Actually, I don't give a hoot about you, Frank."

"Yeah, yore mad all right." Frank scratched his beard sheepishly. "Guess I was a might hard on that girl and the boy."

Jay refused to look up.

"Got my own woman troubles, ya know." Frank moved to sit on a log, hands folded, watching Jay work. "Come on, son . . . so I *am* a heartless, angry, old man . . . I *did* save yore life."

Jay glanced up.

"I was the one who found you and brought you to Elga's cabin."

"That was you?"

Frank nodded. "That was me. Fool thing you done, shoving that outhouse over with Red sittin' in it."

"Well—" Jay lifted another shovelful of snow—"face it; I do a lot of foolish things."

"There ya go, bein' hard on yoreself agin. You was on yore way back to the Mule Head when it happened, wasn't ya?"

"Before I was . . . detained."

"Then what's the problem? You didn't run her off. You was comin' back—or least ya would have if ya hadn't let yore orneriness get the better of yore common sense. Son, you don't fool around with a man Red's size. Ain't anyone ever told ya that?"

Pausing for a moment, Jay's gaze traveled to the mine. "She thinks I deserted her—stalked off and never came back. She didn't have a chance against you and Tucker after that. She gave up her dreams and went back to Denver City."

"Yeah—shore hated to hear that."

Jay met the old prospector's eyes, aware that his injuries were still apparent. "Why would you hate to hear it? That was your plan, wasn't it? Run her off, scare her witless so she'd give up the mine? She'd still be here, Innis, if it wasn't for me. She wasn't scared of any *ghost.*"

Frank hung his head. "Yeah, she's purty spunky."

Jay kept shoveling. It was a while before he spoke. "Have you heard anything about Patience?" he asked softly. "Did she make it back to Denver City all right? Is she well?"

"Hear tell she's well. Got a friend over in Denver City—I've been keepin' up since I knew you couldn't. Her and the boy are stayin' with the pastor and his wife, along with the other girls. She's being taken care of, buddy boy, better'n when she was livin' up here, fightin' that mine."

"Wilson?"

"Wilson? Mick Johnson, a fellow miner, passed through Denver City last week. He says rumor is the boy hates everything—suppose it's his age."

Jay's voice dropped to a ragged whisper. "I love her, Frank."

"Yeah, I know, buddy boy." The old man scratched his head. "I was in love once—didn't turn out much better than you and the girl, but I can shore remember how I felt about her."

Jay rammed the shovel into another drift, angry now. "I fell in love with her. I told myself a thousand times I wouldn't, but I did. Fell in love with both of them. The time we spent here . . ." Jay's eyes traveled the mine area. "We were a family, Frank. God gave me a second family, and I didn't realize or appreciate it."

"Yeah, well, now there's still time to do somethin' about it. Not all's lost. She might be in Denver City, but that ain't the jumpin'-off place. You got a swift horse—go after her."

Jay noticed that Innis crossed his arms when he kept shoveling. "Why are you shovelin' that snow?"

"I have to do something to pass the time."

"Shovelin' snow's only gonna sap yore strength. Better save it, son, for better things."

"Are you ever ashamed of what you did to her?"

When Frank didn't answer, Jay looked up, expecting the old miner to be gone. Instead, he sat there, his arms folded across his bony chest, staring out across the mountains.

"Frank?"

The old man glanced at him, eyes misted over. "Ashamed, you ask. Yeah, I'm ashamed. She's a good woman. Reminded me of someone I used to know. Never deserved what I did to her, and I liked the boy too. Never had a son or grandson. Seemed like you and Wilson sort of filled that need."

Jay stared at Frank in disbelief. "So you blew up the mine with me in it? Thanks a lot, *Dad.*"

Frank shook his head. "You ain't takin' me as serious as you ought to."

"I'll take you serious when you talk serious. You set out to drive us away from the mine."

"Yeah. I did that. Gonna go after her, aren't you, boy?"

Jay knew he'd eventually have to return to Denver City and face Patience. It also meant that he had to explain the thug, the beating, and the gambling debt to the town council. He paused and leaned on the shovel handle. "I haven't a thing to offer her—no gold, no solidarity. Nothing."

"Aw, shucks. Gold ain't no problem. You are gonna go after her, ain't ya? Shame to let a purty little thing like that git away."

"She's better off without me."

Frank shook his head. "Feelin' sorry for yoreself agin."

Maybe he was. Jay had faced the grim reaper and lost the woman he loved. Law didn't pay anything. If anyone had a right to feel sorry for himself, he did. His mind returned to the days of his youth when his family lived on Pop's fees: fresh eggs, vegetables from a grateful patient's garden, a butchered hog come fall, fryers and stewing hens throughout the summer.

There were times when an outbreak of cholera gripped the community and Doc Longer wouldn't see his family for days. When he did come home he'd be so tired he could do little more than eat leftovers and fall into bed for a few hours' sleep. People came and went at all hours of the night. He could never be counted on to be around at important times like Christmas and birthdays.

Delivering babies, tending the terminally ill, hovering over the desperately sick—never enough time for his own family. Law was the same way. Once Jay returned to Denver City his time would belong to the citizens. Patience and Wilson would be better off without him. He wanted wholesome meals on his table, new shoes for his children every winter, a house, and a team of horses to take his family for a Sunday afternoon ride.

Slinging his shovel over his shoulder, Jay walked away from Innis and the dugout.

"Hey . . ." Frank sat up on the log. "You leavin' for good?"

Jay never looked back. He slowly made his way through the deep snow and eventually disappeared over the hilltop.

Seven more days passed before Jay ventured back to the mine. He had vowed he was never going back. Patience was gone, and he sure didn't value Frank's company.

Yet shortly after dawn Sunday morning, he set off in search of her memory. Climbing the steep hill, he made his way slowly down the other side of the incline.

A cold sun glinted off the deep snow. His heavy boots broke through the crusty surface. He plodded toward the mine.

The little dugout looked bleak in the early morning light. What a difference her presence had made.

Sitting down on the log, he stared at the dugout, wondering what Patience and Wilson were doing on this Sunday morning. They'd be in church, worshiping God.

Suddenly he missed the comfort of a worship service. Nelly had been big on going to church, and she'd seen they never missed a meeting. He'd had something to believe in back then, before he'd lost his wife and son and his faith in a loving God.

A hawk soared overhead, riding the air currents. Jay breathed in the cold, clean air, drinking in the beauty of this remote corner of the world. God's world. He started to push the thought away, then paused, unaccustomed to his new feelings. Yes, God's world. The silence was so deep it was like being in a holy place. Like a cathedral.

He watched the hawk, letting his thoughts soar . . . up . . . up . . . into the dazzling blue of the sky. "Are you listening? Was I wrong? Do you really care?"

A sweet, subtle warmth began somewhere in the frozen wasteland inside him, where he kept his memories of Nelly and Brice, spreading outward like the rays of summer sun, thawing, healing.

The truth hit him again with the clarity of church bells. He'd stumbled out of faith, blinded by the pain of losing the two people he'd loved the most. He'd given up on God, but God had never given up on him. It was good to finally trust again.

He sat in silence, letting the peace of this lonely mountaintop seep into his soul. Faith. He'd never lost it; he'd just put it aside for a while. The belief in a loving God who truly cared for his own, that faith was the only thing that could see him through this life. It had taken a young woman and a little boy to make him see the difference.

Cold saturated his bones, aggravating his injuries. Oblivious to the pain, he sat lost in thought.

He'd vowed never to take a risk that involved love again. Never would he take someone into his heart; it wasn't worth the pain. He'd always get hurt. Love would fail him. Erect those barriers. But he was powerless. P had come along and—

"Hey! You! Buddy boy!"

Jay glanced up when he heard Frank's voice. His eyes searched the area for the miner. When was he going to give up and leave him alone?

"In here!"

Jay looked, but Frank, for once, didn't show himself. "What do you want, Frank?"

"I'm trapped."

"You're what?"

"Trapped. Over here."

Now what game was he playing? "Where?"

"In the mine."

Getting up, Jay walked in the direction of the mine. Frank was more trouble than a kid. And more aggravating, he might add. "Where are you?"

"In here."

"Where?"

"Toward the front of the shaft."

"What are you doing in there?"

"Quit talkin' so much and get in here, will ya?"

Turning away, Jay went back to the log. Frank got himself in there— he could get himself out. Jay didn't care what happened to the old fellow.

"Hold on a minute, buddy boy. I got myself a problem this morning. A bad one."

Jay sat back down. "Join the crowd."

"I'm serious. Git back over here."

"No."

"Just git over here!"

Getting up again, Jay walked to the entrance of the sealed shaft. "You are getting on my nerves, Innis."

"I hate to tell you this, but I'm stuck."

"Stuck?"

"Stuck."

"How could you be stuck? You come and go as you want."

"I don't know how it happened. One minute I was moseying through the mine, and the next I was trapped. Cain't move a muscle, buddy boy. You're gonna have to help me."

"What do you expect me to do about it?" Jay wasn't a miracle worker, and he'd had his fill of Frank Innis. In spite of what Frank had said the last time they'd talked, he wasn't convinced the old miner had a change of heart. Innis and Tucker had accomplished what they'd set after. Patience was gone. They should be happy.

"Help me figure out a way to get unstuck."

"The shaft's sealed. I can't get in there. Is there another entrance?"

"Yeah, about three feet from where yore standin'."

He *knew* it.

Jay laughed. "When did you ever think about *my* needs when you were causing all the cave-ins and rigging up the women's picks to knock them senseless, trying to run Patience off? Remind me again, Frank, why I should lift one hand to help you?"

"I'm serious, buddy boy. You gotta do something. I'm a mite uncomfortable."

Jay shifted on one foot. Guilt nagged him. Not five minutes ago he was asking the Lord for forgiveness and mercy. He had to help the old man, even though everything in him wanted to walk away.

"Are you in pain?"

"In a lot of pain. Now get to thinkin'. What are we gonna do about this?"

Kneeling, Jay ran his hands around the entrance, now crumbling. "The dirt's packed pretty tight. I can't get to you."

"Yes, you can. Think."

Jay knelt, his eyes assessing the situation. He could hear Frank clearly—that meant there was an open hole somewhere. "Where are you?"

" 'Bout fifty or so feet inside the shaft. Ya know that outcrop of shale just to the left as you come into the mine?"

"Yes." Jay knew it well. Went by it every time he entered the mine shaft.

"That's where I am. Wedged in between two big rocks."

Rising, Jay looked around for something to dig with, but his shovel seemed to have disappeared.

"You can't *dig* me out," Frank called. "You're gonna have to *blast* me out."

"Blast you out? Why, that would—"

"Kill me?" Frank mocked. "I'm tough as cowhide. I'll survive the blast, but if you leave me here I'll die a slow, agonizing death. Air's runnin' out, buddy boy. Ya have to do something—there's a couple of sticks of dynamite in the dugout. Go get 'em."

Jay glanced toward the dugout, puzzled. "Patience didn't keep explosives in the dugout."

"Just go look," Frank said crossly.

When Jay returned, he was carrying the two sticks of dynamite he'd found in the dugout. They had been lying in the middle of the kitchen table, a placement he found bizarre.

"You find 'em?"

"I found them."

"Good. Tell me when you're gonna light the fuses. I'll plug my ears."

"You better plug more than your ears—" This was insane. He couldn't kill the old man, no matter how tempting the thought. When he lit the dynamite that shaft was going sky-high.

"Jest do what I say! You ain't gonna hurt me!"

"You just said you were in pain!"

"Don't worry 'bout me! Just light the fuses!"

Jay searched his pockets. "I don't have any matches." How was he going to get out of this? Did Innis have a death wish?

"Good grief, boy! Have I picked an idiot to free me? There was matches layin' right next to the dynamite. Didn't ya see 'em?"

Jay stiffened. Name-calling now. Anger surged and he wished he had a match. A box of them. "I didn't see any matches."

"Well, go look."

"Hold on."

"Yeah, like I'm goin' somewhere," Frank muttered.

Jay was back in a minute.

"Got 'em?"

"I have them."

"Get to blastin'."

Jay began to set the charge, praying. *Lord, stop me. Revenge is the devil's tool, and you've been too good to me to let me fall again. I don't know how I'll get him out, but I refuse to light the fuse.*

"Now, you are going to Patience, ain't ya, buddy boy?"

Jay glanced up. "What?"

Suddenly Innis stepped into the open. His eyes twinkled with devilment. Outside the mine; he'd been *outside* the shaft all along. Jay's jaw dropped.

"I said, you *are* gonna marry the little Smith gal, ain't ya?"

"*Innis*—what kind of game are you playing now?" This was getting downright aggravating! Jay straightened, about to walk away, when Frank walked closer, holding a match.

"What's your answer?"

"It's none of your business what I do about Patience and the boy."

"You *are* gonna marry her, ain't ya? You ain't gonna let that pride of yours stand in the way of love, are ya?"

"Okay—yes. Soon as I'm well enough I'm going back to Denver

City. If Patience will have me . . ." He paused. That was a big *if*. Would she have him?

"Gonna take good care of the boy, see that he gits a good education?" Innis asked.

"What's the sudden interest in Patience's and Wilson's futures? You never cared before."

"I told ya. I took a likin' to the boy." The old man's features softened. "I'm old—don't have much time left here on earth, and I shore don't need the gold, so I've been thinkin' that before my days are through I might ought to do something worthwhile."

Jay frowned. "What are you talking about? Because of you and Tucker—"

"Aw—I was jest fillin' time with Silas. Had me a little fun 'hauntin'' the mine, owner after owner. That ole coot prospector wouldn't scare off. Then the woman came along, and I thought to myself, *Frank, you ought not to scare women and children,* so I decided to go to work on you." He scratched his beard. "That didn't work out either—but then I kinda liked the boy—never had any kids myself, and the little tyke's kinda cute with all his animals and his grown-up talk."

Leaning forward, Frank struck a match and touched the end of the fuse. "So, if you're watching, Lord, I'm doin' somethin' nice for a change. Shore hope you make note of it."

Jay backed up, his eyes on the sizzling fuses. "Innis—you're *nuts*. That shaft's going to blow sky-high—"

"I'm ready, buddy boy! Let 'er blow!"

Jay dived for the old prospector, trying to pull him to safety at the same time a thunderous explosion rocked the Mule Head, showering dirt and catapulting debris straight up.

Dust settled and Jay slowly got up, his eyes searching for Frank. *"Frank!"* The name echoed over the mountainside. There wasn't a sign of the old prospector. Dropping to his knees, Jay frantically dug into the shale, trying to locate the old man.

A ray of sun suddenly caught a shining speck on the ground. A moment later a second ray caught another, then another. The brilliancy that suddenly surrounded Jay was blinding.

Scraping up a handful of nuggets, Jay studied the findings. Slowly lifting his head, he looked around, realizing that he was sitting in a pile of more gold than he'd ever seen in his life.

Huge, unbelievable stones covered the ground as far as the eye could see.

Bursting into laughter, he scooped up handfuls of the enormous nuggets, tossing them into the air, delirious with joy. The mother lode! He had hit the *mother lode!*

His laughter died away as his eyes searched for Frank. Had he done this? Had he finally relinquished the gold?

"Frank," he called hesitantly. "Are you still there?"

In the distance he heard distinct footfalls and an unmistakable *heh, heh, heh.*

Jay grinned. Why, that old fool!

Chapter Twenty-Six

J ay's here."

Patience glanced at Wilson from the open oven door, wiping a stray hair out of her eyes. "Who?"

"*Jay.*"

Lugging the heavy roaster to the cooling board, Patience set it down with a thump. "That isn't funny, Wilson."

"I'm not being funny. He's really here."

Patience turned, her heart hammering against her rib cage, halfway believing him. "Where?"

"At the front door. He doesn't look like riffraff anymore, Patience. He looks *rich.*"

"Rich?"

Wilson nodded. "*Really* rich. I've never seen Jay looking so good."

Dropping the hot pads, Patience touched her hair, wishing for a comb. "Dear God, please let it truly be him," she whispered. It had been nearly two months since she'd returned to Denver City, and she hadn't heard a word from him.

Shrugging, Wilson sneaked a bite of the roasted hen. "*Filthy* rich, actually," he murmured.

Racing down the hallway, Patience wondered what he really looked like and immediately decided that it didn't matter! He could be wearing sackcloth and ashes for all she cared. *Please God, let it be him.*

Rounding the corner, Patience came to a sudden halt. Standing before her *was* the most handsome man she had ever seen in her life.

Lily stood in the doorway, her gaze fastened on the handsome sheriff and a goofy grin on her face.

Jay's eyes met hers over Lily's head. Gazing at one another, there was no need for words. His expression told her everything Patience needed to know.

Giving a squeal of joy, she flew into his arms, nearly bowling Lily over in her exuberance.

Clasping her tightly to him, Jay kissed her. Rockets exploded, colored lights flared, and the roar in Patience's ears sounded like a dynamite blast.

"Patience Smith!" Lily gasped.

The taste of him, the feel of him—Patience couldn't get enough! The shameless, passionate embrace was embarrassingly prolonged.

When they finally parted, Patience took both his hands, smiling up at him. "You're a little late."

"I have a good excuse." Leaning forward, he kissed the tip of her nose. "By the way, I love you."

"Mmm," she whispered, returning the embrace. "I love you too."

Quickly and without taking a breath, he told her about his injuries and why he hadn't followed her to Denver City immediately.

Shutting her eyes, she willed back tears. *Thank you, God. I knew there had to be a reason.*

Lily cleared her throat, closing the front door. Realizing her lack of propriety, Patience quickly apologized. "I'm sorry, Lily—it's just . . . I'm so *glad* to see him!"

"Can't blame you," Lily murmured.

Still holding tightly to the sheriff, Patience pulled him inside the parlor, where the pastor, his wife, Mary, and Harper sat. He looked so . . . different today. Dressed in a suit of pearl gray worsted, under a brass-buttoned greatcoat, his snowy white cravat studded with what must surely be a diamond set in pure gold, he bore little resemblance to the scruffy miner or the town sheriff. From the crown of his beaver hat to the toes of his polished boots, he was bandbox fresh and a joy to behold.

"Look, everyone! Sheriff Longer is back."

The minister rose immediately, reaching for Jay's hand. "Good to see you, son! We've been worried about you."

"Thank you, Pastor." Removing his coat, hat, and gloves, Jay handed them to Lily, who had followed them into the parlor. He grinned and winked at the flushed young woman. Once everyone was comfortably seated, Patience reached for Jay's hand, unable to leave him alone.

"Pastor, Mrs. Siddons—I've come to ask for Patience's hand in marriage," Jay began quietly. "I know you're not her parents, but she thinks of you fondly. It would be well and good if you were to grant that permission, but I must warn you, I love this woman with all my heart and soul, and I will marry her no matter what you say." He turned to look at Patience. "Me and God had a misunderstanding for a while, but we've worked it out." He smiled. "Like you say, P, God is good."

"Oh, Jay." Patience was so proud of him she could burst. "You said that so well!"

He nodded, courtly indeed. "Thank you, Miss Smith. I thought I did a rather good job myself."

"Marry her!" The pastor's grin widened. "Why, that's wonderful, son." He glanced at Patience fondly. "You have my and Mother's deepest blessing."

A grin spread across the sheriff's face. "I think you should know that Patience is an extremely wealthy woman, sir. She and Wilson and Lily, Harper, and Mary will want for nothing." His gaze met Patience's. "Absolutely nothing."

Patience covered her mouth with both hands. Rich? Her?

"You hit the mother lode, sweetheart."

"Oh, Jay!" Springing to her feet, she flew back into his arms. There would be time later for him to explain everything. Right now it was enough to know that he loved her enough to marry her—rich or not!

Pastor Siddons smiled. "Wealth is subjective, Jay. Good health, love—"

"Two million isn't, Pastor."

Patience's soft intake of breath filled the stunned silence.

"Two . . . million," Mary repeated lamely. *"Dollars?"*

Jay grinned. "Give or take a few hundred thousand."

"Well, goodness," Harper fanned herself. "Ain't nothin' sub—subject—whatever you said, about *two million dollars!"*

Later, Patience drew Jay into the parsonage kitchen, where they could be alone. The door closed behind them and she turned into his arms.

"Oh, I've missed you so," she whispered. His mouth lowered to take hers. Between patchy kisses, he managed to tell her in greater detail why he had failed to come back that day. He explained how he would have died if Frank Innis hadn't found him and taken him to Elga's house.

"But the money," she whispered. "Were you making that up?"

Chuckling, he held her tightly. "The money is real. Innis gave us the mother lode, darling."

Frowning, Patience looked up at him. "Innis?"

"The man I told you about—the one posing as Gamey O'Keefe's ghost. He admitted he'd been trying to scare us into leaving, so he and Silas Tucker could jump the claim, but seems like Innis felt guilty for what he'd done. He convinced Tucker he'd lied about the mine having the mother lode. He's the one who helped us find the gold."

"Oh," she said lamely. "There really was a man?"

Resting his lips on her hairline, he whispered, "It doesn't matter if you believe there was or wasn't. He believes in us."

Laughing, he kissed her bewilderment away. "There is so much we have to catch up on and to learn about each other. On the way over here I looked up Red and Luther and paid off the gambling debt. I knew you wouldn't mind." He held her closely. "I'll make you and God a solemn promise: I will never wager money again."

"Oh, darling, I love you *so*," she whispered. "Then, we truly are rich?"

"Honey, we can burn money for firewood." He grasped her shoulders, slightly moving her back so he could meet her eyes. "Chappy Hellerman told me you hadn't deserted the mine, that he was holding the deed. Strange, I never saw him around, but apparently he made it known you were away on business."

She smiled. "I never gave up the dream, and I trusted Chappy to guard my secret. When you didn't come back I knew I had to really think about Wilson's future—but deep in my heart I knew you would come for us. If for no other reason you would return to Denver City and your job. I knew when you did, I would chase you shamelessly until you were mine." She kissed him briefly. "What d' you think of them apples?"

"I love them—and I love you more."

Closing her eyes, Patience thought about what the money would mean to Mary, Harper, and Lily. "Thank you, God," she whispered.

"This is all well and good, but what about me?"

Springing back, Patience saw Wilson sitting at the table, calmly stuffing cookies into his mouth.

"What about you?" Jay reached over and rumpled the boy's hair.

"You can have your own zoo now, kid, complete with elephants and giraffes, if you want."

"I'd like an elephant, perhaps one giraffe, but that isn't the point." The child wasn't to be deterred. "I *know* you'll take care of me because Patience will make you."

Jay's tone gentled. "Wilson, I would take care of you regardless, but knowing you, you're about to make a point. What is it?"

"The point is you *hurt my feelings.*"

When Jay glanced at Patience, she shook her head warningly. Wilson had been angry with him from the moment they left the Mule Head. It would take a while for the child to forgive and trust again.

Kneeling beside the table, Jay said softly, "I'm sorry I hurt your feelings. Do you want to tell me what I did so you won't resent me anymore?"

Wilson's countenance turned grave. "Patience and I waited all day for you to meet us, but you didn't come. It was cold, and we waited all day. You didn't come."

"I didn't come because I couldn't. Because Red beat me up. I did a stupid thing, and I paid for it by temporarily losing the two people I love most."

Tears brimmed to Wilson's eyes. "You love *me,* Jay? Honest?"

"Honest." Leaning closer, he said, "Next to P, I love you more than anything in the world. We're going to be a family, Wilson. You, me, and P."

"And now you love God again?"

Jay nodded. "I never stopped loving him—he hurt my feelings, Wilson, like I hurt yours. But now I know he never stopped loving me."

Throwing his arms around Jay's neck, Wilson hugged him. "That day, when you didn't come, I thought it was because you didn't like me."

"Never," Jay assured him. He reached out and took Patience's hand, drawing her into the circle. She smiled back, her love overflowing for this man. "And from now on I won't be pushing over any more outhouses. But that's another story entirely." His eyes met hers. "When you need me, I'll be there for you."

"Always?" P and Wilson parroted.

Drawing the two of them to him, the sheriff whispered, "Always."

Epilogue

Someone knocked on the front door, and Lily hurried to open it, feeling anyone else would be anticlimactic after Jay's arrival. What a day this had been! She swung the door open and stopped with her heart in her throat. There facing her was the best-looking man she'd ever seen. Even more handsome than Jay Longer, to her notion.

"Afternoon, ma'am. The name's Claxton. Cole Claxton."

Lily stared up from her five feet two inches, thinking she hadn't known God made men that tall. For a minute, she longed to be blonde and beautiful, instead of having plain brown eyes and hair the color of maple syrup, to say nothing of the smattering of freckles across her nose. Freckles weren't beautiful.

"M-Mr. Claxton," she stammered.

"I was told I could find my old friend Jay Longer here."

"Oh, yes." Lily opened the door wider. "Come in. I'll get him."

She hurried to the kitchen, surprising Jay and Patience by bursting in on them. "Oh, Sheriff. There's someone here to see you."

Jay turned slowly. "To see me? Who?"

"He said his name was Cole Claxton."

Jay took Patience's hand and hurried through the kitchen and down the hallway to the front door. "Cole! Come in, man. How are you?"

The two shook hands, and Cole's eyes slid past Jay to linger on Lily and her heart fluttered. "Just passing through. Thought I'd stop and say hello."

"I'm glad you did." Jay glanced toward the crowded living room and stepped out on the porch, motioning for the women to follow. They sat down in the rocking chairs Pastor Siddons kept there. A pale sun rose high in the winter sky. Lily pulled her woolen shawl closer, too excited to stay in the house.

Patience and Lily listened as the two men reminisced about past experiences. Lily caught her breath in wonder at the bravery of the lawmen and what they considered harmless escapes. To Lily, they seemed suicidal. Wilson crept out to join them, listening with shining eyes to the tales of adventure. Lily remembered her manners and brought cups of warm cider.

Finally Cole stood up. "Well, it's been nice, but I've got to be on my way." He shook Jay's hand and nodded to Patience and Lily. "Maybe I'll ride through this way again before too many years." He caught Lily's eyes and she felt light-headed. He put on his hat, and said, "Ma'am," and left. She watched him walk down the path, mount his horse, and ride away.

Jay grinned, drawing Patience into his arms. "Lily, don't get any ideas about Cole Claxton. He's married."

She turned to face him, frowning. "Why are all the good men taken?"

Jay threw back his head and laughed. "But he's got a passel of friends who've yet to take the marital plunge—good-looking, ornery men." He reached over and tugged a lock of her hair. "You've got good taste, lady. I've known Cole Claxton for a long time. He's from Missouri. Got two brothers, Cass and Beau—both happily married. The Claxton men are lawmen—best in the country. Only a special woman can lasso men like the Claxtons."

Lily gave him back look for look. "You were a man of the saddle once."

Jay chuckled. "And I was lassoed."

Mary and Harper joined them on the porch. Patience slipped her arms around the two newcomers, and her smile included Lily. "It's so good to be back together again. All of my plans for us have come true. We'll never have to worry again. A lot has happened since we left the orphanage, but our journey is over. We've finally found a home."

She released the women and stepped into Jay's waiting arms. "A real home with real love."

Smiling, Lily's eyes followed Cole Claxton—man of the saddle. He rode out of town, straight and tall. So . . . Mr. Claxton had a passel of unmarried friends . . .

Ornery lawmen.

"Patience, I wouldn't hurt your feelings for the world," she murmured, though nobody noticed. "But don't count this girl out on finding her own true love. Miracles still happen—and I can lasso with the best of them."

A Note from the Author

Dear Friends,

Words cannot express my gratitude for the loyal readers who have followed the Brides of the West. The series started with three books and grew to six. Now we come to the end of the brides' journeys, and though I'm sad to part with this family, I'm satisfied that each woman has found true contentment, whether by marriage to that special man, or—like Mary, Harper, and Lily—through God and the knowledge that life is unique and not everyone finds happiness in the same way.

Now I look ahead to a new HeartQuest series titled Men of the Saddle. Much like the brides, these young men are rugged pioneers who paved the way for freedom, democracy, and yes, love in the Old West. And who knows? Lily might even bump into one of these handsome strangers. . . .

Meanwhile, I'm busy with another fun series for Tyndale House: Morning Shade Mysteries. The stories involve my usual quirky characters, a small (fictional) town in Arkansas, people who love the Lord, and the oddest mysteries. Of course, eighty-seven-year-old Stella Diamond can't let a good mystery lie, so she and the self-appointed, bumbling town constable Hargus Conley bump heads when an occasional strange happening pops up—like the recent bizarre case of the furniture mover. Someone is breaking into homes, rearranging and redecorating! *A Case of Bad Taste* was released in July 2003, and *A Case of Crooked Letters,* the second book in that series, will be available in spring 2004.

God continues to pour out blessings on the Copeland family. My husband and I have purchased a small motor home, and we now camp with good friends as often as our busy schedules allow. We spend a good deal of time shamelessly spoiling our five grandchildren (and kissing their faces off), having picnics and Bible studies with our church family, and each day thanking God for the wonderful life he has given us. Not without its problems, but most assuredly under his watchful care.

Until we meet again—

Lori Copeland